D0400350

THE ICARUS CORPS

THE DARKSIDE WAR | TITAN'S FALL | JUPITER RISING

ZACHARY BROWN

SAGA PRESS
LONDON SYDNEY NEW YORK TORONTO NEW DELHI

1230 AVENUE OF THE AMERICAS, NEW YORK, NEW YORK 10020

This book is a work of fiction. Any references to historical events, real people, or real places are used fictitiously. Other names, characters, places, and events are products of the author's imagination, and any resemblance to actual events or places or persons, living or dead, is entirely coincidental. + + *The Darkside War* and *Titan's Fall* were previously published individually. + + For information about special discounts for bulk purchases, please contact Simon & Schuster Special Sales at 1-866-506-1949 or business@simonandschuster.com. + The Simon & Schuster Speakers Bureau can bring authors to your live event. For more information or to book an event, contact the Simon & Schuster Speakers Bureau at 1-866-248-3049 or visit our website at www.simonspeakers.com. + The text for this book was set in Bembo Infant. + Manufactured in the United States of America + First Saga Press paperback edition July 2017 + 10 9 8 7 6 5 4 3 2 1 + CIP data for this book is available from the Library of Congress. + ISBN 978-1-5344-0235-5

TABLE OF CONTENTS

THE DARKSIDE WAR

ZACHARY BROWN

BOOK ONE OF THE ICARUS CORPS

1

I stood at attention. My boots dug into the sad, scraggly patch of open field that was all that remained of what had once been called Central Park, and I remembered standing in the middle of a baseball field here, once. A long time ago.

Shit, I had to have been, what, three years old?

Our ragged lines formed up between the organic mangrove-like legs of alien spires. The matte-black, treelike structures dwarfed the human-built New York City skyscrapers: our glassy, blocky, primitive efforts to reach toward the sky.

A human sergeant in Colonial Protection Forces gray, a single red shoulder stripe marking his rank in the Accordance, walked up to face the lines of human recruits.

"Listen up, you useless maggots," he shouted, his voice amplified so much it hurt my chest and left my ears ringing. "There are many aliens out there. They come in all sorts of shapes and sizes. You will probably fight beside creatures that will haunt your nightmares long after you leave the service, and they're the good guys."

He paused a moment to let that sink in. Some of those

"good guys" watched us from balconies that jutted out like dark thorns from the slender legs of their buildings, but from down on the ground they were just a collection of distantly tiny, odd shapes to our eyes.

"However, if you want to survive your first encounter with the enemy, there are five aliens that you need to learn to spot on sight. Pay attention now, you might live to see your mama again someday."

The human sergeant held up a black-gloved fist. He raised an index finger.

"Drivers: They're cat-sized and scaly. Those pronged rear feet will sink into the flesh of your back and hook on. That pink ratlike tail? Once it plunges into your spinal cord, you're a brain-dead meat puppet at its total and utter disposal. Ever see a whole squad turned into zombies for the enemy? You will."

Two fingers up. I shifted and wiped the sweat from my forehead. Something like cinnamon wafted through the cool air from one of the nearby portals leading inside.

"Trolls: Yes, they look like rhinoceros that stand on two feet. Either of which could stamp you into a puddle of human goo. That armor? Nothing short of depleted uranium gets through it. I've seen one of these flip a tank. Ever come face-to-face with one, you call in an air strike and run like hell."

Three fingers.

"Raptors: Our enemies decided that a velociraptor with a brain, thumbs, and the running speed of a cheetah wasn't good enough, so they made cyborgs out of them. They also carry rifles. But they smell like chicken if you hit them with a laser."

He smiled when he said that, and held up a fourth finger.

"Crickets: These insectile robots are the first wave. The winged variants provide air support as well. Shoot them to bits. But watch out, those twitching leftovers reassemble as needed. So make sure the bits are really, really tiny, and then shoot them some more."

He uncurled his thumb. His voice changed. More serious. Lowered. I leaned in slightly.

"And lastly: Ghosts. They seem to be in charge, the masters of it all. We think they're covered in advanced adaptive camouflage. They stay out of the fight, and any nearby enemy forces will sacrifice themselves in a suicidal frenzy to protect a ghost. So if you see one, kill it. If you can. No one has ever survived a face-to-face with one; we just get the suit recordings afterward."

A gaggle of civil servants in dark-blue uniforms spilled out of a portal and milled around in clumps, watching us. Three orb-shaped cameras flew overhead, hanging in the air as if gravity were just a minor annoyance as they recorded us.

This was a show, and I knew it: Watch the recruits line up and get processed. I would be on any number of news streams and live shows.

"These are the enemies of the Accordance," the sergeant shouted. "These are *our* enemies. They are the Conglomeration, and they seek to destroy us. So we must destroy them first. We will teach you how. Do you have any questions?"

Yeah, I thought. How long will any of us survive against that?

The sound of chants and protest floated between the buildings: fifty or so licensed protestors in a permit-cleared free-speech zone on the edge of the Accordance Administrative Complex.

Last week, there had been tens of thousands of them.

+ + + +

The protest against alien occupation grew around the edges of the gnarled forest of alien structures. Summer heat beat down, refracting off the windows and buildings, and the determined, angry crowd smelled of sweat, body odor, and street food. Tents lined the sidewalk and spilled onto the street, creating a haphazard fabric city. Barrel fires filled the air with a sharp-tasting haze.

Some thousand people had elbowed me in the ribs or stepped on my feet before I stopped, suddenly transfixed by a pretzel cart along the Harlem side of 110th. Four men in suits on the other side of the Harlem antiterrorist gates eyed me warily as I sidled up to the cart and breathed in the smell of fresh pretzels.

"Devlin?" The voice came from behind a pair of protestors in gray hoodies holding up two halves of a broken globe and waving them in the air.

"Devlin Hart!"

I frowned. I knew the voice. I knew that the caller's name started with a *T.* But I'd been in four different schools just in the last year and a half. My parents kept moving from safe house to safe house.

"Tristan, right?" I asked.

"Yeah!" Tristan ducked under the fractured globe easily and sidestepped people to get closer to me. We'd played soccer. He was a striker, I remembered. Up at the front, compact and fast. He moved through the crowd like he slipped between players on the field: quickly and efficiently. He held a quad-copter drone in one hand.

"What are you doing here?" Tristan asked. And then he laughed as we grabbed hands, half shook. "Right, I didn't mean *here,* at the protest. I meant here in this part of the street. Figured you'd be near your family."

I soaked up the moment of familiarity. I'd liked the three weeks I'd gotten to play on a team. Make some friends. Before my family had been forced to move and hide again. "We're on a food strike."

"That sucks."

"Yeah. No one asked me if I wanted to join." I was just, it seemed, the son of Thomas Hart. *He* was the Great Planner. The leader of the closest thing humanity had anymore to a resistance.

What was a little hunger compared to the Fight? The Fight to get humanity back out from under the thumb of the overlords that had descended from the skies before I was born. That from orbit had destroyed the cities of the world that rose up against them.

"You're protesting?" I asked.

"Recording." Tristan grinned. He held up the quadcopter. "Watch." He threw it into the air. The four propellers buzzed and it hovered in place above us, waiting for instructions.

Tristan circled it around overhead a few times using his phone to pilot it. "A few friends of mine rented a room nearby; we've been flying these things and streaming the video all over. Drop a few ads in, we've been making some spare cash. Everyone's curious to see who blinks first: protestors or Accordance enforcers." He nodded toward the nearby gate leading into Harlem, where the businessmen still stood and stared at the crowds. The gates slid down into the ground and under the sidewalk.

Two struthiforms in lightweight armor walked out in front of the businessmen. Fast and dangerous, they looked like stoic ostriches dressed in ancient Roman armor. But the heavy Accordance-made energy rifles held across their feathered chests in scaly arms were nothing but serious.

"Jesus," I said. Usually the enforcers carried stun guns and prods for protests. These looked ready for war.

The sound of the crowd changed around us. The chants and hive-like buzz of protest shifted, like a changing wind, and built into a low growl as people noticed the escorts.

"Go home," shouted a woman in baggy jeans as she shoved an Earth First poster with a hand-painted version of a simplified, almost cartoonish green globe at the two aliens. The suits behind the guards grimaced and stepped back slightly. The struthiforms moved their feathered hands into the oversize trigger guards of their rifles and stepped forward.

The vendor slammed the windows shut over his hot plates, balled up his apron, and slid into the cab of the rolling cart. My stomach grumbled. The cart rolled away with a whine as the vendor piloted it gently through the crowd and down the crowded street.

The woman with Earth First poster stepped right in front of the struthiforms, her placard high in the air as she blocked their way onto the street.

"Step aside," the struthiform on the left said, voice strong and authoritative via a translation collar on its spindly neck. I could just barely hear the hisses and clicks of its natural language underneath the human voice the collar projected.

"You have no right to order me to do anything."

The standoff created an island of tense silence as people watched the birdlike alien confront the human protestor.

The struthiform on the right hit her in the stomach with its rifle butt, forcing her to double over. Leaning back on one massive leg, the alien pinned her roughly to the ground with the other. The flattened talons grasped her waist as she struggled to get free. The struthiform aimed the rifle at her head. "You will cease your obstruction, or face a penalty," the struthiform said.

Members of the crowd shouted back, anger bursting into the air. More faces turned toward us.

"Quick," I hissed at Tristan. "Buzz them."

"What?"

"Buzz the drumsticks, before the crowd turns on them. Remind the enforcers they're being watched. Live. Or they'll kill someone."

"They might come after *us*."

"Then give me your phone."

"No. No, I'll do it." Tristan swooped the drone down low, skimming above the crowd and stopping it just above the aliens. The fans blew air downward, ruffling the struthiforms' feathers. They glanced up and the one on the left raised its rifle.

A snap of light, pure energy leaping outward from the rifle's barrel, melted the drone right out of the air.

Tristan swore and looked around, ready to run.

But the distraction broke the tension. The struthiform on the right let go of the woman. She wriggled away, leaving her poster on the ground and keeping her hands in the air, her defiance blunted by the show of force.

The struthiforms took the moment to continue through the street, escorting the suited humans toward the midnight-black forest of alien buildings on the other side. Off to do whatever it was civil servants did for Accordance bureaucracy in there.

"I'm sorry about the drone," I said, taking a deep breath of hot air tinged with smoke. I held back a cough.

Tristan shook his head as if it were no big deal. But his hands shook a little as he rubbed them together. "It's okay. They're disposable. I have a couple more."

I swallowed. "I can pay you back." I actually couldn't.

Tristan shook his head. "I'm going back to get another one, but I don't think I'm coming back out into the crowd. It's changing, isn't it? I want to catch it, live. But I should leave."

"Okay." The San Francisco riots had been put down bloodily, so I understood his reluctance to get caught in the middle of something going bad. The New York chapters had practiced discipline. I'd helped train some of the cells. You had to convince people to not raise a finger in the face of violence, to take the beating that would come when enforcers came out with stun guns.

You had to drill them hard to stand in place, militarily, and not flinch. And despite the instincts deep inside you, you could not fight back. Because when you did, like they did in San Francisco, the Accordance had the excuse they needed to use more than nonlethal force.

That discipline didn't come easily to human beings. We could get pissed and riot. We could murder each other. Blow things up and run away. Rage was easy. But calm defiance: tough.

Tristan hesitated. "Hey, if you want, I have some food back in our room. Not a good view of the protest, but we can launch drones. Want to come meet everyone?"

My stomach clenched and gurgled. The press of humanity around us had slipped from celebratory to hostile. Even just pushing through it to get back to the organization tents I was supposed to be hiding in seemed a little dangerous.

"If it turns negative," my mother had whispered to me after San Francisco, "don't worry about me and your father. You get out before the enforcers start creating a line."

Something neither of us had told my father she'd said. Our little secret.

I was already on the fringe, why not get a little more

distance just to be safe? And get something to eat. I'd never promised to be part of their hunger strike.

And I half suspected the hunger strike was bullshit. For a month we'd been huddled in a Yonkers slum, living in a tent not much fancier than the ones pitched on the street here. Since San Francisco, donations to the cause had dried up. We could barely afford food right now.

"I'll come," I said.

We snaked out along 110th, ducked up one of the few ungated North Harlem streets, and got away from the dull roar and heat of bodies. The number of humans faded as we moved farther into Accordance space.

A few more struthiforms in armor moved along the streets. Heavy Accordance security. Human cops in duckling-yellow uniforms followed the struthiforms like little hatchlings, as ordered. We steered clear.

I followed Tristan up the stairs of an old brownstone converted into a hotel advertising housing for "All Species." Two floors up, and then into a corridor where the doors seemed to lean slightly and the fluorescent lights flickered shadows onto the wall. He knocked three times on the door to room 305.

The moment the door cracked open, Tristan bolted inside.

"What are you—"

I ate the following words. Two struthiforms in full midnight-black armor stood in the empty room. They looked at me, dinner-plate-sized eyes not blinking behind their armored visors.

"I'm so sorry," Tristan said from behind them.

"You asshole!" I shouted as he disappeared out the window and down the fire escape.

I spun around to run and came face-to-face with the

compound eyes of a carapoid. The horse-sized beetle of an alien didn't have any armor. It didn't need it. Its bony wings snapped out, filling up the corridor and knocking plaster from the walls. "Surrender peacefully," it warbled.

I scrabbled backward. Another carapoid grabbed me. Its sticklike arms wrapped around my chest and protuberances dug hard against my ribs as it lifted me off my feet into the air.

"Cease struggling," a struthiform standing behind me shouted.

The carapoid twisted and slammed me against the wall to make the point. Breath knocked out of me, my head swimming, I nodded and wiped blood from my nose.

"I'm done."

The carapoid dropped me to the ground, and a struthiform put scaly claws to the back of my neck.

"Devlin Hart, you are to be detained under the Human Antiterror Act 1451-B. Resistance will be met with mortal force."

The other struthiform roughly zip-tied my hands behind my back.

2

I rattled the shackles holding my wrists to the table in the middle of a sterile oval room. Two chairs flanked the table I sat at. Ovoid screens displayed deep ocean water and the room was filled with a faint bubbling sound. A contrast to the simple chain-link holding cells I'd been tossed into outside the building along with hundreds of other protestors swept up in the last several hours.

The door opened. The man in the black Armani suit screamed lawyer. He moved like lawyer. Smiled like lawyer.

"You're not Stephan," I said suspiciously. "Where's my family lawyer?"

The man sat across the table from me. He crossed his hands and gave me the considered, serious look. It came down like a mask, along with a mildly patronizing, lecturing tone. "I'm Gregory Stafford, and I'm your Interceder, not your lawyer. We don't have lawyers anymore, Mr. Hart, you should know better. And I'm assigned to you because there's a conflict of interest in your being represented by your previous Interceder."

"I've been standing inside a chain-link cell for three hours,"

I said. "In the sun. It's too small to sit or lie down in, and too hot to lean against the metal. I want Stephan. I have the right."

"The right?" Stafford looked pityingly at me. "You have no *rights*, Mr. Hart. You are involved in an act of sedition during war. Your parents are due to be executed, and you'll be lucky to be back out in that cage if everything goes well."

I tried to jump out of my chair. I shouted at Stafford, and my manacles crackled with electricity. My back wrenched straight and every muscle in me clamped down hard enough that I tasted blood.

My head struck the white table as I fell forward. I lay slumped, drooling out of the side of my mouth, every muscle in my body screaming.

Stafford leaned forward so he could meet my stunned gaze. "The Accordance has been waiting for the right moment over the last few years. All the while, it has been modeling how best to stop threats to recruitment. Now, all over the world, movements such as your father's have been raided and rolled up. There is no more antioccupation movement. Tomorrow morning, live broadcasts will show leaders of movements and cells being executed for treason. Your question, Devlin, is how you survive the next few hours."

"Tegna Gnarghf," I spat as best I could, still trying to get feeling back into my checks as I moved my jaw around.

"What's that?"

I took a deep breath and tried again. "Tentacle licker."

Stafford's high cheekbones reddened. "Listen, whether you like it or not, the Accordance came here. They have superior weapons. They destroyed DC. They took Manhattan. They sit in every major world capital. We've ceded them the moon, and other planets because we've never even reached them. And in exchange for that legal grant, we get some autonomy. The fact that, under their agreement to follow *some* human protocols, you're considered a minor and will not die with your parents: That's all that keeps you alive. Time to shape up, now, Mr. Hart."

I could sit up now, though the room wobbled and spun around me. I rubbed my eyes and groaned as I tried to process all this. From betrayal to capture. Everything turned upside down so fast. My father had organized peaceful protests, not fought on the streets. This was protest, not the damn Pacification. "What . . ." I gritted my teeth. "What do we do?"

"There are some options." Stafford tapped the table, and documents appeared on the surface. "The main concern the Accordance has is that they're in the middle of a war. It was why the Accordance was even created: defense. And they need recruits. You understand about the war, right?"

"Yes." I rolled my eyes. "We hear it all the time. About the Conglomeration. I've seen the propaganda. Five different species allied against the Accordance." Hopefully Stephan was meeting with my parents right now, trying to think of ways to stop all this. My heart hammered against the back of my throat, and it wasn't just because I'd been zapped. Everything settled onto me like a horrifying weight, trapping me in my chair. You knew the Accordance rule from on high. But then you encountered their boot on your throat, and it was suddenly too real.

"Against us all," Stafford corrected me. "The Accordance protects us. Anything that hurts recruitment, risks lives. Our lives. And your family, Mr. Hart, has risked many. However, recruitment is voluntary. The Accordance understands the value of good public relations. I think I can help you make a case to Accordance judges that executing a minor would be a horrible PR decision on their part."

"But not my parents?" I whispered.

"Just you. I'm sorry." Stafford's lawyerly mask slipped for a moment. I fought to keep seated and still, not wanting another muscle-clenching explosion of electricity to leap through my body.

I slumped farther down into my chair. "The only reason I won't die is because they don't want the bad PR."

"The war out there is real," Stafford said. "Even if it hasn't come to our world yet. If we're lucky, it won't. The Accordance needs fighters. From everyone it protects. We stand together under the Accordance umbrella, or we'll fall to something far worse. So they are being very careful here."

I couldn't imagine something worse than the Accordance. Something that destroyed cities from orbit and marched through the ruins in black power armor, ferreting out the remaining resistance with overwhelming force.

But there was apparently something out in the universe that made the rulers of the Accordance, the squid-like Arvani, shit their tanks. Even if no one on Earth had ever seen it.

And now my parents were going to die because of it.

"My father thought peaceful resistance would work," I told Stafford. "My parents saw what happened during the occupation; they thought this was a better path."

"The Accordance is ruled by aliens, not humans," Stafford said. "The Arvani and the Pcholem do not tolerate dissent, violent or peaceful. And the other species have less power within the Accordance. Your father should have known this; he was jailed for his inability to follow guidelines when teaching Indigenous Mythology."

Indigenous Mythology. My dad taught History 101 at NYU before I'd been born. He still insisted on carrying the old pre-occupation textbooks, big paper-printed monstrosities, around with us as we moved from house to house.

I blinked my eyes several times and looked away. I was so angry with them right now. Angry for spending my childhood never staying in one place. Angry because they always felt there was a higher purpose in their lives, a purpose far higher than anything I could ever mean to them.

What was a child compared to the past glory of humanity that had once ruled itself? I knew my place in the world. In my parent's world.

This was their fault, I thought angrily. *They'd* chosen this. It certainly wasn't my fault. Fuck, I was still hungry because of their choices. Even if I got out of this room, all I had was a hot, smelly tent in Yonkers with its moldy history books to go back to.

I clenched my fists.

They'd stolen themselves away from me a long time ago. So why did this hurt so badly?

I clenched my jaw.

"Our tentacled rulers want good PR," I said softly. They needed the fight to fade away. They needed to hobble the protestors. They needed to kneecap the leaders of the movement.

They needed to kneecap my parents.

Death was one way. "There's another," I said.

"Huh?" Stafford asked.

"There's another way they can neutralize my parents," I said. I knew what it was. That anger I'd been building inside had steered me toward a solution, and now it faded to sadness.

Stafford looked curious. "What do you mean?"

"Me," I said. "You can use me."

Stafford leaned back, then cleared all the documents off the table with a wave of his hand. "I'm listening."

"If I do this, I want to see them. I want to see them today," I said. Because in order to save my family, I would have to first destroy it.

"I can arrange something," Stafford said.

I took a deep breath and paused. Could I do what I was planning?

Yes. To save their lives. I could do this.

I had to. Angry as I might be, what sort of son would I be if I watched them die and didn't try to stop it?

The electrified fence between us prevented any touching. My dad stood in the middle of his cell, avoiding the walls like I had. But he'd spent all day in the sun, and the bags under his eyes from lack of sleep, food, and drink made him look older and frail. His salt-and-pepper hair hung every which way.

He licked bloodied, sun-cracked lips, and hung his head when he saw me enter.

My mother, in the other cell, had managed to fold her legs into a tight cradle so she could sit down, but she also looked frazzled and exhausted. Her normally even brown skin was splotchy with dirt and streaked with blood from a cut on her scalp. Dried blood also stained her shoulders.

"Oh God. Dev!" She tried to stand, but shrank back into her position when the cell sparked. Mine had just been hot, theirs was designed for maximum misery. "You're alive."

"Mom." I put a finger carefully between the spaces in the metal grid so we could touch fingertips gently. "I'm okay."

"I'm so sorry, Dev. We can't even get to talk to Stephan. I'm so sorry. It's very bad. All those Accordance soldiers in armor, they didn't care. They shot people. Right in the street. Live, on camera."

She was shaking. In shock. It must be a war zone on 110th Street, I realized. Other prisoners in the cages looked worse than my parents. Blood-splattered clothes, distant stares.

Gunshot wounds, jagged wounds. Ignored, without medics, some of the protestors trapped out here would die.

"Mom, you know I love you," I said tentatively.

"Of course. They said there was a chance you might . . . not be in the same position we are." Her brown eyes teared up. She whispered now, not wanting my father to listen in. "You have to take that. And don't feel guilty about it. Anything we've done, it's only hurt you. And I'm sorry about that. What we've done, it's us. Okay? It's us. You run, like I told you. You run from all this."

I closed my eyes. "I know." My voice cracked.

"Devlin?" My dad had cocked his head to stare at me. He used his teacher voice, strong and commanding attention even in his state. "What's going on?"

"I can save you." I took a deep breath filled with the smell of blood, unwashed bodies, and sewage. "But I'm going to have to say . . . some things. I'm going to have to do things." I closed my eyes, focusing on the unsteady pressure of my mom's fingertip against mine. A single line of contact. All I would have.

Sometimes I thought about why family members always fought so hard with each other; maybe it was because they were the only ones who could get fully into each other's heads. Dad saw through me instantly. "Don't do what you're thinking," he said. "That's everything we've been fighting against. We're trying to stop you from having to fight their wars for them. You know none of the recruits they've taken off-Earth have come back yet. We're trying to build a different future for you."

"Well, that didn't work too well, did it, Dad?" I snapped. "So what other choice do I have?"

"You have choices. You *always* have choices," he said.

"Like letting you die? What the hell kind of human being would I be if I let my own parents be executed?" I shouted, my voice quavering. Hold it together, I told myself. I bit my lip and calmed down. "There is no choice. The only choice is what you do with the second chance I'm buying you. Maybe you both try to sneak more antioccupation activity in, and I come back and find you dead anyway. Or maybe you get jobs, keep your heads down, and I live to come back and see you again."

Or maybe, I thought into the silence, we all would die for nothing. I opened my burning eyes to look at my angry, confused, hurt parents. Just as I knew they would be.

You're welcome, Stafford, I thought. I'm breaking them. I'm taking it all out from under them. And in some ways, they would consider it worse than death.

"You sign up to fight for the Accordance," my mom said, "then they've trapped you. They've talked you into this. Don't do what they tell you. Don't *collaborate.*"

That word. I pulled my finger back. "I'm sorry."

A struthiform guard opened the gate leading out. Stafford waited for me on the other side. "Time's up," he said, pointedly avoiding looking at any of the prisoners.

"You'll be under house arrest," I told my parents. "You'll get filmed going there. But it will be safe. And good." And it would make them look utterly like they had made a deal, and would undercut their authority in the eyes of the anti-occupation movement.

My dad grabbed the wire mesh. Sparks danced around his fists. He was crying, out of pain from the electrified wire or from my betrayal. I didn't know which. "You don't let them change you, Devlin. You find ways to fight them. In your own way. Like I raised you. You stay *human*!"

3

A human policeman in yellow uniform opened the van door with a crunchy squeak. I looked out warily. Leftovers from the protest filled 110th Street. The ripped pieces of the command tents blew up against stacked metal barricades, along with the detritus of protestors who'd fled.

Or been dragged away.

"You've got two hundred feet to walk on your own." Stafford directed me forward. "We'll be watching you."

The door slammed shut behind me. For the first time in twenty-four hours, sunshine hit my face and free air blew past me. I was free. Free for the two hundred feet between me and the gates of the Accordance Administrative Complex.

I picked my way around the trash and the barricades.

Halfway to the great legs of the administration buildings, I wondered if I could still run.

No. My parents were still in Accordance hands. Running would do nothing. I wasn't really free. These two hundred feet I walked on my own were as much a cage as the heated cage I'd been penned in.

Other volunteers straggled down the street toward the two-story skeletal gates that locked down the forest of the Accordance Administrative Complex against the world around it. Four or five of the volunteers rubbed their wrists, now free of their shackles. "Volunteers." They'd spent time in the fenced cells as well.

I wondered what horrible choices they'd had to make.

A drone buzzed overhead and blasted hot air into my face. We were live for the world to watch. Earth volunteers, signing up to join the Accordance's war against the Conglomeration. Rise, you sons and daughters of Earth, to help the Accordance defend a vulnerable world.

"Look at them," one of my fellow travelers said, acid in her voice. She nodded her head across the street. Ten well-dressed volunteers ambled down from the Harlem gates, where their parents clustered near struthiform guards, waving.

The volunteers waved back at their families, then at the drones in the air.

"I want to punch the shit-eating grins off their entitled faces," the girl next to me muttered. "Our future officer class. My dad says Harlem used to be all human-held. He grew up there. After it was all evacuated and the buildings seized, it became just collaborators and aliens. You look familiar; do I know you?"

"No," I said. Then, "I don't know."

"Keep moving!" Human soldiers in gray uniforms with no sign of rank on their shoulders waited on the other side of the black, bony gates. They herded us into lines that snaked through three booths in the middle of the glassy road, shoving us until we stood where they wanted.

Struthiform officers in red armor with oversize eyes and bobbing heads trotted up and down our lines, their necks undulating this way and that. "Walk through the scanners, hold your breath. Do not move," they ordered.

"Where are the scanners?" I asked.

A feathered arm shoved me forward until I stood on a blue circle in the road between two booths.

A blast of air hit my groin. I gasped. As I crouched and swore, a spinning tube of glass shot up out of the ground around me, then dropped right back down. A struthiform technician in the booth on my right glanced briefly at a three-dimensional skeleton that appeared in the air between him and me. My skeleton. Visible to everyone in line. Then it turned into an image of my skeleton with internal organs. Then my skin filled in. I was naked in front of everyone behind me in line until the technician waved the image away.

"Move!" he ordered.

My embarrassment hadn't even had time to form when the struthiform behind me shoved me forward so that the next recruit could stand in my place.

"Run! Run!" Pushed forward by other recruits and struthiforms yelling at us, we jogged under the shadowed roads and around the great twisted legs of the lower buildings.

A hundred of us stopped as one on a patch of grass. A plaza in the heart of the alien forest of a city buried in the heart of New York. A human sergeant in gray marched up to our front.

I'd seen his type before: on commercial breaks between sports, on public service announcements on screens in delis.

"Listen up, you useless maggots," he shouted, amplified words ringing out throughout the plaza. "There are many aliens out there. They come in all sorts of shapes and sizes. . . ."

Fuck. This was really happening.

I was going to become one of those people who disappeared off into deep Accordance space and had yet to come back.

Sweat trickled down the small of my back as I focused on an orb-shaped drone flying around the crowd for close-ups. I half listened to the description of our five enemies and what they could do to us.

I was going to let myself get shot across space. I was going to leave Earth far, far behind, and go fight a war that would be light-years away. With creatures that I'd never seen with my own eyes.

And I was going to do it for another bunch of alien creatures.

The human sergeant finished his well-rehearsed speech and left. The cameras flew away. Struthiforms yelled at us again. A line formed.

"Hold out your forearm." The man in front of me held what looked like a nail gun.

I did, and then winced as it punctured my skin with a sharp pneumatic hiss. I looked down. A single bead of blood welled up in the center of a tattoo of a stylized Earth with a triangle in the middle. My skin sizzled around it for a second.

"What's this?"

"Your rank and ID. Welcome to the Colonial Protection Forces. Move along."

I stumbled forward. Another annoying orb camera dropped out of the air to eye level and circled around me as a man stepped forward. "Mr. Hart, I'm Vincent Anais, with Colonial Broadcast Agency. If it's okay with you, I'd like to have a moment." His voice indicated he wasn't asking a question. I noticed he had a CPF tattoo on his forearm as well. His had two dots underneath the triangle.

"Um . . ."

"Just relax, smile, and one, two, three. . . . Mr. Hart, what prompted you to volunteer to join the fight against the Conglomeration?"

I licked my lips and tried not to look at the drone and its spiderlike clusters of unblinking camera lenses. "I . . . just want to do my bit to serve, and protect our world."

"And how did your parents feel about this, Mr. Hart? Are they proud you joined the CPF?"

I gritted my teeth. "I think they understand why it was important that I make this choice."

Anais smiled broadly. "So they weren't happy about it?"

"No," I told him. "No, they were not."

"Thank you for your time, Mr. Hart. And thank you for your service. Your world appreciates it."

The drone flew away, and Anais leaned forward. "Off the record, kid: You're going to have to do a lot better than that if you want your family to stay out of trouble."

Kid? Really? He was calling me a kid? *Who the fuck was he?* "I gave you what you needed," I snapped. "I'm here, aren't I? You got me to join, now leave me the hell alone."

Anais grabbed my collar and yanked me forward. When I tried to pull away from him, he tightened his grip. "Listen," he hissed. "I saw you tuning out the speech the sergeant gave back there. You think it's all just words. But what's out there, it's real. There's a black hole of an alien empire out there, reshaping the galaxy for its own purposes. It is old, implacable, and more alien than the aliens around us. The CPF needs minds and bodies to fight for the Accordance. This isn't about your wounded pride, or your family's. It's about something far, far bigger. Your usefulness as a tool to the CPF is just beginning. So get with the fucking program and start selling it, or it's going to get far worse, recruit."

4

Fifteen recruits, dressed up in their grays, stood with me in the train car as the countryside swept by at five hundred miles an hour on the high-speed rail line from New York to Richmond. The sort of high-speed rail that Americans had never been able to build until the Occupation, as Accordance propaganda was always fond of pointing out. "You are about to meet the acting president of the Regional American Council," Anais said.

He walked back and forth in front of us.

"This is a big fucking deal," Anais said slowly. "President Barnett has been an important part of Colonial Administration for a decade now. You will shake his hand. You will answer his questions. Then you will circulate and shake more hands. Be polite, be enthusiastic. Got it?"

"Yes, sir," we shouted back.

Anais sighed and then practically growled back at us. "How many times do I have to tell you there are no 'sirs' here in the CPF! The Arvani don't want tribal honorifics. Drop that shit. And definitely drop that shit in front of any Accordance. Got it?"

"Yes, s—" We choked back the follow-up word as Anais stared us down.

Once Anais left the train car, we relaxed.

I'd expected boot camp. But yesterday I'd been peeled off from my fellow trainees, stuffed into dress grays, and ordered out into an oval courtyard. A wasp-shaped Accordance ship spiraled down out of the sky, engines kicking up grass as it settled on its skids, and Anais had prodded us aboard.

I paused near the heavy door that swung up, looking over at the bulging engine pods sticking out from either side. Deep inside the engines, dark matter collided and swirled around, as advanced to human nuclear technology as a reactor might be to someone accustomed to shoveling coal into a steam-powered engine.

"What's the matter, recruit?" Anais asked. "Never been flying before?"

"Not in an Accordance jumpship," I said.

"Not a jumpship," Anais said. "Jumpships go to orbit. The engines on this aren't powerful enough, though the frame looks similar. We call these hoppers. Intra-atmosphere only."

The engines kicked the ship off the ground, rattling us around inside as we bumped and shook into the air. A few hundred feet up, the pods rotated, and then a subsonic thump shivered through the hopper as we sped up. A minute later the hopper hit supersonic.

After the flight from New York to London, we'd publicly helped other recruits get tattooed and inducted into the Colonial Protection Forces. And I'd been interviewed again about my parents. Again I'd all but disowned them, and talked about my pride in protecting my world. Only this time, with Anais watching me like a hawk.

At the repurposed barracks of Windsor Castle, we'd jogged

around the courtyards for the cameras, waved, and then boarded another Accordance hopper to Jakarta. And then we'd come back to New York for another recruitment drive. I'd done interviews near the steps of the Empire State Building, which had been converted into a barracks for CPF soldiers.

And now we approached the city of Richmond.

"Don't look so glum," Hammond told me. An older recruit, in his twenties, he came from a predominantly Accordance-owned area of Harlem. "Make them happy, you get an early discharge and a spot in civil service. Get a job in Colonial Administration and you're set for life."

DC's ruins swept by our windows. Swamp crept over the rubble of the city. The white, skeletal remains of several walls and some columns flashed by as the rail line cut through the heart of the demolished capital.

"Colonial Administration is for aliens, you idiot," another recruit said from the bar. She shook her head. "You'll work for them, but you're not going to advance up the political chain."

"Sounds about right," I said.

"What the hell do you think you know? They're not going to hand you a position: Your parents are terrorists," Hammond snapped. "In fact, be careful. You screw this up for us, I'll fuck you up so hard you won't even remember your own name. Only reason you're here is to shit on your parents."

I took a deep breath. I wanted to jump across the velvety carpet and punch him in the face.

But if I blew this opportunity, my parents would suffer.

Hammond saw the resignation on my face and laughed. "Thought so."

I stalked out of the train car to try to get some space to myself to stew. I wandered out to look at the other inhabitants headed for Richmond. The rich and powerful, the humans who worked with their alien rulers to help keep everything down here running nice and smoothly. They sipped champagne and chatted about stock prices; their eyes widened when they saw my uniform.

I wasn't on duty. I didn't have to suffer their inane questions and chatter, so I just kept walking. I stopped when I reached the locked doors leading to the alien section of the train.

No humans past this point.

I turned around and walked back.

Acting president Barnett took over the capitol building in Richmond as his private estate when he ascended to power in the Colonial Administration. Through the heavily guarded gates, we could see the tall white building within Accordance-built walls that defended the complex.

Between us and the walls: hundreds of protestors. Not nearly as thick a crowd as New York, but still determined.

"Jesus, you'd think they'd have learned by now," Hammond said.

"Okay recruits," Anais shouted. "You're in after our guests get rolling. Shoulders back, beam with pride, and let's get inside."

"What about the protestors?" I asked. They didn't look disciplined. And they weren't standing in any authorized zone.

Anais looked blankly at me. "What about them?"

Hammond shoved me forward and hissed, "Grow a pair."

We staggered forward. The upper-crust guests roared ahead in armored vehicles, struthiform soldiers running alongside them. Unlike the armor on the soldiers in New York, this black-and-red armor covered the aliens entirely. They ran easily, joints making a loud snicking sound. Powered armor,

I realized. The struthiforms were as protected as the vehicles, and far more dangerous.

It didn't take more than a few seconds for the fifteen of us to fall in line and walk. Our routine fell into place easily, even after just a few days of practice: Wave for camera drones. Look like excited recruits.

Inside there would be good food. All we had to do was shake politicians' hands. Pose next to the human machine that kept Accordance interests on Earth running smoothly.

And all I had to do was try not to think of my parents seeing the images.

"This isn't like the other protests," someone said, eyeing the crowds shouting at us. Usually we heard words like "traitor" or "collaborator." Since the occupation, and then Pacification, most countries had been following the same pattern as the one in the Americas: peaceful protest. Carefully organized, very publicized.

The Pacification came after the occupation, when humanity rose up to fight on the streets and the Accordance responded. At the time I was only five, but I'd watched the grainy, green nighttime livestreams of hunks of rock arcing across the sky to descend on Jeddah, Moscow, and Cleveland. The plumes of debris that kept rising and rising into the air, all that was left of the cities.

The Accordance did not like dissent.

This crowd had worked itself up to spittle-flecking anger.

"Are those flags?" Hammond asked, in shock. "They're illegal."

I recognized the *X* pattern of stars and stripes. "It used to be the flag for the South," I told him.

"Like Old Mexico?" he asked.

He didn't recognize the flag. No one taught indigenous

history anymore. Accordance-approved history downplayed smaller regional history for a big sweep. Indigenous history is not conducive to their desire to create a global human culture and to reduce regionalism.

That was how my father had lost his job at NYU. Teaching US history in too much detail. Not enough focus on the UN and larger regional commonalities, as the Accordance ordered.

"It's nationalistic," Hammond muttered, disgust in his voice.

My father's lecturing voice bubbled to the tip of my tongue as I prepared to educate Hammond. But a bottle of liquid struck the ground in front of us and exploded.

"Molotov cocktail!" someone shouted. Fire spread across the road, separating the line of recruits.

Ahead of us, on the other side of the fire, I saw Anais look back. He spoke into his wrist, annoyed. One of the recruits swore up a storm as he kicked and stamped out his smoldering pants.

The struthiform soldiers snapped back around in unison, flocking together as they loped through the guttering fire left by the bottle's debris. They broke free of their tight cluster a second later as another bottle arced up over the crowd at them.

The foremost struthiform leapt twenty feet into the air, following the arc of the homemade explosive, and scattered protestors when it landed in their midst. A man struck the alien on the back with a tire iron, and the struthiform backhanded him.

I watched the man fly through the air, arms flailing until he hit the wall with a wet sound. He slumped to the ground and didn't move.

"Get over here," Anais shouted. I realized it was the second or third time he'd yelled at us: We'd just frozen in place.

Several gunmen mixed in with the crowd opened fire on

the struthiforms. Bullets thwacked against alien armor over the crackle of little fires left from the Molotov cocktails.

Not all the protestors had been planning violence. Most of them scattered. I fixed on one mother and her son, who looked about eight years old, as they ran past. Her head snapped back and misted red blood in the air around us, then she pitched to the ground.

The kid fell with her, eyes wide and screaming. He scrabbled in the dirty road and picked up a rock.

I ran. Not even thinking twice.

He threw the rock past me at the nearest Accordance soldier. When it struck armor, the struthiform spun and aimed. Shielding the kid behind me, I held my hands up and winced, closing my eyes.

The shot never came.

Anais grabbed my hair and yanked me out of my half crouch. "Move!" he screamed. Struthiform soldiers fell in on either side of us.

Everyone retreated through the gates, which snapped shut after us with startling speed.

"What the hell were you thinking?" Anais shouted at me. "What the fucking hell were you thinking?"

"Sir . . ."

I bit my tongue and let the last part of the word hang in the air as Anais glared at me. "You stood down an Accordance soldier. You're lucky it didn't just shoot you."

"It was going to shoot a child," I said.

"You should have stood aside and let it do what it needed to do," Anais said. He grabbed my elbow hard, the points of his fingers digging into the flesh to bruise muscle as he shoved me up the great steps into the capitol building. Two human guards in light armor stood on either side of the columns.

"Inside," Anais snapped.

One of the recruits sat on the ground, blood covering her grays. A medic squatted next to her, sealing a wound with a spray can of bioglue and checking vitals.

We were in a foyer. I could see that beyond the doors a reception under crystal chandeliers was quietly going on. Men in suits, struthiforms with red command strips located just above their wings on their tailored uniforms. A carapoid lumbered around a corner of the room, moving a large table full of drinks into place.

And I noticed something that made my mouth go dry. A spherical tank of clear water wrapped around the bullet-shaped flesh of what looked like an octopus, but most certainly wasn't.

Arvani. The tentacles under the clear, body-conforming tank were mechanized, wrapped around the Arvani's natural tentacles. They undulated, shifting the tank expertly around as the alien rose up on the tips of its tentacles to look at a human politician eye to eye.

The creators and leaders of the Accordance.

Only a handful of Arvani lived down on the surface. They preferred their space stations, filled with giant pools that let them re-create their oceanic home environs. When they did live on the surface, they preferred the coasts.

A politician ignored the whole reception to stride through the doors toward us. He carried a bottle in one hand, a glass in another. Acting president Barnett, seventy years old, scowled as his pinched, leathery face regarded the scene in his foyer.

Anais left to talk to someone by a marble pedestal. Barnett focused on me. "I just looked over the video. You're the idiot who stood in front of the kid?"

My mouth dry, I nodded.

Barnett motioned me closer. He rubbed absentmindedly at a dry, bloodshot eye. "I have five women waiting for me back in my bedroom. Can you imagine that? A whole damn harem. They're buck naked and standing along the side of the mirrored wall for me. You know how many pills I have to take just to keep up with that? You can't imagine. Maybe you can, you're young. I'll bet you can imagine all sorts of things. Multiply it, son. I've done things that would've shocked even me when I was your age."

This was not what I expected. I also didn't want to think about the president naked and sweaty . . . No. Just no. What the hell was happening?

"You know," Barnett said. "I used to hate people like you."

"Younger . . . ?" I floundered. I saw this man on screens all the time. Yet here he stood in front of me, swaying slightly.

"Brown," Barnett said bluntly. He poured some of the amber alcohol into the glass in his other hand. He drank it like someone thirsty would down a glass of water. "Brown people."

I didn't know what to say to that. I stood and blinked.

"You look tan. Hard to tell. Maybe you're out in the sun too much. Maybe you have a background. Where's your mother from?" Barnett moved closer to me. The smell of alcohol rolled out of his pores. I was surprised his clothes weren't dripping with it.

I didn't want to answer. But this was the acting president of the Americas, and I could recognize the ton of shit I'd stepped into. "Puerto Rico," I stammered.

He nodded knowingly. "Thought so. Latina. Nice. . . . During the occupation, I linked up with my fellow soldiers in units all over the South. We negotiated with the Accordance to stand down. It was the Federal's fight with the ETs, not ours. We saw a chance to rise again, we took it. Now, from Richmond to Tampa, ain't nothing but the right kind of churches, and the right kind of folk. And you know what?"

I shook my head. I didn't.

"We all still have problems. The poverty, that didn't go away. Those people out there, they're still facing seeing their children get drafted. Or 'volunteered.' That's why they're angry. Angry because they can't eat. Because they barely have any work to go around, unless it's for the Accordance. Angry because there's still some war off in the distance. And they're angry at me. I thought it would get better. I was wrong. And now, I know things. The Accordance: They've shown me what's coming. And I'm going to eat, screw, and party until I drop dead. I'd recommend you try the same."

Anais smoothly appeared next to us both. "Mr. President, your presence is needed."

Barnett glanced over at the two Arvani in their mechanized water tanks waiting for him. "Well, fuck. Here we go. Time to be obsequious and do my duty."

Anais held up an open palm with a pair of blue pills in it. "Your personal aide suggested I pass these on."

"Ah." Barnett picked up one of them and eyed it. "You're going to make me sober up. Do you know how much expensive bourbon it took for me to get to where I am right now? Never mind, rhetorical question."

He swallowed the pills dry, blinked, and took a deep breath.

Anais indicated that Barnett should go first, but the president grabbed his shoulder. "The Arvani are going to lecture me. Before I go, Anais, make sure this boy is taken care of. If the Accordance bayoneted a kid out there, that mob outside would have overrun my estate."

"The capitol building, you mean?" Anais prompted.

Barnett waved his hand. "Capitol, estate, personal palace. President, ruler, puppet. My head on a pike: We'll see it happen at some point when they get over the walls. I just would rather have some more fun while there's still some life in me yet without some goddamned Accordance soldier screwing me over early. Struthiforms can't tell the difference between a child and a fully grown human because the walking drumsticks lay eggs and leave them, so they don't even understand what a child is. See, that's the problem with aliens on the ground. They're alien. Which I keep saying. But who the fuck listens to me? I'm just the acting president."

Anais glanced at me. "He can't be in the publicity program. There have to be consequences for what he did."

"Let the CPF give him a chance to prove himself. He stood between a soldier in full armor and a kid. Do your president a solid: Send him to the Hamptons instead of . . . what you're planning."

I looked at them both, but they avoided my eyes.

Anais finally sighed. "Okay, Mr. President. The Hamptons it is."

5

The hopper rattled and shook as it flew us over the American East Coast. I sat on a plain bench with Anais on one side of me, and on the other side an unshaven, older Colonial Protection Forces soldier who looked supremely bored.

I twisted my wrists. The zip ties cut into my skin, but neither of them had cared about my complaints. Right now, I was still technically a prisoner. A recruit who'd gotten in the way of the Accordance military doing their job.

The soldier propped up two prosthetic legs against the bench on the other side, leaned back with crossed arms, and closed his eyes.

"Anais, what about my parents?" I asked.

"What about them?"

"Are they going to be executed, now that everything is changing? What's going to happen?" I was scared that a split-second decision was going to ruin it all. All the sacrifices I'd made. "Anais, please help. If everything I've done is for nothing—"

"Help? Help?" Anais groaned. "I've done nothing but help

you and you've blown it. Who *helped* coach you to sell your story better? Who shepherded you kids around the world? Who ran into the fucking fire to drag your ass out to safety? I did. I did that. Now you're whining about more help. You know what you haven't done? Have you thanked me? Once? Have you ever thought about the fact that all of this isn't just about you?"

I pulled back from his anger. "It's your job," I protested.

"My job is to take willing recruits and parade them around the world for PR purposes. If I really gave a shit about nothing but my job, I'd only take recruits from families that worked closely with the Accordance. I wouldn't have helped you save your parents' lives by letting you into the program. To be honest, I may not be making that mistake again."

I resisted Anais's words. I couldn't find it in my heart to give him credit for doing the good thing. It was the minimum.

And yet. He was right. He could make things simpler. And he hadn't. And that said . . . something.

"As for your parents," Anais said, "I don't see the point in sending a recruit to training knowing his parents are about to die. That shit isn't going to make a good soldier. No, the deal stands. The deal stands because you were on live TV, standing in front of a child. You risked your life to protect, and we're spinning that. You're about to get the promotion that you've been begging for, because you want to protect more than just a child in a riot."

"A promotion?" I was zip-tied and locked to a bench in an Accordance vehicle. There were no portholes, just turbulence and whining motors. I didn't feel like I was getting a promotion.

"Promotion to combat. Real action."

The old soldier on my other side spoke up. "Congratulations, boot. You're about to become cannon fodder. You could have spent your whole enlistment being an actor in uniform. Simple exercises, safe on Earth. Now, no more TV appearances. No champagne with politicians. No handshakes. No jogging along nice boulevards with security."

Anais smiled sadly. "He's right."

The hopper pitched up and shook, the engines whined as we suddenly dumped velocity. The CPF soldier staggered up and slid the side door open with a grunt.

"Your home for the next couple days," he shouted back over the wind.

We glided through the air over the Hamptons. Obstacles littered the beach. The remains of bombed-out mansions used for target practice slumped over into sandy grasses. Bunkers pocked the landscape like inside-out barnacles, hoppers lined up on landing pads around them. Barracks clustered around bulldozed pits, and I saw several squads of humans running in formation.

The hopper slid over it all and dropped the last hundred feet down to the beach, kicking up a maelstrom of sand and water.

Anais cut the zip ties loose and pointed at the door. "If you make it back, look me up," he said, not unkindly. "I'll buy you your first drink."

The soldier grabbed my collar. "Welcome to the first day of the rest of your war," he shouted into my ear.

Then he threw me out of the hopper and into the storm.

I choked and tried to cover my face as wet sand blasted my exposed skin. The hopper eased back into the sky, and the flurry stilled. I wiped caked sand away from my face and stood up.

Four other hoppers slapped down onto the beach. Three or four recruits tumbled out the doors of each hopper, landing awkwardly in the sand and staggering in the blast of air as the vehicles rose back into the sky.

We milled around, pulling closer together as we watched the insectile aircraft skim out over the ocean, then bank south together in formation.

"Anyone know where we're supposed to go next?" a girl nervously asked. She hugged herself, and her wide-eyed fear created a sort of boundary around her. Everyone stepped back, as if worried they might catch it.

We glanced up at the sound of a loud buzz. A carapoid, wings fully extended, finished a ten-foot jump over our heads and landed in the sand near the water.

We all gaped. No one had ever seen one of the beetle-like aliens in armor. It looked like a mobile tank with scuttling feet as it moved toward us, holding a raised baton in one of its knobby hands.

It jammed the stick into a puddle of salt water. The stick sizzled and spat, and the puddle of water exploded from the jolt cast by the mother of all cattle prods.

We all reflexively jumped back. "Jesus," someone muttered. "Is that our drill instructor?"

"What are any of you good for?" the carapoid asked in a hiss augmented by the heavy segments of gray armor molded to its mandibles. They creaked as it moved. "Do you have any survival instincts? Or will you be the first to die when it gets really ugly? Do you have any talents to offer me? Because right now you all seem bewildered and scared, and that's not what I need. But maybe I have trouble interpreting your ugly alien faces and you're all ready to go. Either way, you are here so that we learn where best you might serve."

The carapoid moved over the sand, thudding its way around the group, eyeing us through compound eyes protected by scarred blast-proof goggles backlit with heads-up display information.

It tapped the prod against the armored carapace. Tick, tick, tick.

None of us said anything.

"The Accordance sacrifices much to keep an umbrella over your heads, and you're all cowering on this beach like hatchlings on a mother's stomach," the carapoid said. "So let's shake you loose and see whether you can scuttle on your own, yes?"

We all looked at each other.

Tick. Tick. Tick. "See that pier out there? I'm going to start walking toward it after you. Anyone I catch up with, I'm going to tap to encourage them. Ready? Go."

For a second we all remained frozen. Then the carapoid reached out with the prod and gently tapped the nearest recruit. The tip sizzled and snapped, and electricity danced across his shoulder.

He screamed and leapt into motion, staggering away from the carapoid drill instructor. I needed no similar convincing. I ran.

I'd been on a hunger strike the last week. This week I'd been drinking punch and flying around the world to parade myself as a new recruit. I was jet-lagged and bewildered. Out of breath.

Smaller, faster recruits than me ran past as I struggled to keep to the middle of the pack, highly aware that just a few people struggled on behind me in the wet sand.

Zap! I glanced behind to see the girl with wide eyes eat sand as the carapoid got within reach and tapped her.

She lay facedown on the beach, quivering, as several of the other girls gave her and the drill instructor a wide berth to pelt for the pier. They passed me by; I'd slowed down as I'd looked behind.

I snapped my attention forward and ran like hell, passing a purple-haired girl wearing a leather jacket and jeans. She glanced over at me, and her eyes glinted silver in the sunlight. A couple years older than me, than most of the recruits, she looked pissed, not scared like the rest of us.

We all made it to the piers. I grabbed one of the weathered pylons and panted, holding myself up.

"This won't do," the alien drill instructor said as it trundled up to the heaving, exhausted mess of us scattered around the pylons. It moved around on its many legs to face back down the beach, then turned back to us. "Again!"

It squeezed the prod. Sparks ran threateningly up and down it.

The group took off. But the girl with the silver eyes walked up to the carapoid. "This is stupid," she said calmly.

I stayed to watch, still catching my breath, ready to run like hell.

"What?"

"You've figured out who can run faster," she said. "But what the fuck does that have to do with who can fight the best? Unless you're planning on putting us into battles where we run away from the enemy a lot."

The carapoid rubbed its forehands together, making a cricket-like chirp. "Now, there's some spit," it said. "Well done. You're right. This exercise tells us nothing about you other than who can run the fastest, and that's not all we're looking for. There will be more tests, don't you worry about that. But what it also tells us is—"

It slammed her on the chest with the prod. She fell back against the pylon behind her, but surprisingly kept standing.

From her jacket rose a wisp of smoke, and she quickly shucked it off and let it drop to the sand by her feet.

"It also tells us who follows orders! Now follow my damn orders and run!"

We both took off down the beach.

A boy with thick shoulders stood on a chair in the center of the mess hall. His skin dripped salt water from his grays, and he'd shaved his head down to the scalp to reveal a custom CPF Earth-and-triangle tattoo on the back of his neck.

For the whole day we'd been run back and forth down the beach. Until recruits dropped to the sand and wouldn't move. Until we coughed, our lungs burned, and our muscles gave out.

Human medics checked over recruits with burn marks on their skin as we milled about and eyed the kitchen's empty counters. The food that had been left out had been snapped up by the runners who got to the mess hall first.

Runners like the kid with the South African accent standing on the chair.

"Today, you learned something about yourselves," he shouted at us. "About the warriors you really are. Or aren't. Over the next few days, we will find out who the true fighters are, and who will be our support staff mopping the barracks while we fight to protect Earth!"

“Sounds like a lot of bullshit,” I muttered.

Someone next to me snorted. I hadn’t realized I’d said that out loud. I was more tired than I realized. She nodded though. “His name’s Ken Awojobi. He was on my transport in. His family is in deep with the Accordance. He’s on the officer track, and he knows it. Been training and studying for this his whole life. A chance to serve, gain rank, then come out high for something in Accordance civil service. Maybe run a partition, or something nice like that.”

I wasn’t too tired to smile and hold a hand out. “I’m Devlin,” I said.

“Cee Cee.” Cee Cee was a head shorter than me. She’d pulled her blond hair back in a tight ponytail. The corners of her eyes fluoresced with processor ink tattoos. Extra augmentation.

“What is he doing?” I asked out loud.

Ken had pulled out a pair of clippers. “You, grab him.”

A nearby recruit squirmed and kicked at the two lean recruits pinning him down. Ken grabbed his head and the clippers bit down.

“This is crazy,” I said, looking around for the drill instructor.

“It’s all a test,” Cee Cee said. “Look.” I followed her eyes to the upper corners of the room.

“What?”

“Cameras. I can sense their link-ups.” She tapped the nano-ink beside her eyes. “They’re watching us. All the time. We’re being studied. Smile.”

“Just keep moving and keep people between us and the idiot with the clippers,” I muttered, and tried to put a hand on her lower back. A bit of showmanship that I couldn’t help.

But my plan didn’t work. Ken spotted the movement. He swaggered over and flipped the clippers on and off. “Worried about losing a little hair? Think it'll mess with your good looks?" He glanced at Cee Cee and smiled.

"Look," I said. "They have official barbers; if we're going to get shaved down, they'll do it." Ken didn't need to parade around as if he were in charge. Although, from what Cee Cee said, he probably would end up being in charge anyway.

"Oh, but this is *tradition*," Ken said.

"I don't care," I said. Why was I bristling so much? "It's not your place."

Ken's eyes flashed. "Not my place?"

"Look—" As I said that, Ken grabbed my head with one hand. "Hey!"

"I know who you are, asshole," he hissed. I jerked back from him, the clippers snarling and catching my neck. Hair fell down between us as I twisted away. Two of Ken's "assistants" grabbed my arms. I tried to yank free, but they were strong, their fingers bruising me as they shoved me down onto a table. "Seen you on TV. Seen your parents. You're traitors, anti-Accordance. So you might fool some people, by pretending to join. But anyone who looks closely can see you don't give a shit about all this. You're half-assing it."

Metal ran up my scalp and more hair flurried around me and landed on the table shoved against my face.

"Fuck you." I squirmed and tried to kick backward. I got a knee, and a curse.

"There's some real, actual fight in him," Ken announced to the room. "He's not as much of a pacifist coward as his parents after all." He dug an elbow into the back of my neck and I gasped. The clippers nicked my left ear, and I felt a little trickle of blood run down the lobe.

Ken shoved himself away from me, and I jumped up, my face hot with humiliation. Fists balled, I growled, but he just laughed and stepped away as his newfound groupies made a wall in front of him and shook their heads.

Five recruits now surrounded him like bodyguards.

Six on one. Two of them older, large biceps under their gray T-shirts.

I was going to get my ass handed to me. And Ken knew it. He smiled, daring me to try. Everyone else had seen the logic of not trying it.

Fast. I'd have to get past them and focus on getting just one punch in. One punch to show the room that Ken wasn't invincible. To make a point.

To prove that I wasn't a coward to everyone watching.

"Lights out in two minutes!" a human drill instructor shouted from across the room. "Anyone not in an assigned bunk will spend the night on the beach with me. Your names are on your bunks. Go!"

The larger threat scattered us.

I jogged through the hallway, looking for the bunks, exhausted, hungry, still tense with anger. I stopped when I saw a water fountain.

"We don't have time for that," someone passing me hissed.

I kept drinking water. Until I felt like something in my stomach was going to burst. Part of me was trying to fill that hole the hunger had excavated in me. But I also had another trick up my sleeve.

The end of the corridor opened up into an almost warehouse-sized room. Hundreds of bunk beds in rows in the open area. To the back, bathrooms and showers.

I jumped into my lower bunk. Looked around. "Hey, upstairs," I asked the bunk above me. "Is it all boys in one row and girls in the next?"

"As far as I can see," the voice replied tiredly.

"Huh."

"I wouldn't get out of the bed at night, though." The bed shifted, and a brown face peered over at me. Curved gang sigils marked the massive forearm dangling over the side.

"Why not?"

"Force fields. I got here a day early. Our overlords aren't interested in anyone here getting into trouble at night. We might as well be in a jail cell come lights-out."

And just as he said it, the lights cut out.

There was some muttering chatter between the rows—invitations—and then a sound like a bug getting zapped in one of those bug lights. Someone screamed and swore.

"See?" Upstairs laughed.

"Shit. When do they turn back off?"

"Hoping to make friends with someone you met?"

"No, I drank a lot of water. I'm going to have to pee," I told him. "I wanted to wake up early, but now I'm wondering how I take a piss in the middle of the night."

My bunkmate's face came back over the edge. "Up early," he said thoughtfully. "That's smart. What's your name again? I saw it when I got to the bunk, but forgot."

"Devlin," I said.

"Rakwon." Rakwon extended his hand over the edge of the bed. I shook it. It was a big, strong hand. I felt like a child.

"You play sports?" I asked.

"No. Everyone asks. We run big in my family. I guess it's because my mother's Samoan. Dad's from Queens. My brother played rugby, but quit after he lost a tooth." He laughed. "If you don't piss the bed tonight, wake me up with you. The fields turn off right before breakfast. Getting there first while everyone is getting their bearings is a good idea."

Another loud zap, this time swearing in a decidedly female timbre.

"The fields are up across beds as well. So it's only bunkmates that can move around. Get some sleep, don't pee yourself. Wake me up when you get up."

We converged on breakfast like a barbarian horde, up before the force fields around our bunks dropped out, waiting for the telltale shimmer in the air to fade away.

The line cooks ladled porridge-like goop into divots in our trays. At the end of the counters were squares of what looked like unwrapped energy bars near large baskets of fist-sized gray blobs.

"What is this shit?" I asked.

Rakwon pointed with a spoon at the goop. "Slurry. Made in Accordance vats and perfectly balanced with all the nutrients a human digestive system needs. You can live off it forever."

"And this?" I shoved the gray blob. It wobbled.

"Energy drink, kinda. Sharpens focus. And hydrates. You can eat the film that holds it together." Rakwon bit into his blob and slurped hard to get the liquid out before it dribbled out from the collapsing spheroid. Then, like slurping spaghetti, he sucked the remains in and chewed them.

"It looks like snot."

Rakwon grinned. "Keep the energy bar in your pocket for later," he said, sliding his square into a pocket of his grays. I did the same.

The slurry tasted vaguely like oatmeal . . . if I used my imagination. I spilled most of the lightly coconut-flavored orb juice down my chin. And I didn't care. We'd got in first, got our table, and had food.

"Holy shit," Cee Cee said. I looked up, mouth full of food, to see the girl with silver eyes and purple ponytail pass us by.

"She tried to stand down the instructor on the beach," I said.

"Those eyes." Cee Cee shook her head. "They would've had to tattoo in the nano-ink with a gun right to the open eyeball."

Rakwon stopped eating and put down his plastic fork. I swallowed; my appetite fled as I thought about a needle striking an eyeball.

"No sedation." Cee Cee winced.

The girl wore her grays now. No street gear. No piercings. But she'd somehow not had her hair shaved down. The purple stood out as she walked between the tables. I noticed processor tats ran down her biceps and forearms in galaxy-like swirls and swoops.

"Hey, hey you!" a smiling boy shouted. "Where *you* from?"

She stopped. He stood in her way. They were face-to-face, food tray to food tray. "Bronx," she said.

"Nah, I mean, where are you *from* from?"

"Castle Hill," she said, looking quite unimpressed.

The boy shook his head. "No, no. Like, where are your *parents* from?"

"Wisconsin and Jersey," she said.

"No, no, you know what I mean."

The girl could have blended into a crowd in some South Asian country. She shoved her interrogator and walked around him with a "Get out of my way." Rakwon laughed. "Bronx," he said.

"Better question is, what's her name," Cee Cee murmured. "She's a walking supercomputer with attitude."

The boy didn't get out of her way, though. He moved back to stand in front of her. "You ain't too polite; I'm just asking you a question," he insisted.

She shoved him again with the flat of her hand. He dropped his tray and pushed her right back. Hard enough she flew back and sprawled hard on the ground.

Everyone froze.

Except for the purple-haired girl. She grabbed a nearby chair and kicked a leg out from it. The metal screws broke right off with the impact.

Then she hit him across the side of the face, using the chair leg like a bat.

He dropped to the ground. She kicked him in the ribs twice, then once in the face. She tossed the leg aside and stepped back, hands in the air, as two human drill instructors ran across the room at them. "He needs help," she called out to them. "He fell into that chair really hard."

They tackled her and dragged her away.

"Washed out in one day," someone said in an awed voice.

There was only cold satisfaction on her face, though. Like she was done playing a silly game she hadn't wanted in on to begin with.

"Glad I didn't say good morning to that one," Rakwon muttered.

"She seemed cute and cuddly to me," I said, still staring at the door she'd been dragged out through.

"A real teddy bear," Cee Cee said. "I'm sure you wouldn't mind trying to put an arm around *her* at night."

"I have a feeling it'd be like hugging a porcupine," Rakwon said.

"Move out!" a carapoid drill instructor shouted from the doors. *"Move out!"*

+ + + +

The drill instructor the previous day hadn't lied. We weren't just running up and down the beach. Now we were tested in other areas. In a room with screens mounted on clear plastic stands, I stared at a holographic display of random parts floating in the air.

"This is a puzzle," said the carapoid alien instructor. "You will now solve it. Attention will be paid to how fast you solve it."

Simple enough, I thought, looking at the pieces.

Then I noticed the instructor tugging out a fire hose from a box in the wall.

Wait a second. . . .

"Waterproof screens," Rakwon moaned.

I didn't even have time to swear. A powerful jet of frigid water knocked me back from my console. The carapoid instructor gleefully swept the stream of pounding water across the room. By the time I'd put the three-dimensional puzzle together, my fingers shook so hard I could barely manipulate the images.

To warm us all up, they ran us up and down the beach.

Last ones in didn't get dinner. So I went hungry again.

By lights-out I didn't have the energy to talk to Rakwon. But I did stop to drink enough water to get up early again.

Day three we built a tower out of large logs, and defended it against other teams on the beach. Ken led a team. He buried my face in the sand, choking me. "You're too slow to eat dinner. Chew on sand, coward," he hissed.

Maybe the girl with the purple hair had the right idea. I was going to have to kneecap Ken and get dragged away to a prison to get away from all this.

Rakwon and Cee Cee picked me up to brush the sand off.

I didn't want to meet Cee Cee's eyes. I felt half as tall as I was. But she joined Rakwon and me at breakfast again.

"It is what it is," Rakwon said philosophically, watching me glower. "Ken's officer bound. He's not worth the trouble."

"He's an asshole," I said. He was a collaborator.

But then, everyone here was a collaborator. Me too. I couldn't use that word out loud.

"He's excited to be here and he's well trained," Cee Cee said. "He's a good soldier. We're all ready to kick ass, right, recruit?"

I looked around. All of us in our grays. Training. Running. At Accordance's beck and call. I couldn't tell if Cee Cee was being sardonic or genuinely drinking it all in.

I kept my head down and mouth shut. I just needed to be adequate. So that my parents could live. So that I could survive this.

Just live through it, I told myself. Stay human.

On the fourth day, the mix of alien and human instructors started picking us off for interviews in small offices. I sat in front of a human instructor, a middle-aged man with graying hair and weary lines around his eyes. Behind him, a struthiform instructor rustled feathers and glanced at a screen in his feathered, clawlike hands.

"We've been watching you," the human instructor said. "You're avoiding trouble. Following orders. Getting up early for breakfast: Nice trick with the water fountain. So, now it's time to think about how best you can be of use to the Colonial Protection Forces. How do you envision your future service?"

"I was thinking cook," I told them both. "Peeling potatoes.

Making stews. I could be a great sous-chef for the CPF, I think."

"Cook?" the alien asked.

"I've also heard some armies have bands, right? I used to play flute. . . ." I had the most earnest voice, and kept my face straight. But what else was I going to do? Ask them for the most dangerous position?

I just wanted to show up and do what I'd promised: no more, no less.

The human instructor cut me off. "You're not going to be in a band."

"There's a book in the indigenous literature section of the common library on this base," the struthiform said, craning its neck forward to regard me. "*Catch-22*. The concept behind the title is that you'd have to be crazy to ask for missions and sane if you didn't, but if you were sane you had to fight in the human war. But if you fought, that meant you were crazy, and shouldn't. And if you didn't want to fight, that meant you were sane and had to. See?"

I didn't. I hadn't read it, either. Most human classics had been not banned but "de-emphasized" in schools. There were older, superior Arvani sagas. And shows.

"You done having fun?" the human instructor asked. "Because here's the thing, recruit, it's all going to shit out there. And we're going to need all the bodies we can get."

He waved a hand. The desk between us filled with an orbital image of a world. Greenish clouds and unfamiliar, patchy continents.

"This is happening. Tens of light-years away. But as far as the Accordance is concerned, it's right next door and getting closer every day." The daylight faded; the planet spun into night.

Clusters of circular city lights in the planet's dark flickered. Then died. A cluster here, then another there. When the planet spun back into daylight, pillars of smoke streamed up to join the clouds.

The instructor swiped the image away. Flicked through videos of cities, unnaturally high Accordance spires and more black, treelike skyscrapers slumping over to the ground as their legs splintered and gave out. Bodies flicked by. Struthiforms, carapoids, a long-legged furry thing with surprisingly human-like eyes. The corpses lay still.

"We just lost an entire planet," the instructor said. Something large descended. Eldritch, asymmetrical, a city-sized jellyfish dropping out from the skies. Translucent, and yet it sucked all the light away as it moved.

"Conglomerate host-ship. Atmospheric entry class," the struthiform said coldly.

"Those black, flea-like things coating it, they're living ablative shields. They stick themselves onto the host-ship and use their backs to protect it as it enters the atmosphere. Once it's down, they detach and forage for food."

"Forage?" Millions of crispy shells fell clear of the shivering host-ship. Most broke as they struck the ground. The survivors, steaming hot, ripped into the corpses on the ground.

"The Accordance traced the home world of those creatures," the struthiform said. "They used to be a space-faring civilization. Intelligent. Now they're living heat shields. And that's it. Their monuments dust, their cities lost. Covered in a living shell of Conglomerate computational slurry that's slowly eating its way down into the core of their world. They reshape whole systems to their needs, and entire species to their whims. They love finding new biomes, like Earth's. They'll sample our DNA, investigate, catalog, and then reshape us into whatever they have a need for. They already tried this with the Pcholem once. That's why we need fighters, Devlin. Because we're losing worlds to them. We need more fighters."

The human instructor jumped back in. "Your test scores from the past few days are back. We think you're well suited for one particular arm of the Colonial Protection Forces."

I was still thinking about living ships discarding their heat shields to gobble alien corpses. "What do you think I'm so good at?"

"We're creating an all-human fighting force. Human officers. Human fighters. We need to build human expertise up, and stop depending on Accordance-led human squads so that we can grow the CPF's native strength. You're going to join the first all-human light enhanced infantry regiment."

Light enhanced infantry. Just enough powered armor that a human could keep up with enhanced infantry in the Accordance military. Just enough power that we would be put in the middle of alien-versus-alien action.

These two instructors sounded excited. As if I should be proud of the chance. I bet they sounded like this even when they were handing someone a toilet scrubber and explaining that the recruit's new mission would be to scrub toilets onboard an Accordance space station.

"There's a new training center on the dark side of the moon: Icarus. Named after the crater that surrounds the whole area it sits in," the human instructor said. "Congratulations, you ship out for Icarus tonight."

7

"Listen up!" drill instructors both alien and human shouted at us as we crowded together down on the cold morning beach. "You will bring nothing with you. You will leave all personal objects behind on this beach before getting inside transport craft."

Hoppers flew in over the Long Island Sound. They kicked up saltwater spray as they overflew the beach, and then dropped down to pick up recruits at the front of the line.

"Devlin!"

Rakwon and Cee Cee broke out of line, like many of us milling around the back, to say good-bye. It had been only a few days, and yet it felt like a graduation of some kind as we quickly hugged each other. "Where are you going?" I asked.

"Peacekeeper forces," Rakwon said. "Manhattan. If I keep in line, in a few years I could get a promotion."

"Peacekeeper? They gave me a whole big story about being desperate for soldiers in the CPF."

Rakwon shrugged. "They were talking about the 'repacification' process. We've been out of the news loop here all week. I think there are more riots or something. Well, at least I'll get to see my family on weekends. I can take a message to your family for you, if you want."

"No." They didn't want to hear from me. "What about you, Cee Cee?"

"Recruits: in line!" an instructor shouted.

"Orbital counterforces. Drones and links," Cee Cee shouted as she ran back to her place. "I might even get to fly a Stingray . . . if they pass the human pilots emergency authorization act."

"Good luck," Rakwon said as he ambled quickly away.

"No!" an all-too-familiar voice screamed from behind us all. We turned to see Ken dragged out through the doors and thrown into the sand. He staggered to his feet, lurching back toward the struthiform instructors that had thrown him out. His voice broke with emotion as he screamed, "You can't do this. This isn't how it's supposed to be! I'm from a Landed Family! I was born, and trained, to be an officer. Do you even know how much was invested in me?"

The nearest struthiform slapped him with the back of a feathery hand. Ken fell awkwardly into the sand. "Get in line," the alien snapped.

Ken crawled on his hands and knees, nose dripping blood down onto the sand. In just a single morning he'd fallen a long way from being the strutting leader of his instant crew. He crawled into line behind me, and someone helped him to his feet.

He looked at me with bruised eyes and a swelling lip. "You too?" he asked numbly.

"Light infantry," I confirmed, not quite sure whether I should enjoy his humiliation or hate the aliens that had backhanded him so casually. "I'm going to Icarus."

I wanted to ask if he was okay. But he very obviously wasn't. It was a stupid thing to want to ask. I didn't bother.

Ken swallowed. "You know what happens to human infantry."

"What?"

"We die."

The hoppers landed us at the flowerlike structures of the new Lakita Singh Air and Space Port. Instructors pushed and herded us into a launch terminal, then yelled at us some more.

"This is your buddy," a human instructor said. He shoved a nervous recruit at me. "Put your hand on your buddy's shoulder. Hold tight. Now, you are responsible for your buddy. Anything happens to your buddy, it'll happen to you. When I ask you where your buddy is, you won't tell me, because you'll be holding your buddy's shoulder and it'll be so obvious where he is, you won't have to say anything. Got it?"

I nodded.

The instructor shook his head, like my father when trying to teach me some complex piece of math that I just couldn't quite get the first time around. "You don't nod. You answer with a 'yes' and an 'instructor' in there, son. The Hamptons may be run by aliens that don't allow us to use 'sir,' but we can work around that. You're still CPF. And it'll be all-human CPF for you lot. So my rules apply. Let's try that again: got it?"

"Yes . . . instructor!" I fumbled. His eyes narrowed, then he nodded and moved on to the next recruit.

"What's your name?" my shoulder buddy asked. We were standing awkwardly facing each other, an arm each on a shoulder, like at a dance.

"Devlin. You?"

“Keiko.”

We’d been lined up against the walls of the terminal. This was a wing for launches headed for orbit, not flights around the world. Since the occupation, the Accordance had dismantled most of the smaller airline hubs in favor of incredibly high-speed rail. But international flights and flights to space were still served.

LSP had once been something else, before the aliens had deemed it unusable and demolished it. Another set of letters. “At least,” my father had told me, “they kept a human name on the port.”

Most of the humans in the port flaunted expensive suits and waited in glassed-off areas with subdued lighting. They sat on lounge chairs where attendants came by to take their orders. We watched them eat, laugh, and sashay around.

Someone pushed a pink dog in a stroller back and forth across the waiting area, cooing at it, feeding it tiny snacks.

The hushed, quiet space behind that glass could have been mine. I could have been mixing with those upper-class civilians, enjoying finger food and traveling the world. If I hadn’t thrown away my usefulness as a propaganda tool.

Now . . . I rubbed my short hair.

What was taking so long? We’d been just sitting here for twenty minutes, hands on shoulders, bored.

“Look at that,” Keiko said with wonder in his voice. “I saw her get hauled off for beating a kid up. You saw that, right?”

I leaned far forward. At the very end of the line the girl with silver eyes and still-purple hair sat on the ground as two human instructors conferred over her.

“*Smell* that,” I said, my attention drifting across the hall as my stomach growled.

For those in a hurry, a Brooklyn brownstone had been pulled apart, brick by brick, and painstakingly reassembled in the terminal. And on the steps, in front of it, an "authentic" food cart sold hot dogs and cheeseburgers.

"Did you get a chance to eat before getting shoved out to the beach?" Keiko asked.

"No," I said. "Look, we're about to be shot off to who the hell knows where. We've been drinking balls of juice in round slime containers. Because it's optimal and easy to feed us that way. This might be our last chance to eat something real for a long, long time."

"We have to stay put," Keiko said. "They'll kill us. . . ."

I looked down the line. The instructors were still focused on paperwork and the purple-haired girl. "Last chance," I hissed. "Even if I get in trouble: It'll be all on me. I promise, it'll be worth it."

Recruits on either side had been listening in. "Just grab my shoulder when he goes," someone suggested.

"How you gonna pay?" someone else asked.

I glanced back down the line. The instructors had their backs to me. I let go of Keiko.

"Shit, man, don't do this," he whined.

I lit out away from the group, quickly, just to get distance. Then I walked casually over. "Hey," I called out.

The older lady at the cart looked startled. Her blue eyes darted back and forth. "I can't help you run, son," she hissed. "It's humans-only in this terminal anyway, you can't go anywhere without passing a checkpoint."

"No," I spread my hands. "This is our last chance to get any real food. Before . . ."

She let out a deep breath.

"Look, my father's name is Thomas Hart. I don't have any

way to pay on me, they took everything away, but if you contact him, he'll . . ."

"What do you want?" she asked quickly. She just wanted to get rid of me, I realized.

"Anything I can carry," I said quickly. She slid me a box of doughnuts and five hot dogs on a cardboard tray. I eased back across into the line.

"Holy shit, holy shit," Keiko hissed as I slid back into line. "Holy shit."

"Come on. Pass these along. Hurry up! Drop the box on the floor when we're done, put a doughnut in your pocket, a hot dog in the other." I stuffed my hot dog into my mouth.

Oh man. Never had street food tasted . . . So. Fucking. Good.

"Move on up!" the instructors shouted, turning around, their paperwork done. Actually, no, I realized: A struthiform instructor had arrived. The human instructors had been waiting for the real leadership to show up.

The doughnut scraped sugar on the outside of my pocket, but I wiped it off best I could.

"Let's go! Keep it moving! Get aboard the jumpship." I chewed my hot dog surreptitiously as I passed the instructors waving us through down to our new transport.

The wedge-shaped jumpship's blistered and pockmarked skin, which I'd glimpsed near the docking tube, meant it had seen quite a few reentries. There were no portholes, no screens. Just ribbed metal hull and foam seats for us. Two carapoid pilots sat behind a bulkhead and door, however. They shut it as we entered.

"Buckle in. You should know how to use a buckle. So get it done already! You, sit. Sit there. With your buddy."

Minutes later the ship rose through the air. I could feel engine pods under our feet, and then even heavier Accordance engines kicking on behind us. This was no hopper. The engines behind us growled with energy and shoved us back into our seats. Manhattan's Accordance-spired skyline fell away as we tilted toward the clouds and flew up.

With alacrity. The pressure of acceleration continued to press on my chest. Whenever I thought the squeezing had to stop, it continued to press harder.

Until, with a gasp, it went away.

Weightlessness. A big smile grew on my face, despite myself. There were no portholes, but I knew we were in orbit. I knew that from here, if I could see anything, I'd be looking down at the continents and the curve of the Earth.

"What *the fuck* is this?" an instructor asked, unbuckling herself to rise up into the air to grab at something.

It was a doughnut, trailing sugar glaze in the air.

"What is unauthorized food doing on *my* transport?" the instructor shouted. Her ponytailed hair bobbed behind her as she looked around. "Who did this?"

She only got a series of blank looks from my row.

Another instructor bounced up into the air. "Don't anyone unbuckle. We're going to search you. . . ."

Ken raised a hand. "Instructor: I know!"

"Rat motherfucker," I hissed. I barely had time to say even that. One very angry instructor's face was right up in mine as she positioned herself in the air next to me.

Then the other.

The yelling began, and behind them, Ken held up a doughnut of his own and took a bite with a big smile.

It looked like his natural state of asshole had come back online.

8

Everyone poured excitedly out of the docking tube into Tranquility City. "Hey. Gravity," someone said.

"I can't bounce around like those old astronaut videos. What gives?"

"Antigravity in the floors," Ken announced. "When my family visited Tranquility, they told us humans aren't allowed dense attractor technology."

"Antigravity," someone chimed in.

"Dense. Attractor. Technology," Ken repeated.

That was why the one human space station struggling in orbit still had people floating around in it. And our transport, a cheap craft used to move recruits around, had none either.

But somewhere underfoot, Accordance engineers had laid down a grid of material that pulled us all down toward it. Immensely expensive, and done just so that they could be comfortable here on the moon.

The cargo bay's vaulted ceilings stretched far overhead, like a giant's ribcage. Robotic forklifts with long, articulated, spider-like arms scurried around the football-sized open floor, pulling square containers off five-story racks that they sometimes had to climb up to reach.

"I saw a whole program about the people they flew to the moon to do the construction," Keiko said. This part of the city had been dug out by humans helping run alien-built mining machines. The end of the cargo bay was a massive airlock designed for giants, with train tracks running through it into the bay.

"Okay recruits, keep walking!"

We trooped out of the busy cargo bay in obedient lines and snaked our way into Tranquility City's subways and tunnels. Then up a series of escalators, everyone still making sure to keep a hand on the shoulder of the recruit in front of them.

The familiar architecture of Accordance spires appeared when we broke street level.

"Fuck me," Keiko said. "We're on the surface of the moon."

"Keep moving!" the instructors shouted as we stumbled, looking around.

"Nothing like on a screen," I said, awed and also stumbling after the recruit in front of me.

Translucent material capped the streets between buildings, letting us look up into the black sky. Bright light dripped from luminescent globes and strips, filling shadows and crevices with a soft green light to augment the natural sunlight. Gray hills circled around the city where the streets ended, plunging back underground.

"I thought I'd see stars," someone said.

"Too much light. Washes it out. Just like at a stadium."

"It's Earth," Keiko whispered as we turned the gentle curve of an Accordance skyscraper's base.

It hung in the sky, blue and small. Everyone stopped as

they looked up. The entire line bunched into a crowd. I craned my neck, ignoring the busy street.

"What's that?" someone else asked. A comet-like silver shape high overhead occluded the Earth briefly, casting us in a flitting shadow before moving on.

"A Pcholem ship," someone said. "They came in those ships."

"That *is* a Pcholem. Not a ship. Pcholem."

"What?"

"Move!" a struthiform instructor hissed, coming up alongside us. "Move now."

Carapoids moved around us on the street, and more struthiforms bobbed past to avoid us. The streets ran thick with aliens going about their business. Several water-filled glass bubbles with Arvani inside trundled past.

"It's just us," Keiko said. "We're the only humans out here."

Most humans on the moon worked for the Helium-3 mines, or on Accordance construction.

We kept moving, still looking up for a last glimpse of home, until we passed under another large airlock at the city's edges. Humans glanced at us from several small eateries that lined the edge of the oval common area.

No shiny, green-tinged metal cleaning robots in here. Trash and dirt littered the crosswalks and graffiti filled the walls.

Welcome to the human section.

"I gotta go," Keiko whispered.

"What?"

"Bathroom. We're in a human zone, right? I gotta go."

"The instructors are out for my blood already, now we're going to get noticed again?"

"That's not fair," Keiko said. "As your buddy, I'm going to catch all that shit too. So the least you can do is help me take a dump."

I groaned as Keiko raised a hand and waved.

"What is it?" the nearest instructor asked, her ponytail whipping around.

"I need to use a bathroom, instructor."

"Buddy up. The nearest one is right across the museum. You have ten minutes. If you're not aboard . . ." She let the missing words hang in the air.

I wondered what they did to recruits absent without leave here on the moon. The Accordance owned it outright, now. It didn't belong to humans anymore, even though they could see Tranquility City's lights from Earth.

Humans hadn't been using the planets and their moons, the Accordance had noted. It was better they be developed by a civilization actually able to do so. It would happen anyway. That was the stick. The carrot was the offer to keep autonomy by signing off.

On Earth, humans still demanded the right to run themselves directly despite occupation, and would cause trouble to keep that. Here? The Accordance could do anything they wanted.

Be careful up here, I thought. Make it out the other side.

"Where's the museum, instructor?" Keiko asked.

She pointed between the restaurants across from us. Hand on shoulder, Keiko and I crossed the hundred yards of common area.

The Apollo Cultural Heritage Preservation Site. The pictures I'd seen had never shown it surrounded by a pair of restaurants filled with tired-looking lunar miners in overalls.

On the other side of the translucent doors I saw a familiar boxy shape.

Keiko made a strangled sound. "Bathrooms, here we go." Right outside the museum, between the nearest restaurant and the museum.

“I’m going to let go of your shoulder now,” I said.

“Yeah, whatever.” He scurried inside, and I heard a stall bang shut.

And just on the other side of the wall from where he squatted, something that took humanity decades to create gathered dust in an exhibit. The pinnacle of achievement in outer space. The farthest a human had ever gone from our world. The Apollo Lunar Module descent stage.

The Accordance had crossed stars. We had made it to the moon.

Keiko clamped his hand on my shoulder and I yelped. “You look deep in thought,” he said.

“Yeah, well.”

We crossed back. “What were you thinking so hard on? How much we’re going to kick ass at training camp?”

I opened my mouth to answer, but the response never came. A wave of hot energy smacked into the back of my head with a roar. The explosion came a split second later. Or, at least, my awareness of it did.

Things spun around me until my head smacked into the steel-and-concrete ground.

Everything faded. I lay still, blinking and looking at the world askew.

The roar hadn’t stopped. It kept thundering on. A wind rushed past me up toward the ceiling. I wiped blood on my sleeves and twisted around. “Keiko?” I croaked.

People ran past us, trying to get through the ten-foot-thick doors that trundled toward each other to seal off the human section. They dodged chunks of metal and dirty moon concrete and just barely slid through.

A flurry of sharp dust whipped around, stinging my throat as I tried to pull in a deep breath.

“Recruits: on board, now!” an instructor shouted. “In, in, in!”

“Keiko!” I staggered back in the direction I’d been tossed from and away from the airlock where the instructor stood. “Keiko.”

“Recruit!”

I glanced back. No gray shapes stood in line anymore. They’d all boarded. Gotten safely inside the craft that would take us to our training camp. If I ran there, I might make it in. They would have to shut the door soon, to stop losing air.

Because that was what the wind was: air getting sucked out of the cracked top of the human section. It had been half-buried under one of the hills surrounding Tranquility City, where all the rock and dirt came from.

Keiko lay next to a chunk of roof, a pool of blood slowly spreading around him. I scrabbled over. A supporting beam the size of a car had pinned his leg, bent it, and trapped him in place.

I saw white bone when I looked underneath. And more blood. It kept pulsing out the ruined mangle of flesh.

He stirred slightly, a moan of pain, but his glassy eyes looked through me as I grabbed his bloody hand and squeezed it. “Hold on!” I shouted. “Just hold on.”

I panted and blinked, dizzy and coughing in the dust still whipping around me. How could I stop the bleeding? We didn’t have belts, and there was so much damn blood.

And I could barely focus. Or breathe.

Hands behind me pushed a mask against my face. “Take a deep breath.”

“Okay. . . .” I turned. Silvered eyes, purple hair. Behind a similar emergency rebreathing mask.

“What’s your name?” she asked.

“Devlin,” I murmured. Then stronger as oxygen cleared my head. “Devlin!”

“I’m Amira.” She kicked off one of her boots and unlaced

it. "Give him air too. You take a couple of pulls, give it to him for a couple."

"Right." My senses rushed back as my brain got moving again. Three deep breaths, then I got the mask on Keiko. "Do you know what to do?"

"I'm reading instructions right now," she said, voice muffled behind the rebreather.

The eyes. The nano-ink tattoos. Like Cee Cee, she could ride invisible bandwidth. A hacker. Full of bioware and other computing and neural hardware. She'd be pulling up entries on how to stop bleeding and following the instructions. I took two pulls on the rebreather, then set it back on Keiko's face. I couldn't tell if he was breathing; there was no fog on the glass visor.

"Hands up!" came an order shouted so loud my ears buzzed. Struthiforms in thick, full-black armor and helmets ran at us. "Hands up, don't move."

Amira was trying to get the shoelace around Keiko's thigh and cinch it. Blood soaked the lace, and her fingers dripped red. I moved in front of her and Keiko, my bloody hands in the air. "We're CPF recruits!" I shouted into the thin air. "We need medical attention for—"

The head struthiform in the wedge formation struck me with a wing hand. I crumpled to the ground, dizzied by the hit. It held my face down in Keiko's muddied blood as another Accordance soldier zip-tied my hands.

"If you continue to struggle, you will be shot."

"I don't understand," I gasped, the dizziness creeping back over me. "We're CPF. Why are you doing this?"

Amira looked over, her face also shoved into the ground. "It was a bomb. A human bomb. All humans in Tranquility are getting arrested."

9

Amira wriggled her shoulders, stretched, and then pulled free of the zip tie. She rubbed her wrists and put the tie on the table between us.

"How did you do that?" I asked.

"Isn't your dad Thomas Hart?"

"Yeah."

"And he didn't teach you to cross your wrists and flex before getting zip-tied? Or how to break them off?"

"We never fought the arrests," I told her. The struthiforms that interrogated me in a separate room had retied my hands in front of me. I held them toward her now. "Can you help?"

"I will. But when they are about to come back, you need to put them back on, got it?"

"Definitely. I'll keep them loose around my wrists."

She pushed a fingernail in and somehow released the catch. The tie opened up, and I massaged my hands. "Thank you. Thank you for coming over."

"You looked ready to pass out," she said. "The rebreather

masks were in a locker near the transport's airlock. Didn't feel right watching you die."

I looked down at the brown flakes on my fingers, and on hers. "Did you get the shoelace tied before they pulled us away?"

Amira waited a beat. "No."

"He wasn't breathing." I refused to look up at her. I kept my head down.

"I know."

I took a deep breath. "I didn't go to any regular schools much, we moved too often. I've been in the middle of protests, riots, arrests. I've seen people shot, but carried away by ambulances quickly. I've never seen that much blood before. It's like something from San Francisco."

"Or earlier," Amira said, somewhat nonchalantly. "Before your dad. When the fighting was violent. The paramedics couldn't get in during Pacification."

"You're not *that* much older than me," I said. "You were, what, eight or nine years old then?"

"Yes," she said.

I imagined a young Amira watching a running gun battle in the middle of a burned-out New Jersey. "And now you're fighting for the Accordance?"

Amira's jaw clenched. "Your parents are still alive and resisting. Lucky you. Mine were executed on a street corner. I survived because if you needed a pass, a way into limited movement areas, then you had to talk to little Amira Singh. For a payment I'd help hack and forge anything. My parents had wanted me to help the cause. The whole family invested in the cost of me taking online classes and apprenticing to older hackers, but all those investors had hungry children who needed me as a meal ticket after their parents were shot. Lucky for them I learn fast. Lucky for them I had the education. Unlucky for them, now, that I've been dragged off and they have no one."

She waved her fingers over her eyes and at the silvered swirls on her arms and neck. "Accordance isn't supposed to sell this on Earth, but there are always black markets where less-than-scrupulous aliens can make money selling us what we can't make ourselves. I can tap into Accordance virtual networks and augmented reality feeds. We'll never be full citizens, but I can at least taste a little of their world. When they caught up to me they gave me a choice: a lifetime sentence, or the CPF. *That*'s why I'm here."

"I'm sorry."

"Fuck 'sorry.' Everyone's sorry the Accordance invaded our world. I'm sorry half my neighborhood fought back. Sorry I detected enforcers coming and hid myself, but couldn't warn the rest of my family. We're sorry that kid died in front of us. I'll bet you're sorry you betrayed your parents to serve in the CPF."

She leaned forward and pulled her zip tie closed with her teeth as I stared at her.

"Someone's coming?" I asked, doing the same.

"Under emergency session, acting president Barnett just forced microchip legislation through," Amira said, letting go of the tie. "Everyone is now going to be sorry that Tranquility was bombed by radicals, because if they want to travel, they'll now need to be tagged like the little pets we are. Everyone's fucking sorry, Devlin. It's the state of the universe these days. But at least you tried to help someone next to you, and that's more than we often get."

The door slid open. An Arvani commander in full matte-black battle gear scuttled through the door. Its eight mechanized tentacles tapped the ground as it approached us.

No water in a tank, like civilian Arvani. This armor form-fitted the alien. Pistons and plates hugged the octopus-like form, sliding and shifting with it as it walked toward us.

Shimmering glass covered the large, unblinking eyes. "Call me Commander Zeus. The sound is close to what I like to think my name begins with, and I hear the name holds import, so I will have it. I'm your new instructor. Of all the indignities piled on me of late, my latest is that all the human instructors at the Icarus camp have been dismissed and your training turned over to me. I had to come pick you apes up myself.

"If I could, I'd leave you here to rot. But that would be more paperwork than just hauling myself down here to drag you out of this room. Let's move."

Commander Zeus turned around.

"No," I said, refusing to get up.

The commander pivoted back, a scary rapid uncoiling movement that happened in the blink of an eye, and regarded me. "No?"

"Tell me what happened to Keiko."

The Arvani didn't move for a second. "Dead."

I'd expected that. I didn't expect it to suck the air out of me even though I'd prepared for it.

"We need to do something," I said. I wasn't sure what. Some kind of ceremony. Something.

Zeus knocked the chair out from under me. I hit the ground with a groan, and the commander squatted over me. "One dead recruit is a tiny speck of shit in a whirlpool," the alien said. "There will be more before your time is over. This is the perspective you should curl your limbs around."

"We still have to respect our fallen," I said. "It's what we do."

"The fallen do not care," Commander Zeus said. "And I do not care 'what you do.' But I will tell you what *I* will do. If you do not follow me out of this room, there will be consequences for your dereliction. I'm sure you can imagine them. I do not care what you choose. My duty to protocol here has been made."

Zeus turned around.

Amira grabbed my arm and helped me up.

"Remember Keiko in your own way," she said. "Let it go for now. Don't put you or your family on the list."

"I had to—"

"I know. But you just pissed off Captain Calamari there. The creature that'll be running our whole world for the next few weeks."

"Commander Calamari," I corrected her.

"No." Amira squinted. "I think it's Captain Calamari for me."

10

The commander's tentacles filled most of the free space in the tiny craft that dropped out of the lunar night, leaving Amira and me to push ourselves as far up against the back bench as we could.

Through the large porthole on my side I watched as we arced high over the cratered mountains in the dark, whipping a mile overhead a desolate landscape punctuated by the occasional grid and piping of lunar mining facilities.

There were so many craters. The Earth-facing side of the moon had been smoother with its seas and plains. The dark side looked as if it had been in a long, losing war: billions of years of constant artillery bombardment, ravaged by the vengeance of outer space's constant barrage of rocks from beyond Earth's orbit.

All around me, as far as I could see right now, was the Icarus crater. It was almost sixty miles wide, and we'd been flying over it for the last couple minutes.

"Big railgun," Amira said. I looked out her porthole. A mile-long bridge-like structure ran along the surface. It held a long pipe in its struts rather than a road, though. "A mining facility. They're taking the processed ore chunks and just shooting them in capsules to wherever in orbit they need to go for Accordance projects."

As we watched, lights danced up and down the trusses and a capsule slightly bigger than the craft we sat in hurtled toward the horizon and rose up into orbit.

A minute or two later, another one followed it.

"Your new home." Commander Zeus tapped an armored tip against the curved screen in front of him.

The lights of the Icarus training facility lit up the horizon, then almost blinded me as we crested a hill. The craft shuddered as the commander fired engines to slow our forward motion to a near stop, leaving us hanging just over the complex.

Below us an entire crater had been capped with a clear dome, then filled with ponds, brush, bridges, obstacle courses, and other objects I couldn't identify.

Four petal-shaped complexes spread out around the capped dome, making it look like a giant clover from above. More half-buried cylinders popped up inside nearby craters.

"The dome allows for a variety of conditions," Commander Zeus explained. "We can heat it, chill it, raise the pressure, lower it. Blow wind. Flood it. Put in any number of atmospheres from a variety of planets. We can create storms, hail, winter, summer. We can change the gravity itself via dense attractor base plates buried under the ground. Your living quarters are off to the sides, your commanders live in the quarters one crater over. Be proud: We invested a lot in this for just humans."

We gently struck a landing pad on top of one of the petals. It pulled us inside, the roof closing overhead after it.

The pad came to a shuddering halt near a row of rovers, their massive balloon-like wheels almost touching each other.

"You're just in time," the commander said. "While you've spent a day sitting around doing nothing, your teammates have had a meal, learned where their rooms are, and are getting ready for their first round of Escape the School."

"Escape the School?" Amira asked.

"I'm told it's a rough translation of a concept we Arvani use in our training. I want to see you all in action."

Recruits strung out in a circle in the natural amphitheater to the back of the capped lunar dome.

We slipped in at the back of the line, taking our place. Most of the recruits were in their late teens, like me. Quite a few in their twenties, though. "War's a young man's game," my father had often said. "One where older statesmen send the patriotic young to settle their elders' disagreements with their blood."

I looked around. Lots of thickly muscled arms and strong backs. I felt like the runt in the back. Whatever came next, I guessed I'd have to depend on quick feet and quick thinking.

Commander Zeus descended on a cabled platform from the top of the dome.

He threw a black ball out with one of his tentacles into the muddy grass in front of the recruits. "The moment your fingerprints touch the ball," he shouted, "it registers that you have possession. It also lights up so you can't hide with it."

We all regarded the ball.

"The aim of this test is to show me who can hold on to the ball the longest."

Someone raised a hand. "What happens to those who hold it the shortest? Or who don't get it at all?"

"Your orders," Zeus said, "are to hold on to it the longest."

Amira stood behind me, her arms folded. "You remember the beach on the Hamptons?" I asked her. "We need to get our hands on that thing. Together."

"One against everyone is going to be hell," she agreed. "A bunch of us against everyone else is going to be more survivable."

"Right. Let's find anyone we know."

We started walking around, looking for recruits we recognized from the trip to Tranquility City.

The platform began to rise back up into the air on its cables, lifting Zeus into a catwalk gallery under the dome.

"One last change in the current," the alien commander shouted. "I will be venting the dome's atmosphere until you pass out to see how you function."

I thought about the choking moon dust lacerating my throat as I struggled to breathe back in Tranquility City.

"Hey, it's Doughnuts," a voice called out. Amira pulled a familiar-looking dark-haired recruit along.

"Nico's in," she said.

"What are the rules?" a recruit down the line shouted up at the retreating platform. It was Ken, I realized. "What are we allowed to do?"

There was no reply.

Amira yanked more people over to me. Our hasty team grabbed shoulders in a huddle. I counted ten of us, mostly all recognizable from the ride to the moon. "Here's the idea," I said. "If any of us can grab it, the rest of us huddle around and protect them. We rotate in, get some holding time, until we've all got hands on it. Then we let it go. Yell 'ball' and we'll surround you. Each of us gets five seconds."

"You sure this will work?" the recruit who'd nicknamed me Doughnuts asked.

"No," I said. "We'll get the shit kicked out of us trying to do it. But you think it'll go any better with us trying it alone?"

A horn blared, an unmistakable start signal.

A scrum instantly developed over the ball. Individuals scrapping around the mud to try to hold on. Legs churned, bodies writhed.

One of the recruits staggered out of the mass of bodies, swore, then threw herself back in with a vicious elbow to someone's neck.

"My finger's broken! Help!" A scraggly boy crawled out and held up a hand. Bone stuck out of the side of his finger and blood ran down his wrist.

But no help came down from the gantry. Or from anywhere else.

Ken approached us, a surprisingly humble nervousness obvious in his body language. "Create a wedge," he said. "I think that'll get us in there."

"There is no '*us,*'" I snarled at him, remembering his elbow digging into the back of my neck as he shaved my head, embarrassing me in front of Cee Cee.

He raised his hands, conciliatory. "Look, I'm sorry about the doughnuts."

"Fuck off," I said, and turned my back. I took several deep breaths, watching the dozens of recruits in front of us fighting like a cluster of weasels over the ball. I glanced back and saw Ken walking away, looking for someone else to join forces with.

"We need all the help we can get," Amira muttered to me.

"Fuck him. We don't need *his* help."

"He was right about wedging in," Amira said.

I grunted. "I guess."

"When do we try for it?" the guy who'd called me Doughnuts asked.

I looked over at Amira's silver eyes. "Our instructors are venting air. When do we start getting dizzy?"

The right corner of her mouth pulled back, a half smile as she figured out what I was thinking. The first time I'd seen that. "Five minutes. More or less."

"I want to eat dinner first tonight, if they're pulling that stunt from the Hamptons again," I said. "So we're just going to stand here and take long, deep breaths. Keep yourself oxygenated. We're going to form up in a triangle, and keep our arms locked together. Biggest up at the spear tip, right? If that scrum moves at all, we slowly track it. Amira, can you keep time for us?"

"Nice thinking, Doughnuts."

"It's Devlin," I said. "You are?"

"Grayson."

We linked arms and formed up, like protestors facing an advancing line of enforcers. The hard part would be waiting and holding as Amira ticked off a minute, and then another. I kept up a running patter of positive support, keeping the small squad upbeat about our plan.

"Three minutes," she reported. The scrum broke apart. A recruit with a ripped uniform punched someone in the face and tore free. Blood streamed down his face as he held the ball to his barrel-like chest, cradled in thick, muscular arms. The ball lit up like a small sun as he placed his fingers against it. We all blinked and shielded our eyes.

"Let's get him," Grayson said. We all surged forward a bit.

"Walk!" I shouted. "Walk. Stay together."

A cloud of recruits surged after the recruit with the ball. They ran across the mud toward an obstacle course away from the open clearing we'd assembled in.

Some of the runners looked woozy, but determined.

"Two minutes," Amira called out.

"Breathe deep, walk easy," I said as we shuffled after the prize.

The recruit finally succumbed to the crowds chasing him and went down. The scrum reassembled, occasional figures wrapping themselves around the ball in a fetal position as they got the shit kicked out of them and the ball pried out of their hands.

"One minute."

Screams of injured recruits echoed off the dome and bounced back down at us. I glanced up at the catwalk. Zeus stood on his platform, surveying the chaos but not putting a stop to it.

"It's sleepy time," Amira said.

"Go!" I shouted.

Our wedge struck the scrum hard, scattering bodies and trampling people caught by surprise. We were fresh, not dizzy, and organized.

"Get the ball but don't unlink your arms!" Amira shouted.

"Count to five, then pass it along." I hoped that whoever had snagged it wouldn't hog it, or I'd be screwed.

The center of our huddle lit up, dazzling my eyes as one of the recruits managed to get on his knees to retrieve the ball. Behind me, a knee struck my kidney hard enough that I sagged in place as I gasped.

I hung limp, tears running down my cheeks. Amira yanked me back onto my feet.

"Pass."

The ball was passed to the right as we huddled and weathered a storm of scratches, punches, and attempts to pierce our human wall.

But the air loss was having an affect. The punches were weaker. The roars of rage choked. We were on our knees, arms still linked, heads together, struggling to keep strong.

When Amira awkwardly passed me the ball I hugged it to

my stomach. At the count of four, the Klaxon sounded. We all flopped onto our backs and gasped fresh air as it streamed back into the dome in a rush of wind.

Commander Zeus descended from the sky on the platform, picked around the passed-out humans—sidestepping moaning recruits being tended to by struthiform medics—and ignored the still-standing survivors who eyed him warily.

"I seem to have been stuck with a mass of miserably performing apes!" the Arvani commander shouted. "And while I find you all about as appealing as barnacle growth, I have my duty. So we have a lot of work to do."

I didn't like the sound of that.

Zeus paused in front of me. "You: You performed tolerably. You will pick seven to create your arm."

"My what?"

"Your arm," Zeus repeated. "A collection of fighters. Eight fighters to an arm. You will be their octave."

"Sounds like we're going to be a group of fighting flutists," Amira muttered behind me.

Zeus raised the voice coming from the armor. "Eventually there will be twenty-five arms here on the base. You will learn to lead your arm, and the arms will also learn to fight together and against each other. It is a privilege to be an octave. Grasp it tightly. Hurry to pick your team, or the other octaves will have their choices."

"Amira," I called out.

Zeus moved across the mud. "You: You are an octave."

I didn't pay attention to who the other octaves were. "Grayson." He could keep calling me Doughnuts if he wanted, but he'd held the line.

"Worst game of playground dodgeball ever," he muttered, but came to stand next to me.

I started grabbing recruits, some from our group, others that I'd noticed who'd somehow grabbed time on the ball during the exercise.

Amira tapped me on the shoulder as our team formed. "You have a fan," she said.

Ken stood near a climbing wall, his arm in an inflatable cast and a purple welt over his right eye. He glowered at us, then pointed a finger at a tall recruit. She jogged over to join his team.

Ken pointed at me and flipped me off.

"Family privilege," I grunted. "Welcome to Earth under the occupation. Apparently he gets to be an octave whether he's skilled or not."

Amira raised an eyebrow. "You sure about that?" she asked.

I was.

"Hurry up and pick your team, know-it-all," she murmured. "Pay attention, there are some people you don't want Ken to snag from under you."

11

I had yet to see my bunk, but I guess it didn't matter. I didn't come to Icarus with any belongings. I didn't have anything to put down anywhere.

Zeus clanked his way around the warehouse we'd been ushered to in one of the living quarters off the crater dome, deep in one of the cloverleaf-like areas, eyeing the various arms assembled before him.

"Now that the arms are picked and the octaves are in command, you will suit up in armor," Zeus announced.

My arm shifted, its members slightly excited by the announcement.

I had picked Grayson Stockton, from Leeds, who played rugby before getting recruited out of a tenement in occupied London. He'd literally held me up while we fought for the ball. Another member of the first team, Casimir Sharpe, I'd spotted moving quickly through the mess before he joined us. I wanted that speed on my side.

Amira had pointed out a Viking shield-maiden of a figure towering over half the group near the back. "You'll want

Amabel there for muscle," she said. "The other octaves aren't taking her seriously."

"Yeah." If Amira wanted her, she was with us.

Roger Li, another member of our initial huddle, agreed to come with us. Haselda Madsen was another Amira suggestion. "I sat next to her on the way to Tranquility. She's smart."

"Smart is good," I said.

"She's also spent time in Brazil and Chile. With Roger's Mandarin, you have two of the most common CPF first languages outside of English. The Accordance is pulling a lot of different people together, and that means we have a variety of languages being used. A lot of them know English as a second language, but we can't count on it. There'll be a lot of Chinese-, Indian-, and Spanish-speaking recruits."

Zeus raised an armor-plated tentacle. "Your armor," he announced.

Struthiform officers pushed racks of black armor into the room, the suits swaying on their hooks. Each suit split open, looking like mandibles of black, chitinous insects ready to swallow us.

We stared. The sleek plating and mechanized joints meant this was Accordance military-grade issue. Designed for humans, but illegal on Earth. Even human enforcers didn't get to step into this stuff.

"Check out the patches on the shoulder," Amira said. "At least that's human designed."

A stylized Earthrise had been etched into each shoulder patch. The pockmarked moon in the foreground, Earth rising behind it.

"What are you gawping at?" Zeus shouted. "Get suited up!"

"How?" I asked, tentatively approaching the cracked-open suits.

"Some on-our-feet learning," Amira said.

“Oh, come on.” Amabel laughed. “I’ve seen struthiforms do this on-base outside Charleston when I was four. We’d sneak up to the edge of the base and watch them train.” She strode over, spun around, and put out her arms. Then backed into a hanging suit.

The cuffs snapped to her wrists, legs snapped forward, and the chest closed in. The whole suit gripped her and sealed shut with a hiss, seams disappearing. It readjusted, shaping itself with minor tweaks until it conformed to her size and shape.

She winced. “Okay, that hurts a little.”

“What hurts?” Casimir asked, a little nervously.

Amabel raised her legs, rocking back and forth on the hook. “Come find out,” she challenged.

I walked forward. The suit was alien. Inside I could see the lay of the cut-open human shape it manifested, but that was the only recognizable human element of the suit. The interior of the suit glowed with spiky filaments of some kind of bio-luminescent mold.

I turned around and backed in.

When my arms touched the gauntlets, they startled me by grabbing my wrists. The rest of the suit snapped shut around me, just like Amabel’s had.

Sections readjusted shape, memory metal shifting and pulling in tight to become a heavy second skin. Something pricked my skin, then shoved its way into my lower back. The burning sensation spread up my spine.

I gasped. “That’s invasive.”

Around me the rest of the arm backed into their suits until we all dangled from hooks.

Zeus moved to the front of the mess. “This is a fusion of inferior human technology and the superior workmanship of the Cal Riata.”

"The what?" someone closer to the front asked.

"Arvani that left the depths for the shallows," Zeus told us. "We colonized the lakes and tidal pools of the Arv. We did that by building machines to let us explore land. We are still the leaders of Arvani invention and study. You should consider yourselves honored that I'm stuck here in your backwater."

"He sound a little bitter about being here to you?" Amira asked.

"Hard to tell, the voice is synthesized; but I think you're right," Amabel said.

"This armor," Zeus shouted, drowning out the snapping sound of the suits closing up, "is powered by the same engines as a hopper, just smaller. It can do more than just increase your strength five times over: It features adaptive real-time camouflage, and it can recycle the internal air for a few days as well as liquids for up to a week."

"Ewww." Grayson made a face.

"Your communications have quantum entanglement for security on each arm's own channel, entangled again for a connection back to Command. There are also public radio frequencies for inter-arm—"

A loud crash interrupted Zeus. Someone had leapt off his hook and buried himself in the ceiling. The soft material rained to the floor, and the recruit had obviously not died as he kicked and wiggled around, stuck in the gooey ceiling. Obviously the room was designed with a safety feature.

Zeus didn't look up, just waited a second and then continued. "First, you need to visualize your helmet. This finishes the suit-up process now that there is a neural link with your spinal cord."

I closed my eyes and thought about a helmet. The rim snicked and then something thunked into place. The air around my head filled with the sound of my breathing. I opened my eyes to see the helmet had shot out of the collar and surrounded my head.

"And now I'll release the suits from their racks," Zeus said, his voice filling my helmet. "Move slowly, and cautiously. Do not damage my ceiling any further."

The hook yanked free, and I stumbled forward. Each step jerked oddly, but as I took each one, something about the suit seemed to stop resisting and then overreacting to me. It began to move with me. Anticipate my movements.

By my tenth step, I felt one with the suit and no longer like an awkward toddler staggering forward.

"Hey, this is Amira." Amira's voice startled me by filling the helmet as well. "I know you're all new to this, but just think about where you want to talk to. Think 'Command' and you'll be sending to Zeus. Probably not a good idea unless you have to. Think of your team, or arm I mean, and you'll be on the channel."

Then right over, Zeus came in. "Now it's time to get used to your suits."

A few groans popped out on the public channel from other arms.

Zeus scuttled out of the room and we followed. Down halls, and then out into the domed crater we'd struggled through earlier.

There were no days on the moon, I realized. Zeus would decide when we slept, when we were tired, what we would do.

When was the last time I'd slept? Had it been a couple days? I'd been moving from event to event and wanted to rub my eyes, but the helmet was in the way.

I thought about visualizing it opening. And right as I did so, a whirlwind almost knocked me over.

"Amira here. They dumped the air," Amira reported on the arm's channel. "Everyone helmeted? Call it in."

"I'm here."

Amira sounded annoyed. "Who the fuck is 'I'? I don't know your voice yet. Use your name."

"Sorry. Casimir here."

"Amabel."

"Roger."

"Katrin."

"Grayson."

"Devlin," I said.

"Haselda . . . shit," she grunted. "Just landed on my face. I'm here."

I looked around and saw a figure standing up from a divot in the dirt.

"Welcome back to the training area," Zeus said. "We have prepared an obstacle course for you. First arm to the other side gets dinner. The losing arms get to run back to this side and go hungry. Go!"

"What is their obsession with starving us?" Amira grumbled.

"Let's go," I grunted. "Let's just get this done."

We loped forward along the dirt trail leading to the other side. The first obstacle: a tall stone wall with barbed wire at the top.

"And up we go." Amira leapt nearly fifteen feet into the air, skimmed the barbed wire, and disappeared over the other side. "Careful, water pit on the other side," she reported.

I leapt. I didn't quite coordinate my jump, so I didn't reach the top. I struck the wall, stone broke and crumbled, and I flipped forward, landing in the pit of water upside down and flailing.

A suit landed nearby in an explosion of water, and the

helmeted head turned down to face me. Ken's voice came through on the public channel. "I *thought* that was you, Devlin. Graceful."

I struggled to stand, and Ken shoved past me, checking me easily with a shoulder. I toppled back into the water. "Damn it."

Ken leapt out, streaming water behind him. He hit the ground and flexed his knees, then jumped like a cricket to a spot another twenty feet away.

"Come on, Amira," I called out.

"Let it go," she said. "Haselda's having trouble getting over the wall."

"Casimir, help Haselda," I ordered. "Everyone else, keep up with me." Why was Amira arguing with me over the arm's channel? I was the octave. I was the leader.

I ran after Ken through more pits of mud and water, and then crawled quickly under crisscrossed lasers that sizzled against the suit.

The ghostly word OVERHEAT flashed in the lower right corner of my helmet's screen, some kind of heads-up display popping into my field of vision, but it faded as I crawled away.

I battled through a hell of competing wind and firestorms that buffeted me. Staggered through what looked like a pool of acid, took a running leap, and jumped out over a chasm.

I didn't realize how deep it was until the midpoint of my leap when I looked down, and 800 FEET appeared along with a range finder on the heads-up display.

"Shit." I wouldn't have jumped if I'd realized the fall could kill me.

I'd assumed the training grounds were a safe place. But they weren't. Maybe that acid would have eaten through my suit if I'd taken too long.

No one was playing games here. The Accordance wanted

to train us to fight an enemy they feared. They weren't holding back.

Zeus hadn't cared about Keiko. He didn't care about me. We were aliens to the Arvani. Aliens they needed to train to fight.

Disposable.

I slowed down. Took the obstacles more seriously.

Survive, I thought as I ran toward the wide maw leading out of the crater training grounds. I wanted to survive this.

The remnants of other arms straggled in. My vague fantasy of grabbing Ken in full armor and knocking him down had faded. I was just glad Amira and I had struggled across into the tunnel in one piece.

Zeus thudded across the metal floor. "Where is the rest of your arm?"

"Behind us," I said.

"Unacceptable. Where is Haselda? Have you looked into your arm's welfare? Have you kept it together and used it effectively?"

I looked down at the ground. "No."

"Useless ape," Zeus hissed in my helmet. "You are an octave. Act like it. Everyone, strip out of your armor, that's enough for one day. Hart, you'll be outside running laps without the suit."

I started to work on cracking out of my suit as the rest of my arm caught up. Again, visualizing the action sent the command through whatever had slipped itself into my spine and did the trick. The chest cracked open. Haselda limped in, held up by Casimir.

The large doors leading out to the crater rolled shut. More helmets snapped open and slid down into the suit collars. "Are you okay?" I stopped focusing on trying to get out of my suit and walked over. It resealed itself up the middle of my chest.

Blood ran down Haselda's lips from her nose. She walked past me, looking weary.

"Casimir?"

"She hit the wall headfirst after the first stumble," he said. "And then you left us behind. Nice work, man."

"You know what," I said, temper flaring. "I didn't ask to be an octave. I didn't even fucking ask to be sent here to the moon."

"Let's just get out of the power armor and take our medicine," Casimir said tiredly.

Amira moved in closer, her voice tight. She'd shucked her armor already. The neural interface was easy for her. "They're depending on you, Devlin. And we're going to have a lot of time stuck together."

"Hey!" Ken had his helmet flipped down and walked toward me. "You know what you are? You're a disgrace. You're a coward. You don't deserve the honor of being an octave, because you don't even want it."

It stung because it came too close to the truth, which I knew deep down, but on the surface I exploded. "Hey, asshole. Who ran from Tranquility when the bomb went off? You did. You left Keiko to die."

That hit home. Ken came at me swinging. I put up a gauntleted hand to block his punch, and then smacked into him just as hard.

"Guys!" Amira shouted.

We grappled and swung around. Then separated. "Asshole," I muttered. "You've been at this since the Hamptons. You need to back the fuck off."

"Go back home, traitor."

"Stop it!" Amira snapped, sounding utterly exasperated. She stepped between us, and I pushed her aside to get at Ken.

My forearm struck her with a loud crunch, and both Ken and I froze.

Amira didn't make a sound; she looked annoyed as she collapsed. Then she grabbed her stomach. Her eyes rolled back into her head.

"Amira, oh shit." I dropped to my knees. I was in power armor. Five times as strong. She'd stepped out of hers. "I'm sorry. I'm sorry. It was an accident."

"Step aside." A struthiform shoved past me. Another whipped in next to Amira. Medics.

"Is she okay?"

"Shut up," Zeus said. One of his mechanized tentacles grabbed the back of my armor and yanked me off my feet into the air.

Amira was rolled onto a stretcher, and the struthiforms picked her up and left the room. I struggled to get down and follow her, but Zeus held me up. "Careless," he said. "Useless. You're done. You are no longer octave. Get out of your armor, go outside. Start running. I'll come get you when you're done."

12

No one met my eyes as I walked down the rows of tables with my tray of Accordance human-optimized food. The gray goop and energy spheres wiggled with each step, and the square protein bars slid around the nonstick surface.

I tried to sit with my arm, but Casimir shook his head as I moved to swing my leg over the bench.

"Oh, come on," I snapped. I'd been isolated from everyone for an entire day; wasn't that punishment enough? "You'd all be licking Ken's boots right now if it weren't for me."

"Maybe," Casimir said. "But Amira wouldn't be laid out with crushed ribs, internal bleeding, and maybe worse."

"They said she was going to be okay," I said firmly. Accordance medical technology was near magical. Everything was okay.

Or, at least, I kept telling myself that.

Haselda sighed. "You've got to be kidding me. . . ."

Roger Li shook his head. "You need me to translate?" he asked sharply. "No one is happy with you here."

"This is high school shit," I snapped. "I made a mistake.

I admit it. I fucked up, big. But I'm still part of this arm. I can sit at this table." In fact, I'd pulled this whole group together.

But that didn't mean jack, apparently. Grayson stood up and loomed over me. "Look: We'll train with you, yeah? You're part of this arm. But at this table, right now? You're not *fucking* welcome."

I picked up my tray with its wiggling, alien food, and moved on through the chatter of the mess hall. Faces I vaguely recognized glanced at me, then went back to conversing and eating.

The mess hall was on the rounded edge of the leaflike barrack building radiating out from its hub, the crater. A set of floor-to-ceiling windows looked out over the pitted and pocked lunar dark side. I sat by myself and gazed over the barren gray hills in the distance.

Something twinkled and flew out over the craters and hills, rising as it shot away over the lumpy horizon. A minute later, another twinkling sparkle flung itself out into the darkness. The mass driver over the hill was patiently slinging its pellets of raw material out into orbit, regular as a metronome.

As those pellets circled out from the dark side of the moon, they'd probably come out of the moon's shadow and into the light, and see Earth.

It had been only a couple days since I'd last seen it from Tranquility City, but for some reason time had stretched and everything that had happened there felt like it happened both an hour ago, and forever ago. Every time I thought about seeing Earth over the lunar hills, I felt the punch of an explosion, the rush of air leaving my lungs. Blood on my hands.

Shivering, I poked at an energy sphere until it broke apart and spilled liquid all over the tray.

+ + + +

A simple schedule started to form for us. The last two days we'd been run across the crater, herded, drilled, and yelled at by struthiforms, carapoids, and Arvani instructors in the morning. Or, at least, the first four hours that the lighting throughout the base was on.

In the "afternoon" we had an hour to eat and rest. Most snarfed their food, like I had, so they could use the time for themselves. After I tossed my tray, I straggled behind a small clump of recruits walking back to their bunks.

"Too fucking exhausted," a familiar American voice muttered in front of me: Amabel Lee, who sounded faintly like the acting president but without the creepy factor. "I'm just going to lie down on top of my blanket and die for a half hour. Wake me up?"

"I could wake you up," Casimir said with a tired sort of leering in his voice.

"Don't do that," Amabel said. "I'm too tired to tell if you're joking, flirting, or being creepy."

"My bad," Casimir said.

In the corner near a supply closet, two couples leaned against a crook in the wall and made out haphazardly. Casimir snapped a towel at them. "Asshole," the girl muttered.

We might be exhausted, on the dark side of the moon, monitored by aliens, but that wasn't going to stop human nature in any way, judging by the sounds late at night.

Casimir and Amabel walked into our bunk room. Our whole arm slept here, and there were eight rooms for the eight arms of this wing, housing all sixty-four recruits. After our class proved its worth, we'd been told, more humans would be pulled into the elite Darkside training program, and all four wings would be filled with recruits.

I looked in the room. The bunk near the door would have

been mine, as octave. Instead, Casimir flopped onto it and noticed me.

I nodded neutrally and kept walking past the door. I hadn't planned on lying in uncomfortable silence there, which was all I'd gotten the past two days whenever I was in the room.

The sickbay for this wing was right off the great doors leading into the training crater. The struthiform medics had turned me away each time I'd tried to visit, but this time they let me through.

"I'm here to see Amira Singh," I told the struthiform medic in an alcove by the door.

It looked up from manipulating three-dimensional images of some pink-and-purple alien anatomy. The large ostrichlike face had been reshaped in some horrific accident and then fixed. Parts of its face were artificial, and matte-black patches of machinery pocked the face where fine down should have been. Scars ran up and down the slender neck. "I don't know what an 'amirasing' is," it said.

The struthiform stood up, the thick left leg hissing at it did so. Synthetic. And the winglike hands, also heavily scarred, had some digits ending in prostheses. I took a step back.

"Amira. One of the recruits. That's her name."

It cocked its head, the scraggly feathers above the hard shell of its nose wafting about. The limpid eyes blinked. "I don't know your names."

"Well . . . why not?" I found myself asking, while also mentally slapping myself. Even by alien standards, this one seemed a little off.

"Names don't really matter, now. We are all just feed for the machine." It pointed claws at my chest. "I will fix you, I will tend to you. But I will not learn who you are, because I never wish to have known you. It will only be another emptiness pulled from me if I did that. I will reward you by not burdening you with my own method of self-identification. It is a gift. Say, 'thank you, medic.'"

"Thank you, medic," I stammered. "I guess I hadn't realized you all had names."

"Why, have you never asked one of us?"

"Usually you have your boots on the back of our necks."

The struthiform raised its wings. Shit. I was in trouble. But after a second of it tapping the floor, it lowered them. "Well said. They are so enthusiastic about doing Arvani bidding, aren't they?" It stomped the floor again. "We are scared. Every one of us you meet, that is the last of the clutch."

"What do you mean?"

Wing hands drooped and feathers ruffled. The struthiform sat back down at its station. "Arvani said I would soar the dark skies to protect my clutch. But instead I burned. But in this war, there is nowhere to go back to. Instead, they have pieced me back together and I'm alive once more. And before I burned, I saw my world fall to the Conglomeration. Without the brood nests and mothers, the Thunder Cliffs, the great Joins, there are no more clutches. Arvani tell us we will retake the home world. But, with each battle, it is farther and farther away, and more of us die. Do you think I will see the end of my species, human, or will I die before that happens?"

I stared at him. "I don't . . ."

"The one you seek is in the first room, a member of your arm. I would not go see her, though. There will be greater things to worry about soon, I imagine, and you must save your strength."

"I'd still like to go see her, though," I said.

"Then go." It waved a wing hand.

I hurried before it could change its mind and walked

quickly past shimmering energy curtains and spiderlike machines that hung from cables in the ceiling. Surgical robots that could, in seconds, pull you apart, fix you, reassemble you. Emergency medical pods lay in half-repose, shells open and ready to hug a body, whether carapoid, struthiform, human, or Arvani.

I stopped at the first door and glanced in. Amira lay back, ensconced in a medical pod. Tubes led out from it to plug into the wall.

She was sitting up and talking to Katrin, who loomed over her while Haselda sat on the edge of the pod nodding along. Amira's face looked puffy, and her right arm was purple with bruises. I winced.

Everyone stopped talking when Amira noticed me at the door. Haselda and Katrin looked at me, then back at Amira, looking for a cue.

Amira raised her right hand, and then made a dismissive wave. The door slid shut in front of me.

Message received.

"Heads down!" Casimir shouted as we huddled behind a pile of debris late the next morning. Now our octave, he radiated frustration. We'd been tasked with claiming a muddy pit up the hill that was currently occupied by Ken's arm.

It wasn't going well.

We didn't have real weapons yet. We just had training handguns and rifles.

"We have a full inventory of native-made weaponry," Zeus told us when they'd handed out the training weapons with human handgrips. They looked . . . close to what we expected a weapon to look like, but as if someone had melted them and stretched them. Accordance loved their smooth-flowing organic shapes. "We have native handguns, machine guns, submachine guns, and shotguns. But they all, primitively, use bullets. And we can't train with bullets, can we? Instead, you'll be using human-grip light trainers. One handgun model, one basic rifle with a variety of simulated fire rates. Even though these emulate Accordance weapons, you will be assigned native weaponry for battle. Accordance weapons are for Accordance fighters."

Our training weapons spit out a blue laser light with roughly the same power as a toy pointer you might use to drive a cat crazy.

But sensors all over our suits would shut down the power armor and freeze any part of the suit that got hit. Which was why Katrin was pulling herself up toward us without the use of her legs.

"Grayson, we need to flank them," Casimir said to us. A heavy wind kicked up, scouring us with debris and knocking some of us over.

"Someone needs to help Katrin in," I said.

"They're trying to lure us out," Casimir said. "Ken's arm chose to shoot her in the legs to draw us out."

I knew it was just a training mission, but seeing her slowly pulling herself toward us didn't feel right.

Something zinged overhead. I caught a glimpse of scaly, waving legs and a spiny pink tail.

"What was *that*?" Haselda asked.

Even though I'd only seen it out of the corner of my eye, I knew what it was. We'd had the lessons drilled into us so many times, I'd felt a chill down my back. "Driver," I said. "It was a driver."

"It can't be real," Haselda said.

"No more real than our pistols," Casimir said. "But . . ."

A driver bounded out of the slurry of wind and dirt, smacking into Katrin. "Shit," she grunted. "It's taking over my suit."

Despite myself, I relaxed. Katrin was alive and talking. This might feel real, but she was going to be . . . crap, she was on her feet and bearing down on us.

"Shoot her!" Casimir shouted, as if over the wind, despite the fact that we were all connected and listening via helmets.

I fumbled around and faced Katrin with my rifle. Then I shot her three times, nearly point-blank, as she jumped into our midst.

"Fuck!" She sprawled, perfectly still, between us all.

"I think they're trying to flank us," Amabel said suddenly. She was hunkered down just far enough away that I couldn't see her through the muck whirlwind.

"Where?"

We were clumped together, and vulnerable. Huddling. Waiting for Casimir to start acting instead of reacting.

And Ken's team would be able to pick us off easily in a few bursts of fire.

"I'll look," I said.

"Devlin, wait!" Casimir ordered.

I poked my head around the debris, not above it, flipping through types of imaging on my helmet to see if I could penetrate the artificial storm Zeus had whipped up for us.

Infrared. UV. Something that turned the entire helmet into black-and-white scratches. Was that radar? On thermal, something warm loped at us.

"There," I said, moving my rifle and firing. Once, twice. "Got it!" A driver bounced, lifeless, across the ground toward us.

"Dev!"

Something smacked into me from above the debris pile.

My suit lurched to standing, against my will. My visor went dark.

"Well done," Zeus said into my ear as I was yanked around to fire on my own team. "You've gotten yourself killed and become a walking corpse because neither you nor your arm covered an attack from the air."

It was all over in seconds. The storm faded away, and I regained control of my armor.

Zeus descended from the ceiling to point out to the other arms what we'd done wrong. Ken watched us, triumphant, from farther up the hill.

After we were dismissed, the arm trooped toward the racks by the bay doors leading into our barracks to shuck our armor.

Casimir got up in my face. "That was all on you, Hart," he hissed. "You shot us all."

I should have argued back, but for some reason I couldn't find the energy. Katrin was the first one to try to kill us in that exercise. And we shouldn't have all been huddled behind that rock pile together playing defense.

But I didn't say anything. I was just going to keep my head down and get through it.

In my sweaty grays I headed for lunch, stomach grumbling. This was all play, anyway. There was no blood leaking out of anyone into the dust. No real explosions.

It felt like we were playing on a distant, dreamy stage.

Amira sat at our arm's table. "You guys got your asses handed to you," she said with a half smile.

"Yeah," Casimir grumbled.

"Looks like you could use my help. So I'm back."

Our arm had its full strength back—Amira was okay to train.

The only good thing to happen so far today.

I leaned on the edge of the table, and no one said anything. I kept quiet, and listened to Amira and Casimir break down what had gone wrong.

"You should have kept your head down," Amira said coldly. "That's when it spotted you."

I smiled to myself, kept my face blank, and just nodded. She was talking to me again. That was a step in the right direction.

13

Three days. More drills. More drivers taking over suits and creating chaos within perfectly executed plans. Casimir stopped yelling at me after he ended up shooting us in the back when one landed on him.

A quiet peace developed between my arm and me. I kept my mouth shut, and they let me slowly ease my way back in.

We began to improve. Not as fast as the Arvani instructors wanted, though. Zeus and his two fellow instructors would stomp around the crater's obstacles in their armor to yell at any number of recruits. But by now we knew to sweep the air, the ground, and our perimeter. We could leapfrog our way forward and attack another arm.

Not bad, I thought.

"When do you think they'll give us the real weapons?" Haselda asked at one point. "Instead of the toys."

"We'll be playing laser tag until we stop getting our suits taken over by the mechanical training drivers," Amira said. "Right now toys are all we're ready for."

On the fourth day, all the arms gathered in front of Zeus.

"Four to eight arms," he declared, "make a fist." He pointed at us. "You on the left will be Red Fist. On the right, Yellow Fist."

We stood in the heart of the Yellow Fist.

We broke apart quickly, shepherded to either side of the crater on a run led by struthiform instructors.

"Your job is to take, and hold, the structure in the center of the training grounds." A ragged set of pylons and concrete had extruded itself from the ground. It looked somewhat like an ancient Greek ruin, but with alien curves and script on the broken columns.

"Who's in charge of the team?" someone asked over the general frequency.

"Fist," someone corrected.

"Whatever. Who's in charge?"

"Commander Zeus didn't say."

"We have four octaves; one of us will need to figure it out," Casimir's voice broke in. "Everyone else: Shut up."

There was a pause. Then, "I'm good with Casimir."

"Cas for me."

"The other fist is moving."

"Let's go!" Casimir ordered.

We bounded across the training ground, around caustic pits and mud-filled trenches, making the run back toward the center. It was exhilarating, until a bank of mist began to bubble out of the ground.

We slowed, suddenly unable to see more than a few feet in front of us. The edges of pylons loomed out of the murk at us. An acrid taste, like tear gas, briefly slipped through my suit's air before it switched over to internal recycling of air.

The common channel filled with a few coughs.

"I'm down!" someone cried out.

"Who said that?" Casimir asked, frustration in his voice.

And then the common channel erupted in chaos. Within minutes, Red Fist had taken a chunk out of us as we tried to organize.

Recruits lay scattered in unmoving suits, swearing and apologizing.

Instead of trying to hold the structure, Red Fist had run right through it to come out on our side and cut us in half.

"Now all we have to do is hunt you down and pick you off," said Ken over the common channel, glee in his voice. "Or do you want to just surrender now, Casimir, so we can all head in for lunch early?"

Commander Zeus interrupted, "There's no early lunch; you fight until I call an end to it."

"Casimir," I said on our arm's channel, working very hard to visualize sending the message correctly and not accidentally broadcasting to everyone. "If it's Ken, let me go out there and run around, create some chaos."

"That's a waste," Casimir replied.

"No. Ken hates me. He won't be paying attention if I'm running around shouting at him. Seriously, toss me out there, then counterattack."

Casimir was quiet for a while. I had almost never interrupted his plans, until now. Finally, grudgingly, he said, "Okay."

I leapt out from cover. I was good at sprinting, and the current gravity setting in the crater was comfortable. I ran and shouted on the common channel, "Ken: I'm coming for you!"

Flashes lit up the air around me: people shooting at me. But I ducked and weaved all over the debris at the center like an insane rabbit while shouting obscenities at Ken, wherever he was. Through rubble, underneath, around. I even managed to wing a few people with shots of my own, though after I got too turned around, I stopped shooting to avoid friendly fire.

Ken took the brunt of my shouting without saying a word, while I suggested what horrible things he did to squid-like aliens in return for their blessings.

I kept it up for a good five minutes until a suit struck me from the side and knocked the air clean out of me.

Ken's angry face stared at me, visor to visor. "You call me a tentacle licker one more time . . . ," he growled.

I did worse.

He punched my helmet with armored hands, while I laughed and lay in place. As long as he was focused on me . . .

The glass in my visor cracked slightly. "Hey," I said.

A spiderweb of cracks spread out with the next punch, and gas seeped in. I coughed. "Hey, you're breaking my helmet." I tried to struggle free, but Ken had me pinned, and another member of his fist had my legs.

He punched again, and now the acrid, yellow gas shoved its fingers in and filled my helmet. My eyes teared up, forcing me to close them. I gagged on the foul-tasting air.

"I can't breathe," I yelled. "Get the fuck off me. Get off."

Ken didn't say anything, kept punching, and glass shards hit my face as the visor completely broke. My nose ran, my throat screamed, I tried to hold my breath.

The next punch, I realized, would be to my face. With nothing to protect it, Ken might yet kill me. I rolled slightly over, jamming my face into mud and gas, and Ken continued hitting me, forcing my face down into it.

"That's enough," Zeus said over the common channel. "Red Fist has it."

\+ \+ \+ \+

By lunchtime the next day I had blown the last of the mud out of my nose, but still had the aftereffects of inhaling the gas. I'd spent the night in one of the medical pods, the cold biometallic arms wrapped around my chest as it monitored my lungs for any lasting damage.

Amira joined me to watch the twinkle of the mass driver's launches.

"You okay?" she asked.

"Not looking forward to running; still hurts a little to breathe. But they say I'm ready." I slurped one of the energy spheres. I was getting better at doing it without making a mess of myself. "I'm glad that half-cyborg struthiform wasn't on duty. Did you talk to him?"

"A cheerful one. He refused to tell me his name. It was his 'gift' to me."

"I think I'd be in even more of a foul mood if he'd talked to me while I was laid up there overnight," I said.

Amira laughed. I wasn't sure if the warmth spreading through me came from the drink, or because Amira put a hand on my shoulder. "We didn't win, but that was a smart move," she said.

She let go.

This was a possible reopening of our friendship. I felt relieved, like that simple touch had filled a massive emptiness.

"We keep getting matched up against Ken," Amira said. "You notice that?"

"They're pushing us."

"Zeus is. I had some time laid up in the medic bay to poke around. This isn't standard. Arms should be chosen by randomization for one-on-ones. Zeus keeps overriding. He's having fun with you two."

"Well, it's easy with Ken, isn't it? Just toss him into the situation—"

Amira interrupted. "Get real. You've been just as eager to needle him. What you did yesterday was tactically sound. But don't act like everyone didn't hear everything over the common channel."

I pulled back away from her. "Oh, you're taking *his* side here?"

"Damn it, Devlin, there are no *sides* here," she snapped at me. "There are only humans, who are not part of the Accordance. Who don't get to vote in Accordance affairs, or rise to be in charge. We are a client species. We are their cannon fodder. Ken knows it. You should know it. Spending all your energy worrying about him means you aren't paying attention to the real thorn in your side. So get your head out of your ass."

My ass? I opened my mouth to say something nasty back, and then closed it. Maybe I was tired from whatever they'd injected me with last night. Or maybe having my visor broken and staring a gauntleted punch in the eye changed something. But I bit my lip for once.

"At the very least," Amira said, "not being at each other's throats for the rest of training will make things calmer, yeah? And then he's out of your life, most likely."

Do the time. Get back.

I wasn't going to get back to Earth and my family if Ken punched my face inside out with power armor during a moment where Zeus couldn't stop him.

And besides, I didn't want to endanger Amira's goodwill. So I sighed and got up. "Okay."

I walked past the tables and across the mess hall. People glanced up, then realized my target. Conversation died down, more heads turned.

"Hey . . . ," I said, as earnestly as I could imagine. "Ken."

He turned around. His expression changed, lips tightening,

a controlled anger settling into his jaw. "Come to personally surrender before the next exercise?" he asked. "Get it all over with?"

"No." I thought about sitting next to him, but then thought better of it when I saw that the rest of his arm looked just as hostile. "I wanted to come and . . ." I realized how this looked. I looked weak. Fumbling over my words. Trying to apologize. Trying to patch things up. As everyone stared.

"Beg me to leave you alone?" Ken asked. "Put your hands together and get on your knees, ask pretty please?"

People laughed. I flushed. "You know what, I tried. Fuck you."

I'd tossed a match. I knew it. Ken knew it. He shot up.

"Look, let me take that back," I started to say, trying to fix the crumbling bridge. But Ken shoved me in the chest. I wobbled back on my feet, arms flailing. More laughter.

If I'd ever had any social capital in this room, it was all gone. "Stop pushing me," I hissed. "I'm trying to talk." I should have done this somewhere else, somewhere less public. Small gestures, leading up to a peace. Instead of this grand gesture.

"No one here cares what you have to say," Ken said, and stepped forward to push me again. "Go away."

I stopped his shove, blocking the movement and grabbing his hand.

He looked at me, then stepped right in. With a sudden ferocity, we'd locked. Grappling, we swung around twice, and then Ken threw me. I hit the table, smashing globs of food and bouncing off.

I launched myself forward and got one good hit. Right in the chin. Ken staggered back, and then we both exploded into an uncoordinated mess of punches and kicks, what little training we'd had forgotten as we tried to draw blood. Or at least a concussion.

An armored tentacle wrapped itself around my waist and picked me right off the ground, yanking me away from Ken.

Ken likewise hung two feet over the ground, his legs kicking wildly.

"You useless fucking apes," Zeus said. "You know, on our world Cal Riata like me used to find something shiny. Then we'd dangle it just out of the water by a riverbank until an ape like you would come down to the edge. Then we'd drag you under, drown you, and eat you. I can see the appeal."

I gasped, my waist squeezed so tight I could barely suck in half a breath.

"Let's fight," Zeus said enthusiastically. "This is what you do, right? Constantly war with each other? Squabble for the slightest reasons? It's in your nature. Between the fighting and your sexing each other every spare minute you have, it's a wonder any time is left over for training. So let's see it out."

Our nature? I coughed.

Zeus marched us out into the crater, through the rumbling bay doors, curious recruits following along to see what would happen.

But at a careful distance.

Zeus dropped us on a beam of metal above a frigid pool of water and shoved a stick in each of our hands. "There." He sounded satisfied, or maybe I imagined it. "Now you fight."

He left us shivering on either side of the beam and retreated to watch.

Was this standard? Was it a part of training to set two recruits to fight each other?

Ken moved across the beam toward me.

I kept the sticks in each hand down. "I'm not going to do this; this is crazy."

"Crazy because you know you're about to get your ass kicked."

I moved forward slowly. "This is what Zeus wants. A show."

Ken hit me in the stomach with one of the sticks. I doubled over, but didn't hit back. He frowned, and paused, watching me, waiting for a return strike.

"Hit him!" Zeus shouted, the voice echoing throughout the entire training ground.

Ken glanced over, struggling between wanting to obey the command and having to hit someone not fighting back.

"I'm done," I said. "I don't want to cause any trouble. I just want to focus on getting through this as best I can."

"Shut up!" Zeus ordered. "Listen up, apes, there's no talking on the beam. There's only battle."

Ken gave a halfhearted jab in my direction to see what would happen. I ignored it.

"I'm going to make whoever falls off that beam run around this entire forsaken moon," Zeus said. "With no food. Until you drop and beg for the chance to get back up here again."

Ken swallowed.

"Hit him!" Zeus repeated. "Or I'll extend the punishment to your entire arm as well."

Ken looked at me. "Fight."

"No." I shook my head.

"Asshole," Ken hissed, frustrated, and followed that up with a fast strike to my head.

I wasn't going to perform for the alien. I let the hit knock me off the beam. All the heat fled my body as I struck the water.

Enveloped by the cold, I slid down through the water, trailing blood. The cold made it easy to just lie back and let it happen.

I struck the bottom, fifteen feet below, in a state of calm.

Fuck this shit, I thought.

14

"Unfortunately," said a flat, toneless voice, "I recognize you. I apologize."

I tried to sit up with a gasp, but the familiar alien petals of a medical pod gripped my chest firmly. The struthiform with the burn scars stood in front of me.

"Should I tell you my name?" it asked. "Would that be fair? I know your name now: Devlinhart."

I swallowed. It hurt. Something had been shoved down my throat and pulled out. Maybe I'd inhaled some water? I remembered being yanked out by tentacles and thrown onto the mud by a disgusted Zeus.

"I'm Shriek, of the One Hundred and Fourth Thunder Clutch," the struthiform said. "What was it like?"

"What was what like?" I asked hoarsely.

"Dying," Shriek said conversationally.

I stared at him. "I don't understand."

"The Illustrious Leader, our Commander Zeus, left you in the mud without medical attention for a half hour, where you drowned due to inhalation of water when he yanked you out too quickly."

"The fuck?" I struggled to get out of the pod, suddenly feeling trapped and claustrophobic. The memory of water rushing up through my nostrils and gagging me filled the back of my head. "How long have I been here?"

"A few days. I had you sleep. Your arm is unable to visit; they are too tired. They've been made to run a great deal."

I groaned. "Zeus." If anything had thawed with the arm, it would be frozen again. They would hate me now.

"Far be it from me, a simple rebuilder of broken tissues and bones, a low-ranking survivor who failed to die defending my home, to criticize a great leader like Zeus"—the alien glanced down at a readout—"but such instructing might be considered by some, though it is not my place to say this, somewhat callous and wasteful of life. Luckily for you, I am here."

Shriek leaned forward and delicately tapped my nose with the tip of a finger claw. I jerked back and coughed.

"Yes, lucky for you," the struthiform mused. "And soon you'll be healthy enough to go back to training. And you, too, will be alive and full of vigor, ready to experience what it will be like to lose your own home world. Congratulations on not dying; the Arvani appreciate it."

I shook my head. "Lose our home world?" That didn't make any sense. "The Conglomeration is light-years away. That's why we're going to be shipped far off. Why our volunteers have yet to come back."

"They are light-years away. But what are light-years to beings like the Pcholem, who run the Accordance's starships? They live in the Great Ships, skipping from star to star. And for the Conglomeration, a light-year is a few months' journey. Look at my scars, human. They're closer than you think.

If they found you like we found you, from all the noise you broadcast out to the suns, it will not take them long to come sniffing around to see if your genetic stock will add value to the Conglomeration. I wonder what they will use humans for. I'm told my kind were rapidly evolved into package delivery systems." Shriek held up wing hands and looked at them. "I hear we can fly again now, even though free will has been bred out. I wonder if there is any joy in flying on your own."

Alarms wailed through the sickbay. Shriek snapped around and looked over at another pod. Someone flailed inside it, spitting blood as the head jerked back.

Shriek ran over, waving wing hands and pulling up holographic interfaces and controls. Another struthiform joined him. I watched as they moved furiously around. Aliens, and yet the flurry of doctors around a hurt patient an all too recognizable activity.

Then silence fell. A pale face slumped back in the pod as the machines all withdrew. I stared at the unmoving body on the table.

"Who was that?" I asked. "Who *was* that?"

"Don't ask that," Shriek told me. "You know you shouldn't ask."

Another struthiform checked my pod over, and then released me. I stood by the open bio-mechanical petals, looking over at the cluster of aliens around the limp human body.

"Go!" one of them ordered me firmly. "Now."

I cleared out of the sickbay, slowly walking back through a silent mess hall. The arms' bunks were empty. I found mine and lay down in it, shaken.

I hadn't achieved anything with Ken. I'd shoved the arm into even more trouble. Zeus had an eye on me. It was all a mess. And what for?

Just to survive? I'd watched someone die in a pod that had more medical technology in it than most of Earth had before the invasion. More medical tech than most people still on Earth had.

That shaved head had just lolled. A stranger, but maybe someone I could have met, or gotten to know, while training here.

Was it better to not know their names?

Because we're just cannon fodder for some upcoming clash of two alien civilizations?

I curled up into a ball and shivered. "Fuck."

There was no way out. There was no coming back. I'd been fooling myself. The only way out would be the same way I came, I thought. I remembered landing at the base. The lunar vehicles sitting in rows near where the elevator had stopped.

If I wanted out, I would have to get out.

I had to get ready to get out.

I sat up, looked around, and realized I had nothing to take with me. There was no "getting ready."

If I wanted to live, and not die in some alien war or right here in training, I needed to walk away now.

But going AWOL on the moon was going to be hard. And as soon as I got to Tranquility City I would have to get a message to my parents to run so they could survive, too.

The lunar rovers, blocky and ungainly on their oversize balloon tires, looked like silvered alien beetles on wheels sitting in pools of shadow. Instead of massive compound eyes, there were cab windows. And awkwardly jointed arms folded across their fronts were mechanisms that kept the passengers inside.

The rover nearest the bay airlock opened up when I tapped the door handle, swinging up over my head with a hiss. I jumped in and pulled it shut behind me.

"Okay, that's halfway there," I said aloud. In the cab, what was clearly a key hung from a hook near the dash of somewhat familiar physical controls.

There weren't a lot of vehicles for humans to operate; the industry had been taken over by the Accordance. But I'd been in a few. Seen enough shows. I felt I could run this.

They'd left the keys in the ignition, I thought. Idiots.

I checked to make sure they had human suits inside the locker by the door. I didn't want to make it all the way to Tranquility City, then get stuck because I couldn't sneak in through a quiet airlock.

There was a human-compatible suit in a baggie. I put my own bag of energy bars and liquid food bubbles next to it.

Back in the seat I started puzzling over the controls. I found the language swap screen and watched the panes of information around me reconfigure into English. Alien glyphs shifted into readable figures and icons.

And I would have to figure out how to trigger the vehicle airlock from here to get out onto the lunar surface.

Sitting still, poring over the read me files, I jumped in place when a fist smacked the glass right by my left thigh. "Shit!"

Amira stood in front of the rover, expression inscrutable.

Shit.

15

"You can't open the airlock yourself," Amira said, brushing past me. The rover door shut behind her and sealed with a soft clunk.

"I've got the help files up," I told her. "I'm figuring it out."

We sat down in the two cab chairs, looking out toward the vehicle lock.

"That was a statement, not a question," Amira said.

The entire rover jerked forward. "Got it," I muttered. Just a test, to see if I had it figured out. I could drive the damn thing now.

"The doors require an authorization code," Amira said. "Why do you think they left all the keys inside?"

Damn. "Wait, how do you know they left the keys in?"

"I snuck back here the first night. Took a look around. Always know your landscape. And your exits."

"But you didn't leave," I said.

"Not then."

I looked anywhere but at her. Thinking. Then I stabbed the controls forward. The rover lurched on, picking up speed.

"I watched a recruit die while I was in the sickbay," I told her. Knowing what I knew about Amira, about that nano-ink, if she'd been in here and there was a code, she knew it. "How many more are going to die? That struthiform, the scarred one: It calls itself Shriek? It told me about its dead home world. That the Accordance is slowly losing and falling back. And what are we going to get, for dying for them? Will they leave Earth, finally? Am I crazy for wanting to run?"

"I'm not going to open that door for you. You have no idea how stupid this idea is, do you?"

"I'm not going to slow us down. I know it's on manual now, so as long as I'm pushing these controls we're headed for that lock."

We stared at each other.

I continued, "If you're in the rover and we crash into the wall, you're going to have to come up with some kind of story."

Amira didn't reply. But the massive locks split apart, the gentle thrum of their separation accompanied by a steady rumble and the high-pitched whistle of escaping air.

I let go of the controls and we ground to a halt, half-in and half-out of the locks. The inner door was closing quickly behind us to prevent more air from getting out. I had been holding my breath. Amira was shaking her head.

"I'm masking everything. Including the damn loss-of-air indicators you just set off. By the time they notice what happened, we should have at least a day. You have food with you, water? Suits in the locker?"

"Yes to all three. Do you want to use a suit to get out?"

"No. Take us out."

I stared at her. "You're coming with me?"

"Without me you won't even make it out of the base's

perimeter without setting off every zone alarm out there. Come on, let's go."

Still unsure, I gently moved the rover the rest of the way out. The outer metal maw closed behind us.

My eyes adjusted to the vista of gray hills and pitted craters in the gloom of distant lights. I eased us out and away.

Amira muttered directions to me, guiding us around craters and the bases of hills as she used satellite data to map a course that wouldn't get us stuck somewhere.

"You did the right thing at Tranquility. I like that. But this? A very stupid idea," Amira said. "I just wanted to put that out there."

I'd been tense, waiting for something like that. "It's the only idea that guarantees we don't die in some pointless, far-off, alien war."

"It's a stupid idea for *you*. Your family will pay the ultimate price if you go AWOL here."

I flushed. "Maybe they should've thought about that before becoming terrorists."

"Oh, come on." Amira shook her head. "Even you don't believe that. Protestors, irritants, problem makers. Yeah. But your parents weren't setting off backpack nukes in downtown Atlanta to take out Accordance oversight buildings. And you're lucky to have them. Some of us aren't that lucky. But there are others who will pay a big price if you go all the way with this."

"Who's that?" We dipped into a crater and the tires kicked up dust. It hung in the air behind us for an eerily long time.

"Your arm, asshole. Zeus isn't quite right in the head as it is. What do you think happens to everyone after we're missing? Zeus may be an alien, but I can still spot a sadistic, disaffected shit who's abusing command easily enough."

"That's not an argument for me to go back. I'm done with it. I'm done with it all," I said grimly, looking out over the blasted lunar landscape. Now that we were ten minutes away I'd flicked on the lights. Driving near blind, depending on Amira's instructions and the instruments, had been a bit unnerving.

"It's a good thing I have a strong survival instinct," Amira said. "Because I wouldn't want to be back there when the shit hits the fan. You might toss them under the bus, but you're not taking me down with you. No one drags me down. No one."

A long stretch of flat lunar plain opened up in front of us. "Look," I started to say. But I didn't get to finish arguing about whether I was dragging her down or not. Amira slid out of her seat and jammed a baton up against my neck. "Hey!"

Lightning struck me. It leapt through my spine, up and down my ear, through my head, and out through my nose. I tasted ozone so deep in my sinuses, I breathed, spit, and coughed it.

My entire body spasmed, then seized. I tried to scream but managed only a gargle and fell over onto the floor.

Amira let me hit it, my head bouncing off the metal floorboards. She squatted next to me as I struggled to breathe. Every cell inside me ached and protested. "I survived the Pacification, Devlin. I fought Accordance on the street. I helped lure their foot soldiers in to kill traps as a child. I kept people on the block out of their systems. I kept one step ahead of them for a long, long time. And now that's over. So understand me: I have no love for Accordance. But I can't have you fucking us all over, particularly me, because you had a bad few days and need to mope. Understood?"

I managed a moan.

"At the very least, I'm saving your ass. You know your

tattoo and rank, here on your arm, you know they have a transponder buried in them? It lights up on a ping; that's how I followed you. Wanted to make sure you didn't do anything stupid. Lucky me. But we have to head back before someone realizes you're missing. I can only delay and hide our little unauthorized lunar hike for so long."

She pulled out a couple zip ties. "What . . . ," I managed.

"For your own safety," she said, and zip-tied my arms to my legs. "Don't want you getting jumpy."

"Are you going to turn me in to Zeus?" I demanded sullenly.

Amira sat down and turned the rover around, heading right back for the camp. "As I said, he's a sadistic fuck. I wouldn't do that. But if we get discovered sneaking back in, I'll shove your zip-tied ass out in front of me as chum for that tentacled shark. Got it?"

I swallowed. "Got it."

16

I sat in a small bubble of my own angry silence. My wrists were starting to go numb, and even though Amira had taught me how to get out of them, while electrocuted and lying on the ground, I hadn't been able to move a single muscle.

My fingers hurt at this point. But I wasn't going to ask her for anything. And I particularly wasn't going to beg for my restraints to be loosened because I was uncomfortable.

The gray landscape, most of it shadowy in the dark because we'd killed the lights again, ghosted by the cab windows.

It felt like it was taking longer to get back. I leaned my head against the chair and closed my eyes, drifting off to the thump of the soft tires against lunar dirt.

"What was that?" Amira asked aloud, startling me out of my stupor.

"What?" Damn it. I spoke before remembering I was giving her the angry silent treatment.

She was looking through the upper cab windows. Up at the dark and stars. "Something . . . just grazed the sensors. Like an absence—"

Amira jerked back in her seat, her whole body taut with pain. At the same moment, the rover's interior lights flickered, then shut down. It coasted along on momentum, bouncing over a hole, and came to a stop. Amira grabbed her head and moaned.

"Amira?"

The sounds of fans circulating air faded away. An eerie quiet fell inside the rover.

"Amira?" I was a little freaked out. "Amira, what's wrong?"

We were busted. Fuck. We'd been caught, the rover disabled, and soon Zeus would come striding toward us. I was going to be deep in the shit any second now, and she was going to . . .

Blood streamed from Amira's nose. She rocked back and forth, mewling.

"Amira, are you okay?"

She pulled her hands away and looked at me. I gasped. Blood trickled out of the corners of her eyes, like red tears. "It hurts," she hissed.

"Can you see?"

Amira took a deep breath and wiped her bloody cheeks off with the backs of her wrists. "Yeah. Yeah, I can see. I lost some function, but I can see."

"What the fuck is going on?"

"Some kind of electromagnetic pulse. Anything non-hardened burned out. Some of my ink's military-grade; it's still running. Civilian stuff's mostly shot to shit."

I briefly imagined nano-ink sizzling all throughout her body, wrapped around nerve endings and skin as it bubbled and sparked. I shuddered and twisted my aching hands.

Amira saw the movement. She leaned halfheartedly forward and pulled a knife out of a hip pocket. After cutting me loose, she sort of hung there, holding the other seat and closing her eyes for a moment. "The air isn't being recycled," she said in a shaky voice. "It'll be okay for a while, but we need to check the suits. We'll use the rover's air until it's stale, and while I see if we can get a signal out, then switch to the suits."

I looked over her shoulder. "I don't think that's our biggest problem." This wasn't something Zeus was doing to us, I realized. Not punishment for stealing the rover. Not anything.

She turned. The lip of the crater above us glowed red, reflecting flashes of fiery heat. The horizon lit up, like lightning flickering away in a distant storm.

Then more red flashes danced out in the open, the hellish glow increasing. Balls of fire, dissipating quickly as the air vomited up into the sky, rising into the black night of the lunar dark before fading away.

"That's a lot of air lost to burn that long and high in the open vacuum," I said softly.

"It could be an industrial accident." Amira staggered to her feet. "The mass driver isn't too far away from the base."

"With an electromagnetic pulse? You *said* you sensed something in the sky."

She grabbed my shoulder and limped back toward the suits. "I *thought* I did. It could be anything."

"And the only way to know is to climb up and take a peek. How far away were we? Do you remember?"

Amira opened the locker and touched the nearest suit's collar. Lines throughout the suit glowed briefly yellow. "The suits are hardened, ready for a variety of outside jobs." She breathed with relief, resting her head against the locker's edge.

"There might be painkillers in the first aid kit," I said.

"No." Amira straightened with effort. "Might need it for later. Save it for when we know what's happening."

We pulled the shapeless suits on. Amira pointed out the controls on the left forearm's inner surface. Tap to make the materials tighten and shape to my body. Not too different from the backup manual controls for our fighting armor, really. But this one didn't slither into my back and link up to my thoughts.

"Don't use the common channel or speak while we're out there," Amira warned, before I tapped to make the helmet slide up out of the fabric and lock into place.

I nodded.

We bounded our way across the dust and up the side of the crater. The last hundred feet were steep: a rock climb, though falling would likely not be as dangerous as back on Earth. It was hard to figure out what a dangerous height would be, but we flirted with it.

I mostly worried about missing a handhold in the dark, and we weren't using any lights, even though the suits had built-in spotlights for just this sort of situation.

Huffing, I finally pulled myself up to the rim of ragged rock and looked out over the shadows and dirt between us and the conflagration.

The training base burned. The cap over the entire crater drooped, melting over what structure remained. Blackened spars jutted out in irregular directions.

Something moved above it. A charred, translucent jellyfish. It was massive. Almost as big as the base itself. We watched as bioluminescent light filled its interior, then traveled down through the long tentacles reaching the ground.

The behemoth's surface boiled with movement; not a single space remained still. Tiny sticklike insects fell away like dandruff, a cloud of brown that swooped around and clustered tighter as it dove into the ruins of the base.

I jumped as a hand grabbed my shoulder. "Hey," Amira said. "I'm patching a direct line via physical contact so we can talk."

"Those are crickets," I said. "Easily a hundred of them. This is a Conglomerate attack."

"Raptors are on the ground," she said, and pointed.

She was right. A dozen of them loped over boulders, clad in armor, kicking up dirt as they ran toward the base from where they'd been lowered by a tentacle away from the structures.

"Oh shit." Two rocky humanoid figures walked out from the interior of the Conglomerate ship. They leapt off from the edge of the gelatinous-looking rim, falling slowly at first, then speeding up. They struck the surface, throwing dirt up all around them and leaving small craters from the impact.

"Trolls." Amira's voice quavered, just as mine had.

The two creatures towered over the raptors at their feet as they stood and thudded their way toward the base.

17

More explosions ripped the base as we watched in horror. People we knew were trapped inside. People we knew were dying in there.

"They're switching to heavy jamming," Amira said. "Anticipating that there'd be a lot of hardened equipment around. I can't get the suit's comm systems to make contact with anything."

"So we have no idea if this is happening anywhere else? The moon, Earth, they could all be under attack and we have no idea?"

"We're in the dark," Amira said. And her hand squeezed my shoulder.

"Fuck."

"This isn't a large force, but I don't know what that means. It could mean they're just being detached to mop us up and all the action is elsewhere. Or it could be a sneak attack. And since we're on the other side of the moon, we can't even just wait to see if we spot any explosions on Earth to figure it out."

"We could run until we get out of jamming range," I said.

"And who knows how far that is? We have twenty-four hours of capacity in the suits. We probably blew out most of our air leaving the rover; it didn't have a proper airlock."

Another silent fireball rose above the base as something detonated inside. I flinched. Twenty-four hours of life left. My vision narrowed. What did that even mean?

The suit felt suddenly claustrophobic, my breathing loud and accusatory. Every breath, more air lost. Another lungful closer to a gasping death. "We're fucked," I said.

"We will be," Amira said. "We have twenty-four hours to think of something. To find air. Survive. The longer we keep going, the more options appear."

I looked out over the base, my heart pounding. This couldn't be happening. "For what? To die a few days later? To walk out across the moon and see Earth burning like Shriek said it would? I don't think I want to see that."

The image of an Earthrise came to me, but instead of a rich blue sphere I imagined the Earth burning as it appeared over the lifeless gray lunar surface.

"I'm going to choose life," Amira said. It sounded like her jaw was clenched. Fury filled my helmet as she continued. "Even if it's not for very long. I've fought too goddamned hard for every little scrap I've gotten. I'm not stopping now. I think we might be able to walk to the mines. I'm not sure if we can make it, but I'm betting there are supplies there, for the humans who service the automated launcher."

It was hard to hold two theories in my head at the same time, and try to figure out how to proceed while consulting both possibilities. One: The Earth and the rest of the moon were under attack. In that case, we were just buying time.

But if it wasn't widespread . . .

"Surely you can't attack an entire world without the

Accordance noticing *something,*" I said. Two: only the moon was under attack.

"I was thinking that," Amira said. "Seems unlikely, doesn't it?"

"We need our armor," I said. "The rebreathers will give us enough time to walk out from under the jamming. Or at the least, get us to the mines for sure. How far away are they? Fifteen miles?" It had been hard to tell flying over. But I could see the launches from the base, so the launcher couldn't be too far away.

"Maybe."

"People can walk twenty or thirty miles a day, I think. But there are a lot of craters in the way to scramble through and around. I don't want to end up passing out a few hundred feet away from the entrance of a mine and dying there."

"Our armor is in the middle of a damn firefight," Amira said, pointing at the base.

"Yeah," I said.

"It doesn't look like they're taking prisoners from here. I'm not seeing anyone shooting back."

"We don't know what's going on, but we know the crickets are mostly patrolling, so it's a dozen raptors . . . "

"And two trolls."

"And two trolls." I nodded.

"They'll rip us apart if they see us," Amira said.

"Not if we can get to the armor first." I turned around and looked at her faint face behind the helmet glass. "I'll go while you wait, if you want."

"No. I think you're right. I can't tell for sure if we'd make the mines. It's a coin flip. But there's one thing still in our way." She pointed at the Conglomerate ship. "It'll see us. Any of those weapons it used on the base will make charcoal out of us."

Even as she said that, the organic structure wobbled. It glided out over the base and over toward the Arvani quarters.

"Now we have to run for the base," I said. "It's on the other side."

"Fuck," Amira swore. "Fuck. I know. You're right. I don't like it. Fuck."

I hid my relief. I knew I needed her abilities. Whatever was hopefully left of them. "Then let's do this," I said, with more confidence than I felt.

In the old history books my father had kept, I'd read with disbelief the stories of men in battle during a great world war. Huddling in trenches, they'd be ordered with a whistle to rush over the lip into horrible machine-gun fire and die in horrific numbers.

At the time I couldn't ever imagine anyone being able to move their muscles to stand up from safety and walk toward their own execution.

Yet here I was, moving down the outer slope of a crater toward the open plain between the base and us.

We used boulders and smaller craters for cover as best we could. But it was awkward to scrabble around in the lower gravity of the moon. We'd been mostly training in the artificial higher gravity of the base. It was hard to crawl on your elbows when a single shove could pop you back up to standing.

My helmet was filled with sweat by the time we scraped our way closer, waiting for the large Conglomerate jellyfish of a starship to rise up over the ruined top of the base.

But it was still busy on the other side.

Amira pointed at a large, still-glowing hole in the side of the base. I touched her shoulder. "Can you access anything?"

"Yes. Some of the cameras are able to talk to me, but I'm

low bandwidth. Mainly motion-sensing information, simple stuff."

"So is there anything moving on the other side of that hole?"

"Not unless it's waiting to jump us."

"Ah, shit."

"Better than standing out in the open," Amira said.

We didn't come this far to turn back. We bounced through the breach under the mess hall. I glanced up at the broken windows and saw a body slumped over. No head, just a bloody stump. Frozen blood made a long, ruddy icicle down the side of the black wall above us.

Gravity yanked at us as we stepped into the base. The plates below us were still working.

We skulked carefully around the corridors in silence, discovering more bodies. I didn't want to recognize the faces, and I was starting to understand Shriek's refusal to learn names as twinges of recognition lanced me.

Most of the faces I saw were gnarled into silent screams, struggles to breathe air that never came. Surprise. Fear. Unseeing eyes looking through me.

Long hair in a ponytail behind an emergency rebreather. For a second I wondered if she was passed out and lying down. Until I saw the horrible burn marks.

Some of the recruits had gotten to emergency gear, but then been shot by the Conglomeration.

Amira grabbed my forearm and turned me around. The doors leading out to the corridor had been ripped off. Plates bulged where they'd been forced aside.

"A troll came through here," she said.

The silver walls were covered in splotches of blood where bodies had been smashed against them and mauled.

18

I tapped Amira. "Wait."

I kicked at the yellow emergency box on the wall. Once, twice. The cover was warped, but remained closed.

"Come on!" I hissed to myself.

"Hold a second," Amira said, tapping my shoulder to make contact. "It's locked to recruits. Let me spoof the recognitions."

The warped cover twisted open as she waved a wrist over it, careful not to catch her suit on the sharp edges.

"Take the ax," she said.

"Sweet." I grabbed the ax inside. The handle, made for larger, alien hands, twisted and bulged awkwardly.

But it was a weapon, and holding it made me feel better.

Amira grabbed a can of fire suppressant.

We passed through the utility corridors in the subsections, walking right around clogged emergency airlocks and through gaping holes. Trolls, it seemed, liked punching *through* things. Several times we stepped over the bodies of dead struthiforms near reinforced bulkheads. They'd been waiting for the enemy to come at them through the doors.

Not through the solid walls.

It appeared the trolls had punched through the struthiforms as well. Alien blood saturated the walls and piles of organs lay on the floor.

We were going to have to pass the dorms to get to the armor. How many dead people were inside their rooms?

Amira slowed down ahead of me. I put my hand on her shoulder. "The sensors up ahead are down," she said. "I don't see any movement behind or ahead of the dead spot, though."

"Should I take a peek?" The emergency lighting faded away ahead. A pitch-black corner menaced us.

"My eyes are better," Amira said with gritted teeth. "You can't see in this."

She pushed my hand away and ever so slowly leaned around the corner.

Nothing happened.

I let out a deep breath. "Come on," she said.

We stepped around the corner into the dark. I lit up the corridor with the light on my shoulder, just in case anything dangerous was lurking there.

A crouched form cast a shadow on the gray floor. It turned a reptilian head toward us.

"Shit." Raptor.

The reddish armor jerked as the alien moved away from a body it had been inspecting on the ground and stood.

Amira shoved me back toward the corner, making contact for a second. "Run!"

I was already backpedaling as she passed me by, watching the raptor's long arms pull some kind of rifle up. The beady black eyes stared directly at me, cold and focused. I smacked the light off, plunging the corridor back into darkness, and scrabbled around the corner as a line of pure, coherent energy struck the spot I'd been standing in just a split second before. *"Shit, shit, shit."*

The beam carved up the floor toward the corner, leaving molten metal behind it, until it struck the other side of the wall.

Safely on the other side, I spun around and ran after Amira.

Damn, she was fast. Left, right, I struggled to keep up with her turns. She was using a map in her head of the facility we'd already walked through and was moving us quickly back through it to try to shake the raptor.

But then she abruptly stopped and I stumbled into her. "This corner, make a stand," she gasped. At least she was also out of breath.

"We should run," I said.

"We can't. It's following us. It's catching up. I can't shake it. But I *can* see it. Get ready with the ax. We'll probably only get one chance."

How the fuck was she so calm?

I stood, my own heavy breathing filling the helmet, condensation trickling down it. If there were atmosphere, we would hear footsteps. But now I had to rely on Amira's vision of the raptor through the cameras.

"When I say 'swing,'" she said, "swing. Right at this height. Two feet out into the open corridor."

I shifted on my feet. This was happening. Now.

"Get ready. Three, two, one: Swing!"

Raptors, even in armor, stood only a foot higher than a human. I adjusted the ax and swung on pure faith as hard as I could. And at the end of the swing, the raptor turned the corner. The ax smacked into its faceplate.

It didn't shatter. Instead, the ax rebounded, hard. But the impact clotheslined the raptor, its feet flying out from underneath, and it landed hard on its back.

Amira leapt forward and triggered the fire suppressant. She aimed it at the helmet, and gallons of foam covered the visor the moment she pressed the trigger.

I leapt forward with the ax and chopped at the raptor's helmet again. Foam and ax bounced away as we struggled.

The raptor got to its feet, us clinging to it. Amira dropped the fire can and went for the rifle the raptor was holding. The alien swung around, trying to shake her loose, so I climbed up onto its other arm.

Its vision was obscured from the foam, but it sensed the extra weight and started throwing elbows. The ax went flying, so I punched at its helmet: a useless gesture, but one I hoped at least alarmed the creature. I heard my suit rip as a claw grabbed at me, but I didn't have time to worry about it.

As Amira wrestled with the trigger guard, the rifle jerked up and around my head. I grabbed the barrel, shoving it toward where I though the raptor's chin might be, and my vision exploded with light.

We all three fell together.

My vision returned. There was no helmet anymore. Just a cauterized stump of neck where the armor stopped.

For a moment we lay on the alien's body, breathing hard, grateful to be alive. "We got lucky," Amira said.

"I'll take lucky." My hands shook. Each breath dizzied me. I'd been hit hard in the stomach, maybe broken a rib.

Amira fiddled with the rifle. "Shit. It's security tagged. It won't let me fire it. The rifle only fired because the raptor still had control of it when we were fighting. *Damn it.*"

I wasn't paying full attention. The dizzy feeling was all wrong. It wasn't from getting hit. "I'm losing air," I said, as I realized why the sensation felt so familiar. I remembered the ripping sound when the raptor's mechanical fingers had tried to grab and break me as I wriggled and squirmed. "My suit's ripped."

I patted myself down, panicked, and found the long tear. The suit was trying to compensate by blowing air in for me to breathe as fast as it could. But that spiky, bruised feeling was my skin being exposed to vacuum.

I grabbed the ripped edges and pulled on them, then twisted them around until I could hold the rip somewhat shut.

Losing air still, but not nearly as badly.

The suit began a gentle beep near my ear. Low air warning.

"Quick," Amira said. She picked up the ax as we went past it and pulled me along with her other hand.

I staggered after her, my vision stuttering as I got to my feet. More lefts, more rights, as Amira guided us back through. I hesitated as we plunged into the dark again. And this time I didn't light it up. Let the monsters in the dark come for me. I didn't want to see them.

Amira stopped on the other side.

"We can't take the elevator or big stairs to get up above. Here's the emergency ladder." She lit up a shoulder light.

I stared at the orange ladder on the wall leading up to a hatch. "I only have one hand free."

"It's this or run into crickets. And I think there's a raptor coming down to check on its buddy who's gone mysteriously silent."

"I'm almost out of air."

"So move quickly."

I grabbed the nearest rung.

"Faster," Amira said.

I grunted my way up toward the hatch with little grace and a lot of swearing. "How do I open it?"

Amira was silent, her hand on my ankle. "Shit. Came down

with loss of pressure. There's air on the other side, but it doesn't want to open. Give me a second. Excuse me, hug the ladder."

She pulled herself up behind me, holding me against the ladder and looking up from my back at the hatch. I relaxed against her. I was getting dizzy, and I didn't have the energy to hold on. My hands were shaking, my legs close to giving out. The suit had switched to beeping insistently, and breathing was getting hard.

"Hey, you're getting heavy," she said.

"I'm sorry." I tried to pull myself forward.

Amira grabbed a latch and pumped it six times. "Okay, it's charged." She yanked it out, and the hatch popped open. "Fucking go!"

I launched myself through.

She closed the hatch behind us. I ripped my helmet off, flopped to my side, and took a deep breath of fresh, invigorating air.

Breathing. I would never take it for granted again. Such a basic, beautiful, primal thing.

"We can't stay here," Amira said. "There's movement. And we made a lot of noise. We have to keep out of their sight."

"I know," I said. "Just give me ten seconds to sit here and breathe. That's all I ask."

19

Inside the shadowy storage room Amira and I wasted no time struggling into our armor. She'd piloted us both around distant footsteps, the sounds of plasma fire, and screams to get us here in one piece.

"Never thought I'd be this happy to get back in this damn thing." I leaned into my splayed-open suit and smiled as it wrapped itself around me. I gritted my teeth as the suit wormed its way into my spine, but then relaxed as the neural interface synched up. I clenched a fist, feeling power surge through my forearms.

"Hold still," Amira said. "I'm disabling the training protocols. We don't want the suits locking up in a real fight."

"Shit." I hadn't even thought of that.

"Okay. You're good to go." Amira walked over to the door. Her helmet snapped up out of the collar ring and she held up a finger to silence me.

I snicked my helmet up with a thought.

"What's up?" I asked. With the helmet up, my voice wouldn't

carry. And with our quantum-encrypted comms, no one would be listening in.

"Gunfire. Hear it?"

Not with my own ears. And though I was interfaced with the suit, I wasn't quite as good as Amira at getting it to amplify things like that for me. That was going to be in the training ahead. Training we hadn't gotten to.

But then even I heard the crack, just down the corridor. "Quick, behind the open suits," I said. There were rows and rows of them on their wheeled racks, plugged in to base power and recharging.

Amira moved away from the door and joined me at the very back. We stood like statues in the ready position near several other broken, closed armor sets. I darkened my helmet. "We still don't have any weapons," Amira said.

"All we trained with were toys anyway," I replied. "We have the suits. That gives us a chance. More than we had when going up against them with an ax and no protection. Hopefully they won't even notice us."

The doors slid up, the light from the corridor outside spilling in. Two shadows darted inside. I could hear hushed whispers.

"They're human," Amira said with relief.

"I know." I slid my helmet down. The loud snicking sound made the shadows jump.

"Who's there?" someone hissed nervously.

I stepped forward with a thump, gauntleted hands raised. "Devlin Hart," I whispered.

Someone moved from my right. I hadn't even seen them detach and work around the row of suits. A flashlight blazed into life, and the end of a nasty-looking submachine gun jammed up near my cheek, making me wince.

"That's not a trainer," I muttered.

I turned and found myself face-to-face with Ken. He started laughing. "It's me, Ken Awojobi," he said, as if we hadn't seen each other in years. He grabbed the back of my neck and pulled our foreheads together. "You, you made it. Yes, you are too damn annoying and full of yourself not to. I love it. I am so happy to see you."

"You have real guns," I said, not sure how else to respond but to focus on the obvious. "How did you get them?"

Ken held up a hand and looked back at the door. "Everyone, in," he said with a wave.

More shadows slipped in, and one of them closed the doors. Once they were shut, someone flicked the lights on.

Amira shifted in her full armor behind Ken. He jumped away. "Fuck! How did you do that? I didn't even see you there."

She smiled. "How did you get the guns, Ken?"

Ken tapped the submachine gun. "You like my MP9? I've been waiting for us to go live fire. I wanted to see what our inventory was like, and one of my team members, Boris, was a recruit originally with the class in front of us. Held back for injuries. He knew where the good stuff was, and so did I. We went on a raid. Boris!"

"Incoming," Amira said.

A short recruit with a sharp chin joined our huddle. He held up a phone in one hand. "Raptor team," he confirmed with Amira. She nodded, agreeing.

Boris had a distinct South London accent. I imagined him loitering around an Accordance relief camp in the bombed-out ruins around the Thames, selling trinkets to struthiforms on leave.

Someone cut the lights, and we all tensed as raptors ran by outside.

"Okay," Boris said.

On some unspoken agreement, we didn't turn the lights back on. Amira lit her suit up, using blue shoulder lamps to create a soft pool of light around our sudden conference.

"How'd you get a pair of networked phones?" Amira asked.

"It's like lockdown back at home, isn't it?" Boris said. "Been playing keep-away with ET since I was yea high." He waved a hand near his waist.

"Boris gets you things," Ken said. "He had emergency air under his bed, in case Zeus tried something funny."

"Sadistic fucker," Boris said.

"We got more emergency breathers and hunkered down," Ken said. "Then the explosions and screaming started. We figured out it wasn't a drill."

"Shit went pear shaped," Boris put in. "So we snagged everyone with breathers willing to listen and made a dash for the weapons locker."

"A raptor jumped us on the way out." Ken rubbed his forehead. "It killed five of us before we put it down."

He wasn't bragging. Not trying to score points. He looked shaken mentioning the deaths.

"How many are near the door?" I asked.

"Outside of me and Boris, five others."

So just nine of us in the room. "Have you seen anyone else?"

"Just screams and bodies," Ken rasped. "Efua, you said you saw something?"

One of the other survivors had moved closer in the dark and spoke up. "We did see a cloud of crickets drag Commander Zeus off," she said. "We don't know what happened, though. Normally they don't take you alive . . . they just start firing first."

Commander Zeus must have had some value to them alive, I thought to myself. Unlike the recruits.

"I'd thought, once we had guns we could get armor and then fight back," Ken said softly. "But after that raptor . . . I realized we aren't ready for this. We barely started training. They're seasoned killers. After that encounter, I just wanted to get suited up and find a place to hole up. Fight only if cornered."

I nodded. "Amira and I were going to armor up, then go hide in the mines. See if we could get somewhere safe from there, or find out what's going on. Is it just here? Or is everything under attack?"

Ken looked up. "Like Earth?"

"The Conglomerate is here, and they usually come for whole systems," Amira said.

"Fucking hell," Boris said. "The mines aren't a bad idea."

"Can you really reach out from there to find out what's happening?" Ken asked.

"If anyone can, it's Amira. Anyone have a better idea to stay alive?"

Ken took a deep breath, then shook his head. He looked at Boris, who also shook his head.

Amira held up a hand. "Crickets," she said. "They're going door-to-door."

I turned to Ken. "Give Amira and me the MP9s you and Boris have, you all get into armor, and we'll hold them off."

Ken hesitated for a second, then handed me his submachine gun. He handed me an extra magazine. "Shoot sparingly, not a lot of magazines left. And we lost most of the other weapons in the fight. We just have some handguns passed around now."

Amira pointed at a rack of suits. "Ken, Boris, those suits are all the same arm. We're going to need to stay on the same network that they can't hack so we can chat. Everyone else, just make sure you're all in the same arm."

I stomped my way forward toward the doors and checked the MP9. "Is this the safety?"

Amira leaned forward and flicked up the switch I'd indicated. "Firing mode. Keep it off full automatic for now. Save ammo. The safety is in the trigger on this one. Just keep squeezing."

"Right." I didn't ask how she knew all this, but raised the gun and flipped my helmet up as the sound of skittering outside got louder.

20

The doors jerked up, a slight gap of light appearing before they seized. Amira had her eyes closed, concentrating as she fought to keep the doors from opening. Electrical smoke from burning motors in the doors wafted around us.

A pair of sticklike pincers reached under the door, trying to pull it up.

I stomped them, snapping the limbs clean off.

It was like kicking a beehive. Suddenly the entire gap filled with metal lobster-sized bodies thrashing to get through the gap and into the room.

"They know we're here," Amira grunted.

I aimed the machine gun low and fired along the floor. Pieces of cricket flew off and clattered to the floor with each shot.

"Save the ammo for something bigger!" Ken shouted from the back of the room.

I kept stomping. The door lurched farther open. I grabbed a cricket out of the air with my right hand and slapped it into a wall. It burst into parts and rained to the floor. One of the legs twitched and tried to jam a knifelike tip down into my ankle. I leapt back away and shot it.

Crickets zoomed around the room, bursting past us, seeking to stab anything they could. But everyone had armored up.

Cricket bodies were slammed against walls, pulverized under boots, or just thrown aside as we spilled out into the corridor. "Amira?" I shouted.

"This way."

We retreated from the swarm of metal insects falling over themselves to get at us. I followed Amira, crushing crickets underfoot. How far away was the breach that would get us outside onto the lunar surface? Because then we could really open up and run.

"Stop!" Amira shouted. "Raptors. Backup is coming."

"How many?" Ken asked.

"Four."

No way could we face four raptors.

"Back the way we came," Ken said.

"But . . . ," someone objected.

"He's right!" I shouted. "Come on."

We charged into the boiling mess of crickets, flailing and destroying as many as we could as we ran on. We skidded to a halt at another junction. Amira raised a hand.

More crickets scuttled toward us, some of them bouncing off the walls with eagerness. Why were we stopped?

Then I felt it: a thud in the floor under my boots.

"Troll?" I asked.

Amira turned toward me. Through the helmet I could see her face had gone pale. She nodded.

"Raptors to the back, troll ahead," I said out loud.

“I told you we should have gotten those fucking explosives,” Boris said. “Take them with us.”

I leaned against the wall, feeling each vibration of the troll approaching us. “We can’t get to the breach,” Amira said. “We’re going to have to see if we can outrun them on the training grounds, it’s the only direction left.”

“That’s something.” I started backing down that corridor.

“It’s just buying time,” she said.

“You told me time gives us options.” I was thinking.

“Troll or raptor, not much of an option.”

“No, but we have something they’re not expecting,” I said.

“What’s that?”

“*You*. The facility is still powering up the variable gravity. Can you access it?”

“I think so,” Amira said. “You want me to use the field against them?”

“Captain Calamari did it against us. Should be just as annoying, don’t you think?”

Amira started to jog faster. “Yeah. Yeah. I don’t know how long it will take, though. Ken, take this MP9.”

“We’re going deeper into the base,” I called out. “Cover Amira as best you can, give her space. If you want to get out of here alive, you’ll make sure nothing touches her.”

We burst out of the bay leading onto the center grounds and scattered without thinking. We’d been doing drills on the training field enough that it was instinct.

Only this time it wasn’t a fellow squad coming at us, but real Conglomerate enemies.

“Keep moving,” I said. “We have to buy Amira time.”

“This better work,” Ken grumbled.

Crickets tumbled out after us, some of them unfolding translucent wings and taking to the air. Then came the loping raptors.

I circled around the rim of a crater to get something between us as long lances of focused energy stabbed at us from the raptor's rifles, exploding dirt whenever they hit the ground.

Gunfire answered them. Ken perched on the lip of a boulder, sniping at them. He'd pulled the gun's shoulder stock out and unfolded the forward grip for better aim. The aliens scattered as well, hunting for cover as more accurate fire struck them.

The cap over the grounds had been punctured and melted, so there was no atmosphere. But Amira stood behind us and raised her gauntleted hands. "I'm into the training system's weather control. I think this will only hit them," she muttered to us. "But just in case, hunker down."

Fist-sized hail flung itself out of the sky on the other half of the course. Crickets circling overhead fell, wings suddenly punctured. The raptors huddled, distracted by the pelting chaos.

Without eyes in the sky, with the raptors knocked back, we took the chance to rearrange ourselves, finding the best spots on the course. Spots well-known to us.

One of the raptors broke cover and jumped into the air, looking for us. Amira waved a hand and the raptor twisted. It came right back down to the ground, faster than it had anticipated. It struggled to get to its feet, fighting the suddenly heavy gravity.

Ken fired three quick bursts at it. It reeled back and fell over a ledge, then slid down into the middle of a crater.

"One less raptor to worry about," he said.

But none of us were paying attention. We were all looking

at the rocky creature stooping out from under the bay door and stepping into our arena.

The troll seemed to keep unfolding, getting taller and taller. It took slow, deliberate steps forward.

"I've got gravity cranked all the way up," Amira said. "Overrides and all."

"Can you imagine the world that thing came from?" Ken whispered, somewhat awed.

I didn't want to.

"Anyone see something behind the troll?" Amira asked. "There's something there, right?" Her voice sounded strained. She staggered and fell back. I moved closer to her, leaving cover.

"Amira, what's wrong?" I moved around to look into her visor. She glanced over at me, and I saw blood run down her upper lip. Like it had when the electromagnetic pulse fried the computer chips and her unhardened nano-ink. "Shit. Amira!"

"Look at the troll!" she snapped. "Do you see something near it? I can feel it, all over the network. It's attacking me."

I looked again. Yes, something: a blur moving alongside the legs.

"Yeah. I thought something was in my eye, or on the helmet," Boris said.

"Ghost," Amira said softly. "It's a ghost." Almost too soft to hear.

"Fuck," I said. That's all we needed, the alien that caused all the other aliens to go berserker.

Amira's voice firmed up. "I think I can still work around it. It's everywhere, but I can . . . here we go, get ready to run."

Yellow mists rose from the ground. They swirled around the troll and the raptors and rose quickly. Other gases mixed in, and the entire dome thickened with them.

"Smoke screen. And they're slowed down. Now we run," Amira said.

Ken and Boris hung back to cover us as we bounced to the other side. A big leap with our assisted legs got us onto the scaffolding twenty feet over the grounds. Some awkward climbing and we broke out of the facility.

Another great leap for us, and we were on the lunar surface, bounding for safety in the shadows of the jagged hills and craters around the base.

"Faster!" I shouted at everyone. Over by the Arvani quarters the Conglomerate starship was pulling up its tendrils with surprising swiftness for something its size. Whatever it was.

It began to drift our way.

"I think it's coming for us," I said, just before thick beams of energy lit up the lunar night like searching spotlights, dancing around the battered gray rocks we were trying to hide behind.

21

The barrage melted lunar regolith and threw boulders into the air as rock exploded. Stabbing energy blasts dazzled my eyes as I scrambled for cover.

"They're climbing higher for an angle on us," Ken shouted after a few minutes of chaos and hell.

Someone started whimpering on the arm's channel. I sympathized as I huddled down into the shadows of a niche in a crater. "Stay still," Amira said. "The suits have adaptive camo. They have countermeasures built in for Conglomerate sensors. Heat, UV, color, EM. Just don't move, and the suit has the capacity to hide us. Move and it can't keep up."

I was already gray as the rock around me.

"Everyone should call in," Amira continued in a calming voice. "Who made it out? We didn't have time for names back inside. Who's in our arm?"

"Boris, me, you, and Efua are one arm," Ken said. "The other four are another arm."

If we used the common channel, the Conglomerate would

use the radio chatter to find us. The quantum entanglement only worked for intra-arm communication.

"Which one of us is closest to someone in the other arm?" Amira asked. "Are they moving around?"

"I am," said a voice that wasn't Boris's recognizable accent, Amira, or Ken's deep voice. She recognized the need to identify herself. "Efua here. I'm ten feet away from someone in the other arm. I don't know the person's name, but whoever it is saw us all stop moving and hide, and is copying us."

Good. I hadn't even thought about comm issues. If we'd been supported by properly trained octaves we'd know how to pass communications through from arm to arm, as well as ways to pass information up to leaders.

But we had no idea what we were doing. Amira was our most competent technologist, and she'd been hit by the electromagnetic pulse.

"Efua, can you safely get to this person and touch their armor?" Amira asked. "That'll set up a direct comm link, and you don't have to do anything. The suit should figure it out for you."

"I think so." Efua was silent for a long moment. "I'm going over."

We waited for her to do that. I winced as more energy struck the dirt nearby. But it was random fire.

"Where is everyone?" I asked after a few minutes. I hadn't been paying attention as we'd run for it. I'd dived into a crater a couple hundred feet away from the base. Ken was close to the bottom of the same crater, behind a boulder that had rolled down the slope. I didn't know where anyone else was.

"A little farther ahead on the other side of the ridge," Amira said. "I saw Devlin dive in. I risked the fire to get more distance."

“I’m right next to Devlin,” Ken said flatly.

“Um . . .” Boris cleared his throat. “I’m near the rover bay, hiding behind one of the transport shuttles.”

“You doubled back to the base and moved around to the bay?” Ken asked, beating me by a split second.

“Well,” Boris said, “flying out with a shuttle when they’re distracted might be easier than trying to leg it out, yeah? Also, I thought there might be some useful bits lying around.”

“And?”

“I found a welding torch,” Boris said. There was a faint hint of satisfaction in his voice. “It’s supposedly strong enough to go through walls. I think it might go through raptor armor.”

“Anything else useful?” Ken asked.

“Explosives,” Boris added.

“Where’d you find those?”

“Locked away somewhere I had to use the torch to get at,” Boris said.

“You could have blown yourself up,” Ken snapped.

Boris made a noncommittal sound.

“We’re all in danger,” Amira said. “It’s as good an idea as any. He may yet be the one that makes it out now that the damn ship is trying to melt us into the surface.”

Efua interrupted us. “Okay, I have contact with the other arm. Is there anything you would like me to say to them for you?”

“Stay put,” Ken said. “Tell them about the camouflage, okay?”

“Okay. I am telling them.”

The light show stopped. The ground stopped shaking underneath us.

“What’s happening now?” I asked.

“Want to take a look over the edge?” Ken asked. I couldn’t

tell if he was being sarcastic or not. But someone was going to have to.

"Give me a second," I told him.

"Wait . . ."

I did it slowly, trying to give the suit time to adjust to the change. Hopefully anyone looking at this tiny little space at the crater's lip would see nothing but gray.

"Devlin, what are you doing?"

I tensed, waiting for a bolt of energy to smack into my helmet and take the top of my head clean off. Nothing happened. I kept moving until I finally peered over the edge of the crater.

I stared at the lumpy, bell-shaped head of a troll standing tall farther down the slope of the crater. "Oh shit."

It leapt into the air, passing over me and sailing into the center of the crater.

Ken rolled away from the boulder and started firing at it. The gun silently puffed smoke in the vacuum out of the barrel, and bullets chipped away at the troll's bulky ankles.

"Ken! Run!" Amira bounced onto the tip of the crater. She must have leapt as hard as the suit possibly could, maybe even killing overrides for safety, to make it back from the ridge in a single bound like that.

The large rock she'd been carrying continued on as she smacked into the ground. It struck the troll right in the temple, and the alien swung to look at her.

Ken leapt out of the crater. So did I. But Ken shot at the troll again, clipping it in the head, getting its attention back on us and away from Amira.

"Those bullets aren't doing shit!" I yelled. "They're good for crickets, that's it. We're just pissing it off."

"I know." Ken popped up like a tick, bouncing from boulder

to boulder, zigzagging and staying well away from the troll. "Efua, get your arm to the mining facility while we have the troll's attention!"

The troll stopped trying to catch him and pulled out a large weapon strapped to its back. More cannon than gun. Well, more sawed-off cannon than cannon, really. It was squat and oddly bulky. In fact, it was wider than it was long. A weapon that was almost all mouth.

"Cover!" I yelled. The cannon glowed white and blue, then spat a long line of darkness. Light bent and wobbled around it. The boulder Ken hid behind was plucked right off the ground.

"What the . . ."

Ken swore as he watched the large chunk of rock sucked toward the troll in a cloud of fine gray dirt.

I opened fire. "Jump away, Ken!" I shouted.

Bullets struck the cannon, knocking it sideways just enough that the line of darkness wobbled off to the right. With the cannon beam's hold on it broken, the boulder dropped, and Ken made like a grasshopper, shooting off for the ridge Amira had come from.

"What the hell was that?" he asked.

"I think it's packing something like a portable wormhole in there. A weaponized tractor beam," Amira said. "Ken, keep coming for the ridge, there are places to hide on the other side."

I leapt the other way, heading back for the craters. The troll bounded after me. Every time I landed, I spun off in a new direction, waiting for the line of darkness to reach out and grab me. Or for a giant rocky foot to plaster me against the surface.

I was rabbiting away, swerving this way and that as best I could, but it was slowly, ploddingly, getting closer. It had thrown the wormhole cannon away. Had I broken it?

"Hold on," Boris said. "I think I can distract it a second."

I turned my head back in midleap and saw the sparkle of an explosion in the bay doors. The troll paused the next time it landed, and then turned back for a second.

That's all I needed.

I skimmed low across the landscape and made it over a nearby set of ridges. Once I had lunar mass between me and the troll, I randomly bounced this way and that from hard, rocky surfaces so I didn't leave footprints.

And then I dug in and froze.

No looking over the lip and getting spotted *this* time. The troll was out there stomping on bugs, and I was going to be a good little cockroach and stay put in the dark crevice I'd found.

"Dev?" Amira whispered, even though she didn't need to. "You there?"

"Yeah. Ken?"

"Yeah. Boris?"

No reply.

"Boris?"

A loud grunt, some spitting sounds, and a metallic screech filled our ears. "Boris!" we all shouted.

"I'm still here," Boris panted.

"You okay?"

"I'm happy to report that the welding torch does cut through raptor armor," he said. "However, the downside is a bit limiting: You have to get rather close to them. Hang on."

The silence stretched. And none of us seemed to want to jinx it by saying anything.

Then Boris was back. "I'm sorry, I have to blow something else up."

A very distinct thump came through my helmet.

Amira swore.

"What's wrong?" I asked.

"The other troll just jumped past us, headed toward the mines. I think they spotted some movement."

"Efua?" I called. "Did you hear that?"

She didn't respond.

"There are," Boris interjected, "a bloody shitload of crickets swarming out of here. I'd stay very, very still for a long while."

"Are you going to be okay?" I asked him.

"I think I convinced them I blew myself up. I found a nice hiding spot in the wreckage; they're not pawing through it. So let's just wait for everything to die down, shall we?"

"Sounds like a plan." I was on my back, shoved deep into a crack. I stared at the rock above my helmet.

I'm a shadow, I told the lunar landscape. A shadow in the dark under this rock. A shadow that wasn't going to move for a good long time.

But that wasn't good. I had stopped running. Stopped moving around. Stopped reacting.

I had time to think now.

Time to think about all the recruits' faces that I'd seen mangled and staring past me as I passed them in the airless corridors.

Time to realize that Casimir wasn't going to ever bark orders at me. Katrin wasn't going to give me a disgusted look for breaking Amira's ribs due to my stupidity.

Right now, I'd trade anything for their frosty silence at the table.

I suddenly wish I'd never known their names.

And then I felt horrible for wishing it. I closed my eyes and began to shiver, hoping it wasn't causing my armor to twitch.

"Dig in!" Ken shouted.

The explosions started again. The Conglomerate ship, apparently not wanting to wait for the trolls to dig up every rock and crevice, floated over the landscape. A full-on barrage of furious light and energy danced around us. Rocks jumped and tumbled around me. New craters spewed liquified moon rock up into the dark, where it slowly misted and settled back down to the ground.

22

"You know what I've always wondered?" Boris suddenly broke the silence.

I snapped my eyes open and looked around. The crater was empty. I'd nodded off. I'd needed it. I glanced at the time stamp floating over the visor. I'd been asleep for twenty minutes.

Damn. I could have been killed in my sleep. Melted by one of those explosions from the ship.

"I've always wanted to know what struthiforms think of breakfast burritos," Boris continued.

"What?" Amira's voice sounded crusty and strained.

"It's the eggs, yeah?" Boris sniffed. "I mean, scrambled eggs. They're giant ostriches, how does that look?"

"Well, like us eating a small mammal, like a pig," Ken chimed in.

"Veal," Amira said. "Baby mammal."

"Hmmm . . ." Boris sounded unsure. "I guess so."

I opened my mouth to tell them about Shriek, and that the struthiforms were all dying because they couldn't go back to their home world.

But since we didn't know whether we were about to lose ours, why harsh everyone's mellow? "What does it look like out there? They still hunting us?"

Quiet.

"Hello, can you guys hear me?"

"Devlin"—Amira sounded worried—"what have you been doing the last half hour? Sleeping? We've been calling for you."

"Well . . ." I cleared my throat. "Yes, sorry. I nodded off." The regular rhythm of the bombing had become constant. A background noise.

"Damn," Boris said. "You're all ice. You slept through all that? Shit, I'm still vibrating."

I opened my mouth to reply. To tell them I was so exhausted, I couldn't help it, and that thinking about the dead just on the other side of the ridge was too much.

"They left," Ken reported. "Ten minutes and nothing has moved near me or Amira. No more explosions. No hunting parties."

"Could be a trap," Amira said. "We've been discussing that. Then Boris changed the subject."

"You were all boring me," Boris said. "I'm hiding under shuttle debris, and I can't so much as twitch, and you two are just going around and around. Not discussing. Arguing."

I looked around the crater I'd hidden inside. Nothing.

The debate started up again, Amira assuming that there were at least crickets out hiding away, as still as we were, waiting to get triggered. Ken insisting that he could move around his hiding spot.

I tumbled out onto the dirt and rock. I didn't want to put anyone else at risk, and we couldn't wait here forever. Eventually, someone had to be the first to put themselves in the crosshairs. If there were any.

My joints protested, but after a few seconds of movement, they warmed and loosened up. It felt good to stand.

Nothing moved but me. The attack I'd been half tensing for didn't come.

I scrabbled up to the rim and bounced off across to the ridge. "I'm out in the open," I reported. "Nothing coming after me."

"Shit," Ken said. "I knew it. I'm—"

"Why don't you two stay where you are," I interrupted. "Boris, you too. In case the enemy is waiting for more movement."

"Okay," they muttered.

I slithered up the rim and looked out over toward the Conglomerate ship. It hung over the main base again, tentacles down. There was nothing out on the plain between us but newly pockmarked ground.

"Did Efua make it to the mines?" I asked.

"We are here," Efua said. "We found some air canisters. We think. We're trying to understand how to hook them up to our suits."

"Can you call out from there?"

"No," Efua said. "We are still being jammed."

I looked at the ruins of the base, thinking. "Efua, you said the crickets came and took Commander Zeus away. To the officers' quarters?"

Efua was quiet for a second. "I think so. In that direction, at least."

Amira jumped in. "Zeus's transponder is there. Whether that means Zeus is there or not, I can't say. I'd need to get closer to verify, grab some higher bandwidth, line-of-sight comms."

"What about our rank transponders?" I asked quickly,

thinking back to Amira's lecture that the tattoos had trackers in them.

"I, obviously, killed them a long time ago," Amira said, almost as if she were talking to a child. "Or we'd be toothpaste under troll toes."

Sure. That made sense.

"What are you thinking?" Ken asked.

I looked off in the direction of the launcher. Safety. For now. What would a fighter do here? Hide like a cockroach? Until his air ran out?

Or . . .

Or what?

"Zeus and the other Arvani in their quarters, and the struthiforms, if they're alive, have heavier armor. They're trained for this. They're officers. They know what our options are. They've fought the Conglomerate before. We're untrained recruits. I think we need Zeus back."

"That sadistic bastard?" Ken asked.

"Captain Calamari is crazy," Amira agreed. "But Devlin has a point: We could aim that crazy at the Conglomerate bastards."

Boris laughed. "Captain Calamari? Why didn't I think of that? You even demoted him . . . to an appetizer! We called him Sergeant Suckers. I do have some leftover explosives for getting inside the Arvani quarters."

"Or we can just get me close enough that I can pop the locks. What are you thinking, Devlin?" Amira asked.

"We take our time. Shadow to shadow. Total sneak mode. If it feels risky, don't move. We have our suits, and we have all day to get there. We're going to converge on it from all points. No rush." We were going to be good little stealthy cockroaches. "If we get spotted, scatter and hide again. Once inside, kill anything in our way, get the commander and any other Accordance survivors."

"I like it," Ken said. "We take the fight back to them."

"And what about us?" Efua asked.

"Give us twenty-five hours from now. If we go silent, try to get out from the jamming and get a signal back to Tranquility."

"Good luck," Efua said.

"You too," I replied, and began to slither to the nearest rock.

23

Five hours. Five hours of slinking across the fields of gray waste. Five hours of waiting to get caught. Five hours of tension building. The closer we got to the Arvani officers' quarters, the more I felt like something in the back of my neck was going to snap.

"Worse game of red light, green light ever," Amira said.

One of us would advance, the other watch from a safe position, and the other two would stay hidden.

Foot by foot.

Inch by inch.

We converged on the airlock. Boris bounded up the last few feet, unslinging an arm-sized black claw with four sharp points at the end. The alien welding torch.

"We ready?" I asked.

Boris held up a disk. "I have explosives," he said happily. Then he awkwardly held up the welding torch.

Amira walked up to the doors. "I already said there's no need."

"We'll see." Boris strapped the disk back onto his hip.

Ken stepped forward. "Boris, you and me are in first, we have the guns. Amira, Devlin, come in behind us. Amira: when you're ready."

I got in place behind Ken.

"On three. One, two, three." Amira waved a hand and the airlock doors slid up and open. A cloud of wet air puffed out past us.

We slipped in, the outer door closed behind us, and Amira held up a hand. "There's a raptor on the other side," she said. "Wait a second. He's turning away. And . . . Get ready."

This was it.

I crouched. Ken pulled the MP9 up tight to his shoulder and Boris held up the torch. The four claw points lit up and glowed white-hot. Energy leapt out from each point and met in the air a foot ahead.

"Anytime," Boris said.

"Now." Amira waved her hand and the inner door opened.

Ken jumped into the air. The raptor spun at us, raising a weapon even as Ken arced toward it, firing with quick bursts that did little more than plink off the armor around the raptor's claws. The shielding was too tough.

But Ken had known that going in. He wasn't trying to break the armor. The kinetic energy of each bullet was hitting the raptor's weapon, making it hard to bring the burst of energy to bear on us.

And to give Boris time to close the distance without being carved up.

When Boris struck the raptor, both bodies tumbled end over end. And then he jammed the welding torch up into the raptor's jaw.

The white-hot energy point at the torch's end sizzled and spat as it ate right through the alien's helmet. The inside of the visor filled with steam and heat, then burst open like wet fruit.

Boris shoved the armored corpse off and to the side, jumping up, ready for the next attack.

Nothing.

We stood on metal grating that led down to a very tropical-looking spit of sand, and beyond that a deep pool. Purple-and-black shrubs cluttered around in transparent tubs, their fronds dropping toward the water.

In other rooms leading off from the main common area, I saw water fountains and tiled wading pools.

"I guess it makes sense the Arvani officers' club would look like a bathhouse," Boris said. "Are we going to have to go swimming to find the prisoners?"

"No," Ken said, coming back around a corner. "They're all stacked up along the back of this pool."

Five Arvani bodies had been ripped right out of their traveling armor.

"Beached squid," Amira said.

"Yeah." Their long tentacles were coiled like rope in the sand, which had absorbed enough of their spilled fluids to look somewhat jellied.

"That raptor stacked them up nice and pretty," I observed.

"Movement!" Ken shouted.

Something rippled in the water of the common pool. We moved along the wall, Ken and Boris taking point again. The light of the torch dazzled against the walls and rippled reflections in the wavelets past the sand.

"Come out slowly, or we shoot!" Ken shouted on the common channel.

A familiar, mechanically translated "voice" responded. "Who are you?" Ignoring Ken's command, the familiar vision of Commander Zeus rose out of the water in full armor.

"Commander, we're survivors. We came to rescue you."

Zeus paused on the edge of the waterline and swiveled to regard us. The alien instructor took an extra moment to regard Boris's sizzling weapon. "Well, good. We were taken by surprise and with no weapons. My options have been limited. Do you have any plans for what you are going to do next?"

We all looked at each other. "Rescue you, Commander," I said. "And find out if it's just this base under attack, or if everything is. We escaped the Conglomerate attack, along with some others. They have headed for the mining launch facility. We were hoping, at the least, you would know where to find better weapons. Or what we should do next."

"I see." Zeus rotated around quickly and regarded the dead raptor. "This is the spear tip of a Conglomerate attack force. A special swarm, tasked with gaining ground and holding it secretly. They're mopping up anything left alive now. After that will come other cities on the moon in a rapid sequence, directed from this one. Once consolidated, jamming anything in this moon's orbit, they will use the shadow of your moon's orbit to assemble the attack on your world. They likely feel this is less of a waste than a large fleet attack."

"So Earth isn't under attack?" Ken asked. He sounded relieved. Much like me. I was slumping forward, a heavy weight sliding right off my back. I hadn't even realized I was holding that fear so tightly.

"No," Zeus said. "But it will be. If you don't help me. We're going to trigger a self-destruct sequence, maybe take that ship with the base. Together, we can hurt them back. And we're going to send out a distress call that can punch through that jamming."

Fuck. Yeah. I grinned widely. Boris gave me a thumbs-up.

As we moved, Ken paused. "What about the bodies of the

other Arvani?" he asked. "Is there anything we should do for them?"

Zeus snorted. "They were lower order Gaskation. Never the best of warriors. Leave them where they lie."

I glanced at Amira.

"A bit cold," she said on the arm's private, encrypted network.

"He's a bastard," I said. "But he's our bastard now."

We followed Zeus to the airlock, buoyed and ready to follow orders. And relieved to have someone who knew what was going on to lead us.

24

We all paused in front of the airlock. I took a deep breath. Once more back outside, across the surface in the open.

But Zeus stopped us.

"Down," he said. "There are tunnels." Zeus scuttled across the sand to one of the small wading pools. Spiral stairs on the other side led down into dimly lit, gray tunnels carved smoothly out of the lunar rock. How far down had they dug? The gravity plating had to be under us, and there were grates and more subsystems handling air and water systems.

Zeus sped up ahead of us. We were adjusting to being back under the pull of the base's gravity, fine-tuning our suits' movements.

Armor suddenly slammed into armor when Zeus turned a corner. Zeus staggered back into sight, suddenly lit up by a blast of Conglomerate rifle fire as he battled a raptor. Tentacles writhed and slapped around, and then slowed as they wrapped around the alien.

"I can't shoot," Ken said. "I'll hit them both."

"Don't," Zeus snapped.

Then, slowly and inexorably, Zeus started pulling the raptor apart.

It looked like the armor strained, bending and buckling slightly as he pushed it to the limit of its abilities. And then, with a popping sound, the raptor's arms came off, the armored surface revealing the flesh inside in an explosion of bodily fluids.

The raptor fell down, writhing.

Zeus kicked it aside with a tentacle, smearing the floor underneath. The useless Conglomerate energy rifle, now bent into a right angle, lay on the floor next to it. Zeus had a long scorch mark running up a tentacle. "That should be it," Zeus said. "Keep following me."

As I stepped over the raptor I paused, looking down at it. The reptilian eyes had clouded over, staring up at the ceiling.

I wondered how intelligent it was. Whether the Conglomeration had designed it to never question what it was doing, or if it believed that flying through the dark of space to come to my world had some greater purpose.

What did it think as it lay there dying?

In the quiet, empty corridors of one of the unused wings, Zeus led us through reinforced locks and into another weapons locker.

A much wider variety of weapons sat on racks here. Sig Sauer P250 handguns. M20 rifles in various configurations, more MP9s, and sturdy Mossburg shotguns.

Since I'd used the submachine gun already, I went for what I knew. Boris lowered his flashlight, staring like a kid in a candy store. "Look at all the RPGs," he whispered. "We have some Sierra-272s."

"GR-50." Ken moved toward a mean, heavy-looking rifle clearly meant for snipers; it was as long as he was tall. "That'll put a dent in some raptor armor."

Zeus clanked to the side where there was a wall of Accordance energy weapons. He picked up a pair of organic matte-black smoothed rifles, similar to the ones we'd trained with, and what looked like battery magazines for them. One of his other tentacles snagged something that looked similar to the Sierra RPG Boris was hugging.

"Okay, Commander," Ken said. "What about the comms now?"

Zeus jerked forward. "Commander," the Arvani mused on the common channel. "I hate that human word."

A tentacle slammed a battery pack into each of the two rifles, while another tentacle slung the longer weapon onto its back.

"I am not a commander, I am not a member of a *human* fighting force. Your ranks are irrelevant to me. I am Cal Riata, a master of the schooling force. And, you idiot of an ape, there is no self-destruct sequence. You will not be calling anyone for help."

Zeus raised the pair of rifles at us.

"What?" Ken said, not moving.

"What building has a self-destruct sequence? Has your home ever had one? Have you ever heard of one of your Navy ships having one?"

All of us, lined up in front of him, being yelled at, shifting from foot to foot: I had a strange sense of déjà vu pass through me in a shiver.

Zeus wasn't done ranting at us. And we all instinctively said nothing. "Or are your military forces genuinely stupid enough to feature an actual sequence that could destroy a fighting asset? That you would believe such a thing existed, that would allow one person to blow up this base, indicates your lesser ability to reason. Now, drop those weapons. Or die standing where you are."

I hadn't even gotten a chance to pick one up yet. Everyone else dropped theirs. I stared at Zeus, my stomach feeling like I was falling as my heart raced.

"You're Conglomerate?" Amira asked. "After all those lectures about how dangerous they are?"

"No. No. I'm Cal Riata," Zeus said, moving forward to flick the weapons on the ground away from us with a tentacle tip. "Proud Cal Riata. One of the finest of the Arvani, sent all the way to this backward system to do the scutwork that's beneath my kind. We Cal Riata lead schools of warships. We rain ruin upon our enemies. But I am here, to be overwhelmed fighting the Conglomeration in rear guard action? No. Not me. And not other Cal Riata who have been forced into positions like this. We are not inclined to be on the losing side."

I had led them into this. I'd decided not to run to the mines. Why had they listened to me? And the others! "Efua," I said on our arm's channel quickly. "Efua. Zeus betrayed us. He's Conglomerate. And he knows about you. Hide, get away. You probably don't have much time."

I wanted to throw up in my helmet. This was bad.

"Shit," Efua said, her voice brittle. "Shit. How long do we have? We're pretty deep inside here."

"You're on the losing side," Zeus continued. "They didn't tell you that, but the Accordance has slowly been watching planet after planet fall to the Conglomeration."

Amira answered Efua. "Not long. There are crickets headed your way. I wish I could tell you more. . . . I'm having trouble sneaking around the network. There's something actively blocking me. I think the Conglomeration has taken over the local networks and has counterintrusion coming online. And some of it is really good, it's blocking me out. I'm sorry."

"So now you kill us?" Ken asked.

"Maybe," Zeus said. "You survived. That shows *some* basic innate intelligence and survival instinct. More than I would have suspected from a bunch of air-breathers. So, quit running around underfoot, messing up plans that took many years to carefully craft, and make something of yourselves. Be rulers. The Conglomeration will need humans to help rule. It could be you."

"And what will you rule?" I asked.

"The Pacific Ocean." Zeus's dinner-plate eyes swiveled to lock onto me. "From the turquoise sandy shallows I will frolic in to the true depths that are my right. The depths my ancestors were chased out of by other Arvani a long, long time ago. What do you want? A state? A small country to rule together? This is the moment where you could have it."

I thought about the acting president, staggering around with his rheumy, alcoholic eyes. "The Conglomeration butchered defenseless recruits," I said.

"Soldiers die in war. It was going to happen, sooner or later," Zeus said. "You were never going to all live through this war. Now, I will take you to answer some questions about the rest of your group, and where they are. You will decide what currents to follow from there. Walk forward now. I'll guide you to where you need to be."

"He could have killed us by now," Boris said. "They want something specific out of us."

"Whatever it is, don't give it to them," Ken said. "Maybe they'll eventually get it out of us, but the longer that takes, the more likely the others get out of the mine."

"Zeus already knows they're in the mines around the launcher," I pointed out. "We told him. There are crickets headed that way. What else could they want? We *gave* them the information they need."

We followed our captor in silence for a moment.

"Plans," Amira said.

"What plans?" Ken asked.

"Zeus said we were upsetting long-laid plans. What plans were there? Plans to take Tranquility and the rest of the moon. They're not sure if we warned anyone or not."

I thought about it. "It could be."

"We might trigger them into attacking earlier," Amira said. "And we haven't actually warned anyone yet. And Efua and her . . . team . . . are going to get attacked."

She'd laid it all out. We'd really fucked this up.

I'd really fucked it up.

"I'm sorry," I told the team. If I could have hung my head visibly, I would have.

"Oh, get over yourself," Amira snapped. "We could have walked away from your plan to come in here and rescue this fucker at any time. It made sense. We rolled with it. You aren't some tragic leader we followed blindly to our deaths. Our eyes were open. We just got screwed by this asshole."

Boris clicked over to the common frequency. "So, you think the Conglomeration is better than the Accordance?" He sounded thoughtful.

"By the depths, no," Zeus said. "The Conglomeration is going to strip your species down to its usable genetic core, and then rebuild you into some tool that serves it best. It's a horrific thing. I have made the best of it."

"So the Conglomeration honors agreements?" Boris asked.

"Boris: What are you asking?" Ken snapped.

"What do we know about these invaders?" Boris asked us on the arm's private channel. "We can be second-class people in the Arvani's Accordance, or we can be lesser peoples within the Conglomeration. Either way, Earth is ruled by another alien race. Maybe we should hear their offer out. Maybe—"

"We know the Conglomeration kills unarmed recruits," I said coldly. "The Accordance, for as much as we hate them, at least follows a rule system. They're conquerors, but they leave us alive and intact once we surrender."

"We don't know what the Conglomeration really is, because all we get is what the Accordance told us," Boris said. "The one thing we do know for sure is that the Accordance is their enemy, and the Accordance rules Earth with a fist."

"The Accordance lifted billions out of war and poverty," Ken hissed. "They—"

Boris interrupted, "You say that because your grandfathers and great-grandfathers helped that fist, Ken, and you were handed spoils for helping the victors. They built you entire cities and industries in mere months. You didn't grow up watching the Thames run red with blood. . . ."

"Yeah, and why did people in my part of the world need those things so desperately that they would work with aliens, Boris?" Ken shouted. "Because your ancestors were not fucking helping us catch up, after they'd gone so far on our very backs, with *our* resources."

"Divide and conquer," I said softly, breaking in with a soft voice. "And maybe the Conglomeration will do it again, and Londoners will get the keys to the new civil administration. The easiest way to keep a population subjugated is to have them angry with each other. Or . . . maybe everything every creature has ever said about the Conglomeration is right.

I know the struthiform, Shriek, seemed honest enough. I think, maybe the Conglomeration's worse."

A moment's quiet.

"Maybe," Boris agreed. "But I think, to be honest, after the Conglomeration gets what it wants, there won't be a deal. I think we're dead."

"I think you're right," I said.

We trudged on past the ridges of bulkheads and through corridors.

"We're going to have to try and run, or fight him," Ken said. "I refuse to die without fighting."

I'd been thinking. Trying to imagine how I wanted to die. And I knew I agreed with him. I was terrified. But I wanted to do *something*. I didn't want to walk.

But I could see the appeal. Every minute placidly following Zeus meant another minute alive. And the back of my brain wanted life. It saw every minute of continuing life doing this as part of a chain that might mean more life. It was a groove, and I was following it.

How did I want to die? Fighting? Or delaying for every last minute? A placid participant? I wasn't going to try for glory, because it was likely that no one was ever going to know how I died.

But I didn't want to die stupidly. If I was going to try one last thing, let it be clever. Let it be . . .

I put out my right hand and let the tips of my armored fingers tap the bulkhead of another door. "Amira?" I tried not to look up. "Amira, we're passing bulkheads. I know you're cut out, but can you override them?"

She leaned back slightly, then stopped herself. "Shit," she said. "This wing wasn't damaged, so the bulkheads haven't shut automatically. It's too dangerous to open myself up while trying to get into the Accordance network to try to trigger them."

My heart sank. "You can't even try?"

"There's something prowling around it, hunting. I don't know for sure, but I suspect I'll end up a vegetable if I'm not careful."

"Fuck." I clenched a fist. "Is it the ghost? Is that what it is?"

"Maybe. Damn it. There's something familiar about the presence, like it's not Accordance, but I'm feeling like if I had time and the situation was different, I could pick apart the code and find something I've seen before. I don't know, maybe the Accordance stole technology from them and I'm seeing resonances there. But, never mind that . . . ," Amira said thoughtfully. "Maybe I have a way around needing to get into the network."

"We don't have many bulkhead doors left before we're out to the training grounds," I said.

"Shut up. Just a second. I can't get in, but maybe I can trick one locally."

We turned the last bend. The bay doors leading to the training grounds were just a couple hundred feet ahead in the widening corridor.

Amira grunted. "I can shine a laser at the air sensors," she said. "Convince them that everything went to shit. Drop the door. We have to time it just right. We all have to hang back, just a little, but not so much that Captain Calamari here notices."

"Any objections?" I asked.

"Do it," Ken said. We were getting close to another junction where the corridor bisected another. The last bulkhead before the bay doors.

We slowed. Zeus pulled slightly ahead, then stopped and

half turned to look back at us. He suddenly threw the bulk of his armored body back across the junction, his tentacles churning against the metal floor.

The five-inch-thick bulkhead pressure door slammed down into the top of his armor, pinning him to the floor. I had expected him to be on the other side and was caught flat-footed, not sure whether to run or attack.

"Get his guns!" Ken yelled.

We attacked. Four of Zeus's arms lashed at us, trying to get rifles aimed, while the other four tried to push away from under the door, which had groaned to a halt, lights flashing emergency yellow warning signals. Zeus's skin reacted inside the tank of water, twitching and changing colors like a strobe light. "You fucking apes!"

Zeus shook us around like limp dolls, smacking us against the lip of the pressure door, then against the floor. I tasted salty blood as my head rattled around inside the helmet, my legs fighting to kick a rifle loose as the world snapped dizzyingly around me, then stopped with bone-jarring crunches. "You will die for this. I will flay your skins and use them as *bait*."

When the rifle I'd been kicking at flew across the floor, I continued to hang on, rattling around and trying to hold the tentacle still.

"Got it," Boris said.

"Me too," Ken reported with a clatter.

I let go, smacked into the wall, and staggered back. My armor had been scraped and dented, but still worked.

Zeus dug every single tentacle down into the floor, piercing it and sinking in. Then, slowly, started pulling free of the door.

"Shit."

Amira stepped forward and pointed upward. The pressure door shivered. Smoke drifted from the sides of the walls.

Zeus's tank cracked. The tentacles froze.

The top of the oval tank splintered, and the door lurched down several more inches, cleaving its way in. Blue water slopped out onto the floor, spilling out of the gashes appearing throughout Zeus's armor.

"Do it!" Ken shouted.

Zeus's tentacles started scrabbling again. The back of his armor gurgled, a vomiting sound. Zeus began to frantically pull out of the armor.

The armor gave way in an explosion of fluids, sparks, and screeching. The pressure door slammed into the floor, leaving half a suit and two tentacles in front of us.

We'd been thrown clear of the door by Zeus during the struggle. Boris was the first one to walk forward and lean over the tentacles. "Well, he's going to be limping; there's flesh inside that armor."

"Boris," Amira said in a strangled voice. "Run!"

"What?" He straightened up. I saw his face through the visor. He looked bemused. We'd just won a victory. We'd come back from the brink. Boris wanted a moment.

A blur struck him, moving with inhuman speed from the corridor on the right. It picked him up with ease, as if it were handling a child.

It was an absence of something. Invisible, bending the light around itself and slipping around.

"Ghost!"

They disappeared down the corridor.

"I knew this would come in handy," Boris muttered to the rest of us. "Been saving it for a special occasion. Guys, you'd better run."

"Boris!" I shouted. Amira was picking up one of Zeus's rifles, seeing if she could get it to work. Ken ran forward.

The corridor exploded, knocking Ken back.

"Boris!" Ken screamed, his voice breaking. I couldn't understand whatever he said next. It was in a language I didn't recognize, but a pain in his voice made me shiver. Ken crawled on his hands and knees until I grabbed his ankle.

"We have to run," I said.

Amira grabbed Ken's arm and helped me yank him to his feet, even as he strained to pull away from us.

"We need to get weapons we can use, and get the hell out of here," I said, my voice shaking. "Boris gave us time. Now we need to use it."

25

We had retrieved weapons. The three of us had loaded up everything we could hang off our armor or carry in silence. I had an MP9 hanging from each shoulder, a handgun, and magazines clipped into pinchers up and down my thighs.

Also, after staring at it for a moment, I picked up Boris's cutting torch. Amira paused in front of a shelf, then pulled out what looked like an RPG launcher. But the tube was solid, and ribbed with high-density battery packs and high-energy cabling that crawled in and out of hundreds of ports, giving it a surprisingly cobbled-together look.

I glanced at the labeling on the shelf she'd taken it off. EPC-I was all it said.

Efua broke the silence as we slowly crawled out over the lunar surface for the ridge that would cover us: the far rim of the Icarus crater. "We're pinned down," she informed us, her voice somewhat flat and calm. "There is a raptor outside, and crickets inside. We're trying to use as little ammunition as we can, but eventually . . . the raptor will come for us."

"We're coming," I said solemnly. "But it's going to take a

while to get past the ridge." We were moving from shadow to shadow again, easing our way over the pockmarked surface out of the line of sight of the Conglomerate ship.

"And how long do you think 'a while' might be?" Efua asked.

"It took five hours to cross last time," Amira said. "Plus time to get from the ridge to the mines."

"Five hours," Efua repeated. "Okay. Okay, six hours. We will see you then."

She didn't sound sure of that. She was talking herself into it.

"The ghost isn't dead," Amira whispered. "It's still on the Accordance networks, trying to find me. I have to stay locked down."

"It could be a different ghost," Ken said, speaking for the first time in over an hour.

"It *could* be," Amira agreed. She didn't sound sure.

"Trolls," I said from my spot in the dark. The giant creatures had come around the side of the base, roving back and forth in a crude search pattern.

"They're going to slaughter everyone in Tranquility," Ken said, two hours later. We crouched in separate craters, waiting for the trolls to turn their backs so we could move. "And then they'll come for Earth."

"I know." I was in the clear. I scrabbled over broken rock to leap out from the shadows in the dark. I landed on the tip of a boulder, then swung behind it just before a troll turned and looked my way.

No dust, I pleaded. It had been a long, risky move.

"It didn't see you," Amira said.

I let out a breath.

“Clear to spot for me,” she said a moment later.

I peeked around the boulder and got eyes on both massive aliens.

“What are we going to do?” Ken asked.

“Stay alive,” I said. “Try to get word out. Try to walk out from under this jamming and get Amira to send a message. And you’re good, Amira. Go.”

I saw Amira kangaroo out from boulder to boulder in almost a straight line. The impacts looked brutal, but it kept her from arcing up high over the surface.

Smart. I’d have to try that.

“It’s going to take too long to walk out from under this,” Ken said. “They will move away and attack Tranquility before we have a chance to get within range of something that can hear our suits. We need to take direct action.”

“You’re welcome to pop up and wave at the trolls anytime you want,” I told him. “I don’t want to be toe-paste.”

“There is more than just surviving,” Ken snapped. “The stakes are much higher.”

“Stay alive first,” Amira cautioned. “The longer we do, the more options we can scare up.”

“I just . . . ,” Ken started.

“I know,” Amira said. “Save that. Just hold on to it for later.”

I leaned back against the boulder and looked up over the ridge that we’d been slowly, too slowly, moving closer to.

Something twinkled up into the dark sky between a notch in the rock, then disappeared, blocked from my sight as it was flung into orbit.

“Efua, Devlin here,” I said. “Is the mass driver still launching payloads?”

“Devlin, I hear you, just one moment.” Efua grunted. The sound of something like a slap came through, and tortured metal. Efua panted. "Yes. It just launched. I think the Conglomeration is leaving it alone, so that no one from Tranquility realizes anything is wrong over here."

No gunshots. Her team had to be attacking crickets by their armored hands to save ammunition.

Dangerous. But they were trapped and running low.

Buying time, I thought. All we were doing was buying time. And the end was the same no matter what. We were not going to live through this. Even if we got word out, or hid and survived, eventually our air would run out.

We needed to go about this in a different direction. We needed to stop running and start *thinking*.

I looked back up at the notch where the twinkle of the launch came through.

"I think Ken's right," I said, before I'd even realized it.

"Shit. You too?" Amira sighed. "What are you thinking now? We storm the base?"

"No. We're fucked," I told her. "We're outnumbered. We'd get cut down the moment we popped our heads up. But maybe we can still hurt them. Hurt them enough to get a signal out. When Zeus flew us in, he said the mass driver could change where it delivered packages."

"It's giant artillery," Amira said. "Right in front of us. You're right. But there is a raptor and a shitload of crickets crawling around."

"I didn't say it would be easy. Or guaranteed. But can you access the systems?"

"That's not the biggest problem," Amira said.

What had I missed? "What's the problem?"

"The moment I get into the Accordance systems on that thing, the ghost will know. It's sniffing everything around here. I see why the Accordance uses entangled quantum systems for our team comms, and tries to use regular frequencies as little as possible. Trolls aren't looking, you're a go."

"Moving." I took a deep breath and shot across the surface and up the ridge. I smacked into rocks, some of them tumbling down the base-facing side. "Shit."

On the other side I rabbited again.

"They're focused elsewhere, still good. Still good. Ken: Go!"

I found a bolt-hole on the other side of the slope and watched the horizon.

"Can you trick it?" I asked.

"Go," Ken said.

Amira responded with a grunt. She was moving now. I looked left just in time to see her somersault over the ridge and arc slowly down into the crater. She hit in a plume of dust.

"Get clear of that," Ken said.

She hopped from rock to rock, away from dirt, trying to avoid leaving tracks from the large divot she'd made. "What do you mean, 'trick it'?"

"They're going to know we're attacking and retaking the mass driver and the mines supplying it," I said. "So they're not going to be *that* surprised if you show up on the network. I don't know a ton about systems and networks, but can you trick them into thinking you're trying to break out a signal?"

Amira bounced around some more, then came to a stop. "Maybe," she said thoughtfully.

"As long as they don't realize we're fucking with the mass driver," I said. "We hit their ship, the jamming goes down, we warn everyone."

"And then all hell breaks loose."

"Exactly," I said. "And a lot of lives might be saved."

"We are clear," Ken said, arcing overhead in a long jump

away from the rim. "They are circling back the other way. And I think Devlin has the plan."

"My last one wasn't so hot," I said.

Ken hit dirt. "I want to see that seething mass of Conglomerate shit fall out of the sky and burn. I can't think of any other way to make that happen, and it's a better plan than any I've come up with. Amira, are you willing?"

"You can't do this without me," she said.

"It matters how we choose to die," Ken said.

"Don't lecture me about how to die, Ken. I've seen people throw themselves at a cause and bleed out in the street. I've held arms while basement surgeons try to save a fighter for a cause. When the moment comes, all you have is pain and fear. No one's marching off into it full of fervor and excitement. They beg for their mothers. They beg for relief."

"They scream," Ken agreed softly. "Then they choke, because the air is sucked out of the building. You try to give them air, but some of them wave you away. And then their heads pop, hit by concentrated energy. Hundreds of them. No fervor, Amira. Just survival."

"I'm sorry," she said. "I forgot you were in there when it happened."

"And so was Boris," Ken said. "I want to give them back a taste of what they did. Will you help?"

"Well, we're going to head over there to help Efua out anyway," Amira said. "We might as well try this."

"Good." I stood up and loped along behind them. "Efua, we're coming!"

"I heard your plan," she said. "But you need to hurry."

We picked up the pace as best we could.

26

Crickets swarmed around the pilings, a mechanized cloud of snapping pincers and needle-sharp maws. The launcher itself dwarfed us all. It sat inside a low-lying crater, the breech down at the center and the tip propped up by the ridge a mile away. Accordance engineers had then covered the entire crater in superstructural, organic latticework that created a perfect bowl for the barrel to rest in.

The mile-long barrel could be moved, just as Zeus had said. The lattice below it had gears and pistons the size of buildings under the pilings. A typical Accordance structure: fragile looking, giant, and carved quickly out of a landscape.

"Where are the tunnels to the mines?" Ken asked. "Efua? Can you tell us?"

"She's been quiet for the last forty minutes," Amira said.

"Efua!" Ken repeated.

"She'll answer us if she can," I said.

"Let's try the base of the launcher," Amira said. "There's probably another way in. They'd want to be able to drive things in, but we'll have to walk all the way around the rim of the crater to find it. They have to have something near all that equipment that needs maintaining, though."

"Also, that's where the crickets are swarming from," I agreed. The moving cloud hadn't spotted us peeking down from the ridge at them yet. A small part of me suggested that it would be a good idea to turn and run before they did, that I could still live through this by running.

But where?

"We have to be quick; they could just cluster and overwhelm us." Amira sounded annoyed by the idea, like it was a tactic beneath her.

"Keep them away from your helmet," Ken said. "Don't waste too much of your ammunition. And watch for the raptor. I haven't spotted it yet, have any of you?"

A child-sized cricket scuttled up from under the latticework and leapt into the air. Amira fired once with a handgun, hitting it in the center and scattering pieces, which rained slowly down around us.

The boiling mass at the center of the crater stopped swirling around the mass driver's infrastructure and swirled in our direction.

"Let's go!" I shouted, leaping over the ridge and onto the lattice toward the swarm. "Amira, keep behind us."

"Oh, bullshit," she snapped, angry. I looked up as she leapt over me toward the oncoming rush.

"You're the only one that can program the damn thing!" I shouted.

"Then keep up." Amira jumped again, high and visible to the cricket swarm. They adjusted en masse, shifting to anticipate where she would land.

"Amira!"

At the apex of her jump she swapped from handgun to the

EPC-1 device with all the energy blisters she'd slung on her back. And didn't fire.

It had been a ridiculously tall jump, with not much forward progress. Crickets boiled underneath her, climbing over each other's metallic jointed bodies with artificial eagerness to look upward at her. Jaws snapped, legs readied to stab at her.

Ken changed course, headed toward the growing mountain of crickets. "Get back," Amira snapped as she plummeted down at them.

She triggered the device she held casually at her hip. The energy blisters glowed, the cabling lit up, sparked, and a ring of energy spat from the tip. Everything in my suit dimmed slightly at the same time, and my movements stuttered.

Crickets of various sizes and shapes fizzled and spat, then fell still. Amira plunged into their bodies and slid down a hill of twitching legs. "They're not the only ones who can use electromagnetic pulses," she said triumphantly. "Electronic Pulse Cannon, model 1, for the win. Come on!"

We changed course, zigging and zagging our way down the slope so that crickets could gather and clump for Amira. After two more bursts, and two more piles of twitching crickets, we hit the base.

"So many," I muttered.

"At least we haven't encountered any drivers," Amira said. Just the test ones in training could scatter us.

"Don't jinx us like that." I didn't even want to think of the things jamming their tails into my spine to take me over.

"There's an airlock, and a ramp," Ken said, veering off.

"Right behind you," Amira said.

I came up behind them, making sure something didn't get us while we entered. Amira hopped around, looking for manual overrides.

Three cat-sized crickets, one of them dragging broken legs behind it, leapt over the ramp's edge at us. I shot them down with a few silent, quick bursts of my MP9, then crushed the remains with my heel.

"Okay," Amira said. "We're in."

We piled into the airlock and Amira shut it behind us. Moments later things clattered against it, trying to break through and get to us.

We stood in the space between the two doors for a moment, catching our breath.

Then Amira grabbed a lever and pumped it several times to charge the inner door. "You ready for this?" she asked.

I raised my MP9. "Yes."

I was lying. Anything on the other side knew something was about to come through.

Ken stepped up next to me. "Ready," he said.

Amira pushed the lever back into the wall and the door clunked, then jerked open. A white-hot bolt of lightning blew my vision out as it snapped through the open space and hit Ken. He opened fire even as he flew back, knocked into the outer door.

I stepped forward, firing wildly. Amira's weapon fired, my steps stuttered, and fuzzy static filled my ears. "Got the energy rifle," she said.

The snap of electricity stopped, my helmet visor faded, and my sight returned just in time for me to see a raptor in midleap, tossing its now-ruined weapon to the side.

"Raptor!" Ken shouted, a moment too late.

"Oh—" It struck me, knocking me right back into the airlock. "Shit!"

The thwack of bullets filled the airlock: Amira, on the raptor's back, firing point-blank at its long neck with her handgun. It let go of me and slammed up against the airlock, trying to shake her loose.

Ken staggered to his feet as I fumbled with the welder. I'd seen Boris use it, but it was an alien tool designed for alien hands. For several agonizing seconds, I couldn't figure out how to turn it on as we struggled in the airlock.

Then it lit up, the points converging on the pure point of light, and I swung it up into the tangle of Amira, Ken, and the raptor. I aimed for its chest, but Ken, wrestling with one of its hands, swept past me. The welder cut through his calf and he screamed.

"Shit." I apologized as I slammed the torch into the raptor's chest, not willing to risk also hitting Amira, who struggled on its shoulders, if I aimed for the neck.

Molten armor splashed back against me and covered my shielded wrists. I shoved forward, and the raptor staggered back. "Get away," I warned Amira as I leaned in, feeling the welder bite through armor, then pop through.

Amira rolled away, and I pinned the alien to the wall and buried the weapon deeper with another shove. It stopped trying to claw at me. It slumped forward, pinned as the welder passed through the back of its armor and melted into the wall.

"I think you got it," Amira said. "You can turn it off."

I pulled my thumb off the button and the sizzling faded. I let go, leaving both the alien and the welder hanging from the wall, and turned around. "Ken!"

He stood on one leg, with an arm over Amira's shoulder. "I'm okay," he said, through audibly gritted teeth. I could see sweat dripping from his face through his helmet.

"Shit, man, I'm so fucking sorry."

"You killed it." He grimaced. "That is what matters. And the cut is not so bad. The suit is giving me painkillers and packing the wound with sealant. I can compensate. You can let me go. We must get control of the mass driver."

He pulled away from Amira and wobbled on his own.

"I just need somewhere to patch in locally," Amira said. She sounded tired. They were all running on fumes. Maybe even making mistakes at this point. Small ones, but how straight could you think when you hadn't slept since the attack?

But we couldn't slow anything down now.

"There will be more crickets in here," Ken said. "Go with Amira so she can focus on the things she needs to do. I'll search for Efua and the others."

"Be careful." I wanted to grab his forearm, but he nodded and limped down the corridor. I turned and grabbed the welder with both hands and yanked it. The raptor toppled to the floor.

"This way," Amira said, stepping over it.

"How do you know?"

She pointed to the floor. "Directions in ultraviolet, lines that lead to different points. I can read a little Arvani."

We leapfrogged sloppily and quickly down the corridor, grateful for no surprises but still jumpy in the low red lighting.

Several turns later and a floor below, Amira triggered a set of doors. "Here we go."

Floor-to-ceiling displays cascaded information, including outside views of the launcher. "I thought there'd be *something* in here," I said.

"Shit's automated," Amira said. "This room's for trouble-shooting and maintenance. Watch the doors."

I set up next to them, glancing back at her as she walked to one of the displays and put her palm out. Blue light danced across her arm. "The clock just started," she said. "The ghost knows we are here."

Her fingers began to twitch as she manipulated glyphs in the air.

"Does it know what you're doing?"

"Shhhh. It thinks we're trying to signal out. The jamming just kicked way up."

She went back to work. I kept quiet. But there was a new noise. I amplified it. A sound like metal hail against the outer door.

Crickets trying to get in.

I had to assume she'd locked them out. How many had piled up out there, redirected by the ghost to come knocking?

I swallowed. What else might come join them at the door as I waited.

"I found Efua and the others," Ken said. I could hear in his voice what he was seeing, by the way it cracked slightly and in the soft tone.

"I'm sorry, man." I shook my head. "I'm sorry."

"Amira?" Ken asked sadly.

A long pause. "They're dead?" Amira asked.

"Yes."

She sounded as shattered as Ken did. "I can't do it."

"What do you mean?" Ken and I asked her as one.

"The mountain in the center of that crater the base is in. It's in the way. I can't take out the ship, or them, or the base. I guess I could shoot at the top of the ridge and hope something gets through, but I doubt it. And it'll warn them. They'll have time to move. And I can't aim the launcher higher, like artillery. And that wouldn't work anyway; the moon's gravity is too weak. No matter where you point that fucker, the payload's going to orbit. I'm so sorry, guys. We can't turn it and shoot."

I wanted to slide down, my legs felt so suddenly weak. Out on the other side of the door, the sound of the metallic hail slowly grew louder and more insistent.

27

I looked at the screen that Amira waved into existence. It showed the mass of rock in our way. Not something any of us had thought about: topography. And I'd assumed she could have fired *over* anything. But the gravity was too weak on the moon. Things fired at great speed took a while to curve downward.

Ken made a strangled, frustrated sound. I couldn't blame him.

"We need to get out of here," Amira said.

"No." I held up a hand. "No. We need to brainstorm. We need to slow down. All three of us. There has to be an answer here."

"Damn it," Amira snapped. "Let go of it. We're not going to be heroes. We're not going to save the day. Even if this had worked, we were probably going to die like Efua, trapped in a corridor somewhere. Let's find a place to buy more time, Devlin."

"Take a breath," I said. "You're tired, we've fought these things since we broke into the base. We're still alive, but we're running on adrenaline and will. Let's not make a mistake now, when we've come so far. Come on, let's just stop. We have a launcher—"

"Fire a series of them," Ken suggested. "First one blows up the hilltop. The next one comes through."

"I thought about that," Amira said wearily. "First explosion alerts them. They move."

"Not necessarily," Ken replied.

"No, but I also don't know for sure if the hilltop will break away. It's soft. It might just create a hell of a dust cloud and that's it. I can't model what's going to happen without more time and computing. We're not going to get that. So that's two unknowns."

Small dents were being hammered into the door. A single feeler rammed its way through the gap between the doors, trying to pry them open. I broke it off and stomped on it.

"We have a device that can launch anything we want into orbit," I said. "What else can we do? Launch ourselves? Can you slow it down so we're not instant toothpaste?"

"Wait," Amira said. "Wait a second."

I had a vision of us in armor, in orbit, beaming a weak SOS to anyone who could hear us. "Or maybe we could put an emergency signal on repeat on a suit and put that into orbit," Ken said. "We don't have to load ourselves. We . . . have extra armor here."

"No. Shut up." Amira had her hands up behind her neck. "Orbit. It's about orbit." She was thinking. But we were all so tired.

"What?" A series of loud pops against the doors made me jump. Something fizzled outside. What the hell were the crickets doing out there?

"Orbit." Amira's fingers danced again. She stood in front

of the lights and glyphs like a conductor. Lines flowered out from a central point in the air. "Fucking orbit!"

"This is good, right?" Ken asked. "You have an idea?"

"I hate to say it, but Devlin's right. I was too tired to see it. We're still going to shell the fuck out of that Conglomerate ship." Amira sounded excited.

"How?"

"We're not going to fire right at them, we're going to come at them from behind," Amira said. "The capsules will fire into orbit, all around the moon, and then hit from the other direction. Each capsule contains a ton of ore, and it's going to be moving fast. Each shot will be a slightly different angle, so when it comes back around, it's going to saturate the area. And all at the same fucking time, too."

"Will the ship have time to get away?" I asked. "If the shots come in from orbit."

"Not if I come in low, just above the surface. The moon is very round, it's smaller. I can use topography maps, the first rounds can come in right over the hills. The ship will have seconds to react at the speeds I'm planning."

"I like this," Ken said. "How long will it take to do this?"

"Not long. First capsule just got fired, and it looks good. Just keep those crickets out of the room and I'll start. But we'll need to stay in here until the capsules hit," Amira said.

"Why?"

"The capsules can maneuver. Small adjustments, but if the Conglomeration figure out what we did, they could alter the commands, shift where the rounds hit to somewhere else nearby. If we hold the room, there's a better chance."

I looked at the door. Another small leg had wiggled through and was waving about. I crushed it. "It's going to be dicey."

"All we have to do is last until the capsules come back around. Two hours."

"Two hours." I shook my head. Stay alive for two hours.

More dents appeared in the door.

Maybe.

"Oh . . . ," Amira breathed. "That's not good."

"What?"

She waved one of the images through the air toward me. "Trolls."

Two of them softly trudged through the dirt on the other side of the ridge, a mile away and closing. Crickets loped along with them, some riding on the large, irregular feet.

Farther back, three raptors arced through the lunar night in a triangular formation.

"Reinforcements," I told Ken. "The two trolls. Three raptors. More crickets."

"And the ghost is out there somewhere," Amira said. "I can feel it. Probing. Trying to figure out what I'm up to."

I looked around the room. "When I leave the room, you hide in the floor panels. Crickets can't see you, or they'll report back there's still someone in here. They have to think it's just me and Ken that'll be running around outside."

"It's too dangerous out there," Amira said. "The ghost—"

"Don't use that electromagnetic pulse cannon unless you have to, if you're holding the room. We want to get as much time keeping them guessing as we can," I continued.

"I won't stay in here." Amira raised her hands.

"You have to," I pleaded. "You're systems. You have to make it through this. You have to make sure these fuckers get the hammer dropped on them."

"Fuck!" Amira shouted.

She was right. Running would feel better than hiding and

waiting. It was not her style to hole up in the shadows. But she needed this room. "I'm so sorry. We need to hold the room. We need to pull them away."

"Okay," she said. "Okay. I can power down the suit, hide under the cable runs. I should be able to sneak into the system here and there, keep monitoring things. I'll keep the EPC, if I have to, last ditch, hold the room. Damn it, you two give them a hell of a chase, okay? And we meet up afterward."

"You two are stuck with me for a long while yet." I helped her rip the flooring up. She crawled in, digging down between thick conduit and cables, then I handed her the EPC.

I pushed the floor back down, making sure the panels fit right in and didn't look disturbed.

Crossing my fingers mentally, I approached the doors.

"Be careful," Amira said. "Tell me when to open them."

"Yeah. Careful," I said. I took a deep breath. "Open."

The doors jerked open and crickets poured over each other to get inside at me. I opened fire and leapt through into the boiling mass, yanking clutching limbs free and swearing.

28

I slid around a corner, a wave of crickets nipping at my heels.

"Duck," Ken growled. He stepped around the next corner and raised an MP9 in each hand. I slid, and he opened fire. The chattering sounded distant through my helmet, but I could feel cricket bits and pieces pinging against my armor.

Ken dropped the submachine guns to swap to a handgun as he jumped over me and started smashing remaining crickets against the wall.

They swirled around, keeping away from him, then changed direction and scuttled away in full retreat.

I stood up as Ken limped back my way.

"Now to get outside," he said to me. "And lead them all away. Amira, are you still hidden?"

"Yeah." It was a curt, chopped off "yeah." "Want me to take a look at how close your guests are?"

"Take no risks," Ken said.

Ken and I got into the airlock. We stood on either side of the scorched body of the raptor. Three more of those things were coming for the two of us, I thought. And one almost killed the three of us. "What about your leg?" I asked. "I cut through, didn't I?"

"There was sealant both for my leg, and to secure integrity," Ken said. "It should be fine."

"Should be?"

"Yes." Ken pumped the manual lever, and the door leading back to the corridor shuddered shut.

"Because now's the time for you to turn back," I said.

"Why would I turn back?" Ken asked, incredulous.

"So you don't die out there on the lunar surface when that outer door opens."

Ken stepped forward with a thud and pumped the outward manual lever. "We're hoping they haven't noticed there were three of us, and Amira makes sure to destroy their ship, and many of them. As for you and me . . ." The outer door slid open with a rush of air.

We leapt out, weapons up. But nothing shot back at us. No giant feet stomped us out of existence.

"They're still coming," I said, relieved.

Ken bounded up the latticework alongside the giant barrel. "Come on," he urged.

We hopped and bounced our way up, huffing and puffing until we reached the rim and stopped to look back.

"How's the leg?" I asked.

"The seal holds," Ken replied. We stood on the rock, watching the other side. Waiting.

"Shit, this is intolerable," I said. "My hands are shaking. Just standing here. Jumpy."

"My father fought in the Pacification," Ken said. "He said a lot of war is just standing, waiting for the sudden action that might mean your death."

I guessed Ken's father hadn't been fighting the Accordance. But I didn't say anything, just kept looking at the ridge.

"There." The two trolls crested the other side and paused.

Ken reached back, then flung a grenade that had been stuck to his lower back. It arced accurately over the length of the barrel, across the crater to the other side, and skittered across near the trolls' feet.

Their large heads swiveled our way as the grenade exploded, charring the lattice but not them. One of the wormhole cannons snapped up. Ken and I both leapt away. The rock where we'd stood shivered as it was stripped clean of dirt, then a large chunk ripped free and flew away.

"That got their attention." I hopped around boulders. "Should we split up?"

"No. But be silent. This is now a marathon." Ken sailed away with a giant leap.

I followed.

We fell into a rhythm, an awkward-looking set of jumps alternating leg to leg, assisted by the armor. Occasionally Ken would accidentally key the channel, and I'd hear him grunt in pain as he landed on his left leg and jumped.

I didn't say anything.

We ate up several miles this way, sometimes pausing when one or the other fumbled and wiped out in the dirt. The adaptive camouflage didn't do too much good with this much movement, but after forty minutes on the run we were gray, dirty messes that had to be hard to spot from a distance.

Problem was, the trolls weren't that far in the distance. They were gaining. Every minute they loomed even closer, and the raptors were just behind them.

"When do we make our stand?" I asked, scanning for good

terrain. Some rabbiting, turning around, maybe we could get our hands on one of the raptors.

Maybe.

"I see a lot of jagged hills to the north," Ken said. "Lets—" A blur struck him right at the apex of his jump. He tumbled end over end with it, grappling as they rolled.

I swerved toward them, trying not to look behind us. The trolls would get within wormhole cannon range in twenty seconds easy. I keyed the welder on, lighting up the gray lunar surface with its pure light, tossing shadows everywhere.

Every ounce of me strained as I leapt from a boulder, arrowing right at Ken. I aimed the tip of energy right at the blur, despite not being able to even understand what I was seeing.

"What's happening?" Amira asked. "Is it the ghost?"

At the last second the slippery nothingness twitched. I struck it hard enough to knock Ken loose and started trying to stab it with the welder. It had penetrated raptor armor; maybe it would cut through this. "Run, Ken!" I could feel the ground underneath me shake.

"Guys?"

The nothingness had my wrists. I struggled to pivot the welder, but my wrists were pushed back, and then farther back, until something tore and popped and I couldn't hold the welder anymore.

The welder dropped to the ground and spat dust until something turned it off.

I lay pinned to the ground, looking right through whatever held me there, to the darkness far above. I waited for the killing shot, or blow, but nothing happened. The blur picked me up, and then, slowly, began to walk.

The camouflage on the ghost worked similarly to the

Accordance's: It was bending light around itself to replicate whatever was on the other side. This close, I could see the effect shifting in real time. Accordance armor required you to stay still, but this armor adjusted in time to keep the effect going. And even at six inches away, all I could tell was that the ghost was bipedal.

Whatever was underneath, I still couldn't see.

"Ken?" Amira asked.

"I'm sorry," Ken said. "He saved me from the ghost. But now . . ."

"I'm not dead yet," I said, and then, utterly perplexed, I added, "It's carrying me. Tell my parents—"

"I'm going to come for you!" Ken interrupted.

"No!" I twisted around to look. "The trolls are following me and the ghost, but the raptors are still out looking for you. Wherever you're hidden, just stay put. We're keeping them out of Amira's way still, there's nothing you can do for me."

"But *I* can," Amira said. "You're far enough downrange of the launcher that I might be able to fire on you. I could get the capsules to start maneuvering right out of the barrel to arc down at you and hit the trolls."

"No," I said firmly. "That will warn them that we have control of the launcher. No, let it take me."

"Damn it," Amira snapped. "Listen, give me access to your suit. Just think permission my way, I want in."

"What will that accomplish?"

"Just do it. I've been thinking about the ghost. The Conglomeration, they're thinking creatures. They use machines. And that has to mean similarities. They have assembly language, or ones and zeroes, or something. Input-output ports."

"Can you explain that in plain English?" Ken asked.

"There are maybe even similarities in technology," Amira

continued, and then paused. "Ken, I'm going to use his suit to probe the area around him using our encrypted connection. Thankfully it's impossible for them to tell we're talking over quantum networks."

"Okay, Amira," I said. And willed the permission over my neural connection.

"What do you think you can do?" Ken asked.

Hopefully she would learn something about our enemy, I thought. I looked over at the massive, rock-armored feet of the trolls.

And maybe she could figure out why they were taking me alive.

29

The trolls continued their honor guard position all the way back to the ruins of the base. We stopped under the trailing arms of the jellylike Conglomerate starship. Two raptors ran out of a nearby airlock, danced around the trolls, and tried to grab me. The ghost responded, invisible limbs shoving one of them rudely back.

"You stopped moving," Amira said. "Are you okay?"

"There are two raptors here." They aimed their energy rifles at me. "They seem to be arguing with the ghost."

"About what?"

"I don't know. I don't speak invisible alien," I snapped. "But I think maybe they want me dead."

A massive hand swung from the sky and slapped a raptor. It flew across the dirt and bounced several times, and the second troll stepped forward and crouched aggressively in front of the other raptor.

It slung its rifle and stepped back.

The other raptor stood up and visibly shook itself, then slunk off.

"I've been working hard on updating some heads-up display software to patch in and show you something," Amira said. "You're going to need it. You're in the strike zone and you have five minutes before the barrage starts."

"I'm not getting away," I said. I'd been fighting the ghost all the way here. In addition to broken wrists, I now had contusions all over my body. A slight concussion from rattling my head around left me slightly out of it. The ghost was stronger and faster.

My visor flickered and rebooted. The information about my suit and charge levels faded. It came back on, and the lunar surface around me changed. It was overlit by large pools of red light.

"Red is impact, timers are above them. The arcs are the trajectories."

A four-minute timer hung above the red bull's-eye I stood in. I looked above me. Three minutes until the Conglomerate ship got hit. Lines of silvery thread led away from the center of the impact pools off into the dark sky.

Nine different silver lines led to the alien ship. Another ghostly one appeared as I watched. Each came in from a different angle or vector.

"Now, for getting you away from the ghost, I need you to hug it and get the charge port in your heels firmly against its surface. I'm going to discharge your power into it, and when I do that, it will temporarily overwhelm it. Or startle it. I hope. It's the best I can do."

She sounded so apologetic, I felt duty-bound to respond with energy. But I was tired, and hurting, even despite the painkillers I'd had the suit pump into me. "Thank you, Amira." I looked up. Two minutes.

"If that happens, you run. Stay out of the red zones. Debris is still an issue. You'll have to work hard, the suit will be mostly dead or dying after the discharge of energy."

"Okay."

One of the long tentacles unfurled itself from the starship and reached down for the ground. I watched it descend all the way down to meet us. The flat tip hit the ground in front us, kicking up lunar dust. I gently shifted my feet down, angling them to touch the ghost's invisible surface.

"Tell me when you're ready," Amira said.

Sixty seconds.

The ghost and trolls waited for the dust to settle, then stepped forward onto the flat tip of the tentacle. I pressed my boots firmly against the ghost.

Forty seconds.

The tentacle contracted, transparent musculature showing veins the size of bridge cables pumping fluid underneath its skin, and we slowly rose.

I watched the lunar surface drop away.

Thirty seconds.

"Now," I told Amira.

My boots exploded with arcs of electricity. The ghost danced and writhed in pure blue light, and its viselike grip on me broke.

I shoved off and out from the platform tip of the tentacle and into free fall, streaming electricity as I fell.

When I hit the ground on my back I lay there, the air knocked out of my chest, gasping.

Fifteen seconds. "Did it work?" Amira asked.

"Yes," I hissed. One of the trolls let go of the tentacle and stepped out over the side to fall down after me. I got up. The armor wasn't too heavy, but there was no assistance. It was just me and my own muscle.

The troll struck the ground in front of me.

I turned and ran back the other way in a halfhearted loping bounce. I just needed to get out from under the ship, even if it meant heading farther into the strike zones. The pool I stood in had a countdown of a minute.

Seven seconds. A troll leapt over me and landed in front of me. We faced off.

Five.

It stopped looking at me and glanced up.

Three, two.

One. Something flashed along the silver line so quickly I barely saw it and struck the side of the Conglomerate ship. The entire jellylike structure shivered as the capsule ripped out the other side. Debris hung in the air over us, yanked out of the ship's insides. "It's a hit!" I shouted, and regretted it. Pain spiked through my ribs from the effort.

A figure leapt out away from the tentacle. It was no longer invisible; I could see limbs. Two legs, two arms, a head. The flat gray armor looked mundane now.

The second impact and third hit the Conglomerate ship. It began to move, wobbling and struggling to get away.

"Devlin, run!"

I turned and bounced away, looking at the red pools. Twenty seconds. I veered in a circle, leading the troll around and into it. The now visible ghost followed. I'd burned out its camouflage and gotten away, but it was mobile again. And coming for me. Shit.

Ten.

Amira shouted excitedly. "Kinetic energy is an *angry* bitch!"

The ship was no longer directly overhead and debris was hitting the ground everywhere, pieces of the ship falling away. A whole tentacle detached and draped itself over the base.

Crickets boiled out from the ship and the base, leaping and running for safety.

"Devlin, Ken? Are you okay?"

I doubled back, away from the next target. The troll followed. I stopped at the edge, turned back to it, and raised my hands. The ghost stepped forward, out from under the troll's legs.

The lunar surface exploded as the impact I was waiting for happened. I flew through the air, cartwheeling hard enough to black out, then jar back to life as I struck the surface. I bounced several times.

There was no troll anymore, just a black stain where it had stood. Impacts were hitting constantly, the ground shaking every few seconds as payloads Amira had sent up in various orbits were all now converging to hit at almost the same time, even though they'd been launched at different intervals.

The ghost had been flung with me. It lay still, arms and legs spread at unnatural angles. I crawled over, glancing around at the impact points on Amira's heads-up display to see if it was safe as I worked my way toward safety. Sixty seconds before this area would get hit by another of Amira's capsules.

I looked at the ghost as I passed by, and froze.

His face was covered in blood.

But it was a he.

It was a person.

There was a dead *human being* in Conglomerate armor lying on the ground. The ghost was human.

Was this a trick? What did it mean? Had Conglomerate forces been to Earth? When? Or was it some kind of parallel evolution?

Or was this Conglomerate species molded to look human so it could invade or rule Earth?

I didn't know. I grabbed the body and pulled it along with me, grateful for the lower gravity.

Thirty seconds.

I stumbled and fell as I ran out of the area as best I could and—

Wham!

—another impact threw me clear as I clutched the ghost's body. Rocks and dirt rattled against my armor.

I scrabbled along farther, getting clear of the impact zones. I was on my ass, pulling the ghost after me. I watched the Conglomerate ship fall slowly into the base, vomiting gas and fire as it burned and I scooted slowly away.

My heads-up display flickered and died.

No air scrubbing now. I would just breathe the air left inside until I passed out. I wasn't sure how long that would be, but I was sure it wasn't long enough for me to make it back to the launcher.

I sat on top of the ghost, hoping it was truly dead, and watched the destruction unfold in front of me.

30

"Are you okay?" Ken had to push his helmet's visor against mine for sound to travel between us. A quick and crude way for us to communicate. Sound waves hitting his visor, then mine, then passing back to me. He sounded distant and tinny. "Devlin, say something."

I coughed.

"Amira, he's okay. He has some air still."

But not for much longer, I thought.

"Hold on, Amira gave me an air canister when she sent me to look for you," Ken said. He left and walked around to my side. A loud hiss startled me, and then my head cleared. Fresh air. My apathy at seeing Ken, at still being alive, was swept away.

But with that came the awareness of all the pain I was in. And I couldn't request a new round of painkillers.

Ken came back around and touched helmets again. "I think we can make it to the launcher now. Who is that with you? Is he alive?"

"It's the ghost," I said. "Help me pick it up. My wrists are broken."

"But . . ." Ken pulled away to look closer. He turned back to me, talking, but I couldn't hear him without our helmets touching.

He grabbed my helmet and bumped his visor into mine again. "It's a person."

"I know." I pulled away and tried to reach for the ghost on my elbows and knees. Ken shook his head and picked it up. He slung it over his shoulder and leapt ahead of me.

Of course, his armor was still functional. I struggled to my feet, hard to do without using my hands, and bounded after him as best I could on complaining muscles.

We made better time to the launcher than we had when hiding from the Conglomeration, even though I was slowing Ken down. Nothing swarmed us as we bounced over craters and scrambled up the hills.

Amira waited by the slopes of the launcher's crater. She leapt into our midst and tapped me, then pointed up.

Silver Accordance ships, lean and festooned with shards and spikes that indicated heavy energy weaponry descended from overhead.

The cavalry, it seemed, had arrived.

Armored struthiforms jumped out of opening bay doors and down to the ground. They swarmed over us, knocking us down to the dirt and trussing us with electrified cables that snapped and spat as they touched our armor.

I screamed as my wrists were wrenched tight.

They didn't know what was going on, I told myself. All they know is that the base is destroyed.

The cables were hooked to something that reeled us right up off the ground into the nearest hovering ship. Within seconds we were surrounded by more aggressive struthiforms, who stripped our armor off.

“Get away from the armor,” they shouted.

“We are the good guys,” Ken protested, and got struck in the face. He fell down, bleeding.

Amira twitched, but I shook my head. “Don’t. Don’t do anything. Just stay still.”

“Be quiet!”

“If I get put in a cell after saving *all your asses* I’m going to be really fucking pissed off,” Amira shouted.

One of the struthiforms raised an energy rifle, and Amira turned and glared.

It suddenly had second thoughts. “Sit,” it ordered us. “All three. Sit and do not move.”

We sat on the floor, surrounded by our guards. “Are you okay, Ken?” Amira asked. Ken grunted and kept holding his nose. His leg had started to bleed onto the floor.

I watched two struthiforms drag the ghost away.

“Up now,” a struthiform ordered, prodding us with an armored foot.

“We need medical attention,” I said.

“You will get it at your destination. There are no medical facilities for your kind aboard.” It shoved us forward again. “Move now.”

We were hustled down a ramp and into a jumpship with five struthiform guards and a carapoid pilot.

“They’re bringing someone else aboard,” Ken said, trying to stand up.

“One of the others survived?” A bit of hope lit up in me as I looked for a familiar face under the lump of gray being rushed in by two struthiforms.

And then I recognized the tattered, alien form, even despite the tubes and cocoons of alien medical technology wrapped around its core.

"It's Shriek," I said. And even though the face was alien, burned and jagged, I was glad to see it.

One of the other struthiforms turned to regard me. "You know this one?"

"A medic," I told it.

"We found the medic inside a stove surrounded by bottles of pure oxygen," the struthiform soldier said, and flared its feathers out. "So far, the medic refuses to speak to us."

I snorted.

"Nice to see *he* has medical attention," Ken muttered.

"He's Accordance," Amira whispered. "We're just human."

Minutes later we zipped out of the warship and curved over the remains of the base. I winced as I moved to better see out of the porthole. "Look out your windows," I said. "We did that. We survived the Conglomeration. Whatever happens next, whatever the Accordance does to us, remember this."

Shriek stirred on the stretcher and craned to look at us. "You didn't just survive," the strange alien said. "You destroyed them. You protected your home world. Though, I'm going to be curious what the Pcholem think about all this."

The pieces of the Conglomerate ship were spread out across the fields of lunar dirt around Icarus base. Some of them still glowed red.

31

"Do you remember me?" Vincent Anais asked.

Earth's strong pull weighed on me as I sat, handcuffed to a table in a large room near the very top of an Accordance administrative building. Through the floor-to-ceiling oval window, I could look down at Manhattan's silver skyscrapers spread out around the central cluster of Accordance structures.

"I do," I said solemnly. "Where's my drink?"

Anais rubbed puffy eyes. "I would laugh, but I was woken up and dragged out of bed. Then I was told we were all under attack, and that it might only be a matter of weeks before Earth would be overrun. I'm tired, recruit. And everything has changed."

"Twelve hours ago I was on the moon," I told him. "They put us on an Arvani-only ship. It was called a Manta. I think I saw one on a show once. They mainly go planet to planet, right? The way the other passengers acted, you'd think we had cooties, but armed Arvani officers shut them up. And I have yet to see a doctor." I raised my cuffed hands, trying to ignore the pain that came in waves.

Anais winced. "I'm sorry. It'll be soon."

"This isn't how you treat us. Not after what we *did*."

"What you did is up for interpretation." Anais looked away as he said that. His heart wasn't in it.

"Bullshit. You should be able to pull info out of the wreckage. The black boxes in our armor. The launcher. We told our stories on the way here, with weapons aimed at us."

"All the evidence will be carefully examined. Now, Mister Hart, moving on, where is Amira Singh?"

"I'm sorry, did you misplace her?" I stared right at Anais.

He sighed. "She seems to have, uh, escaped."

"Goodness gracious," I said. "In a secure facility like this she's gone missing? I don't know where she is, but seeing that Ken's still holding emergency medical sealant foam on his wound and my broken wrists are shackled to a table, I can't imagine why she'd turn down your hospitality."

"Has she said anything about her intentions as far as revealing sensitive military information found while at the Icarus base?"

I leaned in. "We caught a *ghost*. That's what this is about. You don't want her revealing what it is."

Anais bit his lip. "Devlin, let's be open here. Don't think you're the first to find out what the ghosts are. The Arvani administrators were all just given updates thirty minutes ago. In those files: updated information about ghosts. Information they didn't know about until now. They are . . . upset that this has been held from them. But Arvani top command has been dealing with this for a lot longer than you can imagine."

"And they're terrified that Amira will release this into the wild."

Anais nodded. "Things have gotten tense here since you left. Something like this would be explosive. Do you understand?"

Always trying to manipulate us, I thought. Even now, with the threat of invasion imminent. "I don't know where Amira is," I said. "But the last thing she told me was that, with the Conglomeration about to attack, she wasn't going to spend her last days in an Accordance cell; she was going to go enjoy them. I think the secret is safe with her."

Good luck, I'd told her when we'd gotten off the Arvani ship. *Don't let them drag you down,* she'd said, and squeezed my forearm.

"And what about you?" Anais asked. "Is the secret safe with you?"

Ken, I realized, they already considered loyal. But I was the other wild card. "It all depends on what's happening next," I said.

Anais waved his hand over the table. The white color faded. I looked at a cloud of rubble and rock, so far on the edge of the solar system that the sun was just a tiny pinprick. A suggestion of light, another star.

In the cold dark, shadows moved. Shapes with purpose.

The perspective whirled back. It was a feed from a fast-moving Accordance drone ghosting past the edge of a massive fleet of organic, irregular shapes. Some of them similar to the one in pieces near Icarus base.

"The Conglomerate forces are massing in the outer Oort cloud, on the far edges of your solar system and past our defenses. You repelled their beachhead, so they are planning a siege now. Accordance ships can't get in or out. They are trapped here with us. They need more recruits. Because the fight is coming to us."

A blast of energy wrenched through the dark and vaporized the drone. The image faded, leaving just the white table.

"The Arvani will move your family out of the political

camp they are currently in and to home custody in upstate New York," the Arvani on the left said. An Arvani tank had crept into the room silently while I was watching the video. I tried not to jump back slightly, thinking of Commander Zeus's slashing, armored tentacles. "If you agree to our conditions."

"I can't go home?" I asked.

"You are needed now more than you were before," said Anais. "Let us promote you to the youngest lieutenant, at twenty, in the CPF."

"I thought I was an octave," I said. "Aren't native ranks not allowed?"

Anais smiled. "We're getting concessions. A fully human officer corps. The chance to use native rank insignia across the force; we're configuring this all on the fly, but taking full advantage of Arvani fear. Let us train you more. Deploy you. Help the CPF fight the Conglomeration. Because they are coming for Earth, Devlin. They're coming for us."

"Get the cuffs off me, and get me a goddamned doctor," I told Anais.

I walked down toward the old financial district, enjoying the freedom to choose any direction, any path I wanted. I had no particular aim in mind, I just wanted to feel the sun on my skin, the breeze on my face. I wanted a hot dog with mustard, or a gyro, or a gelato, just something that wasn't optimally designed to fuel my metabolism.

The city was different now. Smaller, maybe. I'd had a change in perspective. The streets looked grubbier. Earth First tags spray painted on brick corners warned me that walking here in my grays might not be too smart.

There'd been bombings. The repacification hadn't worked. Human ingenuity prevailed as minds bent themselves to making life miserable for collaborators, civil servants, aliens. New York looked like a city under occupation: human enforcers in yellow riot gear in clusters everywhere, looking determined and tired. Armored struthiforms rumbling by on personnel carriers. Broken windows, destroyed buildings. The pockmarks of bullets on facades.

Concentration camps in New Jersey and Long Island. Livestreamed executions. Bombings. The occupation's iron grip was slipping, because the Accordance was pulling its forces into orbit to ready itself for the oncoming invasion.

And who knew how many Conglomerate double agents were already here?

Rumors said the Darkside base attack had opened negotiations between Earth First and the Colonial Administration for a cease-fire. Earth First was trying to decide which enemy to fear more: the one that occupied our world and its moon, or the one that might breed us into hungry heat shields.

I stopped walking around aimlessly and headed toward my appointment at the Empire State Building.

The whole side of the ancient structure had been repainted in Colonial Protection Forces gray with white swirls. And to my surprise, recruits in civilian clothes stood in a line waiting to get into the lobby. A line that wrapped around the block. Once processed, they'd be housed here before going to the Hamptons for selection.

People pointed at me as I walked by. The Accordance had used my image already this morning, broadcasting the story of our fight. Ken and I had become symbols of resistance. They'd left Amira out, as they didn't know what she was going to do next.

Even I wasn't sure I wanted that profile.

But I could use it.

As I stood in front of an auditorium full of wide-eyed recruits, I smiled. If we could fight and survive the Conglomeration, the threat that made Arvani shit their tanks, then we'd be a dangerous force.

The graffiti-spreading Earth First activists outside could cause trouble. But these recruits in front of me? They could turn on the Accordance and gain Earth its independence.

In time.

If we survived.

If I could help build them into the weapons we all needed to be.

I cleared my throat, and heard the sound amplified to three hundred pairs of intent eyes.

"Listen closely," I shouted. "There are many aliens out there. They come in all shapes and sizes. But if you want to survive your first encounter with the enemy, there are five aliens that you will need to spot on sight. Pay attention to me now, and you might live."

32

The hopper rattled and the green hills of upstate New York slid by the open side door. The Empire State base commanding officer had given me leave and let me borrow a hopper piloted by a newly promoted human pilot.

The Accordance was getting nervous, I thought, if they were letting us fly craft now.

I ran a hand down my uniform grays with the single red bar of command on my right shoulder.

What could I tell them about my decision to accept command and collaborate with the enemy?

I understood my father's desire to escape the occupation. I'd seen his desire to see people freed burn inside him since I was a child.

They'd hate what I represented. They would turn their back on me. It would hurt.

But that didn't mean I didn't want to see them.

In some ways, this upcoming visit might end up being the most alien encounter I'd had yet since joining the Colonial Protection Forces.

A long streak of lightning danced across the blue sky. A slow pinprick of light unfurled into a flower of fire that hung in place.

"Lieutenant," the pilot called back at me. "Did you see that?"

"That's orbital," I shouted back. "You hearing anything?"

"Chatter, nothing official." The hopper flared and slowed, spiraling down to land near a road leading into a forest. We arrived at the property my parents had just been moved to. A pair of guards at the end of the road walked toward the hopper as the skids hit gravel.

More pinpricks blossomed in the sky.

"That looks serious," the pilot shouted. "That looks really serious."

"It's probably automated Conglomerate probes against the orbital forts," I said.

"Someone just said the space station got hit. It's lost." The Accordance had refused to put protection around the creaky old human station. Not a military asset or necessity.

Gravel spat against the side of the hopper as the engines pounded at the road.

I looked down the road and bit my lip. "Take us up," I ordered. "Get me to the Hamptons."

The hopper scraped along the road and then got airborne with a screech of power.

My earpiece buzzed. I glanced at my wrist and accepted the call. Only one person would be using an unlisted contact to try to reach me.

Amira's voice filled my right ear suddenly. "Hey, Devlin, you seeing all this?"

"Where have you *been*?" I asked.

She moved past the question. "I just talked to Ken. The Accordance is mobilizing the CPF. No more shipping us off to other worlds, everything is getting set up to fight right here in our own solar system."

"You said 'us.' I thought you'd left."

"I wanted a vacation without anyone giving me orders," Amira said. "Consider it personal leave. They owe me that, after everything they've done. But as much as I hate the Accordance, Devlin, the Conglomeration is worse. You know that."

"I do," I said. "I already agreed to stay in. I've been helping recruit—"

"I know, you've been bunking down at the Empire State barracks. I'm in New Haven, coordinates in a few minutes once I pick a spot. Come pick me up."

"Yes, ma'am," I said crisply.

"Fuck you," she said conversationally. Then hesitated. "Make sure you arm up. People around here don't react well to seeing CPF."

She cut the connection. My wrist buzzed and displayed the coordinates.

The hopper curved around a foothill, and the road leading back toward my parents disappeared.

33

We fell into a buffeting storm, straps holding us secure to the benches in the craft. Outside, Saturn's horrific winds howled and tossed us around.

With each second the pressure squeezed the jumpship more. Outer armor plates pushed in hard enough to make the bulkheads groan.

"There's something out there in the dark," I shouted at everyone, yanking their attention away from the visibly distorting hull plates. "And we are part of an elite force of human fighters striking back against it. Accordance commanders might lead us, but we are a *human* fighting force."

Amira held up three fingers. Touchdown was imminent. Something exploded nearby, jerking the entire craft sideways and smacking us around. Close.

I tapped the stylized Earth and pockmarked moon on my shoulder. "We are the Icarus Corps. And we will make sure our world remains right where it is."

"Damn right," Ken said from the other side of the craft. None of us was sure how well the Accordance would support us. They were keeping their weaponry to themselves, leaving us to fighting with human guns. And if they cut and run, we probably wouldn't stand long against the Conglomeration. "So we will fight. Fight harder than the Accordance. Harder than the Conglomeration. Because they *can* be beat. And we have *everything* on the line."

"And if you think Accordance commanders expect a lot out of you, it's nothing compared to what we expect," Amira said, and made a fist. "Seal up!"

Helmets snapped into place with a hiss.

A second later the craft struck. The ramp dropped open and the interior of the craft filled with reddish, yellow storming air.

"Out."

Explosions blanketed the air above us. A full-on firefight. Arrow-shaped Stingrays darted about as they tried to pierce the crisscross lines of defensive fire, but burst apart and rolled off deep into the clouds.

The sun was a bright daystar from here. Or maybe that was a ship burning in orbit far overhead.

"Cover," Ken said. A twinkling star slammed into the side of the jumpship we'd just exited, ripping it apart. The debris sizzled and sunk into the fleshy surface under our boots.

"No way back but forward." Amira took point and started moving forward.

We stood on the surface of a Conglomerate mining facility. Large, gelatinous, the floating structure in Saturn's clouds stretched ahead of us for a mile. Treelike spines spouted flaring gas, lighting the hellish landscape randomly. Pockmarked ridges in the living hull provided hiding space for hostiles.

"Troll," Amira said, pointing into the distance. The chilling and familiar shape thudded toward us.

"Crickets," Ken reported.

"Okay." I pulled my MP9 up tight and looked around at my team in their black armor. "Let's go show them who they're fucking with."

TITAN'S FALL

ZACHARY BROWN

BOOK TWO OF THE ICARUS CORPS

1

Somewhere high over the methane seas, the jumpship hit turbulence, lurching about in the nitrogen-dense atmosphere of Titan. The churning tossed one of the eight rooks out of her seat in a flail of uncoordinated armored limbs. The alien alloys of her powered armor smacked the industrial metal floor, denting it. I looked down as she scrambled back to her seat with wide green eyes and a flurry of almost-dark hair.

Ken leaned forward against restraints. "Goddammit, we told you to *strap in*!"

We were all lined up against the wall and locked in. Everyone in armor, Ken and me babysitting all eight new additions to the platoon. Four rooks to each wall, Ken and me sitting at the front across from each other.

"Yes sir, Sergeant Awojobi!" the rook shouted, struggling with restraints.

"They gave us morons," Ken said to me, loudly enough for the whole cabin to hear. "Did you morons even go through any training? How hard is it to fucking *strap yourselves in*?"

"Yes sir," the rook mumbled, embarrassed. Everyone else

tried not to make eye contact with Ken or me. The jumpship dropped what felt like a hundred feet, my stomach shoving against my throat.

Titan was feeling punchy today.

Ken was too. "Where in the hell did you all train that we're getting such morons?"

"Icarus, sir. Dark side of the moon. Like you." The tag on her shoulder said KIMMIRUT. I was supposed to have memorized the eight names being sent to bolster the platoon, but hadn't had time to get around to it yet. Mainly because, ironically, the Rockhoppers were understrength and working overtime.

"Like me?" Ken said. "I'm *strapped in*."

I caught Ken's eye and raised an eyebrow. Dark side of the moon. Before the Darkside War, which had been more of an Encounter, Ken would not have taken kindly to the bemused "hey, take it down a notch" look I was giving right now.

But a lot had changed since then. We had an understanding.

I had to suspect Ken still hurt, deep down, over getting Sergeant First Class while I was Lieutenant of a platoon. His family had trained him to be officer class. They were fiercely loyal to the Accordance. I doubted we'd ever have been on speaking terms if not thrown into war together.

"Everyone," Ken ordered, his tone calmer, "check your restraints."

I leaned back and closed my eyes. I didn't want to lose my lunch in front of the rooks. That wasn't going to inspire much in the way of confidence. And Ken would use that against me for days. But the sour mash of standard issue Accordance protein globs in my stomach was not taking this shaking lying down.

"One hour out to Shangri-La Base," the pilot shouted

back at us from the cockpit. Alexis Hiteman had been doing bus duty for us for a couple weeks, running the platoon from point to point with gear as needed. A quiet, just-the-facts flyer, Alexis seemed to relish the chance to get to fly alien hardware by himself, without an Accordance pilot overseeing him. A new development in the Colonial Protection Forces, letting humans get their hands on more and more Accordance hardware as the fight against the Conglomerate spread throughout the outer solar system.

One of the rooks threw up. My stomach clenched sympathetically at the sound of splatter.

Alexis shouted back at us again. "It should get better once we're over the ethane lake and . . . ," he trailed off. There was a sort of "huh" sound in his voice as something caught his attention.

One of the rooks whispered a little too loudly, "It's true, the lieutenant can sleep just about anywhere. I heard he took a nap during the bombardment of Icarus crater!"

The awe was misplaced. I had been up for days straight and had nowhere to run. It had just happened. Could happen to anybody. But someone had leaked the after-action report, which included audio of me snoring while the Conglomerate ship all but destroyed the Icarus crater floor.

Ken laughed. "He's not sleeping, he's just . . ."

I opened my eyes and decided to chime in and educate them. Tell them I was about to toss my breakfast at any moment, and it was okay. Relax them a bit.

At that moment, Alexis yanked the jumpship hard right. The Accordance-made engines howled, and as we pulled massive gees, I could feel my armor compensating by squeezing my legs to force blood back up my body. It felt like a massive hand had just wrapped itself all around the lower half of my body and tried to pop me out of the suit.

"Hiteman!" I shouted.

Everyone on my side of the jumpship was hanging from the restraints, limbs sticking out straight forward, eyes bugging. Then it reversed. I was flat on my back as gravity slammed down on my chest.

The familiar thump and hiss of chaff spitting out of tubes near the back confirmed that this was not turbulence-related. Alexis was jinking hard. These were serious evasive maneuvers, the kind I hadn't felt since we first dropped into Titan.

"Alexis!" I yelled again. I kicked the armor on to pull myself forward against the force of the insanely tight turn and lean into the middle of the aisle so I could look forward through the cabin and up into the open cockpit, out into the murky amber-yellow.

"Damn!" the pilot shouted. "I got a trace, just a blip, of something out in the clouds. Came in for a closer peek so I could pass the contact info back on to HQ, thinking I could sniff a bit closer and save someone else on patrol the trouble. I'm so fucking sorry."

Sorry?

Alexis was sprinting now, the engines at an all-out howl and the entire jumpship shaking. We were moving at orbital-insertion speeds and Alexis had gone quiet again, but I could see his right hand dancing over the panels in a flurry. He was muttering into his mic.

"What the hell is this?" one of the rooks asked, his face ash-pale.

Bang! Something shook the entire jumpship.

"What we got?" Ken shouted forward.

The jumpship started wobbling violently. Alexis grunted. "Some of the little fuckers got us, one engine out."

"This is Titan, it's high ground," I said to Ken. We'd lost Saturn to the Conglomerate. Those floating jellyfish-like starships had taken the atmosphere and held it, but we had the rocks above, and Titan had been held solid for two months now. Up the gravity well, above all those other moons; this was well behind the line.

"I think we have a cricket drone swarm," Alexis shouted back. "But I'm not sure. I've never actually run into a cloud before. Just in training simulations. Never actually been in the air with them."

Point defense systems kicked on. The autoguns started chattering away.

"Can we make it to Shangri-La?" I shouted over the constant firing.

What sounded like large pieces of hail hitting the jumpship filled the cabin, and Ken and I looked at each other.

"Brace for impact," Alexis said, matter-of-factly answering my question. "I'm shutting down the other engine so they don't jam it up. It's just a matter of seconds."

Even as he said it, the roar faded into a whine and then silence. The hail-like sound continued, and then the point defense guns ran out of ammo. The whistle of Titan's thick atmosphere rushing past us was the only sound in the cabin.

"Helmets up!" I ordered as we plummeted. Mine slid up over my head and into place smoothly with the thought. The suit connected into me via some invasive alien tech, tendrils sliding up into my spine to synch nervous systems and armor.

One of the recruits started babbling on the public channel, a mix of fear and swearing.

"Get that off the public channel," Ken snapped.

"Hold your weapons tight," I said as calmly as I could. I was sure my voice quavered slightly.

We hit. My restraints snapped and I flew forward into the bulkhead. I staggered back to my feet and looked around as my brain caught up. It was dark inside and full of debris. Liquid ethane, laced with methane and propane, poured in through rents in the hull. "Mayday, HQ, anyone riding shotgun?"

"Go for HQ."

I stood up. Right before we sank into the ethane lake, I could see the tiny hump of a distant hill. Alexis had ditched us as close to solid ground as he could. "Everyone, secure your weapons and get out."

In the cockpit, Alexis lay crumpled forward, spine twisted. He hadn't been in armor. Ethane gushed in around him as the jumpship settled further and then stopped.

We were in the shallow end of the ethane lake.

"HQ, we're down. Our pilot ditched. Said it was crickets."

There was a pause on the other end. "Coordinates?"

I read them out. "How long for backup?"

"There shouldn't be anything out there, Lieutenant" was the response.

"We need evac and support nonetheless," I said.

"Twenty minutes" was the terse response.

I broke out of a gap in the hull and pushed through helmet-high water. Ken stood farther up the shore ahead of me, hip-deep in it. "Get to shore! Come on!"

He wasn't shouting or berating, Ken was calm under pressure. But he knew what needed to be done. We needed visibility, and quick.

"Alexis?" Ken asked.

"Dead. I want a headcount and weapons count," I said to Ken as I looked around. Far overhead, Titan's permanent layer of haze seemed to cap the orange thickness. And the hydrocarbon-rich clouds below that hadn't vomited out the enemy.

Yet.

"All eight accounted for. Five of them held onto their gear."

The recruits were slogging up onto the shore.

"Who're the squad leaders?"

"Tony, Yusef, raise your hands," Ken ordered over the public channel. They did so.

"Squad leaders, take point," I replied. "The three of you without weapons, fall into the center as the rest of us fan out. Yusef, your squad looks up to the clouds. Tony's squad watches the lake."

"Shouldn't we get back into the jumpship for our weapons?" someone asked.

"We stay the fuck put," Ken growled.

They were nervous. Jumpy. Scared. The Accordance had Titan swept. Orbital defenses in the form of thorny-looking platforms in orbit above us. None of this should have been happening and we all knew it.

"You mayday out to HQ?" Ken asked, private channel.

"Twenty minutes out," I replied. "They said nothing should be out here."

"Well, something is damn well out here and we have to deal with it," Ken replied.

I walked around so that each of the recruits could see me checking them over. On the public channel, I cleared my throat. "Listen up! You've heard this before but let me repeat it: There are many aliens out there. They come in all sorts of shapes and sizes. There are five aliens we need to worry about right now to survive the next twenty minutes before help comes.

"Drivers: They're cat-sized and scaly. Those pronged rear feet will sink into the flesh of your back and hook on. That pink ratlike tail? Once it plunges into your spinal cord, you're a brain-dead meat puppet at its total and utter disposal."

The placid liquid ethane on the other side of the jumpship started to boil.

"Trolls: Yes, they look like rhinoceros that stand on two feet. Either of which could stamp you into a puddle. That bio-armor? Nothing short of depleted uranium gets through it. Keep out of the way."

Insect-like forms swarmed and thrust their way through the lake, surrounding the jumpship as they schooled in our direction.

"Raptors: Our enemies decided that a velociraptor with a brain, thumbs, and a running speed of a cheetah wasn't good enough, so they made cyborgs out of them. They smell like chicken if you hit them with a laser."

Tiny wriggling metal legs glinted in the dim light as they began to surface and skip over the ethane at us.

"Crickets: These insect-like robots are the first wave. The winged variants provide air support as well. Shoot them to bits. But watch out, because the leftovers reassemble as needed. So make sure the bits are really, really tiny, and then shoot them some more. Those of you without weapons, stomp them!"

I didn't have time to talk about Ghosts. The masters of it all. Covered in advanced adaptive camouflage, running the battle in secrecy. Nor was I even allowed to tell these recruits what the Ghosts really were.

"Remember your training!" I shouted as the cloud of crickets churned out of the water to the shoreline. "You know what to do:

"Kill them all!"

2

Ken sat with his legs hanging out of the side of the hopper's open door. It had been chewed up on the approach, holes burned through the skin, but it was still flying. A trio of mantaships surrounded the hopper. Heavy air support.

"That was amazing!" Ken said over the private channel. "There's nothing left but cricket pieces back there."

I sat next to him. We'd both been the last ones in before air support started pounding the crickets.

"Twenty minutes. All we did was not die for twenty minutes."

Ken's helmet turned toward me. "We were warriors! We kicked their ass for twenty minutes."

I picked a piece of cricket out from between my boots and tossed it out over the Titan plains.

"Victory is victory," Ken said. "Enjoy the win."

We rattled in over the Shangri-La basin, scooped out of Titan's surface some thousand years before by a very, very big chunk of rock that hit hard enough to release megatons of force and leave an appropriately sized several-mile-wide crater. Then Titan's thick atmosphere had gone to work on it, smoothing and shallowing out Shangri-La into its current gentle shape, though still surrounded by blunted hills.

The Accordance buried their fortress down in the basin's hills, and now was building anti-spacecraft weapons in the protection of the basin. Each weapon was the size of a skyscraper, four needles aiming ever upward, and much of it still in the middle of construction.

I was jittery. I wanted to shuck my armor and take a long shower. I was tired of living in underground warrens and ethane lakes and amber light and Jupiter and aliens and war.

"What the hell is that?" Ken asked.

I looked over and instantly spotted what he was referring to. As we crested the Shangri-La hills and skimmed over the basin, the hopper had to curve around the vast body of a ship. It didn't look like any of the mantas or troop transports we'd been shuttled around the system on.

The heart of the ship looked like a quarter-mile-long seed with a deep black skin. A long spine further stretched out in the middle of the air forward and to the rear, a bony-looking structure with gridwork encasing it. Misty clouds surrounded that, held in by an outer transparent shell. And for hundreds of feet even more out past that hull, a second shimmering cloud hung in the air, hinting at yet another layer of ship, maybe held in place by force fields of some kind.

I clomped forward as we skimmed over the artificial clouds, and got the pilot's attention on the public channel. "What is that thing?"

"Pcholem ship," the pilot said from behind an emergency respirator. Her skin was peeling around it from exposure to whatever raw hydrocarbons had leaked inside. She should have been in a full encounter suit, but pilots this far from the action hated the bulky interference. It also may have been that she didn't have time to fully suit up, scrambling fast to get to us. "Personnel drop."

There were thousands of figures disembarking from ramps, more vehicles and equipment coming off the massive ship. All joining the tens of thousands of human contractors here on Titan, digging out bunkers for the base, drilling down into the deep rock.

A constant stream of hoppers and jumpships flew in and out, the jumpships heading for orbit, the hoppers for other distant points of Titan.

"We'll need to talk to the pilots on base about Alexis," Ken said as the hopper flared to slow down. "Tell them they need to make sure they're going out in flight suits, see if they can get crash protection gear. Let them know hostiles are slipping down. Just in case HQ doesn't think it warrants a mention."

"Yes, but we also need to ask if they'll be holding a memorial." Ken always focused on the practical. "We need to pay our respects. Alexis paid the price. And got us in close to shore, where we had a good chance."

"Right."

A whole division of the Colonial Protection Forces quartered here. Almost nine thousand armored soldiers. There were more human forces deployed around Titan, but the bulk of them were around Shangri-La.

Welcome home, I thought as we kissed dirt. The Accordance had wanted all this for themselves, no humans out past the moon, the point we'd been unable to cross by ourselves before the Accordance came to Earth.

But now that the Conglomeration had found Earth and the solar system, now that war was in full swing, human workers were everywhere toiling away for the Accordance.

It was necessity. All the planets I'd memorized as a kid, if I just reversed the names, it became a list of places the Conglomeration had taken for itself over the last three months. They'd pushed everything back to Saturn, where we held the moons and bombarded it constantly.

The Accordance needed human boots. And the Icarus Corps, built out of the Colonial Protection Forces, was still being trained and built up.

But the Accordance didn't really trust humans fully. The squid-like Arvani who held the top spot in the Accordance truly didn't regard humans with much more than disdain. We were often left guarding supply routes, protecting machinery. Like the massive weaponry being built here in Shangri-La to safeguard Titan.

Rumors were, something big was being planned for Saturn. Maybe a steady asteroid barrage or nukes. But all of Earth would just be a speck on Saturn's windy clouds. How could you attack something so vast?

Down in the bunkers, barracks lit by eerie Accordance bioluminescence embedded in the walls, I met up with the rest of the platoon. Most of them were waiting in the common room for us, lounging on utilitarian cots. News had spread quickly.

At the front, squad leaders Min Zhao and George Berkhardt jumped up. I nodded at them. "Any of you have a pad?"

Min gave me hers, and I fingerprinted in and snagged my dossier and then looked back at my new additions. They were snapping their helmets back down, and I was looking at tired, relieved faces.

Most of them were older than me. But they seemed younger somehow. And they were looking at me expectantly.

"Tony Chin?" I called out, glancing down at the pad. The squad leader raised a hand. "Over to my left."

He took a few steps over. I glanced at the pad. "Maria Lukin, Lilly Taylor, Yakov Ilyushin, over to Sergeant Chin. Rockhoppers, meet the new Charlie squad! Now, Yusef Obari?"

Yusef likewise raised a hand.

I waved to my right. Yusef moved over. "Aran Patel, Mohamed Cisse, and Suqi Kimmirut, join Mister Obari. Rockhoppers, this is Delta squad." I updated our documents.

Berkhardt moved up. "I can help you with your armor," he said to Tony. "You can call me Chef."

"Chef?"

"George Bork-Bork-Bork Berkhardt," Min Zhao explained.

Berkhardt shrugged. "I can't cook for shit, but I speak a little Swedish. And Sergeant Zhao is 'Max.' Should be obvious where we got the nickname."

"Everyone shuck down and clean your armor, stow your weapons," Ken ordered. "If you have any questions, Chef, Max, or me are here. We have bunk beds ready, look for your last name on the rack. We don't have a dedicated shuckdown room, you take your armor off and plug it in next to your bunk. You're never more than a quick sprint away from your armor, got it?"

"Yessir!" they chorused.

I had been looking over Alpha and Bravo squads. Zizi Dimka, Chandra Khan, and Lana Smalley under Sergeant Berkhardt for Alpha. Sergeant Min Zhao's Bravo squad included Greg Vorhis, Jun Chen and Erica Li. That was almost everyone.

"She's not here," Ken said, seeing me survey the platoon.

"I know."

"She's supposed to be here."

I grunted. "I know."

Erica Li was telling the new platoon members they should turn over any food they'd smuggled in to her. "I'll get them into the platoon safe. That shit is in high demand around here, and unless you've got it locked up, people will steal it. They're that sick of alien dog food."

"If you don't handle it, it will go up the chain," Ken said. "It has to."

"I'll go find her," I snapped.

One of the new platoon members gingerly pulled a chocolate bar out and handed it over to Erica.

"I'll deal with that," Ken said, jerking his head in the direction of the chocolate bar.

"Right." I turned for the stairs up to the surface.

Behind me Ken shouted at Erica. "Froyo! Hand the chocolate back over. Taylor, there is no safe down here for food. *Come on.*"

I found Amira at a northeast hilltop, perched on a slab of rock, watching a hundred or so contractors in simple EVA suits working away at an EMP turret. The gun was a fifty-foot-long barrel with power cables as thick as a car running off down the nearby tunnel, which itself sank deep under Shangri-La.

The barrel had yet to be winched into place.

From her perch I could see the whole Shangri-La basin as well as the job site, now dominated by the cloudy shells of the Pcholem starship sitting the middle of it all.

"You ignoring the platoon open channel?" I asked her.

"I was busy. Welcoming the newbies is not high on the priority list. We talked about this." Her armor was streaked with dirt and peeling paint. What hydrocarbon-filled lakes had she been mucking around in?

"We hit a cricket scout cloud coming back. Lost the jumpship. Lost Alexis."

Amira stood up and turned to look at me. The name patch SINGH was missing its S.

"I told you they'd be coming here," she said.

"Could be a fluke," I said. "Accordance holds orbit. The surface was cleaned before we got moved here, before we lost Saturn. Maybe the crickets snuck through."

"No," Amira said. She stepped close enough that I could see her face behind the helmet. The silvered nano-ink tattoos were bright against her brown skin, and her eyes flashed like a cat's as light caught them. "I can taste them, they're out there, just on the edge. Accordance security says I don't know what I'm talking about, but I think our systems here have been compromised. They won't let me get in and audit them. They don't want humans sullying their systems."

"We're not trained—" I started, trying to bleed some of the anger out. She interrupted me.

"I've been playing with Accordance networks and tech for years. It's better but not infallible. You know that. The Conglomeration snuck past them to get to the moon, and that wasn't supposed to happen. And we took the hit for that."

"I know." I thought back to watching the jellyfish-like Conglomerate ship hovering over our training base. The flash of explosions. Stepping over all the corpses of recruits, reaching for emergency oxygen, the crystalized eyes.

Only three of us survived: Amira, Ken, and me. The heroes of Icarus Base. The survivors of the Darkside War. The three humans who took down an entire Conglomerate starship ourselves.

But it hadn't been just the three of us. There'd been all the others who'd died helping us.

And the new squads who'd died during the drop onto Saturn. And the retreat from Saturn.

"I was hoping you'd come say hi to the fresh meat like everyone else," I said.

"Then you should have ordered me."

"Yeah," I told her. "I should have. But you don't ever listen to me when I do that."

"Well, just because the Accordance has leverage on you through your parents back on Earth and can promote you to be Pet Lieutenant doesn't mean I have the same strings on me. But keep playing your cards right, you can be an Accordance lifer."

"Fuck you, that's uncalled for," I shouted. "The Conglomerate is the worst threat. I'm here to make sure Earth survives."

"Then do you want me sniffing out the Conglomerate threat, or dancing to orders because it makes you look good to HQ? Do you want me to pull back? We're the only platoon out here with a dedicated intelligence officer. I may be under you in rank, but we know what I am. I can go anywhere else and run intel for them, and they'd trip over themselves to have me. I expect this rules-following shit from Ken, not you."

Why the hell did this always have to be so hard? "It's not rules," I explained. "You need to know some of the names and faces who will have your back in the next firefight. They need to know you. That's how it works. We're trying to fashion a team out of all these human bits and pieces. I'll block for you while you go hunting, I just want you to take support with you, get them used to working with you. Alternate the new squads in and out daily while you prowl. I want someone to have your back, is that so wrong?"

Amira turned and looked back out of Shangri-La. "You know, I could be jumping at shadows. Don't put yourself out there on my behalf, I can take the yelling if HQ gets pissed. Say I did it against your recommendation."

"You and I both know there are a lot of shadows out in the universe that want us dead," I told her. "Take the squads with you. I'll hold the line."

3

Armored up and fresh after a day down, I took the Delta squad out for a roll with Alpha alongside. The new additions were adjusting to Titan gravity and getting a little jumpy. Which was understandable. They'd come screaming down out of orbit in a hurry, been shot out of the sky by Conglomerate crickets, stood their ground by a propane lake, and then flown into Shangri-La, where'd they'd met an unimpressed platoon.

Now it was time to stretch their legs and keep their attention focused forward. Amira had taken the other squad out past the hills on one of her glitch hunts, though she hadn't told them that. I'd ordered her to take them with her.

Far, far under our feet as we bounded about the Shangri-La plain, the civilian contractors worked to tend the heart of Shangri-La: an Accordance-made dark matter generator, half a mile deep in the rock. This would power everything from our EMP cannons to the skyscraper anti-spacecraft weapons, which we were told could vaporize a rock the size of Manhattan dropping on us.

Which led you to wonder if there would be any on their way anytime soon.

"The Canadian from up near the Arctic, Suqi," I asked Ken, her wide eyes flashing back into memory, "she got bounced around. Is she okay?"

"Physically. She's still a bit wary of me, I think," Ken said.

"You've watched too many movies. Leadership isn't just yelling."

"And you need to stop letting them stare at you like some movie star," Ken shot back. "You need to give them some tough orders, make them realize what it is we're in the middle of. We need them to be ready, not starstruck."

A message from HQ pinged and scrolled down in the lower left of my helmet's visor. A request for a meeting. "Damn. HQ."

"Yeah?" Ken asked.

"They want an in-person."

"I can have Chef take lead and come with you," Ken offered.

"Nah." I shook my head, even though Ken couldn't see it. There was friction between me and Ken, no doubt. And we'd buried most of it back on the moon. But I still didn't want him to stand there and watch me get chewed out for something he'd warned me would be a problem with that "see, I told you so" look on his face. "It's Amira. They're going to chew on my head a bit, no reason for you to get backsplash. Plus, I need to get Shriek back to our barracks. Keep showing Delta the terrain. I want them to be able to bounce around the basin with their eyes closed. Every loose rock—"

"Every loose rock and every hidey-hole," Ken interrupted, completing the sentence.

\+ + + +

HQ, like our barracks, was just under the surface. So we could boil out on the basin like cockroaches from our crevices if the Conglomeration came at us. It was farther into the center of the basin, underneath the bulk of the Pcholem spaceship that had landed and come to dominate Shangri-La.

Major General Foster didn't spend a lot of time armored up; he was in Colonial Protection Forces gray BDUs, which almost matched the gray coming in at the temples, and he had a perpetually tired look. He stared at me as I clomped into his office. Behind him on the wall was the Icarus Corps logo, the moon and an Earthrise, surrounded by a sawblade-like sun.

Usually, shit ran downhill. Foster would yell at someone lower in rank, and then on down, and eventually a company captain would end up nervously having a "chat" with me. But most of the CPF captains had come in after I'd fought the Conglomeration at the Icarus crater. They didn't want to shout at the hero of the Darkside War.

So now I was standing in front of a major general.

"Lieutenant: why the hell are you wearing armor in my office? You can barely fit through the door."

"Rockhoppers shuck for sleep and showers," I told him. "Never more than ten feet from armor."

Foster stared at me. "You telling me you don't trust how secure my base is?"

"Rockhoppers shuck for sleep and showers," I repeated neutrally.

We stared levelly at each other. Foster may have been my superior and my elder. But my Rockhoppers didn't shuck for anything but sleep and showers.

"Fuck it. I really want to talk about Sergeant Amira Singh," he said, a sour look on his face.

HQ was a giant circle filled with pie slice–shaped offices.

What looked more like the bridge of a spaceship occupied the center: consoles for comms, massive holographic displays with maps of Titan and Shangri-La, as well as theater maps of the whole system. Soldiers coming in and out from various parts of Shangri-La. When I shuffled around Foster's office, I turned my back to all that.

One thing I liked about it: few aliens over us. Our overlords, the Accordance, had basically given Shangri-La over to human oversight.

To Foster's oversight.

Foster didn't like me. He'd worked hard to get human oversight. He'd worked hard to get the Arvani off his back and he didn't want that to change. I was something that might fubar everything he'd gotten set up.

"Amira is—" I began.

"I've explained," Captain Foster said, tapping his glass desk. "You've agreed. She can't be haring off on some intuition based on her unauthorized networking and hacking abilities. I said no unnecessary trips out past our defensive coverage."

"Absolutely, sir," I said, as flat and mechanical as I could.

For a month, Foster'd been demanding that Amira focus on beefing up security. Adding trips to the network against outside interference.

But she'd been doing her own patrols. Heading out past the basin, scouring the plains and lakes in her spare time.

"In two weeks, the farms below go operational. We become a real damn fortress here on Titan. Supplies can't be hit." Foster worried about that a lot. "With EMP cannons up, the antiship batteries, our emplacements on the hills, we are Fortress Shangri-La. We have ammo foundries now. Foundries. We are dug in like a tick on the ass of Titan and we will not be dislodged."

"I get that, sir."

"I don't want a loss of focus. Everyone stays behind the walls. Secure. Safe. We destroy anything that comes over the hills. We keep beefing up the hills. The aliens trying to kill us won't be able to touch us. And the aliens that took over Earth, well, maybe they'll leave us alone as well. This is important!"

That was new. I hadn't pegged Foster, a lifer, as having any ill will toward the Accordance. He was old enough to remember Occupation. The accommodations Earth had made to the aliens as they came down to Earth and changed everything.

Apparently, he saw this base as a place to carve out some space from the Accordance.

That made Foster somehow slightly more likable. I wasn't a lifer. I'd been forced into the CPF because my parents were pacifist protestors against Accordance rule. Join the CPF and they lived under comfortable house arrest. If I hadn't, they would have been executed.

"If you don't rein Sergeant Singh in," Foster warned, getting back to the subject. "I will. Demote her, toss her in a brig, something. I'm done. I have no more patience. Shut her down."

"Absolutely, sir," I said, lying through my teeth.

Up from HQ a level, several carapoids had trundled down out of the Pcholem ship. The pony-sized beetles thudded as they walked, natural armor making them something you gave a wide berth as they unloaded new batches of armor onto carts.

Old-fashioned manual labor: a carapoid could easily lift all several hundred pounds of an entire suit of armor.

Several of the carapoids had chiseled symbols on their backs. Swooping letters and what appeared to be umlauts to my human eyes. I'd never seen that on the carapoids down on Earth. They'd been painted official colors, depending on their roles in the Accordance, to match the uniforms of other Accordance members.

I hung back a bit, thinking to ask, but the carapoids kept busy and didn't slow for an instant as they trucked back up toward the surface. They'd be cycling into the outside without any gear. The carapoids could fold their carapaces tight to themselves and pass up to an hour in some extremely hostile environments. I'd seen them fighting hand to hand out in the clouds of Saturn when stripped of suits by the enemy.

I ranged through a few more tunnels, nodding and stepping aside for officers.

Shangri-La's medical facilities were located inside a spotless white cavern. The Accordance didn't see much point in private rooms for general care; most of their technology resided in the ovoid pods stretched in rows by the hundreds. The floors were grilled, the better to flush away any fluids, and could heat up to render the floor sterile again.

A couple of nearby pods were open, the articulated cutting arms inside flung open, as if the moving scalpels wanted an embrace.

I instinctively veered away.

"Do you require medical assistance?" a voice asked in Mandarin, Spanish, and then English.

I turned. A struthiform had approached me from behind. I'd never really shaken the image of them as somewhat stoic ostriches in Roman armor but with velociraptor-clawed legs that could gut you in a split second.

"I am looking for Shriek, of the One Hundred and Fourth Thunder Clutch," I said. "He's assigned to my platoon."

The struthiform cocked its head, feathers near its beak

shifting as it did so. I could hear the pitched squeak from it before the flattened box on the collar near its throat spoke, translating an alien birdlike language to English for me. "I do not know a Shriek," it said. "And that clutch no longer exists. What do you truly need, human?"

I sighed. "Shriek is the one that refuses to learn names or give them. He has prosthetic limbs, and facial reconstruction, he . . ."

"Oh. That one. Yes, we are ready for him to return to you."

The medic led me through to the quarantine wing, where there were actual offices and private rooms. A group of struthiforms clustered around a display, occasionally reaching out with a wing hand to manipulate a three-dimensional image.

One struthiform stood out among the rest. His face had been reshaped, much of it artificial with matte-black patches of machinery. Synthetic leg, and prosthetic fingers on his wing hand whined as he moved. "Devlin!" he chirped, actually using his own vocal cords to call my name.

"He makes your name-sound," the struthiform next to me muttered. "But he refuses to learn those of his own feather-kind."

"Don't be offended," I whispered as Shriek left his fellow struthiforms to approach me. "He is deeply traumatized. He believes to learn someone's name will only lead to loss."

"It is against my will that a creature as mentally unbalanced as he practices medicine," the struthiform said. "But at least it is not on our own kind."

"A pleasure to meet you, too," I said, my grin at seeing Shriek fading.

"I've been learning more human biology," Shriek said enthusiastically. "I did not realize you could not keep yourselves clean without help of special materials. I will stop trying to cancel your shipments of head-feather-cleaning supplies."

"*You're* the one messing up the shampoo rations," I groaned.

Shriek shook out a wing hand. "I've learned a great deal of specifics about human biology studying here. I'll be a better surgeon for your kind now. Let's not hover overlong, looking at the past, arguing about such petty things as who canceled shampoos," he said.

I was entirely planning to throw him under the bus when we got back to the platoon's quarters. Everyone had been griping about shampoo for weeks.

"Have you met the Pcholem yet?" Shriek asked, abruptly shifting conversational direction. "You should, you are famous. It would be delighted to meet someone exceptional."

"I've never seen Pcholem before," I said. "Where is the pilot?"

Shriek spread his wing hands wide, knocking me back. "You are an ignorant hatchling. Pcholem are not pilots; they are the ships themselves."

Shriek began leading me upward.

"Imagine a seed born in space, unfurling its wings to feel the solar wind. Do you know there's a turtle in a zoo in one of your cities that the Accordance took over management of? It's two hundred years old!"

"That's a jump in topics," I pointed out. "I don't see your point."

"There's the elephant and a fly," Shriek continued. "The fly is tiny, it lives a single day. Very fast, quick in life. One single spin of your blue globe. And then, the great, larger elephant. It lives for decades of your solar years. Around and around the sun. And trees, well, there are trees that are thousands of years old. Great big slow things, they last longer. Do you follow me?"

"No, not really. Shriek, we're getting up to the surface. You need armor. Why the hell aren't you clad? You know the rule: Rockhoppers never—"

"You fear death, hatchling. Good for you. I died all those years ago when I watched the Conglomeration burn my planet. So imagine that seed I told you about stretches its newborn wings wide and soaks up light. It chews up dust from the nebulous vacuum around it, growing the natural biological fusion reactors deep inside its midnight-black skin. And it grows, ponderous and large. And it lasts and lasts, my human."

I nervously checked the air as we walked through two airlock doors held open, a breach that should have led to a lot of rushing air and drama. I decided to leave my helmet down, recessed into the back of my armor.

"Where do they come from?" I asked.

"Where do they come from? We do not know. Maybe they don't come from anywhere. Maybe they are always swimming around. But we know when they're born, their souls are entangled on the quantum level, just like our secure communications equipment in our armor. They're always splitting souls, budding new ones."

Shriek walked out onto the surface of Titan, and all around us a shimmering curtain held back the hydrocarbon atmosphere. We were under the belly of the ship. The Pcholem itself.

"The Pcholem don't just live for hundreds, maybe thousands of years. They won't say. But they travel between the stars with time dilation. So, they have seen civilizations rise and fall, wars gutter out. And always they keep swimming between the stars. Long after I finally admit to death, long after you wither, human, this Pcholem will eat the dark between the stars."

With that said, Shriek waved at the dark, curving belly above us. He walked toward a black tongue of a ramp ahead of us, and the darkness at the end of it.

"This is a war we are in. But even in the mud, and death, and shit, and blood, there is beauty, Devlin. Take a moment to come with me and meet a being that may have been navigating the depths of space before your species could even rub two sticks together."

We stepped onto the ramp. "Are we supposed to be going aboard?" I asked, looking back. There was no security, no Accordance telling me to get back to where I belonged. Just the dark maw ahead.

"No one tells Pcholem what to do. They ask for a favor," Shriek said, marching on ahead of me with purpose. "That seed I told you about, once it grows, the older Pcholem gather around it and bless it with upgrades. Like the nano-ink on your friend, or the armor around you. And with those grafts, it gets the ability to extend itself. They grow, change, adapt, as they find things they want or when they find new technologies that they value and will trade for more things to bolt onto themselves. They'll come down into a gravity well, though they hate it here."

"And this one, it shuttles supplies around for the Arvani?"

Shriek whistled. A derisive sound. "It decided to do this. To bring more supplies here to help Shangri-La. It must have its reasons to pull itself into such a small package of only a mile long, to slim its fields down until all we see is the core."

We walked into the darkness and stopped.

A second later, a green glow suffused the air around us. The gothic arches and swoops of the interior loomed with ghastly shadows.

Then the darkness around us faded away, the walls

becoming translucent. Outside, carapoids continued plodding to unload cargo alongside other human contractors.

"I apologize," a voice said from the darkness above, echoing smoothly around us. "The last time you stood here, you flew from a burning world."

"Hello, Starswept," Shriek said.

"You know its name." I was shocked. Shriek refused to learn names.

"It is one of four in this system," Shriek said. "I think it has come down here because it is smart. They value life above all else. Particularly their own, for they are ancient and each life is a precious thing. They are down here to help the Accordance, to help humans. They'll move us around like pieces on a checkerboard. Supply the pieces. But they won't fight."

"They are pacifists," I said.

"Of a sort," Shriek said. "Corner one, and it will do anything it can to live. But it avoids that corner at most costs."

"Then why are they part of the Accordance?" I asked loudly. "Why live under Arvani bootheels?"

The answer came from the halls of the living ship as Starswept replied. "You have seen the Conglomeration's evil. And Shriek has seen it as well, from this very spot. Is that not a will worth frustrating?"

Something was coming down a hallway toward them in the dark. The green light finally glanced on the body of a carapoid, again with those strange carvings on its carapace. "I hear," Starswept said from around us, "that you humans miss your own food, so the last time I was on Earth, I made a point of acquiring something for you."

The carapoid's thorny arms broke free of the powerful armored wings to hand me a wicker basket filled with boxes of chocolates.

“I’m told,” the Pcholem said, “that this is an appropriate gift between your kind. Is that so?”

I held the basket as delicately as I could between my powered alien-alloy fingers, trying not to break it. “It is.”

“I asked Shriek to bring you here,” the Pcholem said. “You killed the Conglomerate abomination that flew to the lunar satellite of your home world. This is a pure act. An act that Pcholem do not forget. We seek to see all such abominations the Conglomeration has made for interstellar travel destroyed. Know this: You are known among Pcholem, Devlin Hart!”

“I—okay,” I said, stumbling over words. This was getting weird.

In my earpiece, Amira’s voice suddenly kicked in. “Devlin, I need you to get out here. Now. I found something.”

4

I left Shriek holding a basket of chocolate, with orders to get it back to the platoon barracks. Ancient alien ship from beyond the stars or not, Amira finding something meant shit hitting the fan.

Rifle in hand, riding a hopper out that I'd commandeered to bus me out with a grumpy-as-hell pilot, I headed out for her location.

"You're not going to like it," she said. "Foster's going to shit."

"Why?"

"I'm way off base. I'm into Accordance zones of control. The nearest base is Needlepoint, one of the humans-not-allowed places. It's a jurisdictional mess."

"What'd you find?"

"A weak spot in Conglomeration shielding. A buzz. A small bit of leakage. A mistake. But it's under the rock. I got them. I fucking got them. They're here."

"You make the call to HQ?"

There was a pause. "Rubbed their fucking noses in it," Amira said, no small amount of satisfaction in her voice.

"Then phoned in to Accordance channels I'm not even supposed to know exist and gave them coordinates. There is a lot of traffic coming my way."

Even as we flared out over her positions, with the two squads ringing her, I could see even more vehicles converging on us in the sky.

My earpiece started pinging. My helmet filled up with notes from HQ.

Foster was shitting bricks. Accordance too.

I jumped out of the hopper when it was still thirty feet up, cracking the ground underneath me as I landed. Somewhere underneath the rock was something. Something Conglomerate.

Nearby, Accordance forms dropped to the ground as well. The beetle-like forms of several carapoids trundled toward us, massive energy cannons held in their spiky wing hands. Behind them, two squid-like Arvani officers in full armor scuttled over the ground toward us. Their legs kicked up ground-up pebbles in their haste.

I grimaced as they approached.

"Fucking told you so," Amira said on the common channel to everyone arriving.

The Accordance information specialists called it ghost sign. The trace of Conglomerate systems somewhere out there, hidden away. Hinting at the presence of something else on Titan with us.

In the common room, hours later, shucked down and out of armor, Amira held up a cup of a fruit juice and gave a rare celebratory shout. The nano-ink tattoos on her cheeks glinted in the bio-light, and her eyes fluoresced. "They may have kicked us off the site," she said. "But at least they're aware."

I placed the basket of chocolates on a coffee table. I pushed one of the boxes toward Suqi. "No tasteless alien food engineered merely to deliver a balanced nutrient mix for human consumption tonight," I said. This was a party. Or as close as we got in the CPF when deployed.

Suqi lit up. "Is that real chocolate?"

"Help yourself."

"I'm sorry to drag you all out with me for so long," Amira said to everyone. "Consider the juice a thank-you."

One of the new platoon members, Patel, held up his paper cup of fruit punch. "How the hell did you get this?"

Amira smiled. "Don't ask me."

"But seriously, this is real," Patel said, awed.

Amira gave him a blank look, the smile gone. "What'd I say?" She looked around at the new platoon members. "Newbies. I swear, no one say shit, or I'll break fingers."

Patel laughed, but Ken shook his head. "She's not kidding."

The smiles died away and the celebratory mood with it.

Ken raised his cup. "Captain Foster is still angry. We are going to be cleaning toilets for weeks, Rockhoppers. My only regret is that we do not have something alcoholic to put in these drinks."

I nodded. Ken hadn't been the one to get the calls from Foster. And the next morning, I had a meeting. To face HQ anger in all its glory. "Something to make the juice kick, yes," I said. "We could have used Boris."

Ken slumped a little bit. "Yes," he said quietly. I had to lean forward to hear him. "Boris would have figured out how to brew something or smuggle it in."

Even the veteran Rockhoppers glanced at each other, not sure who Boris was.

Ken shook his head and tossed back the fruit juice. "I'm going to turn in," he said softly.

Amira walked over to me and jammed an elbow into my side. "What the hell is wrong with you?" she asked.

"I didn't think it would hit him that hard," I whispered.

"Don't talk about Boris around him yet. He's not ready for that."

"I'm sorry." I looked down at my empty paper cup. This was turning into a dud of a party.

"Also, quit staring at Suqi Kimmirut," Amira said, her voice even lower. "That would really fuck up morale. You're not going to climb the CPF chain of command effectively that way."

I did my best to look outraged. "Since when are you all rules and regs?"

"Look, we don't shit where we eat." Amira's eyes flashed silver and black over her brown cheeks.

"That's crude," I protested.

"Doesn't make it less true."

I changed the subject. "You did good out there. With the Accordance really paying attention, maybe they'll find something instead of it finding them."

"Welcome to the real war," Amira said. "Still think I'm too obsessed with hunting for Conglomerate ghosts?"

"Do you think I'd be happy about getting my face chewed off by HQ if I didn't believe you?" I said.

"Thank you for doing your job, *Lieutenant*." Amira rolled her eyes. But she grabbed my paper cup and refilled it. As close to a thanks as I would ever really get.

And good enough for me.

Lights out, which meant smacking my shins into the bunk bed in the tiny room next to the common area. My armor loomed by the head, Ken's by the foot, and Ken stirred when I hit the double bunks. "Sorry," I whispered.

To accommodate the new squads, we'd shifted things around, gotten more cramped. Lots of doubled bunks. I'd given up my quarters to one of the new squads and moved into a room with Ken and Amira until we could get some extra rooms for the platoon.

Ken started softly snoring again, back to sleep after my jolting the bed.

I could hear Amira hitting her own bunk. As I lay down and looked up at the metal bars above my face, I thought about her CPF chain-of-command jab. Did she think I was a lifer? I raised the triangle-and-globe tattoo of the CPF on my forearm into the air and squinted in the relative dark at it.

The thing was something I didn't want burned into me. I was here because the Conglomeration was worse, because I'd seen them kill on the moon. I'd seen their tools at work in the skies of Saturn.

I hadn't talked to my parents since the war started. I wondered what they thought of their son, the Accordance hero. The last time I heard about them, one of the CPF intelligence officers, Colonel Anais, had told me they'd joined an Earth First group demanding that humans not fight the Conglomeration until the Accordance offered independence.

I could see why they believed that. They hadn't seen the Conglomeration burn through one of *their* friends. The pilot, Alexis, wasn't going to be memorialized by them. They'd never seen a cloud of crickets darken the sky.

Never would, if I could do anything to stop it.

But that wasn't going to stop them from trying to do something crazy back on Earth.

I rubbed my face. I hated this moment. Lying here, waiting to fall asleep, while my brain began to spin and spin.

At least the wind wasn't howling outside, like it had been on Saturn. The refinery we'd taken had never let us sleep due to that constant howl of wind. Left us jumpy, exhausted, making mistakes.

This bed was pleasant.

I looked up at my armor. Almost close enough to reach out and touch. Ammo and rifle at its feet. A guardian knight, recharging itself with its chest open wide and waiting for me to slam on in, looking over me in my sleep.

I never felt safe unless I could see it as I lay still, waiting for sleep. Waiting for the drift.

Amira started to snore.

A thudding sound. Armor moving around. I rolled out of bed. "Who's that?"

Ken sat up, groggy. "What?"

Someone screamed. I jackknifed out of the bed and out to the door. In the bio-light, I saw a figure stagger forward. "Chef!" I yelled, recognizing Berkhardt. "Report."

Berkhardt raised his handgun and pointed it at me. I froze, suddenly unable to move. I'd been fighting with Berkhardt since Titan. Since what felt like forever.

The utterly too-loud crack of a shot slammed through the corridor and Berkhardt's brains blew out the front of his temple.

"Chef!" I couldn't help myself.

One of the new members, Maria Lukin, stood behind Berkhardt's body as it fell forward and hit the ground with a wet thump. Her hands were shaking as she lowered the handgun held in both hands to steady the shot.

Then she moved forward as something slithered off Berkhardt's back. Oily, scales, and pronged rear feet that scrabbled at the floor as it ran down the corridor toward Lukin. The pink tail whipped around for balance.

Lukin fired twice, the corridor lighting up. I flinched each time. The driver flopped to its side.

Her face was pale in the dark. "They said in training he's already dead," she said to me. "They said he's already dead, right?"

I unfroze. "Get in your armor!" I shouted. "Now!"

Maria rabbited away, and I realized that was the first thing I should have done. Rockhopper rules. What the hell was I thinking?

I spun back into the room and started backing into my armor. It wrapped itself shut around me, and there was the suddenly cool sensation of something slithering up my tailbone and neck. The suit linked itself directly to my brain.

"What the fuck were you doing naked out there?" Ken shouted.

I willed the helmet to pop up, and it slid up and over my head and slammed in tight.

I looked left. Amira was in.

"Rockhoppers, armor up!" I shouted, using the suit to amplify my voice. It was quavering. I hoped no one noticed. Chef had been staring right at me in the corridor, I thought. Chef had his brains blown out by *one of us*. That look on Maria Lukin's face. I couldn't shake it. "Don't do anything but fucking armor up!"

The public channel was packed with scared chatter.

Ken calmly cut through the noise. "Quiet, all! Ping me if you're armored and armed and then stay in your room and make sure no one's naked."

“Are we under attack?” Amira asked.

“There was a driver,” I told her and Ken on the command channel. The armored suits used quantum-entangled communications among the officers. The enemy wouldn’t be able to overhear anything here. “It got Chef. Lukin shot it. Him first. Then it.”

“Chef?” Ken sounded shaken.

“She shot him, and then she shot it. Twice,” I repeated tonelessly. “Be ready for anything.”

“I don’t hear anything about orbital defenses being breached,” Amira said. “HQ is silent.”

“Let’s get out there and find out what’s happening,” Ken hissed.

Amira had her EPC-1 slung over her back. A rocket launcher–looking tube with high-density battery running around every bit of spare space and cabling running down the back. The electromagnetic pulse it created stopped Crickets dead cold. Would have been useful on the flight back to Shangri-La.

I looked out into the dark corridors, thinking back to Icarus Base and all the corpses we’d walked through back there. “Alpha squad, Sergeant Berkhardt isn’t with us. Smalley, you’re squad leader.”

Lana Smalley. I could imagine her biting her lip as she processed that. Then a calm “Understood. Chaka, Zizi?”

“We heard,” they said.

“Let’s poke our heads out and take a look around,” I said.

5

Alpha squad was down its sergeant. But as we followed protocols and poured out of the tunnels and up toward the surface, a quick roll call revealed that no one else had gotten hit by a driver. Min Zhao had Bravo assembled and sweeping clear ahead of us. Erica Li, Jun Chen, and Greg Vorhis all had stations along the walls and zones of fire covered.

The new additions clustered in the common room. Charlie and Delta hadn't done any night raid drills yet.

"Okay, our role is to protect one of the smaller artillery positions up on the hill," Ken explained to them. "We're going to head out across the basin. We don't know what's up there, so focus on getting to the rally point."

"Alpha takes lead," I said. "Bravo on the rear. Yusef, you take our left flank, Tony, our right. Follow our pips and stay calm."

There was a ton of general chatter going on. Squads trying to figure out leadership on the open ground above us.

"Devlin, you able to get to HQ and check in?" Ken asked.

I was pinging but getting nothing back. "No," I said. "Command's gone silent. Amira?"

"I'm crawling the network, but it's chaos back there. If I know something, you'll know it."

"Good."

"You think heading for the turret's the best idea?" Ken asked.

"Fall back on orders, assess, and then make a call. If they need us to be there and we aren't . . ."

"Rockhoppers," Smalley called out on the common. "We're moving."

"You think this is it?" Ken asked me as the platoon moved up the tunnel, Amira overriding the airlocks and blowing the air out so we could just run through and out onto the plain.

I looked through the night gloom with the armor's amped-up senses. The giant seed-shaped lump of the Pcholem at the center of the basin blocked most of my field of view, though I could see other squads popping up out of the ground.

We'd come out looking for a fight. And it wasn't here. And it didn't seem about to drop on our heads, either. No matter how I scanned the sky, it came back dead. Though anything that could fly was scrambling up into the air and getting clear of the base.

"You think they're coming for Titan?" I asked. "I don't see anything in the air that isn't ours."

"Not yet," Ken said with conviction. "But they're coming."

I looked around. Nothing but CPF. And scoured rock. "Get on the artillery. Keep them together."

"Where are you going?" Ken asked. I was beginning to split off from the platoon.

"HQ," I told him.

"Don't go alone," Ken said.

I slowed. "Charlie squad, on me. Delta, you're responsible for both flanks; stay in the middle and look both ways before crossing the street, got it? Everyone, keep alert for human hostiles."

There was a pause.

"Human?" someone asked.

"You saw what happened to Chef. I don't think he'll be the last, if this is something serious."

Several bodies lay scattered around the tunnel entrance to HQ. Torn apart. Shot. Blood splattered on the walls. We slowed down as we approached, rifles up, nerves amped as we expected every shadow to jump at us.

A suit of armor lay facedown in one of the airlocks we cycled through. Tendrils of smoke leaked from around the shattered helmet.

"Direct RPG hit?" Patel asked.

Kimmirut leaned over. "No blast marks on the outside."

"Eyes up," I ordered, stepping over.

A bullet smacked into my armor, making it ring inside. I flattened back against the bulkhead of the airlock. Just before I'd ducked back, I'd seen a mess of desks piled up against the HQ entrance in a hasty barricade.

"Hello, the shooter," I called out over the speakers on the suit.

"Oh, thank god!" came the immediate response. "Is everyone else there with you able to talk?"

"No drivers here," I said. "Can we step out and approach?" I put my armored hands out in the air.

"Please! We need help putting out the fires."

We vaulted the barricade, bouncing off the ceiling and coming down into the middle of a mess. Fires raged in three parts of the round command center, and the offices were all already gutted. Five people fought, but the smoke kept them back. Their CPF grays were charred at the arms. One of them had nasty burns on her hands.

"Get the extinguishers from them and get into the middle of the fires. Yank out anything on fire and toss it down the north tunnel," I ordered. "Clear the barricade."

"There might be more attacks . . ."

"The fire will kill you now, attacks might come later. We can make a new one," I said. "Why are you shucked down?"

"We were off duty," the woman with the burned hands said. She was trembling. Shock hitting her. Those hands looked bad. "The drivers hit officers' rooms. There were a lot of officers out here. They cut us off, so we got handguns and retreated back here. Two of us got into armor, but the drivers . . . they can still get their tails through. All we could do was retreat to here and call for help, but it was already on fire. We decided to try and hold it."

I'd changed rooms. Given a squad my room. That driver in our hallway, it had been hunting me.

Damn.

"We just lost all our leadership in one strike," I said. "Anyone have a first aid kit?"

Someone was hunched over at one of the boards, trying to call out. Good thinking. "Anything?"

"Needlepoint's quiet," he said. "I'm trying to figure out how to call up to orbit, but I'm not a comms specialist. I'm trying to figure out the interface."

Mohamed Cisse had flipped his helmet up and pulled me aside. "The woman with the burned hands needs a medical pod."

"We're all staying right here for now, I'm sorry," I said. This was all fucked up. I wanted to rub my forehead. "Get your helmet back up; we don't know what's happening."

"Yes sir."

"Hey, I made contact with the ship!" the man on comms yelled.

I strode over. "The Pcholem?"

"Yeah. What do I tell it?"

"Tell it to leave. We're under attack." If there truly were only four of them in the entire solar system, like Shriek had mentioned, then it was a big sitting duck.

"Cancel that!" Someone in an armored suit with commander's stripes on the shoulder walked down the tunnels at us. "We might need an evac."

"Sir," I said. I started to give an update, but the commander ignored me and pushed aside the person at comms.

The armored helmet snicked down. The commander had her hair pulled back in a ponytail that bobbed as she looked over. "Needlepoint has an automated call for general assistance going out," she said, eyes flicking over the screen. "But all the satellites are up, all orbital defenses and weapons ready, and no breaches have been detected. I'm going to get a line up for instructions."

Gunfire started chattering from a level below us.

The commander's head snapped over to the HQ entrances leading downward. One of the fires inside still burned merrily, but Charlie squad had stomped, extinguished, and ripped out the other two. Her lips pressed tight, she twisted my way and I could see the name on her collar: CHARET. "It's coming up from below," she said. We'd been so focused on being hit from above. But the ghost sign that Amira found had been underground. "Deploy your team *that* way."

She pointed down, but I was already on it. "Charlie squad, we want to block the doors coming in from below."

"What about the fire?" Yusef asked.

"Now!" I shouted. "I want weapons on those two doors!"

+ + + +

The next wave came. Hollow-eyed people running up the corridor at us. The Driven never spoke, but they had weapons. They used them. The hasty barricades of desks we shoved up toward the inner doors shattered under the onslaught of fire.

There were too many. They just kept coming. Bodies, the drivers clutching their shoulders with clawed hands and blood running down the fronts of their shirts.

"I'm out of ammo," a shaken Patel said.

"Punch anything that comes over the barricade," I told him.

Underneath us was an entire complex of contractors. The tens of thousands of civilians who slept assuming we were defending them.

"They waited for the next round of command talent to organize here," Commander Charet said. She had left comms and walked up behind us. She held a duffel bag, which she tossed forward. "I thought I was going to have to blow the airlocks leading out, not the ones leading down."

Patel grabbed the bag. "I've been trained to set explosives," he said.

"Let's give him cover," Charet ordered, and flipped her helmet down.

A driver scrambled up and over the barricade and launched. I fired reflexively at it, trying to pick it out of the air. But it landed right on the back of someone's armor. They flailed around, and the pink tail whipped up, and then down and in. Wriggling micro-tendrils sliding through normally impenetrable alloy until it reached skin. "Yusef!" Suqi screamed, running at him.

He hit her, throwing her back several feet. His helmet slid open and Yusef, eyes wide, coughed blood. He grabbed a grenade off his waist, pulled the pin, and jammed it down his neck, and then his helmet snapped into place and he crouched down.

There was a thud. His armor bowed out from the inside. The helmet cracked open and Yusef Obari fell forward onto the ground, smoke rising from the inside of the husk of his armor.

"Holy fuck."

I could hear the sound of retching on the common channel.

"Patel!" I shouted. "Move!" If we waited any longer, we'd be run over.

Patel was over the barricade with the bag of explosives. Everyone opened up, picking off each body that tried to sprint its way across the corridor down to us. For several minutes, there was only calm breathing and gunshots. No one had to say anything.

Patel didn't even wait to get all the way back to us before hitting the remote detonator now in his hands. The explosion blew him through the barricade, knocked us all on our backs, and left me with a nosebleed.

"Charlie squad, call out."

"Kimmirut here."

"Patel," Patel groaned.

"Cisse."

There was a lot of smoke. I swapped a few different filters over the helmet until I could peer through the smoke and see the way down choked in rubble. "That should hold them a while," I said, my voice breaking slightly. I looked down. My armored hands shook, and I couldn't force them to stop.

Commander Charet grabbed my shoulder and spoke on the common channel. "Patel, is there enough to do a repeat?"

"Yes," he said, staggering to his feet and shoving a heavy desk off of him.

“Anyone not in armor here in HQ can’t go outside. So, you take your squad and get out,” she ordered. “We’ll stay here, keep calling for backup, and get the assholes in orbit to see about lending us a hand. I’ll also see if I can link up with any soldiers stationed downstairs who’re not being Driven.”

“You sure about that?” I asked. “We can keep your guard.”

“Protect your team, Lieutenant,” she said. “Get to the hills, and watch your feet.”

“What about yours?”

She snorted bitterly. “I was taking a shit. Can you believe that? Pants down around my ankles when I heard the screaming. Officers’ quarters. I get there, anyone not in armor, they’re just bloodstains on the wall. This private’s running around in armor, killing anything in sight, driver swinging from his back. Two shots. He goes down and it slithers off his back, but not before hitting me.”

“In full armor?”

“Four broken ribs. I’ve been coughing blood, my left arm doesn’t work, and there’s pain in my abdomen. Only reason I could walk over here was because I jammed myself full of painkillers and let the armor walk me. See where things stand? Get with your platoon, hold the hills, wait for orbital support to get down.”

We loped across the Shangri-La basin as the explosion died away behind us, sealing them into HQ.

“Amira, status?”

“Nice of you to check in. We’re locked in; what’s the state of HQ?”

I filled her in as we ran.

“Holy shit,” she said.

"I know!"

"No, I'm looking out over the basin. You need to run faster. They're coming out of the tunnels into the open now."

A figure in armor lurched toward us. Suqi Kimmirut slowed down, pulled out a rocket launcher she hadn't been able to use inside, and hit it midstride, knocking it back in a ball of fire.

"Don't slow down!" I shouted. Then back on my platoon command channel. "Amira, that gun we're protecting. Can we turn it around to face down into the basin?"

"I like it. We need more manpower."

"Then start recruiting," I ordered.

We hit the foothills. I dared a glance back and saw people only in surface suits, no armor, stumbling out into Titan's atmosphere, compelled by the creatures dug into their backs. They fired weapons randomly. A wasteful wave of humanity tossed against anyone trying to get away.

"Crickets," Mohamed Cisse shouted. A cloud of the small Conglomerate mechanical insects blew out of one of the tunnels near the Pcholem and boiled across the ground toward the Pcholem's open bays.

"Well," a voice said over the common channel. The Pcholem, Starswept, sounded very apologetic. "I'm very sorry to have to do this, but there is heavy Conglomerate weaponry coming online. I must take my leave. I wish you all the best of luck in your current battle."

The living starship hauled itself into the air, fields compressing down around it as the gloom filled with a sudden onslaught of fire and weaponry aimed against the Pcholem. Crickets and human beings slid off in the air to fall down to the ground as Starswept accelerated away.

We were on our own.

6

The basin floor crawled with a flood of human forms and scrabbling Crickets balling up to attack positions in the foothills. Ken perched on a rock to look downslope. "Crickets and drivers," he said. "I'm not seeing any trolls or raptors."

"Yet," I said.

"Yet," Ken agreed. We watched a wave of Conglomeration surge against the lower slopes. Second Platoon struggled to keep them at bay, falling back in careful staggered lines with well-coordinated fire.

"They're rushing us, Amira." I turned back to where Amira, the rest of the platoon, and fifteen other soldiers pulled in from the hilltops were slowly shoving the anti-spacecraft energy weapon into place. It wasn't mounted; Amira had to have it moved onto a large cairn of boulders and rocks hastily built for it.

Barricades at HQ. Rock piles. We were stretching.

Soldiers were pushing up the rear of the barrel and stacking rocks under the cannon's stand to get the weapon aimed down into the basin.

"We have three covering the tunnel," Ken said. "We can't risk blowing the cable down."

"So, we're vulnerable on the hill and from below."

"Just from below now," Amira said. She walked over to stand with us and raised a hand. "Fire!"

The energy cannon fired, a subsonic thud. The air around the tip rippled; energy lanced out. A line of blinding light jumped out to hit the basin. Five at the back were moving the barrel around as Amira started calling out targets.

A halfhearted response came in gunfire. Then a small wave of Crickets swarmed toward the hill. Amira stopped calling out directions and pulled out the EPC-1. Massive clumps of Crickets tumbled to a stop after she fired; the rest veered off and wheeled back toward Shangri-La's tunnels.

Cheers came over the common channel.

"They can still kill the dark matter reactor down there." Amira slung the EPC-1 back over her shoulder.

"And we don't have much in the way of ammo, other than what we carried up here," Ken said.

"We just need to give the folk upstairs enough time to drop reinforcements," I said.

"If the reactor goes offline?" Amira asked on the command channel.

I let out a deep breath. "I don't know."

"Now is the time to figure rally points," Ken said.

"Where?" I asked through gritted teeth. "If they're boiling up out of the ground, where do we go? How do we know where to go? We leave this spot, we walk into what?"

"We sit here and fight to the last?" Amira's voice dripped scorn. "You know my feelings about that crap. I'm here to survive. I'm not here to throw my life away to either the Accordance or the Conglomeration."

I opened my mouth but was cut off by a familiar voice. "Third Platoon, this is Commander Barbera Charet."

Relief washed over me. "HQ, go for Third."

"Upstairs has marching orders, Lieutenant," Charet said. "I need you and your team to detonate the weapons foundry and hold the power plant until the ships get down here."

I looked up at the cannon. "Right now we're holding a hill and directing fire down—"

"I know. That's why I'm choosing you. The foundry has a few bombs big enough to destroy access to it; you'll know what to do." Charet coughed and went silent for a second.

"How long will it take for backup to arrive?" I asked.

Silence.

"HQ?"

The sound of gunfire cracked the channel open. An explosion. "I'm going to have to get back to you," Charet said.

"HQ? HQ? Commander Charet?"

I looked over at Ken and Amira. "We have orders," I said on the common channel. "Charlie, Alpha, you're going to split off with me. We're headed down to take the reactor and hold it until help arrives from upstairs."

"HQ just went down," Amira said up on the command channel.

"And we have orders. We hold the reactor, we can hold the hills. You know, Amira, the only way off this planet is up. Ken, Delta and Bravo stay with you. Keep sweeping the basin."

"There's a good chance anyone going down there dies," Amira said. "It's crawling with Conglomerate forces."

"I've been there before. It makes sense, Amira."

Amira walked over to the tunnel and looked down. "You're going to need someone who can open doors and hold your hand. Also, you don't want to go down this tunnel."

"Why not?"

"They're waiting for you there. They won't be waiting for you somewhere else in the middle of the basin."

I wasn't going to ask or order her. I knew her position. "Okay. We're going downhill. Alpha takes point. Charlie covers our asses."

"You need me to open doors," Amira repeated.

"Let's go, Rockhoppers," I said, with a calmness I didn't feel in any way. And beside me, leaping up over the hilltop and down with us, was Amira.

"Thank you," I said on the command channel.

"I'm thinking, before we blow up the foundry, I want to pick up some more weapons," she said.

We boogied down the tunnel after unleashing lightning from the hilltop along our chosen path to force everything well back. Charred bodies lay around the basin as we pelted down into it, hopping and bouncing our way along.

Amira came in behind us, hitting even higher and longer jumps into the air and firing her EPC-1. She left a swathe of twitching Crickets on the ground.

"Left," I ordered.

We veered and hit the inside of a loading bay, preceded by a hailstorm of our own bullets before we dropped in.

"Amira?"

"I'm worming my way into the networks. No ghost sign."

Good. This was the old routine. The first routine, really. Amira had used all that black-market Accordance nano-ink technology buried under her skin to look around corners, check out surveillance video.

The doors opened and we scooted through. Under Amira's

guidance, we began moving through bulkheads and doors, section by section. One squad would provide cover while the other moved. Then we switched places. Doors opened under Amira's thoughtful pauses, and then we'd keep going.

Left, right, down, someone with a driver on their back attacking us. Kill. Crickets, stomp and kill. Drivers, open fire.

We spent five minutes jammed up near the foundry as one of the Driven came at us in full armor. But we'd known it was there, thanks to Amira.

Amira came around the corner with the EPC-1 and hit the armor, and then ducked out. Zizi Dimka hit it with an RPG, and Chaka sniped the driver right in the head halfway down to the ground.

Amira walked into the foundry and looked around. "Grab all the extra ammo you can stand to carry," she said to everyone. "Level up to something with more punch if you need it. Devlin, the bombs are for jumpships. They will need to be dragged out to this bulkhead, and the next one. Should bury it enough."

Charlie squad sat on the bulkhead doors, covering our asses as we set up. Amira tripped the timers, and then we hoofed it down the corridors again, moving down through the basin's warrens.

The bodies in the corridors weren't soldiers anymore. They were contractors in overalls or simple day clothes. A cross section of humanity, lifted out from different continents with the promise of work and a chance to help keep humanity safe.

Here on Titan, we didn't see all the anti-Conglomeration videos. Having seen battle, we didn't need it. But in downtime, the platoon had uploaded some of what Earth was seeing. The Conglomeration's work on other worlds: stripping them of life and keeping only the forms and genetic material that interested them. The Conglomeration had needs, niches that could be filled, and it would take life and reshape it, mold it, to fit any of those needs.

On the moon, we'd seen living heat shields that lived on the outside of a Conglomerate starship. They'd once been a thinking, intelligent race like ours.

I wondered if these people had come here out of a desire to fight, to help the war effort. Or if they'd been starving in refugee camps run by the Accordance and saw no other way out.

Gunfire. We hit the walls and skidded to stops.

"We're CPF," I called out on the common. "Identify yourself."

"How do we know you're CPF?" came the reply.

"Because we didn't try to kill you," Amira said irritably, and walked around the bulkhead out into the open. She flicked her helmet open. "Now—"

Someone shot at her, the single pop loud and bright in the tight space.

Amira moved, blurringly fast. She grabbed someone in blue overalls and pulled a handgun out of their hand. "I'm going to say that you're having a bad day and a little over-nervous," she said. "That is why I have not killed you. But I am obviously not Conglomerate."

She tossed him back toward a group of people in lab coats, overalls, and day clothes. Behind them were heavy blast windows, control rooms, miles of complex alien machinery plunging down into the ground. Gantries and crosswalks laced the air above the reactor pit.

One of the engineers in an environment suit stepped forward. "Apologies," he said. "We're trying to hold the reactor."

Amira held the handgun out to him. "This should be yours. Who are you?"

"Anton Dismont; I'm one of the chief engineers," he said,

and then waved the gun away. "I'm afraid I'm more likely to kill one of you by accident with that than help. Are you here to save us?"

Amira looked back at me. "Alas," she said. "We've been sent here to help secure the reactor until help arrives."

Dismount slumped a little. "We're still under attack."

"Very much so. For now," I said. Then on the command channel: "Amira, can you get me a big boost on the common so I can get a message out to everyone?"

"Thinking of replacing HQ?"

"Yes. We have the power plant. Now let's start securing the base."

Amira raised an eyebrow.

I gave the mental command, and my helmet snapped open and slid into the back of my armor. "If we have the plant, then the hills are secure. Get me on the common channel, Amira."

I couldn't tell if she shrugged, but her silvered eyes looked upward, as if she was recalling something. "You're live, Lieutenant."

Ignoring her slight mocking tone, I said, "All platoons, this is Devlin Hart. We have the power plant secured. The hills are still ours, even though the Conglomeration has taken the tunnels. But now it's time take back Shangri-La.

"I need volunteer squads to get down here. It will be door by door, but we have a systems specialist that you can coordinate with. Let's flush them the hell back to wherever they came from!"

Amira broke out of her trance, mind running deep inside Shangri-La's networks.

"How many?" I asked.

"Three thousand got into the hills," she said wearily. "Platoons agreed to send down a thousand to try and secure the tunnels."

"And?"

"I got them in," she said. "Staggered opening doors to let them clear through by sections. Most of the cable tunnels are secure. A few hundred are fanning out from those points. They're breaking back into HQ, but it's heavy with drivers and raptors there. And that's about as far as we can go right now. And, Devlin?"

"Yeah?"

"Stop pacing. You're in armor. You're making the engineers nervous."

I stopped and looked around. The civilians were staring at me.

"We need more boots in the tunnels," I said.

"The other officers won't," Amira said. "They want the hills covered. A way out."

"Well, we get HQ back at least," I muttered. "But we can pull this all back."

The sound of gunfire interrupted me. I moved up toward the doors and glanced up the tunnel at Lana Smalley. "Smiley?"

"Clear!"

I stomped back to Amira. "HQ? Anyone alive?"

She smiled. "They found only bodies. They're holding it now, though."

For now.

This was all a balancing act that could go horribly wrong so quickly, I realized. And it would take days, or weeks, to clear everything out down here.

But it was possible.

It was damn possible.

"HQ incoming," Amira said.

"Who's taken command?" I asked.

"The officers are still in the hills. Privates who volunteered to push through," she said. "They have a link upstairs. They're saying other bases are scattering to the plains; they're managing to get uplinks and orbital bombardment support."

"Are we expected to abandon the base as well?" I asked.

"No. If we can hold, we are to stay put. However, other officers on the plains and some Accordance chatter are rumoring something big is up from everyone upstairs."

"Like what?" I asked.

"It's fucking alien high command," Amira said. "They're not going to tell us 'apes,' are they?"

7

Ken popped back into the command channel. "We can't call down orbital strikes on Shangri-La itself; they won't engage until we're out in the open and headed for rally points."

I looked over at Amira. "But HQ is still telling us to stay put?"

She'd been glazed over, off in a world of networks to help coordinate clearing out the tunnels for hours. She looked exhausted.

"Amira?"

"We're still staying put," she said, an edge to her voice. "But raptors are running around everywhere, and everyone's starting to run low on ammunition. We shouldn't have blown the foundry."

"We had orders," I muttered.

Amira didn't bother to respond.

Min Zhao's voice came in on the command channel. The four squad leaders had been keeping quiet, leaving most of the chatter to Amira, Ken, and me. They stayed on their squad's entangled comms mostly. "Everyone, we have a very large breakout that is coming up the foothills."

"How bad?"

"Thirty or forty raptors in armor, a couple drivers, big cloud of crickets," she reported.

"Are you in danger?" I asked.

"They're going after First Platoon. They might have to abandon their spot. But that's not why I'm calling in."

I cocked my head. "What's up, Max?"

"They're being led by an Arvani in armor," she said. "And it's broadcasting on the common. You should hear this."

"Amira, you hearing this?" I asked.

"I'm hunting for the signal," she said. And then the sound kicked on for me.

"Do not resist the Conglomeration," a familiar voice said. "You have lost on all the other worlds you fought for. You will lose here as well. The Conglomeration is stronger than you or the Accordance. But if you surrender now, walk away from your positions, you will have a place in the Conglomeration. A great place. You won't have to live under the pressure of the Accordance's grip. You will have freedom. You can have self-determination. You can have riches."

"That Arvani . . . ," Ken said.

"There is a further bounty, however, for those willing to prove their true allegiance to the new order that comes to this world. A promotion to high status, and the natural benefits that will stick to you with this. The bounty I will give to anyone who hands over the following three humans here: Devlin Hart, Amira Singh, and Ken Awojobi."

"Seems like you've got a fan," Zhao said.

"I killed your kind in great schools on the moon of your homeworld," the voice continued. "I will kill all that oppose me here."

Amira blinked right out of her trance and we stared at each other. "It's Zeus," we both said.

"Zeus?" Lana Smalley asked. "The defector from Icarus Base? That Arvani is dead, along with all the other Conglomeration there."

"Obviously not," Amira said.

"It could be just some other Arvani who went over to the Conglomeration?" Min suggested.

"With a personal vendetta. No. It's Zeus." I was sure of it.

"First Platoon is falling back, they can't hold. We lost the gun."

"This is HQ on the common," came an interruption. "Pickup is coming. Pickup is coming. Get down into the basin, hold off any enemy, and get aboard."

"They're abandoning HQ now," Amira said. "They just don't have the ammo to hold off the raptors in the tunnels. Everyone is running topside."

I wanted to punch something. If we'd been able to dig out the foundry, get more ammo . . . maybe. Amira saw what I was thinking and shook her head.

"Ken, keep on the gun as long as you can to hit anything Conglomerate out on the basin."

"Until the guns are blown, they'll need power," I said. Gunfire chattered from up the tunnel again as Alpha and Charlie stopped something in its tracks that was coming at us. "And there are civilians down here, we'll need to escort them up."

"It's going to be a zoo up there," Amira said.

"I know." I looked around at the unarmored engineers in their bright-yellow plastic-looking vacuum suits and rubbed my forehead. "I know."

Two hilltop anti-spacecraft weapons had been seized by several humans with drivers on their backs, protected by five raptors. They spat lines of energy into the sky, lancing around at the jumpships weaving around to try to get into the basin.

Out in the basin, a flood of yellow vacuum suits and civilians rushed the wasp-like ships the moment they touched ground. There were drivers leaping into the mess, shoving tails down into spines and spinning the civilians around to their own purposes, only to be executed by soldiers in armor.

Raptors boiled out of the tunnels, and CPF soldiers hanging out of the sides of the jumpships opened fire on them.

Several squads stayed on their hills, raking the basin with energy. The scarred rock bubbled and boiled, dead Conglomeration obliterated.

Then the hilltop guns stuttered out and stopped firing.

At least that would let more ships get to ground. But now the basin was a scrum.

"There is not enough transport for the civilians," Ken said as the platoon re-formed in a rough circle near one of the larger jumpships.

"Holy shit," I said, looking at the numbers of people surging around the basin to try to get aboard anything that was flying. "This is a disaster."

"It's happening all over Titan. The Accordance wants soldiers back. It wants to preserve fighting strength. The civilians are extraneous to them," Amira said. "You know they do not value human life."

Over and over on the common channel, pilots were shouting, "Spaces are reserved for armored and fighting personnel first."

Despite that, CPF soldiers were shoving civilians into ships and guarding the basin, expecting them to fly away and come back. Or at least, refusing to jump in first.

"Keep the perimeter," I ordered the entire platoon on the

common channel. "Anyone who wants to get aboard, can. But I'm going to stay right here until they bring down more ships."

"Think hard about that," Amira said on the command channel, her words clipped.

"No," I said. "We're in armor. Hundreds of pounds of protection and enhancement. Three or four days of air. Water. Nutrition dripped right into our bloodstreams. Adaptive camo. We can get out there into the plains and survive for a pickup. Everyone standing out here in yellow is a target. That's time for us to figure out what to do next, time these people will never be able to get for themselves."

Amira shifted on her feet visibly. I could sense the coiled frustration even through the armor. "I don't like this," she said.

"No one is *supposed* to like it," I snapped. "That's why I told you to get aboard if you wanted. I'm not going to stop you. I told you what I'm doing, anyone who wants in can join. I can't force you to do this, particularly when it's against Accordance orders."

"Don't shout at me," she said calmly.

I was freaking out a bit. Because I knew they would all probably follow me out into the plains. Into a giant gamble that we would get picked up later, even if the Conglomeration was overrunning the base.

But this *was* the right thing to do.

"There were so many we never got a chance to save back in Icarus Base," Ken said, surprising me by interrupting us. "Devlin's right. We have time to come up with another solution. They don't. I don't want that on me. Not again."

Thank you, Ken, I mouthed to myself. Thank you.

"I'm not—"

"They're taking off!" someone shouted on the common

channel. The jumpship we'd been guarding powered up. Pebbles and rocks slapped against my armor and rattled as it rose into the air.

A handful of yellow vacuum suits staggered back to their feet and looked up as their way off Titan accelerated out over the hills.

All around the basin, more jumpships rose, scattering to the points of the compass gently and then picking up speed.

"There they go!" said a voice on the common channel. Zeus. "Your heroes. Your leaders. Your soldiers. The Accordance. They've left you all behind. Now what? I will tell you. Now you will learn what it is like to live as true, free humans."

"He's coming downhill," Ken said.

I could see the distant cloud Zeus and his team of raptors were kicking up as they raced down into the basin. A mile and a half away from us in the center of it all.

"Surrender now," Zeus shouted on the common channel. "Sit down with your hands folded and you will live to see a new day for your species. You will learn how the Conglomeration extends its welcome, even to its most bitter enemies like my own species. But remain standing and I *will* cut through you."

"Always a charmer," Amira said.

An engineer in yellow tapped my armor. "What do we do now?" Dismont asked. I could see condensation beading the inside of his mask.

"You all have two choices," I said. "Sit down and surrender, or run with us out into the plains. I don't know how long your air will last."

"What happens if we surrender? We've seen the videos the Accordance plays. But you're CPF. You've been on Saturn. What happens to us?"

All we knew were the same Accordance pieces of propaganda.

Dead planets. The Conglomeration's reshaping entire species into functional forms for their own needs. But we didn't know what happened to the people they captured and ruled over.

The communications from places that fell went silent.

"I don't know," I said. "I truly don't know."

"Then we go with you," Dismont said firmly.

I looked at the dust cloud of the approaching Conglomeration force. "That's assuming we can even get out of here," I said.

We grabbed ammo from squads who were sitting down and folding their arms. "No judgments," I shouted. "Just grab what you can."

Zeus was a mile away now, and the slow picking through surrendering people meant we weren't moving away quickly enough. But I wanted everything we could get our hands on.

"Are we sure none of the ships are coming back down for us?" Tony Chin asked.

"If they were only taking soldiers, something bad might be going down upstairs," Amira said. "I've been trying to patch in, but there's a lot of interference. That can't be a good sign. . . ."

One of the skyscraper-sized anti-orbital guns glowed red. Electricity sparked up its sides, gathering into a house-sized ball at the very tip, and then leapt into the sky.

"I think shit's all fucked up and shit," Lana Smalley said.

"Has anyone seen Shriek?" I asked. He would be able to provide some hints as to what might be happening. He'd seen more of this than any of us.

"He got on the jumpship," Ken said.

"Of course he did," I said.

"We need to move," Amira said. "Not many people standing anymore. We stick out."

"Where are we going?" Dismont asked.

A good question. "If the jumpships aren't coming back down, and everything is up in the air—" I started.

"Not everything," Ken said.

"Can anyone here repair a broken jumpship?" I asked on the common channel.

One of the yellow vacuum suits in our midst raised a hand. "I've worked maintenance before getting promoted down to the power core and retrained. What's broken?"

"We sucked crickets into an engine and then crashed," Ken told him.

"We'll need parts," the engineer said.

"Amira? Where can we find parts?" I asked.

We were all moving as a group, trying to keep the yellow-suited engineers in our midst. Amira broke away for a tunnel. "Downstairs," she said.

After the heavy doors shut behind us, they groaned and started smoking. "What's that about?"

"Slowing Zeus down," Amira said.

We had to make the hard choice of loading up with spare engine parts instead of ammo. We left the guns on the floor. But with a plan at hand, the four squads pulled together quietly.

Mohamed Cisse carried a turbofan on his back like Atlas, the engineers clustered near him, and we formed up around them. Amira led us back up and out. We popped out like groundhogs and ran for the hills. After a few lopes, we started dropping even more gear and just picking up the engineers under our arms so we could leap our way from rock to rock.

A triangular formation of raptors fell in behind us, but Ken took Alpha squad and fell behind a bit. The firefight was intense and brief.

We crested the hills and pelted downhill toward the open plains and the ethane lake where we'd crashed with the new platoon members just a day before.

"Keep up the pace," Ken muttered. "We went down a long way from the base, and the engineers don't have that much air. Don't stop for any Conglomeration, just keep moving."

I didn't respond. I was too busy focusing on each armor-enhanced leap that took us farther away from Shangri-La.

"I think the Conglomeration may be taking orbit," Amira said, looking up from the bank of the ethane lake.

I looked up as well. But there was nothing more than Titan's usual gloom and thick clouds. "How can you tell?"

"I'm listening hard. Through the static. I think I'm feeling some battle chatter. Ship-to-ship stuff."

Three squads got their shoulders under the jumpship and lifted it up. "I think I just shorted something out," Erica Li said. "Someone take my place."

They all staggered the jumpship up out of the liquid ethane, letting it all gush out of the gaps as they waited, and then carried it up onto the bank.

Someone started coughing on the common channel. "Shit, same here, something blew inside my suit. There's smoke."

"Contact," Ken said.

"Take Alpha and engage," I said. "Bravo, Delta, circle up

and keep the ship in the middle. Charlie, you're there to help the engineers move anything heavy."

As everyone scrambled to, I stood by the jumpship and looked out across the ethane lake, half expecting crickets to come boiling out of it again. But there was only stillness.

A moment of calm in the storm. It caught in the back of my throat, like a hiccup. As if I'd still been moving forward and then suddenly braked, and everything came up.

The sound of weapons fire floated over Titan's air, breaking the moment of stillness.

"Ken?" I asked.

"Raptors. Scout team. We've been located," he reported.

"Fall back and tighten up. Charlie, you'll have to help the engineers and shoot anything that gets through. How is the ship looking? How long do we need?"

"Two hours," came the response.

"We have fifteen or twenty minutes before the bad guys hit us," I told them. "Hurry."

The first wave of crickets hit ten minutes later.

The next hour, we ground the crickets down as they came at us. Amira took point, using the EPC-1 to down them in swathes. Anything that got through, we stomped into tiny debris.

But the raptors that came in afterward required bullets and direct confrontation, though some of the mines that Ken had taken the time to lay down killed many in the first batch. There was no running now. We had to keep them from the jumpship as the engineers swore and removed this part and that part.

It didn't take long to run low on ammo, even despite short

bursts and frequent direct confrontation. It took three to four of us to wrestle down a single raptor and break its helmet or shove a grenade into some key part of the Conglomerate armor.

We were losing people. Several engineers dropped in the crossfire. Aran Patel started screaming when Mohamed Cisse jumped out and caught a raptor that leapt into the inner circle. It had swung around and ripped open his armor with the wicked nano-filament blades on its legs. In seconds, Cisse ended up shredded, and his armor scattered around the ground before everyone opened up.

"Out," Min Zhao shouted.

And more and more of the platoon started tossing weapons to the ground.

The sound of a loud belch got me to stare back at the jumpship, as I'd almost forgotten what it was we were doing here.

"Everyone get in," Amira yelled. "I've got power."

"You're flying it?"

"No one else can interface with the systems or has any experience."

We fell back. Charlie squad covered us from the doorway, which now was just Aran Patel and Suqi Kimmirut.

There were too many of us. We crammed into the jumpship face to face.

"Amira?" I asked.

The jumpship's engines leapt up an octave, trying to push us into the air. Instead, we scraped along the rocky ground. Metal screamed and something snapped off the bottom of the jumpship.

Energy beams sliced against the sides of the ship, one of them punching through. Blood and flesh splattered against my helmet. The ship bounced off a boulder, spun slightly, and smacked into something. I wiped blood away just in time to see a yellow vacuum suit spin out of one of the large rents in the side of the jumpship.

"Hold on!" Amira shouted. The jumpship wobbled higher into the air and the ground started to fall away. "I think I'm getting this."

The jumpship shuddered again as we rose slightly higher. Another loud bang from something striking the side made me jump.

Alarms started whooping from the cockpit. "We going to make it?" I asked.

"I'll get back to you on that," Amira said.

9

Saturn filled the sky, massive and roiling with clouds, the rings casting shadows over the clouds we'd struggled to get above.

"I'm getting comms," Amira said. The jumpships had direct quantum-entangled linkups into the Accordance. But the minds on the other side of a call could be halfway across the solar system. Getting answers about what was happening overhead, and convincing them she was for real, had been taking up her time as we continued to spiral farther and farther up toward the clouds.

"I can fly the ship. But I don't know anything about getting a craft like this to orbit," Amira had said when I'd asked her why she was spending so much time trying to call in rather than getting us the hell upstairs.

And the engineers only had rough guesses about how orbital dynamics worked. As they pointed out, we didn't want to run out of fuel trying this. Or end up in the wrong place.

"Okay," Amira said on the command channel. "I've explained

our situation and sent back our fuel levels and dynamics, and Accordance is on the other side talking me through our sequence. It's tricky."

Tricky. It must have been if Amira was happily chatting with Accordance pilots over comms. She was not the type to stop and ask for help.

"There's a ticking clock. The ships in orbit are getting ready to punch out and leave. We have a very limited window to get scooped up in time. We don't have enough fuel to come back down."

"You're saying we may get stranded in orbit," Ken said.

"If we make it, yes," Amira said. The jumpship banked to the right. Yellow and brown clouds far under us appeared through the gaps in the ship's hull, and the wind screamed through the cabin as airflow changed. The entire jumpship flexed and warped.

Swearing cluttered the common channel as everyone tensed, waiting for the jumpship to rip itself apart.

"Amira?"

"Fuck, I know," she said, sounding rattled. "I'm trying to line us up. I'm doing the best I can, but the software is struggling with all the damage and I'm not a pilot; I have no idea how much we can push this. So, we might not make it up. And there might not be anyone there when we get there. But I know I can get us back down to ground."

I was sure the rip in the hull near me had gotten wider. "We should ask on the common channel."

"Oh, really, Lieutenant, it's suddenly a democracy in here after all those orders you've given out of late?"

"I gave everyone an option at the jumpships on the ground, and I notice you stayed. That was your choice," I said.

Amira grunted. "You two idiots would have killed yourselves

down there without me. After all we've been through, you're the closest thing I have to family."

"Sergeant Singh, are you getting all sentimental on me?" I asked. One of the other squad leaders snorted and tried to smother it.

"I've had to carry your asses so much, I feel like a mother duck," Amira said. Then on the common channel: "Hey, everyone, I need you to make a choice: up or down." She outlined the situation as she began to point the jumpship slightly up, gaining more altitude.

There was silence for a while.

"That's a hard call to make," someone said.

"You have ten seconds to aye or nay it," Amira said. "Then our launch window closes."

With a loud shriek, a panel ripped away from the top of the jumpship. I looked up toward the purple darkness of space above us. It looked like an electrical storm far overhead, with lightning dancing from spot to spot in the vacuum up there. It lit up gas clouds, like miniature nebula.

Then one of the tiny dots lit up, the explosion slowly expanding. A ship exploding. I realized the clouds were debris, all backdropped by the massive bulk of Saturn looming over us all, making our life-or-death battles seem insignificant.

"Three, two," Amira said.

"Punch it!" I shouted. "Go, go!"

The jumpship tilted slightly higher and the Accordance-made engines kicked on hard. People clattered around the cabin as a whirlwind kicked up inside. Everything shook hard enough to blur vision. Some started repeating a phrase in a language I didn't recognize, but I knew what they were doing: praying.

After a few terrifying minutes of acceleration, the jumpship rolled over onto its back. An engineer screamed and someone tried to grab at them, and then they were sucked clear out of a new gap in the ship's frame. The yellow figure kicked and wiggled in the air as they fell away behind us.

We were riding the skeleton of a ship to orbit.

The engines kicked out. Titan's clouds passed far underneath us and the curve of the planet-like moon could be seen on the horizon.

"We're still alive," Min Zhao marveled.

"Amira?"

"Shut up and don't talk to me. Orbit mechanics *suck*." The jumpship spun around and the engines fired up, nudging us back down toward the clouds a bit. Then it shifted again, pointing forward and firing. Amira was constantly changing orbit.

Occasionally, Amira would swear.

The entire horizon lit up, something white-hot blazing away. It started to move, gathering speed, and then faded off into the dark. Then another blinding spot did the same.

"Carriers making a run for it," Ken said.

"Hold on," Amira said. "They're coming for us."

"I don't see anything." I looked out the numerous holes in the jumpship around us.

"There we go," Tony Chin said from closer to the front.

Something slipped across the darkness between us and Saturn. Inky blackness slipped off its skin.

"That ours?" I asked.

"Uh-huh," Amira said.

The darkness opened its mouth and revealed a cargo bay full of other jumpships inside. It was moving faster than I realized. "Oh, shit!"

The lip of the cargo bay slammed into the jumpship, which spun all the way around until the back end struck the deck and halted the spin. The ship bounced across the bay, smacking into pillars, and came to a stop up against the back wall of the bay.

Four struthiforms in full armor bounced up to the side of the jumpship and ripped the doors off. "Get out!" they ordered.

The docking bay was closing up like a large mouth after swallowing, Titan disappearing behind it.

Accordance lights began to strobe and flash.

"Launch is imminent. Secure yourselves!" The struthiforms scattered and bolted for safety.

A deep thrum vibrated through the Accordance carrier. Then it launched. Anyone not holding onto something was shoved back to the wall. A damaged jumpship farther up the bay groaned, its tie-downs snapped by our ship on the way in.

"Watch out!" Ken shouted.

The carrier accelerated harder still, gravity pressing down on all of us. The jumpship slid down the bay and slammed into three of the team in armor.

"Everyone okay?" I shouted. "Who got pinned?"

Before they could answer, a beam of light sliced through the cargo bay, burying itself deep in the ship. Everything shuddered, but the carrier kept moving. But now the entire side had been sliced away, and we were all staring out into space. Staring at the beams of light searching and stabbing for us and the other carriers.

We watched the winking lights and explosions of the battle we were accelerating away from and held on tight.

10

We built an impromptu camp at the corner of one of the sealed bays after the acceleration eased and the alarms cut out. Struthiform crew in harness uniforms came by with crude cots.

A veritable cross section of Accordance subjects crowded in around us. Struthiform soldiers in their own powered armor, carapoids lying along the back wall like large lumps of polished rock, and other humans with their gear.

One recognizable struthiform approached us, his scarred and half-machine face blinking at the bright, stadium-like lighting in the docking bay. "I heard your approach to the ship."

Lilly Taylor jumped up. She'd shucked her armor. It was behind her, splayed open like something hungry and half machine, half biological, waiting to eat her again. The bright lights seemed to get soaked up by her skin as she went for Shriek's throat. "You bastard!" She'd spoken before with a more precise, almost British accent. Now I could hear the Kenyan accent coming out with her anger.

Min Zhao was on her feet, grabbing Taylor and spinning her off to the side.

Shriek seemed neither surprised nor concerned, regarding them both with his dinner-plate eyes.

I was on my feet too, leaving my armor behind to back Zhao up. "Thank you, Max."

"Maria is gone. We died trying to get up here. Trying to *save* these civilians," Taylor shouted.

Zhao wrapped Taylor up in a bear hug. "He's an alien, Taylor. We're alien to him. He's a lost soul and he's not going to look at it the same. But he still fixes us up, don't forget that. Okay?"

Taylor crumpled for a moment in Zhao's embrace.

Shriek looked back at me. "This is why I do not learn names," he said coolly. "They die. Now I know the dead one was named Maria. What good is that now for me?"

I groaned. "Fuck, Shriek, now's not the time."

"It's good that she grieves. You should all grieve. Grieve now and let each other go," the cyborg struthiform said. He pointed toward one of the large high-definition displays on the bulkhead wall over our heads. "See that small dot there? The blue one? That is your world. Your Earth. I would find a place on this ship, or wherever we end up, to go and look at it one last time. Because the Conglomeration comes for it, and they'll burn it. And then, eventually, you too."

I pulled Shriek away from the platoon. Alpha and Bravo were used to this shit and just looked annoyed. But Charlie and Delta were ready to kill the medic.

We needed a medic.

"I'm half ready to kill you myself, Shriek," I said, out of earshot. "You might be an alien, but right now you're being a real asshole. Shut up about all that. Did you find Ken?"

"As you requested," Shriek said. "He was shot. It happened on the surface, but he didn't report it to you. His armor kept him stable but was compromised. I assume he didn't want you to worry about taking him into pure vacuum."

I let out a deep breath. "Let me go armor up and we'll go look at him."

"The armor stays in the bay," Shriek said. "Ship rules."

"Rockhoppers don't shuck," I said.

"You're on an Accordance carrier accelerating away from the field of battle," Shriek said. "If you want me to take you to see Ken Awojobi, you shall leave your armor, like any other person who wishes to walk the ship."

I bit my lip. "I'll get Amira."

Ken was cocooned in a medical pod, its spider-like arms tucked neatly away. He sat up as he saw us, pulling coconut-like fibers sinking into the skin on his back out to their limit. "I'm sorry," he said.

"For what?" I shook my head. "Shut up, I don't want to hear about that. I'm just glad you're okay. When you stopped responding, and we didn't know where in the bay you were, we didn't know . . ."

"How is everything?" Ken asked. "How bad? I saw the whole side of the ship get sliced off."

"Maria Lukin, one of the new soldiers," I told him. "She was over there. She saved my life in the corridor, back on Titan. Shot Chef when the driver took him. Shook her up. She was a quick thinker."

There was nowhere to sit. Apparently, aliens didn't expect bedside visitors. Amira folded her arms. "How you feeling?"

Ken nodded. "Better. I'm pretty drugged up. We'll see

when I get released how I really feel, because right now it is warm and very fuzzy, which doesn't feel right. We just barely got out alive. It doesn't even feel real to be sitting here, to be still."

"Barely alive," I agreed. "I think I believed that when the Accordance handed us some resources and weapons, we'd get in there and show them how fucking hard we could fight. I thought, maybe they just didn't have the warrior spirit. Weren't motivated enough. But that was a nightmare. We lost Saturn, and now Titan, too. What's it going to be like when they reach Earth?"

"I get that from Shriek," Ken growled. "I don't want to hear it from you, too. Listen to me: I didn't almost die for nothing just now. We didn't fight for nothing. We're going to go back to Titan. We're going to go back and kick their asses, and I'm going to be first on the ground. Because the Accordance is not going to roll over and surrender. The Accordance is better than that. They are strong. We are lucky they are our allies."

There was no food for humans aboard the carrier. By the end of the second day, the engineers were lying down and taking sleeping pills that Shriek offered them, while the rest of us armored up. The steady nutrient drip jacked into our spines was enough to stave off the worst, but it was strange to just mill around in full armor, conserving power and waiting.

Halfway through the third day, the monitors lit up with something other than the outer ship cameras.

A series of rocky asteroids connected by clear tubes and girders flashed on screen. "These are the Trojans," a familiar voice explained. "These asteroids trail along Saturn in its orbit, and serve as something of a naval yard for our Saturn operations and a rally point for Accordance ships engaged on the Saturn Front."

The asteroid base faded away, and a familiar face appeared on the screen with the triangular CPF logo up behind him.

"It's Colonel Anais," Amira muttered, with all the enthusiasm of someone who found dogshit on the heel of a shoe.

"Here at the Trojan naval base, we will begin preparations to defend against any incursion into trans-Jovian Accordance territory," Anais said. "Your valued participation in the wars around Saturn has helped reduce Conglomeration forces. You have struck a great blow. Now please gather yourselves for the next stage."

"What about Titan?" someone shouted, as if Anais could hear them. "We just leave them all there to die?"

Anais droned on more about future plans and the bravery of the CPF.

"We left a lot of people behind," I muttered to Ken, now recovered and suited up. "What are we doing here? We should be going back to save them."

"We're surviving," Amira said. "We're still here. We can't help them."

"Apparently," Ken said bitterly. The news that we weren't going back to Titan seemed to have shaken him. His previous bravado had faded away as the drugs left his system. But I was still surprised. Ken had joined the CPF to get into the officer corps. He'd wanted this. Badly. He'd been a full believer. In the Accordance, in our role in it.

Looking over at the remains of Charlie and Delta squads, and the tired faces of my platoon, I realized Titan had left us all broken.

11

After several days crammed into a docking bay, filling it with the stench of human and the acrid odor of struthiforms and carapoids, the platoon was moved out from the carrier and into the rock of one of the Trojans.

We were close to the surface. On the second day, one of the walls blew out and sucked half a dozen people away.

The Rockhopper's "no shucking" rule became ironclad. We walked around in armor or huddled together in the carved-out end of a tunnel.

"Millions of miles through outer space, kitted with cutting-edge weapons, and we're sleeping in a cave," Ken noted.

Seven plastic buckets spaced out around our spot captured water dripping slowly, like honey, from a broken pipeline over our heads. Accordance had installed a gravity plate somewhere so we could walk around the asteroid, but it was a third of Earth's gravity. And it was strung through the center of the rock, which meant weird things happened if you turned your neck too quickly or turned a corner.

All night long we lay and listened to the drip, drop, drip.

A few miners came by on the second day with a large auger and some baffles. They'd drilled through the rock, breaking out into the vacuum. As the air whistled away, they calmly installed the baffles, sealant, and then a simple plastic box over the hole.

"We now have an outhouse," Ken pronounced in disbelief.

In full armor, we joined the morning mess call, surrounded by humans covered in dirt finishing their drill shifts. They looked exhausted, haggard. More like zombies than real people.

I remembered on the moon seeing Earth First slogans and general anti-Accordance graffiti.

These people didn't have the energy.

"These conditions are inhumane," Ken muttered.

Amira raised an eyebrow. "You've never heard of the Paris work camps? LA?"

"Those are for terrorists," Ken said. "Agitators."

"This is the Accordance," Amira said. "Half the people on my block were hauled away to work in worse places than this. This is a fucking hotel, Ken."

"They created infrastructure in my country when no one else would bet on us," Ken said. "They changed everything. The way things were before they came? My parents would have died. Of hunger. Or disease. The Accordance did many things for humanity; it's just that the little slice of a percent that stood on the backs of others before the Pacification are upset they are no longer Earth's royalty."

I stood up with a ball of Accordance human-optimized feed in one hand, and a globule of water in the other. Since the retreat, with nothing to do, they'd been circling around each other. Amira, raised on the streets that fought back against occupation, black market nano-ink proudly marking her as hostile, criminal, to the Accordance. Ken, raised by his family to be a part of the officer corps working for the Accordance.

Maybe our friendship had only been that of three people stuck in a foxhole together, trying to survive.

Now we were living in a cave that dripped, shitting into outer space, and eating Accordance glop while we waited for . . .

. . . I wasn't sure what I was waiting for.

Min Zhao waited for me as I got back to our cave and shucked out of the armor. When I stepped out, my paper underclothes soaked and stained with sweat, she said, "We need to figure out how to divide the squads. Charlie . . ."

"Not now, Max. I just need to sit and eat my human kibble."

I sat on my cot and nibbled at the tasteless ball of gray playdough.

Zhao shot me a look, and I sighed. "Seriously, Zhao, leave me the fuck alone."

Looking hurt, she nodded curtly and retreated back down the cave.

Shriek came to find us a few days later, once we'd fallen into a schedule of clomping over to the meals and then getting back to our cave. We cleaned it up as best we could, but we were jockeying against every other soldier among a variety of species stuck in the warrens inside the asteroids the Accordance had pulled together to make the yard.

We were still showering with wet napkins and flushing them out the crude space toilet. Welcome to the Trojan point, where clumps of asteroids followed the majestic ringed planet around in the same orbit. And humans flushed their waste and trash out into the same trailing orbit.

"What are we waiting for?" Ken had asked, and no one had an answer for him.

The Accordance had us in storage for now. We'd been saved from Titan, and now we weren't needed as the spaces on the board got rearranged.

"You need to take advantage of this time," Shriek said. "I can give Amira directions to the human holds. There are places to drink, eat, and enjoy the company of the other humans here. You are no longer on the front wing of the attack, and you need to realize this."

"We've been fighting for a long time, Shriek. You don't need to lecture us," I said.

"You barely survived a full evacuation. You need to spin about in the wind and realize that, just for now, being alive is its own amazing moment," the struthiform said. "Because if you do not, what was the point of trying so hard to stay alive."

"Ostrich ET's gotta point," Amira said.

"Alright, armor up," I said. "We'll go over, check things out."

"No armor," Shriek said.

"Rockhoppers don't shuck," I said.

"Then you stay here, in this damp cave, by yourselves. Well done, humans, you have made staying alive as exciting as a scabby infection."

But I knew with certainty that leaving armor meant leaving us vulnerable. "Bravo, Charlie, Amira, Ken. Let's go investigate."

Groans floated through the cave.

"Tomorrow we switch," I said. "We need people standing by the armor. We will not leave it alone."

Shriek clicked approvingly and led us off through the tunnels and warrens of the asteroid. "This will be good, my little adopted humans," he said happily. "Follow along, follow along."

I was counting the turns back.

Just in case.

Our party came out of the tunnels into a large cavern filled with shanty structures made of leftover plastic panels, recycled paper partitions, all of it rigged with lights clamped onto angular, leaning structures.

People stared out suspiciously from behind peepholes, while in the makeshift alleyways the sound of chatter bounced around.

Due to the low gravity, some of the buildings looked like kids' experimental popsicle-stick buildings. Stories high and bundled together by twine. Yet standing.

Shriek led us through the dense clusters of leaning buildings and into the first floor of a wicker dome with a neon sign that blazed the name from the apex: THE PARLIAMENT.

Inside, where it was hazy due to the light gravity, low-circulating air, and total lack of carbon dioxide scrubbers, people crammed up against tables and the bar.

"What do they serve?" Amira asked. "More Accordance gloop?"

"No," Shriek said. "Rocket fuel."

"What?"

"Or," Shriek said, "more like station-adjustment fuel. I believe there are rockets that use forms of alcohol. Someone, somewhere, managed to confuse the purchase ordering forms for rocket fuel and get alcohol delivered instead. Then the humans handling the loading diverted it."

"How is it that the alien in our platoon figured out where the bar was?" Ken asked.

"When you know you are going to die, you spend time seeking out finer moments," Shriek explained.

"Shriek, shut up," I said. "Before you undo all the goodwill."

Amira looked around the whole bar. "We don't have much to trade."

Shriek swept a wing hand toward the bar at the very center, a circular table filled with humans shifting to and from it. "I have opened a tab for the platoon under my auspices."

Zhao grabbed Shriek's half-metal, half-struthiform head in two hands and kissed the top of the wrinkled, ruined skin. "I've always liked this feathered freak. Haven't I always said I love him?"

"You have never said such a thing," the alien medic protested.

"Oh, well, remember that Min Zhao says she loves you. *Min Zhao!* Come on, Shriek, say my name!"

Shriek shoved her away with an angry hiss.

Aran Patel and Suqi Kimmirut stared at us as we laughed. "Serves the fucking walking chicken right for ditching us," Greg Vorhis muttered from behind Zhao.

"Shriek doesn't want to learn our names," I explained to Suqi. "It upsets him."

"I think," Amira said, gently shoving at us, "we should get to the bar before Shriek changes his fickle little mind about that bar tab."

I managed a seat next to Suqi and listened to the back-and-forth chatter. Aran and Suqi didn't join in, but they took to the simple glasses of clear alcohol quickly enough.

It numbed. It burned. Did what it needed to do. And maybe, if we kept going, we could leave Titan somewhere behind us.

Live for the moment, Shriek had told me. Because that moment is all you'll get.

Five glasses later, I was light-headed enough to realize I'd been carrying something on my back. An invisible weight that melted away, glass by glass.

Suqi was asking something.

"What?" I asked.

"Are you okay?"

I'd been staring at her, I realized. "I'm sorry," I said. I reached out and touched her knee. Shriek was right. You only ever had that minor moment. The now. The now was all we had. Because there was nothing but an uncertain haze in the future.

Suqi's drawn-in breath jolted me. She yanked backward and stood up from the stool. "Sir . . ." She sounded embarrassed and wounded.

Yeah. Half her squad had died in front of her and someone who outranked her had just grabbed her knee.

"Shit, Kimmirut," I mumbled. "I'm sorry."

She shook her head and put the glass down. "I'm going back," she said.

I stood up to follow her and wobbled. "Ah, fuck."

I'd never been a hard partier. My parents had been more concerned with dragging me from tent camps and basements to protests. They organized walkouts and strikes, and there was no time for me to be stupid. Not when you were the Harts' son.

Here I was, playing soldier. Pretending to be a hard-drinking veteran when I was just lucky to have escaped.

But it had been a nice few minutes. The alcohol burning out chains that held me to each of these individuals. Leader. I wasn't a leader, I realized as I stumbled toward Ken. I wasn't raised to be one. Or taught. I'd just lived through a Conglomerate attack on the moon, and the Accordance used me as propaganda.

All I'd done was survive.

I tried to grab Ken's shoulder. To tell him. But Amira

intercepted me and slipped under my shoulder to steady me. "You don't look so good; let's get you back to the bar to lean on."

"You were right," I told her. "I fucked up."

"Come over here and tell me about it."

I twisted back around. Ken was in deep conversation with a monstrously tall man who had muscles on his muscles. The kind you handed the big guns to. "Ken has made a friend."

"It's been hard for him since Boris," Amira said, pushing me back to the bar. "I think he needs to connect. Maybe let off some steam. After all we went through, we all need to let off some steam."

I looked at Amira and then back to Ken. "He's gay?"

"You didn't know?"

I shook my head.

"Devlin. Fuck. You don't pay close attention to the people you lead, do you?" Amira handed me another glass of the clear stuff.

"I didn't ask for it," I said. "Any of it."

"Yet here we are."

I squinted at her. "If we all need to let off steam, have you?"

"Day we docked." Amira sipped at the glass. She didn't say it with satisfaction or relish. There was a sudden grimness to her.

"Do you feel better?" I asked.

"I don't feel worse," she said.

A group of miners off shift had been watching them. One of them got up from his table. "You assholes are here partying," he said loudly, "while friends of mine working back on Titan are dead, you fucking collaborators."

The air in the bar buzzed and snapped with voices that sounded like a set of electrical wires dropped on each other.

Amira let go of her glass and stepped forward. "What did you say?"

The fact that she hadn't sworn left me feeling suddenly sober.

The man had a certain ropiness to him. The muscles that came from spending long hours operating heavy tools deep inside the asteroid. He was covered in a gray dust, and his green eyes seemed ghostly behind all that dust.

"You pieces of shit need to crawl back into that cave you're hiding in," the miner said. "Stay back in there and cower."

I walked over. "Hey, man, we just want to drink in peace."

"Drinks *we* got into this bar. Any of you know how hard that is? Know what's going on back on Earth while you march around for the Accordance? Food riots. Executions. They're standing on our backs for a war we didn't ask for. And here you all are, enjoying a drink on the tab of one of those damn ugly walking chickens. Bunch of fucking useless collaborators."

"Hey," I started to say. They were collaborators too, out here working for the Accordance.

Amira hit him in the chin with the heel of her hand. He stood a foot taller than her, but he went back and flopped onto the table, smacking into it and scattering glasses. She was, apparently, not interested in talking any further.

The miner's four friends launched themselves at us. I still had my hands up when I got hit in the face. I should have gone down. I was not a brawler; I'd barely struggled through training, with Ken constantly singling me out.

But something snapped in me. Trying to calm the situation was no longer an option.

And I wanted to fight. I wanted to break something.

"Dev!" Ken shouted, leaping in.

"Here."

We fell in close to each other, backs in, facing out. Amira had picked up a barstool to use as a club, and two miners were out cold on the ground.

But the rest of the bar had turned against us.

There was a brief moment where we kept formation, but then the melee set in. We were all just brawling. Punching, kicking, rolling and fighting. Just us against the world, skin on skin. In the moment.

Until carapoids broke through the walls. Before the splintered pieces of wood were done falling to the ground, we were getting thrown to the ground and zip-tied with our hands behinds our backs.

I threw up onto the ground in front of me and groaned with pain as a thick pair of carapoid boots kept me shoved against the rocky floor so hard, I waited for a rib to break.

12

The door to the industrial-sized airlock we'd been shoved into rolled open. Amira and I stood up, somewhat unsteadily, shielding our eyes from the bright light. We'd been lying on hard rock for hours in the dark.

Once my eyes adjusted, I could make out that the silhouettes were five carapoids carrying stun guns and eyeing us with their diamond-like eyes. And between them all, a familiar figure. The man who'd dragged me out of a cell and into the Colonial Protection Forces.

"Anais," I growled.

"Colonel Vincent Anais," he corrected. "The first few times we met, I was working in a consulting capacity. Since the increased human independence within the CPF, I now have rank."

"Colonel," I muttered.

"Lieutenant." He smiled. His face was more pinched since the last time I saw him. More lines around his eyes. He carried a somberness around him, now, like an invisible lead cape. "I'd like to say it's good to meet you again, but with you, it is always complicated. You owe me a favor."

Colonel Anais snapped his fingers, and one of the carapoids set a chair down on the ground. Anais straddled it and looked at us all mildly.

"A favor?" I said.

He nodded and his eyes narrowed. "A big favor. Because you're still a lieutenant. Look, I know there's a lot on your shoulders. A platoon, your parents under house arrest because the Accordance needs to keep an eye on them. But you need to remember that it isn't just the Conglomeration that has it out for you, Devlin. You have enemies elsewhere. Captain Zeus's children are very upset that you maimed their mother, and they want your head. They've been waiting for any mistake. You handed it to them. Zeus's line wants you all to live in a cell for the rest of your lives."

"Wait, their *mother*?" I asked.

Ken staggered up to join me and Amira. The full-on hangover and soreness from bruises were leaving us barely able to stand in front of Anais. "Zeus is a traitor!" Ken hissed. "We fought a *traitor* for our lives. Again on Titan."

Anais nodded. "Well, traitor Zeus may be, but Zeus was still Arvani. And Arvani expect to be treated . . . like Arvani. Do you understand?"

Ken rocked in place. "But Zeus killed almost everyone in Icarus Base."

"Mother?" I repeated.

Anais looked from Ken back to me. "Yes. Zeus is male currently. Zeus was female earlier in life. They can change their sex, it is not that shocking, there are creatures that do this on Earth as well."

Ken interrupted. "Who cares about Zeus's sex. Zeus tried to kill us. We are going to be punished for doing our duties?"

"Yes," Anais said. "Zeus's progeny have high status in Arvani command circles. But . . . the CPF is independent. The pressure rolled downhill, and I convinced Command to put you all on shit detail for the rest of the war. You'll be scrubbing toilets, digging rock, and volunteering for dangerous manual labor whenever it comes up."

"They could be traitors, too, like Zeus," Ken said. "They probably are."

Anais shook his head. "I wouldn't say anything like that out loud ever again if you enjoy being alive, Awojobi. Besides, the progeny haven't left Accordance yet. They are full Arvani still, with all the naturally superior rights that being Arvani entails."

Amira's laughter stopped Anais cold. He looked at her, visibly annoyed. She smiled back at him. "Some Accordance will always be more equal than others," she said.

"You're quoting from illegal native literature," Anais said. "Again, not a smart thing to do out loud on your part. George Orwell's books have been burned or ferreted out by virus."

Amira stopped laughing and frowned. She opened her mouth, but Anais held up a hand.

"I've stopped you from being executed or even some of the other plans suggested. You're going to be on a security detail for a while until you can be moved to one of the asteroids that are being drilled out."

"This is bullshit!" Ken snapped, angry and surprising me. Amira put a hand on his shoulder.

"You're right," Anais said. "But before you get shipped off to chip rocks, or worse, there's time. And you never know what will happen between now and then. So, keep your damn heads down. The CPF is underpowered. We need you all alive and functioning. Humanity cannot afford to lose fighters. So, don't give up yet."

Someone behind me burped and groaned.

"Earth is falling apart," Anais said, more softly. "Earth First operatives are gaining more followers. And since the Arvani are diverting military resources to fight, security on Earth is faltering. We are retreating to more secure compounds, like Antarctica or the moon."

We were CPF soldiers, embedded in the Accordance. Going where they needed. We'd gotten whispers and rumors, but this was the first time hearing what had been going on in the year since we'd left. "My parents?" I asked, leaning forward. This all started when the CPF all but kidnapped me and forced me to join.

Anais grimaced. "We don't know where your parents are."

I should have known. I grabbed the desk. "Their safety was the reason I agreed to this hell," I hissed. "I gave you your propaganda victory, the son of the famous dissidents joining the CPF and doing his duty. I played the part. And then some. What the fuck am I doing here if not saving them from Accordance 'justice'?"

My anger didn't even penetrate Anais's almost-bored facade. "You're here because you know that it keeps the Accordance from just bombing any camp they think your parents are hiding in. Because you've seen that there are worse things than Accordance oversight."

"Oversight?" Amira laughed. "Occupation."

"The Conglomeration will literally mine people for what they're worth, and then refashion them into something useful for the goals of their gestalt. You might live, but your children will end up being a biological appendage to their civilization. We've seen them do it to countless worlds. And—"

"What about my family?" Ken interrupted. "What about my brothers and sisters?"

"Your family's role in the Accordance was recognized. They've been relocated to refugee quarters at Tranquility. They're safe."

"Refugees?"

"Be grateful," Anais said. "Sections of Earth are trying to devolve into self-rule. It hasn't happened yet, but the chaos is tricky. In the meantime, I need you all to stay alive, out of trouble, and out of sight of Zeus's family. I know I'm going to need seasoned fighters. I'm telling you about your families in trust. Trust that you'll understand the larger picture. Trust that you are smart enough to know what needs to be done, and that sacrifices have to be made."

Anais stood back up from his chair.

"So, now what?" I asked.

Anais looked at the rest of the platoon clustered up behind me. "Lunch is being served. Go eat, get over your hangovers. Get cleaned up. When you get back, you'll be told where security detail is. Try not to screw up. If you're not doing what you're assigned, you stay right the hell here. You only leave this little cave when you're getting something to eat. Got it?"

"Yes," I said wearily.

Anais stared at me for a while, and I looked blankly at him. Then he nodded, turned around, and left.

"You must be laughing at me now," Ken said to me on the way back to our quarters from lunch an hour later. "To see that you were right about the cost of working with them."

"No," I shook my head. "I'm not laughing."

"It wasn't the wealth we had or my own opportunities. It was the infrastructure. The cities they helped us build. The technologies we gained. The great equalization, after so many decades of underinvestment. Knowing that, with the tools, our countries could be as great as any that had looked down at us in the past. We were never stupid; it was divide and conquer. The Europeans did it between people in the past, Accordance did the same by approaching the developing world and offering them more to sign the treaties that formalized oversight."

I grabbed Ken's shoulder. "I guess Earth First, and my parents, are not going to be welcoming either of us if we ever get back home."

Amira broke the moment as she shoved us from behind. "You weepy little shits."

"Damn, Amira, we wouldn't even be here if you hadn't thrown that punch," I shouted back at her, genuinely angry.

"I'm going to have notes in my file," Ken said.

"Really?" Amira made a face. "You knew the fight was going to happen. I just decided to get it over with and skip the posturing bullshit. None of those miners were going to talk it out and you damn well know it."

"True," Ken said. Then he smiled. "Shame you spent so much time on your ass, Devlin; we could have used the help."

"The fuck?" I was outraged. "I was first to your sides. Both of you ungrateful assholes. I should have walked right out of there and left you for the carapoids."

Amira laughed. "I'm sure your parent's nonviolent methods would have worked in a bar fight."

"We don't know if we don't try," I told her, and my outrage couldn't be maintained; I laughed. "We're all fucked. I'm laughing because I don't know what else I can do."

"I know." We walked side by side, lapsing into silence. Then I grabbed them both in a hug on each side.

Whatever happened, we were going through it all together. Even if it was shit.

Amira said in a lower voice, "When we get back, you need to divvy up the squads and make some choices. You can't keep running away from that. We lost people."

I hadn't wanted to do this. But glancing back at Kimmirut and Patel, I knew she was right. They were trailing behind us all. "Kimmirut with Delta. Patel to Alpha. And four becomes three, just like that."

"Who takes over Alpha?" Ken asked.

"Smiley," I said. Lana Smalley as Sergeant. A few months before, Smiley had been standing in a giant crater carved out of the side of a flying mining platform, frozen and staring up at the clouds above. Now she turned and ran toward problems without Ken or me saying a thing.

"I'll tell them," Ken said.

"Thank you," I whispered, unsure of my own voice suddenly.

"We got through it before," Amira said. "After Saturn."

"I got used to just the two squads. I felt like maybe we should just keep going, letting the Conglomeration kill us, until there was no one left," I said.

"No one is replacing anyone else," Amira said, figuring out exactly what was bothering me.

"I know."

I had come to understand why Shriek refused to learn names.

"Hey!" I looked around. "Where is Shriek?"

"He wasn't human, they didn't jail him. He'll be waiting for us, I'll bet," Amira said.

We were posted to a large airlock, not all that different from the one we were jailed in for what felt like a night. The asteroids here kept to a twenty-hour light cycle, Arvani preferences. Several other asteroids had no gravity and had been filled with water for Arvani officers. Some of the miners had been tasked with stocking pools with shrimp and fish.

Fresh fish sounded better than goop. We weren't going to be getting any, though. Let alone any shrimp cocktail.

On the other side of the airlock was another Pcholem. Our job was to prevent anyone from getting aboard. Or even approaching the airlock doors. But no one had. So, we basically stood in front of the doors. Four hours on, four hours off. Two squads at a time, Bravo and Delta today.

"Where is Amira?" Ken asked.

"Not here," I said.

He shot me an angry frown. "This again? We're going to get into even deeper shit if you don't figure out how to lead."

"It's bullshit, Ken." I folded my arms, my rifle slung over my back, and stared at the roof. We were helmets down, and Ken had lowered his voice so we could talk to each other without being overheard. "We're in bullshit because of other things."

"Yeah, I know that," Ken said. I unfolded my arms and stared at him. But he was looking off down the tunnel thoughtfully. "I know she'll bug out. I know what happens next to us, it is unfair. But you still have the platoon to lead, and you need to figure out how you talk to Amira in front of them or they will all take it as permission to do whatever they wish. And then where will you be?"

Shriek sidled up to us. "There's no one in the tunnel," the alien noted.

"Yeah, hasn't been for hours."

He wrapped his one good wing hand and one mechanical wing hand around each of us. He hadn't even bothered to armor up. "Then let's go in and visit."

I looked at the airlock. The inner doors were ten feet high. "No. We're here to guard it."

"How many times do you get to say 'Greetings!' to a Pcholem in a lifetime?" Shriek asked, leaning in close. "When your world is destroyed and you flee for your lives soon, you'll want to know the beings taking you to safety."

"We are already on thin ice," I said.

"I do not recognize the metaphor," Shriek said. He let go of us and started banging on the doors, his artificial wing hand banging loudly. "Hello, Pcholem! We outside wish permission to come and speak. Let us talk! It is so boring; aren't you bored?"

"Shut up!" Ken hissed. The two squads on duty were turning around and staring at us with various levels of concern.

"This is . . ." I stopped as the doors lurched aside. Air whistled for a second, popping my ears as the air pressure equalized.

I stared down the ramp toward the dark-black, coral-like structures inside. Very different from the smooth gothic arches I was expecting to find. But this was another Pcholem, not the one I'd been on down on Titan.

"Enter," said a voice.

Shriek looked back at us and half bowed with his wing hands out and then turned and started down the ramp.

"Stay on guard," Ken ordered the two squads still staring at us.

"Facing *that* way." I pointed at the tunnel into the asteroid to emphasize his order. "Shriek, get the hell back here." I started down the ramp, and Ken followed.

"This is a bad idea," he said.

"I know."

The airlock doors slowly shut behind us.

13

Green bioluminescence increased until our shadows loomed against the curved walls of the interior of the living alien starship. Our footsteps were muffled, the sound soaked up.

"Please," the Pcholem's voice said, "keep walking to find your companion. I will direct you."

The tunnel's strata shifted, down into a rocky substance. Here and there, we passed through grafted-on metal tubes. We turned as the Pcholem politely requested it. Occasionally, we walked into cathedral-like spaces that hummed with alien machinery. Carapoids looked dully at us and then went back to scurrying around.

We broke out into outer space. Startled, I sent the impulse to snap my helmet up, terrified that the ship, a creature that lived in vacuum, had led us outside by accident.

"You do not need protection," the Pcholem said gently over the common channel. "My fields extend far beyond the visible length of my hull. You are safe."

I saw that Shriek, in no armor, stood out in what looked like empty space a hundred feet away. The stars in the darkness that seemed to yawn before us.

"What should I call you?" I asked, snapping my helmet back down with a snicking sound.

"Unexpected Dust," the Pcholem said.

"May I call you Dust?" I asked.

"No. I said my designation is Unexpected Dust. If I wanted to be designated Dust, I would have told you this when you asked."

I looked at Shriek, who spread his wing hands. "Unexpected Dust is a grandfather to Starswept."

Starswept. The ship that left us on Titan. Because the Pcholem were pacifists, happy to move us around like pawns but not stick around.

I understood humans not wanting to get drawn in. But Pcholem were Accordance. An integral part. I wasn't sure what to think of them. Were they giant cowardly starships? Or just smart?

"Starswept has heard you are visiting me, and gives greetings from the orbit of your birth world," Unexpected Dust said to me.

"You can talk to Starswept?" Amira asked.

"Some time ago, the Conglomeration once bargained with us. They were deep in the gravity wells but had the hard metals and curious things we wanted," Unexpected Dust said. "They helped give us entangled, instant communication. Instead of having to swarm together to keep our minds in synch, we could scatter where we pleased."

That was surprising. We'd never heard this before. None of this was approved Accordance history. I was very interested to find out more. "You worked for the Conglomeration?" I asked.

"We do not 'work' for any species," the living starship told us. "We trade. We move individuals around. We seek mutually beneficial arrangements with anyone broadcasting on radio frequencies displaying coherence. We like to negotiate rights to gas giants in particular, so we were saddened by the loss of the ringed worlds here; they were pretty to swim in."

"But now you're Accordance, right?" I asked.

"We have begun a mutual alliance after the Recent Unpleasantness," said Unexpected Dust.

Shriek nudged me. "They live a long time; they're talking incidents that are almost a hundred years ago."

"What happened?" I asked.

"The Conglomeration happened," the ship said. "They attacked some of us, tried to breed us to create a fleet of ships they could control. But they are a fast species, short-lived. They had no patience. They created the Constructs from our living tissues and histories and technologies. We remember the Pcholem they used, our cousin. And now, whenever the Constructs appear, we can taste, smell, hear those *things* that used to be Pcholem but are not really Pcholem. Perversions. Tortured, mindless, broken and reshaped. For that, we will hate the Conglomeration until the suns fade away and die."

"Those jellyfish-looking starships," Ken said. "Those are the Constructs. They're remade Pcholem."

"Yes. The Conglomeration pollutes all it touches," the starship confirmed. "There are few Pcholem in this galaxy. We are long to mature, hard to create. Each one of us is a precious mind, a unique and ancient structure that we have carefully fashioned ourselves into. To steal something so carefully self-made, to destroy an individual, is abhorrent. For that, we will help the Accordance attack them. We will help you also, in your quest. And we are delighted to meet the humans who fought against the Conglomeration when Starswept was deep in the gravity well and vulnerable. Your gift, your losses, we do not take these lightly. You are known to the Pcholem. Know this."

A carapoid walked up to us with a small package carefully wrapped in a green bow.

"It is my understanding that humans exchange small tokens of appreciation," Unexpected Dust said. "Here is a selection of chocolates. Please enjoy them during your guard duty. Please do visit again."

The carapoid left us, and then the fields we stood on began to darken.

"I think it's time for us to leave now, Shriek," I said.

The struthiform cocked his head at me and shook himself. "Its attention is elsewhere now," he agreed.

As we moved back through the ship toward the airlock, I wondered out loud, "Unexpected Dust?"

"Think about it," Amira said.

"What?"

"You're going faster than light. What's the worst thing that can happen?"

I thought about it for a second. "Oh."

"Is that a depressing name or a bad-ass name?" Ken wondered out loud.

But neither the ship nor Shriek knew.

The airlock doors rumbled back open.

14

Bravo squad had shucked down and were taking turns behind a cheap plastic booth to scrub down with wet wipes. The corridors had gotten thick with people being shifted around, temporarily sleeping in rows near the food halls while they waited for their next orders. The air had gone from smelling like saltpeter and rock to human sweat as unwashed bodies crammed up against each other in the asteroid.

Every level was packed. And when the platoon dallied, they swapped rumors. There was going to be a push to take Titan back. They were being gathered for a retreat back to Earth, skipping right past Jupiter, the belt, and Mars.

Whatever the plans were, they were keeping us in the dark, keeping leaks down.

Ken wanted to go back, I could tell. Wanted another chance at Titan.

But maybe, I thought, beefing up Earth to protect what was most important made sense. Maybe we'd be back within a glance of the blue marble again.

I missed it.

"Hey, Lieutenant." Min Zhao had been up near the rock tunnel for a few seconds.

"What's up, Max?"

She threw something in an easy curve through the air at me. I caught it and looked down. A small drive. "What is this?"

Zhao shrugged. "Smuggle mail. Been handed person to person all the way here. Came in with the new batch shipped up from home."

"Anyone have a screen?"

Vorhis lifted his mattress up. "I'm not supposed to have this," he muttered.

"I know," I said, and plugged the drive in.

I'd asked what this was. But I already had a good idea. My mother's face appeared on the screen. "Hey, son," she said. "Hopefully, this gets to you safely."

I sat down on the ground and put a finger up to the screen.

"By now, you might know we took a chance during the Rochester camp riots to get away from our minders. We don't blame you for what you did. What any son would have done."

But my father was not in the video.

"The Accordance is saying they need fighters. They need our help. So, we're demanding independence. Earth for humans. If they really need our help, now is the time for them to give us our freedom back. I know some might disagree, they might say they're the lesser evil. But can we really lay down our lives just to end up back under the Accordance if we help them win their war?"

Even though it had just been months since we'd been split apart, she looked older. There was a scar on her chin, and she'd cut her hair short. Almost military short. She wore a simple vest with extra pockets.

Were they still protesting? Or had they gone deeper

underground? She was filming her message in a tent, I could see.

She looked thinner.

"Just remember this, Devlin. You've made a name for yourself. You did something amazing out there, on the other side of the moon. People listen to your words. They look up to you. Keep that in mind as you make your decisions. Because we're all going to be making some tough choices soon. For Earth. For everyone. Be safe, son."

I looked up from the blank screen and saw Ken regarding me. Alpha squad was back and shucking. Delta getting ready to walk on out to guard duty.

"They don't know," Ken said. "Yours or mine. They don't know."

"Yours love you and admire you being here," I said. "Not the same."

Ken walked over, still in full armor, as everyone pretended not to listen. "Yeah, they're all in now," he said with a bitter twist of his lip. "My sister died when an Earth First protestor set off a bomb in front of the Cairo Arvani embassy; my father still has a limp. Back then, he was a delegate, trying to broker calm, get what he could for many. After that, it was different. Anyway, they're not that thrilled I'm under the command of the son of known anti-Accordance terrorists."

"You still hold anger about it? Me?"

Ken grimaced. "I buried it for a while. Still hung on to it, maybe even as late as Titan. Now?"

"Now?"

"Don't have any anger to waste," Ken said. "I spent it all on other things. Anything I have left, I'm saving up for Zeus."

"Captain Calamari," I said. Our nickname for the Arvani commander when he'd been in charge of us back on Icarus Base.

“Yes,” Ken said reflectively.

“I doubt we’ll ever see sucker-face again,” I said.

“Everyone should have something they hope for,” Ken said. “Little things that give us a reason to wake up.”

Another shift. Another change. Another day guarding doors. This time not Pcholem but munitions stores. And the corridors were empty. People being moved to carriers.

But not us.

Whatever was going to happen, forward or retreat, was going to happen without the Rockhoppers.

Amira pulled me aside, her eyes flashing slightly from the nano-ink buried deep inside her irises. “Bad news,” she said quietly.

“I don’t want to hear it,” I told her. “Let’s just stand here and wait for whatever’s coming.”

“There’s ghost sign in the network,” she whispered. “Just like back on Titan. I can sense little things. We’re compromised. Hacked. Something. It came aboard with all the new arrivals.”

“What the fuck do you want to do about it?” I asked her, tired. “We’re not on patrol. We’re just supposed to stand here. Report what you’ve found and let it go up channel.”

“*They’re* here,” Amira hissed. “They’re here and that’s what matters. Not how the Accordance deals with it. But how we survive it. You and I both know how the ghosts can get inside a place like this.”

Because they looked just like us, I thought.

Or maybe the ghosts *were* us. The one we’d captured looked like a human. Moved like a human. I’d risked my life to bring the body back, and the Accordance told us we’d be killed if we spilled the secret.

Or maybe the Conglomeration was already changing humans and using them against us.

The dead ghost on the moon hadn't told us anything. The Accordance hadn't told us anything.

We were fighting blind in the middle of a war between two giant civilizations.

"Nobody stays more than a few steps away from armor," I said. "You keep sniffing around. That's all we can do."

"We should be ripping this place apart." Amira folded her arms. "Why do you think we're standing around guarding munitions here?"

"Because even here, Arvani are outnumbered by humans. And the thousands of miners who have Earth First leanings are watching, waiting, and angry," I said. "But we stumble, and Zeus's family rips us apart. The Accordance does execute traitors. If our usefulness ends . . ."

"Finding ghosts is useful," Amira said.

"We sleep near our armor and I make sure we all look the other way when you slip out to go sniffing around," I told her.

Old habits. Old roles. She should be used to them by now.

"Listen, more and more people are being pulled into the asteroids. It's getting crowded. General infantry without armor. Engineers. Technicians. Miners."

"So we stay near armor, we stay near the weapons."

"We need more, Devlin. More information. More Accordance technology. More. Because when they eventually fall all the way back to Earth and then abandon it, we can't roll over."

"Do you think Shriek's people are still fighting back on his homeworld?" I asked. "Because I sure as hell don't."

"We can't just roll over," Amira repeated, and then shut up as Zizi Dimka came around the edge in armor.

"Something you should know," she said to me.

"What's up?"

"We're to all report back to the cave to the new platoon commander," she said.

"New?"

"Squiddie," Zizi said. "Just showed up. I walked over because it's on the command channel and I can listen in on public. Figured you'd want a heads-up on this."

"CPF is human," I said.

"It said something about a riot and emergency powers," Zizi said. "It's agitated. All of us are to get down to the cave."

"Fucking Arvani." I looked around. "Okay, I guess we're leaving the munitions doors unguarded, then." The several feet of thick metal would have to hold shut without us.

15

The Arvani officer waited for us impatiently back at the entrance to our quarters. It wore standard encounter gear for outside the water: sculpted, form-fitting exoskeleton filled with water to keep it alive. Each of its eight arms was surrounded by jointed, powered segments.

But not armor. The exoskeleton was painted gaudy purple, red, and black, with red officer's marks near the Arvani's neck. These were the equivalent of fancy dress uniform for the Arvani when they were out of their pools of water and wandering about.

"You are delaying us!" it snapped. "Shape up, apes, we are required now!"

We all glanced at each other, and then the platoon looked at me and waited for orders.

The Arvani noticed this. His pupils narrowed and a single tentacle pointed at me. "You."

"What authority do you have to order this?" I asked. "The Colonial Protection Force is an independent volunteer organization. You have no command here. Who are you?"

It blew surprised bubbles in its helmet, where the vast bulk of its body resided. A few strange hues flashed across its skin. "I am Commander Sthenos," it bellowed via translation. Another motorized tentacle pulled out a pistol. "Articles of emergency have been declared throughout the interior of this habitat. You will arm up, and you will follow me."

Sthenos stalked across the rock toward the tunnel ways.

"Amira? Riot?" I asked.

"Three habitat levels of chaos," she said, eyes crinkling as she dove into the data. I waved a hand after the alien and nodded at the rest of the platoon. Follow the alien.

"We're not peacekeepers," I said, starting to walk after the Arvani commander. "We're soldiers."

"You are here. You are what we have in this location."

"Where are the carapoids? Struthiforms? Other Arvani?" I fell into pace beside Sthenos.

"They are elsewhere," Sthenos said irritably.

"Where?" I asked. "What's going on?"

"You are not cleared yet," Sthenos said. And I suspected that Sthenos, in his fancy Arvani gear and lack of armor, was probably not in the loop. This was a jumped-up supply clerk with a pistol, or some Arvani given a big title and shoved somewhere they thought wouldn't cause much trouble.

Sthenos didn't know what was going on any more than we did.

None of us had helmeted up yet. "I don't know much about riot control," Amira muttered. "But having been on the other side, I'm going to say that if we jump in with full armor and weapons hot, it's not going to cool things down any."

Shriek moved up to join us. The struthiform was in full armor, something he almost never did when inside an

Accordance structure. "I can hear it," he said. "It does not sound joyous."

"That it does not," I agreed. "Don't shoot; keep close to me. Amira, Ken, keep it low, but pass that around."

Sthenos forged on ahead, his metal-clad legs tapping on the rock as he scuttled along.

"Here we go," Amira warned. "Stay calm."

We burst out into a common cavern, mess halls on either side and the upper floors filled with dormitories accessed by metal walkways. Three thousand filled the common area. The small temporary gardens in the middle were already mud, trampled by angry feet in a packed scrum fighting against a handful of carapoids trying to hold the line.

A few open fires burned in the back, on the other side of the cavern. I helmeted up and peeked through it using the helmet's various displays and filters, but it wasn't being used to hide anything. They were just burning stuff ripped off the walls.

The crowd hissed like water tossed on a hot pan as we moved in.

"Be careful. We're suited up, they're not," I said.

"So, what the fuck are we supposed to do?" That was Zizi on the common channel.

I was still thinking. Looking at the massive press of bodies shoving the carapoids back up toward the wall.

Sthenos strode forward authoritatively and raised his pistol into the air.

"Oh, shit." I stepped forward as the crowd flinched, quieted, and started to stare at us.

"Cease this destructive behavior and return to your designated quarters," the Arvani officer shouted via amplification. The words rolled around the rocky roof, bouncing and echoing off the surfaces.

“We want to be evacuated too,” a short woman in a gray mining uniform shouted. She had a pipe in her hands.

“What are you talking about?” I started to ask, but Sthenos interrupted me with another loud command.

“Disperse or face consequences,” Sthenos shouted.

“Don’t say that,” Amira groaned on the public.

Sthenos snapped back, looking at the platoon.

I moved up past him and lowered my helmet to let the crowd see my face. I was a human being, not Arvani. The armor made us look like faceless machines, doubly so with helmet up. I wanted the crowd to see other human beings. I could hear other helmets snapping open around me as the platoon followed my lead.

Holding both hands up, palms out, I called out, “What evacuation?”

“The Arvani are all leaving. They’ve been boarding ships,” the miner with the pipe said. She stepped forward, suddenly realizing she was the closest thing to the group’s voice. The talking had created a momentary calm in the confrontation. I could see the carapoids edging over to us. I couldn’t tell anything from their expressions—the insect-like mandibles and eyes didn’t lead to much that I could recognize—and they didn’t say anything. “Everyone is running. They’re going to leave us here like they did on Titan. We want on the ships too.”

“There is no exodus,” Sthenos shouted. “You will stay at your posts and do your jobs. The fate of—”

“Fuck you, squiddie!” A bottle arced over the heads of the crowd nearest to us and struck Sthenos. The glass shattered and something oily splattered over the Arvani’s encounter suit.

The Molotov cocktail’s fire had guttered out as it had been thrown, luckily.

"Get behind us," I ordered the Arvani. "You're not helping matters."

But Sthenos spluttered and marched at the crowd. It raised its pistol. "I am *Arvani*, and I saw where that came from," it shouted. "There will be a consequence—"

"Fucking drag him behind us and get that gun out of his hands," I ordered, making a quick decision. We were in armor, but Sthenos would literally get pulled apart by the crowd if he started shooting into it.

Zizi and Aran from Alpha jumped the alien, disarming him and pulling back into the close wall of armor we'd made when forming up against the crowd.

That was a popular move. Cheers and hoots echoed around the cavern, and some laughter.

"This is insubordination," Sthenos screamed at us.

I moved another step forward and addressed the miner who'd been speaking, but loudly enough that everyone near the front of the crowd could hear us. "I don't know what is going on, but we haven't gotten the word to evacuate."

"That doesn't mean it isn't happening," she said.

"That's true," I admitted. "The Arvani are up to something, and they're not sharing. With any of us. Not even their junior officers." I pointed back at Sthenos, who was raging at Amira to try and get his pistol back.

"I don't want to get fucked," she said. "Everyone on Titan got left. People are saying we should talk to the Conglomeration now, broker some kind of deal for when they come. We're tired of being in the dark. We're not their tools."

"I understand," I said. "I know why you're doing it. You have to make your decision. But just know you are right. The Arvani don't care about your lives. Which means that when they come next, it will be like that Arvani back there. They'll start killing us. And in here, there's nowhere to run if they decide pacification is needed."

"Desperate times," she said.

"They are," I said. "But I think if we can keep together, organized, and use all the tools around us, we'll see Earth again. I truly believe that. Now, I'm going to back out through the corridor. You seem like you have some sway around here. See if you can keep them from bringing down something worse?"

"This is the only way they'll pay attention to us," she said. "We roll over, we go back to being in the dark."

"You do what you have to," I said. "But let me say this. The Pcholem, the ship attached to this asteroid, I've talked to it. And I have the impression it can expand and carry a lot. Until it leaves, your ride is going to be with the giant alien starship. Don't spook it. But if you're truly scared, send someone to talk to it. Or camp out near it . . . peacefully and calmly."

She nodded. "Okay."

"We're going to step back now," I said. "And take the carapoids with us. Is that good?"

Some shook their heads, but she nodded.

We backed out down the corridor and then let out held breaths of air as the bulkhead doors shut. One of the carapoids split off and approached us. Strong, spiked, and bony hands waved a pattern in the air. "Gratitude," it said simply. Then the massive beetle-like aliens trumped off down a fork and left us.

"I was hoping for a hug," Zizi said. "But that'll do."

"Give our Arvani officer his pistol back," I said. "Sir, we're sorry, but we had to talk them down."

Sthenos snatched his weapon back and pivoted around to look at all of us. "There will be consequences for your insubordination."

Consequences. Sthenos seemed to like that word a lot.

"I understand," I said. "I will take on responsibility for any reprimands that come as a result of the platoon following my direct orders."

Shriek moved. "The angry human mob has a point," he said. "All this dramatic behavior and running around while we wait for your homeworld to be destroyed is dreadful. Maybe you should broadcast surrender now. I'm sure the Conglomeration are wonderful and snuggly, like a mother on her eggs."

"Now's not the time for your jokes," I said.

"That. Is. Traitorous." Sthenos had frozen in place, staring at Shriek.

Amira groaned as Sthenos stalked toward the struthiform. "No humor," she said.

But Shriek seemed to know what he had done. He turned and faced the Arvani, wing hands folded by his body and his head cocked. "What do you think, Arvani? You didn't exactly help my homeworld, did you? Ran pretty fast once you all realized it was risky. Dragged us along to all your other fights. And here we still are."

"According to the common law of the Accordance unified military agreement," Sthenos said, rattling off the specific law that let him execute someone during a mutiny, "I condemn you to death as an enemy to the Accordance."

Shriek dropped his helmet and stepped forward, large eyes on the Arvani energy pistol. "Do it, seafood," he hissed.

This wasn't happening. I knew Shriek wasn't a fan of the Arvani, but the naked anger usually showed up in other forms. Not suicide by Arvani officer.

Sthenos's tentacle tip moved its grip on the pistol to fire. Amira knocked it clear, the pistol bouncing down the rock corridor. "Treason!" The Arvani spun around and looked at us all. "Detain her and hand me your weapon!"

"No," I said, "We're not going to do that. We need our medic." There was a thud in the distance. I wasn't sure what it was.

"You face the gravest repercussions." Sthenos looked at us all, realizing there was no help to be found, and then bolted for his gun.

"Quick," I shouted, and Ken was already by my side. Amira got there first, though, rocketing off a wall to strike the Arvani in the center of his upper tank. Metal cracked and creaked as she struggled to hold onto him in the middle of the eight flailing tentacles that beat against her armor. She was punching and grabbing at something inside the Arvani encounter suit, ripping it out. The comms. She was silencing his ability to call out. I hadn't even thought about that.

I grabbed tentacles whipping about. "Stop struggling, we just want to talk." In the background, again, another thud. Loud enough that I glanced around, trying to figure out what it was.

There was a keening, bubbling sound. I realized that was an Arvani scream, raw and untranslated. Completely freaking out. Hell, so was I. We'd laid hands on an Arvani officer.

"Rope," Amira said calmly. "Now!"

She was jamming her thumbs into joints in the Arvani's powered legs, crushing the metal until something inside snapped and the limbs stopped moving. Then she bashed in the speakers that let the Arvani speak with her elbow.

Someone passed up some kind of paracord and a roll of utility tape. The alien stuff that was vacuum-rated. Amira and I wrapped the Arvanai's limbs together and then sat down with it between us. I looked at her, the question plain on my face.

"We need to crack him out of this suit and shove him out the shit-lock," she said, referring to our crude bathroom against the asteroid's hull.

"It's a long way from here to there. And . . ." We weren't executing Arvani officers.

"Asshole officers go overboard," Amira said. "Old naval ships. Happened all the time."

"This isn't the age of sail," I hissed.

"It might not be, but we're going to hang if we don't get rid of this."

"Why did you do this?" Shriek asked.

"He was going to shoot you," I said.

"So? This was not your fight." Shriek flicked a wing hand. "And what are the chances that even an Arvani would execute a vested officer of the Accordance?"

"I don't know," I shouted at him. "That's just it! It certainly looked about to shoot to me."

"Even if it did, it would only have cost that Arvani everything and meant no attention would be paid your insubordination." Shriek whistled impatiently. "My life is mine to do with what I please. I have been dead since the moment I watched my homeworld burn. I accepted this long ago. I make choices about how to live, how long to live, and when. *Not you*. Now you are all doomed. This is an utter waste. I am filled with despair that I have known your names."

There was another thud. I looked up as dust filtered through the air, shaken loose by the asteroid shaking. "That's the third time; what is that?"

Then the atmosphere-loss alarms kicked on, the annoying whine piercing my skull and near dizzying me.

16

Helmets snicked up and I got on the public channel. "What the hell was that?"

As if to answer me, an all-call went out, loud and crisp on the public channel. "Hull breach. Full vacuum protocol in effect. Everyone is to be in suits or near aid stations at all times. All CPF are to report up the chain of their command immediately."

"Pressure loss or attack?" I asked Amira.

"They'd call it out if it were battle stations."

"Not on the public. Not with people rioting because they're scared they're about to get left behind like everyone did on Titan." I looked around and then back down at our captured Arvani officer.

"Good point," Amira said. "Let me hop my way up . . . oh, here we go."

"Hello, Third Platoon. This is Colonel Vincent Anais again. I can't reach your temporary Arvani commander, so I'm pinging your command channel."

"Yes sir," I said, and then tried to talk right past his implicit query about the alien tied up by our feet. "What's going on?"

"Congratulations, you stuck around long enough to get off crap detail and for me to need you. There's a full-blown mutiny."

"We just dealt with the rioters," I said. "We calmed them down." Sthenos wriggled about, halfheartedly trying to get out from under our knees where we'd pinned him to the rocky asteroid floor.

Tony Chin was swearing to himself in Mandarin, I realized. What were we doing? "Chin, shut it down," I hissed.

"Not where you are," Anais said, almost over me. "We've had human crews working with Arvani specialists around the clock to finish the Trojan conversions. Very hush-hush, but they've been turning the Trojans into carriers. Low-budget, retrofitted carriers. This is to get the numbers we need back to Titan. To retake what we've lost. But—"

Another thud. We instinctively crouched for a second.

Anais swore. That was new. There was a moment of quiet, and then he came back on. "So, the human crews working on two of the Trojans mutinied. They're ostensibly under an Earth First banner. They've demanded the release of Rina Joseph, Alois Kincaide, and Alan Coatzee from Accordance jails."

I recognized two of those names. Rina and Alois. People who'd once planned protests by my parents' side. I knew them as friendly smiles and laps I'd sat in. I hadn't realized they were jailed. Rotting away under the Accordance.

Anais continued. "But I think they're just panicked. Rumors of impending Conglomeration attacks are everywhere, and they saw what happened on Titan. Which is why we need these ships to get back to Titan, damn it."

"What're the loud noises?" Amira asked.

"We've been exchanging fire. Trying to knock out the weapons they have trained on us. Devlin, we've been keeping what we're doing here secret so that the Conglomeration doesn't know our next play. But now, if they see us shooting at each other here in trailing orbit, they're going to come out before we're ready for them. And it's going to be a big fucking mess. So you're going in. Welcome back to active."

"Why us?" I asked reflexively.

"I need someone who can think quick, think creatively, and not make a bigger mess."

"You're asking us to attack human beings who were building the ships we needed," Ken noted.

"You're attacking them only if they fight back or you can't figure out a way to resolve the situation," Anais replied. "And even if you have to make the worst choice, it could still well save everyone we love back on Earth. I'm not saying the job ahead of you is easy. But we're not here for easy choices; we're here to fight a war."

"What am I authorized to offer them, if they surrender?" I asked.

"*I'm told* we're past that point. I'm told that anyone you take alive, we will keep humanely jailed. Now get to airlock five-B; they're waiting for you. Handle this. Get back in the game."

And then he was gone.

I looked over at Ken and Amira. "We should go. It gives us options."

"Like what? Joining mutineers?" Ken hissed.

"Our choices are to flush the Arvani out a lock and pretend it didn't happen, or get to some kind of transport not controlled by Arvani," Amira said. "He's right, Ken. What do *you* want to do here?"

Ken half crouched in his armor. His face, behind his helmet, was obscured by reflections. I couldn't figure out what he was thinking.

"We can't kill the commander," he said. "Whatever we do, we cannot have the Arvani turn against the CPF. We do this, we destroy the freedom the CPF has gained for itself. We put more than our own lives at risk."

"Options are good," Amira said. "Let's tie our pet squiddie to a chair and get the hell out of here."

Within minutes, Sthenos was lashed tightly to one of the bunks back in our quarters. I turned away from Sthenos to face the platoon and explain the orders we'd just been given. "I won't force any of you to come with us, or force anyone to stay," I said to the entire platoon as they all arranged themselves around me, ready to head out with their full weapons kit and everything else they could think to carry packed and strapped. "You all have the choice."

I had more of a speech planned, but they all knew what was what.

"If we stay, Arvani will string us up to blame," Aran Patel said. "In Chennai, I saw them put an entire sector's police force to death for something a captain did. You made the call, we have to follow. One way or another. There's no real choice. We're expendable to them. You know that."

"Jesus, Patel, you make it sound like he personally sentenced you to death," Erica Li said with a snort.

"Well," Aran said calmly.

He wasn't wrong, I knew.

I was going to apologize, but Ken interrupted. "We've always been facing death when we're given commands. That is the nature of what we do. That is the nature of an order, a decision, when in war. Our choices become how we want to face death."

"Well, I'm not giving up my power armor," Aran said.

"Does anyone wish to stay?" Ken asked.

No one did.

"Then it's airlock five-B. The Arvani might be bastards, but if the Conglomeration figures out we're in the middle of a mutiny, everyone else around here is going to be dead. Let's move!" Ken shouted.

17

We were shot out of airlock five-B in all-too-familiar reentry capsules, little more than a heat shield with some thrusters and a parachute we didn't need. Inside the claustrophobic coffin, my helmet an inch from the heat shield, I tried to relax as we tumbled through the half-mile gap of empty space.

No thrusters to adjust course; that would reveal us. We drifted slowly, like seeds thrown onto the wind.

"First barrage," Anais informed us. "To keep them busy."

We heard nothing. We couldn't, in the cold vacuum. Hundreds of beams of light would be stabbing at the other ships, and missiles would be lobbed. And I waited in the dark of the windowless capsule.

"Chaffing out," Anais said.

We would come with a wave of confusing, glittering dust, bouncing signals every which way around us.

"Okay," Amira said. "What's the plan? We join up with Earth First? Or we take the carrier ship for ourselves?"

"Can *you* fly a carrier ship?" I asked Amira. "Because it

seems like a large number of technicians and specialists are on it right now. The large crews are for a reason?"

"We don't even know if *they* can fly it," Amira said. "All we know is that they took one over."

"But you can't fly one."

Amira was silent for a moment. I imagined her grinding her teeth. "No."

"Then we're going to need to ally ourselves with them. Or . . ."

"Or what?" Ken asked.

"Or we help quell the mutiny and face what comes next," I said. "Because those ships are to retake Titan. To protect Earth. With human crews. There is a war. And what are we going to do? Join the Conglomeration?"

"I will die first," Shriek said.

"We know what they do to planets," Tony Chin said. The three sergeants didn't normally interrupt the squad command channel, but he sounded very sure of his opinion. "I'm not doing that."

"I was just thinking out loud."

"Devlin, pick a course and follow it," Ken snapped. "Lead. You are our leader. This is your job. Embrace it and stop trying to hand it away."

"I'm not going to kill any humans who are putting their lives at risk to do what's right," Amira said. "Putting this mutiny down? I'd rather join it and flip the damn Accordance my middle finger."

"Amira—" The thrusters lit up, shoving me face-first against the inner side of my capsule. Then it peeled itself away from me and I hung in the air for a second, coasting toward a large pitted landscape of rock.

Shriek jumped back in on the common channel. "I will

turn myself over after this. I will claim I did it all. The Arvani—"

"Shriek, shut up," I ordered. "We deal with this first. Then we'll sort that out. Everyone, get your head in *this* game, right here and right now."

"We're here," Ken grunted.

The capsules left us with enough momentum that we gently struck the rock in a rain of tiny silver chaff. Laser light flickered in the air around us, madly trying to carve up the remains of our capsules that still hung above the hull.

"Hopefully, the Accordance won't start shooting too," I said.

We stuck to the hull. Somewhere inside the ship were Accordance gravity plates. I'd felt the faint flip inside my stomach that was the pull of gravity as we'd approached.

It wasn't very strong out here. Moon level, maybe. It would increase as we moved down and in toward the core.

"Contact," Zizi shouted on the common channel. "I found an airlock."

"Devlin, what are we doing?" Lana Smalley asked.

I looked at the twinkling chaos between the Trojans and the crude, rocky carrier we were hanging on to. A split second of thought. "Try not to kill them," I said. "But we're going to put this down and take the carrier."

"For the Accordance?" Amira asked suspiciously. "Or for ourselves?"

"I don't fucking know yet," I said. "But either way, try to keep them alive if you can keep yourselves out of risk."

Then I let go of the side and kicked my way down toward Zizi.

A long arc of light danced across the pits and craters of the rocky hull, lighting everything up with harsh white and casting long shadows. "What the hell was that?"

"They've got hull welders," Zizi said, almost bemused.

"They don't want to let us in through the airlock, apparently."

With a loud bang, I spun around and bounced off rock. I steadied myself. "They're shooting. With what?"

"They've got some kind of jury-rigged rail gun. Three o'clock," Min Zhao said. "Everyone, take cover."

"Don't return fire!" I shouted.

18

I scrabbled my way forward to join someone sheltering behind a dip in the hull. It was Chandra Khan.

"You okay, Chaka?" I asked.

"It's going to be hard to get into that airlock without hurting someone," Khan said.

Amira popped onto the command channel again. "I have another interesting question I think we need to mull."

"Right now?" A piece of metal slammed into the rock hull, sending shards flying everywhere. I winced as the debris rattled against my armor.

"Now's as good a time as any to get our heads straight," Amira said. "We need to know what's happening. What we're doing. And you need to make some calls. Because you're the leader here."

"Okay, what's wrong?" I wanted to rub my forehead.

"Ghost sign," Amira said. "I have to keep my head down; I can't help in the usual ways or it'll spot me. It's strong."

"So the Conglomeration is here," Ken said.

"How is that even possible?" Min Zhao demanded. "They

were buried under the ground on Titan. But how are they on a carrier ship, here in the Trojans? How are they fucking popping up everywhere?"

"Don't worry about how," Ken said, his voice reassuring and calm. "Just worry about the fact that this mutiny is not what it seems."

Things were shifting around again. Our plan to maybe sneak off somehow was fading. If there were Conglomeration here, ghosts here, something else was going on.

"This answers a question I have," Ken said.

"Which is?" I asked.

"Where are the other platoons on this attack?"

I glanced up in the sparkling debris between us and the Trojan docks. No more shooting. No more drama.

"We're it. There were other CPF around that might even have been closer," Amira agreed. "Why us?"

"You think they're suiciding us?" Lana Smalley asked. "Or using us as a diversion? Maybe they already know about Sthenos."

I was lying with my back against the rock hull, still staring out into space. I could hear the tension in my sergeants' voices. Smalley, Chin, and Zhao hadn't attacked their Arvani commander. They'd been taking my orders calmly for long enough. They'd put themselves at risk for so long.

"They sent just us because of the ghost sign," I said on the platoon's common channel, taking the debate out of command loops. "Anais, his techs, they must have spotted it. So they sent us."

"I don't understand," Smalley said.

"When Amira sniffed out the ghost sign back on Titan, it was because she was familiar with the patterns and code," I said.

"Devlin. What are you doing?" Ken sounded nervous. That was a first.

"Time to let the Rockhoppers in on the great big fucking secret," I said. "We captured a ghost. Back at Icarus Crater."

"What?" I wasn't even sure who shouted that in shock. "We're supposed to get clear of them. How?"

"Luck," I said. "But we know what we're fighting. Accordance claims we need to pull back and let heavy forces in. But what they want is to not let humans find out what the ghosts are."

"They're human," Amira said.

"What the fuck are you talking about?" Smalley asked. "What do you mean, human?"

"They look like us. Inside this carrier, it could be anyone. They look like us. Ghosts look like us," Ken said.

"Why haven't you told us these things before?" Smalley continued.

"We were under very strict orders," I said.

"Bullshit! Either we're all in this together, or the three of you are just as useless as the squiddies," Smalley snapped.

"Could they be sending us out here to die with that information?" someone asked.

"I don't know," I said. "But you all need to know what we're facing in there."

There was cursing in four different languages on the common.

"But what does it mean?" Ilyushin asked, frustrated.

"It means they need us," Ken said.

Everyone quieted. "Go on," I said.

"I've been thinking about this since Titan," Ken explained. "The Conglomeration are using humans. Or something that looks human. The Accordance, they're putting us into carrier ships like this one. They're using us to build more ships. They wouldn't be doing all of this, either of them, if they didn't *need* us. The only reason humans took these ships over is because they were *building* them. The Arvani, they just don't have the numbers. There are only a handful of Pcholem in the system. Even the struthiforms are dying off because they lost their homeworld, their nesting grounds."

"How the fuck does that help us right here, right now?" Vorhis asked.

"Because we've assumed, since the day the Accordance came to orbit and pacified Earth, that it was about them. Their tools. Their abilities. Their technology. But the truth is, they're fighting over us right now. That's their weakness."

"How the hell is them ripping us apart to fight over us a weakness?" The common channel devolved into angry voices.

"No," I shouted. "Ken's right."

The common channel settled down.

"Anais sent us in because we know what ghosts are," I said. "We're not joining the Conglomeration. We're not going to slaughter these people either, which is what the Arvani would want. They have skills we're going to need soon."

"When?" Ilyushin asked.

"When humanity gets out from under them all," I said.

"That sounds like Earth First talk," Ilyushin noted.

"Well, I *am* the son of famous Earth First terrorists," I said. "What the hell were they expecting?"

I used my fingertips to skim along the hull.

"Where are you going?" Amira asked.

"To disable anyone firing at us with a homemade rail gun. Then we're going to break in and, bulkhead by bulkhead, carefully retake this place without killing them. We're wearing alien-designed power armor, built to take full combat hits. This is a one-sided battle."

I flung myself over the rocky lip and toward the two spacesuits by the airlock.

"They might get lucky," Amira shouted as slugs slammed into my helmet. For brief seconds, liquid metal streamed down the side of my vision as they obliterated themselves against the shielding.

"True," I said. "So I'll have to move quickly."

And before I'd even finished muttering that, I was between the mutineers. They struggled to draw on me, but I snatched the weapons away, crushed them between my armored fingers, and shook my head.

19

Patel came running down the corridor. "Fire in—"

The explosion came right behind him before he'd finished his warning. The flames enveloped him, throwing him forward and into a nearby bulkhead.

Alpha squad shot forward, Zhao taking point.

"Patel?" I called out.

"Fine," he said. "I'm fine."

"Go back and join Taylor, have Shriek look you over."

"I'm *fine*," Patel gritted.

"Do it anyway."

Patel stood up and moved to the back with our twenty captives. Engineers, miners, maintenance workers, all zip-tied together and looking somewhat dazed. Lilly Taylor sat with them. One of the rail guns had punched through her shin guard. Shriek had filled the hole in her with a gel and pumped some painkillers in, and she was ready to get back into the mix. But I had her guarding the captives.

"Hart?" Zhao called out on the command channel.

"Yes?"

"We have a situation."

I looked down through the clearing smoke. "Yeah?"

We'd cut our way down into the carrier. Delta had our asses covered, and Alpha and Bravo were taking turns blowing up doors and pushing forward. We were rolling up resistance and zip-tying them to each other as we went.

It was slow and tedious corridor work. We'd been at it for an hour.

I kept to the side of the corridor and moved up to the front, crouching down by Erica Li, who was covering with her rifle the next bit we'd have to leapfrog into. She pointed down the corridor. Bulkhead doors were open down the corridor. A straight run.

Too good to be true. We'd been fighting through thick steel door after thick steel door. Designed to frustrate invaders like us and keep the carrier airtight no matter the scenario.

The mutineers had kept them all shut to slow us down.

Now they were throwing out the welcome mat?

Someone slowly put their hands out from behind a bulkhead into the open space. "We want to talk," a voice shouted into the open space between us.

Zhao was lying against the bulkhead, looking straight at me. "Second verbal request," she said.

I closed my eyes and thought the command to slide my helmet back down. My nostrils burned. The acrid smoke from the explosives still in the air seared the back of my throat. Not my brightest move; I could have used the amplification in the suit.

But responding in kind felt like the right move. "Hello," I shouted. "What would you like to talk about?"

"We're willing to talk, but only to someone we choose that you'll have to bring over."

"Okay," I agreed. "Who is it that we have to bring over?"

Zhao lowered her helmet and crabbed over to me. "There's some equipment I'm seeing farther down the corridor," she whispered. "I think it's an even bigger rail gun they've wheeled into place."

"Fucking engineers," I hissed. And then louder. "Who are we bringing over?"

"Devlin Hart," the voice shouted back.

I laughed. I couldn't help it. I looked at Zhao, who shrugged, the action taken up by the heavy armored shoulders.

"Bring us Devlin Hart," the voice shouted. "No armor. Hart can negotiate with us. If anyone in armor steps up, we start shooting."

"You're a popular guy," Amira said.

I stood up.

"What are you doing?" Zhao stiffened.

"Shucking," I said. My armor, at a mental command, began to crack itself open. I stepped forward and out, feeling totally naked in just my gray basic wear.

"Rockhoppers don't shuck," Zhao said.

"They want to talk. I'm going in. Ken, hold the corridor. If I'm not back in an hour, you get to make the big decisions." He came up beside me and I grabbed his armored shoulders, feeling small beside him. "You'll get your platoon, Ken."

His helmet slid away and Ken's dark eyes blinked. "I will not be doing that," he said. "If they capture you, I'll be in to take you back out. You are the commander here."

There was something more I wanted to say, but Amira stalked up next to me and stopped. Her armor began to lean back and peel itself off her.

"They didn't ask for Amira Singh," I told her.

"It's buy-one-get-one-free day for Rockhoppers," she said.

"You're not going in alone. Ghost sign is increasing, I want to get in closer and sniff. I'm not going to sit here while decisions about our future get made down there."

Ghost sign. Right. This wasn't just mutineers we were dealing with. The Conglomeration had its fingerprints on all this.

I stepped out with my hands up. "It's your lucky day," I called out. "Because I'm actually Devlin Hart."

"Bullshit," the voice down the corridor said.

"It's me, I swear," I said. "I'm coming forward with Amira Singh."

A face peeked quickly around the bulkhead. I recognized it. "Mr. Dismont. From Shangri-La Base."

Dismont stepped out into the open as well. "Holy shit, it's really you."

I stepped hesitantly forward. "I'm just going to keep walking forward with my hands where you can see them, Amira as well, and we'll talk."

20

I faced the council of mutineers in a room deep inside the carrier's shielded core after being silently trooped past corridors lined with construction workers holding crude, cobbled-together weapons. Arc welders, unwieldy rail guns, and other contraptions I wasn't sure about.

This was the heart of the insurrection: ten tired engineers, gangly men and women with screens strapped to their forearms, staring at us without saying a thing.

"Why did you call for me?" I finally asked.

"When everyone ran on Titan, you stayed behind," Dismont said. "Many of those engineers were tasked to work here on these carriers. We know who you are. We trust you. We will talk to you. We want you to get us a cease-fire to get us some time."

"What do you think you can do? Run to the Conglomeration?" I asked.

"No," Dismont shook his head, exasperated. "It was never that. Conglomerate messages are all over the networks, I know that. Offers to leave us alone if we defect. Preserve a place for us as we are. Promises of power and technology. Promises of land. We don't buy it."

"Then what the hell is all this?" I asked.

"It began with protest," he told us both. "Understand, since we got here from Titan, they've thrown us into this project full bore. We work long days, and we work dangerous situations. The workers on the carriers are suffering from blowouts, and they're expected to work without suits, as the gloves slow them down. We complained, but nothing changed. Everything was rush-rush. Good men started dying. One, airlock accident; one, a tunnel boring blowout. They kept stacking up. We kept holding services.

"Five hours ago, there was a memorial service for three tunnel borers who died after a seal breach. The Arvani sent carapoids to break it up and get us back to work. We were angry. We broke and fought back, refusing to leave. Demanding better safety. More rest time so mistakes aren't made. We know we're in the middle of a war. It's one thing to risk your life for it. It's another to see our lives spent so cheaply."

That rang true. I glanced over at Amira. She wasn't paying attention. Her eyes were half closed. She was focused on ghost sign.

"So, what's the play?" I asked. "My team was just the first wave of what they can send at you. You going to make a stand here?"

"We're going to run," Dismount said. "We can *fly* this thing, Devlin. All we need is some time."

Amira cocked her head. Something was going on in that invisible world of hers. "And where will you run to?" I asked him.

"We have the entire solar system to hide in. Get away from all this. All we need is time so we can continue getting the engines up. We need you to get us time," Dismont pleaded.

I wanted to join him. Run for somewhere in the dark and hide from everything we'd seen. Everything we'd been asked to do. Forced to do.

"There's a problem with that plan," Amira said, opening her eyes.

Dismont frowned and looked at her. "What's that?"

"The engines aren't ever coming on."

Shit. I recognized Amira's ready stance. It would have looked casual if I hadn't seen it before. She had relaxed a bit, a friendliness in her face. But her feet had moved into a more stable position. Her neck was angled just ever so slightly forward. The faintest grin on the corners of her lips. But behind the silver eyes, there would be nothing but a spring being slowly compressed.

Here we go, I thought, and half turned toward the engineers with the hand-built weapons aimed at us.

Amira snapped forward and twisted behind a nearby engineer, shoving a carbon fiber knife from up between her fingers into the side of his neck. "No one fucking move," she said calmly, pulling him back toward the wall with her so that she could keep everyone in front of them.

"Fuck," I hissed, holding my hands up in the air and stepping between her and the guns.

Dismont was crushed and confused. "Whoa," he shouted, "everyone calm down, calm down. She hasn't hurt Chris."

Yes, I thought. Let's stay cool. "What are you doing with Chris?" I asked Amira.

"Chris is a Conglomeration spy," Amira said. "I've been tracking him. So, I repeat myself: Those engines won't come on. Only your weapons that are facing the Trojans will work. Everything else has been disabled. You're being used."

Dismont stepped hesitantly forward. "That's a hell of an accusation."

"It's what she does," I said. "She finds this stuff. She found them out on Titan. She found them out when they attacked Icarus Base."

I hated invoking Icarus. But the moment I did it, I could see the engineers paying close attention and looking at each other.

"On Icarus Base, Amira tracked the Conglomeration as they attacked. She kept us alive. And if you want to survive, you'd better damn well listen to her," I continued.

"I've worked with Chris inside the engines for a month," one of the mutineers said. "He saved my life down there."

"This is insane," Chris said from behind me. I wanted to turn around and look at Amira. I wanted to mouth the word "ghost?" I wanted to get a nod or a shake of the head so I knew what was standing just behind me.

Instead, I swallowed. "We can test this."

Dismont looked at Chris and Amira and then back to me. "How?"

"I get you your time. I call it in. Time enough for you to fire those engines and see if they work. Or if Amira's right. Time enough to test your weapons, too. Okay? If you can fire them, if everything is good, then we have a second conversation. That sound good?"

Tension hung heavy, but eventually Dismont nodded. Weapons weren't lowered, but they were relaxed.

I slowly turned back to Amira. "Do you want to—"

Chris yanked free of Amira, throwing her back up against the wall with a single shove of the hand. She left a bright ribbon of blood along his throat as she was tossed back and hit the wall with a loud thud. Amira leapt forward after him.

"Hey!" one of the engineers shouted as he stepped in front of Chris.

Chris punched him in the face. Blood sprayed into the air and the man dropped, skull shattered and face a sudden mess of flesh, blood, and brain. Then Chris sprinted through the door.

One of the shocked engineers had the presence of mind to shoot a rail gun a second too late. The bullet smacked the rim of the door.

"Ghost?" I asked.

"Yes. It's mine!" Amira snarled, picking up the knife knocked loose when she'd hit the wall. She exploded out the door.

Dismont was on his knees by the killed engineer. "Jesus," he said, in shock. He put a hand down on the ground, unsteady.

I squatted next to him, trying to ignore the bloody mess that had been a person's head. I put a hand on his shoulder. "Chris isn't what anyone thought. Chris is Conglomerate. A ghost." No sense in fighting to keep all that a secret. It was time to explain things. Because I had no idea how long any of us were going to live now.

"A ghost?" I had the attention of everyone.

"Yes. And it talked you into this mutiny, I'll bet. I'll bet Chris was all over the place, giving you all suggestions. Getting you to trust him. But now we need to figure out why this, why now?" I was betting it meant more shit was about to come down on us. Forget the Accordance wanting our asses. It was Conglomeration about to try and kill us now. "Get control of your ship. It won't be able to meddle with things now that Amira is openly hunting it. Get your scanners up. Open channels to CPF. Surrender. But get yourself facing outward. Get your weapons ready. See what I'm saying?"

Dismont looked at me, eyes wide with tears and rage. "Yes."

Good. Angry was good. "I'm going after Amira. Get my

platoon in here. Call them in. With armor." Rockhoppers didn't shuck.

"I will," I heard Dismont say as I ran out into the corridor.

Where had Amira gone? I ran full tilt until I saw blood. Spatters of it on the ground.

They'd engaged. There was an indentation in one of the walls. I kept running. Found a body, twisted unnaturally and tossed aside. For a second, my breath caught. Then I saw the coveralls. Not Chris. Not Amira. Some unfortunate person, her long hair wet with blood, who had just been in the way.

I dug deep and ran even faster. Then almost tripped over Amira at a corner as I skidded to a stop. She crouched against a wall, covered in blood. For a second, I thought she was crying. I moved slowly toward her.

"Amira?"

She looked at me, shivering. Chris's body was at her feet. Lifeless. His throat had been torn out, and Amira still held wet tissue in one hand.

"Amira?"

The second time, her name got her attention. She looked at me, blood smeared across her face. Shit. She *was* crying.

"You're okay," I said softly to her. "You're okay." I put a hand on her shoulder.

"I know I'm okay," she said. "I'm angry. I tried to capture it alive. I really, really fucking tried. We could have gotten it to talk. Figured it out. But I had to kill it. It got my knife away. It got the upper hand."

I looked down. "You did what you had to."

Amira looked down at her hand and opened it. Then wiped her hand against a thigh. "Fuck, Devlin. I was so close."

I looked at the body. The walls shivered and buckled

slightly; booms echoed through the corridor. "What's that?" I asked.

"Contact," Amira said with a sigh. "We're under attack."

"Who?"

"Everyone, apparently." Atmosphere-loss alarms triggered. Amira wiped the back of her hand against her cheek, smearing more blood around. She took a step forward and buckled.

I grabbed an arm and pulled it over my shoulder, and we ran together for safety.

21

Platoon members turned to look at us as we staggered in. They stared at Amira, and I shook my head. Catching the signal, almost everyone found something else to pay attention to. The engineers did not. Their jaws dropped, unable to take their eyes off the blood-splattered Amira.

Ken thudded over. "Your armor's in the corner," he said. Shriek, helmet down, paced back and forth near one of the walls, raggedy feathers puffed and his head bobbing oddly.

"Shriek, there are people in the corridors who're hurt. See if you can set up treatment, coordinate what you can," I said.

Shriek paused, cocked his head. "Okay," he said. "Thank you."

He took off.

Amira brushed past him and headed right for her armor. I watched her nestling down into the gaping maw of opened armor, and then saw Ken's expression. "What?"

"You've been offline for almost half an hour." He leaned closer. "In the meantime, three Conglomerate ships came in at speed on a high angle of attack. Most of the carriers and human-operated ships did not return fire. Sabotage. Mutinies. Everyone had to scramble to figure out what was happening."

"Situation now?" I beckoned him to follow me as I walked up to my armor.

"They were on an attack run. They've swept through, done the damage. Chatter says something on the order of four or five thousand CPF dead; they're tallying things up." Shit, I thought, as I turned around and backed into my armor. It made contact with the back of my neck, and the stinging sensation of neural synchronization passed as I closed my eyes and tried to pretend that alien technology wasn't wriggling its way into my spinal cord. "We think there might be a slower, secondary-stage attack on the way to take the Trojans. But defenses are getting spun up. Rumor is that some Accordance assets are heading in. But that isn't the big news we need to be worrying about right now."

My armor folded itself around me. I opened my eyes and looked at Ken. "What more do we need to worry about?"

"Anais is coming in. With two platoons. They're on the hull and getting ready to board."

"Is he coming for us?"

"I don't know," Ken said. "I left Delta to be a welcoming party for them. Whatever kind of welcome we need. All he's said to me was to wait for him to board."

"No mention of . . ." I looked around at the engineers making calls and coordinating repairs. The Conglomeration had gotten several good hits in. Amira had routed us around unsafe corridors to get us to the core. I lowered my voice. ". . . our little problem back on the Trojans?"

"No."

"Amira, can you help them with their ship?" That would get her focused on something besides the damn ghost she'd killed. Taking her along to meet Anais right now might not be the best move.

She nodded, a little distant. "Yes. I can do that."

"Thank you." I nodded at Ken. "Let's go see what we need to do about Anais."

"Okay." Once more out into the mess of it all, I thought as Ken's helmet snapped up.

Anais came through a service airlock with his platoons spreading out in front of him like a metallic shockwave. Once the bay was secure, the nervous engineers with their hand-made weapons gently pushed back out into the corridors, I moved forward. A wall of crimson-painted armor parted to let me through.

"Hello, Hart," Anais said, helmet down, looking me over. "You have the ship. Well done."

"I'm not sure—" I started to say.

"Oh, you did well. The leadership of the carrier, who had been under the threat of a Conglomerate spy holding them hostage, contacted us once they were freed and worked to help get systems back online to try and help us fight the attack. Now we're all gearing up for the second wave that's on its way. Couldn't have done it without you, Hart. Well done, soldier."

We were face to face now.

Ken shook his head. "We were supposed to kill them all for you; now you're saying they were never really a mutiny? What the hell is this?"

Anais leaned forward. Then, slowly, he repeated himself. "The leadership of the carrier helped get systems back online to fight the Conglomeration after the hero of the Darkside

War killed a Conglomerate plot to take the carrier over. What do you not understand?"

"The fact that it is not true," Ken gritted.

"But it *is* true," Anais said. "And if you disagree, Ken, you put the lives of every single one of those engineers in here at risk. If they're truly mutineers of their own design, then they're to spend the rest of their lives in jail or face execution for treason against the Accordance. So, Ken, what happened here? Truly?"

"This is playing public relations; this isn't about the war." Ken folded his arms.

Anais leaned in close, grabbing Ken's neck ring. "War *is* public relations, son. It's about how to bring the coffins home. Triumphantly, or secretly. It's about telling everyone at home the enemy is so evil that unless we throw all our might against them, all is lost. It's about convincing ourselves we're all on the same page or it all falls apart. There is no war without PR. Never has been."

"So, you're saying the Conglomeration are not evil?" Ken shot back.

With a laugh, Anais let go of Ken. "Hell no, Awojobi. They're evil as all fuck. What I'm asking is, do you want all these engineers here so we can pilot some of these carriers back to Titan, along with the rest of the CPF, and take back Titan? Or do you want to stand here and debate CPF operational tactics?"

Ken's eyes widened. "We're going back?"

"If your folks will lower their defense screens, I have an entire company waiting to jump out into the dark and over to the hull. We boogie out, but we leave enough hardware back here to keep fighting the next wave of Conglomeration coming for the Trojans. I'm here to retake Shangri-La and rescue more of our people. See the big picture, Awojobi?"

"And we're coming with you?" I asked warily, waiting for some kind of trap to snap shut on us.

Anais turned his focus on me. "You hoping to stay behind, Hart? Or does all this sound too good to be true?"

"Seems like a very sudden reversal of fortune," I said carefully. "All things considered."

"Things like the very strange story that came out of your barracks?" Anais asked.

"What strange story would that be?" I projected nothing but puzzled curiosity. But inside, I felt like I was about to be tossed out of the bottom of a hopper dusting out on a fast drop.

"The unbelievable story of an Arvani officer who claims you disabled his suit and tied him to a bed frame, leaving him there during the attack."

I looked at Anais and cleared my throat. "That's—"

"Can you imagine that?" Anais interrupted. "The heroes of the Darkside War, who fought bitterly to the end on the plains of Shangri-La, the enders of the Trojan mutiny, tying an Arvani officer up like that? No one else could believe it either. His superiors felt a pack of mere humans couldn't be capable of that. It was a tall tale to justify an officer hiding away in a closet during an attack. And the struthiform officers were a bit unimpressed that this Arvani claimed to have been trying to execute a multiply decorated struthiform medic as a defense. Sthenos is no longer a problem."

"What happened?"

"Sthenos has been promoted," Anais said. "A delightful and cushy position that takes our mutual friend back to the moon. No active control of any fighting force ever again. And out of our hair."

"He gets promoted?" Ken hissed. "For incompetence?"

"Do anything like that to a remotely competent Arvani," Anais warned, a blank expression on his face, "you'll be executed within a day. And I'll be the one to explain why you all were traitorous bastards undeserving of the tag 'hero.' Understand, Arvani care about Arvani. So, you got off easy, and mainly because I'm absolutely pleased to find that the Rockhoppers' ability to do the right thing while still following orders is still in effect. That's not always an easy finesse."

"So glad to be there for you." The sarcasm dripped from Ken in the empty space.

Anais continued, ignoring it. "So, you get to go back with me. I'm to take Shangri-La, and I want you in my landing team so that when we broadcast the retaking of Shangri-La, the heroes of the Darkside War are the first on the ground for our cameras. The CPF needs the boost. I need the story. I haven't been putting my own ass on the line here with stunts like taking care of Sthenos because I like you. Got it?"

"We'll be there with you," I said.

"Fantastic," Anais said enthusiastically. "I'm going to give the good news to the rest of your platoon and start bringing everyone aboard. Let's get everyone here fired up to go take back what's ours!"

He headed out to the corridor, surrounded by armor.

"Everything that man says is a lie wrapped in truths to get you to do something he needs," Ken said, watching everyone file out.

"We have a chance to get back to Shangri-La and save people we had to leave behind." I shook my head. "That has to be worth it. We came out the other side of a real mess, Ken."

"We're pawns. All he wants is our triumphant return to the ground. Your celebrity. To get more people to join the CPF."

"They need recruits. We're in a war."

"Fucking Conglomeration," Ken said wearily.

"It doesn't matter how, or why, but we're getting a chance to put a boot up their ass. Let's take it."

Ken nodded. "Yeah. Let's go give Shriek the good news. We're going back into the grinder. He'll love a chance to tell us we're all going to die."

I snorted. "Our cheerful feathered friend owes us all drinks forever; I hope he realizes that."

22

The platoon took over a small hold as the carrier began shaking itself up to speed. We were back to Rockhopper discipline: cleaning off our armor and checking it over. Taking stock of our weapons and sending different squad members off to the other teams to see what we could get from supplies, or beg and borrow from the other platoons that had come aboard.

No one strayed more than a few feet from their armor. Most of us rolled out blankets nearby, ready to jump up and in if needed.

"If CPF are dropping in, what are the others going to be doing?" Amira asked, forty-eight hours after we broke orbit. She had her EPC-1 in her lap and was stenciling bugkiller onto it with spray paint.

"Anais won't say," I told her.

"And that should tell us all something," Ken said.

"They are worried about leaks," Shriek said, lying down near the wall. "Can you blame them? This entire carrier now knows a secret the Arvani have been trying to keep from everyone since the start of the war. Something even I didn't know until Icarus Crater happened."

Amira looked up at one of the slightly warped bulkheads creaking as the carrier continued its acceleration. "There's a good chance this whole thing will fall apart before we even get to Titan. Problem solved."

"These are all desperation moves," Ken said in disgust. "Half-built ships taking hastily picked-up platoons, minimal supplies . . . Our first tactical move on the surface won't be anything that makes sense militarily; it'll be about securing ourselves a photo opportunity. Armed jumpships swooping in to drop off the heroes of the Darkside War. We're ordered to jump out with our helmets transparent. One sniper, one random cricket: we die. For *video*."

The platoon's squads were eavesdropping, I realized. Slowly cleaning weapons or playing cards, with bodies half turned toward us.

"This is a good thing," I said slowly. I'd been turning something over in my mind for a long time. Something Ken said. Something I kept coming back around to.

"Why do you say that?" Amira asked, eyebrow raised.

"Because it means they need us," I said firmly, my voice conversational but carrying. "The Conglomeration, they're using human forces. The Accordance is using us en masse. To reinvade Titan. Ken, you were right earlier. The only reason humans could have taken over these carriers and mutinied was because they were *building* them. We know how they work. Just a generation ago, under Arvani, we knew nothing about their technology. Now we build their ships and run them."

"Under their thumb," Amira said.

"For now. What happens after?" I said. "After the war is won? After we take all this knowledge back to Earth?"

"That's a big if," Ken said. "People like your parents are fighting for the independence movement. Arvani say we can explore home rule after the war, but if they won't give it to us right now, when they need us the most, what makes you believe all that knowledge will be allowed back?"

"If we make sure it goes home," I said. "If we're hard as hell to stop. If we turn this war around. We'll have the tools to demand a seat at the table from the Arvani."

A loud chattering came from Shriek. He stood up and shook his wing hands, raising them up over his head. "I love your human enthusiasm," he said, moving toward me. I pulled back slightly as the struthiform flapped wildly, blowing the air around me until grit from the floor stung my skin.

"Shriek!"

"It'll be an amazing thing to die along with all of you," Shriek said. "Defiant to the end! Well done."

He left the room without his armor.

"Rockhoppers don't shuck!" Zizi yelled after him. But Shriek ignored her.

"It *will* be a tough fight," Ken said soberly. "Zeus is still down there. Waiting for us."

I let out a deep breath. "He trained us. He knows our capabilities."

"And we know his," Amira said. "Another reason I think Anais is keen to have us in the first wave, and under his command."

Ken stood up. "Captain Calamari is a walking corpse. A dead thing which just doesn't know it's dead yet." He looked around the entire room. Anger was building inside him. "I used to think I understood the Arvani. I used to think I knew where and what was best for us all, what my training taught me. I've unlearned all this since the Darkside War. But I shall say this: No matter what happens in Shangri-La, I *will* have my revenge on Zeus. You all have heard this."

Ken's mood had bounced from despair through ennui and on into a general frustration at having his illusions about the Accordance refactored.

But now the old Ken was back.

"Damn squid's going to regret the day it ever heard of the Rockhoppers," Chaka shouted out.

"Hell, yeah." Patel smiled.

23

We blazed through the thick atmosphere of Titan like meteors, heat shields cherry red from the fireballs around us. Inside the jumpship, metal popped and creaked, the hull changing shape due to the intense pressures as the pilot shifted the angle of reentry.

"Helmets," Ken shouted.

I looked up and down the platoon as their faces were obscured by faceplates, suddenly anonymous except for the small nameplates.

Everyone was strapped in.

Everyone quiet, determined.

"Incoming!" the pilot, Gennadiy, warned on the common channel.

"I thought they took most of it out from orbit?" I leaned forward to look up toward the front. The nitrogen clouds flickered, lit up from inside by what looked like lightning.

"The Accordance heavy contingent stopped laying it down and moved out fifteen minutes ago," the pilot said. "Only the CPF carriers are in orbit now."

"What the fuck?" That wasn't supposed to happen. The fireball around us had faded. The pilot shuddered us into another curving turn down into the flashing clouds. "Where'd they go? Is it a retreat?" What were we flying down into without orbital support?

"No, not at that speed. They're repositioning," the pilot grunted.

"Where?"

"I don't know" was the annoyed answer. And then we banked hard again, knocking the breath out of me as the jumpship kept turning. We flipped upside down and the engines lit up. "They were supposed to knock out the anti-orbital weaponry, but we're getting a lot of fucking energy in the air."

We were pointed straight down at the ground and going all out.

"Holy shit!" Vorhis shouted.

"No point in dallying around!" Gennadiy shouted back.

Energy danced across the clouds, hopping from point to point and seeking us out. A dot far below us flared and then faded away in a cloud of debris. A concussive wave slapped the side of the jumpship, punching it twenty feet to the side and denting the hull. The craft began shaking hard enough that my vision blurred.

What sounded like rain pattered against the jumpship. We were diving through the remains of someone else.

Then came the flare-out. My armor kicked in to compensate against the sudden crushing force of the jumpship reversing thrust to prevent us from becoming a stain on the ground; it gripped my body and squeezed to keep blood up near my brain. My vision blurred, a rib cracked, and painkillers rushed in from the armor.

We struck the ground and slid for several hundred feet

through hydrocarbon-rich mud before coming to a stop.

My eyes wide, panting, I yanked myself out of the restraints. "Ken, Shriek, check the platoon status."

"We're way out of our LZ," Amira reported.

I was looking at the map overlay on my helmet already as well. "But we're inside the bowl." The pilot had just pointed down and done the insane thing of running all the anti-orbital weaponry in a straight shot. Pips and information from everyone else showed most of the CPF coming down on the other side of the hills. Or getting shot down on the final approach.

"Anyone else insane enough to try the direct approach?" I asked Gennadiy.

"A few of us decided on it when we realized the anti-spacecraft came back up," he said wearily. "They were getting shot down on final approach as well as in the deorbit. We figured, roll the dice, come in on rails, and skip the fancy dancing. We knew it was just a numbers game."

"Everyone's accounted for," Ken said.

"I'm looking at the maps and seeing heavy fire from these points. Those are the anti-orbital cannons we put in place; the Conglomeration moved some of them around," I said. There were smoking gaps in the hills where we had originally placed them. So, the Accordance had not taken the time to verify that they were melting actual emplacements. Just used the old coordinates and moved on. We showed up and were sliced and diced. "Amira? We get those knocked out, we create the space for any CPF trying to come over the hills to retake Shangri-La."

"Well, sitting here is going to be a bad decision in about a minute," Gennadiy said. "We have incoming. I need to get the hell out to safety."

I thudded my way forward. "Troll." Tons of gray armor plated hide came careening down the nearby slope toward us. "Everyone out!"

"We don't have artillery support here by ourselves," Ken said as I spun around. "Mortars aren't going to slow it down. Or hit it. It's moving too quickly."

"Move out!" I shouted, impatient. "Gennadiy, get out of here, I'm jumping. Amira, give orbital our position and bring in a laser, danger close."

I didn't have to ask twice; as the last of the platoon tumbled out, Gennadiy lit up and took the air. Ken and I jumped out, last of the group, and we were already a hundred feet off the ground in the seconds it took for Gennadiy to take off.

As I fell, I looked over at the approaching troll.

Big alien fucker. Multiple eyes. Something out of a bad dream. All sharp armor plates under that rhino-thick skin. Serrated claws.

"Run!" Ken shouted as he hit ice and dirt to find a squad waiting for us.

"Incoming in three . . . ," Amira said calmly on the common channel.

We bounced out like fleas, straining to push our armor to its limits.

". . . two . . ."

I was in midair and flying.

". . . one."

I curled into a ball and looked back behind me. The orange clouds above us split. Energy lanced down from above instead of leaping upward. The beam of focused energy boiled the ground where it struck, just to the left and forward of the troll that had skidded to a stop in an explosion of gravel. The world hummed and spat.

The beam adjusted course, Amira no doubt whispering instructions. It moved inexorably over the ground, leaving a great scar in its wake. The troll ran, but there was nowhere to hide. The beam of light swallowed it up with a sudden lurch of motion and then kept on moving.

There wasn't even a shadow.

I hit the ground in a sprawl and skidded to a stop on my belly. The orbital energy cannon snapped off. "How long for upstairs to recharge?" I asked.

"Ten minutes," Amira said.

I'd known that we wouldn't be able to walk up the hill behind an apocalyptic finger of energy from the carriers' anti-ship weapons being pointed downward, but I was still disappointed. At least, I thought, they were able to give us support and weren't under attack and needing their energy weapons for survival.

For now.

"Who else made it down into the bowl with us?" I asked.

"First Platoon, Charlie Company," Amira said.

"I saw some other pips scattered around on the tactical when we hit; did they link up with them?"

"No," Amira said.

They'd gone silent. I closed my eyes for a second. "Let's get to First Charlie."

We crunched across a field of dead crickets and toward a twenty-foot-long structure of cricket pieces that had assembled themselves into the form of a robotic worm. Half of its body was stuck inside the hole it had dug to try and surprise First Charlie from below ground.

The platoon had crash-landed in their jumpship and then

dragged it around to the front of the crater to use as a hasty shield as they'd dug in behind it.

"I didn't realize you guys were calling yourselves the Groundhogs," Zizi said on the common channel after we scooted in to join them behind the blackened remains of the canted jumpship. "You dig in any deeper here, you'll have a warren."

"Says the platoon hopping across the basin like fleas on crack to hide with us" came the annoyed retort.

"Zizi, shut up," I ordered. The atmosphere was still dancing with light stabbing out from the hilltops around us. The sky-scraper-sized anti-orbital weaponry that the Accordance had built here in Shangri-La was now being turned against them.

I used the live tactical map on my helmet to find the command pip nearby. Sergeant Natalie Cunningham sounded tired as she leaned in to look through helmets at me. She grabbed my shoulder. The armor-to-armor contact kicked in, giving us a secure line.

"Sorry about the chatter," I said.

"We're actually relieved you're in the shit stew with us," Cunningham said. "We thought we were going to be alone here. What's the plan?"

"Upstairs says we don't have to make a run uphill," Amira said. "It's still clear in orbit, so they can keep pointing down. We point out the new coordinates, they'll melt. Then we see what comes scurrying out. Anais is moving toward Shangri-La; they've rounded up a full company's strength."

"So, where are the Conglomerate ships? The Trojans? And where did the rest of the Accordance ships head to?" I asked.

"Lots of theories, lots of bullshit," Amira said.

I briefed Cunningham, picked some spotters, and sent out a squad each. Zhao took Bravo squad out. The basin had quieted. And the Conglomeration hadn't turned any heavy weaponry on the hills down into here.

Yet. I had Smalley take Alpha squad around our perimeter and start mining it.

We were keyed up, looking around, waiting for another wave of ground assault. But so far, it wasn't coming.

"Incoming," Amira muttered. The slopes behind us lit up. My helmet struggled to compensate as the anti-ship weapons from orbit reached down to the ground. The alien energy weapons under the beams of energy exploded, tortured matte-black and green shards flying across the basin.

No one had to be told to get low as debris larger than a jumpship struck icy gravel.

The light faded. "They're recharging," Amira said. "But that's a third of their capacity, easy."

The jagged tips of the hills were now soft and runny.

"Anais gives us ten minutes before he gets up the neutralized hill," Amira said. "Titan's cold enough, a crust will already be formed on the top. We'll have backup shortly."

"And we're going to need it," Zhao reported from cover against a ravine in one of the hills they'd dug into instead of coming back. "They're coming out of the ground."

I turned. Shielded covers were being blown off tunnel access points. Raptors moved out quickly to establish fields of fire. Then behind them . . . humans in surface suits. Hundreds of them boiled out.

"They're not in armor," Tony Chin said mournfully over the command channel. "All they have to fight with are small arms."

They were going to get slaughtered. I got on Shangri-La's civilian common channel. "This is Lieutenant Devlin Hart," I sent. "Please, you are unprotected and barely armed. Get back into the tunnels. The Colonial Protection Forces have come to ground to rescue you and take back Shangri-La. Remain below."

"The last thing we want is to go back to sitting under the thumb of Arvani lackeys," the response came. "Shangri-La is a free zone for humans. We've held elections, we've built a militia. Now we're going to make a stand."

"What is all that about?" one of Cunningham's soldiers asked.

"Conglomerate propaganda," Ken said with distaste.

"They're willing to die for it," I said. "Look." A wave of blue surface suits ran toward us.

"Lieutenant?" Cunningham asked on the common channel.

"Wait," I said.

The blue line grew larger. Bullets started to smack and splinter nearby rock. One pinged off my shoulder pad.

Someone, Rockhopper or First Charlie—it didn't matter—fired back. A clean shot, center mass. Blood exploded out of the back of one of the many blue suits and hung in the air as the figure stumbled and fell forward. The line continued to run right at us, more and more figures dropping, until they hit the mines.

Dirt fountained up, the ground thudded, and the wall of blue shattered. The dust settled to reveal them taking cover or turning back. Sixty bodies lay still in the scree between us and the main body of blue.

"Do you see that they're willing to die for freedom?" a familiar synthesized voice said on the common channel. "Do you understand what you can all get from the Conglomeration? Something the Accordance will never give you. Self-determination. Which means they're willing to face thugs like you to fight and keep it."

"Zeus," Ken said, voice dripping acid.

"I am willing," Zeus said, "to negotiate with the Conglomeration on your behalves. You can end further bloodshed. You don't have to keep cutting down so many, when you should all be sharing a common cause. The freedom of your kind."

"Where's the asshole?" I asked. "Zhao? What do you see? Do you see any Arvani out on the surface?"

"Spot five raptors, one Arvani in the mix at the center of all the blue. They're hanging close to the tunnels," Zhao reported. "Need us to punch in from the side?"

The moment they did, that I had a feeling Zeus would rabbit down into the tunnels. Somewhere, there'd be a plan to hole up for a siege. "No, this is an opportunity," I said. I looked around. "We need to lure him farther out."

I looked at the hole with the cricket boring machine slumped half out of it. A few of us could cram down in there with armor, right down the damn thing's gullet. "I have an idea," I said on the command channel. "To kill Zeus. But it will take just a few of us and leave us pretty vulnerable."

"I'm in," Ken said quickly.

"Me, too," Amira said.

"Okay, Zhao," I said. "I need a distraction to keep them looking your way while we get up to no good. Don't push too hard, just get Zeus's attention and then get holed up somewhere. Got it?"

"Yes sir!" she said enthusiastically.

24

We ripped our way through the heart of the cricket worm, wriggled our way deep inside, and then pulled the mechanical guts in after ourselves. Zhao was busy moving her squad around the back side of the attack, gaining their attention as she, Li, Chen, and Vorhis leapfrogged around, trying to get in a shot at Zeus or his raptor bodyguards.

"See the solar system," Amira said. "Visit exotic moons. Dig your way into the heart of a giant mechanical worm."

"Zhao? Break it off and get to safety," I ordered. "Smalley, tell Cunningham we're go."

"You sure?" Smalley asked.

"Do it," Ken snapped.

We listened to thuds as Cunningham and the rest of the Rockhoppers moved around the mines to engage. "You're right," Chin reported quickly. "Zeus is rushing us and moving them around behind us through the mines."

"Fall back," I ordered. "Don't forget to pass through the jumpship."

"We got it."

More thudding from around us as the two platoons stampeded back to their bolthole. Then more as they abandoned it and began to slowly retreat back toward the slagged hill. The sound of the firefight lessened as it moved away from us.

"Yeah, several of the raptors are clearing the jumpship," Zhao said. "He's not going to go himself, but he's moved farther away from the tunnel entrance. Think I spooked him."

"That's okay," I said. "We have the tunnel coordinates fixed. The moment Amira calls in the strike, we go all out for Zeus, okay, Zhao?"

"We're ready."

"Okay, Amira," I bit my lip. "Now."

I kicked clear and broke out of the cricket worm, pieces flying out as we ripped the entire thing apart in our haste. A nearby woman in blue fell to the ground writhing, a metal shard in her stomach. The blazing beam of light we'd called down from the sky was just fading away, and a puddle of lava boiled where the tunnel Zeus walked out of had been.

"There!" Ken shouted. I followed his armored finger and saw the scuttling form of the Arvani in armor running all out for the next nearest tunnel and then pulling up short as Zeus saw Zhao's squad cutting the escape off.

Amira and Ken were off, and I followed a second behind. Long arcing leaps through Titan's misty air, ignoring Zeus's hasty shots in our direction. The energy rifle could melt through our armor, but there were too many of us, moving too quickly, for Zeus to target. It sizzled and spat energy near me, but scored no direct hit.

"Ah, shit," Amira gasped.

"You okay?" I shouted. We were all locked on, firing in quick bursts. There was satisfaction in seeing the bullets strike and spark against Zeus's armor as we closed in, both squads converging. One of his legs cracked and leaked fluids, dragging behind him. Then another. Zeus slowed.

"I surrender," Zeus shouted on the common channel.

"Anais says capture only. No kill. We *cannot* kill Zeus," Amira said. "Direct order."

"I surrender!" Zeus shouted again on the common channel.

Ken slammed into Zeus, knocking the energy rifle away. Another shot and more of the alien's legs were immobilized.

"Raptors," Zhao said, sprinting right through us in the other direction.

But they too were skidding to a halt. They threw their weapons to the ground and froze. "They surrender as well," Zeus said.

Up at the top of the slagged hill, an entire company of CPF had crested and was pouring down the slope toward Shangri-La's basin. Over near the foothills, the blue surface-suit army straggled along but lost momentum as it saw the CPF numbers.

Two minutes later, it was done. The battle was over.

Ken dropped to his knees.

I couldn't hear anything; he'd cut his mic.

He started punching the ground, turning rock into gravel, and then gravel into dust.

"This," I said seven hours later, "is utterly ridiculous."

I was in an untouched jumpship just down from orbit. Ken, Amira, and I had gotten on; now it was flying a very quick thirty-second loop around the basin and coming right back toward where we had taken off. All the while, it was pursued by spherical camera drones.

"Cunningham should be in here. Chin, Zhao, and Smalley should be here," I muttered.

The jumpship flared out, smacked dirt, and someone kicked the side door open.

"Do it smartly," Anais ordered.

The three of us stepped up together and then hopped down to the ground. Our boots smacked Titan soil, and we marched toward the cloud of drones. The jumpship took off rapidly, mimicking clearing out of a hot LZ. Much like Gennadiy had just hours ago.

We burst out of the cloud, and Anais held up a hand. "Okay, that's all we need. The heroes of the Darkside War have done it again."

He walked with us down into the tunnels and cycled through. We all flipped our helmets back. "They're still going room to room down there," I said. "Couldn't this have waited?"

"No. Ninety percent of the base is cleared. And because we're going to run that clip out, with an announcement to those hiding in the rest of the base. They'll know who's arrived. And they're going to think twice, Devlin. This'll save lives."

"And boost recruitment back on Earth," Ken said.

And raise Anais's profile in the CPF, I thought.

"We've taken the corridor leading to the destroyed entrance of the weapons foundry," Anais said, switching the subject away. "The Conglomeration was drilling through the debris we left in the way to get to it. Another half a day and they would have broken in and been able to arm people here against us. That attack on the surface would have gone a lot differently. These people might even have been showing up as our enemies elsewhere in the solar system, maybe even Earth. There are a hundred thousand people, here, Devlin. This was a great victory. We've retaken Shangri-La."

"And what are we doing with all those people?" I asked. "They were willing to die for the Conglomeration up there."

"Not all of them volunteered to go topside. We detained those who did. The hostility is under control. Everyone else, we will have to monitor and build new understandings with," Anais said. "But we did it. We're back. We're here. Now, level three has a mess set up and some food dropped. Get fed, rejoin your platoon, and go get some rest. We have a lot of work ahead of us, Devlin. You and I will be talking to a lot of the leaders and people here. Regaining their trust."

Anais clapped me on the shoulder, armor smacking armor, and then turned down a corridor.

"I should have accidentally shot Zeus," Amira said. "Think Anais would be this cheerful if I'd done that?"

"PR wins the war," I said to her. "And he has his PR win, right? Let's go eat. And sleep."

I snapped out of my half-sleep and reached for my rifle. The distant explosion still echoed through the corridors, bouncing from wall to wall. Small arms fire chattered for a few seconds and then fell silent. My armor was on its back, ribs splayed, maw wide and patiently waiting. I lay next to it, head on a blanket against the armpit.

"What is it?" I asked, rubbing my eyes.

"Bomb." Amira was standing by the door in armor, on watch with Delta. "Good to know 'the hostility is under control' still," she said.

"We abandoned them here. The Conglomeration promised them freedom and seemed to give it. Then we came back. I don't think this is going to be easy," I said, voice scratchy from exhaustion.

"We're the assholes," Amira said.

"We're the assholes." I lay my head back down. Two more hours off watch. Then I'd be at the door by the bulkhead in full armor, waiting for something to happen.

"This is what they do," Shriek said, speaking up.

"What?" I asked.

"Divide you. Get you to fight against each other. Give some of you freedom and riches beyond imagination to turn on yourselves. You'll still lose it all. They'll take it. Just like they did my world. You won't rest until it's time to flee between the worlds again. It's nice out there in the dark. Quiet."

"Like the Accordance did when they took Earth?" I asked.

"Shut up," Amira said. "We can argue about which group of aliens is worse when we've had some sleep."

25

Several squads had been tasked with clearing out the burned-out command center. The debris had been dragged out. Teams had scrubbed everything down. Techs were underneath stations hanging cables; someone with an arc welder occasionally lit the room up with sharp searing white light, their exaggerated shadows dancing along the walls. There were bustle and determined hurry everywhere I looked.

"Good to see us back up," Jun Chen muttered, looking around. We'd been called up to command. I'd picked Chen and Vorhis from Bravo squad to run with me.

Anais dwelled at the center of it all, the eye of the CPF hurricane.

But he didn't look all that calm.

In fact, for the first time since I'd ever met him, Anais looked flustered, exhausted, and worried.

"I didn't know you were in command of the operation," I said, joining him at the center of the calm. "I thought General Song would be here."

“The general didn’t make it to ground,” Anais said. “I ended up being the highest-ranked to land.”

I searched my mind for something appropriate to say and came up blank. Instead, I half shrugged in my armor and grunted something vague.

Anais looked at me in the full armor. “Rockhoppers never shuck, right?”

“Yeah.”

“I’m thinking that should go company-wide. Everyone in Shangri-La.”

“Bombs got under your skin?” I asked. “Not enough people turn out waving flags to welcome the CPF back?”

Anais brushed that aside. “It’s not *people* I’m worried about.” He took a deep breath and then rubbed his forehead. Then he looked around as if worrying about anyone hearing him. Decided not to say anything. Then changed his mind again.

I’d never seen such an uncertain Anais before.

“Alien problem?” I prompted.

“The engineers and Zeus set charges in the heavy weaponry. We’re vulnerable from above,” Anais finally told me.

“We have orbit. Four carriers and their anti-ship weapons.”

“What if we lose them?” Anais responded quickly. “I’m asking for replacements, my superiors are saying they won’t be able to bring anything in.”

Trouble in paradise. I suddenly realized that Anais was in the dark with the rest of us. “You don’t know why the Accordance all left us in orbit, do you? They’re shrooming you like the rest of us?”

“Shrooming?”

Too long spent with his tongue up Arvani assholes. I shook my head. “Putting you in the dark, feeding you shit? Like a mushroom.”

"Oh." Anais nodded. "I wouldn't say I don't know what's happening. Come."

We walked across the control center to one of the old officers' cubicles. It had been quickly reinforced with heavy rebar welded into place to create a makeshift jail cell. Zeus sat inside, still in full armor. But his armored tentacles were all manacled to the walls.

"He has enough working environmental equipment to last a week or so if we give him some food here and there," Anais said. "He's talking to us."

"Talking?" I had to bite my lip. I wanted to shoot the Arvani in the faceplate, over and over again until it cracked and his water ran out and he choked in the air.

"They're not going to drop in any equipment to Titan," Zeus said, stirring to stand awkwardly despite the chains holding him in place. "Because they've already written off everything down here. No sense in throwing good after bad."

I whirled on Anais. "By putting this traitor piece of shit here in your command center, you're letting the enemy sit and whisper in your ear."

"You accused me of not knowing where the rest of the fleet went," Anais said. "Here's what I do know. Everything is on a fast burn for Saturn."

"Saturn?"

"But that's not the target. It's a fast burn and then a skip. They're going to whip around and keep going. Not coming back," Anais said.

"They're just going to leave us here?" I asked. "You truly believe that?"

That weight he'd been carrying. I could see what it was. "I think we were a diversion," Anais said wearily.

“You were,” Zeus boomed. “There are too many Conglomeration even on Titan for you to do more than hold Shangri-La for a while before being overrun. They are underground, in other Conglomerate bases. Once the humans here agreed to terms, most of the invasion forces left. I was enough, with my bodyguards.”

I glanced over scornfully. “What, you’re telling us this out of a desire to help?”

“To assist myself, yes,” Zeus said, large octopus-like eyes wide behind the watery glass. “If what Anais says is true, nothing else matters other than my need to get off Titan.”

“So, it is self-preservation?” I raised an eyebrow, dubious.

Zeus shook his shackles. “Titan is lost. Saturn is lost. It is now time to poison the reef to keep it from your enemies. To leave the stain of death upon it forever so that it will be tasted in all the currents nearby, so that all understand what happens when your territory is taken from you.”

Anais and I both moved closer to the welded rebar as one. “What do you mean?” I asked. “What happens next?”

“You’ve already seen it, humans. You’ve seen what happens to the worlds that are taken from the Accordance. It is broadcasted to you all. The Conglomeration do what they can, but they die in the plagues and horror the Accordance unleash so that the Conglomeration *cannot* use those worlds against the Accordance.”

If I wasn’t locked into full armor, I would have wanted to sit down. “The Accordance?”

“If we lose a world,” Zeus explained, “we unleash biological bombs. Weapons that won’t pop and fizzle in a small little area. We unleash something that will destroy *everything*. If the Accordance fleet has left you, if it is burning for Saturn, then everything in the Saturn system dies.

Taking Titan, that was to get the Conglomeration to pay attention here."

"We drop down. We kick things up, and then we go back up to the carriers and run away," I said. "That's how you'll know if the squid's right. If we get ordered back upstairs."

Anais was leaning against the bars, holding himself up on them. "Would they bomb everyone down here? After we leave?"

"The Conglomeration is here," Zeus said simply.

I turned to Anais. "How do you like your masters now?"

"Now is not the time for treasonous talk," he said wearily.

"*When* is it the time?" I asked.

"The traitor is messing with our heads. You were right at the start," Anais said, straightening up. "I shouldn't have chained him up here. Or even talked to him. There are Conglomeration that will be counterattacking. We need to prepare for *that*."

"You have just hours before the call. You know the fleet is swinging close to Saturn," Zeus said on the common channel. "You need to start evacuating now. Get yourselves, and me, well clear of here."

"Get back to your platoon, Lieutenant," Anais ordered, face hardening as he ignored the Arvani. "And stay armored up."

"Rockhoppers don't shuck," I said.

Anais looked at Vorhis and Chen. "They good?"

"Rockhopper solid," I said.

"Leave them guarding Zeus. They don't listen to anything he says. They don't let anyone talk to Zeus."

"You're splitting up my platoon?" I wasn't happy with that.

"I need everyone else putting things back together or sweeping tunnels. I need two on Zeus that have seen the fight."

"I'll do it. But you called me here because I know Zeus," I said. "You wanted that expertise. We trained with Zeus. We fought Zeus. You wanted my opinion. Here it is: The squid is right. You want advice from your heroes of the Darkside War? Get prepared for the worst, not just dug in."

26

I looked at Amira. "It's happening all over again," I said. Some sort of sick, bizarre déjà vu. "We're going to have to abandon Titan. This was all bullshit."

Ken stood up in his armor, a complete look of horror on his face. He looked as sick as I knew I must have. The three of us were in the platoon's chosen barracks, but the squads were out on tunnel duty. Amira and Ken were waiting for me.

Amira didn't look surprised. Or much of anything. She just nodded. "Okay. We're evacuating again?"

"Amira, are you even listening to me?" I snapped.

"Yes. We're abandoning Titan. It's all bullshit." Amira looked from Ken to me. "What?"

"The carriers, the jumpships, we can't get everyone off Titan." I explained it slowly, as if to a child.

Amira sighed. "You studied history, Devlin. Ken, you trained for this. You have to know this happens all the time. This is fucking war. Armies abandon positions. They retreat. They come back. They protect. They abandon. They win. They lose."

“The Accordance is going to destroy everything so that the Conglomeration can’t have it,” I told her.

“They’re salting the fields,” Amira said.

“*We’re* the fields.”

She looked at me. I was wrong; there wasn’t a blankness there. There was an intensity in her silvered eyes. “We always were the resources they were fighting over. That they wanted utter control of. Now we know: The Accordance would rather destroy us than not control us. What does that tell you about your dreams of Earth rule?”

That if they won against the Conglomeration, they wouldn’t gratefully hand us anything.

I stalked around the barracks. “We have to think of something. We have to start getting them off planet now. We need a plan to show Anais so that we’re ready when—”

Armor blared an incoming all-call.

“All platoons to rally point three.” Anais sounded tired, his voice cracking slightly. “Situation Feather. Jumpships incoming.”

Situation Feather. Carry only weapons and ammo. Get to your predetermined point within the next ten minutes. Get there alert and weapons hot.

No, I moaned to myself. No. We were abandoning Shangri-La.

We had to pause. We had to think of something.

“Jun Chen, Alpha Company Third Platoon to anyone listening: Command is under attack. I have wounded. I need assistance now!”

Without a word, we grabbed our weapons and skidded out. I slammed into the wall across from the barracks, shattering rock and leaving gravel in my wake as I sprinted up the tunnel and back toward Command. Ken and Amira rocketed along with me, careening off turns as they raced with me.

"Chen, report!" I shouted.

Nothing from Chen. The chatter of gunfire from up the tunnel turned into loud smacks as bullets bounced off my armor. We ducked behind bulkheads.

"Human," Ken said. "Lead."

"Chen!" I shouted. "How many do you think?"

Amira responded. "Judging from gunfire, four, in the hallway between us and Command."

"Cameras?"

"They knocked them out, I'm blind," Amira said.

What surprises were in store?

"I'll take point. Amira, cover. Ken, right behind me. Tight."

"Got it."

I swung around cover and charged. Acting as a shield for Ken in case there was something more heinous than bullets waiting for us. Conglomerate energy weapons.

The first man with a submachine gun dropped, still backpedaling for cover. His blood splattered against the rock wall. The second screamed as her weapon exploded in her hands, a snap shot from Ken. "Stay behind!" I ordered.

Through and into the command center. "Take left," I said. I swept the room, Ken splitting off from me to sweep left. The emergency lights flickered, illuminating bodies.

Movement. I snapped my rifle up, and two shots cracked. Two bodies slumped forward, grenades of some kind in their hands. "It's Chen; don't shoot!" She stepped out from the shadows without armor, a pair of pistols in hand as she kicked the grenades aside. "That clears the command center."

"Clear," Ken whispered on the command channel.

"Coming," Amira said.

"Where's your armor?" I asked Chen.

"Fucked." She pointed at it. A dissolved hunk of twisted material lying face down on the floor.

"Vorhis?" Ken asked. Amira stepped into Command, covering the way we'd entered.

Chen pointed at another burned-out chunk of armor. "Inside. Didn't get out in time. Screamed a lot. The grenade sticks and starts eating away at the armor. Conglomerate. I got out of the line of fire and shucked while they were cracking Zeus out."

"Which direction?" Ken asked calmly.

"They're going topside," Chen said. She staggered a bit. I saw blood dripping from her side.

"Shriek, get up here or send someone. Chen's wounded. Vorhis is down. There may be more in the command center."

"I regret having known their names," Shriek said.

"Not the time, Shriek," I growled.

"I have cameras," Amira said. "I have Zeus. Topside."

"Chen?" I asked.

"Go," she hissed.

"Shriek's on the way," Ken shouted back at her as we followed Amira back out into the tunnels and then up onto the plains.

"Fourth has eyes on them," Amira said. "They're up on one of the slagged sections of hill. Zeus and three humans are running hard."

"Yeah, I'll bet," Ken said. "But he's not going to be running too fast after you destroyed his joints."

"No, they're helping him across the ground. What are they running to?" Amira asked. "That's what I'm trying to figure out."

"If Zeus wants to commit suicide on the surface, I'm happy to help." Ken leaped out front.

"Hold back, let's encircle," I ordered. "They might have more of those grenades. And we're outside here. Get Fourth down off the hill, Amira."

"That's a polite negative from them," she said. "Anais's orders are still in effect for falling out to the rally point. Jumpships are incoming. Now."

I glanced up. The waspish shapes of jumpships were breaking through the thick clouds and circling overhead like mechanical buzzards.

We had air support. Orbital cannon. What the fuck was Zeus doing out here.

"Crickets!" Ken shouted.

A swarm of mechanical crickets burst out of the ground near the foothills ahead of us. Behind them, through the thick, rapidly spinning cloud, I saw the great maw of another worm-like cricket wriggling free of a freshly chewed hole. The cricket swarm had come in behind it and now surged around the worm.

"That is a large cloud," I said.

"If Zeus gets into that tunnel, leading who knows where, and they plug it behind him, you know we'll never see Zeus again," Ken shouted.

"We can't face off against that many out here," Amira said, slowing down.

But Ken charged on, heading for the edge of the cloud that swirled around Zeus and the three people in surface suits.

"The swarm's not engaging us, just defending," Amira noted.

Ken, ahead of us, pounded toward the roiling boundary of crickets.

"Devlin?" Amira asked.

"Clear us a path, Amira," I said.

"I can't kill them all."

"I know; just get us in there." I sped up, struggling to get to Ken as he hit the wall just as a wave of crickets fell out of the air in front of him, struck by the beam of Amira's EPC-1 at the apex of one of her long jumps. The world around us darkened, light blocked by thousands of small bodies whirling above.

"I'm going to run into the tunnel after I grab him," Ken said, speaking for the first time. The three human escorts spun to attack him, but they were no match for Ken. He bounced and jigged around them, leaving their still bodies on the ground.

I ran through a hailstorm, crickets smacking armor as Ken and I surged through into the eye of the mechanical hurricane. "Can you bring down orbital on us when I call it out?" I asked Amira. Crickets peeled off to follow us, a levitating arm of dark swirling material. But we pushed the armor to its edge as we smacked into Zeus.

"The tunnel, now!" Ken shouted. Ken yanked the Arvani off his tentacles, hugging him to his chest like a prize and not slowing down a bit.

I spun around as I jumped and threw grenades out behind us and then started firing as I flew backward down into the tunnel, not knowing what I was going to hit. The thick, chittering cloud boiled and swerved to follow me in. The large earth-eating cricket machine stirred to life, raising itself up and opening its mouth and then jamming rotating bits into the tunnel head.

"Amira: Fire! Fire! Fire!" I shouted, smacking into the dirt and bouncing. I struggled to keep facing the mouth of the tunnel. Our fire chipped away at the large machine's hungry mouths but did nothing to slow it down as it wriggled toward us.

The ground thumped and shivered. Rocks tumbled and fell down, knocking me aside with their impact.

But the machine kept coming. The orbital energy had probably cut it in half and killed all the crickets outside, but whatever was left came for us.

"Back, back!" I kept fire on it, sparking away.

"Grenades!" Ken warned. Three of them sailed right over my head into the gaping, serrated mouths. I shielded my faceplate as the explosion ripped chunks of crickets out into the air and clattering against us.

It still came at us.

"I'm out," Ken said.

"We're going to have to run," I said.

"And where does this tunnel lead?" Ken asked. "Into more Conglomeration? I'll stand. At least Zeus will die before I do, and that is a victory I'll take."

We stepped back some more, weapons chattering and chipping parts off the machine as it struggled closer. Then it jerked, ripples of motion randomly dancing around the chewing mouths. It slowed, randomly spasming, until it came to a complete stop just ten feet from us.

Several explosions rippled through it, cricket debris falling down from the roof of its throat. Hot fireballs belched from the mouth. Amira kicked through its gullet and pointed her EPC-1 up above her. She fired twice and the machine stopped squirming.

She looked around. "Clear."

We surrounded Zeus. Ken pulled the magazine out of his rifle, checked it, and then rammed it back home. "I have been waiting to do this for a very long time," he said to Zeus on the common channel.

Amira took a step back.

"Ken," I tentatively started, not sure what I was going to say next.

“We kill him here. Say it happened in the chaos,” Ken said.

“I’ve been blocking any transmission on the suits,” Amira said. “This is a dead zone. No one will know for sure what happened in here.”

“We execute someone, we’re stepping over a line,” I warned.

“We were considering running away from the CPF up in the Trojans,” Amira said. “I think, after all we’ve seen, we’re no longer walking within the lines.”

“He deserves to die,” Ken said. “For what he did. To all of them back on Icarus Base.”

If he wanted to do this, I wasn’t going to be able to stop him. I wasn’t going to raise my rifle on him. Not Ken, who’d had my back through hell. Hell with aliens thrown in. I bit my lip and waited with a sick feeling in my stomach.

“STOP!” Anais shouted on the common channel. He scrambled over the remains of the tunneling cricket machine in a blue surface suit. “Do not execute the Arvani officer! We take him prisoner back with us. Arvani will put him on trial.”

Ken stared down the barrel of his rifle at Zeus’s large, liquid eyes.

“That’s a direct order,” Anais said.

“I’m sorry,” Chen said, limping up behind him in a similar surface suit and holding a rifle. “Couldn’t hold him back any more.”

Something like a howl came over the command channel. Ken pushed his rifle forward until it tapped Zeus’s visor. Then he yanked it back and slung it over his shoulder. He grabbed one of Zeus’s tentacles and dragged the Arvani along with him through the slagged mechanical entrails of the cricket machine.

“It’s time to get on the next jumpship up,” Anais ordered. “Each of you, off Titan now. You’re not staying behind to assist. I want you on the first wave. Got it?”

We trudged out of the tunnel and into a burned-out crater above where the crickets had once swirled. Jumpships were lined up inside Shangri-La. Armored CPF waited in lines to get aboard. Burn for orbit. Leave all this behind.

The common channel filled with chatter. People begging for spaces aboard the jumpships. I took a light hop up over our group and scanned the tunnel exits. Thousands of people in blue surface suits were spilling out onto the surface and trying to get to the ships. They were being held back by armored lines of CPF.

"We can't do this," I said to Anais. "You know this is *wrong*."

"Last night, half of those blue suits were trying to bomb us. Now they're begging to go with us? How many of them are Conglomerate spies? How many will turn on us?" Anais stayed close to Zeus, keeping an eye on Ken. "Listen, we've been able to create a list. We have room for a few thousand. We'll take the most qualified with no hint of Conglomerate sympathies."

"Everyone needs them," I told him. "The Conglomeration *and* the Accordance, they came to this system in just a handful of ships. They both need us. They're fighting over us. And we need them too. These people are our future. They know Accordance and Conglomeration technology. Leave them behind, we leave human survival behind, Anais. It's surrender. If we lose these minds, even if they hate us, we lose *everything*."

"We don't have the space," Amira said. "I hate to argue their side. But what's your play?"

We all stopped in front of the closest jumpship.

"You're not in charge here!" Anais shouted. "Get on board!"

"I can't do that," I said. "It's unacceptable."

"This is going to be a hell of a lot more than unacceptable, Lieutenant." Anais hit the front of my armor. "I'm going to charge you with mutiny if you don't get the fuck aboard now! You have your orders!"

I took a deep breath. "Since when is merely following orders an excuse to leave tens of thousands to die? What are we fighting for if we become no different than the things we're fighting? We have to be better than them."

Three rifle shots made me jump. Anais spun around. He looked down at the slumped body of Zeus by his feet and then up at Ken, who was slipping his rifle back under an arm.

"What have you just done, Awojobi?" Anais asked, a hushed shock in his voice.

"He's right," Ken said, sounding totally at peace. "This is mutiny." Ken reached forward with an armored hand and flicked Anais in the temple. Anais slumped to the ground, and Amira reached out to catch him before he could hit it.

"Is he dead?" I asked, dazed.

"Knocked out." She stood up, holding a slumped Anais in her arms. His arms hung loose in the air, and his legs hung over her forearm. "Now what?"

I stared at them both.

27

Amira shifted and slung Anais over her shoulder. "Okay, boss, what now?" she repeated.

"You're looking at me?" I was still in shock. "Me? I didn't . . . I mean, there are other people in charge. We need to go and talk to them. Create a plan."

"Talk. Plan." Amira swept her hands around. "The jump-ships are *here*. Armor's on the ground. This is happening now. What's next, Devlin?"

The line of armor up near the tunnel exits folded back several paces, overwhelmed by the sheer numbers pressing against it. The secondary line pulled weapons. The babble on the common channel was overwhelming. A thunderstorm of voices and panic. The crowd could sense something wrong in the air.

Everyone in armor would get on aboard those ships.

Everyone in blue would stand on the plains of Shangri-La and look upward as the ships burned their way up into the atmosphere and left them behind.

Again.

I took a deep breath. "I don't have the rank."

"It's falling apart anyway," Ken said. "Right in front of us. Command structure."

"Armor's fighting over who gets on the first wave," Amira said.

Ken raised both his hands. "Do you have a plan?"

"No." I shook my head in my helmet.

"All of this is happening because you're pissed off that this is unjust," Amira snapped.

"Because there *has* to be a way to save them." I looked out at the growing crowds. "Because there has to be a better way. Because this is a waste."

"Then *how*?" Amira asked.

"I don't know!" I looked around. "I've been thinking about it. I can't stop trying." We just didn't have *time*.

"Take a moment. What tools do we have?" Ken asked.

"The only damned tool I have is that everyone seems to know who we are. And what good is that?"

"It means everyone will listen to you. The hero of Icarus Base," Ken said. "Yes. Yes. How do we use this?"

"I fucking hate that shit," I said.

"No. You're going to embrace that shit," Ken insisted. "You're going to own it. We must use any weapon we have. What is it Anais said?"

"PR," I blurted.

"PR," Ken repeated. "What do we do with it? Is it enough for us to take command of everything on Shangri-La?"

"I've spent all this time struggling to control just a platoon, Ken. Without your help, I would never have been able to handle all this," I told him. Maybe, I realized, for the first time. "Taking control of all this?"

And then, I thought, losing so many more.

So many more lives that would be my fault when they died.

It was easier to fight and complain when Anais was in charge. It was easier to hate the decisions. Now Ken had made a decision that put me in charge. Now the problems could be mine.

Leadership wasn't just giving orders, though. It was listening. "We're not going to take command of Shangri-La. That's not my place. I can't usurp the chain of command. But there is something else I can do."

"Yes?"

"It's time to leverage the one thing we have that no one else has," I told Ken. "You're right. Get me to the command center. Amira, I need you with us. I need you to boost signals."

"What are you planning to do?" she asked.

"Use our greatest asset to save as many lives as we can," I said.

28

Amira, with Anais still thrown over her shoulders like a bright blue fur coat, moved around the command center, checking equipment over. The emergency lights still flickered, bodies had been pulled to a side of the room, and everyone had left to get to rally points. We'd forced our way through angry blue surface suit crowds to get here.

"It's not time to think about taking over something," I said. "Because then I'm only someone giving the orders. Just different orders. And then my reach is limited to whoever is on the ground. We need to think bigger."

"Bigger?"

"It isn't enough to just have different orders. We need to offer a chance. For all of us. Amira, I want this to go out everywhere. As far as you can boost."

"Titan-wide?"

"Orbit. Beyond. Human forces in the system. Up the quantum-entangled comms, throughout CPF. Anywhere you can get it. Conglomeration. Common channels. Anything and everything."

Amira had stopped. "Everything?"

"Everything," I repeated firmly.

There were moments of clarity. Like when I had crouched in front of a child during the riots outside the acting president's mansion in Richmond to stop him from being shot at. Or deciding to fight back against the Conglomeration at Icarus Base. Moments where I knew what I was doing was right. Regardless of what made sense, or what I'd been told to do.

Stand tall, let history judge. Even if it judges harshly. Something my dad said.

Though he would barely have understood any of the decisions I'd made since leaving to join the CPF. To save his life. My mother's. To buy everyone back home time to live, survive, and move on.

Amira pointed at me. "I'll amplify anything you say on the common channel." She held up four armored fingers.

A babble of noise swept through all the various channels, my head tracking them all automatically thanks to the neural link to the armor.

"Mayday, mayday, mayday . . ."

Emergency squawk.

Two armored fingers.

The squeal of digital code transmission over common analog channels.

And Amira closed her fist.

Silence.

I stood still for a long moment. Then took a deep breath. "To anyone who can hear this: I am Devlin Hart. You may know me as one of the survivors of Icarus Base. I am currently making an emergency call from Shangri-La Base to anyone who can hear me. We need your assistance. We need it now.

“There are almost a hundred thousand citizen contractors here on the base. They are engineers, workers, builders. They are us. They’re our future. Our hope. Our brothers in arms. And the Accordance has ordered us to abandon them *yet again* as we pull out. But this time, it means certain death. The Accordance is about to unleash a weapon to destroy everything on Saturn and its moons. And anything, or anyone, left behind will suffer.

“So, I’m calling on any- and everyone with the capacity to get down from orbit and back, please come. CPF soldiers, you’re being ordered to get aboard jumpships. I’m begging you, get aboard only three at a time, and give everyone else a space. Make the ships come back again and again. Pilots, make more than one trip. Carriers, send everything you have. We cannot leave people here to die like that.

“I swear to you. I will be the last person to leave Shangri-La Base.”

I looked over at Amira. She nodded. “Okay, that’s it.”

Responses began to trickle in. Unauthorized broadcast. Cancel that. Everyone was being ordered into the ships. But there was back chatter. Confusion. It rippled out and around. I could hear my squad leaders checking in with each other as they moved through CPF platoons, moving to convince others this was the right action.

“Come on,” said Ken. “We need to get up there and help.”

Amira gave a thumbs-up. “Chaos is spreading. I’m hearing ships detaching to come down against orders. Command is ordering them back into their berths.”

The first wave of jumpships was already leaving when we got to the surface. On the ground: armor. Lots of it.

“Okay,” I ordered. “Start pinging the incoming ships, find out how many. Then let’s make lines. We have a sense for how many we can cram into each jumpship. Mark every group, and then as they land, assign each group a ship. We board fast. They burn for orbit. Drop them off. Come back down."

"If the Conglomeration attacks now, a lot more of us will die. Soldiers that could have gotten away in that first wave," someone said on the common channel. "Lieutenant Hart, you better fucking hope they don't start picking us off."

"They'll be running," Shriek shouted. "Now that Hart broadcast the Accordance plans. They likely suspected it, but now they'll know for sure."

I swallowed. "I'm worse than a mutineer. I'm an Accordance traitor now. What death does the Accordance have for a traitor?"

"They were willing to destroy every life here," Ken said. "Without qualm. How can they expect loyalty if they're willing to toss our lives aside?"

"Some humans who were helping shuttle other Accordance resources around are coming down now," Amira said.

Seven jumpships burst through the clouds over the plain and landed. CPF troops got aboard, three to each ship, packing blue surface-suited people aboard as tightly as they could. People were lying down on top of each other, holding onto anything they could.

"Any Conglomeration out there?" I asked one of the pilots, standing in front of the cockpit windows and waving.

"You Hart?" he asked.

"Yes. Any Conglomeration?" I repeated.

"Yeah, we've seen some cricket swarms. But they're leaving us alone. Boogying for orbit. Rats off a sinking ship, man."

Two CPF soldiers shoved people on board and then struggled to close the doors. Gravel and ice spattered my armor as the jumpship roared off.

Anais groaned and struggled to sit up. Amira dropped him to the ground. "Anyone have zip ties?" she shouted.

Ken got down on the ground next to her. "I do," he said, and then proceeded to hog-tie Anais.

"What are you doing?" Anais asked groggily. He yanked at the zip ties and looked around. Then he wriggled onto his back to watch the jumpships punching for orbit far overhead.

"Good morning, sir. Nice to have you back," Amira said cheerfully, leaning over him.

Anais stared at her, rightfully suspicious at Amira's sudden sunny use of formal protocol.

"Hart, you're trying to evacuate everyone," Anais said fuzzily. He looked over to me. "Get me off the ground and out of these restraints. I will try to figure out how to fix this if you do it. Now. You have no fucking clue how deep the shit is going to get on this."

"It's the right call," I said softly.

Anais looked to Ken next. "Awojobi, you of all people should understand how horrible this decision is. You're committing treason."

"Me, of all people," Ken said. "I gave my all to the Accordance. My family gave their all. I came here to protect them. To protect them and stop the Conglomeration. Now I see how easily the Accordance would leave them to die."

"There are many examples of countries in war turning their guns on things the enemy might come back to use. This is not sports. There is no honor here in war, only winning or losing," Anais snapped. "And thanks to you, we'll be losing CPF soldiers today."

"We lose if we leave these people to die," I said. "Maybe not today. But we will lose."

"You've read too much indigenous literature. You think

there is honor, that there are rules, in battle? It is a human construct, Lieutenant Hart. And you are caught in the middle of a war between aliens with alien values."

"Maybe. Or maybe that's PR we tell ourselves to commit horrors in war. No one is ever fond of hearing the words 'I was just following orders' when it all settles out. I learned that from reading too much indigenous literature. I think there is only life. The life we lead. And the choices we make in that life define it. So, I don't know if I'm going to live through this, but I know I'm going to make the right fucking choice, Anais. I'm going to save as many lives as I can."

"You can't save them all," Anais said.

The next wave began to circle down out of the clouds. Jumpships darkening the skies.

And yet there were far too few of them to save the surging, panicked crowds of blue. Anais was right. I couldn't save them all.

How many more trips could I get away with before some Accordance officer reasserted control over this and stopped it? Before fear gripped the soldiers on the ground who wanted to get away?

As ships hit the ground, I picked up Anais, slung him over my shoulder, and walked him over to the nearest ship. I packed him in with all the other blue surface suits. "Cut him loose when you get to orbit," I ordered. Then I looked at Amira and Ken. "You two should go."

They didn't answer. They shoved more surface-suited people aboard until the inside of the ship was a mess of limbs and people standing shoulder to shoulder, and then shut the doors on them.

The jumpships began dusting off one by one and following each other back up to orbit.

We were alone on the ground again.

"How many off the ground?" I asked. "Anyone able to keep a headcount?"

"The carriers are saying six thousand, if you include this lift," Amira said.

Didn't seem like enough. But considering that the rally points had only been set up to lift a couple thousand troops back to orbit, it was impressive.

But not impressive enough.

The ground shook. "What's that? Are we expecting that?"

"It's coming from thirty miles away," Amira said. "Not local."

How the hell did she do that? "Anyone on the hills?"

"I can bounce up," Min Zhao said. "I'm close."

"Yeah, let's get some eyes on the hills." The shaking increased, knocking loose a few boulders on the hills. Then it stopped. We all stood around nervously.

"There it is," Amira said.

The form rising up above the hills was familiar. The matte-black jellyfish shape of a Conglomerate starship. And even though it was thirty miles away, it was *big*.

"Everyone get into the tunnels," I shouted. "Or take cover."

We'd stood against one of these on the Earth's moon. I wasn't sure what we could do against it here. We'd gotten lucky that first time.

The alien starship, loaded with an overwhelming Conglomerate force that had attacked us to take Shangri-La, shook off the last pieces of Titan from its shell as it accelerated for orbit, followed by a swarm of crickets that surrounded it like an ominous black mist.

The clouds swallowed it.

"We're no longer *the* tourist destination we once were," Amira said.

+ + + +

The next wave of jumpships came in aggressively. Ten ships that circled around the air above the basin, sniffing and hunting for something.

Me.

They surrounded the three of us and Accordance energy cannon dropped from their bellies, tracking our suits.

Twenty CPF in armor jumped the last hundred feet to the ground and fanned out toward us, weapons drawn.

Lana Smalley jumped in. "What do you need us to do?"

I stepped forward. "We need those jumpships to touch down and take people back to orbit."

"Our orders are to take Lieutenant Devlin Hart, Sergeant First Class Ken Awojobi, and Sergeant Amira Singh into custody and get to orbit," their commander stated. "That is a direct order from Colonel Anais. There will be no more lifts."

"There have to. There are still over ninety thousand people down here. Hell, most of the CPF soldiers are still on the ground," I protested.

"Something you'll have to answer for," the commander said grimly. "But there's no time left, Lieutenant. The Accordance missiles are incoming. There will be no more jumpships to Titan after these ten."

"Then take someone else instead of us. I said I would be the last one standing here. I will keep that promise."

Amira very casually shifted her EPC-1 forward.

"HELLO, DEVLIN HART," a voice boomed on all frequencies. "I HAVE HEARD YOUR MESSAGES. KNOW THAT YOU ARE KNOWN TO US, AND THAT I AM KNOWN TO MANY AS HAPPILY SLINGSHOT, AND I AM HERE TO ASSIST YOU."

29

The Pcholem descended from the clouds with the grace of a large sea creature slipping through murky waters and then lowered itself toward the valley. Its extended invisible fields broke the tips of the hills as it slid overhead and then settled down carefully between us all.

Fleeing CPF soldiers trying to get out from underneath bounced away like tiny fleas, only to find themselves frozen in midair and gently pulled toward the center of the alien starship.

"DEVLIN HART, SO PLEASED TO MEET YOU. COME TO ME!"

Amira raised her hands. "I don't think it's a good idea to ignore the orders of a giant interstellar starship, do you?"

I looked around. "Boost me on the common, if you can."

"On it," she said.

"Everyone, get to the Pcholem starship. Now!" I ordered.

The words had their effect. The tide of blue surface suits broke for Happily Slingshot. And mixed in with them, the dark spots of CPF armor springing their way aboard as well.

"Come on, you can't get back aboard the jumpships now," I shouted. The waspish shapes were turning and heading back for orbit. "Get aboard now, you live. Arrest me later."

The soldiers slung their weapons and ran with us.

How fast could ninety thousand people board a starship hovering just centimeters above Titan's icy, gravelly surface?

Five minutes for everyone to get within the Happily Slingshot's reach. Five minutes before it decided to leave.

Happily Slingshot rose into the air. People shouted in surprise as they were picked up by nothing, held in the living starship's embrace as it took to the air. The arrow-like shape of the ship's core flattened. Spars reached out from over and underneath like fast-growing ribs.

The shields flared as we spiraled up into the clouds, shoving them aside.

"THERE IS LITTLE TIME," Happily Slingshot said over all the common channels, drowning everyone out. "WHEN I HEARD THE CALL, WE ALL REALIZED I WAS CLOSEST. I RACED. I FEARED I WOULD BE TOO LATE. NOW I REJOICE THAT WE ARE ALL MET."

A struthiform shape in armor struggled through the crowds of people standing on what looked like air, and looking down two miles to the tops of Titan's thick clouds, to embrace me. It was Shriek. "Your fame grows wide and far, human." He pulled back his helmet and fluttered his wings. "You did it. You saved all these people."

In the distance, broaching another cloud, another massive jellyfish shape swam for the purple line of orbit.

"ABOMINATION," Happily Slingshot shouted. "I SEE YOU." But the Pcholem did nothing more than shout at it, veering off away from it to keep climbing.

"WE APPROACH ORBIT," Happily Slingshot announced. "WHERE SHALL I BE TAKING YOU, DEVLIN HART?"

That . . . was a good question. I looked at Ken and then Amira. "Thoughts?"

"Earth," they both said. "Get them back to Earth."

Earth. Where they could pass on what they'd learned. Spread more Accordance technology out to our own scientists. These were going to be the seeds of something new.

I wasn't just a kid buying time for my parents now. I was going to make a decision about how to sow the seeds of the Earth that would come after this war. And I had to assume, I had to plan, as if we were going to make it.

Besides, we didn't have supplies or resources to survive long. Even on the Pcholem.

"Earth," I said to Happily Slingshot. "We're going to Earth."

I slid my helmet back and took a breath of fresh air. "The Accordance has me now, though. When we arrive, they'll have me arrested."

Shriek put a wing hand around my shoulder. "But it does not, my human friend. You are far from their grasp now. Even going back."

"What do you mean?" Ken asked.

"You know the Pcholem need people that work for them, to help build and equip them with technology. Upgrades. Their trade networks span many stars. And when they found the Arvani, swimming around in their oceans, they reached down from orbit and gave them so much. They were impressed, you see. The way they were able to build their suits to get onto land. To develop their technology despite being in the water. A feat unparalleled! But in exchange, the Arvani tried to rule them. The war ended with Pcholem withdrawing all. But when the Conglomeration came, and then the Arvani became useful again. The Accordance, an alliance between those who would be swept away. Born out of need. But do not think the Pcholem bow to Arvani. They tolerate them."

"So, you are telling me we are safe if we stay right here?" I said. We were over Titan now. The world a sphere below us. Explosions dotted the night sky below us. Accordance missiles, scouring the planet.

"As safe as anyone can be against the implacable nature of the Conglomeration," Shriek said. "And I think maybe, just maybe, there is a small possibility you might live, Devlin. You'll still see your world burn, of that I have no doubt. But maybe there will still be humanity afterward. Because the Pcholem respect what you just did. Your stand for individual lives. They will be your allies. Do not mistake me: I will not be memorizing all the names of the people in your platoon. But I do not regret knowing yours."

I stared down at the moon below as it receded faster and faster from us. Happily Slingshot had turned on the after-burners, or whatever the alien equivalent was.

"There is a dark stain spreading across that surface," Shriek said. "It will melt anything alive it comes across."

For the next hours, as we passed Saturn's rings, we could see the explosions rippling all throughout the gas clouds of the giant planet. Tiny, from our perspective. But each one lethal with self-replicating cellular violence spreading on the winds.

"Your home world," I asked Shriek. "Was it like this? Was it the Accordance, like Zeus said?"

The struthiform never took his eyes off Saturn. "Did we destroy our nest to save ourselves from the raptors? To gain a little more time to live? Would we have done that to gain a place in the exodus? What rapacious creatures would we be if this were true? Would a life of service to healing even begin to count against such a horror-full choice?"

I let it go.

"I'm thinking about something Zeus said. Back at Icarus. Back at training." Ken changed the subject.

"What?" Amira asked.

"That we all decide on the rules of war, on each side." He looked meaningfully at the flashes on Saturn. "How do you think the Conglomeration will take this? How does that figure into their plans when deciding the next stage of the war against us?"

"The shit's always been this deep between them," Amira said. "We're just now getting caught in the middle."

There was a stain spreading across the face of Saturn: the Accordance weapon spreading. Leaping from organic molecule to molecule. Growing. Eating anything in its way and chewing through the howling winds. Down there, anything living was being consumed and burned, the energy from its death fueling the leap to the next target.

I faced away from Saturn with a shiver and looked into the clean darkness of space. Toward the tiny blue glint I had come from. Things might be getting worse. But we were going home.

Home to Earth.

30

Negotiations began in earnest a day before the Pcholem swung us past the moon and into Earth orbit. They continued even as we fell through the upper atmosphere and down into the blue and the white fluffy clouds of Earth. So vibrant. So rich compared to the orange-saturated hues we'd been living in for so long.

So far removed from the landscapes we'd been fighting in.

And then, underneath us, human steel cities glinting in the sun. Beautiful even when scarred by the gouged-out chunks of matte-black Accordance areas, punctured by their organic thorns of skyscrapers built far higher than human reach, from where they could look down upon us. Over the ruins of Washington DC, flashing past Baltimore, and then approaching New York until we flared out over Pelham Bay Park.

Outside, as the fields withdrew from us all and curled back up into Happily Slingshot's belly, the rush of air smelled of sweet spring. People dropped to their knees and kissed the grass. Someone found a tree to hug. Disbelieving laughter was everywhere.

“ARE YOU SURE OF YOUR CHOICE?” Happily Slingshot asked, one final time.

“Yes,” I told the Pcholem.

“IT WAS A PLEASURE TO KNOW YOUR UNIQUE SELF.” The living starship left the ground and ghosted over the park’s trees and then curved up into the air as it pulled in tighter and tighter on itself, until the massive behemoth that had taken tens of thousands of us from Titan all the way to Earth was little bigger than a pair of jumpships.

It pierced a cloud and disappeared, leaving the massive crowd of humanity on the grass.

As per my conditions, I’d shucked my armor, leaving it thirty paces away. Amira and Ken as well. CPF squads surrounded us, rifles out, keeping the blue-suited crowd back and away. “Disperse!”

And bit by bit, the crowds did just that.

A hopper landed at the edge of the park after coming in low over the trees. Jumpships, belly cannon dropped and swiveling in to target us, came next. The crowds surged to run. Off into the trees, out of the park, down the walkways. Nothing good came of a fast, armed Accordance swoop like that.

I kept my arms in the air as the hopper hit the grass, and Colonel Anais stepped out.

I couldn’t help myself. I flinched. Of course.

He glanced at Ken with a flicker of . . . something. Annoyance. Anger. Laying a note down to come back to something, maybe, but other pressing matters needed to be taken care of. The same for Amira, a wry twitch of his lips.

And then Anais stared at me, eye to eye.

“You managed to get them all home, Hart. Congratulations on the biggest PR coup of the war. A hundred thousand men and women, scooped up from the surface of Titan before certain death. All of whom will be able to help us continue the war effort. So, well done."

I didn't answer. To convince the Accordance not to sweep them all up into camps, to come here to this park, for my platoon to not be disciplined, we had to hand ourselves over.

No hiding on the Pcholem. No running.

"You have me; now what?" I asked. "A show trial? And then?"

Anais swept a hand toward the hopper. I stepped in with Amira and Ken. Anais slid the door shut and tapped the bulkhead behind the pilot.

We took off, heading farther into the city, toward Manhattan's core.

"No trial, Hart. You are the destroyer of abominations. The saver of individual lives. The Pcholem love you. Earth loves you. You have a hundred thousand people who owe you their lives. The CPF troops idolize you. Everyone is watching. Closely. No, we bust you down, it's bad PR."

"So, no jail?" I was having trouble wrapping my head around this after spending three days coming to terms with some horrible fate.

"No martyrdom," Anais said. "Something worse. We're going to promote you."

All three of us stared. "Promote?"

"Captain Devlin Hart, Colonial Protection Forces." Anais leaned forward. "Captain. It sounds nice, doesn't it? But it's just a show. We're promoting you so that you're out of trouble's way. Where you can't command any troops to cause any trouble. We're promoting you up so you're going to sit right outside my office where I always have an eye out on you. Me and you, we're going to be like a married couple, Captain. We're going to be joined at the hip, and we're going to use you to raise so many more recruits for the CPF. They're going to line up like screaming tweens for a concert to see you, and you're going to help us send them back out there. Where you can't go anymore."

"And Amira and Ken?"

Anais nodded. "They're going to train the recruits you bring us. After this little flight, the three of you will never be a team again. They will not get promotions. They're lucky to avoid an execution squad."

I glanced at Ken, but his face showed nothing but contempt for Anais.

Anais looked over my armor undersuit and then opened a small can of black grease. He dabbed his thumb in and smeared it randomly across the shoulders and chest. I jerked back when he smudged my chin and cheek. "Verisimilitude," he said.

"What's going on?"

"They all know you've landed. They saw the Pcholem. They know their families came back safe. It's a parade, Captain. They're all here to see their hero. All those potential recruits and citizens grateful to the Accordance." Anais returned the small can of grease to his pocket. "The Conglomeration has abandoned Saturn and its moons. An armada now assembles. It will come for Jupiter. It will come for Mars. It will come for Earth. We live in desperate times, and we need to fight back. Because if we don't, the Accordance will get aboard those Pcholem and leave."

Anais opened the doors. The crowd on the streets around us roared at the glimpse of us.

I turned back to Amira and Ken. "Thank you. For everything."

"Anytime. Anywhere," Amira said, her silver eyes glinting in the dark of the cabin.

"You are my brother," Ken said, reaching out a hand.

Anais pulled me out of the hopper with him before I could say anything more. The hopper screamed and kicked up the air as it lifted off.

I faced the wild crowds, bewildered.

"Now, captain, wave like our lives depend on it," Anais hissed. "Wave like our world depends on it!"

"I don't feel like I deserve any of this," I said.

"You don't," Anais said into my ear. "But wave anyway. Wave for your platoon. Wave for your family. Just wave, dammit."

I raised a hand as confetti showered down on me, the roar of thousands washing past me.

And I waved.

JUPITER RISING

ZACHARY BROWN

BOOK THREE OF THE ICARUS CORPS

PART ONE

1

I walked into the unlit drill hall. It was dark except for a hint of predawn light coming through the translucent upper windows, but thanks to the nano-ink on my eyes, I could see the man clearly. I didn't need any special tech to pick up the sharp scent of his worry-sweat. That wasn't unusual. Colonel Anais had been chronically stressed for a while.

His sad, deep voice boomed out in the hall. "Sergeant Singh. What have you been doing out so early this fine morning?"

I inhaled, came to attention, spoke quickly. "Warming up before I run with Captain Hart and the recruits. They're not up to standard yet, so I need to push myself."

Colonel Anais liked to snark at me. He was our commanding officer, the man in charge of the recruiting drive-slash-draft of the Colonial Protective Forces. There was a time he'd had good reason to have me executed—hell, he could still have me executed. I forced myself to remember that as I tried to keep my expression from being insubordinate.

"I'm watching you," he said.

I didn't reply to the obvious. He'd been waiting for me

to screw up for months now. On Titan, I'd acquired a reputation for going rogue. At times it worked out for me, and at times it didn't. I felt that Anais regretted having to let me live, but there were more important things than smacking me down for refusing to follow orders. Like the PR machine of the Colonial Protective Forces that kept the war machine fed with eager new recruits. Like the rumors of organized sedition on Earth that grew louder as the Accordance turned its attention to the front lines farther out in the solar system. I knew that Anais had researched me thoroughly and knew my background. Perhaps he wanted me to be a model soldier, but it was more likely that he hoped I'd break and run and lead him and the CPF to the roots of the underground rebellion. I wished it were that simple.

Then he said something unexpected. "I'm going on leave for two weeks. Think you can stay out of trouble . . . and keep your friends out of trouble, too?"

Leave? We were fully at war. I didn't believe him for a minute.

"You'll find everything in place and in order when you return, Colonel Anais," I said. I meant to sound neutral, but a little sarcasm leaked through.

He chose to ignore it. "Good. And, Sergeant, the longer you stay useful to us, the easier it will be to stamp your promotion as approved."

"Colonel?" I asked warily.

He stepped in and spoke menacingly a few inches from my face, drill-sergeant style. "Come on, Singh. We all know your IT skills are beyond most of our specialists. Your qualifications aren't the problem. You are. Prove your loyalty to the CPF, and you'll be allowed to rise in the ranks. Is that clear enough for you?"

I stood my ground. I did not flinch. But for all that, I was still a little surprised. Anais wasn't my favorite person, but, snarking aside, he wasn't a natural bully. "Yes, Colonel."

He drew back, gave a satisfied nod, and went. I watched his back and wondered. What do you really want, Anais? He might be tired of babysitting us and want us to move on—whether as dedicated CPF members or jailed traitors was our choice. But he was clearly pushing me to choose.

Devlin Hart—*Captain* Devlin Hart—arrived just then, in time to sketch a salute to Anais in passing and notice my bemused stare at the Colonel's back. He frowned. "What did you do, Amira."

I raised my hands in innocence. "Nothing . . . this time."

"Then what—"

He stopped short, glancing to the door as Second Lieutenant Mallory Jonse appeared, and the sergeants and their recruits began to file into the drill hall.

"Never mind," said Devlin with regret and resignation. "We'll talk later. Time to start the show."

"Man down! Recruit Regis is down!"

Devlin reacted immediately to the distant wail. "Recruits, mark time! Medic to the rear."

I stopped running, looked back down the line of thirty-odd sweating, gasping recruits that made up Second Platoon Charlie Company, and gave Devlin a glance that was all exasperation. This was an easy morning jog in the second week of easy morning jogs. Why were they so feeble?

Devlin waved Second Lieutenant Jonse over and lowered his voice. "Mal, from now on, when they start dropping, just call it in and let them get picked up by ground crew. We can't delay the training schedule, not today, not next week, not ever."

"Yes, Captain," she agreed. She looked nervous as she ran off, but I didn't feel sorry for her. She was almost as green as the recruits, and even though that wasn't exactly her fault, it made me angry.

"Recruits, take five," Devlin ordered. "Make it count—it's the last you'll get while you're here."

I bit my tongue and turned my back to the recruits. The bleak landscape of low buildings, gridded dikes, and ever-present marsh wasn't much of an improvement. "What a horrorshow," I muttered as Devlin came to stand beside me.

He reached into a pocket and took out a pack of chewing gum. I accepted the stick he offered and we both chewed in silence for a while.

"I'm surprised you're still here," he replied, his tone deeply morose. "I thought you'd find somewhere more exciting to be by now."

"These days, everywhere is exciting," I grumbled.

"There is that," he replied, sounding even more depressed.

I stared at him. "You're not regretting Titan, are you?"

"No!" he said with a sharpness that startled us both. "Of course not," he continued more evenly. "It's just . . . I had something to do. I had a task, a mission."

"This isn't task enough for you?" I said, tracing a broad arc of horizon with an eloquent, sarcastic hand.

We had a lot of names for the Orlando training base. Disney World, New Venice, the Magic Kingdom—those were the ones we said in front of the Accordance and their sympathizers. For bitter days, we used Walt's Water Hell, Bleak Lake, Hastalavista and, when the wind got really fragrant, the Sewer. A rarer name—the Big Mistake. Never heard, no matter how eagerly I listened for it—Ship 503. But it was the Colonial Recruit Training Command, and its purpose was to churn out cannon fodder as fast as possible for the Jupiter theater in the Accordance-Conglomeration War.

Devlin glared at the base, then glared at me. "Fuck off, Amira."

I almost laughed. He was so pissed off, but so self-controlled. We had no choice. Surveillance was built into the DNA of the place, and we refused to perform—not out of any sense of secrecy or privacy, but out of contempt for the watchers. And yet . . . I wondered about that. He'd forced the evacuation of Titan with a little help from one of the ancient spacefaring Pcholem. Could the Accordance be worried that Devlin was perhaps too good at leadership, up to the point of gaining his own allies and coconspirators among the established Accordance species? Why else put him into the reverse-fishbowl environment of CRTC Orlando if not to watch him closely?

But the hero worship was also useful. Devlin Hart had saved a lot of human lives on Titan, and even though the Accordance didn't really care about that, they cared enough to use him and build up the myth around him in order to get more human soldiers to fight their war.

"I could wait it out," Devlin mused, "or I could just take off like you do sometimes. Maybe even find my parents, see what the Earth First movement is up to these days."

I kept my face relaxed, but inside I was ready to slap him. He had courage and intelligence and I owed him my life, but he was still so damn young. I wouldn't put it past him to go AWOL. It wouldn't be the first time he'd done something stupid out of sheer, reckless restlessness, and I had too much on my plate to micromanage his behavior.

I faced him, forced my lips into a smile, and let my eyes spark fury. "Not yet. Be patient. Not yet."

He gave me that look: guarded, uncertain, as if he was measuring out portions of trust onto a carefully calibrated balance. He also looked disappointed, which only irritated me more.

"Recruits!" he barked out suddenly. "End five, on your feet!"

I took a deep breath, exhaled most of my anger, and used the rest to spit my spent chewing gum at the nearest dike. Its darkly translucent surface was made to baffle human vision, but the gray nano-ink over my corneas caught the flinch and furl of tentacles withdrawing from the observation glass. I grinned in childish delight as the offended Arvani spectator swam off.

Fucking squid.

As we jogged along the road back to base, we sighted another platoon, First of Alpha Company, its recruits also visibly struggling with the pace while their sergeant screamed at them. I knew Sergeant Bright well, and in my opinion he didn't live up to his name. He was one of the few people who went beyond loving the shiny tech and new space adventures into full-on, creepy adoration of the Accordance itself. The platoon was well ahead of us, and his lieutenant was nowhere to be seen, probably running with another platoon in the company. We were close enough to see Bright but too far away to do anything. He ran to the back of his group, whipped out an extendable stun baton from his belt, and began to nudge the stragglers with it. Their yelps drew everyone's attention. I was uncomfortably reminded of the first time I met Devlin, both of us running like hell from an alien drill sergeant wielding an electric prod.

I glanced at Devlin. "Idiot," I heard him mutter, and then there was a crash and I turned back to see one of the Alpha recruits sprawled out and twitching with blood running from his nose.

"Shit," I said quietly. A ripple of distraction ran through our ranks. "Keep moving," Jonse yelled. Our medic peeled off to join Bright and his medic with the fallen body, and the other recruits of First Alpha slowed uncertainly.

"Don't stop," Bright roared, waving vigorously toward the entrance of the base. We ran past them and absorbed them as part vanguard, part ragged tail.

Devlin looked over his shoulder with a frown. "Later," I said shortly.

Deal with Bright later. Get these recruits back now. He nodded reluctantly. We ran on.

After a shower and late breakfast, Devlin dragged me with him to visit the Charlie Company recruits in class. He hated going by himself, and unfortunately, I had a light schedule for the first three weeks, so I had became his unofficial adjunct. I understood when I watched Lieutenant Sigurthardottir, the alien biology instructor. Like Anais, she was a CPF consultant turned ranking officer, and as a result was probably one of the oldest lieutenants, but she showed Devlin, the youngest captain, full courtesy and only a little envy. Devlin had risen so far so fast that people still didn't know whether they should brace for his fall or cozy up to him during the early years of a potentially great career.

The recruits were simply in awe, and when Sigurthardottir offered them a chance to show off their training to Captain Hart, enthusiastic hands shot up. She chose a second-row recruit. "MacLeod."

"Drivers!" MacLeod began cheerfully. "Squamous, bare-tailed, body length about twenty inches—" Sigurthardottir glared at him. "Wrong," the recruit acknowledged. "Zero point five meters long, tail length similar, height zero point two five meters, rear talons—"

Devlin was already shaking his head. "Squamous?"

"Uh . . . scaly, Captain."

Devlin looked at the lieutenant. "I see. Let's have the short version—the one they teach you when you first sign up."

A front-row recruit spoke up unprompted. She had not been one of the enthusiastic hand-wavers, and her tone was soft and shy at first. "Drivers: cat-sized, scaly. Rear talons hook into your back, pink tail burrows into your spine—kills the brain and takes over your body. Shoot on sight . . . kill them and whoever they're riding. Trolls: giant rhinos in bio-armor, unstoppable. Evade and call in a strike."

Devlin's attention was caught. He absently nodded approval and the recruit's voice gained confidence and volume as she continued.

"Raptors: opposable thumbs and high intelligence, cyborg-enhanced, fast as a cheetah. Smell tasty when barbecued with a laser gun. Crickets: swarming robot insects, usually the first wave of attack. Shoot them, smash them, crush the pieces, and scatter them wide before they can reassemble—"

"Thank you, Brentley," Sigurthardottir interrupted. "That will do. Captain, of course they have the basics to identify and engage with enemy combatants, but this class teaches much more than that."

Devlin turned to her fully and lowered his voice. "Do they have time for more than that? Do we?"

Sigurthardottir's face moved from respectful tolerance to outright irritation. I decided to make a diversion.

"Excellent work, class. But I think you've got a few gaps in your curriculum. For example, humans: allegedly called wise, more curious than sensible, thrive on adrenaline and make excellent cannon fodder."

The class laughed, Sigurthardottir gave me a startled look, and Devlin stepped back a bit, watching me with a smile.

"Arvani," I continued, mocking. "The Kraken's revenge, our new squid overlords. Struthiforms: the hobos of the galaxy, a terrible warning of what happens when you lose your home planet. But they're pretty cool, especially our feathered friends in Biomech. Carapoids: the less said about those big beetle bullies, the better."

Again, the recruits laughed nervously. They were never quite sure whether I was joking or not. I preferred it that way.

"Pcholem." I paused, came to attention, and said solemnly, "Amazing. Incredible. It is a marvelous thing, to know and be known by a Pcholem. If you survive basic training and get out into space, you may see one up close. It's worth it."

Next to me, Devlin exhaled. Some of the recruits remained uncertain, some kept the military stone face, but a few looked a little dazzled and dreamy at the promise of wonders in outer space.

"Thank you, Sergeant Singh. Lieutenant Sigurthardottir, please continue." Devlin marched us out of the lecture hall before we could sabotage the class further.

Neither of us had said a word about Ghosts.

The day didn't improve. I was working hard but no one knew it. I wasn't officially due to train the recruits until week six, but in the meantime I kept up with the routine stuff: assisting at self-defense training, shuffling personnel files and progress reports, and doing recces for training exercises. That was easy enough, but there was more going on. Six years ago, there had been a flourishing detachment of the Resistance based in Orlando. Now it was part marsh, part drowned city, and all Arvani beneath the surface. Orlando was a wasteland rebuilt, a ground zero of alien malice and climate consequences. Most of the civilian population shifted north to higher and more peaceful ground. Those who stayed behind became furtive and feral. The Arvani started extending their Miami semiaquatic megacity, and people gave up all hope of returning and reclaiming their property.

During every run and recce, I was mapping new information over old. The dike grid was a system of raised water tunnels for Arvani to stroll through and stare at humans in their natural habitat, but once, there had been a human tunnel system for drainage instead of flooding and occasionally for espionage. I was fairly sure it was gone—either sabotaged by the last of the retreating Resistance, or found and repurposed by the Arvani. But the Arvani loved to brag about their conquests, and the Orlando tunnel system was missing from their tally. Either I'd have to credit them with more subtlety than they'd shown so far, or the tunnels had been kept secret.

I had figured out four possible locations for entry points to the old tunnel system, but none of them could be accessed without the Accordance breathing down my neck. I needed help, but I wasn't sure who to trust. Devlin was good to have at your back in battle, but he hadn't really mastered the art of a level head. Ken . . . Ken Awojobi was another kind of problem. He was levelheaded. He knew how to keep his mouth shut and work step by careful step through a long-term strategy. He was also Accordance through and through, even when he hated them.

Like now. I found him in a corridor near the officers' mess, yelling at Staff Sergeant Wu, who worked in accounts. Something about his last paycheck being the wrong amount for his rank. I could see that Wu was about to blow up, so I snagged Ken's arm, telling him I'd been waiting for our lunch appointment, and dragged him off before the situation got worse.

"We don't take our frustrations out on people who are just

following orders," I reminded him as he struggled to calm down.

I liked Ken. We were on opposite sides of the war in some ways, but in others, we'd had the same kind of upbringing, the same kind of internal and external expectations shaping our beliefs and our ambitions. I understood him even when I didn't agree with him, and I knew he was going through a bad patch. I just hoped he'd make it through without doing something to get himself court-martialed and executed. Not that it would be the first time.

"I'm going to keep leaning on them," he told me between mouthfuls of lunch.

I eyed him cautiously as I hunched over my plate of food. The officers' mess had one full wall of observation glass, and although chewing made lipreading a bit harder, it still didn't make sense to talk about certain things in the open.

Ken shrugged at my wariness—he was backing the wall—and kept talking. "They make the rules, fine. So I'll make them follow their own rules."

"Yeah, Ken, I'm not sure it's that simple."

He leaned closer, his face coldly furious. "Listen. Our pay is less than two thirds of the standard Accordance pay for ranking struthiforms, carapoids and Arvani."

"Why are you surprised? We are a client species. This isn't news."

He ignored me and continued his quiet, intense rant. "Our assigned quarters are up to 50 percent smaller than the space granted to other species."

"They are bigger than us," I muttered.

He slammed his knife down on his plate. Miraculously, nothing cracked. "Whose side are you on?"

"Ken, this is the story of your life. I have heard it many

times. The Accordance promises you something: rank, money, power. Instead, they make you a foot soldier, cut your pay, and act like you're disposable and replaceable—because you are and always will be nothing but cannon fodder to them. Once, it mattered to you because it was you and your pride was hurt. Now it matters because you understand that's how the Accordance sees all humans. But you keep going back to them, hoping to find some mythical golden rule that will get them to apologize and try to be decent to us. You keep being a hero and thinking they'll respect you. When are you going to understand that this is a fight you can't win? Why do you keep trying to win their approval? They'll use us, but they'll never accept us, and you are wasting your time on this shit for no fucking reason."

He froze. He looked so stricken that I regretted my words. No—not my words, but perhaps how I had said them.

"Look . . . Ken . . . I'm sorry. It's been a hard day and I need a drink. We need a drink. Let's go." I pushed my chair back and got to my feet.

He looked confused. "Go where?""

I paused and frowned. Mirrors were suspect, and the walls were thin. At high tide you could hear the water sloshing under the flooring. Everywhere there was the sensation of being observed.

"Can I trust you, Ken?" I asked seriously.

He took a moment to wipe his mouth clean with a napkin. "Uh-huh," he mumbled casually, but his eyes were sharp and curious.

"Then follow me."

2

I would have gone mad without the Speakeasy. Through the combined skills of IT and Procurement, a storeroom had been secured, proofed, outfitted, and stocked. Everything was allowed: music, sex, slam poetry, dancing. No fighting, though. The management frowned on anything that could cause damage, and no one wanted to risk being banned from the Speakeasy. I shouldn't have been surprised that Ken didn't know about it. I wondered if it would help him, or if he'd try to use it as leverage in some way. I didn't want to be known as the person that got the Speakeasy shut down.

You could get to the Speakeasy via air duct (back kitchen), through a specific locker in a bank of lockers (gym), or by using the broad and comfortable VIP entrance (by invitation only) in the quartermaster's Narnian cabinet. I chose the lockers. We shuffled sideways along a dark, claustrophobic passageway until my trailing fingers felt the edge of the sliding door that was the bar's main entrance.

"And voilà," I declared, opening the door and pulling a confused and slightly bruised Ken into the dim light.

People looked up warily. Only three mattered—the woman behind the bar, the man sitting at the table nearest the door, and the person who I could not see but knew to be there, on the ledge above the door, pistol drawn and ready. I nodded cautiously to the woman keeping bar; she looked Ken over carefully, then slowly nodded. I exhaled and moved forward.

Ken noticed none of this. He was too busy staring and gaping. I looked to see who was there—various admin personnel both military and civilian, several commissioned and noncommissioned officers, some training sergeants, one anxious corporal who was probably going to be acting sergeant very soon, and, naturally, Devlin, sitting at the bar with a glass of something green and frothy and a ridiculous curly straw.

Ken saw him even before I did. His laugh was mostly rueful but still slightly bitter. "Of course he knows about this before I do. Can't let the hero be left out."

"You're a hero too," I said, trying for some reason to soothe him. "But this place does love a rule-breaking, maverick hero, which Devlin is publicly known to be and you are . . . not. Something you should be grateful for, unless you enjoy execution. What are you having to drink?"

"Surprise me," he murmured, and wandered off to speak to Grant Boone, one of the IT instructors.

I went to the bar and perched half my butt on a stool next to Devlin. "What the hell's in that?" I greeted him with a nod to his glass.

He sipped and made a face before answering. "Don't you know? The newest concoction from our biotech experts. A little nanosludge to seek out and destroy any internal bugs—and you know what kind of bugs I mean. At least that's what the bartender told me. She won't serve me alcohol. Says it'll stunt my brain development."

He sipped again, and I saw his eyes straying. I followed the line and saw he was watching Mal of all people, half-shy, half-competent Second Lieutenant Mallory Jonse, who was still trying to find her feet as a commander of recruits mostly older than she was. She was sitting with a group of training and admin people, looking more relaxed than I'd ever seen her. "Can you please not?" I told him wearily.

"What?" he replied with testy innocence. "We're both officers!"

I signaled the bartender for my usual, then thought of Ken and signaled for two. I'd need something to take the edge off by the time I was done talking. "Okay, Devlin, take a deep breath because I'm about to give you a little lecture about trying to live normal in highly abnormal situations. In short, we can't. Take my parents, for example." I paused for an extra breath, still feeling the burn of the old resentment, and hid it with a nod to the bartender when she slid two glasses toward me. Straight vodka, with an intense herb tonic mixer lending a neon tint.

"They worked together, fought together, but at a certain point they realized they didn't want to be together. One day, my mom said, 'I'm tired of your father,' and that was it. Quietest divorce in the twenty-first century. We barely noticed the difference. They still worked together, fought together. We were too busy surviving to add personal drama to our mix of problems. But she was a grown woman."

"And I am not grown," Devlin replied sarcastically.

I grinned at him. "In some ways, you are not. I don't mean to mock your adolescent urges, but I can see you have a soft spot for girls who look like they need taking care of, and they won't say no to Captain War Hero. You need to choose more wisely. Why not Nalima? From what I've been told, she's professional, discreet, and, from what I hear, very good for relieving tensions without fucking up the chain of command."

He looked vaguely disgusted, as if I was giving him advice on potty training. "I don't need to do that. I can control myself."

"Mm-hm." I held his gaze for a couple of seconds, then flashed a glance over to where Mal was seated. Now she was engaged in a flirty, intimate lean toward a newcomer, a very handsome man, a man with lightly glowing tattoos that twined around and down his forearms and hands to his fingertips.

"Who's that?" Devlin asked sharply.

I took a moment to sip my drink before replying with a sly smile. "That would be Jasen. He's professional, discreet, and, from what I know, very good for relieving tensions—"

"Shut up." He glared at me. He had the nerve to look betrayed.

I snapped, "No, you shut up. It looks like Mal has more sense than you. Don't jeopardize what we're building for a teenage crush that'll last as long as a snow cone in summer."

His glare faded as he scanned the bar with its crowd of rapidly assembling pairs and partners, including Ken cheerfully flirting with the IT lieutenant. "Well, looks like everyone's handling their tension but me."

"Rank has its privileges and its price. If your recreation has to be a little more scheduled than most, so be it. Now, if you'll excuse me, I have an . . . appointment with a friend of Jasen's, and I'd better go after I've given Ken his drink, or I'll be late." I slid off the stool slowly and grabbed my drink and Ken's, smirking with intent to annoy.

He smiled, sort of. At least it wasn't a sneer. "I hate you."

"Good!" I shouted back over my shoulder.

Ken's table was right in front of me, but I hesitated as I approached. The atmosphere had changed. Ken was no longer making nice. He was frowning and stabbing the rough wood of the table with his finger as he spoke forcefully, making some point. Whatever the discussion, Boone's exasperation showed in the sneer on his face and the incredulous tilt of his eyebrow. He leaned away from Ken with a touch of contempt. I wavered, not sure what to do to help the situation, then darted in quickly and plunked down Ken's glass of vodka and tonic right between them. It was loud and it was unexpected and it broke the tension. I gave them both a strained grin.

"What's happening, boys? Let's not annoy the bar staff, okay?"

They looked around and realized for the first time that they were being stared at, hard, by the bartender and security. Brawls were never allowed—that could lead to discovery.

"Talk to your friend," Boone said. His tone could best be described as calm contempt. "He thinks he's the first person to notice how this brave new world works. See if you can stop him from being a hero or a martyr."

He got up to go. I grabbed him by the sleeve. "Boone. Don't be mad."

His expression softened. "Not at you, Amira, but some of us have long memories and little forgiveness for collaborators."

He walked away.

"What the hell does he mean by that?" Ken asked harshly.

I looked into my glass for a moment, wishing for a double shot. "He means that you can't earn trust overnight by telling us what we already know. You can't automatically expect us to follow your lead."

Ken looked angry and hurt. "Oh, so in the game of us-and-them, you've chosen your side already?"

My hand clenched around my glass. "You really need to stop talking about things you don't understand."

I went to join Boone at the bar. He let me sit in silence while my head cooled and bought me another drink when my glass got empty. I didn't turn my head, but I saw when Devlin got up and joined Ken at his table.

"You're not their ma, you know," Boone said.

I made a noise of disgust.

"Hart has potential. He's young and stupid, but he looks out for others. Awojobi is all about his own comfort and status. He only notices injustice when it affects him. You'll want to be careful with that type."

"Boone, don't—"

"I'm not looking to break up your little triumvirate, but you have to be realistic. This isn't what you were trained for. Don't waste time and resources."

My head whirled for a moment to a degree that could not be blamed on alcohol. I blinked, straightened, and snapped at him, "I never do."

He kept thankfully quiet after that. I had a minute or more of peace before he spoke up again. "Amira, that Alpha recruit who got zapped? His name's George Miller. He's dead. I know someone in Biomech who was there when he flatlined a while ago. I think you'd have found out on your own, but when you see his name disappear from the rolls, when you hear that Bright's been transferred, remember what I told you today."

I went suddenly cold. I finished my drink and left the Speakeasy without a nod or smile to anyone. I did have an appointment with Jasen's friend, and my head was warning me not to be late.

I was walking down a hallway—no, I was walking down an alleyway. I was holding someone's hand. I looked up and saw my mother smiling at me, a quick, nervous smile that tried to reassure. I wasn't surprised when the screaming started. I remembered how it happened. Ahead of us, a manhole cover rolled and spun and settled in a series of clangs. Water briefly bubbled up, washing the tarmac dark with salt water, and in the midst of the puddle was a set of writhing limbs, human and Arvani. Those who stood nearby jumped back in shock, a few rushed forward to help, but it was too late. The screaming man was dragged into the flooded foundations of Manhattan with a strength and speed that no one could match. The smear of blood he left behind was quickly diluted and drained back into the sewer.

My mother was one of those who had surged forward, but she stopped, recalled to responsibility by the pull of my weight on her hand. Another hand gripped my arm gently.

"Go, Malika. Call it in, get that breach secured. I'll take Amira to safety."

She let go of my hand. "Go with your grandfather, Amira. I'll be home soon."

My grandfather quickly hustled me away from the noise and the growing crowd. "Come, it's not safe in these alleys. We will walk along the avenue."

We came out of the alley into a blaze of illumination. I blinked until I could see.

"Granddad. They're staring at us."

Tentacles pressed up against a vast length of glass, giving the impression that the squid were holding us in, molding our unbreakable bubble in their grasp. Back then, I didn't know what Arvani curiosity looked like, or laughter, or spite, but I knew that the glass had a dual purpose—to watch us, and to make us see we were being watched.

We observed the alien audience in silence, seconds ticking

by. We could have gone some other route, but my grandfather was always teaching, always delivering a lesson. The Accordance redesign of submerged Wall Street was fascinating. It forced you to understand on a deeper level what invasion was—not simply the presence of strange bodies in a familiar environment, but also the gradual perversion of that environment into something alien and inhospitable that would not support you.

"Let them stare," Granddad replied after a while. "Let them get accustomed to seeing us and underestimating us." And he took my hand and walked with me along the dry half of Wall Street, ignoring the bisecting glass and the Arvani crowds, chatting casually all the way.

"Did I ever tell you about my time on Wall Street? The first time I lost everything, I learned how much people love you when you have money, but when you are poor . . . that's a different story. The second time, I learned that even when you save enough of your reputation and fortune, you can still lose so much self-respect that poverty and neglect would be easier to bear. Now I have changed and grown beyond such mistakes, but it doesn't matter. Money is meaningless now. It was only a way of measuring power. And what is power, Amira? Think about that."

I returned to the present, my hand twitching at my side as memory faded and freed me from my grandfather's clasp. I looked around the hallway quickly. Either no one had seen me zoning out, or I hadn't been acting strangely enough to draw attention. I moved on swiftly to my destination, hit the office door with two brisk knocks, and entered before the "come in" was over. The person behind the desk gave me a worried look.

“I’ve forgotten your name, but Jasen recommended you,” I said in haste.

“Call me Makani,” she replied, standing up and coming around the desk. “What happened to you?”

“Hallucination. Just now.”

“Sit.”

I promptly obeyed. She took my head in her hands and brushed her nano-inked fingertips over the tracings at my temples. “Oh God, when last did you sleep?”

I mumbled something apologetic.

“Idiot,” she said under her breath, more in sorrow than anger. “You should be in Biomech, but since Jasen sent you, I’ll do what I can.”

It didn’t take long to set my ink to maintenance mode, so she left me in a reclining chair to complete the process while she returned to her desk and examined the documents and diagrams flickering over its surface. It looked more like a starship console than a horizontal screen. I would have loved to have a desk like hers, but only IT pros with solid security clearance had any right or excuse to that level of tech. Anais, out of spite or caution, still kept me from official access to some levels. Makani saw my envy and smiled.

“You can’t even take care of the tech you have,” she chided. “What’s filling up your nights? Nightmares? Spying? Don’t be afraid to tell me. I always keep my office clean of bugs and shielded from surveillance.”

I grinned at her. Now my head was feeling steady again, I found I liked her bluntness a lot. “I run.”

She tilted her head in query.

“It’s peaceful outside at night, fewer gawkers and lots of space. I go through the camp and a little beyond it.”

“That’s a lot of running.”

"A lot of running and a bit of fun, especially around the park ruins." I shifted into a more comfortable position, one that kept her clearly in view.

"What are you looking for?" she asked.

An innocent question from a face that was anything but innocent. I thought quickly but not quickly enough, and the pause went on too long. She laughed out loud. "Please. Don't play shy. You're looking for Ship 503."

"What do you know about Ship 503?" I asked quietly.

Makani left her desk and stood in front of my chair. "Hardly anything. The Arvani cleared out Orlando when they built this base—but you know all about that."

"What Ship do you belong to?"

She gave me a respectful nod for getting to the point. "I was with 1220 when I was in Maui. Half landship, half fleet, like most of the coastal ships. But then I came inland for family, and things got complicated." Her eyes closed and she gave a moment of silence to a painful memory. I did not pry further—survivor's courtesy—and waited for her to continue.

"If anyone knows anything about Ships in this area, it's JP, our local IT supplier. You should have a chat with her," she said.

My frown questioned her trust in this stranger source. She turned away and returned to her desk, speaking quietly as she did so. "I'll let her tell you what Ship she hails from. I notice you haven't told me yours."

"Ship 1," I mumbled, embarrassed to speak it out loud. "Thought you knew that."

"Wanted to hear it from you," she said with a grin.

She took a piece of paper from a drawer, wrote down a string of numbers and letters, then tore off the written corner and held it out. "JP's contact. Don't let her attitude faze you. She's all right."

I hopped down from the chair, accepted the paper, glanced at the codename, and handed it back. "Got it. Thanks. Thanks for the reset, too."

She nodded. "Thank me by paying better attention to your personal maintenance."

"That's hard when you don't really trust Biomech," I pointed out.

Her mouth twitched in rueful agreement. "Good people. Compromised tech."

"Oh, you're not going to tell me I'm paranoid?" I challenged her.

She shook her head. "It's not paranoia when your world has been conquered and occupied."

"Noted," I agreed. "See you in the speakeasy sometime?"

"I don't drink. But my door is always open to you."

Was that smile just a little flirtatious? "Noted," I said again, smiling back. Never hurts to have a friend on the safe side of IT and Biomech.

I had JP's codename burning in my brain, and I wanted to find her and talk to her as soon as possible, but I made sleep my mission that night. I didn't want any more hallucinations, and I certainly didn't want to collapse in front of CPF informers who'd carry the tale back to Anais. I shared quarters with Ken, so he knew my night habits, and he pretended to collapse in shock when he saw me getting ready for bed before midnight.

"Glad you've found your sense of humor again," I told him.

He pulled a puppyish sad face. "Sorry. Not for what I said but for how I behaved."

"I think you mean well," I said in half-acceptance of his

half-apology. "But if you want results, you're going to have to revise your methods, because right now they're wack."

"Don't hold back," he said, raising his hands in surrender.

"Do I ever?" I threw my pillow hard at him, he threw it back, and somehow, peace was made.

3

I slept hard, too hard, and woke sluggish and angry in the morning. Ken was already up and out. He taught basic weapons and self-defense to the recruits, but he also doubled up in the Communications department so he could keep up with everything. I didn't envy him. In some ways it was worse hearing firsthand what was happening out there. I understood his bitter mood and desperation to do something, anything, useful.

Devlin was always present for roll call and I was usually on time, but this morning I couldn't care enough to rush. I showed up just as the 2-Charlie recruits were jogging out to start the morning run with Mal in the lead and a couple of medics bringing up the rear in a base cart—those solar-powered amphibious vehicles the CPF had scavenged from defunct golf courses and retooled to more military purposes. Good. No more stopping for dropouts.

Devlin watched them leave, then turned to me, looking grim. I thought I knew why. "Before you lecture me for being late, let me remind you that I'm here to teach basic power armor combat from week six, and the morning run is not one of my responsibilities—"

He cut me off. "It's nothing to do with you. Rai's missing."

"Who?"

He stared at me in horror and disappointment. "When Amira Singh gives a damn, she has names, faces, and background checks for everyone in the room within half an hour. Are you that zoned out that you don't know who the recruits are after two weeks?"

My ears burned with embarrassment. "I've had other things to think about."

"Clearly." Devlin said it in such a superior and chastising way that I stopped feeling ashamed and started feeling annoyed. "Mawusi Rai is one of the fitter recruits. She was doing well in the classroom, too. I'm surprised you haven't noticed her."

"It's coming back to me," I lied, intending to scan the records as soon as the conversation was over. "Who saw her last, and when?"

"Everyone in her troop, and allegedly at lights-out. Mal tried to ping her transponder, but no luck. Says she's still in her bunk when she's clearly not. I'm going to order a check of the base surveillance records."

"Ugh," I said. Using base surveillance to trap a recruit felt like becoming the enemy.

"I know, Amira, but she could be in danger. We have to."

"Let me try. I have resources, and maybe, if we need to, we can keep this quiet so no one gets punished unnecessarily."

Devlin wavered. He trusted me . . . mostly. He also knew that I had ways of doing things that could cause us all to get punished unnecessarily.

"I can be discreet," I said.

“All right,” he groaned, as if already regretting it. “But I still have to report her missing within forty-eight hours, and if Anais finds out about this, it’s my ass on the line. Please help me preserve my ass.”

“Su ass es mi ass,” I told him with a grin. “I’ll preserve them both.”

There were several things I could do immediately. I scanned the recruit records. Mawusi Rai’s face shot and full-body holo sparked only a vague recollection. I’d seen her, but she’d never stood out. She wore her hair in two short braids close to her skull, and her expression was slightly wide-eyed, as might be expected from an excited new recruit who was desperate to impress. She looked young, but they all looked young. The record of her age, last home address, and previous education and training was commonplace and unenlightening.

I went to the recruit barracks while they were still on their run, and there I made a thorough search of what remained of Rai’s kit. One thing stood out—a medical sample vial tucked into the hospital crease of Rai’s neatly made bunk. I snagged a sterile glove from the room’s first aid kit and protected my hand before taking it out. Blood had smeared the inside of the vial to near opacity, but I could still see the contents: a small scrap of something brown with the CPF Earth-and-triangle etched into it.

I stared at it some more, then opened my private channel. “Hey, Ken. Can you ping the Mawusi Rai transponder for me?”

“Devlin already asked, I am pinging it repeatedly as we speak, and I can inform you that, as before, all indications are that Rai is still in her barracks, in her bunk.” His words were clipped with irritation.

“Well, Rai’s transponder is here,” I told him calmly, giving the vial a shake to free the small bit of flayed skin from the coagulating blood on the sides. "But she isn't, so kindly expand your search to include the fitness tracker built into CPF-issue running shoes."

"Will do, ma'am," he replied, still very dry.

"Hey, Ken," I said gently. "We have to do this by the book, but for the next few hours we write the book, understand?"

"It's not just Rai, Amira. I just got news that some biological bombs went missing on the Moon, at Tranquility."

"The bio-bombs they used to wipe Titan and the whole Saturn system? They're storing them that near to Earth?" My shock was naïve, I knew it, but I couldn't help my visceral reaction. It wouldn't take much to erase the last thing I cared about. I thought about Shriek, our struthiform medic and friend. The trauma of world loss had made him eccentric and philosophical. He distanced himself by refusing to learn people's names so they would not be added to the near-interminable list of dead he already held in his memory. What would world loss do to me? I doubted my coping mechanisms would be that benign.

Ken wasn't finished. "It gets worse. The CPF personnel, everyone in charge of administration and security for the missing bio-bombs—they've been executed. Something about fears of infiltration by Earth First freedom fighters."

My heart rate picked up. Of course they'd blame the Earth First movement. It wasn't yet common knowledge that the Conglomeration leaders, the Ghosts, were visually indistinguishable from humans. I remembered the Ghost I'd killed on that carrier amid the Trojans, the asteroid shipyards of the Accordance. He'd fooled a lot of human engineers into useless rebellion before I ripped his carotid out.

I placed the vial carefully on the bed, yanked the gloves off, and wiped my hands roughly against my thighs. Then I took a deep breath. "Ken . . . I get it, but we can't deal with that right now. We have to focus on what's happening here in front of us."

"Understood," he said.

I left the barracks, walking slowly as I ran maps and timings through my head. Was Rai sensible enough to avoid the Arvani field of view? Did she go on foot and under cover, or in plain sight in a stolen cart? I sent out more requests, asking about discrepancies in transport schedules, or missing vehicles. I alerted Jasen and asked him to put the word out on the informal networks. Daytime Jasen was an ordinary admin private, but his nonmilitary standing among the bootleggers and sex workers was near boss level.

I wanted to visit Makani as well, but I still had the unused contact for JP. It would be awkward to go asking for more favors with that still on my to-do list. I quickly sent a message out to the codename and was startled when the reply pinged in not five minutes later.

Warehouse B-6, near the corner of Saxon St. and Normandy Road, west side. Come alone.

A set of coordinates concluded the terse message. Strange location for an IT supplier to hold a meeting, but maybe JP was part of the bootlegger network along with Jasen and Makani—in which case, this was perfectly normal.

And yet . . .

I called Ken again, this time using his personal contact. "Ken, track me, but keep it off the record."

"Excuse me?"

"I'm not going far. I'll take a base cart, make it easier to trace. I'm probably being overcautious, but in case I need backup—"

"No, you're being unusually sensible. I've got you. Go safely."

I went.

The route was short and direct, and it led to an empty parking lot outside a grid of old warehouses. I parked the base cart and allowed myself a moment of nostalgia for the old world.

Before the Arvani flooded out Manhattan and Miami, but after the collapse of the pre-Accordance government, some effort was made to pack up and preserve the bits and pieces of the amusement park industry until it could be restored in better times. Several warehouses were dedicated to the attempt, and some remained unransacked, like vast elephant boneyards with fragments of dismantled rollercoaster track, rusting ride cars and pods with long-forgotten themes, and shipping containers filled with masks, costumes, and other theater paraphernalia.

Warehouse B-6 was a classic example of jumble and rust. At least the metal stairs looked sound. I bypassed the decaying junk in the storage area and headed to the upstairs offices. Following JP's coordinates, I walked along the corridor and peered into doorway after doorway. Empty. Empty. Scattered papers and a solitary orphaned desk drawer. A dead bird, mummified and dusty. Then . . . a figure sitting in an antique, wheeled office chair next to a grimy window, patiently waiting.

I walked through the door and paused. Her face was familiar. "JP. I know you."

No need to question why the CPF hadn't drafted her into their IT department. She was small, barely a meter forty, with bony legs in overlarge jeans and wrists that looked fragile enough to snap with a squeeze. No power armor existed in her size, nor tech suit or space gear of any kind beyond the generic lifepod. I was intrigued to see no visible augmentation, no nano-ink, nothing to hint at any additional boost or edge. But she probably didn't need it. I knew about JP.

"Makani told me you're an IT supplier, but if you're the JP I know, I bet you're more than that."

She stayed seated by the window and looked at me. I stood still, half a meter into the room, waiting to be allowed further in. JP deserved my respect, and my caution, especially on her own turf.

"Come in, Singh," she said finally, her voice flat and without welcome or censure.

I came in a few more steps and remained standing. "Ship 23, am I right?"

She looked out of the window again. "22, but I did start in 23. Didn't get on with my troop commander, so they traded me."

"Is 22 still sailing? Or settled?" I asked. Silence. I decided to push. "Sunk?"

She gave me a glance and a smile. "I'd rather not say in front of your uniform."

"Fair enough," I acknowledged. "What can you say in front of my uniform?"

Her gaze was once more fixed on the window view. "First things first. You have a recruit missing. You should find her."

I blinked. "Any help you can give me with that?"

"No," she replied calmly, "but I might be able to help after."

"A test of my loyalty?"

"Loyalty to what? An idea, a dream? Honesty and effectiveness is the test. Can you do what you say you will do?"

"That depends on what you think I said," I countered, frowning.

"Find her quietly, so no one gets punished unnecessarily."

"Congratulations on your surveillance," I snapped. "And

yes, after twenty-four hours, whether I find her or not, you can be sure I'll come to you again."

"Don't be angry. Think of what you'd do in my position."

"Think of what you'd do in mine."

"I am, which is why I can say two things. First, the commander of Sierra Troop of Ship 97 thanks you for saving him and other key personnel by distracting the CPF with your surrender. Second . . . congrats on your survival. Goodbye, Amira Singh."

I didn't linger. I gave her a curt nod, turned, and left. No running. It wouldn't have been any use. When someone like JP says "congrats on your survival," you should seize the compliment and go while it stays true. IT supplier, intelligence gatherer, probably into contraband as well, but ethical, because she chose to meet me in that abandoned building where my death, if needed, would inconvenience no one but myself.

I got into the base cart and called Ken.

"That was quick," he said. "Got any news?"

"Nothing useful," I half-lied. "Anything from your end?"

"Yep. Anais is coming back tomorrow. Surprise inspection with General TJ Gerrard. Everyone's running around like headless chickens, getting their kit in order."

"Son of a bitch!" Two weeks' leave, my ass.

"Another thing. Your recruit's shoes are moving around, but the location data is scrambled. Time-delayed, sometimes overlapping, and I doubt she can bilocate. She's very likely still on base, but I don't know how much longer that will be true."

"Damn," I said, admiring in spite of my frustration. I was starting to have some suspicions about this recruit. "Have you been sending security to those locations?"

Ken coughed. "I've asked for some quiet checks. We are still keeping this quiet, aren't we?"

"Trying to, Ken. You're sure she hasn't just put her shoes in a box to be shipped around base as a decoy?"

"No, these shoes are being worn, and worn by someone with her biometric data. It could be an elaborate trick, but what I'm seeing is a lot more complicated than simply shifting the shoes around."

"I'll ask some questions at IT," I told him. "See you soon."

"Amira, it's eleven hundred hours. Anais will be back at oh nine hundred hours tomorrow."

"Thanks for the reminder," I said in a tone that was anything but grateful. "Get someone to cover the last hour of your shift and meet me in our quarters. Tell Devlin to come too if he can get free. Be ready to armor up."

I had less than a day left to find her. The CPF was one thing, JP was another, and then there was my own growing irritation at the elusive Ms. Rai. Maybe she was a plant, part of a setup by Anais to see if we could be trusted to do the right thing in his absence. Maybe she had been sent by the Resistance to test my loyalty before giving me access to the Ships. Nothing said she couldn't be both. Either way, I wasn't going to let her beat me.

Nano-ink does what it's supposed to do: adding something extra to what's there or making up for what's lost. But it's also visible, and it creates expectations, which can be good or bad.

I have nano-ink in a few places, but everyone focuses on my eyes. They think I'm doing amazing things with them. Superhero X-ray vision, data from hacked sources drizzling down my field of view, the power to stare into the sun with impunity . . . well, actually, I can do that, but so can any filter in a power armor helmet. Dipping into the IR and UV ends of the visible spectrum is also straightforward. My eyes weren't done just for that.

The nano-ink on my scalp allows me to access just a fraction of the potential of my corneas. Theoretically, with more training and improved tech, I could be doing superhero-level things in twenty, thirty years. Theoretically. I could also buy some corneas grown from my own DNA, get a transplant, and never worry about nano-ink again. No maintenance, no hallucinations when remembered data leaks outside of your dreams, no nosebleeds when you overload your tech.

My hair is another thing that draws attention. Purple—kind of stupid for a resistance fighter who might need to go unnoticed, but it's not for fashion or rebellion. The ink that coats my hair also shields the tech on my scalp from electromagnetic pulse and some—not all—kinds of hacking.

My grandfather used to say that the tools are only as good as the craftsman. Good tech can give you options, but it can't make you a genius if you bring nothing to the table. I started with an edge—my experimental eyes and the circuits that supported them—and I specialized. Some hackers grab and go. The ones I trained with call themselves sneaks, and they don't always use computers to get the job done. They taught me to infiltrate real and virtual environments.

Being in the CPF with that kind of background is a challenge. It's safer to find the official way to do things, or bribe someone with access to get you what you need. I've been stockpiling information for years, and it makes me look quicker or smarter than I am. I have a storehouse of access codes and manuals that I picked up by being in the right place, or talking with the right person. It doesn't matter if the data looks useless or trivial at the time. I can bring up information quickly and work with whatever I have.

Devlin thought I sussed out the power armor within minutes of our first training session. I learned about them months in advance. The Accordance was drafting more and more "volunteers," and I'd wanted to be prepared. It wasn't common knowledge, but it was hardly top-tier intelligence.

I had a theory about power armor.

My job was to train the recruits in handling power armor and larger weapons after they've finished basic physical fitness, zero-g familiarization, and personal weapons training. The course barely scratches the surface. They get most of their real training on the way to the front lines. Earth-based camps are meant to weed out the truly incapable and provide a steady supply of admin and grunts who know how the system works and how to follow orders. Recruits like ours were considered sacrificial lambs, but maybe CPF had let a wolf into the fold, a wolf who knew more about power armor than any recruit should, particularly the cloaking and evasion functions.

I could have marched to the quartermaster and demanded an inventory of the power armor suits. I was the instructor, after all. But, just in case Rai's disappearance and our actions became the subject of an inquiry, I decided to do it in a way that wouldn't have my name attached to any paperwork.

4

I headed for my quarters as fast as I could without actively running. Devlin snagged my arm as our paths crossed outside the mess hall. "You heard?"

"Ken told me. Take it easy."

"Take it easy? You know Anais has been waiting for me to fuck up."

"Come with me. We're going to get Ken, and then we're going to check something out."

Ken was in our room, sitting on his bed in apparent deep thought. He sprang to his feet and gave Devlin a nod that showed both relief and reassurance, then looked at me. "Ready."

I shut the door, leaned against it, and closed my eyes for a moment of intense work. The surveillance protections I'd placed throughout our quarters were less extensive than Makani's but still as sophisticated as I could make them without drawing the official attention of IT and security. Devlin and Ken waited patiently, knowing what I was doing.

"Rai's moving about the base in power armor using

camouflage mode," I said as soon as I could speak.

"Are you sure?" asked Devlin, just as Ken said, "Yeah, that makes sense."

Devlin glanced at him and then back at me, repeating his question silently.

"We're going to check if any of the power armor is missing. If there is, we'll armor up. I'm not risking myself tracking someone who could kill me by mistake."

Finally, Devlin nodded. "Okay. Lead the way."

I climbed onto my ordinary, non-screen, standard-issue desk, and stretched my hands up to slide open a ceiling panel. Putting a finger to my lips, I signaled the other two to join me. Devlin was dumbfounded. Ken simply shook his head at me, but he looked amused when he saw Devlin's face and realized that Devlin had no more idea than he did about this new route. I smirked and swung myself up into the crawlspace. I had learned a lot about the base schematics and access codes when I helped IT and Procurement set up the Speakeasy.

We traveled in silence, dropping out of the crawlspace into a small access corridor and then squeezing through an even smaller hatch to enter a storage hall with rows of power armor hanging empty and open from ceiling hooks.

"What are we looking for?" Devlin asked softly.

"I'll know it when I see it," I said, turning slowly, scanning each row. "There! Notice anything strange?"

Ken spoke first. "That's a closed suit." He reached for his sidearm.

I put out a hand to stop him. "No need."

I ran toward the closed suit, skidded to a stop in front of it, and whipped my hand through the helmet. The illusion vanished. I examined the small decoy projector I had snatched off the suit's hook. Devlin and Ken came running and I held it up for them to see. Then I dropped it, set my heel on it with a harsh crunch, and quickly swept up the remains and dumped them in my pocket.

"Shit," said Ken.

"Uh-huh," I agreed.

Devlin looked pissed. "Okay, armor up. I'm calling this in now."

I opened my mouth, not sure what I was going to say.

"Wait, Devlin." Ken got in first. "We're in Orlando, surrounded by Arvani. It's possible, but improbable, that we've been infiltrated by Ghosts—"

"I would have sensed them," I interrupted, my voice sharp with anger and bad memories.

"Exactly," Ken said soothingly. "So, considering that the threat we're facing is probably entirely human, could we make the most of the little time we have before Anais shows up?"

"Desertion equals execution equals bad PR, and we know how much our dear colonel hates bad PR," I said sarcastically. "He won't mind if you bend the rules for that."

"True," Devlin said, his lip curling in contempt. "Okay, not calling it in, but the armor-up command still stands. If anyone asks, tell them we're going to assess sites for power armor training. And we are. All over this damn base."

"You still have to keep an eye on preparations for the inspection," Ken pointed out.

"PR," I reminded him.

Devlin clenched his jaw so hard we could hear his teeth grind.

Ken clapped him on the shoulder. "Don't worry, Captain. Rai's had plenty of opportunity to assassinate you before, so I doubt that's her goal. But we'll armor up now and be ready for hunting later."

“Ken’s right,” I said. “Besides, there’s someone I need to see.”

We armored up. Apart from training sessions and public appearances, it had been a while since we’d put on armor under threat of real combat. There’s a different hum, a unique vibration to when that suit clicks shut and your blood is singing with adrenaline. We’d crept in like rats; we strode out like giants. Some people eyed us with curiosity, a few even with envy, but people were busy and, above all, they knew not to ask questions in case the answers led to more unwanted tasks.

I made a call and went straight to Jasen’s quarters. I didn’t waste time. As soon as the door slid shut behind me, I shucked my armor. I didn’t stop there. I stripped to my underwear and stuffed each item of clothing and the fragments of the decoy into a clothes hamper at the door and watched the hamper’s readout intently.

“You, of all people, really don’t have to do that.” Jasen’s voice was deep, amused, and relaxed. I waited until I was certain that the decoy was dead and my clothes hadn’t picked up any bugs before I turned around. Like any good and professional pretty boy, he was already naked, and he was lounging with the right amount of casual but artistic sensuality.

“While it’s true that I can bug-scan with the best of them—and you, my dear colleague, are one of the best—today is a day for double-checking.” I walked over and sat at the end of the bed, swinging my legs up and rubbing my feet playfully against his. He had the expected handsome face, but the intelligence and awareness in his eyes were what made me smile. Then something else caught my attention. “Ouch. Gorgeous, but ouch!”

He shrugged with studied unconcern. “Only the best can afford the best.”

“Yes, but . . . may I?”

He nodded permission. I bent closer, taking his penis in hand so I could scrutinize the faintly raised texture of several square centimeters of top-grade nano-ink. It was a dense, beautiful pattern, deceptively artistic, and practically an epidermal supercomputer. On anyone else, placed anywhere else, it would have been glaringly illegal, but on him it was merely a toy's toy, part of the pretty-boy arsenal. Better than studs and ring piercings, too. Less obvious, and much harder to rip out.

"And people freak out about my eyes. Good for you! Did it take long?"

He couldn't suppress a shudder. "Oh yes."

"But it's useful," I stated.

The sexy slipped as he suddenly geeked out. "Oh yes. In all kinds of ways." And he proceeded to tell me, at length and in detail, precisely how useful as I continued to hold and examine his greatest asset with bemused fascination.

At last, and somewhat sheepishly, he wound down and finished his spiel. I released his penis and gave it a politely respectful pat, saying cheerfully, "I like it. A lot. It shows dedication to your craft."

Sneaks and professional pretties have been friends for decades. When the news media shifted from scripted to raw delivery, the established intimacy firms lobbied for special exemptions. Officially, they got slightly better than the standard bathroom-privacy blackout. Unofficially, their richest clients were making sure that they had the training and tech to turn any house or room or closet into an information black hole: everything flowing in, nothing going out. I make a point of getting friendly with the resident pretties wherever I go. They're good people to know, and many of them have heard of me already.

Jasen told me once, "There's a long and rich history of

courtesans as spies. We can go everywhere." They do, and when they do, they carry things with them that would never be stored on a hackable network.

"So," I said, "got anything for me?"

"Come and see."

The professional smile was back in place. I was puzzled, but I played along and leaned in to meet him for a kiss. It was as good as I expected; his lips were sweet and soft, and his tongue gently pushed a datachip into my mouth. I tucked it away between gum and cheek and enjoyed the rest of the kiss.

"Something like that?" he said quietly, pulling away slowly.

"Yes, thank you, that's great," I murmured, a little distracted.

"More?" he asked, and glanced at my hand, which was still resting on his thigh.

I hesitated and considered, but he seemed like an important resource and I didn't want to risk an attachment. Besides, thanks to his dick-tech lecture, I'd already spent twenty minutes, plenty of time for an unremarkable midevening quickie.

"Sorry," I said with true regret. "I want to see you again, soon and often, for work. We'll play another time, when this is behind us. And I have to save up. Can't just pay for the standard rate now you've told me about those additional features."

He nodded, pursing his lips in a brief pout of disappointment. "Yeah. Well, I think Grant's free now if you want—"

"Nah, I'll just—wait, what? Lieutenant Grant Boone?"

"In training. Says he needs the extra funds."

"But he's not . . . never mind. As I was saying, I'll just go for a run."

His expression brightened. "Can I come watch?"

"Some other time," I told him with a grin.

\+ \+ \+ \+

My granddad insisted that I never get used to anything. Not coffee, not alcohol, not sex. Didn't matter how it made me feel, or whether it was good or bad for me. The important thing was to never be dependent on any single thing or person.

And then he trained my body to run, and later they trained my brain to sneak, and I've never been able to shake my need for the adrenaline rush they give me.

I was dressed in freshly debugged clothes and armored up. Jasen's datachip still sat inside my mouth, flush against the epithelial tissue in a wash of saliva, quietly communicating with my nano-ink and dumping loads of data. Anais's location and ETA, power armor override codes, names and times of base cart use, the newest updated schematics for the ever-shifting ways above the ceilings and in the hollow walls. Some of it was old stuff; quite a lot was new. I wondered if my meeting with JP had unlocked another level of access, or whether I was simply being given enough rope to hang myself in the search for Rai. The uncertainty only added to the rush.

When the dump was complete, I checked in with Devlin and Ken. Both were busy with recruits and duties, so I simply updated them as best as I could, given the short time and lack of full privacy. For a moment I thought about leaving my armor in my quarters and running light as I usually did near base, but the thought of encountering Rai in a power suit made the back of my neck prickle. I didn't feel completely dressed until I took out my EMP cannon and slung it over my shoulder. Veteran's privilege. That EPC-1 had been with me for a while—modified, personalized, and best of all, completely liberated from the CPF ordnance records. Messily stenciled lettering spelled out BUGKILLER along its length. I doubted I'd find any crickets to zap, but the cannon would at least slow down anyone with nano-ink or implants.

I waited until after nightfall. I went out, closed my helmet, and started running, trying to guess where I'd go if I had just stolen a suit of armor and was trying not to be conspicuous. I was also sorting the new data by priority, and thinking over my conversation with Jasen, my brain taking simultaneous multiple tracks from the trivial to the technical.

Grant Boone? I'd stopped myself from saying something rude in front of Jasen, but the truth was Grant Boone wasn't really that pretty. To be fair, most of the pros hadn't been born pretty either. They enhanced themselves by various genetic and surgical means to fit a range of aesthetic templates to draw a certain clientele. If Grant was in training and hadn't even bothered with the most rudimentary tweaks to his appearance, then what did that mean? Was he taking advantage of a new fad in sex work? Were the pros now considered too polished and the boy next door preferred? And what did he need funds for?

Suspicion was my natural state of mind. I put this information away as something to check on later and ran to one of my safe spots.

Personal security on base is a challenge. In a place saturated with high-level surveillance, the presence of a blank space is as telling as a piece of incriminating data. You have to hide data so well that there are no missing pieces and the landscape is seamless. I've done so much work for the CPF, for the Accordance, that they know a lot of my old methods. I've had to be creative and find new ways to sneak.

Running helped me find all the places out of sight of Arvani view and beyond the reach of all human and Accordance networks. I was looking for someone else that had found those spaces, something with the familiar signature of Accordance power armor in cloaking mode.

Power armor isn't really made for cloaking. There's a tradeoff between wanting to know where your soldiers are situated and allowing them to hide from the enemy. Somewhere between the two states there would be enough of a trace for me to find the rogue suit.

Tech cuts both ways. There was also enough of a trace for me to be found.

I was knocked sideways, armor clashing against armor with a muffled boom. I grabbed an arm instantly and took my attacker with me, dragging us through dead leaves and brush until we fetched up against the side of a dike. The dike's viewport glass cracked—a satisfying sound. It wouldn't break, though. The base and the dikes were built to stand up to Category 5 and higher. I took the opportunity to slam her helmeted head against the glass, a futile move for any real damage, but I hoped the shock would confuse her.

"I'm not the enemy!" The words came over my private channel and rang in my helmet, too loud and panicky.

I banged helmet to dike again. "I'm not convinced. Prove it."

"We need just one suit. We've been reverse-engineering a lot of shit, but we need to develop our own space armor."

I flipped her onto her back, kept a hand on her shoulder and a knee on her leg, and cued her helmet open with a quick, silent override. She blinked at me, either helpless or pretending to be. My own helmet opened and retracted into its collar, and I gazed directly at her with my best no-bullshit stare. "Who is 'we'?"

She blinked again, looking a little less innocent. "Ships on land, Ships on the sea. You know. Maybe Ships in space very soon. You're the last person who'd want to stop us."

I straightened, shifting my weight as I slowly took control

of the rogue suit, locking all the joints. "You think you know me?"

Shadows fluttered on the other side of the cracked glass. We both glanced sideways at it. Arvani, turning up to see what the noise was, of course. I stood, extended a hand to Rai, and we made a show of her being helped to her feet and the two of us walking away. All the while I was maneuvering the second suit like a marionette. I took us to another safe spot nearby and commanded Rai's suit to turn, face me, and freeze in position.

"Thank you," she began.

"Not yet, Rai. You're trying to take a suit off base. I say 'trying' because you must have discovered pretty quick that this year's improved transponder tech won't let you take base property without raising a hell of an alarm. And somehow you're sure I'll look the other way while you do this."

"Sergeant Singh, you've been in the CPF for a while. It's natural that your loyalties are a little skewed."

"Rude!" I said with a humorless laugh.

Rai dipped her head and was silent for a moment. I recognized the preparation to appeal to my common sense, or better nature, or old loyalties, or something of the sort. "CPF or no CPF," she said, "do you really think humans will have a chance in a galaxy where Accordance and Conglomeration keep the best toys for themselves?"

I remembered something Devlin said—when Earth breaks free of the Accordance, we'll have extra knowledge and tech from when the Arvani forced us to build their ships and fight their battles. My vision was a little darker—should the Accordance turn tail and run, leaving Earth and the solar system to be overrun by the Conglomerate, would we have learned and gained enough to defend ourselves?

"Give me a minute," I said grudgingly.

I stepped away, brought up my helmet again, and engaged the private channel. "Devlin, Ken, I've found her. What now?"

Devlin's voice crackled with stress. "What do you mean, 'what now'? Do you need help bringing her in?"

"Um . . . complicated reasons suggest this might not be best for all concerned. Think of our long-term goals. She's with an anti-Accordance group. Not sure which one yet, but we don't want to piss off potential allies."

He took time for a suffering sigh. "Right. Can you restrain her until midnight? There's still too much happening here, damn Anais and his mind games."

"Ken? How much longer before Anais arrives?"

Ken's voice was calmer but still tense. "Anais is expected at oh eight hundred hours. Trains are running to schedule."

"Of course they are. Okay, I can keep her here till midnight, but that still doesn't answer the question of what we do after that."

"Amira's right, Devlin," Ken said. "If this thing is to be covered up, it's going to take more than us three to do it."

"I won't send a recruit to be executed by the Accordance," I stated. "Don't care if they mean us good or ill. If they've got to be taken out, I'd rather do that myself. Judge, jury, and executioner if needs be."

I heard Devlin exhale slowly. "Amira, I need time. Expect us after midnight. I'll send you a message."

"But—"

"Amira, please."

I nodded, resigned. "All right, Captain. I'll wait for your message and meet you after midnight."

I let my helmet slide back and frowned at my prisoner as I

rechecked the overrides that kept her suit under my command. "Comfortable?' I asked her calmly.

Rai gave an anxious laugh. "That depends on what you're going to do." Her final word emerged at a strangled pitch as I shuffled her suit back a couple more feet into the brush.

"I'm going to wait," I said, settling down where I could see anyone coming from any direction. "And so are you."

5

I'm not ashamed to say that I took a nap. Rai wasn't going anywhere with her suit locked and tethered to me, and my suit kept watch better than a human soldier. Besides, Makani was right; when it came to maintaining my tech, there was no substitute for sleep, especially after such a large data intake.

I woke up at the ping of Devlin's message—he was on his way with Ken. "Rai! Time to stretch your legs."

Rai swore at me, but when I moved her suit, she groaned in relief as her joints flexed and unstiffened. I made the suit bend, twist, and high-step, testing my control and the suit's remote capabilities. I was still at it when Devlin and Ken arrived, fully suited with helmets down. Ken was very surprised when he saw me making Rai dance.

"You can do that?" he said anxiously.

I nodded. "Don't worry. It's a temporary instructor override present in training mode. Hacking into battle-ready suits is not a thing that can happen."

Devlin wasn't interested in chatting. "Come, the rest are waiting for us."

I blinked but hid my curiosity. We followed him to a clearing near the edge of the base—not quite a safe spot, but still fairly well sheltered with screening foliage. What I saw there made me more than blink. I calmly sat Rai and her suit down, locked her in position with helmet open, and spoke privately to Devlin.

"Devlin, what the hell?"

He stubbornly repeated Ken's words. "It's going to take more than three of us to cover this up."

"Yes, but the whole platoon?"

They sat quietly in rows, dressed in PT gear, their expressions variously bemused, irritated, curious, resigned, and worried. Many of the names escaped me. When Devlin accused me of not giving a damn because I couldn't recall who Rai was or what she looked like, he wasn't wrong. I realized I was becoming like Shriek, caring less and less about names that would soon die and be forgotten.

I looked for other officers, but there was only Mal, also in PT gear and unusually grim-faced. That actually made sense. Older, more established officers might be less inclined to mutiny, but Mal could be persuaded, or even pressured.

"Our long-term goals, remember?" Devlin replied. "I can't do CPF propaganda forever, Amira. I've got to plant a seed here, send a message via this group. I can't do it with Anais and his shadows watching me. I'm taking my chance now."

I glanced at Ken, who gave a small, rueful nod to show that they'd argued it out earlier and reached some kind of agreement. I had plenty more to say, but I wasn't going to debate it in the open. "Okay, Captain Hart. The floor is yours." I went and stood by Rai, facing the audience of recruits.

"Listen up, Second Platoon Charlie-C. You have a decision to make."

He'd synced his suit's mike to a handful of transmitters in the audience, a neat trick that meant he didn't have to raise his voice.

"Mawusi Rai stole power armor and went AWOL. Desertion is enough grounds for execution, and theft of defense tech . . . well, that just seals it."

He paused and looked around at them, watching their faces as his words sank in. I was watching them too, checking if there was any recruit who glanced—or refused to glance—at Rai in a significant manner.

"Me and Sergeants Singh and Awojobi—we're the only ones who know the power armor's missing. If it's returned intact, nothing needs to be said. Rai's disappearance lasted less than twenty-four hours, so if a few of you could come up with a reasonable story, there's no need for an official report. What else happens to her . . . is up to you."

The recruits began to speak softly among themselves. They didn't look reassured. "Why should we lie for her?" I made an effort and recognized the speaker as Trey Maslin, an older recruit, older than me. "Doesn't that get more of us in trouble?"

Ken spoke up. "We're already in trouble, Maz, all of us. You've heard about the missing bio-bombs and the CPF soldiers who died because of it. Do you want us to send Rai to be executed?"

I added my bit. "We have to be our own justice. The Accordance doesn't care about human lives."

Maslin laughed humorlessly. "Does it matter if Rai is killed here and now instead of in space months after? We know about the executions, but we've also seen the casualty lists. Is there a difference? Weren't you sending us to be executed anyway?"

His quiet, intense words carried easily throughout the

group, inspiring murmurs of agreement. Devlin began to say something but stammered and stopped. I felt sorry for him. It hadn't even crossed his mind that the recruits might not want to protect their own.

"You should listen to Captain Hart," I said, an edge to my voice. "He made sure no one got left behind on Titan, and that wasn't easy. He's asking you to try to do the same for each other, that's all."

Maslin locked eyes with me, and I didn't like what I saw there. He wasn't impressionable and naïve, and he was letting me know it. "I understand Captain Hart's importance, and yours too." He waved at both me and Ken. "You're not just CPF propaganda. You're a message to humans from the Accordance, and we get it. We really do. Doesn't matter if you want peaceful protest, rebellion, or collaboration," he said, pointing to Devlin, me, and Ken in turn. "Doesn't matter. You end up serving the Accordance regardless."

My blood chilled with fury. I couldn't trust myself to move even as much as a turn of the head, but I could see Devlin's stricken face and hear Ken's sharp exhale, something between pain and laughter. The worst was Rai. She looked at us with pity and nothing more, not even a hint of contempt or anger or fear.

Another voice broke the tension.

"We don't hate you. You're trying to stay alive, and right now you have a good chance at it. Go on. Do what you have to. But we're going to do the same."

More started to speak out, bolder in the masking night.

"The only chance we have for survival is our kids, and their kids."

"Exactly. We're not going to win against them. We've got too many disadvantages. Knowledge, technology. We have to train and prepare generations to come. Maybe they'll make Earth free again."

"I'd rather live, but if I die, at least my CPF pension will pay for my daughter's health and schooling."

"I don't have kids yet, but I left my eggs in storage. My family knows what to do with them if I don't come back."

Ken finally exploded. "You're all just going to give up? Put all your hopes into some vague dream that in the future, we might be more than lowest rung? What about right here, right now?"

We all turned and stared at him—son of collaborators, model CPF soldier, decorated officer—while he ranted as if possessed. When silence finally returned, there was an awkward pause, and then Mal said sadly, "It's gonna be a long game, Sergeant. We thought you knew that."

"Time's ticking," I murmured to Devlin. "Let's wrap this up before emotions get out of hand."

Devlin nodded and raised his voice. "Right! You want Rai to face consequences? Okay. We can make it a lesser charge. Failure to report for duty or something. She never left base grounds, so that's no lie. The power armor, that's our call, and we've decided we're not reporting it."

"No!"

Devlin opened his mouth to reprimand the recruit for the interruption, but a cascade of dissent drowned out his attempt to speak.

"This isn't a battlefield. It won't be that easy to cover up." "You can't maverick your way through this and hope for a medal if your dumb luck holds out!" "We are being watched. They'll know. They always know." "If you won't follow the rules, they'll just replace you with someone who will."

Devlin and Ken moved quickly among the recruits, trying

to bring back silence and order. Rai was laughing quietly beside me. "You see, this is how it starts. Give it a few more decades and we'll be fully tamed, but for now, a little culling of cowardice may be in order."

I know I meant to reply to her. I'm sure I had something biting and insightful in mind. I wish I could remember what I said.

It's not like in the old movies, where the grenade falls in slow motion before unleashing blooming carnage. In real life the grenade falls as it falls, and you're the one stuck in slow motion, scrambling to move through thickened air with lead-booted feet. Somehow, in spite of all that, you're convinced you'll find that burst of superhuman speed needed to swat it away or dive behind something solid. You remember to start screaming at least, so that the pressure doesn't take your ears. You shield your eyes reflexively; they are doubly vulnerable to changes in pressure and impact of debris. If only you had been closer, faster . . . nothing would have worked, nothing could have been quick enough. But even if you had been, it's not a grenade or any kind of explosive you've ever seen. It's a small, flat disc, like a poker chip, easily hidden in the power armor's gauntlet. Rai flicks the device away from you and into the thick of the audience of recruits.

There will be some lost time, some ragged memories around the event. There will always be a lost moment between the curving arc of the disc and the taste of blood in your mouth, the smell of blood in the air, and the slow, dragging sensation of your own body, full length on the ground, uncoordinated and unconnected to your dazed brain.

"Ken! Devlin! Ken!" I couldn't hear myself at first. I struggled into a half crouch and stumbled to the nearest tree.

Its solidity was comforting and it gave me a place to lean as I checked myself over. Stunned but not hurt. Armor intact. Cannon still in place over my shoulder. I straightened up and tried to look around. Dust and smoke clouded everything, but I could see an armor-suited figure lying a few feet away. It definitely wasn't Rai. The stolen suit of power armor was sprawled nearby, open and empty.

The armored figure shifted and cursed in a voice that I could recognize even through the muffled ringing in my ears. Ken. My vision and my wits were returning. That distinctive heat signature moving about in the smoke, that was another power armor suit—Devlin, alive and cursing over the public channel. At least he'd managed to get his helmet up in time.

I crawled over to Ken and helped him sit up while I engaged my own helmet and opened a channel to base. "Biomech. Emergency. Multiple trauma . . . deaths. On my coordinates. Expedite."

A familiar and unwelcome sound cleared my head instantly—the percussion of small-arms fire, the sizzle and crunch of smoke grenades, all of it coming closer. Ken put his helmet up immediately, and we leaned on each other as we scrambled to our feet.

"We're under attack!" I yelled. "Take cover!"

I stretched my senses and sensors, and looked around frantically. The rapidly clearing smoke was becoming less of a factor, but no matter how carefully I scanned, what I saw was unbelievable. There was no advancing line, no armored cart arriving or hopper descending to account for the new combatants appearing from the northeast. They came out of the earth via access hatches. I snatched a moment to check my old and new schematics for the tunnels built by Ship 503 and the dikes constructed by the Arvani. The two webs did not match, but I made a wild guess. Arvani builders had scrapped and salvaged the tunnels of Ship 503 to become the service and maintenance conduits of their system of viewing dikes. It appeared that the survivors of the Ship had retained enough knowledge to turn that to their advantage.

Even IR vision couldn't cut this smoke, but I still got a good glimpse of them. The freedom fighters had manufactured their own armor. It wasn't powered and it didn't have the bulk and solidity of CPF infantry build. This looked like a new and improved version of something the Ships created to defeat the Arvani on their own ground—an amphibious suit designed for stealth, speed, and agility. Its black, drag-reducing skin gleamed in the starlight in alternating, irregular stripes of matte and low glow, and the wide-eyed goggles made the helmet look insectoid. It was as if we'd been invaded by a clutch of aliens from old-time movies.

Ken groaned. "Look! The Arvani!"

The dikes in the middistance suddenly blazed with enhanced bioluminescence, turning our once-sheltered spot into an arena. Arvani were already on the ground in mobile water tanks and power armor, chasing after the humans who had emerged from their realm.

Devlin hailed us over the private channel. "Amira, Ken, protect the recruits. I'm going to head off the invaders."

"Which ones, the Arvani or the humans?" Ken shouted.

I unslung my cannon, pointed it at some armored figures, and fired repeatedly. I was going to take them both out, eight legs and two, and let base security sort out the rest.

I did not see Rai, and trust me, I looked for her.

Five of the recruits were killed instantly; two more died of their injuries minutes later in all the mayhem. There had been about six human guerrillas, no more, who made enough noise and cloud and diversion to extract Rai and leave. The Arvani created a bigger mess by rushing out and charging everything that looked human, which included us, the recruits that could still stand, and the contingent of base security that turned up for round two. Maslin was one of the few who escaped the explosion with only scratches, but he picked up a bad leg break when a couple of civilian Arvani in their water tanks bulldozed randomly through the melee. Finally, base communications got through to Arvani security, who corralled and removed their gung-ho civilian colleagues. The injured were evacuated, the dead were carried away, and by the first light of dawn, there was only scorched and blood-soaked earth.

Four power armor suits were returned to storage. Captain Devlin Hart reported that we had accompanied Second Lieutenant Jonse and Second Platoon Charlie-C on a midnight "morale run." Unfortunately, we ended up in the wrong place at the wrong time when anti-Accordance agitators fled the dikes and tunnels they'd infiltrated, with Arvani civilians and security following in hot pursuit. Unarmed recruits were injured in the clash, with the majority of deaths caused by an explosive device of unknown origin. Recruit Mawusi Rai was missing, presumed captured by the anti-Accordance group. Briefings with base security, communications, and IT revealed that an unspecified tech failure in a section of the perimeter enabled the group to evade capture. Investigations were continuing. Cosigned by Sergeants Singh and Awojobi. The end.

The honor guard saluted as Colonel Anais and General Gerrard disembarked from their hopper, one hour behind schedule. The parade ground was packed: Alpha and Bravo Company present and accounted for, and a slightly ersatz Charlie Company with its spaces filled in by civilian personnel dressed in recruit uniforms. Anais's orders. There was to be no evidence of trouble.

Ken and I stood with the other instructors and senior admin officers lining the main entryway. Anais gave me a brief glare and nod as he passed with the General at his side and Devlin miserably in tow. The General himself was short, round, and looked twice as miserable as Devlin. Then again, if he came bearing more casualty lists, he had reason.

That was it. They went directly into Anais's office, leaving Devlin outside the door. We'd busted our butts for a two-minute showpiece. I should have been glad that Charlie-C hadn't faced closer inspection, but instead I was mad at the utter lack of recognition that something terrible had happened.

"Fucking PR," I grumbled as we dispersed.

Breakfast in the mess hall was a nightmare. Arvani packed the observation glass in a solid, intimidating mass of tentacles and eyes, surpassing the worst of my Manhattan memories. They didn't need to be there. For every Arvani pressed up against the glass like a curious child, there were tens, hundreds, or thousands watching footage of our movements from the comfort of their ocean dwellings. The Arvani were always watching but, like my Granddad said, sometimes they wanted us to know we were being watched.

No one lingered. Ken went first, muttering about needing to check on something in Communications. Devlin and I left soon after. The feeling of constant surveillance persisted even away from the mess hall. Part of that was because it was true, but another part was the presence of the visiting general. An ordinary stroll down the corridor became something to be done with straighter spine and a snappier step. We had become used to carefully self-censoring our conversations, but the weight of the night's events was too much for casual chatter. That weight only grew as I saw something disquieting: Private Jasen Russo walking down an adjacent corridor, flanked by two military police officers and carefully avoiding eye contact with anyone.

"Devlin—" I began.

"Not now. Anais told me to come to his office after breakfast."

I frowned at his brusque tone, but I followed him to Anais's office. The secretary informed us that the Colonel was (fortunately) still busy with General Gerrard and would send for Captain Hart later. We made ourselves scarce before "later" somehow became "now."

"Good. Now I have a few minutes and we need to talk privately," Devlin said.

"My quarters, then," I replied.

The door barely had time to close before Devlin exploded. "Didn't you search her?" he demanded. "Why didn't you search her? How did she get a grenade past you of all people?"

"Right, my mistake," I shot back as I turned away and yanked open my locker. My EPC-1 was in my grab-and-go bag with some clothes and other emergency gear. "And whose idea was it to bring thirty unarmed recruits to the party?"

The door opened again—we flinched, but it was only Ken. "Guys," he warned. "You can still be overheard the old-fashioned way."

I tried to speak calmly. "Rai's gone, but I can find her. I've got a lead—but I won't be able to do much if I stay here."

Devlin's eyes widened as I pulled my bag strap over one shoulder. "You are not going to pull your AWOL shit now. Not after what just happened."

I shook my head at his stubbornness. "We don't have time to dance with Anais and CPF regulations, Devlin. Rai's trail is getting colder."

Exhaustion and stress cracked his voice. "You can't lone-wolf this one, Amira. When are you going to realize that you're part of a team?"

I groaned. He was trying to guilt me, as if I wasn't feeling guilty enough. "Devlin, this isn't the time."

"Bullshit. You think I don't know what you've been doing since we got stuck out here? You're trying to reach your old networks. You've given up on the CPF."

"That's not true," I snapped. "Anais wants to downplay the base security breach. Well, I'm helping. If he asks, tell him I'm investigating."

"No. I'm ordering you not to leave. We work on this together."

"Excuse me?" I said. "Did you just say you're ordering me?"

"People died, Amira, people under our command—"

"Devlin," Ken interrupted Devlin's rant. "Let her go."

We both stared at him.

"I just heard that the Arvani investigation of the breach traced stolen security codes back to our IT department. I'm not sure who really did it, but . . . there's been a confession."

"Jasen," I said.

Ken nodded.

I dropped on the nearest bed and dragged my hands over my tired eyes. "Shit."

"He's covering for his people," Devlin said with sober respect.

"Of course he is." I hammered my fist on the bed. "Dammit! He won't even get CPF justice. The Arvani will take him and execute him."

Ken sat beside me. "That explains why they were so many gawkers today. Hoping to catch our reactions when we got the news."

"Devlin, I've got to find Rai. If anyone has to be executed, I want it to be her. Talk to Anais, tell him Jasen's just a bootlegger. Make him stall."

Devlin raised his eyebrows. "I'll try, but . . . are you sure? If you take down Rai, won't that make enemies of your old friends?"

"They're not friends if they're walking in with bombs."

"Point," Ken said.

Devlin twitched at the tap of a summons. "Anais wants me. I've got to go. Amira . . ." He paused, shook his head, and left without another word.

I blinked, also startled by a message tap. JP—I'd almost forgotten about her, but she hadn't forgotten me.

meet me in New Jacksonville

The message was rushed in content but solidly layered in encryption. I was as cautious with my reply. *Why?*

come and see for Jasen not for Rai

Explain. My counterdemand was met with silence. Ken was staring at me.

I stood up. "I'm going on a recce. I may be some time."

6

Getting out was easy, too easy, thanks to Anais's insistence that the base maintain a veneer of normality during the general's stay. I flashed a two-day leave pass at the guard and got waved through the gate. Makani drove me to the train station and wished me all the best, and that was as much rebellion as she could manage. Although there had been no other arrests after Jasen's confession, IT staff was still under scrutiny and she knew not to stray too far from base.

New Jacksonville was a dangerously confusing place. It was an anomaly, an unplanned modern city packed beyond capacity with the displaced masses who fled north and west after the Arvani flooded most of Florida. Major roads were fairly reliable, but temporary shelters and their access roads came and went as the transient population moved in and then moved on. There was no way to tell where JP was, except to ask.

I'm here, in New Jacksonville. Where are you? Where should I meet you?

Silence. Time to implement Plan B. I turned in place in front of the station, staring, looking lost.

"Miss! Do you want a guide, miss?"

Seven seconds. Not bad, but I'd been faster to the mark in my day. I looked at the boy—no, not a boy, a girl dressed as a boy but not yet comfortable in the costume of big boots, long shorts, and pirate-style embroidered headscarf. "How long have you been in New Jacksonville?"

Wide eyes, wide smile, big lie. "Three years, miss. I know how to get around. Can I carry your bag?"

"No. It's too heavy for you. I need a hostel and a tech shop. Nothing too pricey, I'm not made of credit. How much and what currency?"

The child squinted at me, turning the grin from friendly to fiendish. "Tech shop organizes my credit. See?"

She showed me a nano-ink logo on the back of her hand. I nodded slowly, approving. It was a recognized brand. "Okay. Let's go to the tech shop first."

We walked for a few minutes away from the station along an alley, and then stepped out onto the sidewalk of a busy city street. I stayed in character as naïve traveler, gawking and stopping occasionally. The place was a mess. Not like how New York or Washington DC was a mess—part bombed out, part taken over by alien structures—but in that unique mess that humans make when settled meets nomadic in awkward truce. Mid-rise buildings in the traditional stone, brick, and concrete were extended and linked with platforms of wood and tarp. Some of the tarp was solar-capable and more. I looked more closely at the girl's headscarf, and noticed with all my senses the various shawls, capes and wraps so popular among the pedestrians. New Jacksonville folk wore their tech and their wealth in fabric threaded with golden circuitry. It wasn't uncommon tech, but I'd never seen so many in one place before. Still, it made sense—if you're constantly on the run, you don't want tech you have to stop and grab. That's why I have nano-ink.

The tech shop was located in a clean, midsized building with no auxiliary structures, no squatters, no beggars. Very respectable. They could probably afford to pay for protection and maintenance. The owner was a big man who wore pants and T-shirt in mismatched blacks, a pale purple head wrap, and a brown logo-stamped wristlet with an input interface. He was predictably cautious and not at all brimming with the milk of customer service. "Got any ID?" he asked gruffly. He was staring at a cluster of screens on his wall. They appeared to be security-camera views of the area, and I gave another thought to the crime rate.

"What kind do you take?" I asked.

He looked at me, at my hair actually, and looked away again. "You a CPF groupie?"

My surprise was unfeigned. "Groupie?"

He waved a hand. "Purple hair, like that sergeant. Fashionable, even when it's not the real thing."

"I don't groupie," I said. "What kind of ID do you take?"

"DNA, nano-ink logo, chip. No cards, no papers, no plastic."

I had the CPF enlistment logo, but I wasn't about to use that. I took a risk. "DNA."

At last I became more interesting to him than the screens. He took out a lancet from his wristlet and pressed the STERILIZE button. I nodded when I saw the steam and presented my right hand. He ignored the outstretched palm and jabbed it into the side of my elbow. I hissed but didn't complain. People could secrete pouches of foreign blood in the expected places—fingertips, palms, inner elbow. He checked the result, resterilized, and repeated the process with my right earlobe and below my left collarbone to confirm. There was no double take. There are many Amira Singhs in the world, and I'm sure he never learned the name of that purple-haired sergeant who occasionally showed up in Devlin Hart news clips.

"So, what do you want, Singh?" he asked.

"Communications and news access, the usual channels."

He typed my details into the wristlet, but I caught the assessing glance at my nano-ink, and the silent "yeah right" in his slight smile and eye roll.

"I like to start small in a new place. Shows respect." My tone made it clear that I didn't owe him an explanation, but I was willing to have this casual, neighborly chat.

He nodded in agreement, his gaze still on his wristlet, finished his typing, and handed over a datachip. "You're set. Did Tica guide you all right?"

"Yeah." I looked over at the child, who was leaning on the wall just inside the door, watching the street, probably looking for marks. "She's taking me to a hostel next."

He raised his voice. "Hey, Tica. Show her the Gator Raid." He briefly caught my eye. "Lots of your kind there," he added more quietly.

My kind? Soldiers? Nano-inkers? Sneaks? "Thanks," I said aloud. Then, as I left the shop and followed Tica, it finally clicked: Aggregator Aid. When Accordance tech became the standard, a lot of human service providers and innovators in IT hit rock bottom fast and hard. The Aggregator Aid Association emerged in response—half union, half social club. In some cities, membership was open with IT types in the minority. Interesting that the New Jacksonville one was true to its roots.

Just how true came as a bit of a shock. Tica brought me right into the lobby of the hostel, confirmed my credit deposit by messaging her boss, took an additional credit tip from the concierge because why not, and skipped off without any goodbyes. I looked around the lobby warily. There were just a few people, two or three groups sitting and standing and talking together, but they made me wonder, Is this place a convent? Music and radio DJ patter blared from the corners of the room, suggesting that no, this was not a convent in spite of what appeared to be an exclusively female clientele.

"Yes dear," the concierge prompted, trying to return my wandering attention to her and her desk.

"Uh . . . yes. Can I . . . stay here?" I asked.

Her gaze flitted to the nano-ink on my face and arms. I noticed she even glanced down at my right leg, well covered in thick twill, as if she could see the tattoo there above the knee. "Yes dear, you can stay here. Do you wish to?"

I looked around the lobby again. Older women, mostly. Black shining hair worn in a long single braid. The long wrap, subtly but densely embroidered with tech. Their outfits were varied, but I couldn't shake the sense of some uniformity, as if they'd all grown up in the same neighborhood . . . or institution. I spared a quick, cynical thought that in this case "my kind" meant "of Indian appearance."

"Sorry," I said brightly to the concierge. "Yes. Yes, I would like to stay here. Not sure how long yet."

"Well, let's put you down for a week, and we'll see what happens after that," she said. "Do I register you as Amira Singh or as Sergeant Amira Singh?"

I did a quick revision of the situation. There were suddenly too many eyes turned toward me, too many curious and assessing looks. "Amira Singh," I said firmly to the concierge, ignoring everyone else.

Or trying to. My peripheral vision caught the moment when the silent staring turned to whispering and staring. The concierge merely smiled and blinked rapidly as she processed some invisible information. "I've put you in room 5B with Lia Chaudry and Karina Wilmer. Second floor. You share bathroom facilities with 6B."

As she spoke, I received information packets: directions to 5B, the rules of the hostel, and my invoice for a week's stay. I nodded in thanks and began to walk in the direction of the stairs when the concierge added, "Sorry, dear. You need to pay in advance to get your door code if you're not backed by a corporation or institution. Of course, if you're here as part of the CPF . . ."

I didn't bother to turn around. I stopped and sent the signal to release the credit to the hostel. The invoice instantly updated with a code attached. I kept walking. The room was near the stairs, which I appreciated, and neither Chaudry nor Wilmer were visible, although the privacy screen around the third bed was sealed shut. I passed the unmade bed in the middle of the room and dumped my bag on the bed by the window. I fell next to the bag with a big sigh and closed my eyes.

Sneaking through the networks is easiest when you have another network to work from. The tourist access purchased from the tech shop gave me a decent entry point, but something told me to stay cautious. The first thing I noticed was the privacy screen in the room. Professional-grade, good enough for any sex worker or establishment. Strange to see that level of screening in a hostel. Then I paid attention to the formal networks. Accordance throughout, of course, and as basic as could be expected of a civilian network in a minor city of mostly transients. New York was different. The networks were as solid as the buildings, the surveillance as constant as the threat of anti-Accordance forces and, if I were to imagine the worst, Conglomerate as well.

The informal networks of New Jacksonville were another matter altogether.

I've discovered nooks and niches, hidden places carved out from existing structures and shielded by the normal. I've stumbled over dead spots of unusual silence, light shining through unstopped cracks, static and frequencies appearing and disappearing for no good reason. New Jacksonville was hiding in plain sight as a mosaic of independent micronetworks flashing in and out of existence, shorter than the lifespan of a trace. The natural result of having thousands of semilegal personal networks making brief connections to other personal networks, or something more significant? And there was still no reply from JP.

"Hi."

I got my feet off the bed and under me, moving from prone to standing in a second or two. The speaker backed off nervously until I sat down, then approached again with an outstretched hand.

"I didn't realize you were sleeping. Sorry."

"S'okay. Hi." I shook her hand and glanced past her. The privacy screen on the other side of the room was gone, revealing a neatly made bed, but the middle bed was still unmade. "Amira Singh. You're Wilmer?"

She nodded. She was a lot younger than the regulars. Short hair, no wrap, jeans, and singlet.

"Where's good to eat around here that won't drain my credit?"

She shrugged. "There's a couple of food trucks in the neighborhood that aren't too bad."

I nodded.

"You're in the CPF?" she asked. Her voice had that stressed, hurried sound of suppressed hope.

I grew instantly cautious. "Was. Why?"

She looked down. "My brother got conscripted months ago. I haven't heard from him in weeks."

"CPF doesn't just let go of its conscripts. Have you asked them? He should be in the records. Unless you . . . can't ask them, because you were a conscript too."

She met my eyes again. The soft, shy persona was no more. "Some of us can't dance between loyalties as well as you can, Amira Singh. So, can you help me contact him?"

I frowned. The EPC-1 hidden in my bag was not my only weapon. I pulled my hair out of its ponytail and settled the hair tie around the knuckles of my right hand while idly finger-combing my hair with my left. "That's not a priority for me right now, especially if he doesn't want to be contacted. Have you considered that?"

"There's always a risk of indoctrination. That's why I can't abandon him."

"I dance between loyalties, remember? Are you sure it's safe to ask me?"

"Of course not, but the key word is 'loyalty.' You're known to have a sense of honor. I can offer you something, and if you decide the transaction is worth it, you'll follow through. You always do."

I flexed my hand under the hair tie and tried to smile. "This is a test."

Her smirk said "of course."

"I'm sick of tests. Last one got a lot of people killed, and I'm almost sure that wasn't due to any failure on my part. Do you really have a brother? Were you ever in the CPF?"

“Yes, I was in the CPF. Yes, I have a brother. Yes, it wasn’t your fault.”

I raised my eyebrows. She shrugged apologetically. “We’re not a monolith. We can’t control wildcards.”

“Where’s your wildcard now?” I said with quiet anger. “I can take care of that for you.”

She blinked as if startled, but not by my words. “Later,” she said briefly. She vaulted past me, over my bed, and through the open window. I moved after her as quickly as I could, but I was only in time to see her catch hold of the edge of an adjacent sill and swing to the nearest bit of temporary scaffolding. I took a moment to admire her technique, and also sniff at her use of grip shoes as she scrambled down the poles to the street and took off.

The door opened. I spun around on my bed. Two women came in carrying grease-darkened bags that smelled of sugar, salt, and heaven. They looked surprised to see me and were about to speak, but then my stomach growled, and they laughed. I wasn’t in the mood to laugh yet, but I grinned.

“Hi, I’m Amira. I’m guessing . . . you’re Lia Chaudry?”

It was a guess, but the older one looked most like the regulars with her single braid and embroidered wrap. She nodded and waved a hand at her friend. “Yes, and this is Karina Wilmer. Glad to meet you, Amira.”

I smiled at them. “Glad to meet you both.”

7

"I need a little ink maintenance. Can you recommend a place?"

Tech shop owner guy, who I now knew as Ted, thought for a short while. "The Gator girls should be able to help you out."

"The Gator girls, as you well know, are of old-fashioned corporate stock. They're not hackers or sneaks. I'm not going to upset them by asking them to service my semilegal tats."

I wasn't being facetious. In a few days, they'd made me family, or tried. I'd gotten used to being approached with a new query and a new name. "Are you sure you're not related to Danielle Singh who worked with TLMax Inc on their intel-data project with the fourth-gen geosats?" "No ma'am, never heard of her." "What about Nadira Singh? She was project manager on the last lunar mission before the Occupation. We started as programmers in VYN-8." "No ma'am. I don't believe any of my family were programmers."

Not exactly a lie. We had been trained to compete with programmers, not follow their rules. But at the hostel I followed the rules, kept Bugkiller locked up and hidden in my bag, and wrapped my hair in an ordinary dark-purple scarf. It had no embroidery, no tech, and no other purpose but to hide my hair and make me blend in with all the other scarves and wraps of New Jacksonville.

Ted gave me a worried look. "Semilegal? You mean non-standard tats?"

"I'm looking for an artist," I said vaguely. "Someone who doesn't work in just the corporate or government areas."

His look morphed from worry to vague suspicion, but at last he gave me the contact for "a friend of a friend," and off I went to a seedier side of town. I would get to the ink artist . . . eventually. My real goal was to walk about in some of the areas where the informal network felt most dense and organized. I had to push and hope that something or someone pushed back. I couldn't let myself get distracted with thoughts of Jasen, but I felt stalled and frustrated. Three days after my arrival and there was still no hint of JP's whereabouts, and the strange CPF conscript-deserter hadn't bothered to return with her transaction offer.

I went in lazy on purpose, probing noisily and making sure that anyone with a decent sneak level could hear me coming. The result was the same physically as virtually. People skirted my presence, which only made me madder. I'd come to New Jacksonville with hands up and waving, and no one could be bothered to detain me. Was the Singh name worth nothing now, or had the CPF taint permanently destroyed any chance I had at getting back into my old world? I arrived at the recommended place disgruntled and at a loss. The location was in a proper back alley, half-camouflaged by the fabric sheltering several stalls and carts along the road. The room was empty except for an assistant grooving in a bubble of personal sound as he did some tool maintenance, and the inker himself working on a piece of lab-grown hide stretched on a small easel. He could have been related to Ted—big with muscle turning slowly to fat, a preference for black clothes and bright headscarves, and a suspicious nature that made it difficult for him to make eye contact with strangers until he was sure they were clients.

"What do you need done?" he asked, setting down his stylus and addressing the tats on my left arm.

I raised said arm. "Got some scratches. They may have messed up the connections a bit. Think you can mend it?"

He glanced at me very briefly, then went back to staring at my arm. "These are old."

"Yeah," I confirmed. "I was fighting with something that didn't want to be caught. Healing wasn't a problem, but there's been a 20 percent drop in processing speed."

"Why didn't you use an extra dose of scar suppressant?"

"Couldn't. You know the risks." The suppressant stopped the immune system from rejecting nano-ink as foreign, but post-dose, there was an increased probability of developing cancer in that area.

He took out some tools and scanners and had a proper look at the left tats, and compared them to the right tats to be sure. He shook his head. "This is well within the parameters of normal healing. You don't need me for this."

"Well," I said slowly, "there's also the ink on my leg."

He quirked an eyebrow with weary cynicism. "You don't say. Care to show that to me?"

I undid my pants and dropped them so he could see the palm-sized design above my right knee. He didn't flinch, bless him.

"You've had this a while," he noted. "It's grown with you."

I took a second, more objective look at it. The skin was

slightly raised along each line of ink, but I couldn't see exactly what he was talking about.

"Nonstandard ink costs extra to touch up,'" he mused. "Twice the amount stated on my price list. Also buys my silence, you see."

I hesitated. I wanted to believe I could find Rai and get back to Orlando with no delays or problems, but if not, there would come a time when the CPF stopped paying me. "Maybe later," I said, and put my pants back on.

The assistant collapsed his sound bubble and gave me a strange look, part curiosity, part smugness. I immediately reassessed the threat level. Still just two of them. I edged closer to the door, casual but confident. I didn't stumble, but I did blink when I passed my eyes over the hide in the easel and it sunk in that I was not looking at artificial hide, nor art in progress, but a segment of human skin from which the ink was being slowly separated and unraveled.

Noises came from the street outside. I looked out the door and saw carts and canopies being packed up and moved out at speed. I took a deep breath, preparing to run. Not out, certainly not past the four enforcer types who were now entering the cul-de-sac. I quickly scrambled up a fence, hauled myself onto a roof overhang, and took a short leap from that roof to a nearby second-floor balcony. Lovely decorative bricks edged the building's corners, and I gratefully stepped down them as easily as if they'd been a ladder. There was a cool, shady place under an awning, and I stopped there to stare at the shop window and watched the reflection of the people on the street. It was busy enough to feel safe and clear enough that I wasn't hemmed in.

"Well, are you going to buy something or not?" said a voice testily. A tall, grim-faced woman leaned in the doorway of the store, watching me as if I might break the glass and scamper off with her merchandise.

I focused on the items in the window for the first time. Solar panel textiles, navigation tools and survival kits, everything your modern refugee could desire. "Yeah. You got a nano-ink stylus?"

The woman glared at me. "We don't encourage tats here."

"Okay," I said mildly. I walked away, shaking my head in disbelief.

I returned to the hostel. The concierge greeted me cheerfully and I tried to respond in kind, but she saw my slump and invited me to sit for a moment. I chose a solid, overstuffed chair with back and arms as thick as battlements and let myself brood. In minutes I heard a delicate rattle, and there on a side table was a cup of fragrant Darjeeling, kindly placed there by the concierge. I picked it up with a grateful smile and drank as she made small talk and looked at me with an auntie's concern.

"You know," she said, "my job is not just to help newcomers to the hostel. I also help newcomers to the city. What are you looking for, Amira Singh? If you let me know, I may be able to help."

I put down the half-empty cup. "I can tell you what I wasn't looking for. A sanctuary of retired programmers. Stigmatized nano-ink and ink artists of dubious reputation who collaborate with skinsnatchers. A thin, basic communications network which hasn't granted me so much as a single message, and a rich, shifting, multilayered informal network which I can see but not touch."

"Oh, that does sound frustrating," she agreed, smiling. Smiling, in fact, at my appalled expression and instinctive recoil from the liquid remaining in the cup.

"Don't worry. You'll be a little suggestible, nothing more. You are so very guarded, Amira Singh, and this is a respectable establishment with no place for violent confrontations or illegal tech activities. This is the best way."

"Who are you with?" I mumbled, trying and failing to feel the danger this woman presented.

"Amira, this is New Jacksonville. No one is really 'with' anyone. We define ourselves by who we are not with. For example, the CPF, the government—"

"The Ships?" I guessed wildly.

She laughed softly. "Oh, there are all manner of ships and boats and dinghies about. But no admirals. We are not very fond of admirals."

"Can't have a fleet without an admiral," I mused.

"Exactly so. However, unlike the freedom fighters and demonstrators, we do not draw attention to ourselves and the Accordance does not pay attention to us."

I tried to move, to raise my voice, to have any kind of normal reaction to the conversation. I hated that we were in a public area with people going in and out, and I looked like I was merely having a friendly chat over tea instead of being interrogated against my will.

"What about your rogue dinghies? What about people like Mawusi Rai?"

She pressed her lips together briefly before speaking. "There will always be people who want to fight, or protest, or play soldier, or turn traitor. They become outsiders, able to see but not touch."

"I just want Rai," I confessed. "Do whatever you want in your own time and your own way. I'm not here on CPF business. This is personal. I'm trying to save a friend's life."

She gazed at me with teary eyes. I had never felt more

unnerved in my life by the weight of so much pity. "Amira Singh. I'm sorry. You have a reputation for honor, but so do we. Remember that."

A new presence moved at the edge of my field of vision. I thought I could turn my head, just like I could get up and walk away any time I wanted to . . . but I didn't want to.

"What have you done to her?" JP said.

"What the hell took you so long?" I whispered.

"I need her to come with me. Can she walk?" JP continued, ignoring me.

"Of course," said the concierge. "Just tell her to follow you, but mind you don't take advantage."

JP sighed. "Come with me, Singh."

I stood up. I was steady on my feet, but my will was detached from my body. JP looked me over anxiously, then silently questioned the concierge with a worried glance. "Come," she said again, and stepped slowly toward the door, watching me. I matched her pace and we went by tentative degrees out of the hostel and into a waiting car. JP spoke quietly to the driver and then settled back, not so much ignoring me as avoiding me.

My will was still scattered, but my brain was working. The city center had public transportation along the main roads, and people used hoverboards, scooters, and plain walking for the alleys and tracks. A car meant a location outside of the center, where the old roads still made sense and the suburbs, though cramped, were not yet chaotic.

The car turned into the driveway of a residence. Large grounds, small bungalow—strange, as if the owner had intended to build a mansion but was sidetracked by the tiny detail of alien occupation of Earth. In fact, that was probably exactly what had happened. The driver left us at the front door and disappeared into the dusk. JP took my arm and pulled me inside. I leaned against the wall and blinked slowly as the lights came up to show a living room with bare walls and empty floors.

"Where are we, and why did you take so long?" I asked again. In my head I was screaming demands, but my voice stayed even and unconcerned.

"I got delayed," she said angrily. "I'm sorry, Amira."

That was the second person to tell me sorry in less than an hour. My sense of detachment began to fade. "Why?"

"Jasen is dead. They executed him the day after you left. They've been interrogating IT, Procurement, Transport—it's a mess right now."

"Devlin and Ken. Didn't they tell Anais to wait?" I was trying to yell, but I wasn't there yet.

JP scoffed. "Trust me, this is far, far beyond Anais. Don't waste time blaming him or your friends. The Arvani wanted blood and they got it."

"Standard procedure," I said sadly. My emotions were reconnecting.

"What?" JP was startled, probably surprised that I was finally shedding the zombie state.

"Standard procedure for the Ships. There's always a designated scapegoat to take the fall and move suspicion away from the majority."

JP watched me as I spoke, her hand over her mouth. She drew it away and said, "But Jasen didn't belong to a Ship."

"Doesn't matter. It's a principle of collective survival. Anyone who'd read my grandfather's writings would know about it."

"That's right."

I faced the direction of the new voice. A man with close-cut, graying hair and untidy stubble stood in the darkened doorway leading from the living room. His black silk shirt and black wool suit were both expensive and worn, hinting at past prosperity. I extended the theory of the grounds and bungalow to the person. Probably a billionaire before the Occupation who'd opted for a quiet retirement in a modest hideout rather than rail against the new world order.

"Amira. You don't remember me."

I came closer, frowning. He smiled and waved his hand. I saw the scars like raised welts, signs of nano-ink removed from skin under less than ideal circumstances.

"Not that I expect you to. I met you when you were very little, a few months before I left New York for good. I knew your grandfather. He made quite an impression on me. My name is Alessandro Russo."

"Aren't you hot?' I asked foolishly, not yet recovered from that damn Darjeeling.

He rolled his shoulders under his suit jacket, which had clearly been made when his back had been broader. "I have a . . . condition. I feel the cold easily, even in Florida. Or perhaps I can't let go of the good old days."

His eyes . . . I did recognize those eyes. The Russo family, where the bosses wore all black when on business. "Russo. Jasen was your son?"

"I have no sons," he corrected with a haste that had some emotion behind it that I could not identify. "But yes, Jasen was family."

"Mister Russo wanted to see you," JP mumbled almost guiltily. "Can we go now, sir?"

He gave her a sharp look. "No. Not yet. Amira, I swear on my honor, you may consider this a place of sanctuary. Trust me. There are things you must know."

JP's expression was not reassuring. The guilt was there, but there was also fear—not fear of our present situation, but fear of what I was about to learn. Pure curiosity woke up the last drugged bit of my willpower.

"Lead the way, Mister Russo. I have no reason to trust you, but honor is the only currency we have these days."

He smiled in approval. Then he turned to go into the darkness of the inner house, and I almost choked on my own breath. Tubes and wires ran from the back of the black jacket and trailed along the floor to some unknown connection.

JP watched my reaction impassively. "Go on, Singh. Don't falter now. I know you've seen worse."

8

JP was right. I had seen worse. There were sneaks who grew so absorbed in their work, so convinced that it was essential, that they constructed elaborate cyber-support systems to enable them to work faster and longer. At least Russo could still walk and talk, and his body hadn't atrophied much. I knew many cautionary tales of sneaks discovered and cut loose from their life support, unable to scream, unable to run. Then there were those who were hidden too well and died when their power and nutrient feeds ran out because their caretakers had fled or been killed. A few tried out mobile tank designs like the common Arvani style, but the best sneaks were real-life con artists, escape artists, and runners who'd never let a tube or wire tie them down.

Russo's system filled a room. He had the usual: blood filter, brainwave regulator, nutrient intake and waste outflow, temperature and humidity controls. What was unusual was the presence of additional communications tech. Russo wasn't simply tapping into the existing networks, formal or informal. He had created his own.

"I admired your grandfather immensely," Russo said as he settled into his specialized recliner. It didn't look comfortable, but he claimed it like a throne. "He never let age hold him back. I've been working since I was sixteen. Always wanted to get to the point where golfing and cruises were all I had to worry about, but then the Accordance happened and I had to do something. Fortunately, I had a secret, a useful secret. I had ten clones."

"Ten?" I exclaimed. "Full, functional, illegal clones, not just templates for organs and limbs? What would you be doing with ten clones?"

He smirked, laughing at himself. "Taking on a very expensive bet."

I glanced at JP, begging her silently to confirm that he was insane, but she just shrugged. She'd likely heard the story before.

"I was in Japan, working with colleagues on some international business that turned out very well for all involved. At the concluding celebrations, I got a bit drunk with three high-ranking reps, one Ukrainian, one Irish, one Namibian. We had that age-old debate on nature versus nurture because we were all of us either third or fourth generation in the business. At first it was a bet that, if we each had five random clones raised outside of the family influence, they'd still find their way into our line of work. Then it was a bet that if we kept the influence but fostered the clones in different countries, we'd have a cultural and linguist asset in the family. We went away and sobered up and didn't think about it until the next morning, when the boss of the Japanese syndicate sent each of us a little gift certificate to the top genetics clinic in the hemisphere and a single sentence on the back. 'I dare you.'"

He laughed outright. "I don't know what they dared, but I took my maximum of ten clones and found surrogate mothers and foster families for them in all the key locations. London. Moscow. Lagos. Rome. Los Angeles. Mexico City. Shanghai. Delhi. São Paolo. Tokyo. I figured I'd meet them when they reached eighteen and skim the sinners from the saints."

He grew serious again. "But they reached eighteen in the Year of the Accordance, and everyone's priorities changed. The families, firms, and syndicates found it hard to adjust. Some of my old friends became rebels, some collaborators. A few retired, one killed himself. I went in a completely different direction."

He gestured to another machine. It was unfamiliar, but I was reminded of the easel I'd seen in the inker's studio. Here it was a bank of frames suspended in fluid, and each frame held a section of densely tattooed skin.

JP faced me and spoke almost pleadingly. "This wasn't my idea. Jasen insisted, and Biomech helped with the operation. All I did was arrange delivery."

"Are you saying . . ." My voice failed.

"Yeah. Jasen's computer."

Russo spoke softly, almost kindly. "It's still very experimental, but there is some fascinating research into the extension of human cognition from the individual to the collective via shared nano-ink access. It always worked best with twins. Clones, of course, are as good as twins. I've lost four so far: one to illness, one in an accident, one in battle . . . and one—Jasen—to execution. It hurts, of course, but I've found it's less disruptive when I save the ink from the terminated clone and keep it functioning in the system."

I stared at the four frames. "You cannot be serious."

He looked wistful. "You know what I realized? It's not the crime. It's the risk. It's the small details. It's the information, the thrill of knowing stuff and putting it all together to gain an edge. That's my nature. That's what my clones do, some legally, some illegally. Although I can't say what 'legal' means anymore now that the Accordance is the law."

I heard him, but I couldn't focus on the sense of his words. I felt cold. Scraps of inked skin suspended in biotech frames—why? There were a few rare inks that might be worth stripping from skin once the owner was done with them, but that was a day's work, if so much. Data stored was easily retrievable, so why keep the skin? What artificial intelligence, what shadow-personality could remain in those densely inked patterns?

"Jasen was prepared for this. He doesn't want to you blame yourself." Russo looked at me as kindly as any undertaker, a man acquainted with death, with half-life, with imperfect immortality.

"JP, get me out of here." Perhaps it was the tea getting in a last kick, perhaps it was Russo's use of the present tense, but my stomach was churning.

JP moved quickly, which made me grateful. She grabbed my arm and guided me out. Russo kept to his chair and watched us with a tired smile. "We'll meet again, Amira. You'll know."

Outside was dark, warm, and humid. I braced myself against a pillar of the patio gate, breathed deeply, and forced the sickness down and away.

"Sorry," JP whispered. "I didn't have time to prepare you."

"You work for him?" I asked, my voice wavering between disbelief and disgust.

"Of course not, but he gets the good info. He's so rich, you can't pay him for it. He'll only share it if he likes you. Now he likes you. Use that when you can."

I closed my eyes. If Russo had been some random ex-mobster and not the clone parent of a dead friend, I might have taken it better, but at that moment all I wanted was to go back to the hostel, dodge the concierge, grab my stuff, and figure out what to do next.

A faint, low vibration came from the direction of the main gate. "Our ride is here," JP said.

"Our." I knew she wasn't talking about the transport that brought us to Russo. As the vehicle approached I could see it was not a sleek and quiet car for the streets, but a rumbling off-roader. I scanned it thoroughly and what I found made me laugh. The car was almost devoid of tech, like the ones the military used to make before small-scale EMP shielding became viable. However, the driver was wrapped in various kinds of shielding, like a walking data safe.

The jeep came to a stop and the driver leaned out of the window. He wore glasses—smart glasses, of course, made to mimic everything my own eyes could do and more. "JP?" he asked. Stupid. As if he couldn't see well enough in the dark.

I stayed where I was as JP went around to open the passenger door. "Who are you?" I challenged him.

"What?' Either he was genuinely bewildered, or he was faking it well. Given the little play with the night vision, I chose the latter.

"A human Fort Knox rolls up in an antique car and doesn't expect questions? I asked, who are you?"

He rubbed the side of his glasses. "I'm Jin. I'm an accountant. I have bank-level tech security to protect my clients' data. It's not that serious."

"Oh." I hoped I didn't look as drained and foolish as I felt.

I meekly got into the backseat. From where I sat I could see he wore a long black coat, but his T-shirt had a sparkly pink galaxy graphic across the chest. It was neither mob-boss fashion nor geek chic, but it could be an accountant on his day off.

"Want to go get something to eat?" JP suggested, politely avoiding mention of my mini rant.

"Oh, yes please," I said wearily.

Jin and JP picked at appetizers and talked about me as I blazed through steak, buttery baked potato, deep-fried jalapeños, and a large milkshake.

"She's really hungry," Jin muttered.

"She was drugged," JP said. "Then there was the emotional stress from meeting Russo and hearing about Jasen," she added, lowering her voice although she was sitting right across from me.

"She didn't know?" Jin said, raising his brows so high that his glasses slid down his nose a little. He pushed them up with his forefinger. "Didn't she find out from—"

"I'm right here, you know," I complained halfheartedly as I muffled my words in delicious garlic bread.

"Didn't you find out from your colleagues on base?" he asked me directly.

I stopped chewing, considered them both for a second, and took a risk. "I am not in communication with my colleagues on base. What I am doing here is not what you might call an official activity."

Jin smiled and stared at me through his glasses. "Going rogue?"

"No. Not rogue. 'Unofficial' does not mean 'unsanctioned.' For example, wasn't Jasen one of yours?"

He looked away. "I am Mister Russo's client, nothing more."

Did he mean Jasen or Alessandro? Did it matter? I shook off a shudder and continued between mouthfuls. "Don't you mean he's your client? I thought you were an accountant."

"Even accountants need information. We have a mutually beneficial exchange of services."

"That typical New Jacksonville reluctance to state allegiance to anyone or anything," I grumbled under my breath as I stacked food on my fork.

Jin laughed. "Sergeant Singh, you are no better. You're in the CPF, JP tells me you are looking for Orlando's Ship 503, and you come from a famous line of anti-Accordance rebels. Who are you? Who do you work for? Why should anyone trust you?"

I sighed, drank my milkshake, and appealed to JP. "What do you think, JP? Can I be trusted?"

She smiled. "You have honor."

"Honor isn't the same as trust," Jin noted. "Trust means loyalty to people, honor means loyalty to principles. What's your guiding principle, Amira Singh?"

I wiped my mouth with my napkin, folded it slowly, and gave him the full glare of my inked eyes. "Survival. For as many of us as I can manage."

He took off his glasses and returned my stare without a blink. "I can work with that," he said softly. "If you've finished eating, let's go for a walk."

My grandfather preferred to have his most private conversations in wide-open spaces. He loved tree-filled parks with wide paths. He loved the simple efficiency of a hat or an umbrella to screen audiovisual information from even the most dedicated human and artificial spies.

So I understood completely why Jin was inviting me to

stroll with him and JP under the stars in the field adjacent to the restaurant. We spent a few minutes of idle chat in admiring the proprietor's kitchen gardens and greenhouses, then wandered farther from the buildings in comfortable quiet. I observed JP and Jin, saw how they walked in sync together like a captain and his XO. I wasn't surprised when Jin finally spoke.

"My name is Hideo Pereira. I am in charge of Ship 507, successor to the now-defunct 503 of Orlando and 501 of Miami."

"In charge?" I repeated, testing him. "Someone told me recently that the Ships here have no need of admirals."

"Admirals . . ." He made a dismissing noise, half scorn, half amusement. "But accountants? Everyone needs accountants."

A light wind teased the bottom edge of his knee-length coat, and a little flare, a hint of iridescence, caught my eye. I took time to view and analyze the coat's lining—a full tapestry of matte nano-ink on spidersilk—and then I looked him up and down. "Nice threads—very nice. Accountant, my ass. You're a numbers expert!"

He grinned widely. "So, you believe me now?"

"Oh, I never doubted you, sweetheart, but I still need to know who you're working for."

"What. What am I working for." He stepped closer, no longer joking. "I'm working for the movement started by your grandfather, Bismil Singh. The foundation may be a bit shaky, but I think with a little refining, it could work. It might even be great."

"The foundation was the mutual mistrust of New York's mafias," I scoffed.

"Precisely why it was so shaky. But now we have a single identity—us, and a common enemy—them."

"That's astonishingly simple for a numbers guy."

"Sociology is not my specialty," he admitted, "but the stats don't lie and that's what they're telling me."

"Are they also telling you that some of 'them' look like 'us'?"

The intensity of his gaze went from persuasion to calculation. "How much do you know about that?"

I smiled at him, my sweetest smile. "How much should I know, and how much time do you have to waste on being half-honest with me?"

"I'm about to be all honest with you now." He stopped, went off the path, and pulled up a round cover that looked like part manhole cover, part submarine hatch. "The tunnels here are drier than in Orlando, I promise."

JP waved me forward. Jin—or rather Hideo—disappeared into darkness with the faint clanging sound of booted feet on steel ladder rungs. I followed more cautiously, lacking his familiarity with the entrance. JP brought up the rear and closed the hatch behind her. The moment the cover snapped secure, a dim light illuminated the tunnel. Five meters or more of ladder ended in hard-packed earth floor and slightly brighter lighting. It looked like we were in an underground storehouse. They'd become very popular after the Occupation, when people started to hoard goods due the uncertainty of what an Accordance future might mean for humans. They were still popular because hoarding remained common, and they had many additional uses—hiding illegal broadcast studios and tech, hiding fugitives, hiding weapons.

As we came into a larger room, I guessed that they were probably hiding all three. It wasn't just the size of the place. It was the number of people and the purposefulness of their movements. It was the lateness of the hour and the sense that this was just another ordinary work shift in the day's operations for Ship 507. I hadn't seen anything on this scale since the early days of the Manhattan Resistance, and it filled me with both longing and loss.

"I have so much to show you, Amira Singh," said Hideo. "Let's get started."

9

The underground hideout was illuminated with the warm, dim light of a late sunset, so when Hideo handed me a pair of shades, I looked at him strangely. "Precaution," he explained. "I know what eyes like yours can do, and although I'm willing to give you a tour, I'm not willing to give you all our secrets."

"Fair enough," I said, taking them from him and putting them on. They were immediately irritating and disorienting, limiting not only my range of vision but also my connection to the networks. I hid my discomfort and joked, "Did you have these made just for me?"

"We've been watching you for a long time, Amira," Hideo said with a simple directness that made him sound worryingly ordinary.

A short, slender man dressed in worn khaki approached JP with a datacard in hand. "Moreno, the manifest for the priority incoming finally arrived. We need to sit down and plan the next stage."

JP took the card and glanced quickly at us before saying, "Been busy, Slate. Can you give me ten minutes?"

"I think Sergeant Singh won't mind if you leave her with me," Hideo said. "We'll catch up with you later."

Shades regardless, I picked up several things. The use of my full name, a slight fluttering blink from Slate as he took in that new information, JP's mild frown as she took the polite dismissal as . . . well . . . a dismissal, and the unspoken behavior of the entire group which told me that Accountant Hideo was indeed the man in charge, but in a somewhat mad-scientist kind of way. I'd seen it before in the Resistance and after—sometimes people were known and appreciated for getting results, but they worried you because you couldn't guess what they'd do next, and whether or not it would be to your benefit.

JP nodded and turned to go. Slate gave me a small smile before he followed. Hideo took me gently by the arm, steering me in the opposite direction.

"Juanita Pilar Moreno. Gained quite a reputation for ruthless efficiency years ago, but some people fear she's gone soft now. I think she's just a little burnt out. I give her about two months or less before she starts trying to oust me. Of course, I plan to be gone by then. She could run this place better than I can, and I . . . I need to step up a bit."

I questioned him with a look.

"New goals, new scope. Like I said, the Ships could be great, but we need to stretch ourselves more. I've been running the numbers, and I think it's time to—but more of that after you decide if you want to join us."

It was a carefully planned tour, showing just enough strength and structure without revealing everything. He showed me a fleet of ground vehicles very like the one he drove and a couple of stealth hoppers. I glanced at the ceiling, looking for a hidden hatch to the outside air, but the shades defeated me. I stood in a doorway and saw stores of weapons and ammunition, mostly sidearms, sniper rifles, and basic body armor, but so antiquated as to be almost quaint. Then, as I turned to go, I did a double take and noticed changes, adaptations, tweaks. Hideo pressed me onward before I could take a closer look.

It was a respectable accumulation of materiel, but I was sure it was only the tip of the iceberg. Given what I'd seen of Hideo, JP, and Russo, I suspected the real strength in the operation was intelligence, and the rest was for defense only in case of discovery.

Hideo brought me into a glass-walled office positioned in the center of a bustling hall—very mutually panopticon of him. I see you, you see me. He had no desk. A conference table with twelve chairs dominated the middle of the room, and there was a round, low table off to one side bearing a neatly arranged tea set and ringed with four seating cushions. He invited me to be seated on one of the cushions, then settled himself opposite me and started to make tea. I glanced at the walls, wondering if he changed the transparency levels at any time, then choked back a gasp of pure greed when I realized that the middle third of the wall, all around the office, was an input screen like Makani's desk.

"Okay, you wanted me to impress me; I'm impressed. This Ship is obviously operational. Why do you need me at all?"

Hideo smiled. "Bismil Singh's granddaughter—"

"I'm sure you don't need a figurehead," I interrupted him, "so don't waste our time."

He raised his hands. "Figurehead, no, but people respond to a symbol. Don't tell me you've never used your name to get ahead."

"It can also make you a target," I replied, thinking of my

parents. "It can make you try too hard and risk too much to deal with all the hopes people invest in you."

"True, but you didn't let me finish. Bismil Singh's granddaughter, former member of the Resistance, now sergeant—more or less—in the CPF, has an enviable portfolio. Amira, you have fought on several fronts now: urban centers on Earth, alien and human networks, moons and asteroids and deep space. We need your experience. The Resistance must create a fleet of space-based Ships."

"Why?" I demanded. "Who are you planning to fight? Accordance? Conglomeration?"

"That's step two, Sergeant. The point is, you won't even have a chance to fight if you can't get into the ring." He placed a cup in front of me. "Supplies are so disrupted these days, unless it's something the Accordance can use, of course, but this is the best green tea available. It doesn't compare to my pre-Accordance childhood memories, but does anything?"

"You're trying to duplicate the Icarus Corps. That's only going to create more conflict."

"Duplicate? Are you really comparing our Ships to the space arm of the CPF?"

"You said it yourself, it's as simple as us and them. Where do you put the CPF in that equation?"

Hideo leaned back a bit and drank his tea in temporary retreat. "It was easier," he said finally, "when the CPF was mostly collaborators. Now they have martyrs, lots of martyrs, and a few key heroes. I'm sure I don't need to tell you what strong symbols those are."

Heroes. I thought of Devlin, often screwing up the small things but coming through when it really mattered, principled and loyal, honor and trust together. I missed him, and I wondered whether I could find the same kind of team bond with Hideo and JP that I'd found with him and Ken.

"So, Amira, it comes down to this. Humans must be in space. Will you bet on the Icarus Corps, or on the Resistance?" He pushed away his cup and stood up. "I'll even help you decide."

He went to that massive ribbon of tech that I envied so much and tapped a panel to life. A familiar face appeared. "Slate, this is Hideo. Put Rai on my channel."

The panel switched view so quickly that I missed whether Slate had reacted at all to the request. I saw a small, brightly lit room, empty of furniture, with Mawusi Rai sitting cross-legged on the padded floor. She appeared unhurt and at ease. I felt my jaw tighten.

"Symbols aren't hard to find, Amira. Rai is another descendant of famous leaders. Her grandfather was Mehmed Rai, founder of Ship 9, and her mother was Kira Andrushko of the Black Sea Syndicate, which provided a lot of support to the Resistance in the early days before the full blockade. Rai did indeed try too hard and risk too much, and no one would blame me if I handed her over to you. I won't, but I doubt I could stop you if you really wanted to take her in."

"Not another test," I growled.

"A test, a trap, or an opportunity. Most of all, a way back into the CPF's good graces—success covers a multitude of sins. Or, if you prefer, have your own personal revenge on Rai and take her place in my team."

"Either way, I'd be in debt to you," I noted.

He shrugged as if to say, That's your problem.

I took off the shades, folded them neatly, and placed them next to my cup. "I think it's time for me to leave, Hideo Pereira. Thank you for your hospitality."

"Here," he said, tossing me something. I caught it on reflex, and the hard metal of a car key on a key ring stung my hand.

“Take the jeep back to the hostel. It doesn’t have built-in nav, but I doubt you need it.”

“Thanks. Uh . . . how do I get out?”

Hideo put his hands behind his back and gave me a very sarcastic smile.

I shook my head. “Fine. I’ll be in touch.”

I never get lost. I followed the internal map that my tech traced as Hideo was showing me around. No one tried to stop me, and when I went up the ladder, the hatch cracked open when I was within two rungs of it. I scrambled through, closed it, and after a pause, I gave it a tug. Locked down, of course. Would I be able to find it in the dark again? I looked at it carefully, expanding the spectrum to see if there was any excess heat, any unusual radiation. Then I saw it, invisible to the unaided eye, luminescent in the ultraviolet—a thumb-sized emblem stamped into the hatch, which at first glance looked like a triangle set in a circle, but which I knew from experience to be the sail of a ship on a segment of ocean in a ring of rope. No—not rope. A ring of chain.

I walked back through the fields and past the restaurant’s gardens and greenhouses. The parking lot was almost empty. I went to the jeep and started it up. Hideo didn’t even ask if I could drive a car without autopilot or cruise control. I can, but it’s not that common these days.

I was quite sure that he knew everything about me. That’s why I decided that out of the two options he was offering, I would choose—neither.

The drive back was quiet and incident-free. I braced myself to face the concierge, but she wasn’t there. The desk sported a cheerful sign next to an old brass bell, inviting latecomers to ring for help checking in. I resisted giving it a spiteful flick as I passed, and went straight to my room. One roommate was already in bed, tucked in and motionless. I quietly checked Bugkiller, repacked my bag and secured it, then took a deep breath.

"You're not asleep, Mrs. Chaudry," I said softly. "I can tell."

She sat up. I could faintly see her reproachful frown in the darkness.

"What?" I grumbled. My head felt heavy. I blamed the concierge and her tea.

"Yesterday, a man grabbed me, demanding to know about you." She held out her arm, bruised below the elbow. "We stay here to be safe. If you are doing something dangerous or illegal, you should leave."

"I am leaving." I shifted my vision to a broader spectrum to see her face more clearly . . . and something caught my eye. A scarf lay across Karina Wilmer's bed. It had the usual embedded tech, no surprises there, but it also had a bright ultraviolet logo. Not the 507 logo, but a similar type—a dhow with a single wind-filled sail ringed with pearls.

I took a wild guess. "I'd leave a lot faster if you'd help me with something."

"I don't see how—"

"You have skills. I bet you could help me break into a Ship stronghold and extract a prisoner."

"Why would I do that?"

"Because I still work for the CPF. Because you value your safety. And because you had someone waiting to test me the moment I walked through that door. What's her name, really?"

Silence, then, "Wilmer. Jody Wilmer. She's related to Karina." A small, proud smile. "She talks in riddles, but she rarely lies."

"And you all belong to another Ship. I'm guessing . . . 98, based in Charlotte? Just passing through New Jacksonville?"

"Not really."

Still cautious. I didn't blame her. "Do you know what Ship 507 is planning? Do you agree with them?"

"I don't know the details. We all know how the recruits died, but I don't think they meant to do that."

"No one will believe that if they don't hand over the person who did it. Not the CPF. Not the Accordance. They'll target all the Ships."

She breathed shakily. "What do you want me to do?"

I slung my bag over my shoulder and stood in front of her. "Get Wilmer into 507. She looks like the adventurous type. Let her make some noise, stir up some trouble, then get her out. I'll take care of the rest. Tell her she can reach me with this." I handed her one of my old business cards, comm tech embedded in paper.

"Where are you going?" she asked as I turned away.

"To find a place to sleep. I don't feel safe here."

Nowhere was safe, really, so I did the only sensible thing. I went back to 507, did a little sneaking to get in through another entrance, and slept in the backseat of one of the five hundred jeeps parked and waiting for the revolution.

10

I woke up with a stiff neck to a sharp tapping on the window. It was Wilmer the younger, looking far too relaxed for a covert operation. I wound down the glass and glared at her.

"Well, I'm here," she said.

"I can see that. Let's be clear—what do you expect to get out of this?"

She grinned. "I already told you. Find my brother. Take a message back from me."

"I can try. What else do you want if I can't deliver on that?"

She finally sobered. "Remember Ship 98 helped you. We had to lie dormant for a few years, but when the time comes, put in a good word for us."

"Deal." We shook hands. I took up my bag and got out. The muzzle of the EPC-1 poked out of the top and I paused to adjust the flap over it.

"What are you going to do with that?" Wilmer asked with a tiny hint of "are you crazy" in her tone.

"Wide beam takes out crickets. Narrow beam takes out surveillance tech. Narrow beam needs more aiming accuracy but also has a remote firing option. I'm guessing you took your own precautions or else you wouldn't be standing here chatting."

She pointed to her jacket. "Bulletproof and more. And there's this." She showed me a stun gun. I was relieved. I didn't want collateral damage.

"Good. Your target is being held in a padded cell three levels down. That's an educated guess, by the way, so if I'm wrong or she's been moved, be adaptable. Open the door for her and get out of her way fast. Don't look back."

"Aren't you coming with me?" Wilmer now sounded a little worried. Not accustomed to solo action?

"I have my own target," I replied.

We parted ways and I made for the panopticon office. It was still early, predawn time, and I had calculated that before sunup and after sundown were the likeliest times for Hideo to come in to his second job. I crossed the near-empty hall boldly, walking like a guest rather than an intruder. I could clearly see the signature long black coat moving about in the office during the entire fifteen seconds it took me to cross open space. I stood before the door, and another twenty seconds passed before it opened. Hideo faced me, and the screens behind him fuzzed and flickered.

"Sergeant Singh. I thought from the unusual static that you were on your way to take out Rai, one way or another."

I shrugged. "I'll catch up with Rai later. Right now, you're coming with me."

His mouth twisted in vexation. "JP was right. She said you'd rather be owed than be in debt to anyone. Ah well, that's why we prepare for all eventualities."

"That's one thing we can agree on," I said as I unleashed a microburst from Bugkiller.

Five of the screens grayed out completely. Hideo staggered and the hem of his coat began to smolder. There was a clatter of running and JP, Slate, and five armed security regulars appeared at the office. It was too late; I already had a knife at Hideo's throat.

"You were right, JP," he said cheerfully as he squirmed between the sharpness of the blade and the strength of my hold.

"Didn't want to be," she answered, her eyes regretful as she regarded me. "Amira, just go. Rai's gone, but she won't be hard to find. Let's end it here."

"Hideo's a bigger fish, wouldn't you say? Lots of information and lots of ambition."

JP signaled for a lowering of weapons and raised her arms in surrender to me. "Let's bargain. What do you want?"

"As you said, I can pick up Rai anytime. What I really want is you running this Ship quietly without competing with the CPF, and Hideo with me learning to be useful in less dramatic ways. That's a win for you, I'd say."

"Okay." She nodded, more considering than agreeing. "What about—"

I'll never know what she was going to propose, because just then I got hit with a dart in the hip. I looked at it in alarm as I felt my legs go slack. I clutched Hideo as I fell; the knife sketched a faint red line down his neck and arm.

"Didn't know you had it in you, Rai." That was JP's voice, slightly envious, slightly sarcastic.

My nemesis came into my field of view long enough to stare into my eyes, not gloating but assessing. I watched as she kneeled and pulled out the dart. The pain was a shock. While she still crouched over me, Hideo bent close to her ear and murmured, "This changes nothing, Mawusi. The numbers don't lie." Whatever the phrase meant, it turned her expression from confidence to sorrow.

Hideo straightened up. "I need my tools. She's knocked out some of our security shielding with this." His body shifted as he nudged my bagged EPC-1 with his toe. "Can't risk the CPF tracking down their transponder."

Hands lifted me and placed me on the conference table. I twitched but failed to raise a limb. "Hold her," said Hideo, and the hands pressed me down. A faint reflection in the glass ceiling showed him setting a metal tube to my arm, right against the CPF tattoo over my deltoid. I gave a choked scream as the device ripped the transponder out of my skin. Someone held out a metal bowl; Hideo dropped it in with a ping and wiped the blood from his gloved fingertips with a slight sneer of disgust.

"Get rid of that," he said. "JP, secure the Ship. Find Singh's accomplice. I'll watch over the sergeant."

The room cleared and the sound of footsteps faded into the distance. Hideo frowned at me, not in anger, but as if I was a problem he hadn't had time or data to properly assess.

"You didn't have to take it out," I slurred. "That only makes it worse. You should have disabled it. Simple procedure for someone with your processing power."

He looked away, picked up an inking stylus and scrutinized me again. He traced the tip of the stylus down below the freshly bleeding tattoo, over the nano-ink that coiled around my arms. "You'll thank me someday. I've discovered that this kind of tech is more of a liability than an asset. Do you think you could learn to do without it?"

"Get myself a long coat like yours?"

He smiled. "Maybe. But first, a little pain."

I tried to hit him. He caught my sluggish arm midswing

and said firmly, "I'm going to temporarily restrain you because you do not want me distracted during this operation."

"No, wait." I had nothing to bargain with. "Don't be stupid. If you torture me, I'll tell you pigs fly if that's what I think you want to hear."

He stared in surprise. "Do you really think I'm such a fool as to interrogate so inefficiently? Here's your first lesson, Amira. A human with the right amount of tech is like a computer that can never shut off. I don't have to ask you a thing when I can plug straight into your circuits and download your memories."

I'd been trained to bear a certain amount of pain, but Hideo's linkup hit me like a nasty mix of sleep deprivation and poorly maintained tech. Dreaming in reverse. Hallucinating to order. It was a nauseating violation of will and intelligence that made the physical ties around my wrists and ankles a mere detail of indignity and the probes in my arm tats a simple itch.

I lost track of time and then of the sequence of time. I saw JP, but she was in the deserted office of that Orlando warehouse, in the hostel, in the streets—no, that was a younger image of her, not a memory but some fragment of information from Jasen that had been filed under "later." I tried to break out of it and wake up, but memory blurred with reality and I couldn't trust anything. I thought I was in a hospital bed with diagnostic lines plugged into my body, then I recognized it as the time my arm got broken on the Moon during Icarus training—Devlin's fault, but that was old history. I transitioned to a new scene: sitting in a chair, no lines and no probes, but with bands uncomfortably snug around my wrists, making some new connection to my nano-ink. I was still in the glass office. Hideo stood on the other side of the room, tablet in hand and several lit screens before him. He looked over his shoulder at me, and I was angry, first angry at Devlin for being a child and not a soldier, then angry at Hideo for trapping me in a space where past emotions sliced as sharp as present feelings.

I heard JP's voice, firm and reproachful. "She needs to sleep."

Hideo answered, "Don't worry, I won't damage her, but there's so much! Her memories of her grandfather . . . those alone would keep me occupied for months!"

"She'll never work with us now," JP said.

Hideo made a tutting noise. "Amira Singh is not known for holding grudges when the stakes are high—and they are very high."

"You've crossed a line, Hideo," JP warned. "You're becoming what you fight against. She won't hold a grudge, but she finds you lacking, you're dead to her."

He sighed. "I'll end it soon, I promise."

JP laughed sarcastically. "It might already be too late."

The memories changed direction drastically. Hideo chose to indulge his pet passion and pulled up every possible reference and encounter with my grandfather. I was embarrassed at how much I had forgotten. Many times he had talked to me not as if I were a child, but a confessional, or a diary, or a living excuse to hear his innermost thoughts spoken aloud and made real. Even in the midst of the crushing torrent that Hideo drew from me, certain words stood out and stayed with me, fresh with new context and adult comprehension.

After a meeting with the fractious alliance with mafia leaders, he said to me, "I have approached this situation as if we were facing one enemy, perhaps two. What if I am wrong? What if there is a third enemy, in plain sight, where we refuse to see them?"

It had been a prophetic statement. Manhattan fell to the Accordance not because the Resistance was weak, or the mafias untrustworthy. It fell because the UN Headquarters was locked into the siege. A coalition of diplomats from collaborating countries signed a treaty with the Accordance, deeding their portion of Manhattan property to the alien invaders. It was surprising how much of Manhattan was foreign-owned. The recapture of Manhattan by the Accordance was completely legal by both international and galactic law.

The last time I saw him, he was contemplating martyrdom. He had made the arrangements for his family to escape. I was to leave with my parents for another city and start over. But he would not come. I begged him like a child to forget about being a symbol and come with us. He tried to explain, and his words were more for my parents than for me.

"A dishonorable enemy will always give the double insult. They will rape you, then call you a slut; rob you, then call you a beggar; work you to exhaustion, then call you lazy; scar your body and mind, then call you ugly. An enemy with honor fights hard, kills clean, and remembers your name with respect.

"If you must lose, arrange as best you can to lose to an enemy with honor. War is a little less terrible when honor is mutual. If that becomes impossible, then leave a message in your death for those who will come after you."

I fought against the bands, hating Hideo again for intruding and digging up fossil pain. My grandfather had tried to prepare us all long before the Occupation. There were family legends of cousins and siblings sent out to prove themselves for a year with zero credit and no safety net, not even change for a call to beg to come back home. Most came back, but some didn't, perhaps on purpose. He hadn't been a kind man—fair, yes, but driven in ways that few could understand. Other family rumors spoke of a childhood on the streets, an earlier family lost with his first fortune. They never said how. Murder by rivals was extreme yet possible. A fed-up wife returning to her in-laws with the children was more likely. I never found out. But it made him create a family ethos that only made sense after the Occupation. Otherwise, we might have been labeled dysfunctional and abused. We would have been pitied. Instead, there was a man dancing through my life's experiences, pretending for a moment that he had been born a Singh of the line of Bismil Singh.

The world changed again, as if granting me respite, and I found myself in the Speakeasy, sitting at a table with Ken and Devlin. Ken was examining my wrists, which were bleeding, and Devlin was leaning sideways into my personal space. "Are you all right? Amira?" he kept saying worriedly. "Are you all right?"

"My God, stop asking me that and get me a drink," I snarled at him.

They looked at each other, baffled, and then back at me in concern. I blinked, and the Speakeasy faded away. I was sitting on a white floor, leaning against a white wall, in a place I'd seen before on a screen. I refocused on Ken and Devlin and realized they were neither dressed in uniform nor seated in chairs, but crouched down beside me in power armor with helmets retracted. Ken had an MP9 hanging slack from his shoulder and Devlin held another wavering at half-readiness as he covered the door.

"No. No no no no. Are you really here? Why are you here?"

"You called us," Ken said. "And you should have called us sooner! Look at you!"

"Why would I do that? This is the last place you should be!"

Ken gently picked me up. "Let's get you out of here first."

"I can walk!" I lied angrily. I was weak and dehydrated. The strongest part of me was my voice. I definitely wasn't thinking straight, but I knew something was deeply wrong. "Go without me! Get out now!"

Devlin set his MP9 to his shoulder and put his helmet up. It slowed, stuck halfway, then subsided back into the collar of the suit. "What the hell?" he said, just as Ken swore.

"Suit malfunction," he said, shaking a leg that had a strangely frozen knee joint.

"Quick, give me your weapon," I ordered.

"What?" Ken said, but he started obediently moving the gun from his shoulder. "No, wait . . . what the hell?"

I watched his elbow lock in place. "Bastard! It's too late. I'm sorry. If I called you here, I'm sorry."

The door opened to reveal Hideo in his long coat, JP and Slate in the casual khakis that functioned as Ship uniform, and Rai similarly dressed and very subdued. I figured out from the cursing in stereo from Ken and Devlin that both suits of power armor had locked up fully.

"I would have let the sergeant call you earlier, but it took me a few days to figure out how to expand and improve on her training-suit overrides." As he spoke, he helped me down from Ken's immobile arms and stepped away. My legs gave way and I slumped to the ground. None of them moved to help me up.

"So, JP, I have all of Sergeant Singh's experience and information without relying on her to willingly join us on our terms. Hmm?"

JP nodded in grudging acknowledgement, but her look to me was apologetic.

"And Rai, I have two fully operational suits of power armor and, which is even more important, zero casualties. Mm-hm?"

Rai nodded and swallowed. She looked terrified, and I wondered if she regretted not taking advantage of that brief window for escape I had given her.

Hideo wasn't finished. "And you will notice that in addition to my achieving both of your goals, I have also managed to reach mine earlier than scheduled—the capture of the three heroes of the CPF."

"Capture isn't keeping," Devlin threatened through clenched teeth.

"True," said Hideo. He spread his hands and the armor cracked open. Ken and Devlin half-fell, half-stepped out and immediately rushed to grab me and brace me upright between them.

"You're free to go. You're free to return." Hideo smiled. "But if you try to leave New Jacksonville, you might find that a little difficult. After all, the city is mine."

PART TWO

11

"What are you looking at?" Ken asked, coming to stand beside me.

I shook my head. "Nothing."

It was a half lie. I was staring down at the street from the second-floor window of our new accommodations. The street was a solid, permanent line of fresh paving, part of the original infrastructure. They could have had us hidden away, but they didn't need to. By putting us in plain view, they increased the number of spies that could tell on our movements. I watched people passing by, knowing now to check beyond the visible spectrum. Almost every other headscarf and wrap bore the 507 stamp of allegiance. Once, the sight would have filled me with joy. Now, under house arrest and unsure of the future, I couldn't even concentrate long enough to come up with a single escape plan.

"I really messed up," I said quietly.

Ken rubbed my shoulder soothingly, and I was so depressed that I let him. "It's not over," he said.

I gave him a glare. "I hope you're preparing your excuses

for Anais. Make it my fault. He always felt I would lead you two astray."

"We're not going to do that, Amira," Devlin said.

I turned around. He walked into the room with his hands full of . . . stuff. Wires and transistors and bits and pieces that looked like they'd come from a museum. I examined them as he spread them out on the small dining table.

"Interesting hobby. How long have you been building these?"

He grinned. "Since I learned how to steal the materials."

I turned my back on the window and came closer. Radio was vintage, niche, a toy for children and an obsession for a few committed adults. I'd never had time to play with old tech when all my hours were spent keeping up with the new. "Is this going to help us get out of here?"

"It might. Ken told me that the CPF inherited a large chunk of radio bandwidth from the old, pre-Accordance armed forces." He nodded to Ken to continue.

"We don't use it because our communications tech is much more efficient now, but it's still there, and it's still monitored. Your Ship colleagues have blocked us from the networks, but they won't expect this."

I tried to ignore the sting when he blandly said "your Ship colleagues" and addressed Devlin instead. "Do you have everything you need?"

"Yeah." Devlin squinted doubtfully at the scrap metal on the table. "I think so."

Footsteps sounded on the wooden stairs; someone was coming up from the streetside entrance. Devlin quickly whipped the four corners of the tablecloth up and around his science project and slid the whole bundle under the couch. Only three people walked freely into the townhouse like that—Hideo and JP, of course, and on one nervous occasion, the concierge from the hostel paid us a visit to hand over my mail. I'd scanned her from head to toe and found no mark of allegiance at all, which I found confusing. The mail, or rather her excuse to visit, consisted of my invoice from the hostel and a brief note from Lia Chaudry. The note tersely informed me that Wilmer was fine, they had both left New Jacksonville, and I was not to attempt further contact with them unless they indicated otherwise.

"Good afternoon," Hideo said cheerfully as he came in, much like Devlin had, with laden hands. "I got Southern this time. I hope you don't mind lots of fried starch."

He set the takeaway food containers down on the coffee table in front of the couch. Then he stepped back almost shyly. "The food's safe. Seals intact, nothing tampered with." He swept out an arm to show off the room. "House is clean of bugs, as you already know, Amira. Sorry that I didn't tell you about the shielding."

"It's fine," I said coldly. "I only used a small pulse. It didn't hurt much."

"Yes, and notice how I gave you back your favorite weapon, your . . . Bugkiller." His tone went judgmental for a second, then promptly dialed back to friendly. "You should use the jeep I gave you. I've parked it below; keys are in the ignition."

Ken leaned against the wall and folded his arms. "Could we use it to drive back to Orlando?" he asked sarcastically.

Hideo flashed him a brief apologetic smile and shook his head, then faced me soberly again. "The point is, we are not enemies. We are still us and they are still them. I understand you're not happy with me—hell, JP's furious with me right now—but that doesn't mean we can't look to see where our interests align."

Devlin spoke up, his voice resonant with suppressed rage. "You kidnapped Amira, tortured her, lured us here, and stole our armor, but somehow you think our interests might align?"

Hideo walked up to him and stopped within arm's length, demonstrating a fine balance between showing respect and showing no fear. "Captain Hart, I believe that we take after our parents more than we care to admit. I admire your dedication to human life, which I am sure you learned from your father, Thomas Hart. I admire Amira's tenacity and I would expect nothing less of the granddaughter of Bismil Singh." He looked over his shoulder at Ken for a moment. "You I'm still not sure about, but you're consistent, and that makes you refreshingly predictable." He returned his gaze to Devlin, insistent, persuasive. "All of you have done your best to preserve humanity, however your methods may have varied. I hope one day you can begin to see me in the same light."

Devlin didn't quite relax, but he exhaled slightly, and with that cue Hideo nodded and turned away to focus on me. "We still have much to talk about. JP insists I make amends with you, and I know the only way I can do that is to show you the method in my madness."

"Later," I growled. "I still feel like killing you."

He raised his hands and retreated a couple of steps. "Fair enough. Until the next time."

Ken pushed his point. "But seriously, we've been blocked from the train station, cut off from the networks, and shut in. You expect me to believe you'll let us get in that jeep and just drive about as we please?"

Hideo sighed. "Well, there might be a small tracking function in our jeeps and you might find yourselves slightly herded if you try to go somewhere you should not go, but apart from that you are free to move about. Don't abuse my hospitality."

He dipped his head in farewell and left. We waited for the retreating footsteps and the closing of the door.

"Let's test him," Ken said. "Bring the food—it's picnic time."

"I was hoping you'd say that," Devlin said, kneeling to retrieve his tablecloth-full of archaic tech.

"Of course. Don't you know I'm refreshingly predictable?"

Devlin and I exchanged a slightly scared look at Ken's deceptively gentle tone.

"Hideo knows how to get into people's heads," I warned Ken. "Don't let him get to you."

Ken gave me a look of utter exasperation. "We've been stuck here for two days. Can't I have a little rant?" He paused and said morosely, "I know I'll go down in history as a sell-out. I just hope I can live long enough to do something big enough to change that."

"Whoa, whoa, whoa, enough of this 'live long enough' talk," Devlin said, pushing his hands out as if pushing away the idea of Ken dying. "Let's get out and enjoy some fresh air and food."

We headed north, away from Orlando. I drove out of the confusing tangle of the city center and let Ken take over. He brought us to the edge of the suburbs and then handed over to Devlin, who had the least driving experience out of all of us. Devlin was nervy and overcautious at first, but then he began to get cocky, and the journey grew loud with shouted advice, cursing, and the sudden screech of tires. Ken saved us all by noticing "the perfect picnic spot"—an overgrown lawn in front of an abandoned house. We settled ourselves, cracked the seals on our food, found it still warm and delicious, and demolished it.

"I'm so glad you guys are here," I admitted. "I stretched myself too thin, and I've been out of the game for too long. I should never have gone in without a proper backup plan."

Devlin shot me a look that was pleased, embarrassed, and guilty all at once. Ken's face was amused and smug. "Yes, you shouldn't have. Goodness know where we'd be if we all went running off without a backup plan. Right, Devlin?"

"Shut up," he mumbled. "So, what Ken is trying to say is that he reminded me of the importance of backup before I went sprinting off to save you."

"In his defense, your SOS was a little terrifying," Ken said.

"Still not sure that was me," I said defensively.

"It probably wasn't," Devlin agreed. "I haven't been able to contact base at all. I even tried Anais."

"In Communications, New Jacksonville has a reputation for being a bit of a mess," Ken said. "Unregulated, but not openly lawless. I don't think anyone realized how much was going on beneath the surface."

"Tell me about backup," I insisted.

"Cleland—he's in Comms—was monitoring our power armor. He'll at least be able to report where and when we were captured. I'm not sure if we can count on Anais to send help. He's been very good at sweeping bad news under the rug. So we told Boone to look for us unofficially if that happened, set up our own encryption/decryption protocol and everything."

"That's where the radio comes in. We can build a transmitter and send a nice loud burst in the direction of Orlando. Cleland should be able to pick it up and then we use the jeep's radio to listen for a reply."

"A nice loud burst that Hideo can also pick up." I scoffed.

"Not until it's too late," Devlin said. "The point is, he can't stop what he doesn't expect. And if we move quickly, he can't even prove it was us."

I was silent for a moment. Hideo had proven to be pretty good at expecting all possibilities. "We can try," I said finally.

"I need a couple more days to finish the transmitter, steal an extra battery or two to boost the signal, and scout out locations for the best reception," Devlin said, ticking points off finger by finger.

"Don't we need an antenna?" I asked, imagining a massive steel tower.

Ken nodded to the jeep. "You're looking at it."

"Hmm," I said. I needed to learn the basics of radio so I could stop wasting time on stupid questions.

Our secret science project shaped the days nicely. We went out driving for lunch, always north, always during the day, doing our best to show we could be trusted while clandestinely plotting escape. Devlin's driving improved. Ken taught me what he knew about radio and pointed me to resources for more information. I told them about Jasen's secret life as a spy and a clone. Ken had guessed the first after conversations with Boone, but the clone bit was a shock to both of them. I filled in the rest of the story with Russo in his creepy life-support and data chamber, six living clones scattered about the world and four frames of dead clone tattoos. Jaws went slack. They were genuinely speechless.

Ken recovered first. "Boone didn't know about that, I'm sure of it."

"You and Boone friends now?" I asked cheerfully.

"We found a middle ground," Ken replied with caution.

Devlin took charge of the construction and working of the transmitter. Ken handled the calculations—frequencies, range, power, geography. When they went off into a technical discussion, I was able to follow them, but I preferred to make myself useful browsing the span of the frequency dial on the intact radio in our borrowed jeep. Much of it was silent, as expected, but sometimes intriguing spikes of static would scrape through. I made a note whenever that happened.

At one stage, Ken left Devlin to work solo and turned his attention to my receiving radio. When he was finished, I had more bandwidth and much better reception. I soon found an intermittent hum and warble on the low end of my new scale. A sense of familiarity nagged me. The pattern—and I was sure it was a pattern—plucked an old string of memory.

"You all right, Amira?" Ken asked.

I was doing what I rarely do, projecting information onto a monochrome object in my visual field for a quick and easy read. My eyes would have been twitching rapidly; my face would have been slack as if I was falling asleep. I didn't blame Ken for checking on my welfare.

"Yes," I murmured. "I'm fine."

I tried to find the source of the hum but was only able to narrow it to the entirety of the urban center of New Jacksonville. I felt a click of recognition.

"Guys," I said. "What if the military aren't the only ones interested in all that empty bandwidth?"

Ken frowned and came closer. "I'm listening."

"Listen to this." I removed my earphones and turned up the volume so they could both hear what I was hearing.

Devlin nodded. "Doesn't sound random."

"How long have you been hearing it?" Ken asked me.

"I found it about thirty minutes ago, and I haven't heard it stop yet—" I froze, mouth open, eyes twitching.

"Amira!" Devlin shouted.

"Be quiet! I'm comparing something. I have to be sure. . . . No. . . . This isn't possible."

"What is it, Amira?" Ken asked, speaking calmly.

"Ghost sign," I said miserably. "There's ghost sign transmitting out of New Jacksonville."

"Where?" Ken and Devlin spoke at the same time.

"Everywhere," I said. "All over."

Devlin started to pack up. "You think they've infiltrated the 507?"

"Don't know. I'm sure Hideo doesn't know. I've got to tell him."

Ken put a hand on my shoulder and made me look him in the eye. "How are you going to tell him without also telling him what we've been doing?"

I blinked and shook my head. "I'll figure it out. We need to know for sure what's going on in New Jacksonville. Devlin, how fast can you get us back without killing us?"

"Plenty fast," he said. "Buckle up."

I spent the entire ride back listening to the radio. The hum grew stronger as we approached the city center, but I couldn't pinpoint a location. The volume and pitch began to fluctuate as we passed some buildings, but when Devlin brushed against a loose awning, the radio shrieked like a banshee.

"Stop the jeep," I shouted. I swung out of the back before he braked fully, and went to touch the awning. People stared at me; I nodded at them with my best eccentric-but-not-dangerous smile and they kept going. Except one.

"Excuse me, miss," I asked the young girl who continued to gawk at me. "Can I borrow your scarf for a moment?"

She frowned at me. "Naw. It's real expensive tech. Took me ages to save up for it."

"No problem. I don't have to touch it. Could you just . . . trail a corner of it over this jeep?"

She gave me a slightly scared, very wary look, but Devlin smiled winningly at her. Still wary, as if expecting a trick, she let the tip drag against the driver's-side door. We all jumped back at the radio's static scream. Ken hurried to turn the volume down.

"Whoa," she said, and did it again. "That's wild."

"Thanks," I said and jumped back into my seat. "Come on, guys. Let's get back inside."

They knew enough not to ask me anything until we were behind the closed doors and safe shielding of our house arrest. "Well?" Ken said.

"Every piece of woven tech, every stitch of fabric in this city is transmitting ghost sign."

"That's . . . a lot," Devlin said with stunned understatement.

"I think it's reading whatever's being processed in the threads. The fabric acts as a transducer and vibrates to send out data at a frequency that can be picked up by a radio receiver at a distance."

"Can they do that to nano-ink tattoos?" Devlin said quickly.

"No!" I replied instantly. It was a horrible thought, and I knew I was reacting emotionally. I made myself calm down and consider it for a little longer. "No. I'm not feeling any buzzing in my skin and I didn't set the radio screamer off, so probably no."

Ken lowered his head, frowning in deep thought. "Devlin, I need your help. We've got to find out everything we can about this new ghost sign and package it in a message for the CPF. That means we have to figure out how to send something more complicated than SOS."

"And I'm going to pay Hideo a visit," I said. They both

looked at me, the same question in their eyes. "Don't worry. I'll tell him about the ghost sign but not the radio. Not until we can get our own message to base."

"Leave the jeep here," Devlin said, and then he winked. "But return with another one if you can."

I grinned. "Will do, Captain."

12

JP met me at the entrance with Slate and two others—a woman and a man who were both taller and broader than me. They all formed up and politely escorted me into 507. "Consider the size of this welcoming party a measure of our respect and an acknowledgment that we have a way to go to earn each other's trust," JP said.

"Noted," I replied. "I have no hard feelings towards you, JP."

"And Hideo?" she asked.

"Some things are more important than trust or hard feelings. I have something to tell Hideo, and I want you to hear it." I turned to Slate. "You're the top Comms and IT man, right? I'm going to need you there, too."

Slate's eyes widened—curiosity, excitement, and something else. I wondered for a moment if he knew what I was going to say, but by then we were already at Hideo's glass office. The two security personnel stationed themselves on either side of the door and the rest of us passed through.

Hideo was already seated at the conference table. He gave

me a rueful look as I seated myself opposite him. "I thought you still wanted to kill me."

"It can wait," I said. "Something came up."

First I told them about the Ghosts. Everyone knew by now about the different types of Conglomerate alien, so I didn't waste time. I only reminded them that Ghosts were the de facto rulers of the Conglomerate, and that they were masters of camouflage, never seen.

They nodded. No surprises yet.

Then I told them what I had learned firsthand during my time in the CPF, information that the Accordance was still suppressing. I told them that I had seen Ghosts, and they were indistinguishable from humans.

Interest all around, but not shock. Hideo leaned forward with a slight smile on his face. His hands clasped together on the table, almost, but not quite, rubbing together in satisfaction. "We heard a few things after Titan . . . mutiny, strange behavior, imposters. Yes, do go on, Sergeant Singh."

Carefully removing any mention of radio, I explained to them about ghost sign. Slate grimaced almost impatiently as I covered what seemed to be old ground for him. I raced to my conclusion. "The Accordance has detectors to scan for ghost sign. I don't need any detectors. I can sense it."

JP sat back and stared at me in dismay. In contrast, Hideo lit up with joy. "You understand! You confess it! I thought I would have to convince you, but this is more than I hoped for—"

"What?" I interrupted quietly, dumbfounded at his reaction. "What are you talking about?"

"You know why the aliens are dangerous, why we have to keep ourselves free of their technology and influence. You've experienced it firsthand."

"No . . . still confused here," I admitted reluctantly. I glanced quickly at Slate—like JP, he had drawn back as if carefully removing himself from the discussion to come.

Hideo took a deep breath, pressed the tips of his steepled fingers to his mouth for a brief moment, then focused intently on me. "How do you sense ghost sign, Sergeant Singh?"

I tried to put it into words, but the best I could manage was a comparison. "It feels like when I'm near someone with military-grade nano-ink. There's a little spillover, a little feedback, but with ghost sign, the patterns are . . . different. Foreign."

Hideo looked at his hands and began to speak in a low, steady tone. "As you may or may not already know, the Accordance military-grade nano-ink, with its higher resistance to radiation and biological attack, is a bioink engineered from Arvani ink and synthesized Ghost neuromelanin."

He took a moment to look up and view my reaction—a slow blink. "Oh. You did not know that. Well. To continue. The few black market nano-inks which rival military-grade ink have been manufactured from squid ink and a blend of human and Ghost neuromelanin—actual Ghost neuromelanin, not synthesized. You are able to sense Ghosts because you are able to detect their neuromelanin, the original of a variant that you yourself possess."

I tried to keep my face blank. The idea that human techs and tat-artists had reverse-engineered military-grade nano-ink did not surprise me, but the substitution of real Ghost neuromelanin for the synthesized version was . . . disturbing, to say the least.

Hideo continued to gaze at me, his face all concern. "Do you understand what I am saying, Amira? Do you understand why we keep our processing power in our threads and not in our skin?"

 Slate cleared his throat. I turned to him. He raised his arm and slid his sleeve back to show me his forearm and its thin, raised scars.

"Safer to remove old ink," he said. "Best to avoid ink at all, really. We're still not sure about the long-term effects on human DNA."

"This . . . isn't the conversation I was planning to have," I said carefully. "But let me ask one thing. Is your aversion to alien ink moral, or aesthetic, or are you adding Earth First purity concerns to your—"

"Amira," Hideo cut me off, sounding a little sad. "Remember how I forced you to recall what I wanted to know? Imagine the Ghosts being able to do that. Why should we use a technology that they know far better than us? How can we possibly shield ourselves from mental invasion, or worse?"

Slate cleared his throat again. "Have you ever had hallucinations so real, it felt like you'd gone back in time?"

I frowned at him. "That's just ordinary overload from too much input and too little sleep."

He pulled his sleeve down. "Yes, with ordinary overload you get a glimpse, perhaps a full flashback. But when you wake up and you can't remember how many days have passed . . ." He fell silent, stared into space, and rubbed his face tiredly with both hands.

JP continued for him. "And when you wake up, you're not thinking straight."

I could feel my calm mask start to slip. I'd always wondered how that one Ghost I'd killed had been able to convince so many humans to mutiny against the Accordance. "Okay, pause a moment. I came here to tell you that I'm sensing strong ghost sign in New Jacksonville. You're saying you already know?"

"Ghost sign? Here?" JP shook her head. "Impossible."

I was taken aback. "Why impossible? Slate said—"

"That was a long time ago, in another place," Slate clarified. "JP's right. It's impossible. We scan for Ghost neuromelanin. Nano-ink isn't very popular here, and the few who have tats stick to the standard inks with no trace of alien additives."

Hideo was watching us talk, his hands still, his gaze shifting from face to face.

"There's another way for bootleg military-grade ink to be made safe but still functional," JP told me. "Remove the tattoo intact, get a skin graft, set up the tat in a biotech frame. That's allowed."

I remembered Russo, but more than that, I remembered the tattoo artist and the framed patch of skin he'd been tending. I now wondered whether the gang had been called to remove my tattoos for me before I became a liability.

Hideo spoke up at last. "In fact, Amira, you are our greatest risk right now, but here you sit, in the heart of our stronghold. We know ghost sign well enough to protect ourselves. You are safe here."

"No," I insisted. "You said it yourself: their technology is beyond us. I know I'm picking up that pattern. A Ghost doesn't have to be physically present to spy on you."

Slate gave a smile of pride. "The New Jacksonville networks are almost spyproof. Have you had any luck breaking in, Sergeant Singh?"

"I have not," I replied soberly. "The units of the network are small, the connections are fleeting, and the encoding is as personal as the fingerprints of a million people. I would need to find a way to get each unit to transmit its data directly to me, use a huge amount of processing power to decode and analyze each transmission, and reassemble the mosaic from the fragments. It is completely beyond me."

I stood up, leaned over, and delivered my best, most dramatic last word. "I do not think it is beyond the Conglomeration."

I walked to the door.

"Wait, Amira," JP said softly.

I hesitated.

"Hideo, whether Amira is right or wrong, we need to pay attention . . . especially now."

Silence. I looked back over my shoulder. Hideo was looking at his hands again, pressing and rubbing his fingertips.

"You know I've run the scenarios," he said to JP almost petulantly.

"You've run scenarios with the known data. You've always said to watch out for the unknown."

"JP, your goal is to ensure the safety of 507. I understand that, but you know my priorities go beyond any single Ship. I think it's time. I am handing over command to you forthwith so we can concentrate on our key responsibilities. I only ask that you keep our three heroes under guard for a little longer."

JP gave me a quick, slightly troubled glance, but she replied immediately and with firm resolve. "I can do that."

Hideo also glanced at me then continued to speak to JP. "I hope that Amira may find it easier to consider returning to the Ships if I am gone. Captain Hart is less likely to join, but he may become a useful ally like your friend Jasen. Do as you see fit."

My honor guard assembled and walked me out. I wondered whether that performance of public transfer of power had been a trick to gain my sympathy and trust, or to distract me from the fact that my ghost sign warning would not be treated with any particular urgency.

JP offered to drive me back. I suspected she wanted to talk to me privately, but instead of indulging my curiosity, I remembered Devlin and asked instead to borrow another jeep.

Besides, I needed to think. I needed to talk to Ken and Devlin before deciding what to do, and I didn't want JP to ask me about loyalties before then.

I settled myself in the jeep. Slate walked away from his colleagues and came to my window. "Listen to me. We're not purity fanatics. This isn't just ideology. You need to get rid of your non-standard tats as soon as possible."

"Look, Slate—"

"I'm serious. What I said, about DNA changes? I'm the walking proof. Scan me and I register as part Ghost."

I tried to shake my head at that, but he took hold of my shoulder and stared me down. "So do you, Sergeant Singh. I tested you myself when Hideo had you restrained."

I shrugged his hand away and drew back, angry at the reminder of what I'd been put through, and extremely discomfited at the idea that the enemy was living in me, part of me, like an old sci-fi horror.

"Years ago, I was part of an astromining crew. Our rig was found drifting . . . and me in the only functioning lifepod. Thought it was my fault . . . couldn't figure out how. Now I know."

"I'm sorry about what happened to you, Slate." It was sympathy and warning together. I refused to discuss it further.

He nodded in acceptance of both sentiments. "Call me Michael." His small, shy smile turned abruptly to more of a bitter rictus. "We're practically kin, after all."

I returned to find the house quiet. Not silent—I could hear both Ken's voice and Devlin's—but the volume was strangely subdued, and the sequence of speech respectfully paced, unlike their usual stepping on each other's heels, overlapping and interrupting.

When I got up the stairs, I understood why. The concierge

was back for another visit. She was settled comfortably in an armchair with a steaming mug on the side table. Devlin sat opposite her on the couch with his elbows tucked in and his knees pressed together as he held his own mug with an effort at good deportment. Ken leaned hands-free against the windowsill, his face and frame relaxed but wary as he watched his dangerous guest. We exchanged a quick look—What is this? I have no clue.

"More mail for me?" I asked her sarcastically.

She absorbed my animosity without reaction, looking up at me with that gentle, pale-blue gaze framed by light-gray, wispy hair. Nothing else about her was soft. Her face was thin-featured Anglo-Indian, and she was aging to bones and whipcord instead of matronly plumpness. I realized I disliked her as much as I disliked Hideo, and for the same reason. She was cool and arrogant and she had bested me because I'd underestimated her.

"I was just having a chat with Devlin here. I knew his parents quite well, but I'm not surprised he doesn't remember me. Peaceful protest did not suit me, so I left very soon. I should have waited a little longer. Now I hear they're at one of the Earth First camps. I wonder if their pacifism survived."

"Were you ever in a Ship?" I asked directly.

"No. I didn't understand their methods—no protests, no counterattacks, just slow, careful organization."

"My guess is that you joined Earth First," Ken said.

She smiled brightly at him. "Before it was cool! Yes, I was one of the first terrorists. I wasn't a James Bond type with guns and suits, but it's amazing how far an old lady can get with a cardigan and a cup of tea."

I emitted a sharp, bitter "ha!" She dipped her head modestly to half-hide an expression of pride.

"Why are you here, ma'am? Talking to us, I mean," Ken asked politely.

She sighed and grew serious. "I think Hideo made a mistake bringing you two here, no matter how much he wanted to get his hands on power armor. I want to be sure we don't end up at cross-purposes. You may have discovered that there's an important shipment heading to New York tomorrow night. I want you to leave it alone."

"Or?" I asked as I frantically thought, Shipment? What shipment? Is that the armor being sent out? Is it something else?

She paused, drank a little from her mug, and set it down. First she addressed Devlin. "For you, the carrot. If you promise not to interfere, we can arrange for you to see your parents."

I saw the flicker of hope followed by deep hurt in Devlin's eyes and I hated her a little more. She turned to Ken.

"For you, the stick is very complicated. Your brothers and sisters are under protection in Tranquility City. We wouldn't presume to threaten them, but . . ." She paused and considered her words carefully. ". . . There are many of us in the CPF, and it would be so easy to reach them. I don't believe in murder myself. You can only kill a man's family once, and then you have no hold left over him. But there are many who want revenge on all collaborators, and under such circumstances, protection often fails."

Ken's jaw clenched tight. He stared at her until she looked away, almost but not quite discomfited.

"Amira, I have nothing you want and no one to threaten on your behalf, so for you—truth. That shipment is a small part of a symbolic strike that will send a message to both Accordance and Conglomeration that humans are not helpless. When they see we can do them real damage, then the negotiations can begin."

"My father would never agree to that," Devlin protested.

"Your father had his chance to try another way. It hasn't worked. Now, regardless of ideology, everyone is assembling under the Earth First banner. I look forward to the day when the officers of the CPF can openly claim us. Until then, all I ask is that you look the other way."

"You ask a lot," Ken said, his voice so low and dangerous, it was almost a growl.

I swooped in and snatched up the mug of tea from her side. "I think etiquette demands that you leave us while we consider the terms of your blackmail."

She pressed her lips together ruefully. "Of course."

I showed her to the door.

I spent a few minutes rechecking the room for surveillance devices. I had faith in Hideo's sense of hospitality and courtesy, but not hers. "Clear," I said shortly, and flopped down on the couch. "I told them about the ghost sign. They didn't believe me."

Devlin exhaled and stood up. "Transmitter is ready, receiver is calibrated, extra battery . . ." He gave me a glance; I nodded. ". . . is here. Let's go. Let's get as far away as we can, send out a signal, and get some support."

Ken kept still in contrast to Devlin's nervous energy. He quietly asked, "And the shipment? The planned attack?"

Devlin stood in front of him and spoke just as quietly. "One thing at a time. We're not the only ones who can stop them. Forget about what she said."

"You guys go on without me. Like she said, she has nothing on me, so let me handle it. I need to be sure that Ghosts don't have a part in this." I told them what I'd learned from Slate about the composition of nano-ink and my suspicions about the Ghost-led mutiny we'd crushed. "We tell Anais this, he informs the Accordance, and they'll kill whoever's involved without asking questions. If the Ghosts are making humans do their dirty work, I have to find a way to stop it. I have to investigate that shipment."

"What about you?" Ken demanded. "We saw what Hideo did to you through your nano-ink, and now you're saying that Ghosts could use it to turn you into some kind of puppet? We're not leaving you on your own."

"We're sticking together," Devlin agreed. "You said it yourself, you need us. You can't do this solo and you don't have to."

I bowed my head, remembering Slate's words, the look in his eyes. I imagined what it could be like, becoming something you could not depend on. "It could be dangerous," I admitted reluctantly. "If I can't trust myself—"

"Don't trust yourself, then," Devlin said. "Trust us. My father once told me that family isn't who you like, it's who you trust. We're family, Amira, and no one can bargain that away, not even you."

I glanced at Ken. He had the most to lose. He came up to me, leaned over, and gripped my shoulder, giving me a gentle, reassuring shake. "You heard him. Family."

I blinked away the embarrassing moisture that blurred my vision. "Understood. We go together."

13

There was one last errand on my list before I could leave New Jacksonville for good. Returning to that bungalow felt like revisiting my friend's death, but desperation drove me.

"You came back."

His eyes looked a little sad, a little hopeful. However rich the life he lived through his other selves, his own body was doomed to the loneliness of the static life-support machine. I understood that, but I had neither time nor energy to feel sorry for him.

"I need your help."

He put a hand high on the doorjamb and leaned in casually—both resting and posing. I recalled Jasen doing that same lean midway through a workout to draw attention to his abs.

"What would you like?" he asked calmly.

"Everything you can give me on 507 and their New York connections and activities. Any reports or rumors of Conglomerate presence on Earth. Techniques to isolate or disable nano-ink."

He pursed his lips and gave a slow nod. "Anything else?"

I stopped and considered, then said slowly, "As much as you're willing and able to give me."

"I'm willing, but you may not be able," he said. "I don't have to tell you about indexing fatigue."

Another term for input-overload hallucinations. "No. I know about that firsthand."

He straightened. "Come in."

I followed him into his inner room. I avoided looking at the machines and focused on his face as he settled into his recliner. "How much will this cost me?"

"You can owe me. I think I'd like that." He grimaced at my unimpressed glare. "I'm kidding. Call it a gift from an old man who's done a lot of bad things in the past and wants to do better."

"If things go the way I think they will, a lot of people will owe you."

"Hm." His face went pleased and smug all at once. "Never been a hero. That'll be nice. Now pay attention. I'm giving you three shots of data. The first is about 507 and New York. The second includes the Conglomeration and the nano-ink and some extra stuff I think you might find interesting. The third is entirely miscellaneous information which I hope will be useful to you at some point. That's as much as I think you can safely take."

I started to say something. "I'm not done yet," he admonished me. "It would take you months to look over all this. I'm also giving you a program and a patch. The program will index everything and alert you when input from your environment cues data in the records. Good for unfamiliar faces or finding a back door quick. It's challenging, but I think you have the training to handle it. Now, the patch . . . the patch is very important."

“What does it do?” I asked, frowning.

“It’ll make you sleep, and you will need to sleep. Don’t skip this part. I like you and I don’t want to see you get hurt.”

“How long?”

“Forty-eight hours or so, not counting food and bathroom breaks. Unless you’d like to stay here and download in comfort. I can hook you up.”

“Thanks,” I said doubtfully, “but I don’t have time.”

“Your loss.” A freshly packaged triple shot—three datachips in a neat row—ejected from a nearby console. He took them out, placed a sealed patch on top like a round mini–band aid, and handed it to me. “Shots go in the mouth, patch goes inside your elbow. The patch is a slow time-release, so if you need to be awake, set an alarm, peel it off, and give yourself at least an hour for full recovery. Ten minutes if it’s just a snack or a piss.”

I took the packet carefully. “Side effects?” I asked.

“Don’t drink alcohol. Don’t operate heavy machinery. Hydrate.”

Gratitude made me take a moment. “Are you going to be okay here?”

He shrugged. “For now. If things get too exciting, I have other retreat locations. Packing is a drag, but I have the staff support to manage it.”

“Good. Thank you.”

He smiled. “Anytime.”

Devlin and Ken were waiting outside in the jeep. I pocketed my information and swung myself into the back. “Let’s go.”

“We should get to the transmission point in about forty minutes,” Devlin told us.

“Do you want to take a nap?” Ken asked me worriedly. “I can drive.”

Devlin's driving was still a little jerky when he was caught off guard, so I understood the question. I looked up at the starlight. "It's barely twenty-two hundred. Are you going to mother-hen me all the way to New York?"

"You said to make sure you slept regularly," Devlin noted reproachfully.

The packet felt hot in my hand. "You don't have to worry about that. I got something from Russo that should help."

I briefly told them about the shots and the prescribed sleep. I mentioned how to wake me up in an emergency and we settled on a schedule of breaks during the day and an uninterrupted block of at least eight hours at night. When we reached the transmission point, I slid the first datachip into my mouth, applied the patch to my elbow, and got comfortably comatose in the back.

The first wake-break was at early dawn the following morning. Devlin gave me a moment, then put a box of juice and a pastry in my hand. I shifted upright and heard a rustling; there were shopping bags wedged all around me.

"Extra clothes. Rations for the trip," Devlin explained. "We didn't want to risk you going hungry. How are you feeling? Any smarter?"

I made a face at him and removed the emptied datachip from my cheek. "What do you need to know?"

"Shipment time, route, vehicles in use. Whatever you can give us."

I twitched. Each word sparked a strange sensation between memory and déjà vu. I tried to access what I needed, but it blurred and slipped away. "Give me a minute."

Devlin settled back with his own box of juice. "The radio transmission went well. Ken picked up an acknowledgement message before we had to shift. We'll check in later. He thinks it may take them a while to do a full decode. We warned them to look for radio ghost sign." His face went sour for a moment. "Reported our power armor stolen. Added our speculation about terrorist activity planned for New York." The corner of his mouth curled up. "We blamed Rai and Earth First for that. We're not turning in your friends yet."

"Yeah, my friends," I said with slightly weary sarcasm. "They'll start looking for us soon. The tracking function in the jeep is purposely low-tech to match the design. It's basically a proximity warning. The moment we go beyond the suburbs of New Jacksonville, it'll activate."

"And the shipment?" Devlin asked me again.

"Twenty-one hundred. They're heading north along 301, then diverting to the bypass road that parallels the train route. Three jeeps, one van."

"Good!" He jumped up, excited. "I'll brief Ken. Go back to sleep."

Ken supervised the next few breaks, partly because he was catching up on sleep himself after a long night with the radios. By afternoon I'd already absorbed the other two shots, and I was feeling strange. I had no flashbacks or hallucinations, but I had overwhelming anxiety that only calmed down when I reapplied the sedative of the patch. Devlin gave me a few worried looks. Ken said nothing, but before he took his last nap before nighttime, he put the backseat fully down, making space for both of us. We slept back-to-back, and sleep came quickly, aided by his warmth and heartbeat.

I woke up from that sleep before dawn of the next day. The jeep was on the move, and from the smoothness I thought at first that Ken was driving. I quickly revised my thought—it was the smoothness of a well-maintained road, something that New Jacksonville did not have in abundance, nor the between-cities network, slowly crumbling in favor of the well-maintained, well-monitored railways. I opened my eyes and sat up slightly.

The driver glanced over his shoulder at me—it was Devlin—and shushed me softly. "Don't wake Ken. He's taking over after we pass Charlotte."

"What are you doing?" I whispered furiously.

"Ken's idea. We timed our departure with the other jeeps, so we look like we're part of the shipment escort. We think it's working! Besides, unless the concierge told your friends about the little talk she had with us, they'll expect us to go south, not north." He paused. "Anything new?"

"No," I grumbled. "Don't get us caught."

"Nah. The road's busy and I'm keeping my distance."

"Good. They'll have a stop near Richmond. I think it's one of the Earth First camps, so don't go wandering in behind them."

He didn't look back again, but I could hear his grin in his voice. "Thank you."

"Hear anything new on the radio?"

His positivity dimmed. "No. We're well out of range. We'll report in when we get to New York."

Perhaps he said something else, but by then I was asleep again.

I woke up a couple of hours later in the middle of a tense exchange between Devlin and Ken. "She can't do this, she needs rest. I can get there, check for our armor, and get back in seconds, and if anyone tries to stop me, you just drive in and distract them."

"Like, ram them?" Devlin sounded too eager.

“No, fool,” Ken said critically. “A sideswipe at most. We’re trying to keep out of trouble.”

I tried to open my eyes, but in addition to the heaviness, there was a painfully bright light flashing red and bluish-white somewhere on the highway. I tried to speak to Ken, but the passenger door slammed and he was gone.

“What’s happening?” I groaned. I sat up and slowly peeled away the patch.

Devlin was startled, but he recovered quickly. “Accident. Doesn’t look serious, but traffic’s backed up.”

“I mean Ken. Where is he going?” I blinked, finally managed to focus, and raised my voice suddenly. “Why has he got Bugkiller?”

“Quiet,” Devlin said. “He’s going to check out the van.”

Ken wasn’t the only one walking on the road. Others had left their vehicles to get closer and see what was causing the blockage. I fumbled to get my door open. “No, not the van. Van’s a decoy. Second and third jeep.”

“Shit. I’ll go get him.” He hopped out of the jeep before I could open my mouth to protest and sprinted ahead to yank Ken to the side of the road, which was dark and shaggy with overgrown brush. Between the flashing lights and other people moving about, I soon lost sight of them.

They weren’t hard to miss when they came back. They were running with three other figures chasing on their heels. Devlin reached the jeep first, jumped in, and started to shift gears before the door was fully closed. Ken slowed to sweep a wide pulse at them, as if killing crickets, then made a mighty sprint to get in the passenger side before Devlin reversed at speed down the empty shoulder of the highway.

“The hell?” I said inarticulately.

“Not now, Amira! Give us an escape, a side road, anything!”

I glanced around, quickly estimating our location from the signage I could see. "Access road, five . . . six hundred meters back. Faster if we jump the ditch about—now!"

Devlin reacted instantly. I was beginning to realize that his style of driving was naturally combat-oriented. We sailed a short distance, struck earth hard and aslant, and then the tires gripped and we were gone, flying down a nearly empty lane on the edge of a half-abandoned town.

"What just happened?" I shouted at the front of the jeep. "Hand over my EPC!"

Ken handed it clumsily back to me. "Sorry. At least I took out their comms for a while."

"What were you two doing?"

"We thought we might have a chance to grab our armor," Devlin answered testily. "I feel naked out here."

"The jeeps don't have our armor. They're carrying bombs," Ken said tersely. Devlin nodded, his face grim. "Biological bombs," Ken clarified. Devlin's head whipped around and he stared at Ken in shock. Ken put a steadying hand on the steering wheel as the jeep veered.

"Slow down," I said, not sure which one of them I was talking to. "You saw actual bio-bombs being transported in those jeeps? Are you sure?"

"I'm sure. I looked at everything to do with that case, every document, every report. If I can remember the names and faces of each and every one of the CPF personnel who were executed when the bombs went missing, I can sure as hell remember what those damn bombs look like."

"I don't know. . . . I imagined they'd be . . . bigger, or . . . spiky or something," Devlin said softly.

"No," Ken said. "Relatively small and extremely well designed."

"How many did you see?" I asked.

Ken shrugged. "We didn't have time to count. Maybe two in that one jeep?"

I thought and calculated. Two bombs per jeep, six in total. "That's nowhere near enough to wipe out Earth. It's supposed to be a symbolic strike against the Accordance. Central Park for sure. Where else would you choose? Newark?"

"You don't know?" Devlin almost yelled.

"I'm still indexing!" I yelled back. "Besides, the exact locations of their targets might be a little more classified than the number of jeeps they're using!"

Ken interrupted our squabble. "We can't count on just six, and we can't count on it being symbolic. What if Ghosts have tricked the Earth First leaders into using these particular bombs instead of human weapons? Maybe they have no idea how dangerous they are."

I shook my head. "They hate alien tech like it's their religion. If they're using bio-bombs, it has to be because humans haven't developed an equivalent weapon."

"This is beyond us," Devlin stated. "We send a full report to New York as soon as possible, get backup, and let the colonels and generals take over and earn their pay."

I hesitated. I knew he was right and the stakes were too high, but I knew that those colonels and generals would react with executions before investigations. If that let the Conglomeration off free, nothing would be solved in the long term. "We do both. Report it to the CPF as soon as we can, but find out where these bombs are going and why. I want to question them, Devlin. I want them to look me in the eye and say they really intended to wipe out all life on the only planet we have."

Devlin thought for a moment, then nodded. "Agreed.

Now get that patch back on. You've got twenty hours of sleep left."

They woke me at dawn.

"Sorry, Amira," Devlin said. "We got a message from Orlando to rendezvous here."

I squinted at Ken. "You said we were out of range."

"Ionospheric bounce happened. Just around Richmond," he said shortly. "We're a couple of hours out of Washington, DC, but we've been told to stay out and wait here."

That was fine by me. Washington's streets were crawling with carapoids and power-armored Arvani, and I still wasn't sure whether I was a sergeant or a deserter.

Moving slowly, I got out of the jeep. We'd stopped in a huge, empty parking lot in front of the decaying remains of an ancient mall. "We're kinda exposed out here. Are you sure it's safe?"

"No," Ken replied. He was clearly in a mood.

A familiar noise made us all look up. "Here he comes," said Devlin.

Of course. Well before the hopper grounded, I knew who would be stepping out to greet us. Devlin and Ken came to attention reflexively. I stayed slumped against the side of the jeep.

"Gentlemen," said Anais with a nod. He looked at me. "And you. Still recovering from the torture?"

"Yeah," I said. "Something like that." I waved weakly toward the single pilot in the hopper. "You're travelling light."

He braced his shoulders, shrugging away tension, and I could see that his facade of weary cynicism was stretched to the snapping point. "I'm expected in New York very soon and this is an unscheduled diversion, so I'll keep this short."

He held out a small screen at eye level. "Watch."

The tiny figure on screen had exchanged his cheerful galaxy-print T-shirt for a neutral gray tunic, but the long black coat was the same as ever.

"I am the accountant for Earth First," said Hideo, "and today is a day of reckoning."

14

We viewed the full message twice in silence. "Nice of them to warn us officially," Ken said, "but do they know they're dealing with bio-bombs?"

Anais gave him a sharp and slightly worried look. "Ah. So you figured that out. No, that's not clear from the message."

"Any demands? Prisoner releases, mutual cease-fire, anything?" Devlin queried.

"Nothing," Anais said. He looked strangely satisfied at the question.

I stood upright and steady. "No, not this time. It never worked before, so this time they're going to strike first and make demands after. There's bound to be an escalation. That's why it's symbolic. It's just the beginning."

Anais turned to me. "You've got a good grasp of tactics. Pity about your loyalties—"

"What do you expect us to do?" Ken interrupted. He sounded completely fed up, way past disillusionment and out the other side.

Anais looked at me. "She won't listen to me, but she'll do

what she can for you, and I think she's got the insider's edge. I want her to use it, no questions asked. I'm unleashing everything in my arsenal to shut this down. I don't have a choice."

Devlin cleared his throat. "Uh, sir, although Sergeant Singh is indeed a remarkable asset, we have no armor, no weapons, nothing."

Anais slapped a hand to his forehead. "Of course. How could I forget." He jogged back to the hopper and returned with two holstered pistols and a couple of comm buttons, which he handed to Ken and Devlin. "There you go. Can't say I never do anything for you." He glanced at me. "None for you. I can cover my ass where these two are concerned. You're a little too high-risk."

He turned back to Devlin. "Succeed and prove you're more than a PR captain. Fail and we all die. See you in New York."

He vaulted back into the hopper, signed a thumbs-up to the pilot, and they took off in flurry of dust and leaves.

"Not if I see you first," Ken said with deadly calm as he buckled on the gun and settled it over his hip.

Devlin exchanged a glance with me. "Okay. Ken, let's hit the road. Amira, anything new for us? I'd like to jump ahead instead of trailing behind for a change."

"Yes. You'll like this one. I think I know where they're taking the Central Park bomb."

I didn't risk putting on the patch again. I needed another sixteen hours of sleep, but I couldn't afford even half of that. Five hours later, I woke to the noise and smell of the Turnpike Tunnel. "Already?" I grumbled as I stretched as thoroughly as possible in the confined space of the backseat.

"Be grateful," Ken said soberly as he navigated the traffic. "What if the Turnpike's a target?"

I didn't answer. The broad glass stripe that showed the Newark Spaceport on the Tunnel's west side had just come into view. I watched it go past silently. "Lots of possibilities, Ken. For now, let's focus on the Central Park destination."

"Okay," Devlin said, "but let's be clear on something. This is your mission. You're in charge, you take us in, you try to reason with whoever's there or take them down or whatever. But if at any point you can no longer command, then Ken is in charge of finding and disabling the bombs and I'm in charge of getting us the hell out of there."

Ken nodded firmly; they'd probably been discussing it while I was sleeping. I felt a bit strange. Proud, I guess, because Devlin had really earned my respect as a soldier and a captain, and Ken's too, when neither of us gave respect lightly. And weirdly happy, because this time, I was traveling with backup, and for a stupid moment I thought I almost wouldn't mind dying if I could go down fighting with them.

"Okay," I said.

Manhattan was a strange combination of Accordance luxury and human slum. Anais had warned us, long before we returned to Earth, that security concerns had led to the creation of separate areas for Accordance citizens. It didn't surprise me—my grandfather considered such things inevitable—but it was still striking. We were going deep into a new slum, through what used to be the Upper West Side. The spires of the Hudson River were not as high as those rooted in what had once been Central Park, but their skybridges vaulted over the crumbling Upper West Side to connect to the greater structures at the center of Manhattan. They looked like flying buttresses of a magnificent cathedral, and the human buildings below like the forgotten detritus of another age.

I guided Ken along streets with cracked tarmac flooded

with a noisome mix of brackish water and sewage. We came at last to the back of a high-rise building with the lower levels boarded up and well graffitied.

"This is it. Used for a short while as a holding facility. Then the Arvani started their sea reclamation project and Riverside South became unsafe, so it was abandoned. And look."

I pointed. There was another jeep, identical to ours, parked nearby in three inches of water. Ken, unprompted, parked right behind it. We got out and stood on the dry sidewalk—three CPF officers who once strode in power armor reduced to civvies, a couple of pistols, and an EPC-1.

Devlin drew his gun. I rested my hand on it and pushed it back under his jacket. "Don't be nervous. I'm linked up to the street cameras, and we're clear. Let's not draw attention to ourselves."

Ken stopped in front of a metal door with a dark square of glass set at handle height, but with no handle nor any visible lock. "But can we get in without drawing attention to ourselves?"

"Thanks to Mister Russo, it seems I've got some access codes," I said cheerfully, waving my wrist over the glass screen. The door swung outward and spilled forth dank and unwelcoming air. I stepped in fearlessly, feeling like I knew this building. "Lights," I said, and like magic the lights came up. "Air," I continued. Beside me, Devlin began to gag. "Okay, no air," I said quickly, cringing from the smell of rot that infested the ventilation system. "Let's try . . . windows. Hmmm. Okay, override safety for floors two and above."

"Better," Devlin said cautiously, drawing his gun at last.

Ken did the same, moving to my other side. I walked forward, looking through the cameras ahead, checking the schematics in my head, going through the maze, becoming the maze. I hesitated at the elevator, comparing camera views to schematics floor by floor so I could figure out where to go.

"Floors twelve through fourteen," I mused aloud. "No cells, all admin areas and offices—yes!"

"What is it? Do you see them?" Devlin whispered anxiously.

The surveillance system was showing three men standing by an open window, arguing over the unexpected opening of said window. One of them turned away in exasperation, pulled out a gun, and started to march toward the elevator. I inhaled sharply.

"Quick, lower your guns," I said. "I'm going to use the intercom, and I don't want them to see a threat."

After a quick glance between them, Ken and Devlin lowered their weapons. I took a deep breath and opened the public channel.

"Michael Slate, it's Amira Singh. I'm here, I'm unarmed, and I want to talk to you."

"Did JP send you?" he demanded.

We were on the thirteenth floor, standing outside the elevator, facing a large, empty room with floor-to-ceiling windows. Slate paced up and down in front of us. His face was sweating and gray with fear, and his grip on his sidearm was a little too tight. Behind him and near the open windows were two figures in black denim, one tall and lanky, the other shorter and stocky. They were unknown to me, but I noted the familiar stamp of Ship 1 tattooed on the back of their right hands. They had set up a small cannon, and the bomb lay beside it, still unloaded, a smooth, matte-black capsule about half a meter long and thirty centimeters wide.

"No. JP doesn't know I'm here." I wondered if they'd fallen out, but I didn't have time to find out. "Slate, the bombs you have, you don't want to use them. You don't want them anywhere near Earth, trust me."

"Why?" he asked suspiciously.

"Because they'll kill everything within an eight-kilometer radius, that's why," Ken said sarcastically. "The Accordance may take a small hit, but you'll have a lot of human blood on your hands."

Slate shook his head. "It's a trick."

The shorter member of the Ship 1 crew had been eyeing us quietly, but at that she spoke up. "Can you prove it?"

Devlin answered. "We were there when they were used to wipe out all life on Saturn and its moons. We've seen what they can do."

"Wait," I said, noticing something on the woman's wrist. "You've got nano-ink?" I thought quickly, made some connections. "You're Emilia Lang, right? Nate Russo. . . . You know Russo. He can vouch for what I'm saying. Contact him now. Ask him about the thirty-eight CPF staff on Tranquility who were executed a while ago. This is why. Someone stole those bombs, smuggled them in from the Moon, and brought them here. I don't think their aim was to kill only aliens."

"Yeah," Lang agreed, shooting a nasty look at Slate. "Because that would be stupid, right?"

Slate's pale face flushed with sudden anger. "You believe her, just like that?"

Emilia laughed. "Apart from the fact that this is Amira Singh, who needs believing when you can just check the facts?" She turned to her crewmate. "We've been played."

I kept pushing. "You've got leaders. Let them decide. Call JP." Something in Slate's eyes made me add, "But I'm guessing she wasn't in agreement with this in the first place. Where's Hideo? Let him run the numbers, with the full info this time."

The intercom suddenly sizzled, which made me jump because I had nothing to do with it. Ken and Devlin reacted to my surprise and went alert, but the other three showed a different kind of tension.

"It's starting," Slate said with deep relief.

A voice sounded through the intercom. I realized two things very quickly: first, that the cause was a citywide override of public channels; and second, that the voice belonged to Rai.

"I am Mawusi Rai, and I speak for Earth First. My message is to humanity. This is the hour of reckoning. At noon, bombs that target alien biology will detonate in cities around the globe. Stay calm and seek safety until the hour is past and the invaders are eradicated. This is the revolution."

"Thirty minutes till noon," Ken noted dispassionately.

I turned to Emilia Lang. "Make it stop. Call whoever's in charge and get them to send out the order."

She smiled. "The Ships of Manhattan have already decided to stand down. We'll have to see how many others agree with us."

"Newark Spaceport is dead to our comm network," Slate said. "Too much interference. If you want me to stop them, I have to leave now."

I tried to read his expression, but he gazed back steadily with nothing more than a trace of resignation. "Go, then," I said.

He took off to the elevators. Lang barely glanced at him as he went. She was distracted by the view outside the window.

"So much for 'stay calm,'" she remarked.

Her crewmate spoke for the first time—a long string of swear words. We watched as the skies filled with public and private transport: metro transit shuttles filled to capacity and skipping their designated stops, corporate hoppers going off route and running wild like spooked smugglers. A blare of sirens below suggested that the streets were no better.

"Slate's going to get caught in that," I mused.

Devlin came to my side and spoke quietly. "Don't worry. I called it in and Anais says they're on it. We should get out of here while we can."

"What about this?" Ken said, pointing at the inert bomb.

"We don't want it," Lang exclaimed, backing away with her hands up.

"Take it to Empire State," I told Devlin. "They can secure it and then it's their problem."

Suddenly, I was in a combat crouch with Bugkiller at the ready and no memory of what had set me off. Then I felt it, ominously increasing in volume like a distant stampede thundering closer and closer.

"Ghost sign!" I yelled.

"Where?" Ken yelled back, pointing his gun at the closed doors of the elevator.

"I don't know!" I cried out in frustration, scanning the floors below and above as quickly as I could. Empty, all of them.

The enterprising Lang quickly packed up the bomb in a large backpack, settled and buckled it on securely, and leapt behind Devlin for cover. Her crewmate was still trying to disassemble the launcher, his back to the window. Twelve black lines came tumbling down, slicing the view into segments; twelve figures zipped down and stopped abruptly, spider-like on the end of each line. The tall young man of Ship 1 turned at last, but too late. The first Ghost into the building plucked him up contemptuously with one hand and tossed him through the window into thin air. That was all it could manage; a second later Devlin's shot snapped its head back, and it tumbled to the ground.

"Stairs! Stairs!" I shouted. "Get her out of here!"

Lang was temporarily frozen by the sudden mayhem, but she found her legs fast, sprinting off ahead of Ken. I found time to jam Bugkiller into the throat of another Ghost, and threw its body at a cluster of them. Ken got off a couple of shots too, but I didn't stop to see where they landed. I was the last to burst through the stairwell door. I reflexively shut it, sealed it, and brought down a second security door in a trio of satisfying clangs.

"Yes, ma'am!" Lang exclaimed in admiration. I stared at her in surprise. She appeared to be the type of person who knew how to work on adrenaline, even when clearly scared shitless. "Here," she said, pulling a Glock out of her jacket and offering it to me. "You'll get more out of this than I will. I'll concentrate on running."

"Good idea. We can't stay here. I've jammed the elevators and shut down the other stairwell, but they can still break through the windows."

Something thumped loudly against the door and we all jumped, but it held as designed. "Down or up?" Ken asked.

"Lang," I said urgently. "Your tats. Standard ink, or something extra?"

"Standard," she answered promptly after a single bewildered blink.

"Right. You, Ken, and Devlin, down. I'll watch and keep the doors open for you. Get to Empire State. I'll meet you there when I can. Me, up. I'm the blip on their radar. I'm the decoy."

"Shit, Amira, no," Ken began.

"Devlin put me in charge," I said, looking at Devlin. "One last lone wolf, right?"

Devlin's eyes had that hurt look, but he set his jaw and nodded. "See you on the other side, Amira. C'mon guys, let's go!"

My head felt like a split screen with a quiet game of chess on one side and a raucous melee on the other. I'd guessed right. More sobering, Hideo was right. I could sense Ghosts because they could sense me. Devlin, Ken, and Lang all but tiptoed from the building unassailed as I quietly opened and closed doors for them. Meanwhile, I sprinted up two flights of stairs, grimly conscious that the elevator doors had already been forced open. I couldn't stay in the stairwell forever. I exited on the fifteenth floor and dashed out into the open. Here was a true panopticon: three open floors of glass-walled cells and an interior observation tower. The view over the river was gorgeous, like a pleasant retreat for white-collar crime. I headed for that west-wall view. There were no cells there, only an open space that had been meant for a dining hall.

I heard pounding heels behind me. Camera scans and a glance over my shoulder showed nine Ghosts coming out of the elevator in the central tower. A laser clipped my heels with a nasty sizzle. I snarled and put Bugkiller on full blast. Lang was right. Running hard and aiming a pistol did not really mix, but I could wide-beam an EPC-1, aim behind me, and hit the side of a barn.

An unearthly scream made me stumble as I ran up three steps to the hall level. I looked long enough to see one of the Ghosts writhing on the ground with eyes and nose streaming blood. I felt a chill, remembering the piercing pain when the same happened to me at Icarus, and then I was glad, because it meant that at least some of them were vulnerable to electromagnetic pulse. There were no more lasers, at least. I reached the windows and paused. This was the tricky bit.

I took a deep breath and everything slowed. Seven Ghosts

were still coming toward me; I steadied myself, aimed, and shot down two. One Ghost was meters ahead of the rest. It held a slab of thick glass scavenged from a downstairs window as a shield and ran fearlessly against the bullets while the others took cover. I shot at the glass twice and clinically observed the crumple and shatter. Then, when the Ghost was still flinching and distracted, I ran toward it, shot it in the knee, and drove my foot into the other knee. While it was still screaming, I took it down and dislocated both shoulders. I grabbed it around the waist with my free arm, looked west to the windows, and carefully emptied my magazine into the corners of one large window. Throwing the gun away, I clutched the twitching Ghost tightly to me and began to run.

We hit the weakened glass with all the speed and mass I'd hoped for. The crushed window bowed out and fell away from the building with us on top of it. We fell free for three full seconds, an eternity of terror, while I spun override codes in my head, sent out commands, and braced myself for the crash.

There's really no soft landing to a hopper in flight, even with three centimeters of glass and a Ghost's body to cushion you. I hit hard enough for the blood to well up in my mouth, hard enough for my ears to ring louder than the passengers' panicked shrieking. The side door opened at my command, and I tilted the hopper slightly so we could slide safely in.

The passengers scattered from nearby seats and cowered as far away from us as possible. I barely glanced at them. I spat blood and sat on the floor next to the moaning Ghost with the wind from the open door clearing the daze from my mind.

"Why are you here?" I asked quietly.

It moaned and turned its head away. I lost patience and leaned my palm on one wrecked shoulder. It gave a bubbling scream.

“How long have you been here on Earth? What’s the plan? Answer me!” I started with a shout, but my voice lost power and breath by the last word. I pressed a hand to my ribs and winced.

“You are the plan,” the Ghost whispered.

“Explain,” I demanded. “Don’t speak riddles or I’ll throw you out the door.”

“Raw DNA,” said the Ghost. “Your DNA. This is the tool we use to master the empty reaches, to spread life throughout the universe. Human DNA, it is so, so sweet. Such a sharp tool, such a marvelous prize. You waste your life here on Earth. We can mold you to do so much more, send you to so many places. The Accordance knows it too. There is a high price on the indigenous blood of Earth. You are the very cream of the doomed, but you still think you can fight us.” It bared its bloody teeth at me in a smile of weary defiance.

I was momentarily shaken. “That’s a lie. You’re human. Use your own DNA.”

“I am but a small sample of something much larger. The Ghost is zealous to become all things. Our present form is useful to the whole, but it is just a small part. And no matter what happens here, we have already won. The solar system will be reshaped. We will have our breeding hives. It is our destiny to fill the universe with all forms, changed to fit their places in the great universal order. You stopped the Hive once, and now we know your tricks. You cannot stop us this time.”

My head was spinning again. The Ghost saw my distraction and lunged up. I couldn’t believe its tolerance for pain. It flung an arm up desperately and somehow got a grip on the emergency override near the door. Sparks flew from the lever and the hopper lurched. I threw command after command at the hopper, and all I could sense was the dying of the control system as circuit after circuit faded out.

I seized the Ghost to pull it away. The open door and the turbulence made it easy to bring the Ghost over the edge and let it fall.

"I'm not a tool. I'm not a thing. I'm a person!" I yelled after it.

The hopper began to spiral down, down. Cursing long and loud, I scrambled to an empty seat and secured myself. I looked apologetically at the panicked passengers. "Brace yourse—"

15

I tried not to wince as the EMT pressed the edges of the laceration together and applied a liquid seal. My skin tingled for a couple of seconds, and that was it. "Head wounds always look worse than they are. Sit for a while if you need to, but get the hell out of here."

I murmured thanks, looked at the continuing gridlock, and sighed. "Easier said than done."

The hopper had crashed on the riverbank, spun, slid, and pushed up a twisted dune of mud, which luckily made a great makeshift emergency slide. By the time the walking wounded left the wreckage, most of us were smeared to anonymity—not that anyone cared to turn me in. The piers were visible at walking distance and there were hovercraft ferrying people away more swiftly than ground transport and more safely than air. Those who could move joined the crowds surging westward toward the ferries.

My destination lay east, and I had no choice but to walk.

I got slowly to my feet. Bugkiller was still on my back, only slightly battered but dangerously choked with mud. I'd have to do a deep clean and full maintenance check before I could risk firing her again. I tried to shift her strap slightly and grimaced as pain crescendoed in my left wrist.

I left the river-washed tail end of West Seventy-third Street, managed two blocks more inland, and then it hit.

I was caught by surprise. I was dazed from the crash and so focused on getting back to Ken and Devlin that I'd forgotten about Newark. I was also completely unaware of the effect of a single bio-bomb in an oxygen-rich atmosphere with plenty of stuff to kill. First, a puff blew through the air, far softer than a shockwave, then another and another as displaced air rushed from the bomb's ground zero and was replaced instead by a spreading, roiling darkness. It moved faster than mere smoke, as if obeying some other laws of physics. The sun dimmed. The screaming around me gained a new terror and a far higher volume as the strange wind whipped in all directions.

I dragged my hair out of my face, fighting the pounding of my heart and a desperate impulse to run, and squinted southwest at the shadow. "Dammit, Slate," I muttered. "Eight kilometers. I'm in the clear, there's no need to run, we're well beyond the danger. Eight K, eight K, eight K . . . come on!"

The shadow slowed. Miniature lightning glittered at its boundary. I had the vague sense that, if the blast from two bio-bombs combined, things would get rapidly and exponentially worse, but this one was solo, isolated, and the biosphere fought back, compressing the stain to a standstill.

I carefully leaned a shoulder against the nearest building and exhaled, shaking. My forehead rested on cool glass. I drew back and focused on my reflection. One-third blood and two-thirds mud, both half-dried and mingled. The stripe where the EMT had cleaned and dressed my forehead stood out like a bar of sanity peeking through nightmare. I drew back further and read the sign PHARMACY.

"I gotta eat," I said to myself, and went into the store.

When I say "went," I mean I quietly reset the entry codes, opened the door, and slipped inside. It would take a lot more than an evacuation order and a couple of bio-bombs to shut down New York commerce. The store's sensors easily accepted my ID and credit as I took up first aid supplies and soap for myself, and cleaning supplies for Bugkiller. I found a bathroom at the back and washed my hands and my face, strapped up my wrist, shrugged in resignation at my torn, stained clothes, and gave Bugkiller a quick wipe-down before rolling her up in a towel and stashing her in a packable duffel. Inside my mouth was still tender, though no longer bleeding, so I swished some antiseptic mouthwash before sitting in the pharmacy's small cafe and settling down to a meal of yogurt and pudding. I ate slowly because my hands were still shaking.

The staff had evacuated too quickly to lower security shutters, so I was able to look though the café's window at scenes of slow apocalypse. Slow traffic became stalled traffic as people abandoned their vehicles and fled on foot to the soundtrack of wailing EMS sirens. Above the streets was no better. The city's overburdened autopilot air control was dealing with the rush of flight plans by enforcing holding patterns. I saw a couple of illegal and risky ultralights darting through. West and south no longer appeared to be desirable, only north, and the river was the path to follow.

I scanned the news feeds. It . . . wasn't good. Several cities and locations were designated targets, and most received some form of public warning beforehand. I suspected that the percentage of human population at the target might have influenced that decision. At zero hour, many of the bombs did not go off. Lang's message and Ship 1's example had counted. But in other cities where the bombs went off, the warnings came too late. Casualties were estimated in the millions. Quarantine containment shields were being put in place, and transport systems were disrupted all over the world.

"Targets were carefully selected to maximize alien deaths and destruction of Accordance capital without significant damage to the biosphere. Symbolic, and strategic . . . even when one key variable was wrong, the estimate of human deaths."

I turned my head at the sound of the unexpected voice. Slate sat beside me with a blank expression, staring out at the confusion in the street. His face was gray and his khakis strangely faded, as if he were an aged Polaroid. I frowned at him in puzzlement.

"Slate? I thought you were dead."

He stared at me impassively. "I thought you were the decoy."

I woke up gasping with vanilla pudding smushed halfway up my nostrils.

I rushed back to the bathroom, gripped the sink, and stared at myself in the mirror. My hands weren't shaking anymore, and my thoughts were sharp and clear. I had to get rid of my non-standard ink. Slate and Hideo had never really convinced me, but a pack of Ghosts hunting me by the scent of my ink was pretty damn convincing.

I filled the sink with liquid solvent and contemplated the purple of my hair. The color was not and had never been caused by dye. A pink microveneer of EMP-shielding nano-ink coated my hair, which helped protect the standard nano-ink in my scalp. I got it done in my early teens after my first run-in with an EMP pulse left me half-blind and incapacitated with chronic pain for weeks. It had cost me five months' earnings back then, and I never expected to regret it.

I started to work. The oily solvent slicked my fingers as I gripped and pulled. Color unraveled from each hair shaft and plopped into the sink in a gloopy mass. I took my time and tried to be thorough. It was strange to see myself with dark hair again. That felt like a disguise, not the purple. The purple was my declaration, my warning of who I was and what I had done to become that person. Now I could have changed places with any of the ladies from the Gator hostel without anyone noticing . . . except I wasn't sure I was like the concierge, able to work magic with a cardigan and a teacup and a ladylike little smile.

The drain was blocked. I ran the water, but the purple would not be diluted and refused to go down. My lip curled in disgust as I scooped the jellied mess out of the sink, mixed it with paper and tissue like papier-mâché, and hid it in the trash. Then I shampooed my hair thoroughly, washing it clean of solvent and Ghost-based tech. It lay flat on my skull and dripped water below my shoulders. I wrapped it up in a towel and stared at myself. I looked pathetic, lost, and unfamiliar.

No time to indulge in self-pity. I took off the towel, ran my fingers through my damp hair, and started a mental inventory. All my scalp and face ink was civilian or military standard, and so were my eyes and arms. That could stay. Before being drafted into the CPF, I had bootleg tech in my piercings and jewelry. Most got confiscated. I managed to save a few, but they were long gone—lost on the journey from the Moon to Titan to Earth again.

Some things I couldn't be sure of. I'd had pins implanted for broken bones in the past, the kind designed to be absorbed and integrated into the healing bone. I was pretty sure I'd ingested something illegal and semi-permanent for the lining of my gut. I needed a full body scan and genetic screening to be sure I was clean . . . and if Slate was right, I might still be tainted. I might always be tainted.

I didn't like feeling helpless. There was one thing I could do, so I did it. I took a sterilized blade, sat down, and carefully sliced out the ridged tattoo above my knee. The site was flayed raw when I finished, so I slapped a burn bandage on it and took a small breather until my hands stopped shaking again. For the first time in a while, I missed my power armor. I made do with a dose of painkillers and stim pills instead, promising myself I would sleep later. When there was time. When it was safe.

Lang found me twenty minutes later on Fifty-seventh and Ninth. I was limping along determinedly, navigating the busy sidewalks, and obsessively checking the frozen stain in the southwest quadrant of the sky. I was so distracted that she was almost in front of me when I noticed her. Out of breath, cheeks ruddy, eyes wide—her adrenaline was still running high. She'd looked older and more seasoned when I first saw her, but now I could see she was young, maybe five years younger than me. Seventeen . . . seventeen was young? But Devlin was only nineteen, and my own seventeen had been—I shook my head, dismissing the train of thought. There was no normal seventeen for anyone anymore.

"Your boys have the . . . thing. They sent me to find you because they've got duties and can't get away right now. Said to tell you . . . Anais?"

I grimaced. "Understood."

"So I'm to hide you until they can get free. Here, this comm is for you."

She handed me a button comm very similar to the one Anais had denied me earlier. I tried to find a clean place to hang it and ended up plaiting it into my hair at my left temple. Lang lit up approvingly.

"Nice. I like your hair, by the way. Got tired of the purple?"

"Yeah. It was time for a change—wait, what's going on?"

A squad of armored carapoids was literally clearing the road by pushing vehicles aside. Behind them, a troop of struthiforms armed with energy rifles was going through cautiously, stopping to apply a tag to every door of every building. They moved tactically, one struthiform tagging while another did the duty of watching and covering. I'd grown accustomed to the struthiforms in Biomed with their brusque but sincere caring, so it shook me to see a rifle butt used to club away a half-dazed man who didn't move off the sidewalk fast enough.

"Shit," Lang said. "They got here fast. Listen."

The lead struthiform was broadcasting loudly through her translation collar. "Remain calm and return to your residences. A sundown curfew is in now effect. Transgressors will be shot on sight."

"Once I would have called that harsh, but now I've seen what Ghosts look like? Makes complete sense to me," Lang remarked. "Let's get out of here. Not much further to go."

I followed her silently. I was processing both old and new information. The civilian networks were buzzing about the curfew, the gridlock, and the inky void around Newark Spaceport. Over it all lay a desperation that suggested no one knew what was going on. That didn't surprise me. If Earth First knew what the bio-bombs would do but still went ahead with the operation, or worse yet, if they were collaborating with the Conglomeration, that meant they'd lied to the Ships and nonviolent protesters who'd joined them. I could imagine quite a lot of organizational upheaval and infighting if that was the case, and there would be no unified voice for a while. But if Earth First was as clueless, if they were all only just realizing they had been duped by aliens while claiming to reject all things alien, that would stir up a different kind of fear and mistrust while causing the same disruption.

The military networks sang a completely different tune in two-part harmony. The CPF side was ordering all enlisted personnel to report to base for screening and reprocessing. The Accordance was sending out the alert about Ghosts on Earth and increasing security levels on all bases throughout the solar system. But there was another line in the mix: the joint CPF and Accordance public message which denounced Earth First terrorists, repeated the curfew order, and said nothing at all about Ghosts.

Lang stopped short. Every screen, every electronic billboard, had suddenly lit up with a screech of snowy static. The image settled and grew sharp. It was Rai again, full-face and larger than life.

"This is Mawusi Rai."

At first I was expecting an Earth First rant, either gloating or shifting blame according to what the propagandists had decided, but in the pause that followed, I quickly reassessed what I was viewing. Something was wrong. A tension vibrated in her voice, the kind of tension that comes from suppressed terror. The camera view opened slightly to show that her hands bound in front of her and her clothing was streaked with drying blood.

Another voice repeated the words in the resonant tone of a translation collar. "This is Mawusi Rai of Earth First, who planted the bombs in Manhattan and Newark. The penalty for mass murder is death."

The energy rifle off camera was too far away to transmit any sound. Both Lang and I jumped as Rai's head exploded without warning into a half-cooked mess of bone and meat. Her body slumped down and out of sight. After a second, the empty frame faded and the transmission ended.

"Poor Rai," I murmured. "It was only a matter of time."

"Execution by suicide mission?" Lang asked shakily.

I thought about Hideo's words to Rai. This changes nothing, Mawusi. The numbers don't lie. "I think so," I said. It was one of the harsher traditions of the Manhattan Resistance, and I'd seen it continue in some of the Ships as well.

The weak stim pills from the drugstore were already wearing off, but I forced myself to pick up the pace. We went through neighborhoods that had already been tagged, and the sprinkling of orange discs looked like a blight. I knew the tags were part of the surveillance network the Accordance was rolling out over Manhattan to flush out the Conglomeration and keep closer watch on human activity. I knew they also worked well as visual propaganda, an obvious "we are watching" that would be both psychologically and technologically effective. As we passed streets with increasingly more aliens and fewer humans, I couldn't help but notice that there were no humans at all among the Accordance soldiers. I glanced up and realized that the airspace was clearer, but now it was all military hoppers and jumpships.

Lang read my thoughts from the direction of my frowns. "Uh-huh. Looks like another Manhattan siege, but this time, the aliens are on the inside."

16

Devlin ticked off his points finger by finger. "Attacks on training bases, several resistance movements joining Earth First, and most of all, Ghosts sighted in Manhattan—"

"Most of all," Ken repeated dryly. He was sitting on my right, Devlin on my left, both trying to sit comfortably on the too-soft bed. They didn't have a choice. Lang's bedroom was pretty much mattress-sized, and the tiny living room/kitchenette was at capacity with two unoccupied suits of power armor. Their weapons lay at the foot of the bed along with a thoroughly cleaned Bugkiller. Lang stood in the doorway of the bedroom, supposedly on guard, but also partly listening and partly admiring the boys in their underthings.

"All reasons for what's happening now. It's not just a curfew and more surveillance. They're shutting down Orlando and merging it into Empire State. More Accordance troops are being flown in via God knows where because they're not telling us—"

"They're not even telling Anais. He is pissed—"

"—and when I start feeling sorry for Anais, it means the

times are dark indeed." Devlin exhaled sharply, paused for a moment of contemplation, then looked back at me worriedly. "Have you slept?"

I waved a reassuring hand at him. "Shower, clean clothes, and nap all managed, thanks to Lang and her friends. Don't worry about me. What about you? Are you even allowed to be out?"

"In power armor, yes," Devlin said. "Rank has its privileges."

Ken made a rude noise.

"We have yet to see a Ghost in Accordance power armor," Devlin insisted. "So, yes, being of the rank and training that permits the use of power armor is a privilege."

"Anais miss me yet?" I asked cheekily.

"Anais is busy being the buffer for a lot of shit being thrown our way," Ken said soberly. "The CPF may notice you're AWOL after they're done reprocessing everyone, but for now, you're safe. Anais has better things to do than be petty about you."

I gave him a surprised look. He sounded really stressed. He met my gaze and sighed. "Sorry. I've been working with him, trying to see if there are any other incidences of lost or stolen materiel that might prove we have a serious Ghost infiltration on our hands. Anais, Gerrard, there's a group of them that have been covering for us for a good while now. The biobombs were too big a deal not to be noticed, but . . ."

Devlin picked up the story. "The concierge wasn't bluffing. I'm really not sure about Anais, but I think there are a few officers in the CPF who have some kind of connection to Earth First. It might be as slight as mild sympathy, or we might have a general who's a full Earth First spy."

"Is that good news or bad news?" I asked doubtfully.

"Yesterday, I would have said bad. Today? The most I can

manage is a 'maybe.' You see, if there are Earth First plants in the CPF, then why didn't they warn them about the bio-bombs? Why didn't they warn them about the Ghosts?"

I lay still, feeling my mind spark with little connecting pieces of information. There was a subtlety to the indexing program that I was just beginning to notice now that I'd finally completed the prescribed sleep cycles. Even ordinary conversation provided it with enough cues to curate relevant information and set it to the side of my consciousness for me to dip into without distraction.

"The CPF has known about the Ghosts since we encountered them on Icarus," I said. "I bet Earth First has been aware for a while. The discovery about Ghost neuromelanin in bootleg tattoos was made around the same time, so that's when the backlash against alien tech began. The bio-bombs were first used on Titan. That was only a couple of months ago, and although everyone now knows what they can do, few people know what the bombs look like. That's one of the reasons the Accordance was so quick to execute that many staff when they went missing."

I sat up and started to talk faster as the pieces fit together in my brain. "I don't think we have a serious Ghost infiltration on Earth. I don't even think we have one in the CPF. Remember the ghost sign in New Jacksonville? That radio signal could be picked up anywhere, another continent, even the Moon and beyond. It doesn't mean the Ghosts are here.

"We need to look at nonmilitary organizations that have a presence in space. Mining companies, research institutes, engineering consultants—they don't have the specialized tech and the ingrained paranoia to look out for ghost sign like we do. Michael Slate was an example of an early, crude takeover, but remember good old Chris, who was working beside those engineers and saving lives and making friends? I bet there are plenty of other crews who have a mate like that—never encountered on Earth before or after the job, just turns up one day and fits right in."

"And then, even though they don't go back to Earth, the ones that they subvert do," Devlin said.

"Exactly. And I'm noticing a trend. Small group, high-risk environment where trust and bonding are part of survival, low-security location where it's easy to appear and disappear. Ghosts can't operate in New York. Huge, settled population, constantly tracked and monitored with every food purchase, every residential rental—they'd stand out."

"But Amira," Ken said slowly, "what about the Ghosts we fought?"

I said nothing at first. My mind was replaying my conversation with the Ghost and highlighting the things I did not want to hear. "They're not based here. They weren't trained to blend in." My mouth went dry. "Ken, what happens when a single bio-bomb goes off, like at Newark?"

Ken watched me closely. "The area is dead, like a blast zone without the physical damage, but it will recover. I'm not sure of the time frame. Months. Maybe years."

"The last Ghost I fought told me we will have our breeding hives. Is that how it starts? Sterilize and seal the area, then bring in what you want?"

His eyes widened. "Planetwide eradication of life depends on the chain reaction of several bio-bombs with overlapping destruction ranges. Space them out well enough . . . and yes, a bio-bomb is only a sterilization tool."

"The Ghosts are exploiting the situation," Devlin guessed. "It doesn't matter whether or not they led Earth First to the bombs. All they had to do was make sure they had control over the target locations so they could take advantage of the aftermath."

"Because their influence, even over someone like Slate, is not total. We saw those engineers. Even a Ghost couldn't make them go against their natures. They persuade, they manipulate, they lie, but they can't compel." I found that comforting, but then my cynical side silently warned me not to get complacent.

Ken looked at Devlin and tapped his wrist. "Time."

Devlin stood up. "We gotta go. Anais wants us at a meeting."

"This late?" I asked.

"It's been tomorrow in Shanghai for a while," Ken pointed out.

Shanghai. That city was almost entirely Arvani, the Miami of the east. It hadn't been an Earth First target . . . probably too difficult to smuggle in a bio-bomb. According to the newsfeeds, Beijing hadn't been so lucky. A large chunk of their Accordance enclave was gone for good.

Lang helped Ken and Devlin suit up without shattering her aged chipboard furniture and maneuvered them with care and patience, one at a time, out of the front door. I left the bedroom, got myself a drink from Lang's small fridge, and stood in the cool breeze from the window. The weather wasn't all that warm, but four human bodies and two suits of power armor could be a tad overpowering in a small space.

"It's only ten thirty," Lang said. "Do you want to go out? I thought you might like to meet some of my Ship mates, or if you want to meet up with people you know, that's cool too."

She was enthusiastic and awake and so completely unconcerned about any Accordance-enforced curfew that I was sorry to disappoint her. "Since I got drafted into the

CPF, I've tried to keep face-to-face contact with my old Ship mates to a minimum. I'm sure you can understand why."

"Oh, yeah, I understand."

She didn't really, because I didn't tell her. After Icarus, I went briefly AWOL in New Haven, hoping to slot back into my old networks. The timing was bad. The news of the Conglomerate attack was all over the feeds, and though I was still anonymous to the public (Anais never liked using me for PR, sensible man), I was too well-known as a soldier to be welcome. I paid a few courtesy visits, bartered some useful information, and limped back to the CPF. Post-Titan was much worse because I couldn't avoid getting caught up in the PR machine, but I suppose something in me still hoped, which was how I ended up searching for Ship 503 in my spare time.

Being in Manhattan where the Ships first began was like coming home, but with all the upheaval and shifting loyalties, I just didn't want to push my luck.

I silently finished my drink, gathered up my courage, and spoke in a quieter, more formal tone. "I'm sorry about your Ship mate. Sorry we couldn't save him back there."

"Oh. It's all right." She laughed mockingly at her own words. "I mean, of course it's not all right, but . . . he's not the first, and he won't be the last, y'know?"

I was about to ask his name, but she went suddenly tense, staring at the curtain as it moved in the slight breeze. I instinctively put down the glass and picked up a kitchen knife. She pulled a gun from her belt, and I felt a lot less guilty when I saw it was a newer, better model than the one she'd given me, the one I'd thrown away.

"Get off the fire escape," she ordered the half-open

window. "They'll shoot you out there and I'll shoot you in here. Choose!"

The would-be intruder cautiously nudged his way past the curtain with his hands up. Hideo. In Manhattan. With his fucking coat and all.

"Fuck! You!" I shouted. I threw the knife—not at his head like I really wanted to, but hard into the nearby kitchen sink.

"Is it a Ghost?" Lang yelped, aiming her gun steadily at his head.

"No, just a damn fool traitor," I snapped.

Hideo kept his hands up and nodded slowly. "I deserve that. Part of it. Not the traitor part. I may have miscalculated somewhat. Missing variables will do that to you."

"Lang, I take it back. I'd love to meet up with your Ship mates. I remember O'Connell—he's fairly high up in the ranks now, isn't he? He can authorize this moron's execution. I'd do it myself, but I wouldn't want to rob you guys of the pleasure."

"Don't be hasty," Hideo said gravely. "I'm afraid this isn't over yet."

I dragged my hands over my face, spun around, kicked the wall a couple of times to release my growing desire to punch him, and turned to him again. "What have you done?" I asked him quietly.

"I know where the rest of the bio-bombs are set."

I froze. Staring at the wall, I scanned the information. The Accordance had never revealed how many of the bombs went missing. I had accounted for thirty on Earth, nine of which exploded on time and on target in spite of our best efforts, and twenty-one that had been seized and secured and were now on their way off-planet once more. I hoped.

"How many bombs came to Earth, Hideo?" I queried politely.

"Thirty."

I breathed again in relief. Two seconds—then another thought choked the breath in my throat. "How many bombs were stolen from the Accordance?" I whispered.

"Three hundred," he admitted. "Two hundred and seventy bombs never came to Earth. They were kept off-planet, closer to their final destination."

"Which is?" I pressed him.

"The Jupiter front. Io, Ganymede, Callisto, Europa, and all free-floating structures and battleships in the area."

"That's all that stands between us and the Conglomeration. Why would you even think to do that?" Lang said. Her voice shook, but her hands didn't, and the gun was still aimed at his head.

"We didn't. It was meant as a bluff, the real opener to negotiations. The first stage was to prove we had them and we were prepared to used them. The second stage was never meant to be more than a threat to hold their attention."

"Oh, Hideo," I said. "I do believe you will have their complete attention on this."

"I don't blame you for hating me, Amira, but you owe me too." Two feet from a bullet and he was still cocky as hell.

"How do you figure that?" I sneered at him.

He slowly reached out a finger and touched my clean, natural hair. "You freed yourself. You listened to me."

He was so full of it. I owed more to Slate and Russo and even the Ghosts that chased me. I began to tell him so, but he cut me off.

"And you still need me, at least until all those missing biobombs are tracked down and made safe."

I gritted my teeth and breathed deeply. "Lang?"

"Yes, ma'am," came the crisp reply.

"You seemed very comfortable about breaking curfew just now. How quickly can we get this joker to Empire State?"

"Half an hour if he cooperates. An hour if he doesn't. There are a couple of abandoned walkways between here and there, so we won't be on the streets for long."

"Hear that, Hideo? Cooperate."

I switched on the comm and called up both Devlin and Ken on a private channel. Ken answered quickly in a hushed voice. "Amira, is everything all right? This isn't a good time."

"Hideo," I answered in a flat tone.

"Here?"

"With me, here, right now. And it gets worse." I told him quickly about the location of the rest of the missing bio-bombs.

Several long seconds passed before Ken spoke again. "A little context. Devlin and I are at a briefing with Anais and General Gerrard. We are about to go into a teleconference to convince a bunch of scared Arvani that disbanding the CPF and processing all humans into vast internment camps is, in fact, not the best way to deal with the Ghost problem."

My only reply to that was a long exhale.

"I have to tell them," Ken said. "I have to tell them right now."

"Of course. And I'm bringing Hideo in."

"Good. We may need a bargaining chip."

There was one more thing I had to do. I dropped an invitation message at JP's contact codename. I didn't have long to wait before my comm buzzed with an incoming.

"You're still alive." The relief in JP's voice was flattering.

"Trying to stay that way. I wanted to let you know that your old boss is here in front of me."

She hissed out a breath. "Is he, now. I hadn't heard from him, but I thank him for that. The last thing we need is to be tied to his failure. We'll have to stay peaceful and polite for a while to build back some cred. We lost a lot of good people on his gamble."

I thought about Slate. "I'm sorry, JP. What can you tell me that won't shock any eavesdropping grandmas?" I wasn't sure how much she'd been able to do about the Conglomerate surveillance in New Jacksonville.

She sighed. "Not much. Our mutual friend already gave you all the good stuff. I'll try to send along what I can via one of his more mobile seconds. It may take a little time."

"I appreciate it. Stay safe." I broke the connection and reflected for a moment before speaking. "Lang, I know about the walkways. I can get to Empire State. This might be a good time for you to bow out if you want to."

Lang shook her head, still concentrating on keeping Hideo within her sights. "I'm kind of interested in seeing where this goes." She flashed me a quick, challenging glance. "If you don't think I'll be in your way, that is."

I smiled and allowed myself to feel a tiny bit of optimism. "Not at all."

I remembered the networks of old walkways very well. Most had been closed long before the Accordance came. Many did not survive the Arvani's aggressive aquaforming of Lower Manhattan. Naturally, we avoided the sewers. The Arvani had constructed their own underwater pathways, but that didn't mean we wouldn't run into a rogue Arvani hunting an illegal trophy of human bones.

Some of the streets had utility tunnels below, narrow but passable. Some didn't, forcing us to cross aboveground with the help of my enhanced vision and Lang's knowledge of where surveillance lapsed and the line of sight failed. Hideo shut up and followed our mute signals with the obedience of sensible self-preservation. We counted four squads of curfew enforcers on our way, most of them struthiforms, all of them armed and jittery.

The fourth group kept us pinned down behind a dumpster for several minutes while they waited as one of them fussed over an energy rifle. I breathed deeply and quietly, forcing myself to be patient as I listened to their voices chirping and clicking without benefit of translation collar.

Then I frowned. Something floated into my consciousness like an auditory hallucination, a low, tired grumble.

". . . typical Arvani selfishness. They only care about their own safety. They don't care about what it's like for us to be deployed within sight of that evil stain."

I focused, and the translation grew clearer. Another struthiform spoke angrily. "Leave it. We report her and her rifle missing, that's all."

"But what if it's discovered and used by a human?"

I peeked out and glanced at them. Lang put a warning hand on my shoulder, but I was already back under cover. The struthiform who was speaking was trying to disable an energy rifle—not her own, which was riding securely on a sling at her back.

"What if! Sixteen of our soldiers have been reported missing since the curfew was announced, and I think there will be more. The stress is too great. We should have sent for more carapoid troops—"

"The Arvani are saving those to guard their own gates," came another sour comment from the first grumbler. "We are more 'dexterous' and 'land-adapted.' They'll keep shipping us in until every human on this planet has its own personal guard."

"I won't be here to see that," the angry voice declared.

There was a collective hum of shock and slightly admiring awe. "Mutiny!" said the grumbler, sounding far more cheerful.

"Not today."

That final voice was a commanding voice, and it returned the other struthiforms to military order and silence.

"It's done," said the struthiform who was tampering with the energy rifle.

They moved away quickly, not at a sprint, which would have encouraged me to do the same, but with enough urgency to make me signal to the others to brace themselves. We lay in agonizing anticipation for several seconds and then we heard:

paff

And that was it. I looked around the dumpster again and saw the abandoned rifle on the ground, smoking and glowing slightly around the trigger area, not ruined but definitely not usable.

I did a quick scan of the surroundings, swooped down, and grabbed the weapon. "Let's take it," I said, holding it and waving it cautiously to cool it down. "It looks like enough of a threat in the dark."

"Time to get back underground again," Lang muttered.

It wasn't until we were once more in a passageway, splashing through brackish water and construction debris, that Hideo spoke up and said, "Aren't you going to share what you heard back there?"

"I don't speak any struthiform languages," I said truthfully.

"Bullshit. I know what it looks like when someone is listening and thinking. JP's friend got you some alien dictionaries?"

I hesitated. "Maybe," I said at last, and briefly told them what the struthiforms had been arguing about.

"Interesting," said Hideo, and he sounded like he meant it.

"We're here," said Lang. She stopped at a locked metal door. "We have to wait a while. I have to send a message to our Ship contact inside, and she'll let us in as soon as she can."

"No need," I said. The access codes were already surfacing thanks to Russo's index, and I didn't want to waste any time.

17

At least one of Russo's clones had been in the CPF, and for all I knew, there might be others. It made sense that the index was full of all the military codes and schematics I'd ever known in addition to many I'd coveted and never managed to find. It certainly made my job easier, but that didn't stop me from feeling a deep professional jealousy.

Two other things helped. First, the Empire State barracks had a larger-than-usual number of civilians in the corridors, people stranded by the attacks and then the curfew. They were literally in the corridors, sitting and lying on standard-issue bedrolls and clutching their small children, pets, briefcases, or bottled water. Second, whenever I was recognized, it was with a blink or a nod, but otherwise silence. Respect for my part in Ken and Devlin's fame? Ship infiltrators in the CPF giving me space to work? Whatever the reason, I appreciated it.

A quick comms check confirmed that Ken and Devlin were still in their meeting. I decided to be bold. I got a full set of uniform and kit from the quartermaster and even requested and got a few accessories to complement Lang's sober denim, the uniform and camouflage of the urban Ship. For Hideo, nothing but zip ties for his ankles and wrists. He gave me a considering look.

"You're in no position to argue," I told him. "Be glad it's not worse."

"It's not that. It's your choice of uniform. Interesting."

At first I didn't know what he meant, but then I glanced down at myself and realized that I had put on the grays of the CPF but kept the black denim jacket borrowed from Lang. A standard-issue sidearm was on my belt, but the unorthodox Bugkiller was in her usual position at my back. Lang wasn't much better, with her Ship outfit under CPF webbing, civilian-issue sidearm, and the burnt-out Accordance energy rifle slung over one shoulder.

"Whatever works, Hideo," I said dismissively.

"Precisely. Now, if I may I ask, where are we going?"

"A place where you'll be perfectly safe," I replied.

Perhaps I was showing off a bit, but I had the schematics and I had the codes, so I broke the three of us into the office that had been assigned to Anais and sat down on the old wooden desk to wait. Lang stood nervously by the window and looked out occasionally at the deserted streets, and Hideo sat quietly next to her with wrists bound and ankles zip-tied to the chair legs.

I jumped to my feet. The camera at the office door showed Anais, Devlin, and Ken approaching. They wore dress uniform, not grays, which said something about the kind of meeting they'd attended.

Anais was talking angrily, and I smiled as he came into range of the door's mic with a sharp demand: "Singh. Where is she?"

"Sir? I don't—"

Anais interrupted Ken. "Don't lie to me! You didn't want to name names in front of the general, fine—but I know she's involved. Call her, bring her in, and tell her she has one job—to watch that slimy accountant and make sure he's not on his second double-cross."

"But, Colonel—"

"Hart, from the very first day we met, our relationship has been all about me trying my damnedest to keep you alive. Why must you make it so hard? I want Singh here! She's the real brains of your little trio."

I almost snorted out loud at Devlin's wounded look.

"You can count on us to carry out your orders to the best of our ability, Colonel Anais," Ken said smoothly.

Anais glared at him and flung the door open.

"And voilà," Ken continued, unable to resist.

"Colonel," I said neutrally, standing respectfully though not quite at attention.

Anais rolled his eyes at the audacity of the universe, went to his chair, and sat down. "I'm dying to hear your solutions to the problem you've brought to our door, Sergeant Singh."

He was communicating on many different levels: ignoring both Lang and Hideo, calling me Sergeant, sitting slumped and relaxed as if our "problem" wasn't really that serious. I was confused and I looked back at Ken and Devlin for clarification.

Devlin explained. "We couldn't tell the Arvani anything. Gerrard barely managed to talk them down from internment camps to screening and microchipping."

"Which makes this an internal CPF matter," Anais confirmed. "Of course, the CPF is meant to be a subordinate part of the Accordance, which makes it a little difficult to sneak around and quash a battle before it's even begun." He leaned forward and said with intensity, "You got an army, Singh? Let me be specific—do you have a space-ready, equipped force that can help us clean up this mistake?"

I held my breath for a moment. Lang and I exchanged a glance. The Ships were not ready. They were an indigenous resistance movement, tied to the planet and the people, and Hideo's dream of expanding into the stars was nascent and unformed.

Anais watched us looking at each other, and when he sat back again, his slump seemed more like defeat than relaxation. "I thought so. Well, that narrows my options, but hey, at least I have options. All of you, get out of here. Get some sleep. Singh, you're in charge of the accountant. Can your deputy be trusted to stand guard over him?"

I questioned Lang with a silent look. She nodded, but the way she bit her lip and the split second before the nod told me that she knew I was asking her about more than nursemaiding Hideo. "Yes," I answered Anais with confidence.

"Good. Because in a short while I'm going to call you three for a meeting, and I'll want the accountant safely watched elsewhere."

"It's almost midnight," said Devlin. He clearly wasn't complaining about the hour. He was voicing what we all wanted to know—what was Anais going to try to cook up while we were napping?

"Yes, and by morning, one way or another, Gerrard and I will send a force to Jupiter. If we do it right, it won't be shot out of the sky by the Accordance. If we don't . . ." He shrugged tiredly. "Go—no, wait. . . ." He held out a hand to Lang. "I think it's high time I confiscated that energy rifle. And now you can go."

We went.

+ + + +

We slept for about two hours before the call came. Surprisingly, it wasn't a summons to Anais's office but to a windowless interrogation room. When we got there, Anais was not alone. He was pacing up and down before a small table, which had the defective energy rifle laid out on it like a trophy. Two chairs faced the door and one chair was set on the opposite side. One of the door-facing chairs was occupied by a CPF major whose face was so unfamiliar that I had to scan the global records to find out that she was from a European division. She looked far more awake than all of us put together, but she only nodded in greeting and let Anais do the talking.

"Hart, Awojobi, Singh, you stand here behind us. Don't say anything unless I tell you to. This is a delicate situation and I have no idea which way things will shift."

"Perhaps you could give us a little more information, sir?" Ken said. As usual, his courtesy to Anais was heavily laced with sarcasm.

Anais stopped pacing. "We're about to meet with someone who does have a space-ready force. The struthiforms aren't happy about working this close to the bio-bomb blast area, and there have been a significant number of actual and threatened desertions. I want to turn that to my advantage."

"And what is our purpose? Decoration?" Devlin asked, matching Ken's sarcasm.

"Precisely. The three heroes of the Accordance, obediently lined up behind me. It's an easy task; try not to blow it."

We shuffled into position. Anais continued to pace. Then everyone jumped as the door opened again. A struthiform commander entered and slowly looked us over, considering. Her gaze came to rest on the energy rifle, and I think we all held our breath. At last, having thoroughly considered, she closed the door behind her and sat at the single chair.

Anais sat down and rested his hands on the table. "I'm grateful that you agreed to meet with me, but I must know—how much of this discussion will get back to the Arvani?"

"The Arvani are hiding in their underwater strongholds, issuing their orders from a distance." The bland tones of the translation collar didn't convey bitterness well, but the commander's body language made up for the lack. "We can talk without their interference. State your case. Who are you to negotiate with us?"

Anais leaned back in his chair. He had the dangerously calm look of someone who has finally been pushed past all caring. "Well, this the Cowardly Lion, and this is the Scarecrow . . ." he said, waving at Ken and me in turn. "And you've all heard of the Tin Man here. And then there's me, a country boy whose only desire is to get back home to Kansas some day."

"I do not understand," the struthiform commander said coldly.

"Don't you? You haven't spoken your name and rank once in this place. You're not gonna get mine on record."

"She can have my name," said the major. "Will that be enough to start with?"

The struthiform commander looked the major up and down. I might scoff at Colonel Anais and his PR in public, but I have to admit privately that he is a warped genius of human and alien psychology. He had not chosen a random colleague. The major was almost a head taller than Anais, and her graying hair was cut short in a feathered style. Female struthiforms tend to be larger than males, and most of them took on combat and command roles while the males filled support positions in IT and medicine. I had a feeling that the commander was meeting her first human female officer over two meters tall, and she was pleased with what she saw.

The commander dipped her head. "I am Eeshak, Fourth Mother of the Seventy-ninth Red Rain Clutch, and Commander of Accordance Landed Force 417."

The major inclined her head in reply. "And I am Major Buchanan of the CPF. Also Margaret Buchanan, Chief of the Name and Arms of Buchanan, Countess of Stormont . . . not that any of that matters anymore, but when you introduced yourself, I admit I felt a little naked. How do you do."

No translator could convey all that, but again, the body language filled in. Authority, respect, and an interest in getting the job done. Eeshak mirrored Buchanan's slight forward lean. Anais, still sitting back as if purposely removing himself from the interaction, observed with a very small, slightly hopeful smile.

"Major," said the commander. "I think we can understand each other. Let us discuss tactics."

At the end of the meeting we had an agreement and a plan. Commander Eeshak would lend us the use of her courier ships to get to the Jupiter front as quickly as possible. The slower troop transports assigned to take bomb-fatigued struthiforms away from Earth would also include a detachment of CPF soldiers if we needed to call for reinforcements. Jumpships would be available to take CPF troops to any of Jupiter's moons, but the struthiforms would stay in orbit and well away from any bomb threat.

Commander Eeshak had also insisted that one of the transports be outfitted as a hospital ship capable of screening large numbers of humans, CPF and civilians, for signs of alien tech. In addition, she assured us that a confidential message would be sent out to all struthiform medics at the front, expanding their official Accordance directive from simply looking out for Ghosts to examining all humans for any trace of Ghost DNA.

I went cold at the reminder. I had to get myself properly checked out.

I couldn't understand why the Commander appeared to be so pleased. She was providing us with everything we needed at great risk to her reputation and the lives of her soldiers. But then my fears faded when she admitted:

"This will restore the honor of those hatchlings who felt they had no choice but to desert. We no longer have a place to run to, but we can at least help you save your nests."

I like to think that Commander Eeshak knew enough about humans to understand why the tiny room suddenly grew noisy with sniffing and throat-clearing.

She left to start the plan rolling, and we returned to the relative comfort of Anais's office for more debriefing. For this meeting, Anais called in Hideo and Lang so that Hideo could tell Major Buchanan firsthand about his part in the bio-bomb conspiracy. In turn, we learned that Major Buchanan was a Conglomerate alien specialist, probably one of those who'd written the lengthy, detailed, boring texts that Sigurthardottir assigned to our poor recruits. That accounted for her ease with Commander Eeshak, and it also explained why she was in New York. She had been present at the autopsies of the Ghosts who died fighting us over the bio-bomb.

"Four bodies of human appearance were recovered," she said. "Two were shot with CPF weapons. One had a crushed larynx. The fourth . . . well, it's hard to tell precisely what killed the fourth. I'd credit the crushed skull from a high fall, but there were several other broken bones that helped it along."

"The shots were Ken and Devlin," Lang said helpfully. "Amira got one in the throat."

Major Buchanan raised a thin blond eyebrow with interest. "And the fourth?"

I described how the fourth Ghost had obtained its injuries.

She stared at me for a while, her expression unreadable. Then she turned to Anais. "I'll take on your consultant and her two attachés."

"Actually, I think I'm still a sergeant . . ." I began.

She gave me a look. "Sergeants get to follow my orders. Consultants get listened to."

"Consultant it is," I agreed.

"Oh, good," Anais said dryly. "I've been trying to find a way to kick Singh out of the CPF since her first AWOL jaunt."

Buchanan laughed. "Come now, Colonel. Where I come from, we always reward successful and innovative breaking of the rules."

"The key word in there is 'successful,'" Anais pointed out. "It's great getting rewarded for being successful . . . until suddenly one day you're not and the body count is more than anyone can overlook."

Everyone avoided looking at Hideo, but he was the black hole in the room, effortlessly absorbing our silent judgement. I felt a little nudge, not Russo's index this time but my own intuition. Failure could be managed. By seeking me out and linking himself to me, Hideo had bought himself a ticket to his best chance for absolution via suicide mission. Would he care if he took out half the CPF for his grand final act? Would it matter to him if Ken, Devlin, and I were collateral damage along the way, or had he factored that willingly into his overall risk assessment?

He sat meekly, head down, ever compliant, but for a moment he looked up, caught my eye, and smiled in a way that I could not interpret.

PART THREE

18

"Let us see what we have here. Oooh, that is nasty." The struthiform medic on our courier ship was bossy and slightly contemptuous of humans, and it showed with every word and gesture.

"I was pressed for time," I tried to say with dignity, but the end of the sentence rose up into the treble of a pained yelp.

"Keep still," the medic said impatiently. "You left fragments in there. They can partially dissolve, travel into the bloodstream, and act as accretion points for thrombosis. It is a miracle you did not kill yourself."

"Blood clot—oww! Nghhhh! Can't you give me an anesthetic?" I said, finally snapping.

"No," the medic replied with obscene cheer. "We cannot have your nerves dulled for this procedure."

I gritted my teeth and thought instead about where I'd rather be—with Ken and Devlin, carefully and thoroughly interrogating Hideo about the precise location of the bio-bombs and Earth First infiltrators on the Jupiter front. But Buchanan had assigned them to work on Hideo while the medic worked on me. Perhaps she had already detected that he could get under my skin with a single word. Perhaps Devlin and Ken had told her about the torture. I felt a little resentful about that. I might have had the occasional daydream about subjecting Hideo to the same kind of mental flaying he'd put me through, but I wouldn't indulge myself and jeopardize the mission.

When I finally emerged from sickbay, bruised and limping, I was surprised and pleased to see Ken and Devlin waiting outside for me. "Finished grilling Hideo already?" I asked with mock disappointment as I headed towards my quarters.

"Sort of," Devlin said with a tight smile. His eyes flickered up and down, checking me over, and I instinctively straightened and tried to look less in pain. "The good news is, the biobombs haven't reached Jupiter's moon—yet. The bad news—"

Ken interrupted. "The bad news is that the infiltrators are spread throughout the fleet. We don't have much time and we need to cut this off at the head, but Hideo can't pinpoint where the orders will be coming from."

"But," Devlin added, "he claims he can figure it out with time and more data."

"He could be stalling," I said.

"We know," Ken agreed, "but we're going to make it work for us. We're on course to encounter our first CPF troopship, and we're going to use it to test our Ghost Reclamation Protocol. Order them to match flight path and prepare for boarding. Isolate the command staff and bring our medics on board to screen them. Return screened personnel to command and proceed with the rest of the crew. It has to be done quickly and without public broadcast so that any Ghosts present won't have time to react."

"And Buchanan says she's prepared to offer amnesty to

any Earth First or Ship infiltrators as long as they help us in our investigations," Devlin said.

"That's kind of her, but I hope she realizes that not everyone will take that amnesty."

"I think she expects you to help with identifying infiltrators. You've got inside knowledge and . . . stuff . . ." Devlin stammered to a halt at the look on my face.

"I'm not prepared to do that," I stated bluntly. "If they fight us, if they confront us, then we've got grounds to detain them. If they're saying nothing and doing nothing, I won't be an informer."

Ken tried to smooth over the awkward moment with a calm voice. "And should they confront us, we're going to tag them with a band for monitoring and restraint. We don't want to overflow the brig, and besides, we'll need all hands if the Conglomerate brings the fight to us."

I thought for a moment. "Fine," I said at last. "We'll make it work."

"Good," Devlin said. "We have ten hours to get ready for contact."

The boarding party looked eclectic, but it had been carefully chosen. Devlin and Ken led a squad of ten in power armor. I would have preferred more, but with the limitations of a courier ship, we didn't have more, and the point of the reclamation protocol was to be as inconspicuous as possible.

I decided not to wear power armor, which shocked Devlin. I explained to him that until I had time to figure out how Hideo managed to reset the power armor mode from combat to training and, more importantly, work on a solution to stop it from happening mid-battle, I'd prefer to entrust my safety to light security armor, a sidearm, and Bugkiller.

"Should we be worried?" Ken asked.

"No," I reassured him. "That level of control only works at close range and on one suit at a time, so if you keep the squad tight and communicate quickly, you should be able to stomp on anyone who tries it."

Hideo was not permitted to attend and Lang stayed behind to guard him. Major Buchanan kept command of the courier, and so the rest of the team consisted of twenty struthiform medics in light armor led by a junior commander called Ikvar.

Buchanan put me in charge. I wasn't sure how I felt about that, but she took time to explain.

"It's very simple, Ms. Singh. You are an excellent coordinating point for the action. You possess an accumulation of military intelligence that few can match, and you have the personal technology to tap into every camera and control panel on the ship. Plus, you can tell us where the Ghosts are."

I opened my mouth and closed it again. This didn't seem like a good time to share my doubts about my ability to detect ghost sign after my amateur and professional tech-cleansing.

At first it went smoothly. Our transit vessel was accepted into the docking bay, and the welcoming crew was scanned and briefed about the situation. Ken took five soldiers to escort half the medics to the bridge to begin screening the command crew while the rest of us waited in the docking bay. I say the rest of us, but I was busy looking ahead throughout the ship, trying to pick up the electronic patterns of ghost sign. I checked and double-checked. Nothing. No Conglomeration signals or messages going out or coming in. I relaxed just a little.

"Bridge has been secured. All personnel are clean and

none admit to belonging to Earth First or any other subversive organization." Ken's voice ran from cheerful hope to dry sarcasm.

"Noted, Sergeant Awojobi," I replied formally. "Let me speak to the commanding officer."

There was a short pause, then a brisk voice. "Commander Boris Ivchenko here."

Stupidly, I felt a pang at the familiar first name, reminding me of one of the many fallen at Icarus. "Commander, this is Ms. Amira Singh, consultant under Major Buchanan. We specialize in the study of Conglomerate aliens. Sergeant Awojobi has explained the situation to you?"

"He has," came the terse reply.

"All is well, Commander, and you are still in charge. I am asking your permission to send a contingent of medics to your sickbay. We can set up our main screening center there. If you could then order all personnel to sickbay in small groups, we should be able to clear your entire crew. There is no need to alarm them with details. We will organize for them to be briefed in sickbay."

He gave a relieved sigh. "You have my permission, Ms. Singh. I want this to be over and done with. I don't feel comfortable knowing that my ship could be compromised."

I quietly echoed his sigh. I hadn't been sure how CPF officers would react to our mini-takeover. I had to thank Major Buchanan. Putting me in charge, having someone with a civilian title and position make requests instead of demands—that might well have made our job easier.

"I only have one question. You mentioned screening all my personnel, and that is in order, but what about the refugees?"

"The who?" I said blankly.

"The refugees of Newark, Beijing, Cape Town, and a few

other places. We found them a few days ago in a fleet of jumpships and orbital shuttles about to run out of fuel. We were going to drop them off at Ceres to get civilian transport back to Earth. We have about three thousand on board. What do you want us to do with them?"

I gaped for a full three seconds before I gathered enough breath and sense for a reply. "Commander, kindly secure all entry to the hold. I would also like to recommend that you secure the bridge after the sergeant and his troops leave. We will proceed for now with screening the crew and get back to you promptly."

I dropped the link to the Commander and spoke on a private channel to Devlin, Ken, and Ikvar. "Gentlemen, we can start stage two. Ken, take your squad and medics to sickbay. Devlin will join you there with his squad and the remaining medics."

"Acknowledged," Ken replied, "but where will you be?"

I touched Bugkiller lightly to reassure myself. "I'll be around, preparing the ground for stage three."

"The protocol doesn't have a stage three," Ikvar said suspiciously.

"It does now."

I waited until at least two thirds of the crew had been scanned, giving us more medics, faster screening, and more reinforcements that we could trust. Devlin and Ken handed over security responsibilities to the crew and left Ikvar to supervise the screening. When they arrived, I was in the same position I'd been in for almost an hour—in front of the main doors to the hold, standing still and focusing furiously on several different cameras in the vast space.

"I'm a little distracted," I warned them. "Pay attention.

Inside the hold looks like a cross between a three-day music festival and a tent city. Bedrolls, portable toilets, lots of privacy screens. Obstacles, poor lines of sight, and plenty of potential for collateral damage."

"Sounds like a tactical nightmare," Devlin muttered.

"Exactly. We can screen them in sickbay in small groups like we did for the crew, but there's no military discipline here. People will question, they will argue, and they will simply refuse to go."

"So tell them the truth," Ken said. "Let's walk in, shut the door behind us, and just talk to people. They're already scared and far from home. Let's not make this into an incident."

Devlin grinned at him. "Are you planning a 'heroes of the Accordance' performance?"

Ken smiled as if embarrassed. "Could be."

I looked at them in disbelief. Months of being pressured into PR, and now they were acting like they actually enjoyed it?

And that was stage three: Ken and Devlin working the vast crowd, signing autographs and taking pictures, and politely asking them to pay a visit to sickbay as quickly as possible.

"Where's the girl with the purple hair?" I heard someone ask as they went past me with a double-autographed T-shirt. She shook the shirt in frustration. "I wanted the full set!"

I turned away hastily and began to cross-check faces to my database. There were a few Ship members. No need to declare their presence; they were only civilians, after all. I made note of at least two criminals—one wanted for document forgery, the other for human trafficking. I would have been tempted to spare the forger, but his record showed that forgery was mild in comparison to his past transgressions.

I stopped dead. Slate?

Hunched against a wall, half-hidden behind a suspended

sheet, bundled in a blanket . . . it was Slate. He was barely recognizable. He'd ditched his Ship uniform for more neutral civvies and his face was bruised gray with insomnia.

He didn't look at all surprised. He smiled sadly. "Amira. I knew you were coming."

I stood in front of him, concentrating hard. The EMP shielding in the hold was thick, and there was nothing in the patterns of communication going back and forth that hinted at anything alien. And yet . . . when I faced Michael Slate, I could sense that suppressed vibration, that slight pulse that whispered ghost sign.

"I need backup," I said urgently over my comm as I raised my sidearm and pointed it at Slate, ignoring the startled noises behind me as people scrambled to get away from us.

He raised his hands in surrender. "Whoa, wait a minute. Are you arresting me?"

"I'm asking the questions, Slate. How did you get here?"

His expression hardened. "Evacuating with a group of scared struthiforms just ahead of the bio-bomb blast. Burning out our fuel too fast because we were desperate to get out of range. Drifting for hours. How did you get here? On that fancy courier ship?"

"Ordinarily, I would say I'm glad to see you alive, but before I do that, I really have to know—where do your loyalties lie? With JP? Hideo? Elsewhere? Because I'm sniffing ghost sign around you and that's new for me."

He sagged, looking vulnerable and helpless as Ken and Devlin joined me, imposing in their power armor. "We discussed this before. I told you that traces will always remain."

"That's not an answer. I need to know if you're a Ghost spy. Can you prove that you're not?"

He shook his head. "The traces are slight. There's nothing

left for them to manipulate. It's just a scar. You're as likely to be a spy as I am."

"That's a lovely theory, but I don't see the proof. Either way, since I'm still not sure which side you've chosen, I'll err on the side of caution." I turned to Ken. "Band him."

Slate grinned as Ken affixed the restraining band to his ankle. "Fine. Don't trust me. But what about you? Why should they trust you and not me?"

I stopped and glared at him. "Ken," I said quietly, holding out my wrist.

Ken shot a worried look at Devlin and received in answer a frown followed by a slow nod. Ken fumbled a bit but finally managed to get the band secured around my wrist. Cold pin-pricks tingled into my nerves and around my nano-ink.

"There," I said. Slate was shocked into silence. I gave him a cold smile. "Oh, you thought this was a game? It's not. When it comes to our survival as a species, I don't play games, not even with myself."

I walked away and quickly opened a private channel. "Ikvar, Ken, Devlin, I have to go back. Can you handle it from here?"

"Certainly," said Ikvar, "but—"

"Good. Ikvar, you have command." I left the hold without another word, with only a slightly raised hand when Devlin attempted to follow me. I had to get to sickbay and figure out what was going on with me and what I could do about it.

19

"Ahh, yes," said my least favorite struthiform medic, squinting at a set of medical readouts and images on a grid of wall screens. He refused to give me his name, so I had started to think of him as the Anti-Shriek. "This is fascinating. I can see the permanent change has been well established."

"Explain," I said, gritting my teeth to hold onto my patience.

"You are right. Your genetic signature has shifted, but whether it is due to Ghost interference, I cannot tell. Regardless, it would be impossible for you or anyone to sense a particular kind of DNA."

"What do you mean? What else could it be if I'm still sensing ghost sign?"

The Anti-Shriek paused to ponder. "You first met the Slate person on Earth?"

I nodded.

"Did you sense anything at that time?"

"I didn't, no," I said with a frown.

"If I may, I have some information that might help?" Hideo said, appearing in the door of sickbay. He was wearing his apologetic persona, which meant that his hands were clasped in front of him in a gesture that was both supplicating and calculated to show off the new restraint band on his wrist.

"Come in," said the medic. "You are the dangerous fool who brought the bio-bombs to Earth? Such a historic moment to meet you."

The words made me smile, but Hideo's wince made me grin outright, and for a moment I liked the medic a little better.

Hideo ignored the medic and spoke directly to me. "I believe you didn't sense anything from Slate because he wore special clothing which acted as shielding. Nothing out, nothing in. It was designed to ensure that what little remained of his nano-ink could not receive anything harmful from a Conglomerate source. At the time I thought it more placebo than practical, but perhaps it did have some effect."

"Okay, that makes sense," I said, feeling instantly depressed. I'd tried to cut the invader out of me and I'd failed.

"I can make something like that for you," Hideo continued.

I tilted my head and raised an eyebrow, skeptical but willing to hear him out.

"You already know that I have a similar layer in my coat to shield my threads. EM pulse, covert data extraction—it protects from all these things, and maybe Ghosts, too."

My despair lifted immediately. All I needed was to know there was something I could do. "I know how your shielding works. I can make it myself, but thanks for the idea."

He winced again at the rejection. "I owe you a lot."

It sounded like an apology. I stared at him silently until he turned to go.

The medic yelled after him, "You owe me too, foolish human. You owe us all. Where is our compensation?"

I bit my lip, caught between agreement and concern. I wanted Hideo to regret his life choices, but not so much that death looked preferable. "Hush," I told the medic. "Let him finish what he's here to do. After that, we'll both give him hell."

"Oh, I would enjoy that. Let that be a promise between us."

"No name, no promise." It was worth a try.

"I would not burden you with that responsibility. Call me Wei. That is a common enough human name."

"All right, thank you, Wei—but why is a name a responsibility?"

Wei went very still for a moment. I realized I'd probably asked something stupid and he was bracing himself to answer calmly. "One's full, unique name is central to the ceremonies of birth and death. I have seen this even for humans."

I was about to risk asking him just how important it was to struthiforms when Devlin appeared. "Got a moment?" he asked, his gaze skittering nervously over the masses of unfamiliar information on the screens.

I said goodbye to Anti-Shriek Wei and joined Devlin. "Where to?"

"Pre-debriefing at Buchanan's," he answered. "What the hell were you thinking back there with the band? No, don't tell me. Wait till Ken gets in."

We had barely settled ourselves in the small meeting room before Ken came in demanding, "What the hell was that nonsense with the band?"

Devlin gave me a smug "I told you so" look.

I raised my hands. "No, but seriously, did you guys really think I was going to put myself under CPF control? Ken, I've sent the key for my band to your private contact. Devlin, I've given you a backup in case Ken can't reach me for some reason. The band won't respond to the standard restraint codes, so keep those keys safe because they're the only way to take me down if I go rogue."

Before they could argue, Buchanan walked in with Ikvar. She sat at the head of the table and Ikvar sat beside me. "First run of the reclamation protocol has been completed. I've seen the footage, but before I say anything—Ms. Singh, why did you transfer command and leave early?"

"I had reason to believe that I might be compromised and went immediately to sickbay to review my medical data," I explained.

"I see," Buchanan said. "Are you?"

"Apparently not, but precautions have been taken."

She eyed the band. "I am aware of some of those precautions. Ms. Singh, can you tell me why the code for the band on your wrist does not appear on my list of detainees? Do you perchance have other precautions in place that are not mere theater?"

"Yes ma'am," I replied. I admired her wording. She had said just enough and framed it with plenty of wiggle room for both of us in case of any future inquiries.

"Splendid. Based on information from Commander Ivchenko, I have decided to proceed with the protocol as follows. The commander is granting us a detachment of medics and officers to train for our next encounter. A small contingent of our medics led by Subcommander Ikvar will join Ivchenko's crew on a mission to secure Ceres. Ikvar will remain on Ceres to establish and maintain a medical base to screen, clean, and band humans as required. Ivchenko will divert to encounter the nearest CPF or civilian transport in the vicinity and begin the process anew."

I really admired how she'd taken hold of the word "encounter." Friendly meeting or military engagement—let the Accordance propagandists decide.

Buchanan leaned forward and addressed me. "I heard about your theory that Ghost infiltration started in the mining communities. If you're right, we have to screen every human in the asteroid belt, no matter how long it takes."

Ikvar nodded in agreement. "With respect, until that is done it will be hard for any of us to trust a human face."

Ken frowned. "Are you saying you want us to do what the Arvani are doing for Earth and the Moon? Register and record every human and monitor their movements?"

"I don't believe it will come to that," Buchanan said evenly. "Awareness and regular screening should be enough to protect the smaller space communities. The banding is only a temporary measure for declared dissidents and any who demonstrate unclear loyalties."

Ken looked doubtful. I stiffened slightly but kept my expression blank. Neither of us said anything. Devlin stared at the major, so obviously radiating attention and obedience that it almost made things worse.

"Our next encounter," Buchanan continued, raising her voice slightly and closing off the previous topic. "Another troopship, but this one has a much higher probability of Earth First infiltration. As for Ghosts, that remains to be seen. Ms. Singh, can I count on you to identify the dissidents and get the information we need to find the lead ship? Now that you have taken precautions, there should be no need for you to abandon your post midmission."

Ouch. The only real difference between sergeant and consultant was that the reprimands were delivered with pointed politeness and no swearing. I preferred the swearing. "Of course, Major Buchanan," I said.

+ + + +

There was time for me to deal with my distrust of power armor. I enlisted Ken and Devlin's help and they practiced being my puppets in one of the holds where we wouldn't be disturbed.

"I thought you would bring Hideo in," Devlin said at one point.

"He's the source of most of our problems. I don't want him around when I find the solutions. He's not getting any information out of me again. Ever."

"Okay," Devlin said. "Can you unlock my leg now? It's going numb."

I froze and unfroze them both several times, did some recalibrating, and then finally managed to fail to freeze them. I grinned. "Got it."

"Cool! What was it?" Devlin asked.

"Hideo got hold of the codes for training mode, probably via Russo, but that's not enough, because the codes are changed regularly. He must have worked out the algorithm for how they're cycled. I increased the change frequency for your suits and I'll do the same for mine."

"Good," Ken said. "I'm not comfortable with you going into a space battle without armor."

"Speaking of armor," Devlin said, "can you tell us about this?" He waved his hand at my new accessories.

I opened my mouth to explain, hesitated, then pressed on. "One useful idea from Hideo. The mesh shields my ink from EMP attack and data theft. Might also hide me from Ghosts. I'm not sure about that, but I guess I'll find out soon."

"Looks snazzy," Ken teased.

I shrugged, but I was secretly pleased. They were kind of snazzy. The arm protectors, which covered from wrist to bicep, were constructed from fine mesh lined with black spidersilk. The latter had taken a good chunk out of my credit, but to my surprise and joy, my consultant's wages were up to the task. I decided to show off a little.

"The hood does this—which is kind of helpful now that my hair tangles so easily without the tech overlay."

Taking hold of the cowl around my neck, I stretched the back edge over my head and down to my forehead and the front edge up and over my chin and mouth. All nano-ink was covered except my eyes. I felt like a superhero. I didn't want to look at a camera image to confirm. The feeling was enough, and the boys cheered for me like it was true.

There was another bit of shielding, the patch tied over my bandaged, slowly healing wound, but I didn't feel like showing that off.

Mastering both the power armor and shielding issues made me more cheerful than I'd felt in weeks . . . months! It was the best stress-reliever I could hope for since there was no bar on the courier beyond the major's private cabinet for diplomatic occasions. I wondered if she had anything special to break out when we'd successfully completed our mission.

In an uncanny echo of my thoughts, Devlin got a call from Buchanan. He left the hold briskly while Ken and I followed at a slower pace. Ken paused by the open door and looked back at me. He'd retracted his helmet, so I could clearly see that his expression was very worried.

I stopped next to him. "What's wrong, Ken?"

"I . . . uh . . . can't help but notice that you gave me the primary key and Devlin the backup."

"Yeah, that's right," I said. I had no idea where he was going with this.

"Then whatever happens here, whether we win or lose, I think I should stick with you."

 My eyes opened wide. "Ken, I didn't give you the key

to obligate you. We can always find a way around that. I don't know where I might end up, but it might not be in the CPF—and I know how important the CPF is to you and your family."

"Yes. But now I'm wondering whether the CPF is where I should be. It isn't what I expected it to be, and it won't become what I hoped it could be. Not yet, not for a long while."

I was struck by his seriousness. "Are you telling me you're going to ditch the CPF and everything you've been working for? The equal pay, the full citizenship—you're going to walk away from that fight?" I knew my words were provocative, but I needed to be sure he'd thought it through.

"It's not a fight when you don't even have the power to negotiate," he said. "Hideo Pereira is a misguided son of a bitch, but he's got one thing right. The Accordance won't take us seriously unless we're an established, independent space power."

I raised my hands. "Whoa, whoa, hold up there. Are you saying you expect me to continue what Hideo screwed up? Launch the Ships of the Manhattan Resistance into space?"

He only smiled. "I think you're capable of many amazing things, but one step at a time, Amira. Don't worry about that yet."

The smile abruptly dropped away and his face changed to an expression of self-loathing. "You should hate me, like Devlin did at the start. I started off with one set of loyalties, and here I am, thinking about shifting again. How can I ask you to depend on me when I can barely trust myself?"

Shaking my head, I replied with confidence, "Your motives never changed. You've always wanted justice for the oppressed, a voice for the silenced. Your methods, your allies, those all changed but that's never changed. I respect you for that, Ken Awojobi."

For one scary moment I thought he was getting choked up, but he got control over himself, cleared his throat, and gathered me up in a careful hug. My mesh-clad arms screeched slightly against his armor and we both laughed.

We were in our quarters when Devlin walked in after his meeting with Buchanan. His face was enough warning that trouble was back on our menu.

"Well," he said, "shit just hit the fan back on Earth. The Accordance is now officially aware of our mission, by which I mean the Arvani finally got their act together."

"Why didn't Buchanan call us all in?" Ken demanded. "If this is going to impact the mission—"

Devlin looked away uneasily. "She had her reasons." He sat down on his bunk, braced his elbows on his knees, and clasped his hands. "Our alliance with the struthiforms is a complication they didn't expect, so they're trying something a little different. They're offering full Accordance citizenship to the CPF officers involved. Gerrard, Anais, Buchanan . . . me. That's it."

He was looking at Ken almost apologetically. It was a painful irony that the two had come from opposite sides, traveled from enemies to friends to brothers, and yet along that journey, Devlin had managed to overshadow Ken in everything that Ken wanted—rank, fame, and now full recognition from the Accordance.

I spoke to break the tension. "They're trying to save face and make it look like they were in charge all along. What does Buchanan think of the offer? Is she going to accept it for herself?"

Devlin shook her head. "She wouldn't say. She told me there were benefits and drawbacks and she believed I was smart enough to figure them out for myself."

"Take it," Ken said.

"Wha—" Devlin's mouth opened and closed before he could find enough breath to say weakly, "You can't be serious."

"Full citizenship for a human? Deadly serious. Be a citizen. Be an Accordance captain, not a client CPF client captain. Set a precedent. They do it once for you, they'll do it again for others."

"But at what cost? Everything my father worked for, subverted, and twisted to prop up the Accordance? I can't do it. It's bad enough that I wear this uniform. I can't do that to him. The last thing he told me . . . he said 'stay human.' If I do this willingly, he'll never understand. He'll think I've given up."

Ken's mouth twisted into a pained smile. "I know how you feel. If my family knew what I was thinking now, they'd say I was betraying everything we stood for."

"How long do you have to decide?" I asked Devlin.

He shrugged. "Buchanan didn't say. I don't think Anais and Gerrard are in a position to refuse up at Empire State, but maybe I could stall until this mission is over. Who knows, if I screw up badly enough, they might retract the offer."

I gave him a glare for even suggesting such a thing. "Try to see the bigger picture, Devlin. We really, really want this mission to go well."

"Yeah . . . sorry. Got a little carried away."

The room went silent I looked at them. Devlin brooded with head down. Ken stared blankly at the wall. We'd been happy just forty minutes earlier. I really wanted a drink.

20

Ten minutes into stage two and we were already running for our lives.

"Devlin, there's a service corridor . . . nearest entrance about fifty meters aft of your location. See if you and your squad can squeeze into it."

"Seen," he answered, terse and out of breath. "Yes, we're in."

"Good. Ken, is the bridge secure?"

"For now, yes."

"Tell the enviro-technical officer to stand by to seal doors 5-12 and 6-12 and cut oxygen supply between them. On my command."

I kept running. Fortunately, ballistic weapons were not used on troopships. That was planetside weaponry, with lots of gravity and room for things to behave as expected. Unfortunately, someone had a small but powerful laser. I ran as hard as I could, grateful as hell for my solid, dependable power armor.

I reached 6-12 and dived through. "Now," I yelled. I enjoyed the percussion that followed. First, like a complex triple tap, 5-12 slammed shut, 6-12 followed, and I tumbled to the ground and slid hard against the wall. Then the sound of bodies slamming into the closed door, unable to stop or slow down in time. Finally, a gentle background hiss for the dominant theme of those same bodies falling to the floor unconscious.

My enjoyment faded. There was one drum out of step, a persistent banging on 6-12 long after the initial series of floor thumps and well after the hissing of the gas died away.

"Ken, Devlin? Problem. We have a Ghost."

I had tried to be careful about showing off my knowledge of access codes, especially for a mission that involved us taking over the ships of our own military, albeit for good cause. But this time I didn't hesitate to seize control of a camera and broadcast the images to the bridge as proof that our actions were completely necessary.

A man, or what appeared to be a man, stood on the other side of door 6-12, banging on the metal with both fists . . . and denting it, too. Behind him, about five humans sprawled in blissful oblivion. It was pretty clear that one of those things was not like the others. The truly painful thing was that he was wearing CPF grays.

"Ken, get them to find out who he is impersonating and how and when the switch was made. There's no way he went through base training on Earth or the Moon without attracting attention."

"On it," Ken said.

I got up, metaphorically brushed myself off, and leaned my right hand on door 6-12. "Ken, ask the ETO to open 6-12 on my command."

"Wait, what?" Devlin cut in. "I'm on my way, Amira. Give me two minutes."

"No time. I've killed four Ghosts without benefit of power

armor. With power armor? Shouldn't be too hard. And . . . now!"

The door slid open far more slowly than it had closed, giving the Ghost time to seize the edge and rip the entire panel away. Bugkiller rode across my chest, pulsing out a steady wave of selective pain and destruction, and the Ghost wasn't expecting it at such close quarters. He staggered back. I braced my hands on either side of the doorway and planted both feet hard in his sternum. He flew down the corridor and hit door 5-12 solidly.

"Try to take one alive," Buchanan had told me before we boarded. I was wondering as I moved forward what could possibly incapacitate a Ghost. Lack of oxygen did nothing, and all my previous engagements with them suggested you had to pretty much kill them to stop them, and even then they'd be punching out their death throes.

I did the only thing I could think of—put Bugkiller on high, focused blast and pointed it directly at the Ghost's head.

I cut my helmet's audio to the outside to block the screaming, but I was forced to watch the writhing and the convulsions. My skin prickled in sympathy, remembering the burning agony of electromagnetic pulse against unshielded nano-ink.

"Amira? Did you get it?" Devlin voice came through on my private channel.

"Uh . . . yeah. Send a couple of medics to my location." I came closer to the Ghost's curled-up body, taking care not to step in the blood, and snapped a set of old-fashioned metal cuffs on its ankles and wrists. I found the laser clipped to his belt—an engineering tool modified for use in combat—and attached it to Bugkiller's sling instead.

I backed away, carefully keeping my eye on the Ghost in case it found a second wind, and startled the bejeezus out of myself by bumping into Devlin.

“I’m here,” he said unnecessarily. “How did it go?”

“It’s still alive, but I don’t know for how long. I’m experimenting with what Bugkiller can do, but I haven’t had time to test it scientifically.”

There was an awkward silence during which I realized Devlin was giving me a very strange, almost fearful look. “Oh, come on, Devlin. Scientific doesn’t mean using human or even Ghost test subjects. There are tons of biosimulations that will give me the information I need.”

We stepped aside and let the medics carry the Ghost away, doubly restrained to a stretcher. One medic stayed behind with oxygen to help the rest of the slowly reviving crew. We both retracted our helmets and Devlin dispatched his squad to sickbay to help the medics finish off stage two.

On the way back to the bridge, Devlin said, “I still don’t get it. I remember when some of your tats got burned out by electromagnetic pulse on the Moon.”

“Yeah. Those were done with standard civilian nano-ink. I had them retouched afterwards with hardened nano-ink.”

“All right, I think I remember, but tell me again what that means.”

“Hardened nano-ink is usually either military nano-ink, which contains Arvani ink, or bootleg nano-ink, which contains squid ink. Unfortunately, the bootleg version swaps the synthesized Ghost neuromelanin in military nano-ink for the real stuff. Using human neuromelanin alone, like in standard civilian nano-ink, wouldn’t work for reasons that are too long to explain right now.”

“So, if Ghost neuromelanin is used to make hardened nano-ink, then a Ghost is like . . . a massive walking nano-ink tattoo?”

“Sort of, yeah. But lacking squid or Arvani ink, so still vulnerable to EMP and other kinds of attack.”

"Okay, but vulnerabilities aside, does that mean they're like supercomputers?"

I thought about it for a while. "It makes them very efficient physically, and they've also got some weird mental stuff going on that lets them get into networks, or into people's heads if those people have bootleg ink. But tattoos are probably still superior because it's not just about the ink, but also the design, density, and location of the tattoo. What, Devlin—are you trying to figure out if I'm stronger than a Ghost?"

He looked over his shoulder with a smile and nod to where the medics had departed with the Ghost. "I know you're stronger than Ghosts. You've proved it every time. I'm just trying to understand how all this affects you."

"Oh. Okay. Most of my tats are hardened military nano-ink now. The mesh is for extra protection, and power armor seals the deal. Besides, I've gotten pretty good at aiming Bugkiller so I never shoot myself in the foot."

"That's useful information, but not exactly what I wanted to know."

Thankfully, Ken interrupted before I had to answer. "Amira, they're asking for you in sickbay."

I frowned in puzzlement, wondering what it could be about, and really, really hoping it had nothing to do with the Ghost I'd just taken down. "Right, Ken, on my way."

It had nothing to do with the Ghost, at least not directly. Wei had sent out the summons. I soon discovered that Wei loved research. He walked with me along lines of crew members waiting for screening or cleaning, and monitored my physiological reactions via sensors. I felt awkward and fraudulent and I told him so.

"Not a word," he ordered. "Not even a hint. I will be able to deduce everything from your data."

I waited impatiently while he ran the results against the crew medical records. I watched the small feathers on his wing hands quivering in frustration. "What?" I demanded.

"I have a theory. Interviews should confirm it. Do you have another duty to perform elsewhere? You are disrupting my workflow."

"Okay, Professor Wei," I said sarcastically. "Call me when you want me."

In a couple of hours, stage two was finished and the mission was formally completed. Devlin, Ken, and I went back to the courier for our debriefing with Major Buchanan. The longest part came when I described how we had neutralized the group of rogue crew and their Ghost leader. Buchanan listened with full attention and asked several questions that focused on the behavior of the human crew, the strength and endurance of the Ghost, my modifications of Bugkiller, and how soon and how much the Ghost had bled.

"We're going to have to try some of those modifications on our EPC-2s. Ms. Singh, can I trouble you to prepare a report for the Munitions division of R&D? Any time before our next troopship encounter should be fine."

"Yes, Major," I said, biting back a sigh. Reprimands and now paperwork.

When the meeting ended and we filed out, something made me linger at the door. I looked back at her. "Major Buchanan?"

"Yes, Ms. Singh, what is it?"

"You've researched Conglomerate aliens. You must know things we don't."

She twitched the corner of her mouth in frustration. "Not

about Ghosts, thanks to the Accordance. They've been loth to share data. Positively stingy."

"Could a full citizen of the Accordance get the data? One of the struthiform medics . . . or maybe even a human?"

Buchanan stiffened and fixed me with a long, cold stare. "My my, you three really are joined at the hip, aren't you."

I half-regretted my words, but I made myself stare back unrepentantly.

Buchanan gave a shrug of resignation. "We will try our best to obtain information using whatever channels are available to us. However, that does not mean we won't continue our own investigations. I think you've been operating in this business long enough to know that the line between information and propaganda is very, very fine."

"Understood, Major Buchanan." I left the room, feeling a little more motivated to write up that report.

Devlin and Ken were using the time between troopship encounters to work on a 3-D projection of known troopship positions, and discussing the most efficient schedule to bring the reclamation protocol to the ships that Hideo had most recently marked as having the highest probability of Ghost infiltration. No chance of distraction from them. I found my own task and gave Bugkiller a thorough maintenance overhaul, a soothing, mechanical job that gave me room to pull up and organize the information I would need for our next troopship encounter. I was so absorbed that when Wei called me, I was annoyed at the disruption of my workflow.

Ken noticed my irritation. "Sickbay again? You want me to come with you?"

I hadn't even noticed when they stopped working. "Sure, why not."

“What did you find?” I asked Wei without ceremony as I entered sickbay.

His eyes were serious. “The presence of Ghost neuromelanin nano-ink does not correlate with your physical reaction to sensing Ghost-sign. However,” he continued, “there is another factor you have not considered.”

I was sure he’d timed his words for the simple pleasure of watching my face fall, so I was a bit snappish when I replied. “What factor?”

“Ghost contact. You have killed several? Touched their blood, sweat, tears, saliva? Or perhaps skin-to-skin is sufficient to do it.”

“Do what? Dammit, Wei, stop talking riddles.”

“Trigger the genetic modification process. The tainted nano-ink is only a first step. It has to be activated, and I believe that contact with a Ghost is the missing factor. Only then will the DNA changes begin to manifest.”

I was speechless. I remembered the Ghost’s bloody, defiant gloating before I threw it out of the hopper. I remembered Chris—such a stupid, fucking, overcommon name—Ghost-Chris, fighting me with relentless fury until he was dead and I was covered in his blood. Ken put a hand on my shoulder, steadying me.

Wei was either unaware of my distress or chose to ignore it. “Every individual who tested positive for Ghost neuromelanin and showed changes in DNA provoked a clear reaction from you—but I admit, the sample size is far too small to date. I would appreciate your assistance in continuing this line of research. In the meantime, I have advised Major Buchanan that individuals manifesting DNA variation should be banded.” He waved at my wrist. “After all, you have led by example.”

That gave me an additional pang. Buchanan was right. Accepting the band had been mere theater, and giving the keys to Ken and Devlin didn't mean much when I had the knowledge and means to find ways to nullify all monitoring and all keys. I thanked Wei sincerely but without enthusiasm, and left with my thoughts whirling. We went back to quarters. Ken shook his head in response to Devlin's raised eyebrows. They both watched in silence as I sat on my bunk and absently picked up Bugkiller again.

"Want to talk about it?" Ken said at last.

"Not sure what there is to talk about," I said slowly. "Nothing I can change. Nothing I would have done differently."

"We can figure out something. Find a cure, whatever," Devlin insisted.

"Thanks, Devlin, but if I put you guys in danger, you need to look out for yourselves." I looked up from Bugkiller and eyed them sternly. "I mean it."

They gave me their best military disobedience faces, that expression that says, "I hear your illegal order but I plan for your sake and mine to pretend I never heard it."

"Fine," I grumbled. "Do what you want, but don't blame me."

An alarm went off, easing the heaviness of the moment.

"Time to suit up," Devlin said. "Round three of Ghost-hunting is upon us."

The tiny quarters that Emilia Lang shared with Hideo had one huge advantage. When Hideo was in session with Ken and Devlin elsewhere, it became the most secure spot on the ship. "Sorry for burdening you with Hideo this long," I told her. "And thanks for tidying up my report for me. I didn't mean to drag you all the way out here to be babysitter and secretary, honest."

Lang did not look at all burdened. She still had the bright, starry-eyed expression of a newbie fascinated by the unfamiliar. "I'm no Ghost-hunter," she said. "I'm happy to stay on this courier and babysit. Speaking of which, here are the names you wanted."

She handed me a tiny but heavily shielded datachip. "Good," I said. "This helps."

Buchanan would have rebanded me as a traitor if I hadn't thrown her a bone or two, so I developed my own protocol. Before each encounter, I got the crew lists in advance and passed them to Lang to go over with Hideo. They returned to me a modified list identifying every Earth First spy and every Ship member who had been tapped for execution by suicide by their Ship leaders, and those were the names I saved to satisfy Buchanan that I was doing my job. I didn't use all of them. I plugged them into Russo's index and used any extra information that came up to pare the numbers down. Buchanan kept her word and only used bands, but a few times, I surprised her by revealing a hidden criminal record and advising prosecution and the brig.

Some people go into space to find adventure, some go to see wonders. Some search for a better life, some get drafted into wars they never asked for. And then there are those who mess up life on Earth so badly that they literally have nowhere else to run.

My private protocol didn't always run smoothly. During one encounter, a Ship mate I'd last seen in New Haven tried to approach me. I stared blankly past her, hefted Bugkiller a little higher, and made sure the band on my wrist was positioned right between our faces. She got the message, and that message spread. The next group of trainees for the reclamation protocol included a member of Ship 1. Showing great sense, he completely bypassed me and went to Lang. They exchanged information, and suddenly Hideo's estimates became much more precise.

"Just accept it," I told a skeptical Ken. "We found a way to cooperate that doesn't require surrender or amnesty."

Busy as I was, Wei still made me walk the lines at each troopship's sickbay so he could add to his data and refine his theory. I put a big outlier spike in his readings when I turned a corner and saw Devlin happily chatting with Shriek. Our favorite struthiform medic was unmistakable with his black prosthetics—wing hand, leg, and face—that rebuilt his battle-ruined form into one functional piece. I shouted his name and came over.

"Amira!" he shouted in answer. "Congratulations on your continuing existence! Devlin has been telling me your adventures."

Devlin was giving me a strange look. "Why didn't you tell us Shriek was here?"

"I didn't know," I admitted. "I've been concentrating on the human lists." I felt embarrassed. That was the kind of mistake Hideo would have made.

Wei rattled his pinions, the human equivalent of a finger snap. "Ms. Singh, we have work to do. Could you please return to the lines?"

"Wait a moment, Wei; you have to meet this medic. He specializes in human medicine."

Wei approached us, looking dubious. "Hm," he said regarding Shriek absently, his brain still deep in work mode. "I have heard of you. Come talk to me after I finish this round of screening. Ms. Singh, the lines?"

I sighed. "Duty calls. Good seeing you again, Shriek. Congrats on your continued existence as well."

I knew that other struthiforms didn't always get along with Shriek, finding his eccentricities and quirks for coping with trauma too much to take. However, Wei was not like other struthiforms. They began a conversation on comparative medicine, and to no one's surprise, Shriek joined the next batch of medics for reclamation training.

21

While things were going smoothly in some areas, trouble was brewing elsewhere. We had to drop a troopship from the schedule when we discovered it was engaged in a firefight with a Conglomeration ship. Later, when we passed where it had been, we found nothing but debris. It was Hideo's idea to risk a look and then do a scan of the area.

"We don't want any stray bombs floating in this area," he said. "That kind of minefield benefits no one."

Hideo was in his element. He had fully recovered from the embarrassment of misjudging the bio-bomb attacks on Earth and was back to his calculating, pragmatic, oblivious self.

News came via the swift, secure quantum-entangled comms that Conglomerate forces had succeeded in taking over Io. That merited a special briefing in Major Buchanan's meeting room. We were all in shock. Hideo showed only relief.

"We can cross that off our list of targets the Ghosts are likely to bomb," he said cheerfully, ignoring our weary, angry, incredulous, and, in at least two cases, murderous glares.

The Accordance still had Callisto, Ganymede, and Europa and everything beyond, but the boundaries were slowly shifting. Battle was raging in Europa's orbit, with the Conglomerate forces on the verge of winning. I noted cynically that it was mainly CPF ships holding the line while Accordance ships were fleeing and withdrawing to the outer moons. No wonder they used up our recruits so quickly.

Major Buchanan was starting to lose patience with Hideo.

"We're in a courier. We're not prepared to fight a Conglomerate ship, and yet you're leading us deeper and deeper into the most desperate battles of the Jupiter front. Mister Pereira, for your own preservation, not to mention the preservation of this entire crew, could you please identify our final target?"

"Almost there," he insisted. "I've narrowed it down to a convoy of five troopships bound for Callisto."

"Tell me something," Ken interjected. "When you and your friends cooked up this marvelous idea, did you have a clue how things were really going at the front?"

"What do you mean?" Hideo asked stiffly.

"I mean your tactics would work if you were imagining a line, with Accordance on one side and Conglomeration on the other, like a neat WWI trench. You could threaten Accordance ships behind the line and get attention. Or if the moon bases were secure, you could make an example of one by detonating a bomb nearby. But that's not the case. CPF are fighting hand-to-hand with crickets and raptors on Ganymede's base. Conglomerate ships are all around Europa and they've claimed space around Callisto. You've got a muddle, not a line. You said it yourself: no Ghost is going to detonate a bio-bomb where the Conglomeration have won or are winning. In addition, no Ghost is going to persuade even the most radical

Earth First fighter to take out a CPF or Accordance ship that's blocking the Conglomeration's path to Earth."

Hideo squirmed. "We may have . . . misunderstood the realities of the war."

"We may have misunderstood the motives," Devlin said very quietly.

We all looked at him. His face was tired and he avoided our eyes as he spoke. "I thought about what you said, Amira. You studied the human personnel files and forgot to check for Shriek. That's the pattern. They've been distracting us. They scared the Arvani so they stopped thinking about Jupiter and started worrying about every human face on Earth possibly hiding a Ghost. They scared the struthiforms by using the weapon that killed their planet—and the Arvani made it worse by pushing struthiform units to serve near blast zones. They scared us. They made us distrust ourselves. Notice how we all reacted, turning our attention inward?"

He looked up at last. "What's going on out there that they don't want us to see?"

"Oh, God, Devlin, Ken. I think you're right." So much for coats dense with processing threads, high-tech tattoos, and experimental indexes. The grunts of the operation had figured it out.

"Sure as hell don't want to be," Devlin answered. "How do we find out for certain?"

"Accordance surveillance has become very short-range and battle-focused," Major Buchanan admitted. "We've lost stations and outposts that would have given us the information we need."

"Let's ask the astronomers and the miners," I suggested. "They've got probes from decades back all around the Solar System."

I used the quantum-entangled comms to send out desperate calls for access codes and information, messaging every Ship member I could reach: miners, soldiers, medics, scientists. The word spread and data began flooding back so profusely that I begged Wei for his multiscreen display in sickbay. A crowd gathered there, watching images coalesce from grainy monochrome to vivid life. I toggled the filters on different screens so the non-augmented eyes could see the full picture.

"What's that?" asked Wei, pointing a wing hand.

"That" was something I had never seen before. A shadow scraped across the clouds of Jupiter, like a slash from a knife. The source was a massive, translucent spindle in orbit trailing a line to another orbiting spindle. I brought up the contrast, making the structures more visible. Six linked gigantic spindles orbited Jupiter like a garland of light and lace. As we continued to look, one of the spindles ejected a spear-like object which pierced the Jovian atmosphere and disappeared. Another spindle did the same. The spindles were shooting chunks of material into Jupiter at regular intervals.

We gazed at the images, baffled.

"I think I know," Shriek said in a hushed tone. "But . . . I do not understand. I saw structures like these orbiting a star before it died, destroyed by the Conglomeration."

"Jupiter isn't a star, so how would that work?" Devlin asked, frowning.

Major Buchanan was already on her feet. "Send this information to every Accordance and CPF ship and station. We need to get back control of our fleet and stop running scared. Mister Pereira, your convoy of five is next. Which ship do we take?"

"I think I'd better come with you for this one," Hideo said.

Everyone looked at him as if he had sprouted feathers and spoken in a rare struthiform dialect.

"Hear me out. First, I'd like to point out my continuing good behavior and full cooperation . . ."

Major Buchanan's look of complete boredom made him pause a bit.

". . . and second, to be honest, although I have better data, I'm still uncertain about a few key things. If I'm there, if I ask the right people the right questions, I can pinpoint where we can target our main strike."

Major Buchanan wearily rubbed her nose bridge and said, "He can go. He's banded and you have the keys. If he gives you any trouble, any trouble at all, you have my permission to push him out of an airlock." She paused and considered for a moment. "But save his coat. I'll find someone who knows how to use it."

Hideo turned a little gray at the blunt sincerity of her words.

Emilia Lang got a kit upgrade to space-ready, unpowered body armor with helmet and energy pistol. I assembled a full range of code keys to disable or discipline Hideo. We boarded and proceeded with stage one: waiting in the docking bay while Ken went with his squad and medics to brief the ship's commander and secure the bridge. I listened to the conversation over the public channel and began to frown. The commander wasn't satisfied with Ken's explanation of our mission and was insisting on speaking to his superior.

I opened a private channel. "Ken, don't argue. Tell him I'm on my way." I looked around at the rest of the team. "Devlin, you're in charge here. Keep listening in on the channel. Hideo, Lang, you're with me."

We entered the bridge, three of us plus a single security escort from the ship's own docking crew. The atmosphere on the bridge was tense, and there was a clear space between Ken and his team and the rest of the bridge staff. The commander was actually backing us, even though he must have heard us arrive. At first, I understood: he was directing a bridge on alert, scanning for Conglomeration forces. Views of the other ships of the convoy appeared all around us on huge screens; orders and information went back and forth between them. A line of empty vacuum suits lined an alcove at the back, waiting for the call to action stations. I understood that he couldn't drop everything immediately and notice our presence, but then he ignored us for too long and I grew irritated.

Ken spoke up at last, an edge of exasperation in his voice. "Commander Nguyen, this is Amira Singh, Hideo Pereira—"

The commander didn't wait for the end of the sentence. He turned, drew, and fired all at once. Lang, who was naturally closest, jumped in front of Hideo and both of them were punched back by the force of the energy discharge. They hit the floor with a hard thump.

Hideo flung an arm past his human shield. There was a loud, tearing noise and a smell of singed fabric and burned meat. I sent a code to his band to stop him, but it was too late. The commander fell. Medics raced to him, but they soon stepped away. A jagged, cauterized scar marked where the laser had penetrated his chest. I recognized the weapon as the one I'd taken off the Ghost.

"What the hell!" I screamed. "Hideo?"

Lang scrambled away from Hideo as he lay slumped and twitching under the effect of the restraining band. He was shaken, not triumphant, and his voice trembled a little as he said, "Dinh Tuan Nguyen, one of the highest-ranking Earth First moles in the CPF and almost certainly carrying some illegal ink. Sorry I didn't tell you earlier, but I had to see for myself. You'd better warn everyone to be on the lookout for a bio-bomb."

I snarled wordlessly, ripped the pilfered laser from his limp hand, and immediately sent a message to Devlin with the command to hold position. Ken was fully occupied, trying with weaponless hands to convince the other officers on the bridge that we were not the enemy.

I looked around at the chaos and braced myself to call Major Buchanan. "We need to adjust the protocol now. A key figure in the process is dead."

"Who?" she demanded.

"Dinh Tuan Nguyen, the ship's commander. Hideo claims he was an Earth First mole. If that's true, I have to go bomb-hunting, but I don't know if the crew will cooperate. We may need backup."

Buchanan's answer came quickly. "Call the ship's medical officers to the bridge. If you can persuade them, you'll be fine. I'm on my way."

The connection cut just as I opened my mouth to protest as only a consultant could. She had the gall to make me feel like shit for rushing off to sickbay during the first encounter, but here she was, about to position herself in the line of fire and effectively putting all of our eggs into one basket. I felt extremely uncomfortable about that.

"All medical officers to the bridge," I said over the ship's public channel. Switching to private, I added, "Devlin, send a squad to take the rest of our medics to sickbay and then escort the ship's medical officers to the bridge. Be on the alert." I turned to Lang. "Lang!"

"Fucking bastard . . ." She was standing, weapon at the ready, with her eyes were still on the unrepentant Hideo.

"Lang!" I grabbed her shoulders and shook her. "Forget him! You're one of the few people on this ship who knows what a bio-bomb looks like. You're with me!"

In the corridors we became just another pair of bodies rushing from point A to point B, the perfect camouflage. I wished I'd had time to train Lang to operate a power suit. We could have been running faster. She could have been picking up audio. I retracted my helmet so she could hear what was happening on the public channels.

"Hideo, where to? Make yourself useful, dammit."

"Three possible locations. Commander's cabin, private storage, or somewhere in general munitions storage."

"Pick one," I said, unmoved by the stress in his voice.

"Try the private storage. Best odds. The net weight of container 237-D1 doesn't match the declared contents."

I found the storage area easily. Lang quickly pointed out the container and turned to me, saying, "Do you have access co—"

Before she could finish her sentence, I stepped forward and struck the container door once with the edge of my armored hand. The door slid and fell off its runners with a scream of dragging metal. I shone a light in. "Lang?"

She went in quickly. She might have been shaking slightly, but that was Lang, channeling her adrenaline to good use. "I see it. It's . . ."

The silence went on for too long. "What? Is it armed?"

"No. No, none of them are."

Them. I maneuvered myself, my weapons, and my armor through the small opening. Lang was silently facing a wall of sixteen stacked bio-bombs.

I deeply regretted the ruined, unclosable door.

"Ken? Devlin?" I called out on private channel. "Got a moment?"

22

The physical evidence of the bio-bombs changed everything. Buchanan arrived, calm and collected in crisp combat dress and a lightly armored vacuum suit, and went immediately into conference with the second-in-command, a Major Frederick Diop. I sat at Buchanan's side and tried to explain what we knew, and by then we had the full backing of the medics as well. But it wasn't quite enough.

Major Diop slapped his hand hard on the table. "All right. I believe you—but that changes nothing! We don't have time for your conspiracy theories. Give our medics the information they need and we'll screen our own crew."

"And all the officers?" I interjected.

"We're minutes from engaging with Conglomeration forces. Our officers don't need the distraction!"

Buchanan and I shared a worried look. She tried again. "Major, if you would just consider—"

"Until I see that you have full Accordance clearance for this mission, I don't have to consider one damn thing. Good day, Major Buchanan. This is a ship at war. Kindly return to your courier and withdraw to a safer location."

"The bio-bombs, sir?" I begged him.

"They stay with us. They are disarmed and we do not know how to arm them. I can't think of anything safer than that. And next time, try to avoid wantonly destroying CPF property."

I was confused until I realized he meant the door I'd broken open. Buchanan shot me a reproachful look.

"Major Diop," she said, "the point is that you may yet encounter a soldier claiming to be in the CPF who does know how to arm those bombs. Can you take that risk?"

"Yes, because it is mine to take. Security, escort Major Buchanan and her people off our ship."

We had almost reached the docking bay when the sergeant in charge of our escort suddenly ordered a halt and stepped away to mutter quietly into his comm. The conversation went on for some time, and we gathered into small, puzzled groups and started up our own murmuring. The troops looked unhappy, but they let us murmur.

"Now what?" said Ken. "A change of heart?"

"I doubt it," Major Buchanan said, frowning at the sergeant. "They'd better not detain us. They have no authority for that."

I sifted through every channel I could access. "Another courier just docked. Accordance. I wonder if we can get some backing now."

Hideo laughed. His body still twitched occasionally from the aftereffects of the band. "That's unusually sanguine of you."

The sergeant returned to stand in front of Major Buchanan. "I have orders to take you back to the bridge."

"Have you been told why? Can we be told why?"

The sergeant ignored her and the squad started to quickly herd us back the way we came. I started to say something to Devlin, then stopped suddenly, distracted.

"What is it?" he whispered.

"Ghost sign. It's faint, but . . ." I stopped and drifted through the crowd, back where I'd first noticed the sensation, but after an initial increase, the feeling faded away.

I went back to Devlin, cursing. "Gone now," I said.

"I get it," Devlin said. "The Ghost must know we can't carry out the protocol. It's got a lot more to gain by lying low and waiting for us to leave."

"You're right," I said. "And I bet you we're going to get that 'battle stations' excuse more and more as we get closer. The protocol is a failure."

"Don't exaggerate. We've created a Ghost-free buffer behind us in the fleet. That's going to help."

Before we reached the bridge, the sergeant had his squad divide us: me, Ken, Devlin, and Major Buchanan ahead and everyone else in the back.

"Just you four. You're the ones they're asking for" was all he said before the doors opened and we could see for ourselves who had done the asking.

I felt cold. There were two Arvani on the bridge, one in armor, the other in a civilian tank. Major Diop was talking to them, but he immediately looked up when we came in.

"Excellent, thank you, Sergeant. I was afraid you'd left already. It appears the Accordance is very interested in you after all."

I wasn't feeling very sanguine now. The cold feeling in my stomach wouldn't go away.

"Thank you Major Diop," the armored Arvani commander said. "We will take over from here. Ken Awojobi, you are a suspect in the disappearance of Commander Zeus in the evacuation of Titan. Is there anything you wish to tell us?"

"No," Ken stated. "I have nothing to say."

"I see." The Arvani commander moved closer to Ken, examining him curiously with large, liquid eyes. "Our Family ordered an in-depth investigation into the whereabouts of our mother, who was last seen on Titan. Colonel Vincent Anais has submitted a deposition in which he claims that during the confusion of the evacuation, you shot and killed Commander Zeus, then incapacitated Colonel Anais with a blow to the skull. How do you respond to these charges?"

Devlin was incredulous. "Anais took this long to say something? Don't you find that a little fishy?"

"We understand that head injuries in humans may cause amnesia. Fortunately, we were able to corroborate at least part of his account using archived footage from a jumpship in the vicinity. We are awaiting your answer to the charges." The civilian Arvani's reply was coldly offended—was it the term "fishy" or Ken's general air of disrespect?

"Yes, I killed Zeus."

"Ken!" I was sure the Arvani were bluffing about how much the jumpship footage had actually shown, but none of that mattered if Ken was going to hand them a confession on a platter. "Shut up!"

The Arvani commander ignored us and spoke to Major Buchanan. "Your association with this criminal is unfortunate. I would advise you to make a decision on our offer. You have delayed long enough."

"If I delayed, it was because more important things were happening," the major replied sweetly. "I have known my answer from the moment the offer was made. I'm afraid it's out of the question."

Both Arvani, civilian and military, went speechless. The commander recovered first. "You would refuse the privilege of being a citizen of the Accordance? You are a client species! You are nothing! It is a great honor we are extending to you, one that you do not deserve, and you are refusing it?"

"I categorically refuse it," she replied.

For a moment I stopped agonizing over Ken's fate. The scene in front of me was too delicious not to be enjoyed.

"These are side matters," Major Diop said wearily. "Can we please concentrate on the battle on our doorstep?"

"Can we also focus on the intruders in our midst?" Buchanan shot back. "Winning won't be much fun if you don't have a place to return to."

"We are aware of your mission," said the Arvani commander, "but it is no longer necessary. The Accordance is now prepared to implement wide-ranging measures throughout the CPF to eradicate all traitors and Conglomerate spies."

Glances were exchanged among the humans on the bridge. Clearly, I was no longer the only one with a coldness in the pit of my belly.

"You are no longer needed in this area, Major Buchanan. You are hereby ordered to take all your personnel, board your courier, and return to Earth. This order supersedes any directions given by General Gerrard and Colonel Anais, and as you have refused full citizenship, you have no right to appeal. That is all."

"But what about our mother's murderer?" the civilian Arvani asked abruptly.

The Arvani commander hesitated, then spoke gently to his civilian kin. "Awojobi will face trial on Earth. The military process must be respected. Do not worry. We will be allowed to attend his execution."

Major Diop gave us a look of pure sympathy and regret. No one in the CPF who knew anything about Zeus's treachery blamed Ken for his actions, but Zeus's children were too influential in the Accordance and their revenge would not be denied.

A klaxon went off, making us all tense up. "Essential personnel only! Everyone else, clear the bridge," Major Diop shouted.

The bridge crew moved swiftly into their vacuum suits and returned to stations. I automatically raised the helmet on my power armor and noted that Devlin and Ken did the same. The bridge did clear somewhat, but the three of us lingered with Major Buchanan, which was a good thing because we were able to catch her when the first shock wave from an energy discharge jarred the bridge.

She thanked us for our help and apologized for her lack of preparation. "I came over in such a rush, I dressed for diplomacy, not war."

"I wanted to witness justice," the civilian Arvani wailed. "I did not come here to die!"

The Arvani commander looked momentarily at a loss, then snapped at Major Diop, "You must retreat to the outer moons!"

"I must stay with the convoy," he shouted back.

"Are you disobeying my orders? I will have you stripped of rank! I will have you executed!"

Major Buchanan drew us away from the argument and spoke quickly. "Amira, take the lads and get off this ship now. Board the second-last ship of the convoy, kill any Ghosts you find there, then get out. Tell everyone you can to get away from here as quickly as possible. I don't have time to explain, but it's going to be bad. Now go!"

It shouldn't be easy for three fully armored adults to slip out without being noticed, but we did just that while the Arvani and Major Diop clashed over command and the ship rocked as it was grazed with energy beams. I took one last look over my shoulder and saw Major Buchanan securing herself in a seat near a view screen and sealing up the helmet of her vacuum suit. She gave me a nod and a thumbs-up.

Then we ran.

We took the courier and sheltered on the side of the convoy that was opposite the Conglomerate's energy weapons. Then we held a meeting to discuss Buchanan's orders and our next move.

Hideo spoke hastily before I could start. "I've added the most recent data to my algorithms. The center of the rebellion should be found—"

"On the second-to-last ship of the convoy," I interrupted him. "Yes, we know. Major Buchanan figured it out just now on the bridge." He visibly deflated as I continued. "She ordered us to terminate the Ghosts on board, then get the hell out. I think that's a good plan. All in favor?"

Through the sound of chiming yeas, Hideo raised his voice. "I want to come."

"Not again," Ken growled.

"I'm serious. I have to be there. I know who's in command. I can tell you if they're being controlled."

I realized I was happier having him at arm's length than letting him stay on the courier. I wouldn't put it past him to hijack it. "Okay, but you'll have to leave that behind."

"What?" Hideo asked uncertainly.

"The coat! Long coats and vacuum suits don't mix, and we're in the middle of hull-destroying activity. Use a patch or a chip or tie a wrap around your head, but ditch the long coat if you want to come."

He opted for the pirate-style head tie, and we gave him the same body armor that Lang had—a little more than a vacuum suit, but a lot less than power armor. No weapon. I was still mad about the laser.

Before we boarded the jumpship, Ken pulled me aside. "Are you sure Lang can do this?"

"She's from Ship 1, deepest Manhattan. She's tough."

"Yes, but this is a different kind of warfare," he noted.

"I still want Hideo watched and I don't have time to do it myself," I told him. "She did really well last time. Quick thinking. None of us expected the laser, but now she'll be on full alert."

Still looking doubtful, Ken let it drop.

Shriek's voice sounded over our private channels. "Diop is moving away from the convoy. The Arvani have won the power struggle."

"Oh, fuck," I said with quiet understatement. "We should get moving, then."

I was the last to board, and Wei the last to leave the docking bay. I grabbed his wing hand. "You're in command now. Take this courier as far away from the action as you can. Run to Ceres. We'll meet you there when we're done."

Wei's beak opened and closed wordlessly. Finally, he said with weak indignation, "I should hope so. My research is nowhere near completed."

"Approaching target in five minutes," Shriek warned.

We could have jumped over the space using heatshields and thrusters, but that would have ruled out Hideo and Lang. Besides, I wanted that getaway jumpship stationed nearby. I don't believe in suicide missions. We coasted out of the bay on minimum power, drifted parallel with the troopship, then landed on the hull and engaged magnet anchors.

I spoke softly over our secure public channel. "Lang, you're with me. Hideo's with Devlin and Ken. Don't panic. We've done EVAs hundreds of times. We'll keep you moving."

We tethered the two novices to our suits and walked to the nearest airlock. Their helmets were opaque so they wouldn't pause in awe or terror at the vastness of space, but we could see Callisto and Jupiter hanging over our heads. I felt an imaginary pull, like the attraction of a cliff's edge, and then I was opening the airlock and nudging Lang inside. We found ourselves in a small service bay with maintenance vehicles and spare parts.

"Hideo?" I queried.

"Straight to the bridge," he answered.

We fell into a natural formation: me and Devlin at the front with Bugkiller and energy weapons ready, Hideo and Lang in the middle, and Ken covering the rear. We ran into a sergeant with a full platoon and braced ourselves to either fast-talk or shoot ourselves out, but the sergeant put her hands up and spoke quickly.

"No, no, we're with you! Sergeant Danner, Ship 209. Glad to see you, Amira Singh. It's been crazy around here. Let's burn out this infection for once and for all."

Lang and I exchanged grins, part relief, part reassurance.

Danner paused at the door to the bridge and looked at us. "I'll go in first. Be ready for anything."

The door opened and we were escorted in.

"Commander, there's someone who wants to speak with you," Danner said. She stood to the side and let me face him, but her stance and the direction of her weapon was as ambiguous as the intent of the troops around us, both prisoning and protecting.

The commander looked at me. I knew his name. He was Keith Martins, an ordinary person of ordinary appearance, and a high-ranking Earth First operative. Had I met him before, in the earlier days of the reclamation protocol, I would not have withheld his name from Buchanan. There was much in the man's history and reputation to fear, Ghosts or no Ghosts.

23

"Amira Singh," he said.

"Have we met?" I replied coldly.

"In a manner of speaking. We all know you."

I realized what was familiar about this man. I had never seen him, never spoken to him before, but his voice, his phrasing, his very sneer all reminded me of that Ghost who smiled at me with bloody teeth and told me I would never win. But the Ghost sign coming from him was faint, a mere echo.

"Where's your master?" I said, trying to provoke him. "Send for him. I don't talk to puppets."

"Do you think we are Drivers?" he countered. "We do not make puppets, we craft tools."

I didn't waste words on him. I simply put Bugkiller on full blast and watched as he fell at my feet, disoriented.

Ghost sign crackled like lightning at the back of my neck. I spun around, my pistol up, but it was already too close. I dented its helmet with the butt of the pistol and rolled back, kicking my legs out at knee level. The crack and the scream were satisfying, but my own armor slowed, temporarily drained by the clash with armor of equal hardness. I floundered on the floor for precious seconds as the Ghost limped upright and slashed an armored hand toward my head. Devlin struck him from the side at a full run.

"Get him!"

I don't know who shouted, but when I looked at where the Ghost had fallen, I could only see boots—power armor boots, vacuum suit boots, chunky security-style and bright-yellow scientist gear, all kicking and stamping and growing more and more sprayed and smeared with red.

It was surreal—too much of a relief to be a nightmare, and too gory and spontaneous to be a comfort. I thought for sure I was hallucinating when I saw something scuttle at the edge of my field of vision.

Then I bolted upright, swung Bugkiller around and set to wide beam. "Devlin! Ken! We've got crickets!"

It felt like ages since I'd used the settings for maximum cricket kill. I got to my feet, still slightly slowed but powering up again, and focused on scything through the wave of skittering black. People ran from the crushed corpse of the Ghost. One crew member in a vacuum suit lost his footing and tumbled into the seething mass with a gurgling scream.

"They're coming out of the storage compartments," Devlin yelled, stamping a few to bits and kicking the pieces away. I spun about furiously, diligently sweeping the bridge with my wide beam until the floor no longer danced.

Ken looked down the corridor from the bridge. "We got more than crickets. I need backup! Double line!" He disappeared from view with power-suited troops following, and within seconds, I heard them firing. The familiar smell of seared raptor filled the air.

I glanced and saw that Sergeant Danner was covering

the other bridge entrance, and then my attention was caught by the main view screen. The third ship of the convoy was turning, and tilting its energy cannons toward us. The other ships were also moving off course, as if they'd suddenly lost direction. Conglomerate fire struck one solidly, shearing off a large piece of hull. A puff of debris and fragmented armoring clouded the once-clean black of space. Around Callisto, the line of CPF ships began to drift out of formation. The only ships that moved with purpose were Accordance, running as fast as they could to the outer moons, and Conglomeration, advancing for the kill.

Devlin was at my side. "They're out of control!" he shouted.

"Yeah," I agreed, watching as the third ship turned its cannons away, paused to reconsider, then re-aimed them directly at us. "But someone needs to be in control, or we're all sitting ducks out here. Hideo! I'm going to open all comms and channels. I need you to boost me as far as you can."

"Done," he said. "The System is listening, Amira Singh. Go."

"Colonial Protective Forces! Ships of the Manhattan Resistance! All humans fighting against the Conglomeration. I am Amira Singh. Listen to me!"

The sound of fighting faded away under the hollow roaring in my head. I hated making speeches and I didn't know how to persuade, but I had seconds to do just that.

"You know me! You've received my messages! You know we've been fighting Ghosts. They look like us. They make you believe they're on your side, but it's a lie. Their leader is dead! If you fight each other now, you're worse than traitors, you're fools!"

The bottom half of the main view screen fragmented into tens then hundreds of talking heads, incoming calls and messages declaring support, screaming defiance, cursing the Accordance and the Conglomeration both, howling in despair.

I switched channels. "This isn't working," I said to Devlin privately. "It's mayhem. Whatever happens from here, the CPF is a shambles. This is a real rebellion and I can't stop it."

"Don't stop it—lead it. They're soldiers. All they need is one clear order they can agree on. Give them that and we'll work out the rest later. You can do this, Amira. You don't know your own power. You're already a legend."

I stared at him, stunned by the intensity of his words. We'd all done that trick at one point or another, given outrageous praise in the heat of battle, hoping to give someone enough strength and daring to take the shot, hold the line, make that last stand. But he sounded like he meant it, and as I looked back at the mosaic of faces, I realized he might be right. Most of them I'd never met, and some of them I'd never even heard of, but they all knew Amira Singh. I had to use that.

I switched back to my vast audience. "There is another way. I'm ordering you—stay alive. Stop fighting for other people and start fighting for yourselves. Retreat to the asteroid belts. Seize what you can and build your own bases. Strike from there. Strike the Accordance when they treat us like inferiors. Strike the Conglomeration for using us as their tools. Grab your damn independence and stop taking orders from above. Make your own worlds there, and be ready to move when the time is right."

It was one of the best speeches I'd ever been forced to make, and yet the mosaic argued back, their allegiances varied and shifting—Earth First, Accordance, Conglomeration, and every combination possible. I had no more words. I stared at Devlin helplessly.

"Amira," Ken shouted on my private channel. "They're too

many raptors out here. We're going to have to fall back and seal off the bridge."

"Amira," Hideo warned, "it looks like the Conglomeration ships are moving to cut us off from retreating."

"Amira!" Shriek's voice caught my full attention. He was aboard the courier, well away from the unfolding clusterfuck. What could be so important that he had to call me?

"Jupiter! Look at Jupiter! It has begun!"

Instinctively, I flung up an image full-screen. Everyone could see it, on the bridge, in the fleet, probably in the entire Solar System if they were on the right channel. The clouds of Jupiter were churning like storms on fast-forward. The spindles no longer ringed Jupiter with a mere thread; they had spun a larger sphere to embrace Jupiter in a net of lightning raining down lances of some dark energy or matter.

"Buchanan was right," murmured Devlin.

"Oh, God," Hideo moaned. "It's going to explode."

I tried to shut him out, but I could not look away from the screen as Jupiter's surface began to bubble and crease. "Get past the Conglomerate ships," I pleaded to whoever was still listening. "Break through and retreat to the asteroid belt. Meet me at Ceres, now that you know who your real allies are. Now move if you want to survive! Run!"

Our own ship was the first to move, peeling off from the others at top speed. We should have been coordinating our movements and covering fire, improving everyone's chances at retreat, but this was desperate and unplanned. We were fleeing something worse than Conglomerate firepower. The ship shuddered as energy cannon raked the hull, leaving gaping holes that let in the peaceful light of Callisto and the angry turmoil of Jupiter.

We journeyed on, our atmosphere lost to the vacuum, trailing bits of hull, dead raptors and cricket fragments in our wake. The ship was rapidly becoming a shell. Danner issued the call for nonessential personnel to abandon ship. Hideo and Lang looked to us, thoroughly freaked out.

"We've got a jumpship, remember?" Devlin said to them. "We're going to catch up with the courier and get out of here. This ship has the firepower but the courier has the speed, and that's what we need right now."

We ran out, keeping Hideo and Lang between us as before, but this time to help them over the obstacles and pitfalls of the buckled floor and shredded walls. I had that cold feeling growing in my stomach again, and when the corridor cut off into empty space, I felt resigned rather than afraid.

"Tether," I asked Ken. He hooked one end to his suit and gave the other to me. I put Bugkiller on my back and used both hands to swing carefully around the torn-open hull. I pushed off and swung back, and both Devlin and Ken easily hauled me in.

"Jumpship's still there," I said, breathing a little quickly. "We did the EVA in, we can do it out, too. Only difference is no airlock."

"No airlock needed," Devlin agreed.

Our novices looked panicked. "Guys," said Lang. "I don't think I can do this."

Ken unsnapped the tether. "Come on, Emilia. You go between me and Amira. Devlin can handle Hideo."

"Change of plan," Devlin suggested. "Let me go ahead and bring the jumpship to you. Shortens the walk in case of accidents." He pointed at the silent blooms of energy cannon that lit the sky, some close enough for their shockwaves to thud against our armor.

"Yes," I agreed, tethering Hideo to my suit. "You'll be fine with Ken, Lang, and we're not going far."

It wasn't far, but it was treacherous. Devlin used both tether and powered leaps to tarzan his way to the jumpship. We scrambled along with less style, helping Hideo and Lang around sharp edges and spikes of ripped hull and twisted hatches that swayed open and clapped shut as the ship shifted under every hammering strike.

The danger came from the last place we expected—a blowout inside the ship. Not ashamed to say I screamed as hard as Lang when the blast scoured past us. I locked my armor down hard to whatever would grip and felt the tug of the stretched tether as Hideo was blown off the ship. Lang spun off too, but at an angle. The tether between her and Ken sliced hard against embedded shrapnel and snapped.

I stopped screaming. Lang continued.

"Devlin!" Ken bellowed. "Go get Lang."

"Getting there," Devlin said. The jumpship disengaged from the hull and eased toward the unarmored figures, one free, one tethered. Hideo swung helplessly but managed to face the jumpship and brace himself before he slammed into its side. Then, to my shock, he leaped again, pushing himself toward Lang. They didn't collide—his aim wasn't precise enough for that—but he was close enough for Lang to snatch hold of the tether as it arced past her. They came together in a dizzy little scramble. I went weak with relief.

Ken nodded up to the open door of the hovering jumpship. "Let's go!"

I put all the force of my muscles and the last of the suit's power packs into a leap toward the jumpship. Ken was slightly ahead, and he hit the sill first and pulled me over the edge. Then he began to haul on the tether, bringing Lang and Hideo in.

We could never agree on what happened next.

Hideo had unclipped himself from the tether and hooked it onto Lang; that much was clear. But then Ken thought it was his fault, that he'd yanked the tether so hard with the augmented strength of his armor that Hideo was unable to hold on. Lang thought it was her fault, that she'd flailed and accidentally kicked Hideo away. But I was the only one able to see his face, the fear in his expression suddenly turning to peace as if he had made up his mind, the gentle push he gave Lang to speed her toward us, and the closing of his eyes as he let himself go. Ken pulled Lang into the jumpship. I kept looking out until the moment Hideo floated into a fast-moving plume of jetsam and disappeared in a mist of red droplets.

The three of us clutched each other, the tether tangling our limbs as we sprawled out on the floor. Devlin looked back at us through the cabin glass. "Everyone in?" His gaze flickered, counting one body short.

I struggled upright and slammed the door shut and sealed. Ken gave him a weary thumbs-up. "Everyone in," he said firmly. "Let's get the hell out of here."

Jupiter continued its dying throes long after we rejoined the courier and set course for Ceres. We didn't pause for lengthy, emotional reunions. We were running flat out, keeping watch behind us. When Shriek recommended that we land on an asteroid's sunward side and brace ourselves, we did so without argument. The shock wave of Jupiter's transformation battered the small rock, but we were safe and alive. We took off from the asteroid and spared a moment to look back at the new red sun.

I tried to access the probes I'd used before, but of course

they had burnt out. We assembled the data from a few distant stations and tried to make sense of the images.

"Everything from Io outwards is still intact," Lang noted. "It's a miracle."

"No," said Wei. "A carefully controlled plan."

"I still don't understand what that plan is. I'm sure they have easier ways to push back the battle lines. Why go to the effort of turning Jupiter into a sun?" Ken remarked.

We looked at the red light and wondered in silence. Nobody had an answer.

24

The refugees from Earth who came to Ceres rarely visited the surface. Hollowed-out asteroids in the style of the Trojan carriers had been connected to the existing orbital station. They were nowhere as bad as the ones we'd lived in before we lost Titan. The toilets were properly designed, the food looked and tasted like humans were meant to eat it, and the walls were thick and securely sealed so it was safe to walk around unsuited. Still, it wasn't the best place for a family reunion, which was why I was with Ken in the Botanical Domes, an impressive park designed and maintained by the Consolidated Miners' Group for their executives on Ceres.

Three figures stood by a pond ahead of us, the space between them close and intimate. There was embracing, the sound of laughter, hands wiping away tears. I had no idea how they got to Ceres—maybe swept up in a stampede of evacuating struthiforms, or part of an Earth First team who, like me, didn't believe in suicide missions. Whatever the reason, Devlin Hart was finally seeing his parents again.

We went slowly along the path, ready to meet the famous

Harts but hesitant to violate their privacy. "How's your family, Ken?" I asked cautiously. "Have you heard from them?"

"Still safe in Tranquility," he answered. "No Ghosts, no Earth First assassins." He nodded at the Harts. "Maybe your dear old concierge keeps her promises."

I blinked. I hadn't thought of that.

We weren't close enough to hear what the Harts were saying to each other, but we did notice when the volume of the discussion went from "happy excitement" to "worrying disagreement." Ken and I both stopped where we were, about sixty meters away from the trio, and turned around quickly.

"Uh . . . that doesn't sound good," I whispered.

"What do we do? They've already seen us coming."

"Let's stay right here and pretend to be talking," I suggested.

For the most awkward five minutes of my life, I pretended not to listen as Devlin's parents argued and he pleaded. At last, his mother left them and came up the path, striding angrily past us without a second look. Devlin and his father followed her, but slowly. There was only one way out of the park, after all.

When they reached us, no one dared speak first. Ken and I looked at each other, completely at a loss.

"Devlin, do you want me to . . . I can go . . ." I didn't know what I was trying to say, but Devlin understood.

"Please," he said. "I have to go with my father. The Accordance has offered him full citizenship with some conditions. We're going to accept."

"Oh" was all I managed. His words knocked the breath out of me.

Thomas Hart raised his chin, not in defiance, not in guilt, but with weary resignation. "I didn't ask for it. TJ, an old student of mine, he thinks I can do more fighting within the system than against it. It wasn't an easy decision." His eyes went to Devlin, who was standing with his head down, biting his lip as if trying not to let tears fall. "But my son thinks we might be able to make a difference together."

"Sir," Ken said, his voice low and intense. "Do whatever you can however you can. It's going to be a long game, but trust me when I say we are on the same side."

Devlin looked up with a small sound of relief, half laugh, half gasp, and Ken immediately stepped forward and gripped his shoulders. "Brothers," he reminded him with a firm shake.

"Brothers," Devlin replied, gripping back just as strongly before pulling him into a hug.

Devlin's father watched them, and his smile was bittersweet. I looked down the path, and I could see Mrs. Hart still walking away.

"Excuse me," I muttered, and began to run.

When I caught up with her, she refused to stop, but she did slow down a little. I walked on for a bit to catch my breath and settle my thoughts.

"Mrs. Hart," I began.

"Rodriguez," she snapped. "My name is Linda Rodriguez. Devlin told me that you agree with this?"

I almost stumbled, taken aback. "Well, there are pros and cons. Why are you walking away from him? He's your son! And that's your husband!"

She glanced over her shoulder, but the regret showing in her eyes wasn't strong enough to make her stop or go back. "Thomas and I have been drifting apart for a while. We can't walk the same road anymore. But you wouldn't understand that. Your parents were such a model revolutionary pair."

"No ma'am," I said, a little edge creeping into my voice.

"They separated, actually, but they kept working together. Love and ideology are different things. You're walking away from your family because you disagree with their choices? Because they'll be Accordance citizens?"

"You dare ask me that? Your parents tried to bomb the Accordance in Atlanta and they were executed for it! By your same precious Accordance!"

Execution by suicide mission. "Yes," I said tiredly. "I know. They were set up. Groups like Earth First don't forgive mistakes any more than the Accordance does. Remember that. Would you prefer to face a firing squad of your enemies or know that your friends left you to die?"

She didn't answer. She was so angry, she was shaking.

"Look, me and Ken, we're trying to find a middle way. If you ever need sanctuary, from friends or enemies, send me a message. I'll find you. I'll always help you . . . for Devlin's sake."

She stopped. We had reached the exit building. "Goodbye, Amira Singh," she said.

"Wait, Linda. Where will you go? Can you at least tell me that?"

She left without once looking back at me.

Days later, we went to the orbital station to see Devlin off. He had to return to duty, his father had already left for Earth, and about his mother he said nothing. We were all three as cheerful as a funeral.

Devlin tried to lighten the mood. "This isn't goodbye," he told us firmly. "I just have to get some annoying PR out of the way, and then they're sending me back into space. I'll come see you guys, honest. We've still got a lot to do together."

"PR, huh?" Ken said. "Do me a favor, kick Anais up the ass for me."

Devlin snorted. "Consider it done."

"And my regards to Buchanan, if they'll let you see her," I added.

Devlin sobered. In spite of everything she'd done to save us, Buchanan's rejection of citizenship and support of Major Diop had put her firmly on the Accordance shit list. "I'll try," he said.

We left as soon as Devlin boarded, and ran into Chief Engineer Abreham Selassie, the man who ran the orbital station, just as we were returning from the departure gate. A younger man in a CPF uniform was with him. "Good to see you Ken, Amira," Chief Selassie greeted us. "We've been looking for you."

Something nudged my brain. I ran a search, pulled up a file and an image, and said coolly, "Lieutenant Wilmer, you should really contact your sister."

The lieutenant's eyes widened. "How did you know about that?"

"About what?"

"I just sent a message off to Jody. First time in months. When they shipped me out, it didn't make any sense trying to reach her. She got out at the right time and I didn't want to risk them finding her. Now I'm with the CPF Resistance, I don't have to worry about that." His smile glowed with admiration. "You really do know everything."

I shrugged modestly. "Not everything. I don't know why you came looking for us."

He pulled himself together. "Oh, yes. Ms. Singh, Sergeant Awojobi, we want to show you something."

I didn't like the way they said my name. "Sergeant" had its own baggage, and "Amira" was too personal, but my grandfather's surname came with the gravity of legend and possibility and was turning into a title. Buchanan of the Buchanans, Singh of the Singhs, Keeper of the Name and Pride and Hope. Was that how clans and dynasties began?

The CPF lieutenant and the chief engineer took me and Ken through several heavily secured and coded doors. My curiosity increased at every new barrier, and perhaps a little fear as well. I had an inkling, and when I exchanged a worried glance with Ken, I knew he had that same inkling.

The journey terminated in a large bunker. Lieutenant Wilmer flipped the large switch at the last door and bright light filled every corner of the storage space. About one hundred black capsules were arranged in a perfect square with seven more ranged in a short file at one side. Bitter, bitter medicine that I did not want to have on my hands, but it was as I'd feared, and there was no way to get rid of them.

"How, exactly," Ken asked gravely, "did these come to be here?"

Wilmer answered. "CPF Resistance brought them in, salvaged from the battlefield debris before the Conglomeration chased us off. We weren't about to hand them back to the Accordance."

"Wilmer, are they . . . ?" I questioned.

"Disarmed, Ms. Singh."

"And what would it take to arm them?"

He waved an arm to a set of boxes stacked at the back. "Those bits and pieces."

I turned to the engineer. "Chief Selassie?"

His mouth twitched, but he gave the full answer I wanted. "Timing and proximity device, fuse for primary detonation, precision mixer, damper for the pre-detonation phase, fuse for the main detonation, and the lock for the main casing."

"Thank you, Chief Selassie. Lieutenant Wilmer, I want

'those bits and pieces' on a ship in two hours. I'll give you the precise coordinates in a while, but I can tell you now that your destination will be the asteroid that maintains the farthest mean distance from Ceres while not actually passing close to any Conglomeration bases."

"And if you don't mind, Chief Selassie," Ken added, "we'd rather store the bio-bomb capsules in one of the uninhabited asteroids, at a reasonable distance from the orbital station."

"Please do," he begged us. He looked around at the bunker. "I want this room cleared. I have other plans for it."

At first we had no official titles. People asked us questions, we discussed the matter with each other, and we gave them answers. There was so much to do that everyone cooperated and collaborated and the hierarchy shook itself out naturally. Ken and I stuck together, and that too felt natural. We brought together two very different worlds: the Ships and the CPF.

The status of the CPF within the asteroid belt was undefined and evolving. Roughly two thirds of the CPF that fled the Jupiter front continued to operate within the Accordance establishment. The remainder settled semi-permanently in the asteroid belt and went slightly . . . rogue. I met plenty of CPF officers and enlisted who declared they would never take orders from the Accordance again, but who also insisted that they were still very much a part of the Colonial Protective Forces. Others drifted back and forth across the boundary of allegiance, depending on their location and inclination. CPF headquarters on Earth had to figure out how to juggle the degrees of insubordination, and mostly they took the Anais route. Those whose actions could not be ignored or covered up were sentenced to demotion, exile, or death, but many careers were salvaged in various creative ways. I still hated

Anais for dropping Ken into the shit without warning, but I could admit to being impressed at the glorious whirlwind of spin, PR, and general misdirection that framed the post-Jupiter days.

And so the CPF Resistance was born. The name began as a quasi-joke, but it was reused with increasing seriousness until eventually it stuck.

The situation on Ceres finally settled down enough that we were assigned permanent places to work and live. Two of the top brass, Sergeant Danner and General Mohr, took great pleasure in showing me to my new office. Office. What a weird fate for a street-running sneak.

The writing on the door said, AMIRA SINGH. DIRECTOR.

I tried to stop them. "You're not putting me in charge!"

"Oh no, of course not," said General Mohr with a slightly patronizing smile. "We're still in charge. You're just the person who will make sure that our decisions coordinate. You have the information at your fingertips and skill to assess it and advise us objectively. Hence 'Director.'"

"She's a Singh," Sergeant Danner growled. "The Ships know her and respect her. She'll be in charge."

Ironically, although Sergeant Danner was subordinate to General Mohr in the CPF, she outranked him in the hierarchy of the Ships. I closed my office door and left them still arguing. A week later, it was confirmed that the Ships of Earth and the Generals of the CPF had voted me in as Director of the CPF Resistance. At first, I wasn't sure if I was a figurehead, but the staggering amount of work that descended on me later suggested not.

Ken Awojobi, dishonorably discharged ex-sergeant of the CPF and fugitive from Accordance justice, was placed in charge of military operations with the rank of commander in the CPF Resistance. Part of it was because he'd rallied everyone together and shown the best grasp of tactics during the retreat and restructuring, but mainly it was the best, strongest "fuck you" they could give to the Accordance in general and the Arvani in particular. So, he was a bit of a figurehead, like me, but to my surprise, he didn't care.

"If there's anything this war has taught me, it's that opportunity counts as much as ability. I'm going to seize this opportunity, Amira," he told me. "I don't believe in much anymore, but there's a reason we survived Icarus. There's a reason we've ended up where we are. I'm here and I'll do my best with what I've been given, whether I've earned it or not."

"I think you'll be amazing," Lang said shyly.

We were in a private area of the main orbital station, looking through the huge viewport at the sights. The station was in the center of a construction boom: the number of docks and ports was being increased and structures added to link and delink massive Trojan-style asteroid carriers to the station's main hub.

Watching the ongoing expansion provided a pleasant distraction for a day off, but we were there for a reason. I had seen it coming and tried to ignore it, but I couldn't avoid it anymore. Emilia Lang wanted to go home.

I tried one last time to persuade her. "Lang, we need people like you—"

"This isn't for me," she interrupted. "Space, aliens, everyone and everything trying to kill you. It's stressful."

"But you always acted like you were handling it," I said.

She grimaced. "Yeah. I'm really good at acting, but any more of this and I'll start screaming some day and I won't stop."

"Look!" Ken exclaimed.

A long, slow shadow moved over the orbital station, dimming the light of both suns and giving an illusion of chill to the air. It was one of the Pcholem, arriving to take the struthiforms who fled from Earth to their new settlement on Mars. The sight of them always made me feel like my head was being turned inside out. Here was something too huge, too incredible to be limited by mere risk assessment, indexing, or mathematics. I could be cynical about many things, but not about the Pcholem.

"Look," I echoed. "Look, Emilia."

Silence. I glanced at her. There was awe in her eyes, as in ours, but it came closer to terror than delight.

I cleared my throat. "Hey, Lang, before I forget, this is for you."

I handed her a soft, cloth-wrapped package. She took it with a puzzled frown, but after two experimental squishes she winced and gave me a slightly pained look. "His coat?"

"Waste not, want not. If you don't need it, I'm sure you can find someone in Ship 1 who can use it. And you've more than earned the right to keep your kit, so we packed that up for you and sent it with the rest of your stuff."

Ken gave her a gentle hug. "Take care, Emilia. I hope you'll at least visit someday."

She smiled at us. "Someday, I will. Thanks for an incredible adventure."

We watched sadly as she walked away. Ken nudged me. "Time for a drink?"

"Oh yes," I agreed.

Infrastructure on the orbital station was too recent and too well recorded for anything to be really secret, but if you knew the mining community and they liked you well enough, you got access to some of the secure tunnels and private bunkers. Ken and I wandered down a few levels and passed through a few code-locked doors until we found ourselves in a familiar space now greatly transformed to new purpose.

The room cheered; glasses were raised in salute. We waved sheepishly in reply.

"Come in, come in," said Chief Selassie. He was behind the bar, slowly and expertly pulling a pint. "Have a seat. Tell me, what's your pleasure?"

25

It was hard to adjust to a public life. There were so many faces, but unlike recruits who could be kept at a respectful distance and moved at your command, these faces all wanted something and wouldn't go away. Ken tried to act as filter for the unnecessary meetings, the people who asked to see me and speak to me for their own satisfaction and not for anything to do with the establishment of the CPF Resistance. It was never enough. I felt myself getting wearier and stupider until I learned to schedule time for data-scanning and naps.

Occasionally, out of all the many faces, I got back something unexpected.

Chief Selassie introduced me to the administrator of a small mining operation. His name—Heath Buchanan. Refreshingly, he had no awe of me nor of the Singh name. He wanted to hear all about my time serving with Major Buchanan, who he had known well and was distantly related to but had never personally met.

"Was it true that you were present on the day she refused the Union?" he asked in a voice that vibrated with awe.

“You mean when she turned down the Accordance’s offer of full citizenship? Yes, I was there, but—”

“No, Director Singh, it was much more than that. If she had accepted citizenship with her standing as Chief of the Name and Arms, it would have had consequences for all those affiliated with the Name. She refused on behalf of the Buchanans and their septs.”

My mouth dropped open. I remembered when she first introduced herself, all that pomp, but then she’d said “not that it matters anymore.” “But I thought her title was a ceremonial thing, heritage and history with nothing political?”

“It was once,” he acknowledged, “but after the Accordance came, we became a lot more political. I think you know a bit about that sort of thing yourself.”

I discovered much later that the date of the Refusal of the Union became an unofficial holiday in Scotland and Eire. That made me smile. I hadn’t always agreed with Buchanan’s decisions, but she had both style and substance.

Another day, Ken and I sat down with the Chair of the Consolidated Mining Group to discuss supplying raw ores, minerals, and scrap to a shipbuilding and mining support services company that was their largest client. The wheels of commerce whirled on in the midst of war. The company was represented at the meeting by its COO, Tan Sri Dr. Diana Chen. I was keeping my mouth shut, letting the specialists talk and only intervening to agree with Ken when he gave the military viewpoint.

Chen’s interest in the military appeared to go only so far as the protection of her company’s supply chain, so I was pretty startled when she turned to me and said. “Amira Singh. Any relation to Mia Gopwani-Singh who worked on the Ceres rig infrastructure project?”

"Uh, no, Tan Sri Dr. Chen. That was before my time."

"Just Dr. Chen is fine. You have an impressive operation here, Director Singh. Your commander is quite the young Alexander."

Ken looked flustered at the praise. I almost laughed aloud. "He is indispensable to me, Dr. Chen. Please don't try to steal him."

"I wouldn't dare. I want to see what he accomplishes with your forces in ten years' time. And you, my dear, are a community builder extraordinaire. What you have done is equivalent to founding a country."

It was Ken's turn to enjoy my discomfort. I muttered a brief, ineloquent thanks, which made Dr. Chen add, "More the rough pioneer than the seasoned diplomat, but it's early days. Very early days. You've left one very important post vacant. He's running your military and you're building a nation, but there's no one in charge of your corporate empire." She raised an apologetic hand to the Chair of the Consolidated Mining Group. "No offense to your colleague, but I am talking about more than mining. Fortunately, I am prepared to offer myself for the position."

Dr. Chen was right. I was rough around the edges, more comfortable with swearing than small talk, and I could feel myself getting ready to tell this rich bitch what she could do with her cloying politeness and unbelievable arrogance. But before Ken could jump in to stop me, even before the Chair could give me a pleading glance, Russo's index kicked me in the brain, dropped a stack of data, and basically informed me just how capable and sought-after Tan Sri Dr. Diana Chen was and how much of an idiot I would be if I turned her down, far less insulted her.

I closed my gaping mouth, got to my feet, and extended my hand. "Dr. Chen, I can honestly say it would be an honor."

One of the best meetings happened after I'd had a stressful day with wall-to-wall problems that everyone expected me to fix in minutes without swearing at anyone. I was so tired that I was napping in my office to gather up the strength to go home to bed. Ken woke me with a message that a new arrival to Ceres wanted to meet me. I was ready to unload the words I'd suppressed earlier, but then I read the words "and JP sends her regards."

I got up and quickly pulled my untidy hair back in a ponytail. I was still half-asleep, and for some reason when I opened the door, I was sure JP was going to be standing on the other side . . .

. . . and it wasn't her. It was someone else.

"Jasen?" I shook my head and mentally kicked myself. "Sorry. Sorry, that was . . . uh . . . which one are you?"

He didn't look offended. He waited until I finished babbling, then calmly shook hands. "I'm Sikander. Sorry I took so long. It's been an interesting journey."

His hand was rich with nano-ink tattoos. I stopped shaking it and started staring at it—intricate coiling designs in gray, blue, and gold, highly functional art.

"Um . . . I have been screened. Thoroughly," he said uncertainly. Now he looked offended.

"Yeah, right, of course. Sorry. Very nice designs." I pulled my hand away and crossed my arms. "You . . . don't look exactly like Jasen."

"He was the LA guy; he had a lot of work done. Nose and . . . um . . . other things. Should I come back later? I have a datachip for you, but I can leave it with you. Here." He set it gingerly on my desk. "Take your time with it. Goodbye."

He backed away and left at speed, almost bumping into Ken, who had just entered the office.

Ken raised his eyebrows. "Short meeting?"

I glared at him. "There's a reason I have naptime. How long is he staying for?"

"His clearance says six weeks, then back to Earth. New Delhi, in fact."

I yawned. "Good. We'll have time to prepare some confidential dispatches to send with him. He's the perfect walking hub for our intra-System communications. JP is a gem."

It never really stopped being weird, but it worked. Every two months or so, depending on how much was happening, JP would put together a massive file of the best data from the Ships and Russo's networks and send it with a Russo clone. Moscow, Lagos, Rome, Mexico City, Delhi, and São Paolo—those were the origins of the six living clones, but after years of working with the Ships, they'd traveled all over and grown comfortable with the semi-nomadic life.

The clone would hang around for a bit, then go back to Earth with written and eyewitness reports. I learned to deal with it. None of them were Jasen, but then again, none of them matched the creepiness of their progenitor. Ken once innocently suggested that I should occasionally hook up to a sleep-nutrition stabilizer, to make sure I didn't get whacked out by all my duties plus my constant processing of information. Man, that fight was epic. He only forgave me after I showed him images of Russo's new mobile support system and calmly explained the slippery-slope seduction of the purely internal world. The resemblance to the tanks used by civilian Arvani was a natural coincidence of basic design, but it still got his attention, and he never disturbed my naptime again.

"How's the terrain?" I shouted over the noise and vibration in my helmet.

"Challenging, but my God, what a view!" Ken sounded blissed out. Four months out of the CPF and he was flourishing. The young Alexander finally had room to stretch his wings, and it was glorious to see.

He'd brought me out to start the workday by test-driving Dr. Chen's newest invention, the qamutrike: a single-occupant trike/tank/hopper designed to skim ice, crawl up rock, and jet from surface to orbital station or ship to ship. I was the first-timer going slowly, and Ken was the maverick pushing the envelope. If I squinted, I could see his trike high on an icy crest, poised to look Earthward.

"Yeah," I said. "I bet it's beautiful. We should get back. Devlin and the others will be here soon."

"You go ahead. I'll be in within the hour."

I left him to his mediations and returned to base. It doesn't matter how much you trust the dedication of your guards, the rigor of your security procedures, and your own ability to kick butt—when you open the door to your quarters and hear a strange snore in the dark, you will freak the hell out. I quickly got ahold of myself, looked carefully in the infrared, then laughed and brought all the lights on full force.

"What? I'm awake! I'm up!" Devlin jumped up from my couch, blinking and flailing like an overexcited struthiform.

I threw my jacket at him, then my helmet. "Oww!" he yelled as the helmet bounced off his elbow.

"You scared me shitless!" I yelled back.

He laughed. "I scared the Ghostslayer herself? Whoa, gotta add that to my resume."

"What are you doing here so early?"

"Sleeping," he answered innocently. "I don't get much sleep these days."

I looked him over. For all his complaining, he didn't look

all that haggard. In fact, he looked good and grown up. He'd nearly finished his journey from hunger strikes and struggling adolescence to the full strength of a seasoned adult soldier. "They've been feeding you well, at least."

He sat down on the couch again, leaned forward, and got serious. "Accordance spy probes have been set up on some of Jupiter's moons, and your help with that has been very much appreciated. We're finally going to be able to look at what the Conglomeration is up to. Would you like to come and see for yourself?"

I grinned. "I can clear my schedule for that."

We sent a message to Ken to meet us at the main dock. I had an embarrassingly happy reunion moment with Shriek and Wei, and then they all showed off their ship to me: a stealth-equipped, boosted jumpship with all kinds of interesting capabilities. It looked like it could hold a company, but today it was just us and the pilot and a payload of surveillance and cloaking tech. I wanted to steal the plans for Dr. Chen to commission something similar for us, but I realized it would be better to just ask her in case it was a model her former colleagues were making in one of their many subsidiary companies.

Just as the pilot was pointing out the individual, heat-shielded lifepods recessed into the ship's hull, Ken came through the dockside airlock and parked his qamutrike nearby. He took off his helmet and walked toward us with the relaxed strut of someone who has started the day well and intends that to continue. "Devlin, Shriek, Wei! Good to see you!"

"Isn't that Ken Awojobi, who murdered that Arvani commander on Titan and deserted at the battle of Callisto?" the unnamed pilot whispered excitedly.

Everyone turned to stare at her.

Devlin spoke slowly, as if to a child. "He's a close friend, a trusted colleague, and our guest for this mission."

"But, Captain Hart, you cannot mean that we should—"

"Are you questioning the word of a highly decorated officer and honored citizen of the Accordance?" Wei said sternly.

"Ken Awojobi? Can't find that name in the CPF personnel records," I said with the utter confidence of truth.

"So be quiet, you boldfaced tentacle-licker," Shriek added.

We all snickered at that while the poor young struthiform pilot flattened her feathers and tried to make herself look smaller.

Ken reached us as we were still smirking. "What's so funny?" he asked.

"Nothing important. Want to go hunting?" Devlin asked instead.

His face lit up. "Where, Jupiter? Sun-B?"

"Or, as we rebels sometimes call it, Sun-Ra," I added.

Devlin gave him a huge grin and a nod.

Ken let out a whoop. "Hell yeah! Let's see what the bastards are up to!"

Stealth limited our speed, but at last we reached the Hildas asteroids and began to connect to the probes. It took a little more time for us to establish secure communication to the surveillance network and to use that communication to find and pinpoint areas of interest.

The data came tumbling in. There had been a lot of changes. I felt my heart beat faster, as if it was warning me in advance that I should run.

Wei stopped poring over the data and began to keen in terror. The pilot glanced at him with scared eyes, but she kept silent.

"What does that mean?" I asked sharply, choosing anger instead of panic. "What's going on?"

"I think it means that Wei also recognizes the infrastructure," Shriek said. His voice sounded as if it were coming from a great distance, and his face was too calm. "The Conglomeration have built genetic refactoring pits and breeding hives. The signature is unmistakable."

"You mean we didn't win?" Devlin said. "They got what they wanted?"

"They didn't get Earth," Ken said harshly.

"Earth was never the target! It was a diversion. The target was the troops on the ships, the miners and engineers and everyone that got swept up when we ran from Jupiter. We failed!" Devlin's voice didn't rise above a whisper, but the anguish in his tone hit harder than a shout.

I said nothing. I scanned the readings, absorbing the data and learning as fast as I could. Wei continued his soft cries, distracting me, until I put out a hand and absently began to stroke his arm and smooth the bristling pinions over his clenched wing hand. "Wei. What does this variable mean? Can we calculate pit volumes from this distance, Wei? We've got a lot of work to do, and I need you to teach me. How many probes are out there? Should we launch more, to improve the data?"

"Amira," Ken said softly.

"It's okay, Ken. I'm okay. We can beat them. We've got to work a little harder, a little longer, but we've got a fleet. We've got an empire! We can win this!"

I felt the warmth and weight of Devlin's hand on my shoulder. "We can," he said, his voice stronger and steady. "We've done it before with less. We'll win."

Shriek blinked and nodded, looking at us clear-eyed and

hopeful. "Yes. This is true. I have been with you from the start and I am still alive. I believe you can."

Our ragged, traumatized little family reassured each other with a word, with a touch, with the comfort of facts, with the sunward view of our still-standing domain. But we did not forget where we were. It was dangerous to linger.

Ken spoke to the pilot. "We've seen enough. Take us back."

"Yes, Commander," she answered. "Setting course for Ceres."